BENJAMIN DISRAELI
(At the Age of 22)
The Author, it is Stated, Took His Own
Character as the Original of
His Hero,
Vivian Grey

"At this moment, how many a powerful noble wants only wit to be a Minister; and what wants Vivian Grey to attain the same end? That noble's influence. When two persons can so materially assist each other, why are they not brought together? . . . I have the mind for the conception. . . . There wants but one thing more: courage, pure, perfect courage."

—Vivian Grey, page 21.

AUTHOR OF "VIVIAN GREY."

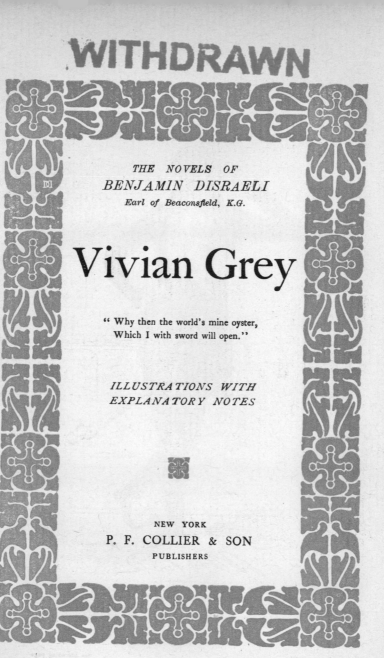

THE NOVELS OF
BENJAMIN DISRAELI
Earl of Beaconsfield, K.G.

Vivian Grey

" Why then the world's mine oyster,
Which I with sword will open."

ILLUSTRATIONS WITH
EXPLANATORY NOTES

NEW YORK
P. F. COLLIER & SON
PUBLISHERS

ADVERTISEMENT

Books written by boys (1825-26), which pretend to give a picture of manners, and to deal in knowledge of human nature, must necessarily be founded on affectation. They can be, at the best, but the results of imagination, acting upon knowledge not acquired by experience. Of such circumstances, exaggeration is a necessary consequence, and false taste accompanies exaggeration. Nor is it necessary to remark that a total want of art must be observed in their pages, for that is a failing incident to all first efforts. When the writers of such books are not again heard of, the works, even if ever noticed, are soon forgotten, and so there is no great harm done. But when their authors subsequently become eminent, such works often obtain a peculiar interest, and are sought for from causes irrespective of their merits. Such productions should be exempt from criticism and should be looked upon as a kind of literary lusus.

These observations apply to "Vivian Grey." For more than a quarter of a century its author has refused to reprint it; but the action of the foreign presses in the present day, especially in the United States and Germany, renders an author no longer the master of his own will. It has, therefore, been thought best to include it in this general edition of his works, and so it is hoped that it will be read with an indulgent recollection of the conditions under which it was produced.

November, 1853.

VIVIAN GREY

BOOK I

CHAPTER I

WE are not aware that the infancy of Vivian Grey was distinguished by any extraordinary incident. The solicitude of the most affectionate of mothers, and the care of the most attentive of nurses, did their best to injure an excellent constitution. But Vivian was an only child, and these exertions were therefore excusable. For the first five years of his life, with his curly locks and his fancy dress, he was the pride of his own and the envy of all neighboring establishments; but, in process of time, the spirit of boyism began to develop itself, and Vivian not only would brush his hair straight and rebel against his nurse, but actually insisted upon being—breeched! At this crisis it was discovered that he had been spoiled, and it was determined that he should be sent to school. Mr. Grey observed, also, that the child was nearly ten years old, and did not know his alphabet, and Mrs. Grey remarked that he was getting ugly. The fate of Vivian was decided.

"I am told, my dear," observed Mrs. Grey, one day after dinner to her husband, "I am told, my dear, that Dr. Flummery's would do very well for Vivian. Nothing can exceed the attention which is paid to the pupils. There are sixteen young ladies, all the daughters of clergymen, merely to attend to the morals and the linen; terms moderate: 100 guineas per annum, for all under six years of age, and few extras, only for fencing, pure milk, and the guitar. Mrs. Metcalf has both her boys there, and she says their progress is astonishing! Percy Metcalf, she assures me, was quite as backward as Vivian; indeed, backwarder; and so was Dudley, who was taught at home on the new system, by a pictorial alphabet, and who persisted to the last, notwithstanding all the exertions of Miss Barrett, in spelling A-P-E, monkey, merely because over the word there was a monster munching an apple.

"And quite right in the child, my dear. Pictorial alphabet! pictorial fool's head!"

"But what do you say to Flummery's, Horace?"

"My dear, do what you like. I never trouble myself, you know, about these matters;" and Mr. Grey refreshed himself, after this domestic attack, with a glass of claret.

Mr. Grey was a gentleman who had succeeded, when the heat of youth was over, to the enjoyment of a life estate of some two thousand a year. He was a man of lettered tastes, and had hailed with no slight pleasure his succession to a fortune which, though limited in its duration, was still a great thing for a young lounger about town, not only with no profession, but with a mind unfitted for every species of business. Grey, to the astonishment of his former friends, the wits, made an excellent domestic match; and, leaving the whole management of his household to his lady, felt himself as independent in his magnificent library as if he had never ceased to be that true freeman, A MAN OF CHAMBERS.

The young Vivian had not, by the cares which fathers are always heirs to, yet reminded his parent that children were anything else but playthings. The intercourse between father and son was, of course, extremely limited; for Vivian was, as yet, the mother's child; Mr. Grey's parental duties being confined to giving his son a daily glass of claret, pulling his ears with all the awkwardness of literary affection, and trusting to God "that the urchin would never scribble."

"I won't go to school, mamma," bawled Vivian.

"But you must, my love," answered Mrs. Grey; "all good boys go to school;" and in the plenitude of a mother's love she tried to make her offspring's hair curl.

"I won't have my hair curl, mamma; the boys will laugh at me," rebawled the beauty.

"Now who could have told the child that?" monologized mamma, with all a mamma's admiration.

"Charles Appleyard told me so; his hair curled, and the boys called him girl. Papa! give me some more claret; I won't go to school."

CHAPTER II

THREE or four years passed over, and the mind of Vivian Grey astonishingly developed itself. He had long ceased to wear frills, had broached the subject of boots three or four times, made a sad inroad during the holidays in Mr. Grey's bottle of claret, and was reported as having once sworn at the butler. The young gentleman began also to hint, during every vacation, that the fellows at Flummery's were somewhat too small for his companionship, and (first bud of puppyism!) the former advocate of straight hair now expended a portion of his infant income in the purchase of Macassar, and began to cultivate his curls. Mrs. Grey could not entertain for a moment the idea of her son's associating with children, the eldest of whom (to adopt his own account) was not above eight years old; so Flummery, it was determined, he should leave. But where to go? Mr. Grey was for Eton, but his lady was one of those women whom nothing in the world can persuade that a public school is anything else but a place where boys are roasted alive; and so with tears, and taunts, and supplications, the point of private education was conceded.

At length it was resolved that the only hope should remain at home a season, until some plan should be devised for the cultivation of his promising understanding. During this year Vivian became a somewhat more constant intruder into the library than heretofore; and living so much among books, he was insensibly attracted to those silent companions that speak so eloquently.

How far the character of the parent may influence the character of the child, the metaphysician must decide. Certainly the character of Vivian Grey underwent, at this period of his life, a sensible change. Doubtless, constant communion with a mind highly refined, severely cultivated, and much experienced, can not but produce a beneficial impression, even upon a mind formed and upon principles developed: how infinitely more powerful must the influence of such communion be upon a youthful heart, ardent, innocent, and unpracticed! As Vivian was not to figure in the microcosm of a public school, a place for which, from his temper, he was almost better fitted than any young genius whom the playing fields of Eton or the hills of Winton can remember, there was some difficulty in fixing upon his future Academus. Mr. Grey's two axioms were, first, that no one so young as his son should settle in the metropolis, and that Vivian must consequently not have a private tutor; and, secondly, that all private schools were quite worthless; and, therefore, there was every probability of Vivian not receiving any education whatever.

At length, an exception to axiom second started up in the establishment of Mr. Dallas. This gentleman was a clergyman, a profound Grecian, and a poor man. He had edited the "Alcestis," and married his laundress; lost money by his edition, and his fellowship by his match. In a few days the hall of Mr. Grey's London mansion was filled with all sorts of portmanteaus, trunks, and traveling cases, directed in a boy's sprawling hand to "Vivian Grey, Esquire, at the Reverend Everard Dallas, Burnsley Vicarage, Hants."

"God bless you, my boy! write to your mother soon, and remember your Journal."

CHAPTER III

THE rumor of the arrival of a "new fellow" circulated with rapidity through the inmates of Burnsley Vicarage, and about fifty young devils were preparing to quiz the new-comer, when the school-room door opened, and Mr. Dallas, accompanied by Vivian, entered.

"A dandy, by Jove!" whispered St. Leger Smith. "What a knowing set out!" squeaked Johnson secundus. "Mammysick!" growled Barlow primus. This last exclamation was, however, a scandalous libel, for certainly no being ever stood in a pedagogue's presence with more perfect *sangfroid*, and with a bolder front, than did, at this moment, Vivian Grey.

One principle in Mr. Dallas's system was always to introduce a new-comer in school-hours. He was thus carried immediately *in medias res*, and the curiosity of his co-mates being in a great degree satisfied at the time when that curiosity could not personally annoy him, the new-comer was, of course, much better prepared to make his way when the absence of the ruler became a signal for some oral communication with "the arrival."

However, in the present instance the young savages at Burnsley Vicarage had caught a Tartar; and in a very few days Vivian Grey was decidedly the most popular fellow in the school. He was "so dashing! so devilish good-tempered! so completely up to everything!" The magnates of the land were certainly rather jealous of his success, but their very sneers bore witness to his popularity. "Cursed puppy," whispered St. Leger Smith. "Thinks himself knowing," squeaked Johnson secundus. "Thinks himself witty," growled Barlow primus.

Notwithstanding this cabal, days rolled on at Burnsley Vicarage only to witness the increase of Vivian's popularity. Although more deficient than most of his own age in accurate classical attainments, he found himself, in talents and various acquirements, immeasurably their superior. And singular is it that at school distinction in such points is ten thousand times more admired by the multitude than the most profound knowledge of Greek metres, or the most accurate acquaintance with the value of Roman coins. Vivian Grey's English verses and Vivian Grey's English themes were the subject of universal commendation. Some young lads made copies of these productions, to enrich, at the Christmas holidays, their sisters' albums; while the whole school were scribbling embryo prize-poems, epics of twenty lines on "the Ruins of Pæstum" and "the Temple of Minerva"; "Agrigentum," and "the Cascade of Terni." Vivian's productions at this time would probably have been rejected by the commonest twopenny publication about town, yet they turned the brain of the whole school; while fellows who were writing Latin Dissertations and Greek Odes, which might have made the fortune of the Classical Journal, were looked on by the multitude as being as great dunderheads as themselves. Such is the advantage which, even in this artificial world, everything that is genuine has over everything that is false and forced. The dunderheads who wrote "good Latin" and "Attic Greek" did it by a process by means of which the youngest fellow in the school was conscious he could, if he chose, attain the same perfection. Vivian Grey's verses were unlike anything which had yet appeared in the literary Annals of Burnsley Vicarage, and that which was quite novel was naturally thought quite excellent.

There is no place in the world where greater homage is paid to talent than an English school. At a public school, indeed, if a youth of great talents be blessed with an amiable and generous disposition, he ought not to envy the Minister of England. If any captain of Eton or prefect of Winchester be reading these pages, let him dispassionately consider in what situation of life he can rationally expect that it will be in his power to exercise such influence, to have such opportunities of obliging others, and be so confident of an affectionate and grateful return. Ay, there's the rub! Bitter thought! that gratitude should cease the moment we become men.

And sure I am that Vivian Grey was loved as ardently and as faithfully as you might expect from innocent young hearts. His slight accomplishments were the standard of all perfection, his sayings were the soul of all good fellowship, and his opinion the guide in any crisis which occurred in the monotonous existence of the little commonwealth. And time flew gayly on.

One winter evening, as Vivian, with some of his particular cronies, were standing round the school-room fire, they began, as all schoolboys do when it grows rather dark and they grow rather sentimental, to talk of HOME.

"Twelve weeks more," said Augustus Etherege; "twelve weeks more, and we are free! The glorious day should be celebrated."

"A feast, a feast!" exclaimed Poynings.

"A feast is but the work of a night," said Vivian Grey: "something more stirring for me! What say you to private theatricals?"

The proposition was, of course, received with enthusiasm, and it was not until they had unanimously agreed to act that they universally remembered that acting was not allowed. And then they consulted whether they should ask Dallas, and then they remembered that Dallas had been asked fifty times, and then they "supposed they must give it up"; and then Vivian Grey made a proposition which the rest were secretly sighing for, but which they were afraid to make themselves; he proposed that they should act without asking Dallas. "Well, then, we'll do it without asking him," said Vivian; "nothing is allowed in this life, and everything is done: in town there is a thing called the French play, and that is not allowed, yet my aunt has got a private box there. Trust me for acting, but what shall we perform?"

This question was, as usual, the fruitful source of jarring opinions. One proposed "Othello," chiefly because it would be so easy to black a face with a burned cork. Another was for "Hamlet," solely because he wanted to act the ghost, which he proposed doing in white shorts and a night-cap. A third was for "Julius Cæsar," because the murder scene would be such fun.

"No! no!" said Vivian, tired at these various and varying proposals, "this will never do. Out upon Tragedies; let's have a Comedy!"

"A Comedy! a Comedy! oh! how delightful!"

CHAPTER IV

AFTER an immense number of propositions, and an equal number of repetitions, Dr. Hoadley's bustling drama was fixed upon. Vivian was to act Ranger, Augustus Etherege was to personate Clarinda, because he was a fair boy and always blushing; and the rest of the characters found able representatives. Every half-holiday was devoted to rehearsals, and nothing could exceed the amusement and thorough fun which all the preparations elicited. All went well; Vivian wrote a pathetic prologue and a witty epilogue. Etherege got on capitally in the mask scene, and Poynings was quite perfect in Jack Maggot. There was, of course, some difficulty in keeping all things in order, but then Vivian Grey was such an excellent manager! and then, with infinite tact, the said manager conciliated the Classics, for he allowed St. Leger Smith to select a Greek motto, from the Andromache, for the front of the theatre; and Johnson secundus and Barlow primus were complimented by being allowed to act the chairmen.

But alas! in the midst of all this sunshine, the seeds of

discord and dissension were fast flourishing. Mr. Dallas himself was always so absorbed in some freshly-imported German commentator that it was a fixed principle with him never to trouble himself with anything that concerned his pupils "out of school hours." The consequence was, that certain powers were necessarily delegated to a certain set of beings called USHERS.

The usherian rule had, however, always been comparatively light at Burnsley Vicarage, for the good Dallas, never for a moment intrusting the duties of tuition to a third person, engaged these deputies merely as a sort of police, to regulate the bodies, rather than the minds, of his youthful subjects. One of the first principles of the new theory introduced into the establishment of Burnsley Vicarage by Mr. Vivian Grey was, that the ushers were to be considered by the boys as a species of upper servants; were to be treated with civility, certainly, as all servants are by gentlemen; but that no further attention was to be paid them, and that any fellow voluntarily conversing with an usher was to be cut dead by the whole school. This pleasant arrangement was no secret to those whom it most immediately concerned, and, of course, rendered Vivian rather a favorite with them. These men had not the tact to conciliate the boy, and were, notwithstanding, too much afraid of his influence in the school to attack him openly; so they waited with that patience which insulted beings can alone endure.

One of these creatures must not be forgotten; his name was Mallett; he was a perfect specimen of the genuine usher. The monster wore a black coat and waistcoat; the residue of his costume was of that mysterious color known by the name of pepper-and-salt. He was a pallid wretch with a pug nose, white teeth, and marked with the small-pox; long, greasy black hair, and small, black, beady eyes. This demon watched the progress of the theatrical company with eyes gloating with vengeance. No attempt had been made to keep the fact of the rehearsal a secret from the police; no objection, on their part, had as yet been made; the twelve weeks diminished to six; Ranger had secretly ordered a dress from town, and was to get a steel-handled sword from Fentum's for Jack Maggot; and everything was proceeding with delightful success, when one morning, as Mr. Dallas was apparently about to take his departure, with a volume of Becker's Thucydides under his arm, the respected Dominie stopped, and thus harangued: "I am informed that a great deal is going on in this family with which it is intended that I shall be kept unacquainted. It is not my intention to name anybody or anything at present; but I must say that of late the temper of this family has sadly changed. Whether there be any seditious stranger among you or not, I shall not at present even endeavor to discover; but I will warn my old friends of their new ones"; and so saying, the Dominie withdrew.

All eyes were immediately fixed on Vivian, and the faces of the Classics were triumphant with smiles; those of the manager's particular friends, the Romantics, we may call them, were clouded; but who shall describe the countenance of Mallett? In a moment the school broke up with an agitated and tumultuous uproar. "No stranger!" shouted St. Leger Smith; "no stranger!" vociferated a prepared gang. Vivian's friends were silent, for they hesitated to accept for their leader the insulting title. Those who were neither Vivian's friends nor in the secret, weak creatures who side always with the strongest, immediately swelled the insulting chorus of Mr. St. Leger Smith. That worthy, emboldened by his success and the smiles of Mallett, contained himself no longer: "Down with the manager!" he cried. His satellites chorused. But now Vivian rushed forward. "Mr. Smith, I thank you for being so definite; take that!" and he struck Smith with such force that the Cleon staggered and fell; but Smith instantly recovered, and a ring was instantly formed. To a common observer, the combatants were unequally matched; for Smith was a burly, big-limbed animal, alike superior to Grey in years and strength. But Vivian, though delicate in frame and more youthful, was full his match in spirit, and, thanks to being a Cockney! ten times his match in science. He had not built a white greatcoat or drunk blue ruin at Ben Burn's for nothing!

Oh! how beautifully he fought! how admirably straight he hit! and his stops quick as lightning! and his followings up confounding his adversary with their painful celerity! Smith, alike puzzled and punished, yet proud in his strength, hit round, and wild, and false, and foamed like a furious elephant. For ten successive rounds the result was dubious; but in the eleventh the strength of Smith began to fail him, and the men were more fairly matched. "Go it, Ranger! go it, Ranger!" halloed the Greyites; "No stranger! no stranger!" eagerly bawled the more numerous party. "Smith's floored, by Jove!" exclaimed Poynings, who was Grey's second. "At it again! at it again!" exclaimed all. And now, when Smith must certainly have given in, suddenly stepped forward Mr. Mallett, accompanied by—Dallas!

"How, Mr. Grey! No answer, sir; I understand that you have always an answer ready. I do not quote Scripture lightly, Mr. Grey; but 'Take heed that you offend not, even with your tongue.' Now, sir, to your room."

When Vivian Grey again joined his companions, he found himself almost universally shunned. Etherege and Poynings were the only individuals who met him with their former frankness. "A horrible row, Grey," said the latter. "After you went, the Doctor harangued the whole school, and swears you have seduced and ruined us all; everything was happiness until you came, etc. Mallett is of course at the bottom of the whole business: but what can we do? Dallas says you have the tongue of a serpent, and that he will not trust himself to hear your defence. Infamous shame! I swear! And now every fellow has got a story against you: some say you are a dandy, others want to know whether the next piece performed at your theatre will be 'The Stranger'; as for myself and Etherege, we shall leave in a few weeks, and it does not signify to us; but what the devil you're to do next half, by Jove, I can't say. If I were you, I would not return."

"Not return, eh! but that will I, though; and we shall see who, in future, can complain of the sweetness of my voice! Ungrateful fools!"

CHAPTER V

THE vacation was over, and Vivian returned to Burnsley Vicarage. He bowed cavalierly to Mr. Dallas on his arrival, and immediately sauntered up into the school-room, where he found a tolerable quantity of wretches looking as miserable as schoolboys who have left their pleasant homes generally do for some four-and-twenty hours. "How d'ye do,

Grey? How d'ye do, Grey?" burst from a knot of unhappy fellows, who would have felt quite delighted had their newly arrived co-mate condescended to entertain them, as usual, with some capital good story fresh from town. But they were disappointed.

"We can make room for you at the fire, Grey," said Theophilus King.

"I thank you, I am not cold."

"I suppose you know that Poynings and Etherege don't come back, Grey?"

"Everybody knew that last half:" and so he walked on.

"Grey, Grey!" halloed King, "don't go into the dining-room; Mallett is there alone, and told us not to disturb him. By Jove, the fellow is going in: there will be a greater row this half between Grey and Mallett than ever."

Days, the heavy first days of the half, rolled on, and all the citizens of the little commonwealth had returned.

"What a dull half this will be!" said Eardley; "how one misses Grey's set! After all, they kept the school alive: Poynings was a first-rate fellow, and Etherege so deuced good-natured! I wonder whom Grey will crony with this half; have you seen him and Dallas speak together yet? He cut the Doctor quite dead at Greek to-day."

"Why, Eardley! Eardley! there is Grey walking round playing fields with Mallett!" halloed a sawney who was killing the half-holiday by looking out of the window.

"The devil! I say, Matthews, whose flute is that? It is a devilish handsome one!"

"It's Grey's! I clean it for him," squeaked a little boy. "He gives me sixpence a week!"

"Oh, you sneak!" said one.

"Cut him over!" said another.

"Roast him!" cried a third.

"To whom are you going to take the flute!" asked a fourth.

"To Mallett," squeaked the little fellow. "Grey lends his flute to Mallett every day."

"Grey lends his flute to Mallett! The deuce he does! So Grey and Mallett are going to crony!"

A wild exclamation burst forth from the little party; and

away each of them ran, to spread in all directions the astounding intelligence.

If the rule of the ushers had hitherto been light at Burnsley Vicarage, its character was materially changed during this half-year. The vexatious and tyrannical influence of Mallett was now experienced in all directions, meeting and interfering with the comforts of the boys in every possible manner. His malice was accompanied, too, by a tact which could not have been expected from his vulgar mind, and which, at the same time, could not have been produced by the experience of one in his situation. It was quite evident to the whole community that his conduct was dictated by another mind, and that that mind was one versed in all the secrets of a schoolboy's life, and acquainted with all the workings of a schoolboy's mind: a species of knowledge which no pedagogue in the world ever yet attained. There was no difficulty in discovering whose was the power behind the throne. Vivian Grey was the perpetual companion of Mallett in his walks, and even in the school; he shunned also the converse of every one of the boys, and did not affect to conceal that his quarrel was universal. Superior power, exercised by a superior mind, was for a long time more than a match even for the united exertions of the whole school. If any one complained, Mallett's written answer (and such Dallas always required) was immediately ready, explaining everything in the most satisfactory manner, and refuting every complaint with the most triumphant spirit. Dallas, of course, supported his deputy, and was soon equally detested. This tyranny had continued through a great part of the long half-year, and the spirit of the school was almost broken, when a fresh outrage occurred, of such a nature that the nearly enslaved multitude conspired.

The plot was admirably formed. On the first bell ringing for school, the door was to be immediately barred, to prevent the entrance of Dallas. Instant vengeance was then to be taken on Mallett and his companion—the sneak! the spy! the traitor! The bell rang: the door was barred: four stout fellows seized on Mallett, four rushed to Vivian Grey: but stop: he sprang upon his desk, and, placing his back against the wall, held a pistol at the foremost: "Not an inch nearer, Smith, or I fire. Let me not, however, balk your vengeance on yon-

der hound: if I could suggest any refinements in torture, they
would be at your service." Vivian Grey smiled, while the
horrid cries of Mallett indicated that the boys were "roasting"
him. He then walked to the door and admitted the barred-out
Dominie. Silence was restored. There was an explanation
and no defence; and Vivian Grey was expelled. .

CHAPTER VI

VIVIAN was now seventeen; and the system of private education having so decidedly failed, it was resolved that
he should spend the years antecedent to his going to Oxford
at home. Nothing could be a greater failure than the first
weeks of his "course of study." He was perpetually violating the sanctity of the drawing-room by the presence of Scapu-
las and Hederics, and outraging the propriety of morning visitors by bursting into his mother's boudoir with lexicons and
slippers.

"Vivian, my dear," said his father to him one day, "this
will never do; you must adopt some system for your studies,
and some locality for your reading. Have a room to yourself; set apart certain hours in the day for your books, and
allow no consideration on earth to influence you to violate their
sacredness; and above all, my dear boy, keep your papers in
order. I find a dissertation on 'The Commerce of Carthage'
stuck in my large paper copy of Dibdin's Decameron, and an
'Essay on the Metaphysics of Music' (pray, my dear fellow,
beware of magazine scribbling) cracking the back of Mont-
fauçon's 'Monarchie.' "

Vivian apologized, promised, protested, and finally sat
down "TO READ." He had laid the foundations of accurate
classical knowledge under the tuition of the learned Dallas;
and twelve hours a day and self-banishment from society overcame, in twelve months, the ill effects of his imperfect education. The result of this extraordinary exertion may be conceived. At the end of twelve months, Vivian, like many other
young enthusiasts, had discovered that all the wit and wisdom
of the world were concentrated in some fifty antique volumes,
and he treated the unlucky moderns with the most sublime

spirit of hauteur imaginable. A chorus in the Medea, that painted the radiant sky of Attica, disgusted him with the foggy atmosphere of Great Britain; and while Mrs. Grey was meditating a visit to Brighton, her son was dreaming of the gulf of Salamis. The spectre in the Persæ was his only model for a ghost, and the furies in the Orestes were his perfection of tragical machinery.

Most ingenious and educated youths have fallen into the same error, but few have ever carried such feelings to the excess that Vivian Grey did; for while his mind was daily becoming more enervated under the beautiful but baneful influence of Classic Reverie, the youth lighted upon PLATO.

Wonderful is it that while the whole soul of Vivian Grey seemed concentrated and wrapped in the glorious pages of the Athenian; while, with keen and almost inspired curiosity, he searched, and followed up, and meditated upon, the definite mystery, the indefinite development; while his spirit alternately bowed in trembling and in admiration, as he seemed to be listening to the secrets of the Universe revealed in the glorious melodies of an immortal voice; wonderful is it, I say, that the writer, the study of whose works appeared to the young scholar, in the reveling of his enthusiasm, to be the sole object for which man was born and had his being, was the cause by which Vivian Grey was saved from being all his life a dreaming scholar.

Determined to spare no exertions, and to neglect no means, by which he might enter into the very penetralia of his mighty master's meaning, Vivian determined to attack the latter Platonists. These were a race of men of whose existence he knew merely by the references to their productions which were sprinkled in the commentaries of his "best editions." In the pride of boyish learning, Vivian had limited his library to Classics, and the proud leaders of the later schools did not consequently grace his diminutive bookcase. In this dilemma he flew to his father, and confessed by his request that his favorites were not all-sufficient.

"Father! I wish to make myself master of the latter Platonists. I want Plotinus, and Porphyry, and Iamblichus, and Syrianus, and Maximus Tyrius, and Proclus, and Hierocles, and Sallustius, and Damascius."

Mr. Grey stared at his son, and laughed.

"My dear Vivian! are you quite convinced that the authors you ask for are all pure Platonists? or have not some of them placed the great end rather in practical than theoretic virtue, and thereby violated the first principles of your master? which would be shocking. Are you sure, too, that these gentlemen have actually 'withdrawn the sacred veil, which covers from profane eyes the luminous spectacles'? Are you quite convinced that every one of these worthies lived at least five hundred years after the great master? for I need not tell so profound a Platonist as yourself that it was not till that period that even glimpses of the great master's meaning were discovered. Strange! that TIME should alike favor the philosophy of theory and the philosophy of facts. Mr. Vivian Grey, benefiting, I presume, by the lapse of further centuries, is about to complete the great work which Proclus and Porphyry commenced."

"My dear sir! you are pleased to be amusing this morning."

"My dear boy! I smile, but not with joy. Sit down, and let us have a little conversation together. Father and son, and father and son on such terms as we are, should really communicate oftener together than we do. It has been, perhaps, my fault; it shall not be so again."

"My dear sir!"

"Nay, nay, it shall be my fault now. Whose it shall be in future, Vivian, time will show. My dear Vivian, you have now spent upward of a year under this roof, and your conduct has been as correct as the most rigid parent might require. I have not wished to interfere with the progress of your mind, and I regret it. I have been negligent, but not wilfully so. I do regret it; because, whatever may be your powers, Vivian, I at least have the advantage of experience. I see you smile at a word which I so often use. Well, well, were I to talk to you forever, you would not understand what I mean by that single word. The time will come when you will deem that single word everything. Ardent youths in their closets, Vivian, too often fancy that they are peculiar beings; and I have no reason to believe that you are an exception to the general rule. In passing one whole year of your life, as you have done, you doubtless imagine that you have been spending your hours in a manner which no others have done before. Trust me, my boy, thousands have done the same; and, what is of still more importance, thousands are doing, and will do, the same. Take the advice of one who has committed as many, ay, more follies than yourself; but who would bless the hour that he had been a fool if his experience might be of benefit to his beloved son."

"My father!"

"Nay, don't agitate yourself; we are consulting together. Let us see what is to be done. Try to ascertain, when you are alone, what may be the chief objects of your existence in this world. I want you to take no theological dogmas for granted, nor to satisfy your doubts by ceasing to think; but, whether we are in this world in a state of probation for another, or whether we cease altogether when we cease to breathe, human feelings tell me that we have some duties to perform; to our fellow-creatures, to our friends, to ourselves. Pray tell me, my dear boy, what possible good your perusal of the latter Platonists can produce to either of these three interests? I trust that my child is not one of those who look with a glazed eye on the welfare of their fellow-men, and who would dream away a useless life by idle puzzles of the brain; creatures who consider their existence as an unprofitable mystery, and yet are afraid to die. You will find Plotinus in the fourth shelf of the next room, Vivian."

CHAPTER VII

IN England, personal distinction is the only passport to the society of the great. Whether this distinction arise from fortune, family, or talent, is immaterial; but certain it is, to enter into high society, a man must either have blood, a million, or a genius.

The reputation of Mr. Grey had always made him an honored guest among the powerful and the great. It was for this reason that he had always been anxious that his son should be at home as little as possible; for he feared for a youth the fascination of London society. Although busied with his studies, and professing "not to visit," Vivian could not avoid occasionally finding himself in company in which boys should never be seen; and, what was still worse, from a certain social spirit, an indefinable tact with which Nature had endowed him, this boy of nineteen began to think this society delightful. Most persons of his age would have passed through the ordeal with perfect safety; they would have entered certain rooms, at certain hours, with stiff cravats, and Nugee coats, and black velvet waistcoats; and after having annoyed all those who condescended to know of their existence, with their red hands and their white gloves, they would have retired to a corner of the room, and conversationized with any stray four-year-older not yet sent to bed.

But Vivian Grey was a graceful, lively lad, with just enough of dandyism to preserve him from committing gaucheries, and with a devil of a tongue. All men will agree with me that the only rival to be feared by a man of spirit is a clever boy. What makes them so popular with women it is difficult to explain; however, Lady Julia Knighton, and Mrs. Frank Delmington, and half a score of dames of fashion, were always patronizing our hero, who found an evening spent in their society not altogether dull, for there is no fascination so irresistible to a boy as the smile of a married woman. Vivian had passed such a recluse life for the last two years and a half that he had quite forgotten that he was once considered an agreeable fellow; and so, determined to discover what right he ever had to such a reputation, he dashed into all these amourettes in beautiful style.

But Vivian Grey was a young and tender plant in a moral hothouse. His character was developing itself too soon. Although his evenings were now generally passed in the manner we have alluded to, this boy was, during the rest of the day, a hard and indefatigable student; and having now got through an immense series of historical reading, he had stumbled upon a branch of study certainly the most delightful in the world; but, for a boy, as certainly the most perilous, THE STUDY OF POLITICS.

And now everything was solved! the inexplicable longings of his soul, which had so often perplexed him, were at length explained. The want, the indefinable want, which he had so constantly experienced, was at last supplied; the grand object on which to bring the powers of his mind to bear and work was at last provided. He paced his chamber in an agitated spirit, and panted for the Senate.

It may be asked, what was the evil of all this? and the reader will, perhaps, murmur something about an honorable spirit and youthful ambition. The evil was great. The time drew nigh for Vivian to leave his home for Oxford, that is, for him to commence his long preparation for entering on his career in life. And now this person, who was about to be a pupil, this stripling, who was going to begin his education, had all the desires of a matured mind, of an experienced man, but without maturity and without experience. He was already a cunning reader of human hearts; and felt conscious that his was a tongue which was born to guide human beings. The idea of Oxford to such an individual was an insult!

CHAPTER VIII

WE must endeavor to trace, if possible, more accurately the workings of Vivian Grey's mind at this period of his existence. In the plenitude of his ambition, he stopped one day to inquire in what manner he could obtain his magnificent ends.

"The Bar: pooh! law and bad jokes till we are forty; and then, with the most brilliant success, the prospect of gout and a coronet. Besides, to succeed as an advocate, I must be a great lawyer; and, to be a great lawyer, I must give up my chance of being a great man. The Services in war time are fit only for desperadoes (and that truly am I); but, in peace, are fit only for fools. The Church is more rational. Let me see: I should certainly like to act Wolsey; but the thousand and one chances against me! And truly I feel my destiny should not be on a chance. Were I the son of a millionaire, or a noble, I might have all. Curse on my lot! that the want of a few rascal counters, and the possession of a little rascal blood, should mar my fortunes!"

Such was the general tenor of Vivian's thoughts, until, musing himself almost into madness, he at last made, as he conceived, the Grand Discovery. Riches are Power, says the

Economist; and is not Intellect? asks the Philosopher. And yet, while the influence of the millionaire is instantly felt in all classes of society, how is it that "Noble Mind" so often leaves us unknown and unhonored? Why have there been statesmen who have never ruled, and heroes who have never conquered? Why have glorious philosophers died in a garret? and why have there been poets whose only admirer has been Nature in her echoes? It must be that these beings have thought only of themselves, and, constant and elaborate students of their own glorious natures, have forgotten or disdained the study of all others. Yes! we must mix with the herd; we must enter into their feelings; we must humor their weaknesses; we must sympathize with the sorrows that we do not feel; and share the merriment of fools. Oh, yes! to rule men, we must be men; to prove that we are strong, we must be weak; to prove that we are giants, we must be dwarfs; even as the Eastern Genie was hid in the charmed bottle. Our wisdom must be concealed under folly, and our constancy under caprice.

"I have been often struck by the ancient tales of Jupiter's visits to the earth. In these fanciful adventures, the god bore no indication of the Thunderer's glory; but was a man of low estate, a herdsman, a hind, often even an animal. A mighty spirit has in Tradition, Time's great moralist, perused 'the wisdom of the ancients.' Even in the same spirit, I would explain Jove's terrestrial visitings. For, to govern man, even the god appeared to feel as a man; and sometimes as a beast was apparently influenced by their vilest passions. Mankind, then, is my great game.

"At this moment, how many a powerful noble wants only wit to be a Minister; and what wants Vivian Grey to attain the same end? That noble's influence. When two persons can so materially assist each other, why are they not brought together? Shall I, because my birth balks my fancy, shall I pass my life a moping misanthrope in an old chateau? Supposing I am in contact with this magnifico, am I prepared? Now, let me probe my very soul. Does my cheek blanch? I have the mind for the conception; and I can perform right skilfully upon the most splendid of musical instruments, the human voice, to make those conceptions beloved by others. There wants but one thing more: courage, pure, perfect courage; and does Vivian Grey know fear?" He laughed an answer of bitterest derision.

CHAPTER IX

IS it surprising that Vivian Grey, with a mind teeming with such feelings, should view the approach of the season for his departure to Oxford with sentiments of disgust? After hours of bitter meditation, he sought his father; he made him acquainted with his feelings, but concealed from him his actual views, and dwelt on the misery of being thrown back in life, at a period when society seemed instinct with a spirit peculiarly active, and when so many openings were daily offered to the adventurous and the bold.

"Vivian," said Mr. Grey, "beware of endeavoring to become a great man in a hurry. One such attempt in ten thousand may succeed: these are fearful odds. Admirer as you are of Lord Bacon, you may perhaps remember a certain parable of his, called 'Memnon, or a youth too forward.' I hope you are not going to be one of those sons of Aurora, 'who, puffed up with the glittering show of vanity and ostentation, attempt actions above their strength.'

"You talk to me about the peculiarly active spirit of society; if the spirit of society be so peculiarly active, Mr. Vivian Grey should beware lest it outstrip him. Is neglecting to mature your mind, my boy, exactly the way to win the race? This is an age of unsettled opinions and contested principles; in the very measures of our administration, the speculative spirit of the present day is, to say the least, not impalpable. Nay, don't start, my dear fellow, and look the very Prosopopeia of Political Economy! I know exactly what you are going to say; but, if you please, we will leave Turgot and Galileo to Mr. Canning and the House of Commons, or your Cousin Hargrave and his Debating Society. However, jesting apart, get your hat, and walk with me as far as Evans's, where I have promised to look in, to see the Mazarin Bible, and we will talk this affair over as we go along.

"I am no bigot, you know, Vivian. I am not one of those

who wish to oppose the application of refined philosophy to the common business of life. We are, I hope, an improving race; there is room, I am sure, for great improvement, and the perfectibility of man is certainly a pretty dream. (How well that Union Club House comes out now, since they have made the opening); but, although we may have steam kitchens, human nature is, I imagine, much the same this moment, that we are walking in Pall Mall East, as it was some thousand years ago, when as wise men were walking on the banks of the Ilyssus. When our moral powers increase in proportion to our physical ones, then huzza for the perfectibility of man! and respectable, idle loungers like you and I, Vivian, may then have a chance of walking in the streets of London without having their heels trodden upon, a ceremony which I have this moment undergone. In the present day we are all studying science, and none of us are studying ourselves. This is not exactly the Socratic process; and as for the γνωθι σεαυτον of the more ancient Athenian, that principle is quite out of fashion in the nineteenth century (I believe that's the phrase). Self is the only person whom we know nothing about.

"But, my dear Vivian, as to the immediate point of our consideration. In my library, uninfluenced and uncontrolled by passion or by party, I can not but see that it is utterly impossible that all that we are wishing and striving for can take place, without some, without much evil. In ten years' time, perhaps, or less, the fever will have subsided, and in ten years' time, or less, your intellect will be matured. Now, my good sir, instead of talking about the active spirit of the age, and the opportunities offered to the adventurous and the bold, ought you not rather to congratulate yourself that a great change is effecting at a period of your life when you need not, individually, be subjected to the possibility of being injured by its operation; and when you are preparing your mind to take advantage of the system, when that system is matured and organized?

"As to your request, it assuredly is one of the most modest, and the most rational, that I have lately been favored with. Although I would much rather that any influence which I may exercise over your mind should be the effect of my advice as your friend than of my authority as your father, still I really feel it my duty, parentally, to protest against this crude proposition of yours. However, if you choose to lose a term or two, do. Don't blame me, you know, if afterward you repent it."

Here dashed by the gorgeous equipage of Mrs. Ormolu, the wife of a man who was working all the gold and silver mines in Christendom. "Ah! my dear Vivian," said Mr. Grey, "it is this which has turned all your brains. In this age every one is striving to make an immense fortune, and what is most terrific, at the same time a speedy one. This thirst for sudden wealth it is which engenders the extravagant conceptions, and fosters that wild spirit of speculation which is now stalking abroad; and which, like the Dæmon in Frankenstein, not only fearfully wanders over the whole wide face of nature, but grins in the imagined solitude of our secret chambers. Oh! my son, it is for the young men of the present day that I tremble; seduced by the temporary success of a few children of fortune, I observe that their minds recoil from the prospects which are held forth by the ordinary, and, mark me, by the only modes of acquiring property, fair trade, and honorable professions. It is for you and your companions that I fear. God grant that there may not be a moral as well as a political disorganization! God grant that our youth, the hope of our state, may not be lost to us! For, oh! my son, the wisest has said, 'He that maketh haste to be rich shall not be innocent.' Let us step into Clarke's and take an ice."

BOOK II

CHAPTER I

THE Marquess of Carabas started in life as the cadet of a noble family. The earl, his father, like the woodman in the fairy tale, was blessed with three sons: the first was an idiot, and was destined for the Coronet; the second was a man of business, and was educated for the Commons; the third was a roué, and was shipped to the Colonies.

The present Marquess, then the Honorable Sidney Lorraine, prospered in his political career. He was servile, and pompous, and indefatigable, and loquacious, so whispered the world: his friends hailed him as, at once, a courtier and a sage, a man of business and an orator. After reveling in his fair proportion of commissionerships, and under-secretaryships, and the rest of the milk and honey of the political Canaan, the apex of the pyramid of his ambition was at length visible, for Sidney Lorraine became President of a Board, and wriggled into the adytum of the cabinet.

At this moment his idiot brother died. To compensate for his loss of office, and to secure his votes, the Earl of Carabas was promoted in the peerage, and was presented with some magnificent office, meaning nothing; swelling with dignity, and void of duties. As years rolled on, various changes took place in the administration, of which his Lordship was once a component part; and the ministry, to their surprise, getting popular, found that the command of the Carabas interest was not of such vital importance to them as heretofore, and so his Lordship was voted a bore, and got shelved. Not that his Lordship was bereaved of his splendid office, or that anything occurred, indeed, by which the uninitiated might have been led to suppose that the beams of his Lordship's consequence were shorn; but the Marquess's secret applications at the Treasury were no longer listened to, and pert under-secretaries settled their cravats, and whispered "that the Carabas interest was gone by."

The noble Marquess was not insensible to his situation, for he was what the world calls ambitious; but the vigor of his faculties had vanished beneath the united influence of years and indolence and ill-humor; for his Lordship, to avoid ennui, had quarreled with his son, and then, having lost his only friend, had quarreled with himself.

Such was the distinguished individual who graced, one day at the latter end of the season of 18—, the classic board of Horace Grey, Esquire. The reader will, perhaps, be astonished that such a man as his Lordship should be the guest of such a man as our hero's father; but the truth is, the Marquess of Carabas had just been disappointed in an attempt on the chair of the President of the Royal Society, which, for want of something better to do, he was ambitious of filling, and this was a conciliatory visit to one of the most distinguished members of that body, and one who had voted against him with particular enthusiasm. The Marquess, still a politician, was now, as he imagined, securing his host's vote for a future St. Andrew's day.

The cuisine of Mr. Grey was superb; for although an enthusiastic advocate for the cultivation of the mind, he was an equally ardent supporter of the cultivation of the body. Indeed, the necessary dependence of the sanity of the one on the good keeping of the other was one of his favorite theories, and one which, this day, he was supporting with pleasant and facetious reasoning. His Lordship was delighted with his new friend, and still more delighted with his new friend's theory. The Marquess himself was, indeed, quite of the same opinion as Mr. Grey; for he never made a speech without previously taking a sandwich, and would have sunk under the estimates a thousand times, had it not been for the juicy friendship of the fruit of Portugal.

The guests were not numerous. A regius professor of Greek; an officer just escaped from Sockatoo; a man of science, and two M.P.'s with his Lordship; the host, and Mr. Vivian Grey, constituted the party. Oh, no! there were two others. There was a Mr. John Brown, a fashionable poet, and who, ashamed of his own name, published his melodies under the more euphonious and romantic title of "Clarence Devonshire"; and there was a Mr. Thomas Smith, a fashionable nov-

elist; that is to say, a person who occasionally publishes three
volumes, one-half of which contain the adventures of a young
gentleman in the country, and the other volume and a half the
adventures of the same young gentleman in the metropolis; a
sort of writer, whose constant tattle about beer and billiards,
and eating soup, and the horribility of "committing" puns, give
truly an admirable and accurate idea of the conversation of
the refined society of the refined metropolis of Great Britain.
These two last gentlemen were "pets" of Mrs. Grey.

The conversation may be conceived. Each person was of
course prepared with a certain quota of information, without
which no man in London is morally entitled to dine out; and
when the quota was expended, the amiable host took the burden upon his own shoulders, and endeavored, as the phrase
goes, to draw out his guests.

Oh, London dinners! empty artificial nothings! and that
beings can be found, and those too the flower of the land, who,
day after day, can act the same parts in the same dull, dreary
farce! The officer had discoursed sufficiently about "his intimate friend, the Soudan," and about the chain armor of the
Sockatoo cuirassiers; and one of the M.P.'s, who was in the
Guards, had been defeated in a ridiculous attempt to prove
that the breast-plates of the household troops of Great Britain
were superior to those of the household troops of Timtomtoo.
Mrs. Grey, to whose opinion both parties deferred, gave it in
favor of the Soudan. And the man of science had lectured
about a machine which might destroy fifteen square feet of
human beings in a second, and yet be carried in the waistcoat
pocket. And the classic, who, for a professor, was quite a man
of the world, had the latest news of the new Herculaneum
process, and was of opinion that, if they could but succeed in
unrolling a certain suspicious-looking scroll, we might be so
fortunate as to possess a minute treatise on, etc., etc., etc. In
short, all had said their say. There was a dead pause, and
Mrs. Grey looked at her husband, and rose.

How singular it is that when this move takes place every
one appears to be relieved, and yet every one of any experience must be quite aware that the dead bore work is only
about to commence. Howbeit, all filled their glasses, and the
peer, at the top of the table, began to talk politics. I am sure

I can not tell what the weighty subject was that was broached by the ex-minister; for I did not dine with Grey that day; and had I done so, I should have been equally ignorant, for I am a dull man, and always sleep at dinner. However, the subject was political, the claret flew round, and a stormy argument commenced. The Marquess was decidedly wrong, and was sadly badgered by the civil M.P. and the professor. The host, who was of no party, supported his guest as long as possible, and then left him to his fate. The military M.P. fled to the drawing-room to philander with Mrs. Grey; and the man of science and the African had already retired to the intellectual idiocy of a May Fair "At Home." The novelist was silent, for he was studying a scene; and the poet was absent, for he was musing a sonnet.

The Marquess, refuted, had recourse to contradiction, and was too acute a man to be insensible to the forlornness of his situation; when, at this moment, a voice proceeded from the end of the table from a young gentleman who had hitherto preserved a profound silence, but whose silence, if the company were to have judged from the tones of his voice, and the matter of his communication, did not altogether proceed from a want of confidence in his own abilities. "In my opinion," said Mr. Vivian Grey, as he sat lounging in his father's vacated seat, "in my opinion his Lordship has been misunderstood; and it is, as is generally the case, from a slight verbal misconception in the commencement of this argument that the whole of this difference arises."

The eyes of the Marquess sparkled, and the mouth of the Marquess was closed. His Lordship was delighted that his reputation might yet be saved; but as he was not perfectly acquainted in what manner that salvation was to be effected, he prudently left the battle to his youthful champion.

Mr. Vivian Grey proceeded with the utmost *sangfroid;* he commented upon expressions, split and subtilized words, insinuated opinions, and finally quoted a whole passage of Bolingbroke to prove that the opinion of the most noble the Marquess of Carabas was one of the soundest, wisest, and most convincing of opinions that ever was promulgated by mortal man. The tables were turned, the guests looked astounded, the Marquess settled his ruffles, and perpetually exclaimed, "Exactly what I meant!" and his opponents, full of wine and quite puzzled, gave in.

It was a rule with Vivian Grey never to advance any opinion as his own. He had been too deep a student of human nature not to be aware that the opinions of a boy of twenty, however sound, and however correct, stand but a poor chance of being adopted by his elder, though feebler, fellow-creatures. In attaining any end, it was therefore his system always to advance his opinion as that of some eminent and considered personage; and when, under the sanction of this name, the opinion or advice was entertained and listened to, Vivian Grey had no fear that he could prove its correctness and its expediency. He possessed also the singular faculty of being able to improvise quotations, that is, he could unpremeditatedly clothe his conceptions in language characteristic of the style of any particular author; and Vivian Grey was reputed in the world as having the most astonishing memory that ever existed; for there was scarcely a subject of discussion in which he did not gain the victory, by the great names he enlisted on his side of the argument. His father was aware of the existence of this dangerous faculty, and had often remonstrated with his son on the use of it. On the present occasion, when the buzz had somewhat subsided, Mr. Grey looked smiling to his son, and said, "Vivian, my dear, can you tell me in what work of Bolingbroke I can find the eloquent passage you have just quoted?" "Ask Mr. Hargrave, sir," replied the son, with perfect coolness; then, turning to the member, "You know, Mr. Hargrave, you are reputed the most profound political student in the House, and more intimately acquainted than any other person with the works of Bolingbroke."

Mr. Hargrave knew no such thing; but he was a weak man, and, seduced by the compliment, he was afraid to prove himself unworthy of it by confessing his ignorance of the passage.

Coffee was announced.

Vivian did not let the peer escape him in the drawing-room. He soon managed to enter into conversation with him; and certainly the Marquess of Carabas never found a more entertaining companion. Vivian discoursed on a new Venetian liqueur, and taught the Marquess how to mull Moselle, an oper-

ation of which the Marquess had never heard (as who has?);
and then the flood of anecdotes, and little innocent personali-
ties, and the compliments so exquisitely introduced that they
scarcely appeared to be compliments; and the voice so pleasant,
and conciliating, and the quotation from the Marquess's own
speech; and the wonderful art of which the Marquess was not
aware, by which, during all this time, the lively, chattering,
amusing, elegant conversationalist, so full of scandal, politics,
and cookery, did not so much appear to be Mr. Vivian Grey as
the Marquess of Carabas himself.

"Well, I must be gone," said the fascinated noble; "I really
have not felt in such spirits for some time; I almost fear I
have been vulgar enough to be amusing, eh! eh! eh! but you
young men are sad fellows, eh! eh! eh! Don't forget to call
on me; good-evening! and Mr. Vivian Grey! Mr. Vivian
Grey!" said his Lordship, returning, "you will not forget the
receipt you promised me for making tomahawk punch."

"Certainly not, my Lord," said the young man; "only it
must be invented first," thought Vivian, as he took up his
light to retire. "But never mind, never mind:

> Chapeau bas! chapeau bas!
> Glorie au Marquis de Carabas!!"

CHAPTER II

A FEW days after the dinner at Mr. Grey's, as the Marquess of Carabas was sitting in his library, and sighing,
in the fulness of his ennui, as he looked on his large library
table, once triply covered with official communications, now
thinly besprinkled with a stray parliamentary paper or two,
his steward's accounts, and a few letters from some grumbling
tenants, Mr. Vivian Grey was announced.

"I fear I am intruding on your Lordship, but I really could
not refrain from bringing you the receipt I promised."

"Most happy to see ye, most happy to see ye."

"This is exactly the correct receipt, my Lord. TO EVERY
TWO BOTTLES OF STILL CHAMPAGNE, ONE PINT OF CURAÇOA."
The Peer's eyes glistened, and his companion proceeded: "ONE

PINT OF CURAÇOA; CATCH THE AROMA OF A POUND OF GREEN
TEA, AND DASH THE WHOLE WITH GLENLIVET."

"Splendid!" ejaculated the Marquess.

"The nice point, however, which it is impossible to define
in a receipt, is catching the aroma. What sort of a genius
is your Lordship's chef?"

"First-rate! Laporte *is* a genius."

"Well, my Lord! I shall be most happy to superintend the
first concoction for you; and remember particularly," said
Vivian, rising, "remember it must be iced."

"Certainly, my dear fellow; but pray don't think of going
yet."

"I am very sorry, my Lord; but such a pressure of en-
gagements; your Lordship's kindness is so great, and, really,
I fear that at this moment especially your Lordship can
scarcely be in a humor for my trifling."

"Why this moment especially, Mr. Vivian Grey?"

"Oh, my Lord! I am perfectly aware of your Lordship's
talents for business; but still I had conceived that the delicate
situation in which your Lordship is now placed, requiring
such anxious attention, such—"

"Delicate situation! anxious attention! Why, man! you
speak riddles. I certainly have a great deal of business to
transact: people are so obstinate, or so foolish, they will consult me, certainly; and certainly I feel it my duty, Mr. Vivian
Grey; I feel it the duty, sir, of every Peer in this happy country
(here his Lordship got parliamentary) : yes, sir, I feel it due
to my character, to my family, to, to, to assist with my advice
all those who think fit to consult me." Splendid peroration!

"Oh, my Lord!" carelessly remarked Vivian, "I thought it
was a mere *on dit.*"

"Thought what, my dear sir? you really quite perplex me."

"I mean to say, my lord; I, I thought it was impossible the
overtures had been made."

"Overtures, Mr. Vivian Grey?"

"Yes, my Lord! Overtures; has not your Lordship seen
the 'Post'? But I knew it was impossible; I said so, I—"

"Said what, Mr. Vivian Grey?"

"Said that the whole paragraph was unfounded."

"Paragraph! what paragraph," and his Lordship rose and

rang the library bell with vehemence: "Sadler, bring me the 'Morning Post.'"

The servant entered with the paper. Mr. Vivian Grey seized it from his hands before it reached the Marquess, and glancing his eye over it with the rapidity of lightning, doubled up the sheet in a convenient readable form, and pushing it into his Lordship's hands, exclaimed, "There, my Lord! there, that will explain all."

His Lordship read:

"We are informed that some alteration in the composition of the present administration is in contemplation; Lord Past Century, it is said, will retire; Mr. Liberal Principles will have the ——; and Mr. Charlatan Gas the ——. A noble Peer, whose practiced talents have already benefited the nation, and who, on vacating his seat in the Cabinet, was elevated in the Peerage, is reported as having had certain overtures made him, the nature of which may be conceived, but which, under present circumstances, it would be indelicate in us to hint at."

It would have been impossible for a hawk to watch its quarry with eyes of more fixed and anxious earnestness than did Vivian Grey the Marquess of Carabas, as his Lordship's eyes wandered over the paragraph. Vivian drew his chair close to the table opposite to the Marquess, and when the paragraph was read their eyes met.

"Utterly untrue," whispered the Peer, with an agitated voice, and with a countenance which, for a moment, seemed intellectual. "But why Mr. Vivian Grey should deem the fact of such overtures having been made 'impossible,' I confess, astonishes me."

"Impossible, my Lord!"

"Ay, Mr. Grey, impossible, that was your word."

"Oh, my Lord! what should I know about these matters?"

"Nay, nay, Mr. Grey, something must have been floating in your mind: why impossible, why impossible? Did your father think so?"

"My father! Oh! no, he never thinks about these matters; ours is not a political family; I am not sure that he ever looks at a newspaper."

"But, my dear Mr. Grey, you would not have used the word without some meaning. Why did you think it impossible? impossible is such a peculiar word." And here the Marquess looked up with great earnestness to a portrait of himself, which hung over the fireplace. It was one of Sir Thomas's happiest efforts; but it was not the happiness of the likeness, or the beauty of the painting, which now attracted his Lordship's attention; he thought only of the costume in which he appeared in that portrait: the court dress of a Cabinet Minister. "Impossible, Mr. Grey, you must confess, is a very peculiar word," reiterated his Lordship.

"I said impossible, my Lord, because I did conceive that, had your Lordship been of a disposition to which such overtures might have been made with any probability of success, the Marquess of Carabas would have been in a situation which would have precluded the possibility of those overtures being made at all."

"Hah!" and the Marquess nearly started from his seat.

"Yes, my Lord, I am a young, an inexperienced young man, ignorant of the world's ways; doubtless I was wrong, but I have much to learn," and his voice faltered; "but I did conceive that, having power at his command, the Marquess of Carabas did not exercise it, merely because he despised it: but what should I know of such matters, my Lord?"

"Is power a thing so easily to be despised, young man?" asked the Marquess. His eye rested on a vote of thanks from the "Merchants and Bankers of London to the Right Honorable Sydney Lorraine, President," etc., etc., etc., which, splendidly emblazoned, and gilt, and framed, and glazed, was suspended opposite the President's portrait.

"Oh, no! my Lord, you mistake me," eagerly burst forth Vivian. "I am no cold-blooded philosopher that would despise that for which, in my opinion, men, real men, should alone exist. Power! Oh! what sleepless nights, what days of hot anxiety! what exertions of mind and body! what travail! what hatred! what fierce encounters! what dangers of all possible kinds, would I not endure with a joyous spirit to gain it! But such, my Lord, I thought were feelings peculiar to inexperienced young men; and seeing you, my Lord, so situated that you might command all and everything, and yet living as you do, I was naturally led to believe that the object of my adoration was a vain glittering bawble, of which those who could possess it knew the utter worthlessness."

The Peer sat in a musing mood, playing the Devil's tattoo on the library table; at last he raised his eyes, and said in a low whisper, "Are you so certain that I can command all and everything?"

"All and everything! did I say all and everything? Really, my Lord, you scan my expressions so critically! but I see your Lordship is smiling at my boyish nonsense! and really I feel that I have already wasted too much of your Lordship's valuable time, and displayed too much of my own ignorance."

"My dear sir! I am not aware that I was smiling."

"Oh! your Lordship is so very kind."

"But, my dear sir! you are really laboring under a great mistake. I am desirous, I am particularly desirous, of having your opinion upon this subject."

"My opinion, my Lord! what should my opinion be but an echo of the circle in which I live, but a faithful representation of the feelings of general society?"

"And, Mr. Grey, I should be glad to know what can possibly be more interesting to me than a faithful representation of the feelings of general society on this subject?"

"The many, my Lord, are not always right."

"Mr. Grey, the many are not often wrong. Come, my dear sir, do me the favor of being frank, and let me know why the public is of opinion that all and everything are in my power, for such, after all, were your words."

"If I did use them, my Lord, it was because I was thinking, as I often do, what, after all, in this country is public life? Is it not a race in which the swiftest must surely win the prize; and is not that prize power? Has not your Lordship treasure? There is your moral steam which can work the world. Has not your Lordship treasure's most splendid consequence, pure blood and aristocratic influence? The Millionaire has in his possession the seeds of everything, but he must wait for half a century till his descendant finds himself in your Lordship's state; till he is yclept noble, and then he starts fair in the grand course. All these advantages your Lordship has apparently at hand, with the additional advantage (and one, oh! how great!) of having already proved to your country that you know how to rule."

There was a dead silence, which at length the Marquess

broke: "There is much in what you say; but I can not conceal it from myself, I have no wish to conceal it from you; I am not what I was." Oh, ambition! art thou the parent of truth?

"Ah! my Lord!" eagerly rejoined Vivian, "here is the terrible error into which you great statesmen have always fallen. Think you not that intellect is as much a purchasable article as fine parks and fair castles? With your Lordship's tried and splendid talents, everything might be done; but, in my opinion, if, instead of a practiced, an experienced, and wary Statesman, I was now addressing an idiot Earl, I should not see that the great end might not equally be consummated."

"Say you so, my merry man, and how?"

"Why, my Lord: but, but I feel that I am trespassing on your Lordship's time, otherwise I think I could show why society is of opinion that your Lordship can do all and everything; how, indeed, your Lordship might, in a very short time, be Prime Minister."

"No, Mr. Grey; this conversation must be finished. I will just give orders that we may not be disturbed, and then we shall proceed immediately. Come, now! your manner takes me, and we shall converse in the spirit of the most perfect confidence."

Here, as the Marquess settled at the same time his chair and his countenance, and looked as anxious as if Majesty itself were consulting him on the formation of a ministry, in burst the Marchioness, notwithstanding all the remonstrances, entreaties, threats, and supplications of Mr. Sadler.

Her Ladyship had been what they style a splendid woman; that was now past, although, with the aid of cashmeres, diamonds, and turbans, her general appearance was still striking. Her Ladyship was not remarkable for anything save a correct taste for poodles, parrots, and bijouterie, and a proper admiration of Theodore Hook and John Bull.

"Oh! Marquess," exclaimed her Ladyship, and a favorite green parrot, which came flying in after its accustomed perch, her Ladyship's left shoulder, shrieked at the same time in concert. "Oh! Marquess, my poor Julie! You know we have noticed how nervous she has been for some days past, and I had just given her a saucer of arrowroot and milk, and she seemed a little easier, and I said to Miss Graves, 'I really do think she is a leetle better,' and Miss Graves said, 'Yes, my Lady, I hope she is'; when just as we flattered ourselves that the dear little creature was enjoying a quiet sleep, Miss Graves called out, 'Oh, my Lady! my Lady! Julie's in a fit!' and when I turned round she was lying on her back, kicking, with her eyes shut." And here the Marchioness detected Mr. Grey, and gave him as sublime a stare as might be expected from a lady patroness of Almack's.

"The Marchioness, Mr. Vivian Grey, my love, I assure you we are engaged in a most important, a most—"

"Oh! I would not disturb you for the world, only if you will just tell me what you think ought to be done; leeches, or a warm bath; or shall I send for Doctor Blue Pill?"

The Marquess looked a little annoyed, as if he wished her Ladyship in her own room again. He was almost meditating a gentle reprimand, vexed that his grave young friend should have witnessed this frivolous intrusion, when that accomplished stripling, to the astonishment of the future minister, immediately recommended "the warm bath," and then lectured, with equal rapidity and erudition, on dogs and their diseases in general.

The Marchioness retired, "easier in her mind about Julie than she had been for some days," as Vivian assured her "that it was not apoplexy, but only the first symptom of an epidemic." And as she retired, she murmured her gratitude gracefully to Julie's young physician.

"Now, Mr. Grey," said his Lordship, endeavoring to recover his dignity, "we were discussing the public sentiments you know on a certain point, when this unfortunate interruption—"

Vivian had not much difficulty in collecting his ideas, and he proceeded, not as displeased as his Lordship with the domestic scene.

"I need not remind your Lordship that the two great parties into which this State is divided are apparently very unequally proportioned. Your Lordship well knows how the party to which your Lordship is said to belong: your Lordship knows, I imagine, how that is constituted. We have nothing to do with the other. My Lord, I must speak out. No thinking man—and such, I trust, Vivian Grey is—no thinking man can for a moment suppose, that your Lordship's heart is very warm in the cause of a party which, for I will not mince my words, has betrayed you. How is it, it is asked by thinking men, how is it that the Marquess of Carabas is the tool of a faction?"

The Marquess breathed aloud, "They say so, do they?"

"Why, my Lord, listen even to your servants in your own hall, need I say more? How, then! is this opinion true? Let us look to your conduct to the party to which you are said to belong. Your votes are theirs, your influence is theirs; and for all this, what return, my Lord Marquess, what return? My Lord, I am not rash enough to suppose that your Lordship, alone and unsupported, can make yourself the arbiter of this country's destinies. It would be ridiculous to entertain such an idea for a second. The existence of such a man would not be endured by the nation for a second. But, my Lord, union is strength. Nay, my Lord, start not; I am not going to advise you to throw yourself into the arms of opposition; leave such advice for greenhorns. I am not going to adopt a line of conduct which would, for a moment, compromise the consistency of your high character; leave such advice for fools. My Lord, it is to preserve your consistency, it is to vindicate your high character, it is to make the Marquess of Carabas perform the duties which society requires from him, that I, Vivian Grey, a member of that society, and a humble friend of your Lordship, speak so boldly."

"My friend," said the agitated Peer, "you can not speak too boldly. My mind opens to you. I have felt, I have long felt, that I was not what I ought to be, that I was not what society requires me to be; but where is your remedy? what is the line of conduct that I should pursue?"

"The remedy, my Lord! I never conceived, for a moment, that there was any doubt of the existence of means to attain all and everything. I think that was your Lordship's phrase. I only hesitated as to the existence of the inclination on the part of your Lordship."

"You can not doubt it now," said the Peer, in a low voice; and then his Lordship looked anxiously round the room, as if he feared that there had been some mysterious witness to his whisper.

"My Lord," said Vivian, and he drew his chair close to the
Marquess, "the plan is shortly this. There are others in a similar situation with yourself. All thinking men know, your
Lordship knows still better, that there are others equally influential, equally ill-treated. How is it that I see no concert
among these individuals? How is it that, jealous of each
other, or each trusting that he may ultimately prove an exception to the system of which he is a victim; how is it, I say,
that you look with cold hearts on each other's situation? My
Lord Marquess, it is at the head of these that I would place
you; it is these that I would have act with you; and this is
the union which is strength."

"You are right, you are right: there is Courtown, but we
do not speak; there is Beaconsfield, but we are not intimate;
but much might be done."

"My Lord, you must not be daunted at a few difficulties,
or at a little exertion. But as for Courtown, or Beaconsfield,
or fifty other offended men, if it can be shown to them that
their interest is to be your Lordship's friend, trust me that ere
six months are over they will have pledged their troth. Leave
all this to me, give me your Lordship's name," said Vivian,
whispering most earnestly in the Marquess's ear, and laying
his hand upon his Lordship's arm; "give me your Lordship's
name and your Lordship's influence, and I will take upon myself the whole organization of the Carabas party."

"The Carabas party! Ah! we must think more of this."

The Marquess's eyes smiled with triumph, as he shook
Vivian cordially by the hand, and begged him to call upon
him on the morrow.

CHAPTER III

THE intercourse between the Marquess and Vivian after
this interview was constant. No dinner-party was
thought perfect at Carabas House without the presence of the
young gentleman; and as the Marchioness was delighted with
the perpetual presence of an individual whom she could always
consult about Julie, there was apparently no domestic obstacle
to Vivian's remaining in high favor.

The Earl of Eglamour, the only child in whom were concentrated all the hopes of the illustrious House of Lorraine, was in Italy. The only remaining member of the domestic circle who was wanting was the Honorable Mrs. Felix Lorraine, the wife of the Marquess's younger brother. This lady, exhausted by the gayety of the season, had left town somewhat earlier than she usually did, and was inhaling fresh air, and studying botany, at the magnificent seat of the Carabas family, Chateau Desir, at which splendid place Vivian was to pass the summer.

In the meantime all was sunshine with Vivian Grey. His noble friend and himself were in perpetual converse, and constantly engaged in deep consultation. As yet, the world knew nothing, except that, according to the Marquess of Carabas, "Vivian Grey was the most astonishingly clever and prodigiously accomplished fellow that ever breathed"; and, as the Marquess always added, "resembled himself very much when he was young."

But it must not be supposed that Vivian was to all the world the fascinating creature that he was to the Marquess of Carabas. Many complained that he was reserved, silent, satirical, and haughty. But the truth was, Vivian Grey often asked himself, "Who is to be my enemy to-morrow?" He was too cunning a master of the human mind not to be aware of the quicksands upon which all greenhorns strike; he knew too well the danger of unnecessary intimacy. A smile for a friend, and a sneer for the world, is the way to govern mankind, and such was the motto of Vivian Grey.

CHAPTER IV

HOW shall we describe Chateau Desir, that place fit for all princes? In the midst of a park of great extent, and eminent for scenery as varied as might please nature's most capricious lover; in the midst of green lawns and deep winding glens, and cooling streams, and wild forest, and soft woodland, there was gradually formed an elevation, on which was situate a mansion of great size, and of that bastard but pictu-

resque style of architecture called the Italian Gothic. The
date of its erection was about the middle of the sixteenth century. You entered by a noble gateway, in which the pointed
style still predominated, but in various parts of which, the
Ionic column, and the prominent keystone, and other creations
of Roman architecture, intermingled with the expiring Gothic,
into a large quadrangle, to which the square casement windows, and the triangular pediments or gable ends supplying
the place of battlements, gave a varied and Italian feature. In
the centre of the court, from a vast marble basin, the rim of
which was enriched by a splendidly sculptured lotus border,
rose a marble group representing Amphitrite with her marine
attendants, whose sounding shells and coral sceptres sent forth
their subject element in sparkling showers. This work, the
chef-d'œuvre of a celebrated artist of Vicenza, had been purchased by Valerian, first Lord Carabas, who, having spent the
greater part of his life as the representative of his monarch
at the Ducal Court of Venice, at length returned to his native
country, and in the creation of Chateau Desir endeavored to
find some consolation for the loss of his beautiful villa on the
banks of the Adige.

Over the gateway there rose a turreted tower, the small
square window of which, notwithstanding its stout stanchions,
illumined the muniment room of the House of Carabas. In
the spandrils of the gateway and in many other parts of the
building might be seen the arms of the family; while the tall
twisted stocks of chimneys, which appeared to spring from all
parts of the roof, were carved and built in such curious and
quaint devices that they were rather an ornament than an
excrescence. When you entered the quadrangle, you found
one side solely occupied by the old hall, the huge carved rafters
of whose oak roof rested on corbels of the family supporters
against the walls. Those walls were of stone, but covered
half-way from the ground with a paneling of curiously carved
oak; whence were suspended, in massy frames, the family portraits, painted by Dutch and Italian artists. Near the dais,
or upper part of the hall, there projected an oriel window,
which, as you beheld, you scarcely knew what most to admire,
the radiancy of its painted panes or the fantastic richness of
Gothic ornament, which was profusely lavished in every part

of its masonry. Here too the Gothic pendant and the Gothic fan-work were intermingled with the Italian arabesques, which, at the time of the building of the Chateau, had been recently introduced into England by Hans Holbein and John of Padua.

How wild and fanciful are those ancient arabesques! Here at Chateau Desir, in the paneling of the old hall, might you see fantastic scrolls separated by bodies ending in termini, and whose heads supported the Ionic volute, while the arch, which appeared to spring from these capitals, had, for a keystone, heads more monstrous than those of the fabled animals of Ctesias; or so ludicrous, that you forgot the classic griffin in the grotesque conception of the Italian artist. Here was a gibbering monkey, there a grinning pulcinello; now you viewed a chattering devil, which might have figured in the "Temptation of St. Anthony;" and now a mournful, mystic, bearded countenance, which might have flitted in the back scene of a "Witches' Sabbath."

A long gallery wound through the upper story of two other sides of the quadrangle, and beneath were the show suite of apartments with a sight of which the admiring eyes of curious tourists were occasionally delighted.

The gray stone walls of this antique edifice were, in many places, thickly covered with ivy and other parasitical plants, the deep green of whose verdure beautifully contrasted with the scarlet glories of the pyrus japonica, which gracefully clustered round the windows of the lower chambers. The mansion itself was immediately surrounded by numerous ancient forest trees. There was the elm with its rich branches bending down like clustering grapes; there was the wide spreading oak with its roots fantastically gnarled; there was the ash, with its smooth bark and elegant leaf; and the silver beech, and the gracile birch; and the dark fir, affording with its rough foliage a contrast to the trunks of its more beautiful companions, or shooting far above their branches, with the spirit of freedom worthy of a rough child of the mountains.

Around the Castle were extensive pleasure-grounds, which realized the romance of the "Gardens of Verulam." And truly, as you wandered through their enchanting paths there seemed no end to their various beauties, and no exhaustion of their perpetual novelty. Green retreats succeeded to winding walks; from the shady berçeau you vaulted on the noble terrace; and if, for an instant, you felt wearied by treading the velvet lawn, you might rest in a mossy cell, while your mind was soothed by the soft music of falling waters. Now your curious eyes were greeted by Oriental animals, basking in a sunny paddock; and when you turned from the white-footed antelope and the dark-eyed gazelle, you viewed an aviary of such extent, that within its trellised walls the imprisoned songsters could build, in the free branches of a tree, their natural nests.

"O fair scene!" thought Vivian Grey, as he approached, on a fine summer's afternoon, the splendid Chateau. "O fair scene! doubly fair to those who quit for thee the thronged and agitated city. And can it be that those who exist within this enchanted domain can think of anything but sweet air, and do aught but revel in the breath of perfumed flowers?" And here he gained the garden-gate: so he stopped his soliloquy, and gave his horse to his groom.

CHAPTER V

THE Marquess had preceded Vivian in his arrival about three or four days, and of course, to use the common phrase, the establishment "was quite settled." It was, indeed, to avoid the possibility of witnessing the domestic arrangements of a nobleman in any other point of view save that of perfection, that Vivian had declined accompanying his noble friend to the Chateau. Mr. Grey, junior, was an epicurean, and all epicureans will quite agree with me that his conduct on this head was extremely wise. I am not very nice myself about these matters; but there are, we all know, a thousand little things that go wrong on the arrivals of even the best regulated families; and to mention no others, for any rational being voluntarily to encounter the awful gaping of an English family, who have traveled one hundred miles in ten successive hours, appears to me to be little short of madness.

"Grey, my boy, quite happy to see ye! later than I expected; first bell rings in five minutes. Sadler will show you your room. Your father, I hope, quite well?"

Such was the salutation of the Marquess; and Vivian accordingly retired to arrange his toilet.

The first bell rang, and the second bell rang, and Vivian was seated at the dinner-table. He bowed to the Marchioness, and asked after her poodle, and gazed with some little curiosity at the vacant chair opposite him.

"Mrs. Felix Lorraine, Mr. Vivian Grey," said the Marquess, as a lady entered the room.

Now, although we are of those historians who are of opinion that the nature of the personages they celebrate should be developed rather by a recital of their conduct than by a set character on their introduction, it is nevertheless incumbent upon us to devote a few lines to the lady who has just entered, which the reader will be as good as to get through, while she is accepting an offer of some white soup; by this means he will lose none of the conversation.

The Honorable Felix Lorraine we have before described as a roué. After having passed through a career with tolerable credit, which would have blasted the character of any vulgar personage, Felix Lorraine ended by pigeoning a young nobleman, whom, for that purpose, he had made his intimate friend. The affair got wind; after due examination, was proclaimed "too bad," and the guilty personage was visited with the heaviest vengeance of modern society; he was expelled his club. By this unfortunate exposure, Mr. Felix Lorraine was obliged to give up a match, which was on the tapis, with the celebrated Miss Mexico, on whose million he had determined to set up a character and a chariot, and at the same time pension his mistress, and subscribe to the Society for the Suppression of Vice. Felix left England for the Continent, and in due time was made drum-major at Barbadoes, or fiscal at Ceylon, or something of that kind. While he loitered in Europe, he made a conquest of the heart of the daughter of some German baron, and after six weeks passed in the most affectionate manner, the happy couple performing their respective duties with perfect propriety, Felix left Germany for his colonial appointment, and also left his lady behind him.

Mr. Lorraine had duly and dutifully informed his family of his marriage; and they, as amiably and affectionately, had never answered his letters, which he never expected they would. Profiting by their example, he never answered his wife's, who, in due time, to the horror of the Marquess, landed in England, and claimed the protection of her "beloved husband's family." The Marquess vowed he would never see her; the lady, however, one morning gained admittance, and from that moment she had never quitted her brother-in-law's roof, and not only had never quitted it, but now made the greatest favor of her staying.

The extraordinary influence which Mrs. Felix Lorraine possessed was certainly not owing to her beauty, for the lady opposite Vivian Grey had apparently no claims to admiration on the score of her personal qualifications. Her complexion was bad and her features were indifferent, and these characteristics were not rendered less uninterestingly conspicuous by, what makes an otherwise ugly woman quite the reverse, namely, a pair of expressive eyes; for certainly this epithet could not be applied to those of Mrs. Felix Lorraine, which gazed in all the vacancy of German listlessness.

The lady did bow to Mr. Grey, and that was all; and then she negligently spooned her soup, and then, after much parade, sent it away untouched. Vivian was not under the necessity of paying any immediate courtesy to his opposite neighbor, whose silence, he perceived, was for the nonce, and consequently for him. But the day was hot, and Vivian had been fatigued by his ride, and the Marquess's champagne was excellent; and so, at last, the floodgates of his speech burst, and talk he did. He complimented her Ladyship's poodle, quoted German to Mrs. Felix Lorraine, and taught the Marquess to eat cabinet pudding with curaçoa sauce (a custom which, by the bye, I recommend to all); and then his stories, his scandal, and his sentiment; stories for the Marquess, scandal for the Marchioness, and sentiment for the Marquess's sister! That lady, who began to find out her man, had no mind to be longer silent, and although a perfect mistress of the English language, began to articulate a horrible patois, that she might not be mistaken for an Englishwoman, an occurrence which she particularly dreaded. But now came her punishment, for Vivian saw the effect which he had produced on Mrs. Felix Lorraine, and that Mrs. Felix Lorraine now wished to produce a corresponding effect upon him, and this he was determined she should not do;

so new stories followed, and new compliments ensued, and finally he anticipated her sentences, and sometimes her thoughts. The lady sat silent and admiring! At last the important meal was finished, and the time came when good dull English dames retire; but of this habit Mrs. Felix Lorraine did not approve, and although she had not yet prevailed upon Lady Carabas to adopt her ideas on field-days, still, when alone, the good-natured Marchioness had given in, and to save herself from hearing the din of male voices at a time at which during her whole life she had been unaccustomed to them, the Marchioness of Carabas dozed. Her worthy spouse, who was prevented, by the presence of Mrs. Felix Lorraine, from talking politics with Vivian, passed the bottle pretty briskly, and then, conjecturing that "from the sunset we should have a fine day to-morrow," fell back in his easy-chair, and snored.

Mrs. Felix Lorraine looked at her noble relatives, and shrugged up her shoulders with an air which baffleth all description. "Mr. Grey, I congratulate you on this hospitable reception; you see we treat you quite *en famille*. Come! 'tis a fine evening; you have seen as yet but little of Chateau Desir: we may as well enjoy the fine air on the terrace."

CHAPTER VI

"YOU must know, Mr. Grey, that this is my favorite walk, and I therefore expect that it will be yours."

"It can not indeed fail to be such, the favorite as it alike is of nature and Mrs. Felix Lorraine."

"On my word, a very pretty sentence! And who taught you, young sir, to bandy words so fairly?"

"I never can open my mouth, except in the presence of a woman," observed Vivian, with impudent mendacity; and he looked interesting and innocent.

"Indeed! And what do you know about such wicked work as talking to women?" and here Mrs. Felix Lorraine imitated Vivian's sentimental voice. "Do you know," she continued, "I feel quite happy that you have come down here; I begin to think that we shall be great friends."

"Nothing appears to me more evident," said Vivian.

"How delicious is friendship," exclaimed Mrs. Felix Lorraine; "delightful sentiment that prevents life from being a curse! Have you a friend, Mr. Vivian Grey?"

"Before I answer that question, I should like to know what meaning Mrs. Felix Lorraine attaches to that important monosyllable, friend."

"Oh, you want a definition. I hate definitions; and of all the definitions in the world, the one I have been most unfortunate in has been a definition of friendship; I might say" (and here her voice sank), "I might say of all the sentiments in the world, friendship is the one which has been most fatal to me; but I must not inoculate you with my bad spirits; bad spirits are not for young blood like yours, leave them to old persons like myself."

"Old!" said Vivian, in a proper tone of surprise.

"Old! ay, old; how old do you think I am?"

"You may have seen twenty summers," gallantly conjectured Vivian.

The lady looked pleased, and almost insinuated that she had seen one or two more.

"A clever woman," thought Vivian, "but vain; I hardly know what to think of her."

"Mr. Grey, I fear you find me in bad spirits to-day; but alas! I—I have cause. Although we see each other to-day for the first time, yet there is something in your manner, something in the expression of your eyes, that make me believe my happiness is not altogether a matter of indifference to you." These words, uttered in one of the sweetest voices by which ever human being was fascinated, were slowly and deliberately spoken, as if it were intended that they should rest on the ear of the object to whom they were addressed.

"My dearest madam! it is impossible that I can have but one sentiment with regard to you, that of—"

"Of what, Mr. Grey?"

"Of solicitude for your welfare."

The lady gently took the arm of the young man, and then with an agitated voice, and a troubled spirit, dwelt upon the unhappiness of her lot, and the cruelty of her fortunes. Her husband's indifference was the sorrowful theme of her lamentations; and she ended by asking Mr. Vivian Grey's advice as to the line of conduct which she should pursue with regard to him; first duly informing Vivian that this was the only time and he the only person to whom this subject had been ever mentioned.

"And why should I mention it here, and to whom? The Marquess is the best of men, but—" and here she looked up in Vivian's face, and spoke volumes; "and the Marchioness is the most amiable of women: at least, I suppose her lap-dog thinks so."

The advice of Vivian was concise. He sent the husband to the devil in two seconds, and insisted upon the wife's not thinking of him for another moment; and then the lady dried her eyes, and promised to do her best.

"And now," said Mrs. Felix Lorraine, "I must talk about your own affairs. I think your plan excellent."

"Plan, madam!"

"Yes, plan, sir! the Marquess has told me all. I have no head for politics, Mr. Grey; but if I can not assist you in managing the nation, I perhaps may in managing the family, and my services are at your command. Believe me, you will have enough to do: there, I pledge you my troth. Do you think it a pretty hand?"

Vivian did think it a very pretty hand, and he performed due courtesies in a becoming style.

"And now, good even to you," said the lady; "this little gate leads to my apartments. You will have no difficulty in finding your way back." So saying, she disappeared.

CHAPTER VII

THE first week at Chateau Desir passed pleasantly enough. Vivian's morning was amply occupied in maturing with the Marquess the grand principles of the new political system: in weighing interests, in balancing connections, and settling "what side was to be taken on the great questions?" Oh, politics, thou splendid juggle! The whole business, although so magnificent in its result, appeared very easy to the two counselors, for it was one of the first principles of Mr. Vivian Grey that everything was possible. Men did fail in life, to be sure, and after all, very little was done by the generality; but still all these failures, and all this inefficiency, might be traced to a want of physical and mental courage. Some men were bold in their conceptions, and splendid heads at a grand system, but then, when the day of battle came, they turned out very cowards; while others, who had nerve enough to stand the brunt of the hottest fire, were utterly ignorant of military tactics, and fell before the destroyer, like the brave untutored Indians before the civilized European. Now Vivian Grey was conscious that there was at least one person in the world who was no craven either in body or in mind, and so he had long come to the comfortable conclusion that it was impossible that his career could be anything but the most brilliant. And truly, employed as he now was, with a peer of the realm, in a solemn consultation on that realm's most important interests, at a time when creatures of his age were moping in Halls and Colleges, is it to be wondered at that he began to imagine that his theory was borne out by experience and by fact? Not that it must be supposed, even for a moment, that Vivian Grey was what the world calls conceited. Oh, no! he knew the measure of his own mind, and had fathomed the depth of his powers with equal skill and impartiality; but in the process he could not but feel that he could conceive much, and dare do more.

We said the first week at Chateau Desir passed pleasantly enough; and so it did, for Vivian's soul reveled in the morning councils on his future fortunes with as much eager joy as a young courser tries the turf, preliminary to running for the plate. And then, in the evening, were moonlit walks with Mrs. Felix Lorraine! And then the lady abused England so prettily, and initiated her companion in all the secrets of German Courts, and sang beautiful French songs, and told the legends of her native land in such an interesting, semi-serious tone that Vivian almost imagined that she believed them; and then she would take him beside the luminous lake in the park, and vow it looked just like the dark-blue Rhine! and then she remembered Germany, and grew sad, and abused her husband; and then she taught Vivian the guitar and some other fooleries besides.

CHAPTER VIII

THE second week of Vivian's visit had come round, and the flag waved proudly on the proud tower of Chateau Desir, indicating to the admiring country that the most noble Sidney, Marquess of Carabas, held public days twice a week at his grand castle. And now came the neighboring peer, full of grace and gravity, and the mellow baronet, with his hearty laugh, and the jolly country squire, and the middling gentry, and the jobbing attorney, and the flourishing country surveyor; some honoring by their presence, some who felt the obligation equal, and others bending before the noble host, as if paying him adoration was almost an equal pleasure with that of guzzling his venison pasties and quaffing his bright wines.

Independently of all these periodical visitors, the house was full of permanent ones. There were the Viscount and Viscountess Courtown and their three daughters, and Lord and Lady Beaconsfield and their three sons, and Sir Berdmore and Lady Scrope, and Colonel Delmington of the Guards, and Lady Louisa Manvers and her daughter Julia. Lady Louisa was the only sister of the Marquess, a widow, proud and penniless.

To all these distinguished personages Vivian was introduced by the Marquess as "a monstrous clever young man, and his Lordship's most particular friend," and then the noble Carabas left the game in his young friend's hands.

And right well Vivian did his duty. In a week's time it would have been hard to decide with whom of the family of the Courtowns Vivian was the greatest favorite. He rode with the Viscount, who was a good horseman, and was driven by his Lady, who was a good whip; and when he had sufficiently admired the *tout ensemble* of her Ladyship's pony phaeton, he intrusted her, "in confidence," with some ideas of his own about martingales, a subject which he assured her

3   Vol. 1

Ladyship "had been the object of his mature consideration." The three honorable Misses were the most difficult part of the business; but he talked sentiment with the first, sketched with the second, and romped with the third.

Ere the Beaconsfields could be jealous of the influence of the Courtowns, Mr. Vivian Grey had promised his Lordship, who was a collector of medals, a unique which had never yet been heard of: and her Ladyship, who was a collector of autographs, the private letters of every man of genius that ever had been heard of. In this division of the Carabas guests he was not bored with a family; for sons he always made it a rule to cut dead; they are the members of a family who, on an average, are generally very uninfluential, for, on an average, they are fools enough to think it very knowing to be very disagreeable. So the wise man but little loves them, but woe to the fool who neglects the daughters!

Sir Berdmore Scrope Vivian found a more unmanageable personage; for the baronet was confoundedly shrewd, and without a particle of sentiment in his composition. It was a great thing, however, to gain him; for Sir Berdmore was a leading country gentleman, and having quarreled with Ministers about the corn laws, had been counted disaffected ever since. The baronet, however, although a bold man to the world, was luckily henpecked; so Vivian made love to the wife and secured the husband.

CHAPTER IX

I THINK that Julia Manvers was really the most beautiful creature that ever smiled in this fair world. Such a symmetrically formed shape, such perfect features, such a radiant complexion, such luxuriant auburn hair, and such blue eyes, lighted up by a smile of such mind and meaning, have seldom blessed the gaze of admiring man! Vivian Grey, fresh as he was, was not exactly the creature to lose his heart very speedily. He looked upon marriage as a comedy in which, sooner or later, he was, as a well-paid actor, to play his part; and could it have advanced his views one jot he would have married the Princess Caraboo to-morrow. But of all wives in the world, a young and handsome one was that which he most dreaded; and how a statesman who was wedded to a beautiful woman could possibly perform his duties to the public did most exceedingly puzzle him. Notwithstanding these sentiments, however, Vivian began to think that there really could be no harm in talking to so beautiful a creature as Julia, and a little conversation with her would, he felt, be no unpleasing relief to the difficult duties in which he was involved.

To the astonishment of the Honorable Buckhurst Stanhope, eldest son of Lord Beaconsfield, Mr. Vivian Grey, who had never yet condescended to acknowledge his existence, asked him one morning, with the most fascinating of smiles and with the most conciliating voice, "whether they should ride together." The young heir-apparent looked stiff and assented. He arrived again at Chateau Desir in a couple of hours, desperately enamored of the eldest Miss Courtown. The sacrifice of two mornings to the Honorable Dormer Stanhope and the Honorable Gregory Stanhope sent them home equally captivated by the remaining sisters. Having thus, like a man of honor, provided for the amusement of his former friends, the three Miss Courtowns, Vivian left Mrs. Felix Lorraine to the Colonel, whose mustache, by the bye, that lady considerably patronized; and then, having excited a universal feeling of gallantry among the elders, Vivian found his whole day at the service of Julia Manvers.

"Miss Manvers, I think that you and I are the only faithful subjects in this Castle of Indolence. Here am I lounging on an ottoman, my ambition reaching only so far as the possession of a chibouque, whose aromatic and circling wreaths, I candidly confess, I dare not here excite; and you, of course, much too knowing to be doing anything on the first of August save dreaming of races, archery feats, and county balls: the three most delightful things which the country can boast, either for man, woman, or child."

"Of course, you except sporting for yourself, shooting especially, I suppose."

"Shooting, oh! ah! there is such a thing. No, I am no shot; not that I have not in my time cultivated a Manton; but the truth is, having, at an early age, mistaken my intimate friend for a cock pheasant, I sent a whole crowd of fours into his face, and thereby spoiled one of the prettiest countenances in Christendom; so I gave up the field. Besides, as Tom Moore says, I have so much to do in the country that, for my part, I really have no time for killing birds and jumping over ditches: good work enough for country squires, who must, like all others, have their hours of excitement. Mine are of a different nature, and boast a different locality; and so when I come into the country, 'tis for pleasant air, and beautiful trees, and winding streams; things which, of course, those who live among them all the year round do not suspect to be lovely and adorable creations. Don't you agree with Tom Moore, Miss Manvers?"

"Oh, of course! but I think it is very improper, that habit, which every one has, of calling a man of such eminence as the author of 'Lalla Rookh' *Tom* Moore."

"I wish he could but hear you! But, suppose I were to quote *Mr.* Moore, or *Mr. Thomas* Moore, would you have the most distant conception whom I meant? Certainly not. By the bye, did you ever hear the pretty name they gave him at Paris?"

"No, what was it?"

"One day Moore and Rogers went to call on Denon. Rogers gave their names to the Swiss, Monsieur Rogers et Monsieur Moore. The Swiss dashed open the library door, and, to the great surprise of the illustrious antiquary, announced Monsieur l'Amour! While Denon was doubting whether the God of Love was really paying him a visit or not, Rogers entered. I should like to have seen Denon's face!"

"And Monsieur Denon did take a portrait of Mr. Rogers as Cupid, I believe?"

"Come, madam, 'no scandal about Queen Elizabeth.' Mr. Rogers is one of the most elegant-minded men in the country.'"

"Nay! do not lecture me with such a laughing face, or else your moral will be utterly thrown away."

"Ah! you have Retsch's 'Faust' there. I did not expect on a drawing-room table at Chateau Desir to see anything so old, and so excellent. I thought the third edition of 'Tremaine' would be a very fair specimen of your ancient literature, and Major Denham's hair-breadth escapes of your modern. There was an excellent story about, on the return of Denham and

Clapperton. The travelers took different routes, in order to arrive at the same point of destination. In his wanderings the Major came unto an unheard-of lake, which, with the spirit which they of the Guards surely approved, he christened 'Lake Waterloo.' Clapperton arrived a few days after him; and the pool was immediately rebaptized 'Lake Trafalgar.' There was a hot quarrel in consequence. Now, if I had been there, I would have arranged matters, by proposing as a title, to meet the views of all parties, 'The United Service Lake.' "

"That would have been happy."

"How beautiful Margaret is," said Vivian, rising from his ottoman, and seating himself on the sofa by the lady. "I always think that this is the only Personification where Art has not rendered Innocence insipid."

"Do you think so?"

"Why, take Una in the Wilderness, or Goody Two Shoes. These, I believe, were the most innocent persons that ever existed, and I am sure you will agree with me, they always look the most insipid. Nay, perhaps I was wrong in what I said; perhaps it is Insipidity that always looks innocent, not Innocence always insipid."

"How can you refine so, when the thermometer is at 100°! Pray, tell me some more stories."

"I can not, I am in a refining humor: I could almost lecture to-day at the Royal Institution. You would not call these exactly Prosopopeias of Innocence?" said Vivian, turning over a bundle of Stewart Newton's beauties, languishing, and lithographed. "Newton, I suppose, like Lady Wortley Montagu, is of opinion that the face is not the most beautiful part of woman; at least, if I am to judge from these elaborate ankles. Now, the countenance of this Donna, forsooth, has a drowsy placidity worthy of the easy chair she is lolling in, and yet her ankle would not disgrace the contorted frame of the most pious fakir."

"Well! I am an admirer of Newton's paintings."

"Oh! so am I. He is certainly a cleverish fellow, but rather too much among the blues; a set, of whom, I would venture to say, Miss Manvers knoweth little about."

"Oh, not the least! Mamma does not visit that way. What are they?"

"Oh, very powerful people! though 'Mamma does not visit that way.' Their words are Ukases as far as Curzon Street, and very Decretals in the general vicinity of May Fair; but you shall have a further description another time. How those rooks bore! I hate staying with ancient families; you are always cawed to death. If ever you write a novel, Miss Manvers, mind you have a rookery in it. Since 'Tremaine' and Washington Irving, nothing will go down without."

"By the bye, who is the author of 'Tremaine'?"

"It is either Mr. Ryder, or Mr. Spencer Percival, or Mr. Dyson, or Miss Dyson, or Mr. Bowles, or the Duke of Buckingham, or Mr. Ward, or a young officer in the Guards, or an old clergyman in the North of England, or a middle-aged barrister on the Midland Circuit."

"Mr. Grey, I wish you could get me an autograph of Mr. Washington Irving; I want it for a particular friend."

"Give me a pen and ink; I will write you one immediately."

"Ridiculous!"

"There! now you have made me blot Faustus."

At this moment the room door suddenly opened, and as suddenly shut.

"Who was that?"

"Mephistophiles, or Mrs. Felix Lorraine; one or the other, perhaps both."

"What!"

"What do you think of Mrs. Felix Lorraine, Miss Manvers?"

"Oh! I think her a very amusing woman, a very clever woman, a very—but—"

"But what?"

"But I can not exactly make her out."

"Nor I; she is a dark riddle; and, although I am a very Œdipus, I confess I have not yet unraveled it. Come, there is Washington Irving's autograph for you; read it; is it not quite in character? Shall I write any more? One of Sir Walter's, or Mr. Southey's, or Mr. Milman's, or Mr. Disraeli's? or shall I sprawl a Byron?"

"I really can not sanction such unprincipled conduct. You may make me one of Sir Walter's, however."

"Poor Washington!" said Vivian, writing. "I knew him

well. He always slept at dinner. One day, as he was dining
at Mr. Hallam's, they took him, when asleep, to Lady Jersey's;
and, to see the Sieur Geoffrey, they say, when he opened his
eyes in the illumined saloons, was really quite admirable!
quite an Arabian tale!"

"How delightful! I should have so liked to have seen him!
He seems quite forgotten now in England. How came we to
talk of him?"

"Forgotten! Oh! he spoiled his elegant talents in writing
German and Italian twaddle with all the rawness of a Yankee.
He ought never to have left America, at least in literature;
there was an uncontested and glorious field for him. He
should have been managing director of the Hudson Bay Company, and lived all his life among the beavers."

"I think there is nothing more pleasant than talking over
the season, in the country, in August."

"Nothing more agreeable. It was dull though, last season, very dull; I think the game can not be kept going another
year. If it were not for the General Election, we really must
have a war for variety's sake. Peace gets quite a bore.
Everybody you dine with has a good cook, and gives you a
dozen different wines, all perfect. We can not bear this any
longer; all the lights and shadows of life are lost. The only
good thing I heard this year was an ancient gentlewoman
going up to Gunter and asking him for 'the receipt for that
white stuff,' pointing to his Roman punch. I, who am a great
man for receipts, gave it her immediately: 'One hod of mortar
to one bottle of Noyau.' "

"And did she thank you?"

"Thank me! ay, truly; and pushed a card into my hand, so
thick and sharp that it cut through my glove. I wore my arm
in a sling for a month afterward."

"And what was the card?"

"Oh, you need not look so arch. The old lady was not even
a faithless duenna. It was an invitation to an assembly, or
something of the kind, at a place, somewhere, as Theodore
Hook or Mr. Croker would say, 'between Mesopotamia and
Russell Square.' "

"Pray, Mr. Grey, is it true that all the houses in Russell
Square are tenantless?"

"Quite true; the Marquess of Tavistock has given up the county in consequence. A perfect shame, is it not? Let us write it up."

"An admirable plan! but we will take the houses first, at a pepper-corn rent."

"What a pity, Miss Manvers, the fashion has gone out of selling one's self to the devil."

"Good gracious, Mr. Grey!"

"On my honor, I am quite serious. It does appear to me to be a very great pity. What a capital plan for younger brothers! It is a kind of thing I have been trying to do all my life, and never could succeed. I began at school with toasted cheese and a pitchfork; and since then I have invoked, with all the eloquence of Goethe, the evil one in the solitude of the Hartz, but without success. I think I should make an excellent bargain with him: of course I do not mean that ugly vulgar savage with a fiery tail. Oh, no! Satan himself for me, a perfect gentleman! Or Belial: Belial would be the most delightful. He is the fine genius of the Inferno, I imagine, the Beranger of Pandemonium."

"I really can not listen to such nonsense one moment longer. What would you have if Belial were here?"

"Let us see. Now, you shall act the spirit, and I, Vivian Grey. I wish we had a short-hand writer here to take down the Incantation Scene. We would send it to Arnold. *Commençons* Spirit! I will have a fair castle."

The lady bowed.

"I will have a palace in town."

The lady bowed.

"I will have a fair wife. Why, Miss Manvers, you forget to bow!"

"I really beg your pardon!"

"Come, this is a novel way of making an offer, and, I hope, a successful one."

"Julia, my dear," cried a voice in the veranda, "Julia, my dear, I want you to walk with me."

"Say you are engaged with the Marchioness," whispered Vivian, with a low but distinct voice; his eyes fixed on the table, and his lips not appearing to move.

"Mamma, I am—"

"I want you immediately and particularly, Julia," cried Lady Louisa, in an earnest voice.

"I am coming, I am coming. You see I must go."

CHAPTER X

"CONFUSION on that old hag! Her eye looked evil on me, at the very moment! Although a pretty wife is really the destruction of a young man's prospects, still, in the present case, the niece of my friend, my patron, high family, perfectly unexceptionable, etc., etc., etc. Such blue eyes! upon my honor, this must be an exception to the general rule." Here a light step attracted his attention, and, on turning round, he found Mrs. Felix Lorraine at his elbow.

"Oh! you are here, Mr. Grey, acting the solitaire in the park! I want your opinion about a passage in "Hermann und Dorothea.'"

"My opinion is always at your service; but, if the passage is not perfectly clear to Mrs. Felix Lorraine, it will be perfectly obscure, I am convinced, to me."

"Ah! yes, of course. Oh, dear! after all my trouble, I have forgotten my book. How mortifying! Well, I will show it to you after dinner: adieu! and, by the bye, Mr. Grey, as I am here, I may as well advise you not to spoil all the Marquess's timber by carving a certain person's name on his park trees. I think your plans in that quarter are admirable. I have been walking with Lady Louisa the whole morning, and you can not think how I puffed you! Courage, Cavalier, and we shall soon be connected, not only in friendship, but in blood."

The next morning, at breakfast, Vivian was surprised to find that the Manvers party was suddenly about to leave the Castle. All were disconsolate at their departure: for there was to be a grand entertainment at Chateau Desir that very day, but particularly Mrs. Felix Lorraine and Mr. Vivian Grey. The sudden departure was accounted for by the arrival of "unexpected," etc., etc., etc. There was no hope; the green post-chariot was at the door, a feeble promise of a speedy return; Julia's eyes were filled with tears. Vivian was springing forward to press her hand, and bear her to the carriage, when

Mrs. Felix Lorraine seized his arm, vowed she was going to faint, and, ere she could recover herself, or loosen her grasp, the Manvers were gone.

CHAPTER XI

THE gloom which the parting had diffused over all countenances was quite dispelled when the Marquess entered.

"Lady Carabas," said he, "you must prepare for many visitors to-day. There are the Amershams, and Lord Alhambra, and Ernest Clay, and twenty other young heroes, who, duly informed that the Miss Courtowns were honoring us with their presence, are pouring in from all quarters; is it not so, Juliana?" gallantly asked the Marquess of Miss Courtown: "but who do you think is coming besides?"

"Who, who?" exclaimed all.

"Nay, you shall guess," said the Peer.

"The Duke of Waterloo?" guessed Cynthia Courtown, the romp.

"Prince Hungary?" asked her sister Laura.

"Is it a gentleman?" asked Mrs. Felix Lorraine.

"No, no, you are all wrong, and all very stupid. It is Mrs. Million."

"Oh, how delightful!" said Cynthia.

"Oh, how annoying!" said the Marchioness.

"You need not look so agitated, my love," said the Marquess; "I have written to Mrs. Million to say that we shall be most happy to see her; but as the Castle is very full, she must not come with five carriages-and-four, as she did last year."

"And will Mrs. Million dine with us in the hall, Marquess?" asked Cynthia Courtown.

"Mrs. Million will do what she likes; I only know that I shall dine in the Hall, whatever happens, and whoever comes; and so, I suppose, will Miss Cynthia Courtown."

Vivian rode out alone, immediately after breakfast, to cure his melancholy by a gallop.

Returning home, he intended to look in at a pretty farmhouse, where lived one John Conyers, a great friend of Vivian's. This man had, about a fortnight ago, been of essential service to our hero, when a vicious horse, which he was endeavoring to cure of some ugly tricks, had nearly terminated his mortal career.

"Why are you crying so, my boy?" asked Vivian of a little Conyers who was sobbing bitterly at the door. He was answered only with desperate sobs.

"Oh, 'tis your honor," said a decent looking woman, who came out of the house; "I thought they had come back again."

"Come back again! why, what is the matter, dame?"

"Oh! your honor, we're in sad distress; there's been a seizure this morning, and I'm mortal fear'd the good man's beside himself."

"Good heavens! why did you not come to the Castle?"

"Oh! your honor, we a'nt his Lordship's tenants no longer; there's been a change for Purley Mill, and now we're Lord Mounteney's people. John Conyers has been behindhand ever since he had the fever, but Mr. Sedgwick always gave time: but Lord Mounteney's gem'man says the system's bad, and so he'll put an end to it; and so all's gone, your honor; all's gone, and I'm mortal fear'd the good man's beside himself."

"And who is Lord Mounteney's man of business?"

"Mr. Stapylton Toad," sobbed the good dame.

"Here, boy, leave off crying, and hold my horse; keep your hold tight, but give him rein, he'll be quiet enough then. I will see honest John, dame."

"I'm sure your honor's very kind, but I'm mortal fear'd the good man's beside himself, and he's apt to do very violent things when the fit's on him. He hasn't been so bad since young Barton behaved so wickedly to his sister."

"Never mind! there is nothing like a friend's face in the hour of sorrow."

"I wouldn't advise your honor," said the good dame. "It's an awful hour when the fit's on him; he knows not friend or foe, and scarcely knows me, your honor."

"Never mind, I'll see him."

Vivian entered the house; but who shall describe the scene of desolation! The room was entirely stripped; there was nothing left save the bare whitewashed walls and the red-tiled flooring. The room was darkened; and seated on an old block of wood, which had been pulled out of the orchard, since the bailiff had left, was John Conyers. The fire was out, but his feet were still among the ashes. His head was buried in his hands, and bowed down nearly to his knees. The eldest girl, a fine sensible child of about thirteen, was sitting with two brothers on the floor in a corner of the room, motionless, their faces grave, and still as death, but tearless. Three young children, of an age too tender to know grief, were acting unmeaning gambols near the door.

"Oh! pray beware, your honor," earnestly whispered the poor dame, as she entered the cottage with the visitor.

Vivian walked up with a silent step to the end of the room where Conyers was sitting. He remembered this little room, when he thought it the very model of the abode of an English husbandman. The neat row of plates, and the well-scoured utensils, and the fine old Dutch clock, and the ancient and amusing ballad, purchased at some neighboring fair, or of some itinerant bibliopole, and pinned against the wall, all gone!

"Conyers!" exclaimed Vivian.

There was no answer, nor did the miserable man appear in the slightest degree to be sensible of Vivian's presence.

"My good John!"

The man raised his head from its resting-place, and turned to the spot whence the voice proceeded. There was such an unnatural fire in his eyes that Vivian's spirit almost quailed. His alarm was not decreased when he perceived that the master of the cottage did not recognize him. The fearful stare was, however, short, and again the sufferer's face was hid.

The wife was advancing, but Vivian waved his hand to her to withdraw, and she accordingly fell into the background; but her fixed eye did not leave her husband for a second.

"John Conyers, it is your friend, Mr. Vivian Grey, who is here," said Vivian.

"Grey!" moaned the husbandman; "Grey! who is he?"

"Your friend, John Conyers. Do you quite forget me?" said Vivian advancing, and with a tone which Vivian Grey could alone assume.

"I think I have seen you, and you were kind," and the face was again hid.

"And always will be kind, John. I have come to com-

HARRIET MELLON
Born 1777; Died 1837
Mrs. Thomas Coutts, Later Duchess of
St. Albans
Prototype of "Mrs. Million"

Mrs. Million, who, as the Gotha Almanac says, "takes precedence of all Archduchesses, Grand Duchesses, Princesses, Landgravines, Margravines, Palgravines, etc., etc., etc."
—*Page 65.*

Mrs Coutts.

Vivian Grey

See preceding page

fort you. I thought that a friend's voice would do you good.
Come, cheer up, my man!" and Vivian dared to touch him.
His hand was not repulsed. "Do you remember what good
service you did me when I rode white-footed Moll? Why,
I was much worse off then than you are now; and yet, you see,
a friend came and saved me. You must not give way so, my
good fellow. After all, a little management will set everything
right," and he took the husbandman's sturdy hand.

"I do remember you," he faintly cried. "You were always
very kind."

"And always will be, John; always to friends like you.
Come, come, cheer up and look about you, and let the sun-
beam enter your cottage:" and Vivian beckoned to his wife to
open the closed shutter.

Conyers stared around him, but his eye rested only on bare
walls, and the big tear coursed down his hardy cheek.

"Nay, never mind, man," said Vivian, "we will soon have
chairs and tables again. And as for the rent, think no more
about that at present."

The husbandman looked up, and then burst into weeping.
Vivian could scarcely hold down his convulsed frame on the
rugged seat; but the wife advanced from the back of the room,
and her husband's head rested against her bosom. Vivian held
his honest hand, and the eldest girl rose unbidden from her
silent sorrow, and clung to her father's knee.

"The fit is over," whispered the wife. "There, there,
there's a man, all is now well;" and Vivian left him resting
on his wife's bosom.

"Here, you curly-headed rascal, scamper down to the village immediately, and bring up a basket of something to eat;
and tell Morgan Price that Mr. Grey says he is to send up a
couple of beds and some chairs here immediately, and some
plates and dishes, and everything else, and don't forget some
ale." So saying, Vivian flung the urchin a sovereign.

"And now, dame, for Heaven's sake light the fire. As
for the rent, John, do not waste this trifle on that," whispered
Vivian, slipping his purse into his hand, "for I will see Stapylton Toad, and get time. Why, woman, you'll never strike a
light, if your tears drop so fast into the tinder-box. Here, give
it me. You are not fit to work to-day. And how is the trout

in Ravely Mead, John, this hot weather? You know you
never kept your promise with me. Oh! you are a sad fellow!
There! there's a spark! I wonder why old Toad did not take
the tinder-box. It is a very ʳaluable piece of property, at least
to us. Run and get me some wood, that's a good boy. And
so white-footed Moll is past all recovery? Well, she was a
pretty creature! There, that will do famously," said Vivian,
fanning the flame with his hat. "See, it mounts well! And
now, God bless you all! for I am an hour too late, and must
scamper for my very life."

CHAPTER XII

MRS. MILLION arrived, and kept her promise; only
three carriages-and-four! Out of the first descended the
mighty lady herself, with some noble friends, who formed the
most distinguished part of her suite: out of the second came
her physician, Dr. Sly; her toad-eater, Miss Gusset; her secretary, and her page. The third carriage bore her groom of the
chambers, and three female attendants. There were only two
men servants to each equipage; nothing could be more moderate, or, as Miss Gusset said, "in better taste."

Mrs. Million, after having granted the Marquess a private
interview in her private apartments, signified her imperial
intention of dining in public, which, as she had arrived late,
she trusted she might do in her traveling dress. The Marquess kotowed like a first-rate mandarin, and vowed "that her
will was his conduct."

The whole suite of apartments was thrown open, and was
crowded with guests. Mrs. Million entered; she was leaning
on the Marquess's arm, and in a traveling dress, namely, a
crimson silk pelisse, hat and feathers, with diamond ear-rings,
and a rope of gold round her neck. A train of about twelve
persons, consisting of her noble fellow-travelers, toad-eaters,
physicians, secretaries, etc., etc., etc., followed. The entrée of
Her Majesty could not have created a greater sensation than
did that of Mrs. Million. All fell back. Gartered peers, and
starred ambassadors, and baronets with blood older than the
creation, and squires, to the antiquity of whose veins chaos

was a novelty; all retreated, with eyes that scarcely dared to leave the ground; even Sir Plantagenet Pure, whose family had refused a peerage regularly every century, now, for the first time in his life, seemed cowed, and in an awkward retreat to make way for the approaching presence, got entangled with the Mameluke boots of my Lord Alhambra.

At last a sofa was gained, and the great lady was seated, and the sensation having somewhat subsided, conversation was resumed; and the mighty Mrs. Million was not slightly abused, particularly by those who had bowed lowest at her entrée; and now the Marquess of Carabas, as was wittily observed by Mr. Septimus Sessions, a pert young barrister, "went the circuit," that is to say, made the grand tour of the suite of apartments, making remarks to every one of his guests, and keeping up his influence in the county.

"Ah, my Lord Alhambra! this is too kind; and how is your excellent father, and my good friend? Sir Plantagenet, yours most sincerely! we shall have no difficulty about that right of common. Mr. Leverton, I hope you find the new plow work well; your son, sir, will do the county honor. Sir Godfrey, I saw Barton upon that point, as I promised. Lady Julia, I am rejoiced to see ye at Chateau Desir, more blooming than ever! Good Mr. Stapylton Toad, so that little change was effected! My Lord Devildrain, this is a pleasure indeed!"

"Why, Ernest Clay," said Mr. Buckhurst Stanhope, "I thought Alhambra wore a turban; I am quite disappointed."

"Not in the country, Stanhope; here he only sits cross-legged on an ottoman, and carves his venison with an ataghan."

"Well, I am glad he does not wear a turban; that would be bad taste, I think," said Fool Stanhope. "Have you read his poem?"

"A little. He sent me a copy, and as I am in the habit of lighting my pipe or so occasionally with a leaf, why, I can not help occasionally seeing a line: it seems quite first-rate."

"Indeed!" said Fool Stanhope; "I must get it."

"My dear Puff! I am quite glad to find you here," said Mr. Cayenne, a celebrated reviewer, to Mr. Partenopex Puff, a small author and smaller wit. "Have you seen Middle Ages lately?"

"Not very lately," drawled Mr. Partenopex. "I breakfasted with him before I left town, and met a Professor Bopp there, a very interesting man, and Principal of the celebrated University of Heligoland, the model of the London."

"Ah, indeed! talking of the London, is Foaming Fudge to come in for Cloudland?"

"Doubtless! Oh! he is a prodigious fellow! What do you think Booby says? He says that Foaming Fudge can do more than any man in Great Britain; that he had one day to plead in the King's Bench, spout at a tavern, speak in the House, and fight a duel; and that he found time for everything but the last."

"Excellent!" laughed Mr. Cayenne.

Mr. Partenopex Puff was reputed, in a certain set, a sayer of good things, but he was a modest wit, and generally fathered his bon mots on his valet Booby, his monkey, or his parrot.

"I saw you in the last number," said Cayenne. "From the quotations from your own works, I imagine the review of your own book was by yourself?"

"What do you think Booby said?"

"Mr. Puff, allow me to introduce you to Lord Alhambra," said Ernest Clay, by which means Mr. Puff's servant's last good thing was lost.

"Mr. Clay, are you an archer?" asked Cynthia Courtown.

"No, fair Dian; but I can act Endymion."

"I don't know what you mean. Go away."

"Aubrey Vere, welcome to ——shire. Have you seen Prima Donna?"

"No; is he here? How did you like his last song in the 'Age'?"

"His last song! Poor! pooh! he only supplies the scandal."

"Groves," said Sir Hanway Etherington, "have you seen the newspaper this morning? Baron Crupper has tried fifteen men for horse-stealing at York, and acquitted every one."

"Well, then, Sir Hanway, I think his Lordship's remarkable wrong; for when a man gets a horse to suit him, if he loses it, 'tisn't so easy to suit himself again. That's the ground I stand upon."

All this time the Marquess of Carabas had wanted Vivian Grey twenty times, but that gentleman had not appeared. The important moment arrived, and his Lordship offered his arm to Mrs. Million, who, as the Gotha Almanac says, "takes precedence of all Archduchesses, Grand Duchesses, Duchesses, Princesses, Landgravines, Margravines, Palsgravines," etc., etc., etc.

CHAPTER XIII

IN their passage to the Hall, the Marquess and Mrs. Million met Vivian Grey, booted and spurred, and covered with mud.

"Oh! Mrs. Million—Mr. Vivian Grey. How is this, my dear fellow? you will be too late."

"Immense honor!" said Vivian, bowing to the ground to the lady. "Oh! my Lord, I was late, and made a short cut over Fearnley Bog. It has proved a very Moscow expedition. However, I am keeping you. I shall be in time for the guava and liqueurs, and you know that is the only refreshment I ever take."

"Who is that, Marquess?" asked Mrs. Million.

"That is Mr. Vivian Grey, the most monstrous clever young man, and nicest fellow I know."

"He does, indeed, seem a very nice young man," said Mrs. Million.

Some steam process should be invented for arranging guests when they are above five hundred. In the present instance all went wrong when they entered the Hall; but, at last, the arrangements, which, of course, were of the simplest nature, were comprehended, and the guests were seated. There were three tables, each stretching down the Hall; the dais was occupied by a military band. The number of guests, the contrast between the antique chamber and their modern costumes, the music, the various liveried menials, all combined to produce a whole, which at the same time was very striking, and "in remarkable good taste."

In process of time, Mr. Vivian Grey made his entrance. There were a few vacant seats at the bottom of the table, "luckily for him," as kindly remarked Mr. Grumbleton. To the astonishment and indignation, however, of this worthy squire, the late comer passed by the unoccupied position, and proceeded onward with undaunted coolness, until he came to about the middle of the middle table, and which was nearly the best situation in the Hall.

"Beautiful Cynthia," said Vivian Grey, softly and sweetly whispering in Miss Courtown's ear, "I am sure you will give up your place to me; you have nerve enough, you know, for anything, and would no more care for standing out than I for sitting in." There is nothing like giving a romp credit for a little boldness. To keep up her character she will out-Herod Herod.

"Oh! Grey, is it you? certainly, you shall have my place immediately; but I am not sure that we can not make room for you. Dormer Stanhope, room must be made for Grey, or I shall leave the table immediately. You men!" said the hoyden, turning round to a set of surrounding servants, "push this form down and put a chair between."

The men obeyed. All who sat lower in the table on Miss Cynthia Courtown's side than that lady were suddenly propelled downward about the distance of two feet. Dr. Sly, who was flourishing a carving-knife and fork, preparatory to dissecting a gorgeous haunch, had these fearful instruments suddenly precipitated into a trifle, from whose sugared trellis-work he found great difficulty in extricating them; while Miss Gusset, who was on the point of cooling herself with some exquisite iced jelly, found her frigid portion as suddenly transformed into a plate of peculiarly ardent curry, the property, but a moment before, of old Colonel Rangoon. Everything, however, receives a civil reception from a toad-eater, so Miss Gusset burned herself to death by devouring a composition which would have reduced any one to ashes who had not fought against Bundoolah.

"Now that is what I call a sensible arrangement; what could go off better?" said Vivian.

"You may think so, sir," said Mr. Boreall, a sharp-nosed and conceited-looking man, who, having got among a set whom he did not the least understand, was determined to take up Dr. Sly's quarrel, merely for the sake of conversation. "You, I say, sir, may think it so, but I rather imagine that the ladies and gentlemen lower down can hardly think it a sensible arrangement"; and here Boreall looked as if he had done his duty, in giving a young man a proper reproof.

Vivian glanced a look of annihilation. "I had reckoned upon two deaths, sir, when I entered the Hall, and finding, as I do, that the whole business has apparently gone off without any fatal accident, why, I think the circumstances bear me out in my expression."

Mr. Boreall was one of those unfortunate men who always take things to the letter: he consequently looked amazed, and exclaimed, "Two deaths, sir?"

"Yes, sir, two deaths; I reckoned, of course, on some corpulent parent being crushed to death in the scuffle, and then I should have had to shoot his son through the head for his filial satisfaction. Dormer Stanhope, I never thanked you for exerting yourself: send me that fricandeau you have just helped yourself to."

Dormer, who was, as Vivian well knew, something of an epicure, looked rather annoyed, but by this time he was accustomed to Vivian Grey, and sent him the portion he had intended for himself. Could epicure do more?"

"Whom are we among, bright Cynthia?" asked Vivian.

"Oh! an odd set," said the lady, looking dignified; "but you know we can be exclusive."

"Exclusive! pooh! trash! Talk to everybody; it looks as if you were going to stand for the county. Have we any of the millionaires near us?"

"The Doctor and Toady are lower down."

"Where is Mrs. Felix Lorraine?"

"At the opposite table, with Ernest Clay."

"Oh! there is Alhambra, next to Dormer Stanhope. Lord Alhambra, I am quite rejoiced to see you."

"Ah! Mr. Grey, I am quite rejoiced to see you. How is your father?"

"Extremely well; he is at Paris; I heard from him yesterday. Do you ever see the 'Weimar Literary Gazette,' my Lord?"

"No; why?"

"There is an admirable review of your poem in the last number I have received."

The young nobleman looked agitated.

"I think, by the style," continued Vivian, "that it is by Goëthe. It is really delightful to see the oldest poet in

Europe dilating on the brilliancy of a new star on the poetical horizon."

This was uttered with a perfectly grave voice, and now the young nobleman blushed. "Who is *Gewter?*" asked Mr. Boreall, who possessed such a thirst for knowledge that he never allowed an opportunity to escape him of displaying his ignorance.

"A celebrated German writer," lisped the modest Miss Macdonald.

"I never heard his name," persevered the indefatigable Boreall; "how do you spell it?"

"G O E T H E," relisped modesty.

"Oh! *Goty!*" exclaimed the querist. "I know him well: he wrote the 'Sorrows of Werther.'"

"Did he indeed, sir?" asked Vivian, with the most innocent and inquiring face.

"Oh! don't you know that?" said Boreall; "and poor stuff it is!"

"Lord Alhambra! I will take a glass of Johannisberg with you, if the Marquess's wines are in the state they should be:

"'The Crescent warriors sipped their sherbet spiced,
For Christian men the various wines were *iced.*'"

I always think that those are two of the best lines in your Lordship's poem," said Vivian.

His Lordship did not exactly remember them: it would have been a wonder if he had: but he thought Vivian Grey the most delightful fellow he ever met, and determined to ask him to Helicon Castle for the Christmas holidays.

"Flat! flat!" said Vivian, as he dwelt upon the flavor of the Rhine's glory. "Not exactly from the favorite bin of Prince Metternich, I think. By the bye, Dormer Stanhope, you have a taste that way; I will tell you two secrets, which never forget: decant your Johannisberg, and ice your Maraschino. Ay, do not stare, my dear Gastronome, but do it."

"Oh, Vivian! why did not you come and speak to me?" exclaimed a lady who was sitting at the side opposite Vivian, but higher in the table.

"Ah! adorable Lady Julia! and so you were done on the gray filly."

"Done!" said the sporting beauty, with pouting lips; "but it is a long story, and I will tell it you another time."

"Ah! do. How is Sir Peter?"

"Oh! he has had a fit or two since you saw him last."

"Poor old gentleman! let us drink his health. Do you know Lady Julia Knighton?" asked Vivian of his neighbor. "This Hall is bearable to dine in; but I once breakfasted here, and I never shall forget the ludicrous effect produced by the sun through the oriel window. Such complexions! Every one looked like a prize-fighter ten days after a battle. After all, painted glass is a bore; I wish the Marquess would have it knocked out, and have it plated."

"Knock out the painted glass!" said Mr. Boreall; "well, I must confess, I can not agree with you."

"I should have been extremely surprised if you could. If you do not insult that man, Miss Courtown, in ten minutes I shall be no more. I have already a nervous fever."

"May I have the honor of taking a glass of champagne with you, Mr. Grey?" said Boreall.

"Mr. Grey, indeed!" muttered Vivian: "Sir, I never drink anything but brandy."

"Allow me to give *you* some champagne, Miss," resumed Boreall, as he attacked the modest Miss Macdonald; "champagne, you know," continued he, with a smile of agonizing courtesy, "is quite the lady's wine."

"Cynthia Courtown," whispered Vivian with a sepulchral voice, " 'tis all over with me: I have been thinking what would come next. This is too much: I am already dead. Have Boreall arrested; the chain of circumstantial evidence is very strong."

"Baker!" said Vivian, turning to a servant, "go and inquire if Mr. Stapylton Toad dines at the Castle to-day."

A flourish of trumpets announced the rise of the Marchioness of Carabas, and in a few minutes the most ornamental portion of the guests had disappeared. The gentlemen made a general "move up," and Vivian found himself opposite his friend, Mr. Hargrave.

"Ah! Mr. Hargrave, how d'ye do? What do you think of the Secretary's state paper?"

"A magnificent composition, and quite unanswerable. I

was just speaking of it to my friend here, Mr. Metternich Scribe. Allow me to introduce you to Mr. Metternich Scribe."

"Mr. Metternich Scribe—Mr. Vivian Grey!" and here Mr. Hargrave introduced Vivian to an effeminate-looking, perfumed young man, with a handsome, unmeaning face and very white hands; in short, as dapper a little diplomatist as ever tattled about the Congress of Verona, smirked at Lady Almack's supper after the Opera, or vowed "that Richmond Terrace was a most convenient situation for official men."

"We have had it with us some time before the public received it," said the future under-secretary, with a look at once condescending and conceited.

"Have you?" said Vivian: "Well, it does your office credit. It is a singular thing that Canning and Croker are the only official men who can write grammar."

The dismayed young gentleman of the Foreign Office was about to mince a repartee, when Vivian left his seat, for he had a great deal of business to transact. "Mr. Leverton," said he, accosting a flourishing grazier, "I have received a letter from my friend, M. de Noé. He is desirous of purchasing some Leicestershires for his estate in Burgundy. Pray, may I take the liberty of introducing his agent to you?"

Mr. Leverton was delighted.

"I also wanted to see you about some other little business. Let me see, what was it? Never mind, I will take my wine here, if you make room for me; I shall remember it, I dare say, soon. Oh! by the bye: ah! that was it. Stapylton Toad; Mr. Stapylton Toad; I want to know all about Mr. Stapylton Toad. I dare say you can tell me. A friend of mine intends to consult him on some parliamentary business, and he wishes to know something about him before he calls."

We will condense, for the benefit of the reader, the information of Mr. Leverton.

Stapylton Toad had not the honor of being acquainted with his father's name; but as the son found himself, at an early age, apprenticed to a solicitor of eminence, he was of opinion that his parent must have been respectable. Respectable! mysterious word! Stapylton was a diligent and faithful clerk, but was not so fortunate in his apprenticeship as the celebrated

Whittington, for his master had no daughter and many sons; in consequence of which, Stapylton, not being able to become his master's partner, became his master's rival.

On the door of one of the shabbiest houses in Jermyn Street the name of Mr. Stapylton Toad for a long time figured, magnificently engraved on a broad brass plate. There was nothing, however, otherwise in the appearance of the establishment which indicated that Mr. Toad's progress was very rapid, or his professional career extraordinarily prosperous. In an outward office one solitary clerk was seen, oftener stirring his office fire than wasting his master's ink; and Mr. Toad was known by his brother attorneys as a gentleman who was not recorded in the courts as ever having conducted a single cause. In a few years, however, a story was added to the Jermyn Street abode, which, new pointed and new painted, began to assume a mansion-like appearance. The house door was also thrown open, for the solitary clerk no longer found time to answer the often agitated bell; and the eyes of the entering client were now saluted by a gorgeous green baize office door; the imposing appearance of which was only equaled by Mr. Toad's new private portal, splendid with a brass knocker and patent varnish. And now his brother attorneys began to wonder "how Toad got on! and who Toad's clients were!"

A few more years rolled over, and Mr. Toad was seen riding in the Park at a classical hour, attended by a groom in a classical livery. And now "the profession" wondered still more, and significant looks were interchanged by "the respectable houses": and flourishing practitioners in the city shrugged up their shoulders, and talked mysteriously of "money business," and "some odd work in annuities." In spite, however, of the charitable surmises of his brother lawyers, it must be confessed that nothing of even an equivocal nature ever transpired against the character of the flourishing Mr. Toad, who, to complete the mortification of his less successful rivals, married, and at the same time moved from Jermyn Street to Cavendish Square. The new residence of Mr. Toad had previously been the mansion of a noble client, and one whom, as the world said, Mr. Toad "had got out of difficulties." This significant phrase will probably throw some light upon the nature of the mysterious business of our prosperous practitioner. Noble lords who have been in difficulties will not much wonder at the prosperity of those who get them out.

About this time Mr. Toad became acquainted with Lord Mounteney, a nobleman in great distress, with fifty thousand per annum. His Lordship "really did not know how he had got involevd: he never gamed, he was not married, and his consequent expenses had never been unreasonable: he was not extraordinarily negligent; quite the reverse: was something of a man of business, remembered once looking over his accounts; and yet, in spite of his regular and correct career, found himself quite involved, and must leave England."

The arrangement of the Mounteney property was the crowning stroke of Mr. Stapylton Toad's professional celebrity. His Lordship was not under the necessity of quitting England, and found himself in the course of five years in the receipt of a clear rental of five-and-twenty thousand per annum. His Lordship was in raptures; and Stapylton Toad purchased an elegant villa in Surrey, and became a Member of Parliament. Goodburn Park, for such was the name of Mr. Toad's country residence, in spite of its double lodges and patent park paling, was not, to Mr. Toad, a very expensive purchase; for he "took it off the hands" of a distressed client who wanted an immediate supply, "merely to convenience him," and, consequently, became the purchaser at about half its real value. "Attorneys," as Bustle the auctioneer says, "have *such* opportunities!"

Mr. Toad's career in the House was as correct as his conduct out of it. After ten years' regular attendance, the boldest conjecturer would not have dared to define his political principles. It was a rule with Stapylton Toad never to commit himself. Once, indeed, he wrote an able pamphlet on the Corn Laws, which excited the dire indignation of the Political Economy Club. But Stapylton cared little for their subtle confutations and their loudly expressed contempt. He had obliged the country gentlemen of England, and ensured the return, at the next election, of Lord Mounteney's brother for the county. At this general election, also, Stapylton Toad's purpose in entering the House became rather more manifest; for it was found, to the surprise of the whole country, that there was scarcely a place in England—county, town or borough—in which Mr. Stapylton Toad did not possess some influence. In short, it was discovered that Mr. Stapylton Toad had "a first-rate parliamentary business"; that nothing could be done without his co-operation, and everything with it. In spite of his prosperity, Stapylton had the good sense never to retire from business, and even to refuse a baronetcy; on condition, however, that it should be offered to his son.

Stapylton, like the rest of mankind, had his weak points. The late Marquess of Almack's was wont to manage him very happily, and Toad was always introducing that minister's opinion of his importance. " 'My time is quite at your service, General,' although the poor dear Marquess used to say, 'Mr. Stapylton Toad, your time is mine.' He knew the business I had to get through!" The family portraits also, in ostentatious frames, now adorned the dining-room of his London mansion; and it was amusing to hear the worthy M.P. dilate upon his likeness to his respected father.

"You see, my Lord," Stapylton would say, pointing to a dark, dingy picture of a gentleman in a rich court dress, "you see, my Lord, it is not in a very good light, and it certainly is a very dark picture, by Hudson; all Hudson's pictures were dark. But if I were six inches taller, and could hold the light just there, I think your Lordship would be astonished at the resemblance; but it's a dark picture, certainly it is dark; all Hudson's pictures were."

CHAPTER XIV

THE Cavaliers have left the ancient Hall, and the old pictures frown only upon empty tables. The Marquess immediately gained a seat by Mrs. Million, and was soon engrossed in deep converse with that illustrious lady. In one room, the most eminent and exclusive, headed by Mrs. Felix Lorraine, were now winding through the soothing mazes of a slow waltz, and now whirling, with all the rapidity of Eastern dervishes, to true double Wien time. In another saloon, the tedious tactics of quadrilles commanded the exertions of less civilized beings: here Liberal Snake, the celebrated political economist, was lecturing to a knot of alarmed country gentlemen; and there an Italian improvisatore poured forth to an admiring audience all the dulness of his inspiration. Vivian Grey was holding an earnest conversation in one of the recesses with Mr. Stapylton Toad. He had already charmed that worthy by the deep interest which he took in everything relating to elections and the House of Commons, and now they were hard at work on the Corn Laws. Although they agreed upon the main points, and Vivian's ideas upon this important subject had, of course, been adopted after studying Mr. Toad's "most luminous and convincing pamphlet," still there were a few minor points on which Vivian "was obliged to confess" that "he did not exactly see his way." Mr. Toad was astonished, but argumentative, and, of course, in due time, had made a convert of his companion; "a young man," as he afterward remarked to Lord Mounteney, "in whom he knew not which most to admire, the soundness of his own views, or the candor with which he treated those of others." If you wish to win a man's heart, allow him to confute you.

"I think, Mr. Grey, you must admit that my definition of labor is the correct one?" said Mr. Toad, looking earnestly in Vivian's face, his finger just presuming to feel a button.

"That exertion of mind or body which is not the involuntary effect of the influence of natural sensations," slowly repeated Vivian, as if his whole soul was concentrated in each monosyllable. "Y-e-s, Mr. Toad, I do admit it."

"Then, my dear sir, the rest follows of course," triumphantly exclaimed the member; "don't you see it?"

"Although I admit the correctness of your definition, Mr. Toad, I am not free to confess that I am ex-act-ly convinced of the soundness of your conclusion," said Vivian in a musing mood.

"But, my dear sir, I am surprised that you don't see that—"

"Stop, Mr. Toad," eagerly exclaimed Vivian; "I see my error. I misconceived your meaning: you are right, sir; your definition is correct."

"I was confident that I should convince you, Mr. Grey."

"This conversation, I assure you, Mr. Toad, has been to me a peculiarly satisfactory one. Indeed, sir, I have long wished to have the honor of making your acquaintance. When but a boy, I remember, at my father's table, the late Marquess of Almack's—"

"Yes, Mr. Grey."

"One of the ablest men, Mr. Toad, after all, that this country ever produced."

"Oh, poor dear man!"

"I remember his observing to a friend of mine, who was at that time desirous of getting into the House: 'Hargrave,' said his Lordship, 'if you want any information upon points of practical politics'; that was his phrase; you remember, Mr. Toad, that his Lordship was peculiar in his phrases?"

"Oh! yes, poor dear man; but you were observing, Mr. Grey—"

"Ay, ay! 'If you want any information,' said his Lordship, 'on such points, there is only one man in the kingdom whom you should consult, and he is one of the soundest heads I know, and that is Stapylton Toad, the member for Mounteney'; you know you were in for Mounteney then, Mr. Toad."

"I was, and accepted the Chilterns to make room for Augustus Clay, Ernest Clay's brother, who was so involved that the only way to keep him out of the House of Correction was to get him into the House of Commons. But the Marquess said so, eh?"

"Ay, and much more, which I scarcely can remember;" and then followed a long dissertation on the character of the noble statesman, and his views as to the agricultural interest, and the importance of the agricultural interest; and then a delicate hint was thrown out as to "how delightful it would be to write a pamphlet together" on this mighty agricultural interest; and then came a panegyric on the character of country gentlemen, and English yeomen, and the importance of keeping up the old English spirit in the peasantry, etc.. etc.. etc., etc.; and then, when Vivian had led Mr. Toad to deliver a splendid and patriotic oration on this point, he "just remembered (quite apropos to the sentiments which Mr. Toad had just delivered, and which, he did not hesitate to say, 'did equal honor to his head and heart') that there was a little point, which, if it was not trespassing too much on Mr. Toad's attention, he would just submit to him"; and then he mentioned poor John Conyers's case, although "he felt convinced, from

Mr. Toad's well-known benevolent character, that it was quite unnecessary for him to do so, as he felt assured that it would be remedied immediately it fell under his cognizance; but then Mr. Toad had really so much business to transact that perhaps these slight matters might occasionally not be submitted to him," etc., etc., etc.

What could Stapylton Toad do but, after a little amiable grumbling about "bad system and bad precedent," promise everything that Vivian Grey required?

"Mr. Vivian Grey," said Mrs. Felix Lorraine, "I can not understand why you have been talking to Mr. Toad so long. Will you waltz?"

Before Vivian could answer, a tittering, so audible that it might almost be termed a shout, burst forth from the whole room. Cynthia Courtown had stolen behind Lord Alhambra, as he was sitting on an ottoman à la Turque, and had folded a cashmere shawl round his head with a most Oriental tie. His Lordship, who, notwithstanding his eccentricities, was really a very amiable man, bore his blushing honors with a gracious dignity worthy of a descendant of the Abencerrages. The sensation which this incident occasioned favored Vivian's escape from Mrs. Felix, for he had not left Mr. Stapylton Toad with any intention of waltzing.

But he had hardly escaped from the waltzers ere he found himself in danger of being involved in a much more laborious duty; for now he stumbled on the Political Economist, and he was earnestly requested by the contending theorists to assume the office of moderator. Emboldened by his success, Liberal Snake had had the hardihood to attack a personage of whose character he was not utterly ignorant, but on whom he was extremely desirous of "making an impression." This important person was Sir Christopher Mowbray, who, upon the lecturer presuming to inform him "what rent was," damned himself several times from sheer astonishment at the impudence of the fellow. I don't wish to be coarse, but Sir Christopher is a great man, and the sayings of great men, particularly when they are representative of the sentiment of a species, should not pass unrecorded.

Sir Christopher Mowbray is member for the county of ——; and member for the county he intends to be next election, although he is in his seventy-ninth year, for he can still follow a fox with as plucky a heart and with as stout a voice as any squire in Christendom. Sir Christopher, it must be confessed, is rather peculiar in his ideas. His grandson, Peregrine Mowbray, who is as pert a genius as the applause of a common-room ever yet spoiled, and as sublime an orator as the cheerings of the Union ever yet inspired, says "the Baronet is not up to the nineteenth century"; and perhaps this phrase will give the reader a more significant idea of Sir Christopher Mowbray than a character as long and as labored as the most perfect of my Lord Clarendon's. The truth is, the good Baronet had no idea of "liberal principles," or anything else of that school. His most peculiar characteristic is a singular habit which he has got of styling political economists French Smugglers. Nobody has ever yet succeeded in extracting a reason from him for this singular appellation, and even if you angle with the most exquisite skill for the desired definition, Sir Christopher immediately salutes you with a volley of oaths, and damns French wines, Bible Societies, and Mr. Huskisson. Sir Christopher for half a century has supported in the senate, with equal sedulousness and silence, the constitution and the corn laws; he is perfectly aware of "the present perilous state of the country," and watches with great interest all "the plans and plots" of this enlightened age. The only thing which he does not exactly comprehend is the London University. This affair really puzzles the worthy gentleman, who could as easily fancy a county member not being a freeholder as a university not being at Oxford or Cambridge. Indeed to this hour the old gentleman believes that the old business is "a hoax"; and if you tell him that, far from the plan partaking of the visionary nature he conceives, there are actually four acres of very valuable land purchased near White Conduit House for the erection, and that there is little apprehension that, in the course of a century, the wooden poles which are now stuck about the ground will not be as fair and flourishing as the most leafy bowers of New College Gardens, the old gentleman looks up to heaven, as if determined not to be taken in, and leaning back in his chair, sends forth a sceptical and smiling "No! no! no! that won't do."

Vivian extricated himself with as much grace as possible

from the toils of the Economist, and indeed, like a skilful general, turned this little rencontre to account in accomplishing the very end for the attainment of which he had declined waltzing with Mrs. Felix Lorraine.

"My dear Lord," said Vivian, addressing the Marquess, who was still by the side of Mrs. Million. "I am going to commit a most ungallant act; but you great men must pay a tax for your dignity. I am going to disturb you. You are wanted by half the county! What could possibly induce you ever to allow a Political Economist to enter Chateau Desir? There are, at least, three baronets and four squires in despair, writhing under the tortures of Liberal Snake. They have deputed me to request your assistance, to save them from being defeated in the presence of half their tenantry; and I think, my lord," said Vivian, with a serious voice, "if you could possibly contrive to interfere, it would be desirable. That lecturing knave never knows when to stop, and he is actually insulting men before whom, after all, he ought not dare to open his lips. I see that your Lordship is naturally not very much inclined to quit your present occupation, in order to act moderator to a set of brawlers; but come, you shall not be quite sacrificed to the county. I will give up the waltz in which I was engaged, and keep your seat until your return."

The Marquess, who was always "keeping up county influence," was very shocked at the obstreperous conduct of Liberal Snake. Indeed he had viewed the arrival of this worthy with no smiling countenance, but what could he say, as he came in the suite of Lord Pert, who was writing, with the lecturer's assistance, a little pamphlet on the Currency? Apologizing to Mrs. Million, and promising to return as soon as possible and lead her to the music-room, the Marquess retired, with the determination of annihilating one of the stoutest members of the Political Economy Club.

Vivian began by apologizing to Mrs. Million for disturbing her progress to the Hall by his sudden arrival before dinner; and then for a quarter of an hour poured forth the usual quantity of piquant anecdotes and insidious compliments. Mrs. Million found Vivian's conversation no disagreeable relief to the pompous prosiness of his predecessor.

And now, having succeeded in commanding Mrs. Million's

attention by that general art of pleasing which was for all the world, and which was, of course, formed upon his general experience of human nature, Vivian began to make his advances to Mrs. Million's feelings by a particular art of pleasing; that is, an art which was for the particular person alone whom he was at any time addressing, and which was founded on his particular knowledge of that person's character.

"How beautiful the old Hall looked to-day! It is a scene which can only be met with in ancient families."

"Ah! there is nothing like old families!" remarked Mrs. Million, with all the awkward feelings of a parvenu.

"Do you think so?" said Vivian; "I once thought so myself, but I confess that my opinion is greatly changed. After all, what is noble blood? My eye is now resting on a crowd of nobles; and yet, being among them, do we treat them in a manner differing in any way from that which we should employ to individuals of a lower caste who were equally uninteresting?"

"Certainly not," said Mrs. Million.

"The height of the ambition of the less exalted ranks is to be noble, because they conceive to be noble implies to be superior; associating in their minds, as they always do, a preeminence over their equals. But to be noble among nobles, where is the pre-eminence?"

"Where indeed?" said Mrs. Million; and she thought of herself, sitting the most considered personage in this grand castle, and yet with sufficiently base blood flowing in her veins.

"And thus, in the highest circles," continued Vivian, "a man is of course not valued because he is a Marquess or a Duke; but because he is a great warrior, or a great statesman, or very fashionable, or very witty. In all classes but the highest, a peer, however unbefriended by nature or by fortune, becomes a man of a certain rate of consequence; but to be a person of consequence in the highest class requires something else besides high blood."

"I quite agree with you in your sentiments, Mr. Grey. Now what character or what situation in life would you choose, if you had the power of making your choice?"

"That is really a most metaphysical question. As is the custom of all young men, I have sometimes, in my reveries, imagined what I conceived to be a lot of pure happiness: and yet Mrs. Million will perhaps be astonished that I was neither to be nobly born nor to acquire nobility; that I was not to be a statesman, or a poet, or a warrior, or a merchant, nor indeed any profession, not even a professional dandy."

"Oh! love in a cottage, I suppose," interrupted Mrs. Million.

"Neither love in a cottage, nor science in a cell."

"Oh! pray tell me what it is."

"What it is? Oh! Lord Mayor of London, I suppose; that is the only situation which answers to my oracular description."

"Then you have been joking all this time!"

"Not at all. Come then, let us imagine this perfect lot. In the first place, I would be born in the middle classes of society, or even lower, because I would wish my character to be impartially developed. I would be born to no hereditary prejudices, no hereditary passions. My course in life should not be carved out by the example of a grandfather, nor my ideas modeled to a preconceived system of family perfection. Do you like my first principle, Mrs. Million?"

"I must hear everything before I give an opinion."

"When, therefore, my mind was formed, I would wish to become the proprietor of a princely fortune."

"Yes!" eagerly exclaimed Mrs. Million.

"And now would come the moral singularity of my fate. If I had gained this fortune by commerce, or in any other similar mode, my disposition, before the creation of this fortune, would naturally have been formed, and been permanently developed; and my mind would have been similarly affected, had I succeeded to some ducal father; for I should then, in all probability, have inherited some family line of conduct, both moral and political. But under the circumstances I have imagined the result would be far different. I should then be in the singular situation of possessing, at the same time, unbounded wealth, and the whole powers and natural feelings of my mind unoppressed and unshackled. Oh! how splendid would be my career! I would not allow the change in my condition to exercise any influence on my natural disposition. I would experience the same passions and be subject to the same feelings, only they should be exercised and influential in a wider sphere. Then would be seen the influence of great wealth, directed by a disposition similar to that of the generality of men, inasmuch as it had been formed like that of the generality of men; and consequently, one much better acquainted with their feelings, their habits, and their wishes. Such a lot would indeed be princely! Such a lot would infallibly ensure the affection and respect of the great majority of mankind; and, supported by them, what should I care if I were misunderstood by a few fools and abused by a few knaves?"

Here came the Marquess to lead the lady to the concert. As she quitted her seat, a smile, beaming with graciousness, rewarded her youthful companion. "Ah!" thought Mrs. Million, "I go to the concert, but leave sweeter music than can possibly meet me there. What is the magic of these words? It is not flattery; such is not the language of Miss Gusset! It is not a *rifacimento* of compliments; such is not the style with which I am saluted by the Duke of Doze and the Earl of Leatherdale! Apparently I have heard a young philosopher delivering his sentiments upon an abstract point in human life; and yet have I not listened to a brilliant apology for my own character, and a triumphant defence of my own conduct? Of course it was unintentional; and yet how agreeable to be unintentionally defended!" So mused Mrs. Million, and she made a thousand vows not to let a day pass over without obtaining a pledge from Vivian Grey to visit her on their return to the metropolis.

Vivian remained in his seat for some time after the departure of his companion. "On my honor, I have half a mind to desert my embryo faction and number myself in her gorgeous retinue. Let me see. What part should I act? her secretary, or her toad-eater, or her physician, or her cook? or shall I be her page? Methinks I should make a pretty page, and hand a chased goblet as gracefully as any monkey that ever bent his knee in a lady's chamber. Well! at any rate, there is this chance to be kept back, as the gambler does his last trump, or the cunning fencer his last ruse."

He rose to offer his arm to some stray fair one; for crowds were now hurrying to pineapples and lobster salads: that is to say, supper was ready in the Long Gallery.

In a moment Vivian's arm was locked in that of Mrs. Felix Lorraine.

"Oh, Mr. Grey, I have got a much better ghost story than even that of the Leyden Professor for you; but I am so wearied with waltzing that I must tell it you to-morrow. How came you to be so late this morning? Have you been paying many calls to-day? I quite missed you at dinner. Do you think Ernest Clay handsome? I dare not repeat what Lady Scrope said of you! You are an admirer of Lady Julia Knighton, I believe? I do not much like this plan of supping in the Long Gallery; it is a favorite locale of mine, and I have no idea of my private promenade being invaded by the uninteresting presence of trifles and Italian creams. Have you been telling Mrs. Million that she was very witty?" asked Vivian's companion, with a significant look.

CHAPTER XV

SWEET reader! you know what a Toady is? That agreeable animal which you meet every day in civilized society. But perhaps you have not speculated very curiously upon this interesting race. So much the worse! for you can not live many lustres without finding it of some service to be a little acquainted with their habits.

The world in general is under a mistake as to the nature of these vermin. They are by no means characterized by that similarity of disposition for which your common observer gives them credit. There are Toadies of all possible natures.

There is your Commonplace Toady, who merely echoes its feeder's commonplace observations. There is your Playing-up Toady, who, unconscious to its feeder, is always playing up to its feeder's weaknesses; and, as the taste of that feeder varies, accordingly provides its cates and confitures. A little bit of scandal for a dashing widow, or a pious little hymn for a sainted one; the secret history of a newly discovered gas for a May Fair feeder, and an interesting anecdote about a

Newgate bobcap or a Penitentiary apron for a charitable one.
Then there is your Drawing-out Toady, who omits no opportunity of giving you a chance of being victorious in an argument where there is no contest, and a dispute where there is
no difference; and then there is—but we detest essay writing,
so we introduce you at once to a party of these vermin. If
you wish to enjoy a curious sight, you must watch the Toadies
when they are unembarrassed by the almost perpetual presence
of their breeders; when they are animated by "the spirit of
freedom"; when, like Curran's Negro, the chain bursts by the
impulse of their swelling veins. The great singularity is the
struggle between their natural and their acquired feelings: the
eager opportunity which they seize of revenging their volun-
tary bondage, by their secret taunts, on their adopted task-
masters, and the servility which they habitually mix up even
with their scandal. Like veritable Grimalkins, they fawn upon
their victims previous to the festival; compliment them upon
the length of their whiskers and the delicacy of their limbs
prior to excoriating them, and dwelling on the flavor of their
crashed bones. 'Tis a beautiful scene, and ten thousand
times more piquant than the humors of a Servants' Hall, or
the most grotesque and glorious moments of high life below
stairs.

"Dear Miss Graves," said Miss Gusset, "you can't imagine
how terrified I was at that horrible green parrot flying upon
my head! I declare it pulled out three locks of hair."

"Horrible green parrot, my dear madam! Why, it was
sent to my Lady by Prince Xtmnprqtosklw, and never shall
I forget the agitation we were in about that parrot. I thought
it would never have got to the Chateau, for the Prince could
only send his carriage with it as far as Toadcaster. Luckily
my Lady's youngest brother, who was staying at Desir, happened to get drowned at the time; and so Davenport, very
clever of him! sent her on in my Lord Dormer's hearse."

"In the hearse! Good heavens, Miss Graves! How could
you think of green parrots at such an awful moment? I should
have been in fits for three days; eh! Dr. Sly?"

"Certainly you would, madam; your nerves are very
delicate."

"Well! I, for my part, never could see much use in giving

up to one's feelings. It is all very well for commoners," rather rudely exclaimed the Marchioness's Toady; "but we did not choose to expose ourselves to the servants when the old General died this year. Everything went on as usual. Her Ladyship attended Almack's; my Lord took his seat in the House; and I looked in at Lady Doubtful's, where we do not visit, but where the Marchioness wishes to be civil."

"We do not visit Lady Doubtful either," replied Miss Gusset: "she had not a card for our *fête champêtre*. I was so sorry you were not in town. It was so delightful!"

"Do tell me who was there? I quite long to know all about it. I saw some account of it. Everything seemed to go off so well. Do tell me who was there?"

"Oh! there was plenty of Royalty at the head of the list. Really I can not go into particulars, but everybody was there who is anybody; eh! Dr. Sly?"

"Certainly, madam. The pines were most admirable. There are few people for whom I entertain a higher esteem than Mr. Gunter."

"The Marchioness seems very fond of her parrot, Miss Graves; but she is a sweet woman!"

"Oh, a dear, amiable creature! but I can not think how she can bear the eternal screaming of that noisy bird."

"Nor I, indeed. Well, thank goodness, Mrs. Million has no pets; eh! Dr. Sly?"

"Certainly. I am clearly of opinion that it can not be wholesome to have so many animals about a house. Besides which, I have noticed that the Marchioness always selects the nicest morsels for that little poodle; and I am also clearly of opinion, Miss Graves, that the fit it had the other day arose from repletion."

"I have no doubt of it in the world. She consumes three pounds of arrowroot weekly and two pounds of the finest loaf sugar, which I have the trouble of grating every Monday morning. Mrs. Million appears to be a most amiable woman, Miss Gusset?"

"Quite perfection; so charitable, so intellectual, such a soul! It is a pity, though, her manner is so abrupt; she really does not appear to advantage sometimes; eh! Dr. Sly?"

The Toady's Toady bowed assent as usual. "Well," rejoined Miss Graves, "that is rather a fault of the dear Marchioness, a little want of consideration for another's feelings; but she means nothing."

"Oh, no! nor Mrs. Million, dear creature! She means nothing; though, I dare say, not knowing her so well as we do; eh! Dr. Sly? you were a little surprised at the way in which she spoke to me at dinner."

"All people have their oddities, Miss Gusset. I am sure the Marchioness is not aware how she tries my patience about that little wretch Julie. I had to rub her with warm flannels for an hour and a half before the fire this morning; that is that Vivian Grey's doing."

"Who is this Mr. Grey, Miss Graves?"

"Who, indeed! Some young man the Marquess has picked up, and who comes lecturing here about poodles and parrots, and thinking himself quite Lord Paramount, I can assure you. I am surprised that the Marchioness, who is a most sensible woman, can patronize such conduct a moment; but whenever she begins to see through him the young gentleman has always got a story about a bracelet, or a bandeau, and quite turns her head."

"Very disagreeable, I am sure."

"Some people are so easily managed! By the bye, Miss Gusset, who could have advised Mrs. Million to wear crimson? So large as she is, it does not at all suit her. I suppose it's a favorite color."

"Dear Miss Graves, you are always so insinuating. What can Miss Graves mean; eh! Dr. Sly?"

A Lord Burleigh shake of the head.

"Cynthia Courtown seems as lively as ever," said Miss Gusset.

"Yes, lively enough; but I wish her manner was less brusque."

"Brusque, indeed! you may well say so. She nearly pushed me down in the Hall; and when I looked as if I thought she might have given me a little more room, she tossed her head and said, 'Beg pardon, never saw you!'"

"I wonder what Lord Alhambra sees in that girl?"

"Oh! those forward misses always take the men."

"Well," said Miss Graves, "I have no notion that it will

come to anything; I am sure, I, for one, hope not," added she, with all a Toady's venom.

"The Marquess seems to keep a remarkably good table," said the physician. "There was a haunch to-day, which I really think was the finest haunch I ever met with; but that little move at dinner; it was, to say the least, very ill-timed."

"Yes, that was Vivian Grey again," said Miss Graves, very indignantly.

So you have got the Beaconsfields here, Miss Graves! Nice, unaffected, quiet people."

"Yes, very quiet."

"As you say, Miss Graves, very quiet, but a little heavy."

"Yes, heavy enough."

"If you had but seen the quantity of pineapples that boy Dormer Stanhope devoured at our *fête champêtre!* but I have the comfort of knowing that they made him very ill; eh! Dr. Sly?"

"Oh! he learned that from his uncle," said Miss Graves; "it is quite disgusting to see how that Vivian Grey encourages him."

"What an elegant, accomplished woman Mrs. Felix Lorraine seems to be, Miss Graves! I suppose the Marchioness is very fond of her?"

"Oh, yes; the Marchioness is so good-natured that I dare say she thinks very well of Mrs. Felix Lorraine. She thinks well of every one; but I believe Mrs. Felix is rather a greater favorite with the Marquess."

"O—h!" drawled out Miss Gusset with a very significant tone. "I suppose she is one of your playing-up ladies. I think you told me she was only on a visit here."

"A pretty long visit, though, for a sister-in-law, if sister-in-law she be. As I was saying to the Marchioness the other day, when Mrs. Felix offended her so violently by tramping on the dear little Julie, if it came into a court of justice I should like to see the proof; that's all. At any rate, it is pretty evident that Mr. Lorraine has had enough of his bargain."

"Quite evident, I think; eh! Dr. Sly? Those German women never make good English wives," continued Miss Gusset, with all a Toady's patriotism.

"Talking of wives, did not you think Lady Julia spoke very strangely of Sir Peter after dinner to-day? I hate that Lady Julia, if it be only for petting Vivian Grey so."

"Yes, indeed, it is quite enough to make one sick; eh! Dr. Sly?"

The doctor shook his head mournfully, remembering the haunch.

"They say Ernest Clay is in sad difficulties, Miss Gusset."

"Well, I always expected his dash would end in that. Those wild harum-scarum men are monstrous disagreeable; I like a person of some reflection; eh! Dr. Sly?"

Before the doctor could bow his usual assent there entered a pretty little page, very daintily attired in a fancy dress of green and silver. Twirling his richly-chased dirk with one tiny white hand, and at the same time playing with a pet curl which was picturesquely flowing over his forehead, he advanced with ambling gait to Miss Gusset, and, in a mincing voice and courtly phrase, summoned her to the imperial presence.

The lady's features immediately assumed the expression which befitted the approaching interview, and in a moment Miss Graves and the physician were left alone.

"Very amiable young woman Miss Gusset appears to be, Dr. Sly?"

"Oh! the most amiable being in the world; I owe her the greatest obligations."

"So gentle in her manners."

"Oh, yes, so gentle."

"So considerate for everybody."

"Oh, yes! so considerate," echoed the Aberdeen M.D.

"I am afraid, though, she must sometimes meet with people who do not exactly understand her character; such extraordinary consideration for others is sometimes liable to misconstruction."

"Very sensibly remarked, Miss Graves. I am sure Miss Gusset means well; and that kind of thing is all very admirable in its way; but, but—"

"But what, Dr. Sly?"

"Why, I was merely going to hazard an observation that, according to my feelings, that is, to my own peculiar view

of the case, I should prefer some people thinking more about
their own business, and, and, but I mean nothing."

"Oh, no, of course not, Dr. Sly! You know we always
except our own immediate friends, at least when we can be
sure they are our friends; but, as you were saying, or going
to say, those persons who are so very anxious about other
people's affairs are not always the most agreeable persons in
the world to live with. It certainly did strike me that that
interference of Miss Gusset's about Julie to-day was, to say
the least, very odd."

"Oh, my dear madam! when you know her as well as I
do, you will see she is always ready to put in a word."

"Well! do you know, Dr. Sly, between ourselves, that was
exactly my impression; and she is then very, very, I do not
exactly mean to say meddling or inquisitive; but, but you understand me, Dr. Sly?"

"Perfectly; and if I were to speak my mind, which I do
not hesitate to do in confidence to you, Miss Graves, I really
should say that she has the most jealous, irritable, malicious,
meddling, and at the same time fawning, disposition that I
ever met with in the whole course of my life, and I speak
from experience."

"Well, do you know, Dr. Sly, from all I have seen, that
was exactly my impression; therefore I have been particularly careful not to commit myself to such a person."

"Ah! Miss Graves! if all ladies were like you! O—h!"

"My dear Dr. Sly!"

CHAPTER XVI

VIVIAN had duly acquainted the Marquess with the successful progress of his negotiations with their intended
partisans, and Lord Carabas had himself conversed with them
singly on the important subject. It was thought proper, however, in this stage of the proceedings, that the persons inter-
'ested should meet together; and so the two Lords, and Sir
Berdmore, and Vivian were invited to dine with the Marquess
alone, and in his library.

There was abundance of dumb-waiters and other inventions by which the ease of the guests might be consulted, without risking even their secret looks to the gaze of liveried menials. The Marquess's gentleman sat in an ante-chamber, in case human aid might be necessary, and everything, as his Lordship averred, was "on the same system as the Cabinet Dinners."

In the ancient kingdom of England it hath ever been the custom to dine previously to transacting business. This habit is one of those few which are not contingent upon the mutable fancies of fashion, and at this day we see Cabinet Dinners and Vestry Dinners alike proving the correctness of our assertion. Whether the custom really expedites the completion or the general progress of the business which gives rise to it is a grave question, which we do not feel qualified to decide. Certain it is that very often, after the *dinner*, an appointment is made for the transaction of the *business* on the following morning: at the same time it must be remembered that, had it not been for the opportunity which the banquet afforded of developing the convivial qualities of the guests, and drawing out, by the assistance of generous wine, their most kindly sentiments and most engaging feelings, it is very probable that the appointment for the transaction of the business would never have been made at all.

There certainly was every appearance that "the great business," as the Marquess styled it, would not be very much advanced by the cabinet dinner at Chateau Desir. For, in the first place, the table was laden "with every delicacy of the season," and really, when a man is either going to talk sense, fight a duel, or make his will, nothing should be seen at dinner save cutlets and the lightest Bordeaux. And, in the second place, it must be confessed that, when it came to the point of all the parties interested meeting, the Marquess's courage somewhat misgave him. Not that any particular reason occurred to him which would have induced him to yield one jot of the theory of his sentiments, but the putting them in practice rather made him nervous. In short, he was as convinced as ever that he was an ill-used man, of great influence and abilities; but then he remembered his agreeable sinecure and his dignified office, and he might not succeed. The thought did not please.

But here they were all assembled; receding was impossible; and so the Marquess took a glass of claret, and felt more courageous.

"My Lords and Gentlemen," he began, "although I have myself taken the opportunity of communicating to you singly my thoughts upon a certain subject, and although, if I am rightly informed, my excellent young friend has communicated to you more fully upon that subject; yet, my Lords and Gentlemen, I beg to remark that this is the first time that we have collectively assembled to consult on the possibility of certain views, upon the propriety of their nature, and the expediency of their adoption." (Here the claret passed.) "The present state of parties," the Marquess continued, "has doubtless for a long time engaged your attention. It is very peculiar, and although the result has been gradually arrived at, it is nevertheless, now that it is realized, startling, and not, I apprehend, very satisfactory. There are few distinctions now between the two sides of the House of Commons, very different from the times in which most, I believe all, of us, my Lords and Gentlemen, were members of that assembly. The question then naturally arises, why a certain body of individuals, who now represent no opinions, should arrogate to themselves the entire government and control of the country? A second question would occur, how they contrive to succeed in such an assumption? They succeed clearly because the party who placed them in power, because they represented certain opinions, still continue to them their support. Some of the most influential members of that party, I am bold to say, may be found in this room. I don't know, if the boroughs of Lord Courtown and Lord Beaconsfield were withdrawn at a critical division, what might be the result. I am quite sure that if the forty country gentlemen who follow, I believe I am justified in saying, our friend Sir Berdmore, and wisely follow him, were to declare their opposition to any particular tax, the present men would be beaten, as they have been beaten before. I was myself a member of the government when so beaten, and I know what Lord Liverpool said the next morning. Lord Liverpool said the next morning, 'Forty country gentlemen, if they choose, might repeal every tax in the Budget.' Under these circumstances, my Lords and Gentlemen, it becomes us, in my opinion, to consider our situation. I am far from wishing to witness any general change, or, indeed, very wide reconstruction of the present administration. I think the interests of the country require that the general tenor of their system should be supported; but there are members of that administration whose claims to that distinction appear to me more than questionable, while at the same time there are individuals excluded, personages of great influence and recognized talents, who ought no longer, in my opinion, to occupy a position in the background. Mr. Vivian Grey, a gentleman whom I have the honor to call my particular friend, and who, I believe, has had already the pleasure of incidentally conversing with you on the matters to which I have referred, has given great attention to this important subject. He is a younger man than any of us, and certainly has much better lungs than I have. I will take the liberty, therefore, of requesting him to put the case in its completeness before us."

A great deal of "desultory conversation," as it is styled, relative to the great topic of debate, now occurred. When the blood of the party was tolerably warmed, Vivian addressed them. The tenor of his oration may be imagined. He developed the new political principles, demonstrated the mistake under the baneful influence of which they had so long suffered, promised them place, and power, and patronage, and personal consideration, if they would only act on the principles which he recommended, in the most flowing language and the most melodious voice in which the glories of ambition were ever yet chanted. There was a buzz of admiration when the flattering music ceased; the Marquess smiled triumphantly, as if to say, "Didn't I tell you he was a monstrous clever fellow?" and the whole business seemed settled. Lord Courtown gave in a bumper, *"Mr. Vivian Grey, and success to his maiden speech!"* and Vivian replied by proposing *"The New Union!"* At last, Sir Berdmore, the coolest of them all, raised his voice: "He quite agreed with Mr. Grey in the principles which he had developed; and, for his own part, he was free to confess that he had perfect confidence in that gentleman's very brilliant abilities, and augured from their exertion complete and triumphant success. At the same time, he felt it his duty to remark to their Lordships, and also to that gentleman, that the House of Commons was a new scene to him; and he put it, whether they were quite convinced that they were sufficiently strong as regarded talent in that assembly. He could not take it upon himself to offer to become the leader of the party. Mr. Grey might be capable of undertaking that charge, but still, it must be remembered that in that assembly he was as yet untried. He made no apology to Mr. Grey for speaking his mind so freely; he was sure that his motives could not be misinterpreted. If their Lordships, on the whole, were of opinion that this charge should be intrusted to him, he, Sir Berdmore, having the greatest confidence in Mr. Grey's abilities, would certainly support him to the utmost."

"He can do anything," said the Marquess.

"He is a surprising clever man!" said Lord Courtown.

"He is a surprising clever man!" echoed Lord Beaconsfield.

"Stop, my Lords," said Vivian; "your good opinion deserves my gratitude, but these important matters do indeed require a moment's consideration. I trust that Sir Berdmore Scrope does not imagine that I am the vain idiot to be offended at his most excellent remarks, even for a moment. Are we not met here for the common good, and to consult for the success of the common cause? Whatever my talents are, they are at your service, and in your service will I venture anything; but surely, my Lords, you will not unnecessarily intrust this great business to a raw hand! I need only aver that I am ready to follow any leader who can play his great part in a becoming manner."

"Noble!" said the Marquess.

But who was the leader to be? Sir Berdmore frankly confessed that he had none to propose; and the Viscount and the Baron were quite silent.

"Gentlemen!" exclaimed the Marquess, "Gentlemen! there is a man who could do our bidding." The eyes of every guest were fixed on the haranguing host.

"Gentlemen, fill your glasses. I give you our leader, Mr. Frederick Cleveland!"

"Cleveland!" every one exclaimed. A glass of claret fell from Lord Courtown's hand; Lord Beaconsfield stopped as he was about to fill his glass, and stood gaping at the Marquess with the decanter in his hand; and Sir Berdmore stared on the

table, as men do when something unexpected and astounding
has occurred at dinner which seems past all their management.
"Cleveland!" exclaimed the guests.

"I should as soon have expected you to have given us
Lucifer!" said Lord Courtown.

"Or the present Secretary!" said Lord Beaconsfield.

"Or yourself," said Sir Berdmore.

"And does any one maintain that Frederick Cleveland is
not capable of driving out a much stronger Government than
he will have to cope with?" demanded the Marquess with a
rather fierce air.

"We do not deny Mr. Cleveland's powers, my Lord; we
only humbly beg to suggest that it appears to us that, of all
the persons in the world, the man with whom Mr. Cleveland
would be least inclined to coalesce would be the Marquess of
Carabas."

The Marquess looked somewhat blank.

"Gentlemen," said Vivian, "do not despair; it is enough for
me to know that there is a man who is capable of doing our
work. Be he animate man or incarnate fiend, provided he can
be found within this realm, I pledge myself that within ten
days he is drinking my noble friend's health at this very
board."

The Marquess said "Bravo," the rest smiled, and rose from
the table in some confusion. Little more was said on the
"great business." The guests took refuge in coffee and a glass
of liqueur. The pledge was, however, apparently accepted, and
Lord Carabas and Vivian were soon left alone. The Marquess
seemed agitated by Vivian's offer and engagement. "This is
a grave business," he said; "you hardly know, my dear Vivian,
what you have undertaken; but, if anybody can succeed, you
will. We must talk of this to-morrow. There are some obstacles, and I should once have thought, invincible. I can not
conceive what made me mention his name; but it has been
often in my mind since you first spoke to me. You and he
together, we might carry everything before us. But there are
some obstacles; no doubt there are some obstacles. You heard
what Courtown said, a man who does not make difficulties, and
Beaconsfield, a man who does not say much. Courtown called
him Lucifer. He is Lucifer. But, by Jove, you are the man

to overcome obstacles. We must talk of it to-morrow. So now, my dear fellow, good-night!"

"What have I done?" thought Vivian; "I am sure that Lucifer may know, for I do not. This Cleveland is, I suppose, after all, but a man. I saw the feeble fools were wavering, and, to save all, made a leap in the dark. Well! is my skull cracked? *Nous verrons.* How hot either this room or my blood is! Come, for some fresh air (he opened the library window). How fresh and soft it is! Just the night for the balcony. Hah! music! I can not mistake that voice. Singular woman! I will just walk on till I am beneath her window."

Vivian accordingly proceeded along the balcony, which extended down one whole side of the Chateau. While he was looking at the moon he stumbled against some one. It was Colonel Delmington. He apologized to the militaire for treading on his toes, and wondered "how the devil he got there!"

BOOK III

CHAPTER I

FREDERICK CLEVELAND was educated at Eton and at Cambridge; and after having proved, both at the school and the university, that he possessed talents of a high order, he had the courage, in order to perfect them, to immure himself for three years in a German university. It was impossible, therefore, for two minds to have been cultivated on more contrary systems than those of Frederick Cleveland and Vivian Grey. The systems on which they had been educated were not, however, more discordant than the respective tempers of the pupils. With that of Vivian Grey the reader is now somewhat acquainted. It has been shown that he was one precociously convinced of the necessity of managing mankind, by studying their tempers and humoring their weaknesses. Cleveland turned from the Book of Nature with contempt, and although his was a mind of extraordinary acuteness, he was, at three-and-thirty, as ignorant of the workings of the human heart as when, in the innocence of boyhood, he first reached Eton.

Although possessed of no fortune, from his connections and the reputation of his abilities, he entered Parliament at an early age. His success was eminent. It was at this period that he formed a great intimacy with the present Marquess of Carabas, then Under-Secretary of State. His exertions for the party to which Mr. Under-Secretary Lorraine belonged were unremitting; and it was mainly through their influence that a great promotion took place in the official appointments of the party. When the hour of reward came, Mr. Lorraine and his friends unfortunately forgot their youthful champion. He remonstrated, and they smiled: he reminded them of private friendship, and they answered him with political expediency. Mr. Cleveland went down to the House, and attacked his old co-mates in a spirit of unexampled bitterness. He examined in review the various members of the party that had deserted him. They trembled on their seats, while they writhed beneath the keenness of his satire: but when the orator came to Mr. President Lorraine, he flourished the tomahawk on high like a wild Indian chieftain; and the attack was so awfully severe, so overpowering, so annihilating, that even this hackneyed and hardened official trembled, turned pale, and quitted the House. Cleveland's triumph was splendid, but it was only for a night. Disgusted with mankind, he scouted the thousand offers of political connections which crowded upon him; and having succeeded in making an arrangement with his creditors, he accepted the Chiltern Hundreds.

By the interest of his friends he procured a judicial situation of sufficient emolument, but of local duty; and to fulfil this duty he was obliged to reside in North Wales. The locality, indeed, suited him well, for he was sick of the world at nine-and-twenty; and, carrying his beautiful and newly-married wife from the world, which without him she could not love, Mr. Cleveland enjoyed all the luxuries of a cottage *ornée* in the most romantic part of the Principality. Here were born unto him a son and daughter, beautiful children, upon whom the father lavished all the affection which Nature had intended for the world.

Four years had Cleveland now passed in his solitude, an

unhappy man. A thousand times during the first year of his retirement he cursed the moment of excitement which had banished him from the world; for he found himself without resources, and restless as a curbed courser. Like many men who are born to be orators, like Curran and like Fox, Cleveland was not blessed, or cursed, with the faculty of composition; and indeed, had his pen been that of a ready writer, pique would have prevented him from delighting or instructing a world whose nature he endeavored to persuade himself was base, and whose applause ought, consequently, to be valueless. In the second year he endeavored to while away his time by interesting himself in those pursuits which Nature has kindly provided for country gentlemen. Farming kept him alive for a while; but, at length, his was the prize ox; and, having gained a cup, he got wearied of kine too prime for eating, wheat too fine for the composition of the staff of life, and plows so ingeniously contrived that the very ingenuity prevented them from being useful. Cleveland was now seen wandering over the moors and mountains, with a gun over his shoulder and a couple of dogs at his heels; but ennui returned in spite of his patent percussion: and so, at length, tired of being a sportsman, he almost became what he had fancied himself in an hour of passion, a misanthrope.

After having been closeted with Lord Carabas for a considerable time the morning after the cabinet dinner, Vivian left Chateau Desir.

He traveled night and day, until he arrived in the vicinity of Mr. Cleveland's abode. What was he to do now? After some deliberation, he despatched a note to Mr. Cleveland, informing him "that he (Mr. Grey) was the bearer to Mr. Cleveland of a 'communication of importance.' Under the circumstances of the case, he observed that he had declined bringing any letters of introduction. He was quite aware, therefore, that he should have no right to complain if he had to travel back three hundred miles without having the honor of an interview; but he trusted that this necessary breach of etiquette would be overlooked."

The note produced the desired effect, and an appointment was made for Mr. Grey to call at Kenrich Lodge on the following morning.

Vivian, as he entered the room, took a rapid glance at its master. Mr. Cleveland was tall and distinguished, with a face which might have been a model for manly beauty. He came forward to receive Vivian with a Newfoundland dog on one side and a large black greyhound on the other; and the two animals, after having elaborately examined the stranger, divided between them the luxuries of the rug. The reception which Mr. Cleveland gave our hero was cold and constrained; but it did not appear to be purposely uncivil, and Vivian flattered himself that his manner was not unusually stiff.

"I do not know whether I have the honor of addressing the son of Mr. Horace Grey?" said Mr. Cleveland, with a frowning countenance, which was intended to be courteous.

"I have that honor."

"Your father, sir, is a most amiable and able man. I had the pleasure of his acquaintance when I was in London, many years ago, at a time when Mr. Vivian Grey was not intrusted, I rather imagine, with missions 'of importance.'" Although Mr. Cleveland smiled when he said this, his smile was anything but a gracious one. The subdued satire of his keen eye burst out for an instant, and he looked as if he would have said, "Who is this younker who is trespassing upon my retirement?"

Vivian had, unbidden, seated himself by the side of Mr. Cleveland's library table; and, not knowing exactly how to proceed, was employing himself by making a calculation whether there were more black than white spots on the body of the old Newfoundland, who was now apparently happily slumbering.

"Well, sir!" continued the Newfoundland's master, "the nature of your communication? I am fond of coming to the point."

Now this was precisely the thing which Vivian had determined not to do; and so he diplomatized, in order to gain time. "In stating, Mr. Cleveland, that the communication which I had to make was one of importance, I beg to be understood that it was with reference merely to my opinion of its nature that that phrase was used, and not as relative to the possible, or, allow me to say, the probable, opinion of Mr. Cleveland."

5

"Well, sir !" said that gentleman, with a somewhat disappointed air.

"As to the purport or nature of the communication, it is," said Vivian, with one of his sweetest cadences and looking up to Mr. Cleveland's face with an eye expressive of all kindness, "it is of a political nature."

"Well, sir !" again exclaimed Cleveland, looking very anxious, and moving restlessly on his library chair.

"When we take into consideration, Mr. Cleveland, the present aspect of the political world, when we call to mind the present situation of the two great political parties, you will not be surprised, I feel confident, when I mention that certain personages have thought that the season was at hand when a move might be made in the political world with very considerable effect—"

"Mr. Grey, what am I to understand?" interrupted Mr. Cleveland, who began to suspect that the envoy was no greenhorn.

"I feel confident, Mr. Cleveland, that I am doing very imperfect justice to the mission with which I am intrusted ; but, sir, you must be aware that the delicate nature of such disclosures, and—"

"Mr. Grey, I feel confident that you do not doubt my honor ; and, as for the rest, the world has, I believe, some foolish tales about me ; but, believe me, you shall be listened to with patience. I am certain that, whatever may be the communication, Mr. Vivian Grey is a gentleman who will do its merits justice."

And now Vivian, having succeeded in exciting Cleveland's curiosity and securing himself the certainty of a hearing, and having also made a favorable impression, dropped the diplomatist altogether, and was explicit enough for a Spartan.

"Certain Noblemen and Gentlemen of eminence and influence, hitherto considered as props of the —— party, are about to take a novel and decided course next Session. It is to obtain the aid and personal co-operation of Mr. Cleveland that I am now in Wales."

"Mr. Grey, I have promised to listen to you with patience : you are too young a man to know much, perhaps, of the history of so insignificant a personage as myself, otherwise you

would have been aware that there is no subject in the world
on which I am less inclined to converse than that of politics.
If I were entitled to take such a liberty, I would recommend
you to think of them as little as I do; but enough of this. Who
is the mover of the party?"

"My Lord Courtown is a distinguished member of it."

"Courtown, Courtown; powerful enough: but surely the
good Viscount's skull is not exactly the head for the chief of
a cabal?"

"There is my Lord Beaconsfield."

"Powerful, too; but a dolt."

"Well," thought Vivian, "it must out at last; and so to it
boldly. And, Mr. Cleveland, there is little fear that we may
secure the great influence and tried talents of the Marquess of
Carabas."

"The Marquess of Carabas!" almost shrieked Mr. Cleveland, as he started from his seat and paced the room with
hurried steps; and the greyhound and the Newfoundland
jumped up from the rug, shook themselves, growled, and then
imitated their master in promenading the apartment, but with
more dignified and stately paces. "The Marquess of Carabas!
Now, Mr. Grey, speak to me with the frankness which one
gentleman should use to another; is the Marquess of Carabas
privy to this application?"

"He himself proposed it."

"Then he is baser than even I conceived. Mr. Grey, I am
a man spare of my speech to those with whom I am unacquainted, and the world calls me a soured, malicious man.
And yet, when I think for a moment that one so young as you
are, endowed as I must suppose with no ordinary talents, and
actuated as I will believe with a pure and honorable spirit,
should be the dupe, or tool, or even present friend of such a
creature as this perjured Peer, it gives me a pang."

"Mr. Cleveland," said Vivian, "I am grateful for your
kindness; and although we may probably part, in a few hours,
never to meet again, I will speak to you with the frankness
which you have merited, and to which I feel you are entitled.
I am not the dupe of the Marquess of Carabas; I am not, I
trust, the dupe or tool of any one whatever. Believe me, sir,
there is that at work in England which, taken at the tide, may

lead on to fortune. I see this, sir; I, a young man, uncommitted in political principles, unconnected in public life, feeling some confidence, I confess, in my own abilities, but desirous of availing myself, at the same time, of the powers of others. Thus situated, I find myself working for the same end as my Lord Carabas and twenty other men of similar calibre, mental and moral; and, sir, am I to play the hermit in the drama of life because, perchance, my fellow-actors may be sometimes fools, and occasionally knaves? If the Marquess of Carabas has done you the ill service which Fame says he has, your sweetest revenge will be to make him your tool; your most perfect triumph, to rise to power by his influence.

"I confess that I am desirous of finding in you the companion of my career. Your splendid talents have long commanded my admiration; and, as you have given me credit for something like good feeling, I will say that my wish to find in you a colleague is greatly increased when I see that those splendid talents are even the least estimable points in Mr. Cleveland's character. But, sir, perhaps all this time I am in error; perhaps Mr. Cleveland is, as the world reports him, no longer the ambitious being who once commanded the admiration of a listening Senate; perhaps, convinced of the vanity of human wishes, Mr. Cleveland would rather devote his attention to the furtherance of the interests of his immediate circle; and, having schooled his intellect in the universities of two nations, is probably content to pass the hours of his life in meditating on the quarrels of a country village."

Vivian ceased. Cleveland heard him with his head resting on both his arms. He started at the last expression, and something like a blush suffused his cheek, but he did not reply. At last he jumped up and rang the bell. "Come, Mr. Grey," said he, "I am in no humor for politics this morning. You must not, at any rate, visit Wales for nothing. Morris! send down to the village for this gentleman's luggage. Even we cottagers have a bed for a friend, Mr. Grey: come, and I will introduce you to my wife."

CHAPTER II

AND Vivian was now an inmate of Kenrich Lodge. It would have been difficult to have conceived a life of more pure happiness than that which was apparently enjoyed by its gifted master. A beautiful wife and lovely children, and a romantic situation, and an income sufficient not only for their own but for the wants of their necessitous neighbors; what more could man wish? Answer me, thou inexplicable myriad of sensations, which the world calls human nature!

Three days passed over in delightful converse. It was so long since Cleveland had seen any one fresh from the former scenes of his life that the company of any one would have been agreeable; but here was a companion who knew every one, everything, full of wit and anecdote, and literature and fashion; and then so engaging in his manners, and with such a winning voice.

The heart of Cleveland relented; his stern manner gave way; all his former warm and generous feeling gained the ascendant; he was in turn amusing, communicative, and engaging. Finding that he could please another, he began to be pleased himself. The nature of the business upon which Vivian was his guest rendered confidence necessary; confidence begets kindness. In a few days Vivian necessarily became more acquainted with Mr. Cleveland's disposition and situation than if they had been acquainted for as many years; in short,

> They talked with open heart and tongue,
> Affectionate and true,
> A pair of friends.

Vivian, for some time, dwelt upon everything but the immediate subject of his mission; but when, after the experience of a few days, their hearts were open to each other, and they had mutually begun to discover that there was a most astonishing similarity in their principles, their tastes, their feelings, then the magician poured forth his incantation, and raised the once-laid ghost of Cleveland's ambition. The recluse agreed to take the lead of the Carabas party. He was to leave Wales immediately, and resign his place; in return for which the nephew of Lord Courtown was immediately to give up, in his favor, an office of considerable emolument; and, having thus provided some certainty for his family, Frederick Cleveland prepared himself to combat for a more important office.

CHAPTER III

"IS Mr. Cleveland handsome?" asked Mrs. Felix Lorraine of Vivian, immediately on his return, "and what color are his eyes?"

"Upon my honor, I have not the least recollection of ever looking at them; but I believe he is not blind."

"How foolish you are! now tell me, pray, *point de moquerie*, is he amusing?"

"What does Mrs. Felix Lorraine mean by amusing?" asked Vivian.

"Oh! you always tease me with your definitions; go away, I will quarrel with you."

"By the bye, Mrs. Felix Lorraine, how is Colonel Delmington?"

Vivian redeemed his pledge: Mr. Cleveland arrived. It was the wish of the Marquess, if possible, not to meet his old friend till dinner-time. He thought that, surrounded by his guests, certain awkward senatorial reminiscences might be got over. But, unfortunately, Mr. Cleveland arrived about an hour before dinner, and, as it was a cold autumnal day, most of the visitors who were staying at Chateau Desir were assembled in the drawing-room. The Marquess sallied forward to receive his guest with a most dignified countenance and a most aristocratic step; but, before he got half-way, his coronation pace degenerated into a strut, and then into a shamble, and with an awkward and confused countenance, half impudent and half flinching, he held forward his left hand to his newly arrived visitor. Mr. Cleveland looked terrifically courteous and amiably arrogant. He greeted the Marquess with a smile at once gracious and grim, and looked something like Goliath, as you see the Philistine depicted in some old German painting, looking down upon the pigmy fighting men of Israel.

As is generally the custom when there is a great deal to be arranged and many points to be settled, days flew over, and very little of the future system of the party was matured. Vivian made one or two ineffectual struggles to bring the Marquess to a business-like habit of mind, but his Lordship never dared to trust himself alone with Cleveland, and, indeed, almost lost the power of speech when in presence of the future leader of his party; so, in the morning, the Marquess played off the two Lords and Sir Berdmore against his former friend, and then, to compensate for not meeting Mr. Cleveland in the morning, he was particularly courteous to him at dinner-time, and asked him always "how he liked his ride?" and invariably took wine with him. As for the rest of the day, he had particularly requested his faithful counselor, Mrs. Felix Lorraine, "for God's sake to take this man off his shoulders"; and so that lady, with her usual kindness, and merely to oblige his Lordship, was good enough to patronize Mr. Cleveland, and on the fourth day was taking a moonlit walk with him.

Mr. Cleveland had now been ten days at Chateau Desir, and was to take his departure the next morning for Wales, in order to arrange everything for his immediate settlement in the metropolis. Every point of importance was postponed until their meeting in London. Mr. Cleveland only agreed to take the lead of the party in the Commons, and received the personal pledge of Lord Courtown as to the promised office.

It was a September day, and to escape from the excessive heat of the sun, and at the same time to enjoy the freshness of the air, Vivian was writing his letters in the conservatory, which opened into one of the drawing-rooms. The numerous party which then honored the Chateau with their presence were out, as he conceived, on a picnic excursion to the Elfin's Well, a beautiful spot about ten miles off; and among the adventurers were, as he imagined, Mrs. Felix Lorraine and Mr. Cleveland.

Vivian was rather surprised at hearing voices in the adjoining room, and he was still more so when, on looking round, he found that the sounds proceeded from the very two individuals whom he thought were far away. Some tall American plants concealed him from their view, but he observed all that passed distinctly, and a singular scene it was. Mrs. Felix Lorraine was on her knees at the feet of Mr. Cleveland; her countenance indicated the most contrary passions, contending, as it were, for mastery; supplication, anger, and, shall I call it, love? Her companion's countenance was hid, but it was evident that it was not wreathed with smiles: there were a few hurried sentences uttered, and then both quitted the room at different doors, the lady in despair and the gentleman in disgust.

CHAPTER IV

AND now Chateau Desir was almost deserted. Mrs. Million continued her progress northward. The Courtowns, and the Beaconsfields, and the Scropes quitted immediately after Mr. Cleveland; and when the families that form the material of the visiting corps retire, the nameless nothings that are always lounging about the country mansions of the great, such as artists, tourists, authors, and other live stock, soon disappear. Mr. Vivian Grey agreed to stay another fortnight, at the particular request of the Marquess.

Very few days had passed ere Vivian was exceedingly struck at the decided change which suddenly took place in his Lordship's general demeanor toward him.

The Marquess grew reserved and uncommunicative, scarcely mentioning "the great business" which had previously been the sole subject of his conversation but to find fault with some arrangement, and exhibiting, whenever his name was mentioned, a marked acrimony against Mr. Cleveland. This rapid change alarmed as much as it astonished Vivian, and he mentioned his feelings and observations to Mrs. Felix Lorraine. That lady agreed with him that something certainly was wrong; but could not, unfortunately, afford him any clew to the mystery. She expressed the liveliest solicitude that any misunderstanding should be put an end to, and offered her services for that purpose.

In spite, however, of her well-expressed anxiety, Vivian had his own ideas on the subject; and, determined to unravel the affair, he had recourse to the Marchioness.

"I hope your Ladyship is well to-day. I had a letter from Count Caumont this morning. He tells me that he has got the prettiest poodle from Paris that you can possibly conceive! waltzes like an angel, and acts proverbs on its hind feet."

Her Ladyship's eyes glistened with admiration.

"I have told Caumont to send it me down immediately, and I shall then have the pleasure of presenting it to your Ladyship."

Her Ladyship's eyes sparkled with delight.

"I think," continued Vivian, "I shall take a ride to-day. By the bye, how is the Marquess? he seems in low spirits lately."

"Oh, Mr. Grey! I do not know what you have done to him," said her Ladyship, settling at least a dozen bracelets; "but, but—"

"But what?"

"He thinks; he thinks—"

"Thinks what, dear lady?"

"That you have entered into a combination, Mr. Grey."

"Entered into a combination!"

"Yes, Mr. Grey! a conspiracy, a conspiracy against the Marquess, with Mr. Cleveland. He thinks that you have made him serve your purpose, and now you are going to get rid of him."

"Well, that is excellent; and what else does he think?"

"He thinks you talk too loud," said the Marchioness, still working at her bracelets.

"Well! that is shockingly vulgar! Allow me to recommend your Ladyship to alter the order of those bracelets, and place the blue and silver against the maroon. You may depend upon it, that is the true Vienna order. And what else does the Marquess say?"

"He thinks you are generally too authoritative. Not that I think so, Mr. Grey: I am sure your conduct to me has been most courteous. The blue and silver next to the maroon, did you say? Yes; certainly it does look better. I have no doubt the Marquess is quite wrong, and I dare say you will set things right immediately. You will remember the pretty poodle, Mr. Grey? and you will not tell the Marquess I mentioned anything."

"Oh! certainly not. I will give orders for them to book an inside place for the poodle, and send him down by the coach immediately. I must be off now. Remember the blue and silver next to the maroon. Good-morning to your Ladyship."

"Mrs. Felix Lorraine, I am your most obedient slave," said Vivian Grey, as he met that lady on the landing-place. "I can see no reason why I should not drive you this bright day to the Elfin's Well; we have long had an agreement to go there."

The lady smiled a gracious assent; the pony phaeton was immediately ordered.

"How pleasant Lady Courtown and I used to discourse about martingales! I think I invented one, did I not? Pray, Mrs. Felix Lorraine, can you tell me what a martinagle is? for upon my honor I have forgotten, or never knew."

"If you found a martingale for the mother, Vivian, it had been well if you had found a curb for the daughter. Poor Cynthia! I had intended once to advise the Marchioness to interfere; but one forgets these things."

"One does. Oh, Mrs. Felix!" exclaimed Vivian, "I told your admirable story of the Leyden Professor to Mrs. Cleveland. It is universally agreed to be the best ghost-story extant. I think you said you knew the Professor."

"Well! I have seen him often, and heard the story from his own lips. And, as I mentioned before, far from being superstitious, he was an *esprit fort*. Do you know, Mr. Grey, I have such an interesting packet from Germany to-day; from my cousin, Baron Rodenstein. But I must keep all the stories for the evening; come to my boudoir, and I will read them to you. There is one tale which I am sure will make a convert even of you. It happened to Rodenstein himself, and within these three months," added the lady in a serious tone. "The Rodensteins are a singular family. My mother was a Rodenstein. Do you think this beautiful?" said Mrs. Felix, showing

Vivian a small miniature which was attached to a chain round her neck. It was the portrait of a youth habited in the costume of a German student. His rich brown hair was flowing over his shoulders, and his dark blue eyes beamed with such a look of mysterious inspiration that they might have befitted a young prophet.

"Very, very beautiful!"

"'Tis Max, Max Rodenstein," said the lady, with a faltering voice. "He was killed at Leipsic, at the head of a band of his friends and fellow-students. Oh, Mr. Grey! this is a fair work of art, but if you had but seen the prototype you would have gazed on this as on a dim and washed-out drawing. There was one portrait, indeed, which did him more justice; but then that portrait was not the production of mortal pencil."

Vivian looked at his companion with a somewhat astonished air, but Mrs. Felix Lorraine's countenance was as little indicative of jesting as that of the young student whose miniature rested on her bosom.

"Did you say *not* the production of a mortal hand, Mrs. Felix Lorraine?"

"I am afraid I shall weary you with my stories, but the one I am about to tell is so well evidenced that I think even Mr. Vivian Grey will hear it without a sneer."

"A sneer! Oh, lady-love, do I ever sneer?"

"Max Rodenstein was the glory of his house. A being so beautiful in body and in soul you can not imagine, and I will not attempt to describe. This miniature has given you some faint idea of his image, and yet this is only the copy of a copy. The only wish of the Baroness Rodenstein which never could be accomplished was the possession of a portrait of her youngest son, for no consideration could induce Max to allow his likeness to be taken. His old nurse had always told him that the moment his portrait was taken he would die. The condition upon which such a beautiful being was allowed to remain in the world was, she always said, that his beauty should not be imitated. About three months before the battle of Leipsic, when Max was absent at the University, which was nearly four hundred miles from Rodenstein Castle, there arrived one morning a large case directed to the Baroness. On opening it it was found to contain a picture, the portrait of her son. The coloring was so vivid, the general execution so miraculous, that for some moments they forgot to wonder at the incident in their admiration of the work of art. In one corner of the picture, in small characters yet fresh, was an inscription, which on examining they found consisted of these words: 'Painted last night. Now, lady, thou hast thy wish.' My aunt sank into the Baron's arms.

"In silence and in trembling the wonderful portrait was suspended over the fireplace of my aunt's favorite apartment. The next day they received letters from Max. He was quite well, but mentioned nothing of the mysterious painting.

"Three months afterward, as a lady was sitting alone in the Baroness's room, and gazing on the portrait of him she loved right dearly, she suddenly started from her seat, and would have shrieked, had not an indefinable sensation prevented her. The eyes of the portrait moved. The lady stood leaning on a chair, pale, and trembling like an aspen, but gazing steadfastly on the animated portrait. It was no illusion of a heated fancy; again the eyelids trembled, there was a melancholy smile, and then they closed. The clock of Rodenstein Castle struck three. Between astonishment and fear the lady was tearless. Three days afterward came the news of the battle of Leipsic, and at the very moment that the eyes of the portrait closed Max Rodenstein had been pierced by a Polish lancer."

"And who was this wonderful lady, the witness of this wonderful incident?" asked Vivian.

"That lady was myself."

There was something so singular in the tone of Mrs. Felix Lorraine's voice, and so peculiar in the expression of her countenance, as she uttered these words, that the jest died on Vivian's tongue; and, for want of something better to do, he lashed the little ponies, which were already scampering at their full speed.

The road to the Elfin's Well ran through the wildest parts of the park; and after an hour and a half's drive they reached the fairy spot. It was a beautiful and pellucid spring, that bubbled up in a small wild dell, which, nurtured by the flowing stream, was singularly fresh and green. Above the spring had been erected a Gothic arch of gray stone, round which grew a few fine birch-trees. In short, Nature had intended the spot for picnics. There was fine water, and an interesting tradition; and as the parties always bring, or always should bring, a trained punster, champagne, and cold pasties, what more ought Nature to have provided?

"Come, Mrs. Lorraine, I will tie Gypsy to this ash, and then you and I will rest ourselves beneath these birch-trees, just where the fairies dance."

"Oh, delightful!"

"Now, truly, we should have some book of beautiful poetry to while away an hour. You will blame me for not bringing one. Do not. I would sooner listen to your voice; and, indeed, there is a subject on which I wish to ask your particular advice."

"*Is* there?"

"I have been thinking that this is a somewhat rash step of the Marquess; this throwing himself into the arms of his former bitterest enemy, Cleveland."

"You really think so?"

"Why, Mrs. Lorraine, does it appear to you to be the most prudent course of action which could have been conceived?"

"Certainly not."

"You agree with me, then, that there is, if not cause for regret at this engagement, at least for reflection on its probable consequences?"

"I quite agree with you."

"I know you do. I have had some conversation with the Marquess upon this subject this very morning."

"Have you?" eagerly exclaimed the lady, and she looked pale and breathed short.

"Ay; and he tells me you have made some very sensible observations on the subject. 'Tis pity they were not made before Mr. Cleveland left; the mischief might then have been prevented."

"I certainly have made some observations."

"And very kind of you. What a blessing for the Marquess to have such a friend!"

"I spoke to him," said Mrs. Felix, with a more assured tone, "in much the same spirit as you have been addressing me. It does, indeed, seem a most imprudent act, and I thought it my duty to tell him so."

"Ay, no doubt; but how came you, lady fair, to imagine that *I* was also a person to be dreaded by his Lordship; *I*, Vivian Grey?"

"Did I say *you?*" asked the lady, pale as death.

"Did you not, Mrs. Felix Lorraine? Have you not, regardless of my interests, in the most unwarrantable and unjustifiable manner; have you not, to gratify some private pique which you entertain against Mr. Cleveland; have you not, I ask you, poisoned the Marquess's mind against one who never did aught to you but what was kind and honorable?"

"I have been imprudent; I confess it; I have spoken somewhat loosely."

"Now, listen to me once more," and Vivian grasped her hand. "What has passed between you and Mr. Cleveland it is not for me to inquire. I give you my word of honor that he never mentioned your name to me. I can scarcely understand how any man could have incurred the deadly hatred which you appear to entertain for him. I repeat, I can contemplate no situation in which you could be placed together which would justify such behavior. It could not be justified, even if he had spurned you while—kneeling at his feet."

Mrs. Felix Lorraine shrieked and fainted. A sprinkling from the fairy stream soon recovered her. "Spare me! spare me!" she faintly cried: "say nothing of what you have seen."

"Mrs. Lorraine, I have no wish. I have spoken thus explicitly that we may not again misunderstand each other. I have spoken thus explicitly, I say, that I may not be under the necessity of speaking again, for if I speak again it must not be to Mrs. Felix Lorraine. There is my hand; and now let the Elfin's Well be blotted out of our memories."

Vivian drove rapidly home, and endeavored to talk in his usual tone and with his usual spirit; but his companion could not be excited. Once, ay, twice, she pressed his hand, and as he assisted her from the phaeton she murmured something like a blessing. She ran upstairs immediately. Vivian had to give some directions about the ponies; Gypsy was ill, or Fanny had a cold, or something of the kind; and so he was detained for about a quarter of an hour before the house, speaking most learnedly to grooms, and consulting on cases with a skilled gravity worthy of Professor Coleman.

When he entered the house he found the luncheon prepared, and Mrs. Felix pressed him earnestly to take some refreshment. He was indeed wearied, and agreed to take a glass of hock and seltzer.

"Let me mix it for you," said Mrs. Felix; "do you like sugar?"

Tired with his drive, Vivian Grey was leaning on the mantelpiece, with his eyes vacantly gazing on the looking-glass which rested on the marble slab. It was by pure accident that, reflected in the mirror, he distinctly beheld Mrs. Felix Lorraine open a small silver box, and throw some powder into the tumbler which she was preparing for him. She was leaning down, with her back almost turned to the glass, but still Vivian saw it distinctly. A sickness came over him, and ere he could recover himself his Hebe tapped him on the shoulder.

"Here, drink, drink while it is effervescent."

"I can not drink," said Vivian, "I am not thirsty; I am too hot; I am anything—"

"How foolish you are! It will be quite spoiled."

"No, no; the dog shall have it. Here, Fidele, you look thirsty enough; come here—"

"Mr. Grey, I do not mix tumblers for dogs," said the lady, rather agitated: "if you will not take it," and she held it once more before him, "here it goes forever." So saying she emptied the tumbler into a large globe of glass, in which some gold and silver fish were swimming their endless rounds.

CHAPTER V

THIS last specimen of Mrs. Felix Lorraine was somewhat too much even for the steeled nerves of Vivian Grey, and he sought his chamber for relief.

"Is it possible? Can I believe my senses? Or has some demon, as we read of in old tales, mocked me in a magic mirror? I can believe anything. Oh! my heart is very sick! I once imagined that I was using this woman for my purpose. Is it possible that aught of good can come to one who is forced to make use of such evil instruments as these? A horrible thought sometimes comes over my spirit. I fancy that in this mysterious foreigner, that in this woman, I have met a kind of double of myself. The same wonderful knowledge of the human mind, the same sweetness of voice, the same miraculous management which has brought us both under the same roof: yet do I find her the most abandoned of all beings; a creature guilty of that which, even in this guilty age, I thought was obsolete. And is it possible that I am like her? that I can resemble her? that even the indefinite shadow of my most unhallowed thought can for a moment be as vile as her righteousness? Oh, God! the system of my existence seems to stop. I can not breathe." He flung himself upon his bed, and felt for a moment as if he had quaffed the poisoned draught so lately offered.

"It is not so; it can not be so; it shall not be so! In seeking the Marquess I was unquestionably impelled by a mere feeling of self-interest; but I have advised him to no course of action in which his welfare is not equally consulted with my own. Indeed, if not principle, interest would make me act faithfully toward him, for my fortunes are bound up in his. But am I entitled, I, who can lose nothing, am I entitled to play with other men's fortunes? Am I all this time deceiving myself with some wretched sophistry? Am I, then, an intellectual Don Juan, reckless of human minds, as he was of human bodies; a spiritual libertine? But why this wild declamation? Whatever I have done, it is too late to recede; even this very moment delay is destruction, for now it is not a question as to the ultimate prosperity of our worldly prospects, but the immediate safety of our very bodies. Poison! Oh, God! oh, God! Away with all fear, all repentance, all thought of past, all reckoning of future. If I be the Juan that I fancied myself, then Heaven be praised! I have a confidant in all my trouble; the most faithful of counselors, the craftiest of valets; a Leporello often tried and never found wanting; my own good mind. And now, thou female fiend! the battle is to the strongest; and I see right well that the struggle between two such spirits will be a long and a fearful

one. Woe, I say, to the vanquished! You must be dealt with
by arts which even yourself can not conceive. Your boasted
knowledge of human nature shall not again stand you in stead;
for, mark me, from henceforward Vivian Grey's conduct
toward you shall have no precedent in human nature."

As Vivian re-entered the drawing-room he met a servant
carrying in the globe of gold and silver fishes.

"What, still in your pelisse, Mrs. Lorraine!" said Vivian.
"Nay, I hardly wonder at it, for surely a prettier pelisse never
yet fitted prettier form. You have certainly a most admirable
taste in dress; and this the more surprises me, for it is generally your plain personage that is the most *recherché* in frills
and fans and flounces."

The lady smiled.

"Oh! by the bye," continued her companion, "I have a letter
from Cleveland this morning. I wonder how any misunderstanding could possibly have existed between you, for he
speaks of you in such terms."

"What does he say?" was the quick question.

"Oh! what does he say?" drawled out Vivian; and he
yawned, and was most provokingly uncommunicative.

"Come, come, Mr. Grey, do tell me."

"Oh! tell you, certainly. Come, let us walk together in
the conservatory:" so saying, he took the lady by the hand,
and they left the room.

"And now for the letter, Mr. Grey."

"Ay, now for the letter;" and Vivian slowly drew an epistle
from his pocket, and therefrom read some exceedingly sweet
passages, which made Mrs. Felix Lorraine's very heart-blood
tingle. Considering that Vivian Grey had never in his life received a single letter from Mr. Cleveland, this was tolerably
well: but he was always an admirable improvisatore! "I am
sure that when Cleveland comes to town everything will be
explained; I am sure, at least, that it will not be my fault if
you are not the best friends. I am heroic in saying all this,
Mrs. Lorraine; there was a time when (and here Vivian seemed
so agitated that he could scarcely proceed), there was a time
when I could have called that man liar who would have
prophesied that Vivian Grey could have assisted another in
riveting the affections of Mrs. Felix Lorraine. But enough

of this. I am a weak, inexperienced boy, and misinterpret, perhaps, that which is merely the compassionate kindness natural to all women into a feeling of a higher nature. But I must learn to contain myself; I really do feel quite ashamed of my behavior about the tumbler to-day. To act with such unwarrantable unkindness, merely because I had remembered that you once performed the same kind office for Colonel Delmington, was indeed too bad."

"Colonel Delmington is a vain, empty-headed fool. Do not think of him, my dear Mr. Grey," said Mrs. Felix, with a countenance beaming with smiles.

"Well, I will not; and I will try to behave like a man; like a man of the world, I should say. But indeed you must excuse the warm feelings of a youth; and truly, when I call to mind the first days of our acquaintance, and then remember that our moonlit walks are gone forever, and that our—"

"Nay, do not believe so, my dear Vivian; believe me, as I ever shall be, your friend, your—"

"I will, I will, my dear, my own Amalia!"

CHAPTER VI

IT was an autumnal night; the wind was capricious and changeable as a petted beauty, or an Italian greyhound, or a shot silk. Now the breeze blew so fresh that the white clouds dashed along the sky as if they bore a band of witches too late for their Sabbath meeting, or some other mischief; and now, lulled and soft as the breath of a slumbering infant, you might almost have fancied it Midsummer Eve; and the bright moon, with her starry court, reigned undisturbed in the light blue sky. Vivian Grey was leaning against an old beech-tree in the most secluded part of the park, and was gazing on the moon.

Oh, thou bright moon! thou object of my first love! thou shalt not escape an invocation, although perchance at this very moment some varlet sonneteer is prating of "the boy Endymion" and "thy silver bow." Here to thee, Queen of the Night! in whatever name thou most delightest! Or Bendis, as they hailed thee in rugged Thrace; or Bubastis, as they howled to thee in mysterious Egypt; or Dian, as they sacrificed to thee in gorgeous Rome; or Artemis, as they sighed to thee on the bright plains of ever-glorious Greece! Why is it that all men gaze on thee? Why is it that all men love thee? Why is it that all men worship thee?

Shine on, shine on, sultana of the soul! the Passions are thy eunuch slaves, Ambition gazes on thee, and his burning brow is cooled, and his fitful pulse is calm. Grief wanders in her moonlit walk and sheds no tear; and when thy crescent smiles the lustre of Joy's reveling eyes is dusked. Quick Anger, in thy light, forgets revenge; and even dove-eyed Hope feeds on no future joys when gazing on the miracle of thy beauty.

Shine on, shine on! although a pure Virgin, thou art the mighty mother of all abstraction! The eye of the weary peasant returning from his daily toil, and the rapt gaze of the inspired poet, are alike fixed on thee; thou stillest the roar of marching armies, and who can doubt thy influence o'er the waves who has witnessed the wide Atlantic sleeping under thy silver beam?

Shine on, shine on! they say thou art Earth's satellite; yet when I gaze on thee my thoughts are not of thy suzerain. They teach us that thy power is a fable, and that thy divinity is a dream. Oh, thou bright Queen! I will be no traitor to thy sweet authority; and verily, I will not believe that thy influence o'er our hearts is, at this moment, less potent than when we worshiped in thy glittering fane of Ephesus, or trembled at the dark horrors of thine Arician rites. Then, hail to thee, Queen of the Night! Hail to thee, Diana, Triformis; Cynthia, Orthia, Taurica; ever mighty, ever lovely, ever holy! Hail! hail! hail!

Were I a metaphysician, I would tell you why Vivian Grey had been gazing two hours on the moon; for I could then present you with a most logical programme of the march of his ideas, since he whispered his last honeyed speech in the ear of Mrs. Felix Lorraine, at dinner-time, until this very moment, when he did not even remember that such a being as Mrs. Felix Lorraine breathed. Glory to the metaphysician's all-perfect theory! When they can tell me why, at a bright ban-

quet, the thought of death has flashed across my mind, who
fear not death; when they can tell me why, at the burial of my
beloved friend, when my very heart-strings seemed bursting,
my sorrow has been mocked by the involuntary remembrance
of ludicrous adventures and grotesque tales; when they can
tell me why, in a dark mountain pass, I have thought of an
absent woman's eyes; or why, when in the very act of squeez-
ing the third lime into a beaker of Burgundy cup, my memory
hath been of lean apothecaries and their vile drugs; why then,
I say again, glory to the metaphysician's all-perfect theory!
and fare you well, sweet world, and you, my merry masters,
whom, perhaps, I have studied somewhat too cunningly: *nosce
teipsum* shall be my motto. I will doff my traveling cap, and
on with the monk's cowl.

There are mysterious moments in some men's lives when
the faces of human beings are very agony to them, and when
the sound of the human voice is jarring as discordant music.
These fits are not the consequence of violent or contending
passions: they grow not out of sorrow, or joy, or hope, or fear,
or hatred, or despair. For in the hour of affliction the tones of
our fellow-creatures are ravishing as the most delicate lute;
and in the flush moment of joy where is the smiler who loves
not a witness to his revelry or a listener to his good fortune?
Fear makes us feel our humanity, and then we fly to men, and
Hope is the parent of kindness. The misanthrope and the
reckless are neither agitated nor agonized. It is in these moments that men find in Nature that congeniality of spirit which
they seek for in vain in their own species. It is in these moments that we sit by the side of a waterfall and listen to its
music the live-long day. It is in these moments that we gaze
upon the moon. It is in these moments that Nature becomes
our Egeria; and, refreshed and renovated by this beautiful
communion, we return to the world better enabled to fight our
parts in the hot war of passions, to perform the great duties
for which man appeared to have been created, to love, to hate,
to slander, and to slay.

It was past midnight, and Vivian was at a considerable
distance from the Chateau. He proposed entering by a side
door, which led into the billiard-room, and from thence, crossing the Long Gallery, he could easily reach his apartment with-

out disturbing any of the household. His way led through the little gate at which he had parted with Mrs. Felix Lorraine on the first day of their meeting.

As he softly opened the door which led into the Long Gallery he found he was not alone: leaning against one of the casements was a female. Her profile was to Vivian as he entered, and the moon, which shone bright through the window, lighted up a countenance which he might be excused for not immediately recognizing as that of Mrs. Felix Lorraine. She was gazing steadfastly, but her eye did not seem fixed upon any particular object. Her features appeared convulsed, but their contortions were not momentary, and, pale as death, a hideous grin seemed chiseled on her idiot countenance.

Vivian scarcely knew whether to stay or to retire. Desirous not to disturb her, he determined not even to breathe; and, as is generally the case, his very exertions to be silent made him nervous, and to save himself from being stifled he coughed.

Mrs. Lorraine immediately started and stared wildly around her, and when her eye caught Vivian's there was a sound in her throat something like the death-rattle.

"Who are you?" she eagerly asked.

"A friend," said Vivian Grey.

"How came you here?" and she rushed forward and wildly seized his hand, and then she muttered to herself, " 'Tis flesh."

"I have been playing, I fear, the mooncalf to-night; and find that, though I am a late watcher, I am not a solitary one."

Mrs. Lorraine stared earnestly at him, and then she endeavored to assume her usual expression of countenance; but the effort was too much for her. She dropped Vivian's arm, and buried her face in her own hands. Vivian was retiring, when she again looked up. "Where are you going?" she asked, with a quick voice.

"To sleep, as I would advise all: 'tis much past midnight."

"You say not the truth. The brightness of your eye belies the sentence of your tongue. You are not for sleep."

"Pardon me, dear Mrs. Lorraine; I really have been yawning for the last hour," said Vivian, and he moved on.

"You are speaking to one who takes her answer from the eye, which does not deceive, and from the speaking lineaments of the face, which are Truth's witnesses. Keep your voice for those who can credit man's words. You will go, then? What! are you afraid of a woman because ' 'tis past midnight,' and you are in an old gallery?"

"Fear, Mrs. Lorraine, is not a word in my vocabulary."

"The words in your vocabulary are few, boy! as are the years of your age. He who sent you here this night sent you here not to slumber. Come thither!" and she led Vivian to the window: "what see you?"

"I see Nature at rest, Mrs. Lorraine; and I would fain follow the example of beasts, birds, and fishes."

"Yet gaze upon this scene one second. See the distant hills, how beautifully their rich covering is tinted with the moonbeam! These nearer fir-trees, how radiantly their black skeleton forms are tipped with silver; and the old and thickly foliaged oaks bathed in light! and the purple lake reflecting in its lustrous bosom another heaven! Is it not a fair scene?"

"Beautiful! most beautiful!"

"Yet, Vivian, where is the being for whom all this beauty exists? Where is your mighty creature, Man? The peasant on his rough couch enjoys, perchance, slavery's only service-money, sweet sleep; or, waking in the night, curses at the same time his lot and his lord. And that lord is restless on some downy couch; his night thoughts, not of this sheeny lake and this bright moon, but of some miserable creation of man's artifice, some mighty nothing, which Nature knows not of, some offspring of her bastard child, Society. Why, then, is Nature loveliest when man looks not on her? For whom, then, Vivian Grey, is this scene so fair?"

"For poets, lady; for philosophers; for all those superior spirits who require some relaxation from the world's toils; spirits who only commingle with humanity on the condition that they may sometimes commune with Nature."

"Superior spirits: say you?" and here they paced the gallery. "When Valerian, first Lord Carabas, raised this fair castle; when, profuse for his posterity, all the genius of Italian art and Italian artists was lavished on this English palace; when the stuffs and statues, the marbles and the mirrors, the tapestry, and the carvings, and the paintings of Genoa, and Florence, and Venice, and Padua, and Vicenza, were obtained

by him at miraculous cost, and with still more miraculous toil;
what think you would have been his sensations if, while his
soul was reveling in the futurity of his descendants, keeping
their state in this splendid pile, some wizard had foretold to
him that, ere three centuries could elapse, the fortunes of his
mighty family would be the sport of two individuals; one of
them a foreigner, unconnected in blood, or connected only in
hatred; and the other a young adventurer, alike unconnected
with his race, in blood or in love; a being ruling all things
by the power of his own genius, and reckless of all consequences save his own prosperity? If the future had been
revealed to my great ancestor, the Lord Valerian, think you,
Vivian Grey, that you and I should be walking in this Long
Gallery?"

"Really, Mrs. Lorraine, I have been so interested in discovering what people think in the nineteenth century that I
have had but little time to speculate on the possible opinions
of an old gentleman who flourished in the sixteenth."

"You may sneer, sir; but I ask you, if there are spirits
so superior to that of the slumbering Lord of this castle as
those of Vivian Grey and Amalia Lorraine, why may there
not be spirits proportionately superior to our own?"

"If you are keeping me from my bed, Mrs. Lorraine,
merely to lecture my conceit by proving that there are in
this world wiser heads than that of Vivian Grey, on my
honor you are giving yourself a great deal of unnecessary
trouble."

"You will misunderstand me, then, you wilful boy!"

"Nay, lady, I will not affect to misunderstand your meaning; but I recognize, you know full well, no intermediate
essence between my own good soul and that ineffable and
omnipotent spirit in whose existence philosophers and priests
alike agree."

"Omnipotent and ineffable essence! Leave such words to
scholars and to schoolboys! And think you that such indefinite
nothings, such unmeaning abstractions, can influence beings
whose veins are full of blood, bubbling like this?" And here
she grasped Vivian with a feverish hand. "Omnipotent and
ineffable essence! Oh! I have lived in a land where every
mountain, and every stream, and every wood, and every ruin,

has its legend and its peculiar spirit; a land in whose dark
forests the midnight hunter, with his spirit-shout, scares the
slumbers of the trembling serf: a land from whose winding
rivers the fair-haired Undine welcomes the belated traveler to
her fond and fatal embrace; and you talk to me of omnipotent
and ineffable essences! Miserable mocker! It is not true,
Vivian Grey; you are but echoing the world's deceit, and even
at this hour of the night you dare not speak as you do think.
You worship no omnipotent and ineffable essence; you believe in no omnipotent and ineffable essence. Shrined in
the secret chamber of your soul there is an image before
which you bow down in adoration, and that image is YOUR-
SELF. And truly, when I do gaze upon your radiant eyes," and
here the lady's tone became more terrestrial; "and truly, when
I do look upon your luxuriant curls," and here the lady's small
white hand played like lightning through Vivian's dark hair;
"and truly, when I do remember the beauty of your all-perfect
form, I can not deem your self-worship a false idolatry," and
here the lady's arms were locked round Vivian's neck, and
her head rested on his bosom.

"Oh, Amalia! it would be far better for you to rest here
than to think of that of which the knowledge is vanity."

"Vanity!" shrieked Mrs. Lorraine, and she violently loosened her embrace, and extricated herself from the arm which,
rather in courtesy than in kindness, had been wound round her.
delicate waist: "Vanity! Oh! if you knew but what I know;
oh! if you had but seen what I have seen;" and here her voice
failed her, and she stood motionless in the moonshine, with
averted head and outstretched arms.

"Amalia! this is madness; for Heaven's sake calm yourself!"

"Calm myself! Yes, it is madness; very, very madness!
'tis the madness of the fascinated bird; 'tis the madness of
the murderer who is voluntarily broken on the wheel; 'tis
the madness of the fawn that gazes with adoration on the
lurid glare of the anaconda's eye; 'tis the madness of woman
who flies to the arms of her Fate;" and here she sprang like
a tigress round Vivian's neck, her long light hair bursting from
its bands, and clustering down her shoulders.

And here was Vivian Grey, at past midnight, in this old

gallery, with this wild woman clinging round his neck. The figures in the ancient tapestry looked living in the moon, and immediately opposite him was one compartment of some old mythological tale, in which were represented grinning, in grim majesty, the Fates.

The wind now rose again, and the clouds which had vanished began to reassemble in the heavens. As the blue sky was gradually covering, the gigantic figures of Clotho, Lachesis, and Atropos became as gradually dimmer and dimmer, and the grasp of Vivian's fearful burden looser and looser. At last the moon was entirely hid, the figures of the Fates vanished, and Mrs. Felix Lorraine sank lifeless into his arms.

Vivian groped his way with difficulty to the nearest window, the very one at which she was leaning when he first entered the gallery. He played with her wild curls; he whispered to her in a voice sweeter than the sweetest serenade; but she only raised her eyes from his breast and stared wildly at him, and then clung round his neck with, if possible, a tighter grasp.

For nearly half an hour did Vivian stand leaning against the window, with his mystic and motionless companion. At length the wind again fell; there was a break in the sky, and a single star appeared in the midst of the clouds, surrounded with a little heaven of azure.

"See there, see there!" the lady cried, and then she unlocked her arms. "What would you give, Vivian Grey, to read that star?"

"Am I more interested in that star, Amalia, than in any other of the bright host?" asked Vivian with a serious tone, for he thought it necessary to humor his companion.

"Are you not? is it not the star of your destiny?"

"Are you learned in all the learning of the Chaldeans, too?"

"Oh, no, no, no!" slowly murmured Mrs. Lorraine, and then she started: but Vivian seized her arms, and prevented her from again clasping his neck.

"I must keep these pretty hands close prisoners," he said, smiling, "unless you promise to behave with more moderation. Come, my Amalia! you shall be my instructress! Why am I so interested in this brilliant star?" and holding her hands in one of his, he wound his arm round her waist, and whispered her such words as he thought might calm her troubled spirit. The wildness of her eyes gradually gave way; at length she raised them to Vivian with a look of meek tenderness, and her head sank upon his breast.

"It shines, it shines, it shines, Vivian!" she softly whispered; "glory to thee and woe to me! Nay, you need not hold my hands; I will not harm you. I can not ; 'tis no use. Oh, Vivian! when we first met, how little did I know to whom I pledged myself!"

"Amalia, forget these wild fancies; estrange yourself from the wild belief which has exercised so baneful an influence, not only over your mind, but over the very soul of the land from which you come. Recognize in me only your friend, and leave the other world to those who value it more, or more deserve it. Does not this fair earth contain sufficient of interest and enjoyment?"

"Oh, Vivian! you speak with a sweet voice, but with a sceptic's spirit. You know not what I know."

"Tell me, then, my Amalia; let me share your secrets, provided they be your sorrows."

"Almost within this hour, and in this park, there has happened that which—" and here her voice died, and she looked fearfully round her.

"Nay, fear not; no one can harm you here, no one shall harm you. Rest upon me, and tell me all thy grief."

"I dare not, I can not tell you."

"Nay, thou shalt."

"I can not speak; your eye scares me. Are you mocking me? I can not speak if you look so at me."

"I will not look on you; I will gaze on yonder star. Now speak on."

"Oh, Vivian, there is a custom in my native land: the world calls it an unhallowed one; you, in your proud spirit, will call it a vain one. But you would not deem it vain if you were the woman now resting on your bosom. At certain hours of particular nights, and with peculiar ceremonies, which I need not here mention, we do believe that in a lake or other standing water fate reveals itself to the solitary votary. Oh, Vivian, I have been too long a searcher after this fearful

science; and this very night, agitated in spirit, I sought yon
water. The wind was in the right direction, and everything
concurred in favoring a propitious divination. I knelt down
to gaze on the lake. I had always been accustomed to view my
own figure performing some future action, or engaged in some
future scene of my life. I gazed, but I saw nothing but a
brilliant star. I looked up into the heavens, but the star was
not there, and the clouds were driving quick across the sky.
More than usually agitated by this singular occurrence, I
gazed once more; and just at the moment when with breathless
and fearful expectation I waited the revelation of my immediate destiny there flitted a figure across the water. It was
there only for the breathing of a second, and as it passed it
mocked me." Here Mrs. Lorraine writhed in Vivian's arms;
her features were molded in the same unnatural expression
as when he first entered the gallery, and the hideous grin was
again sculptured on her countenance. Her whole frame was
in such a state of agitation that she rose up and down in Vivian's arms, and it was only with the exertion of his whole
strength that he could retain her.

"Why, Amalia, this, this was nothing; your own figure."

"No, not my own; it was yours!"

Uttering a piercing shriek, which echoed through the winding gallery, she swooned.

Vivian gazed on her in a state of momentary stupefaction,
for the extraordinary scene had begun to influence his own
nerves. And now he heard the tread of distant feet, and a
light shone through the keyhole of the nearest door. The
fearful shriek had alarmed some of the household. What was
to be done? In desperation Vivian caught the lady up in his
arms, and dashing out of an opposite door bore her to her
chamber.

CHAPTER VII

WHAT is this chapter to be about? Come, I am inclined
to be courteous! You shall choose the subject of it.
What shall it be, sentiment or scandal? a love scene or a lay
sermon? You will not choose? Then we must open the note
which Vivian, in the morning, found on his pillow:

"Did you hear the horrid shriek last night? It must have disturbed every one. I think it must have been one of the South American birds which Captain Tropic gave the Marchioness. Do not they sometimes favor the world with these nocturnal shriekings? Is not there a passage in Spix apropos to this?   A——."

"Did you hear the shriek last night, Mr. Grey?" asked the Marchioness, as Vivian entered the breakfast-room.

"Oh, yes! Mr. Grey, did you hear the shriek?" asked Miss Graves.

"Who did not?"

"What could it be?" said the Marchioness.

"What could it be?" said Miss Graves.

"What should it be; a cat in a gutter, or a sick cow, or a toad dying to be devoured, Miss Graves?"

Always snub toadies and led captains. It is only your greenhorns who endeavor to make their way by fawning and cringing to every member of the establishment. It is a miserable mistake. No one likes his dependants to be treated with respect, for such treatment affords an unpleasant contrast to his own conduct. Besides, it makes the toady's blood unruly. There are three persons, mind you, to be attended to: my lord, or my lady, as the case may be (usually the latter), the pet daughter, and the pet dog. I throw out these hints *en passant,* for my principal objects in writing this work are to amuse myself and to instruct society. In some future book, probably the twentieth or twenty-fifth, when the plot begins to wear threadbare, and we can afford a digression, I may give a chapter on Domestic Tactics.

"My dear Marchioness," continued Vivian, "see there; I have kept my promise, there is your bracelet. How is Julie to-day?"

"Poor dear, I hope she is better."

"Oh! yes, poor Julie! I think she is better."

"I do not know that, Miss Graves," said her Ladyship, somewhat tartly, not at all approving of a toady thinking. "I am afraid that scream last night must have disturbed her. Oh, dear, Mr. Grey, I am afraid she will be ill again."

Miss Graves looked mournful, and lifted up her eyes and hands to Heaven, but did not dare to speak this time.

"I thought she looked a little heavy about the eyes this morning," said the Marchioness, apparently very agitated; "and I have heard from Eglamour this post; he is not well, too; I think everybody is ill now; he has caught a fever going to see the ruins of Pæstum. I wonder why people go to see ruins!"

"I wonder, indeed," said Miss Graves; "I never could see anything in a ruin."

"Oh, Mr. Grey!" continued the Marchioness, "I really am afraid Julie is going to be very ill."

"Let Miss Graves pull her tail and give her a little mustard seed: she will be better to-morrow."

"Remember that, Miss Graves."

"Oh! y-e-s, my Lady!"

"Mrs. Felix," said the Marchioness, as that lady entered the room, "you are late to-day; I always reckon upon you as a supporter of an early breakfast at Desir."

"I have been half round the park."

"Did you hear the scream, Mrs. Felix?"

"Do you know what it was, Marchioness?"

"No; do you?"

"See the reward of early rising and a walk before breakfast. It was one of your new American birds, and it has half torn down your aviary."

"One of the new Americans? Oh, the naughty thing; and has it broken the new fancy wirework?"

Here a little odd-looking, snuffy old man, with a brown scratch wig, who had been very busily employed the whole breakfast-time with a cold game pie, the bones of which Vivian observed him most scientifically pick and polish, laid down his knife and fork, and addressed the Marchioness with an air of great interest.

"Pray, will your Ladyship have the goodness to inform me what bird this is?"

The Marchioness looked astounded at any one presuming to ask her a question; and then she drawled, "Mr. Grey, you know everything: tell this gentleman what some bird is."

Now this gentleman was Mr. Mackaw, the most celebrated
ornithologist extant, and who had written a treatise on Brazilian paroquets, in three volumes folio. Heh ad arrived late
at the Chateau the preceding night, and, although he had the
honor of presenting his letter of introduction to the Marquess,
this morning was the first time he had been seen by any of the
party present, who were of course profoundly ignorant of his
character.

"Oh! we were talking of some South American bird given
to the Marchioness by the famous Captain Tropic; you know
him, perhaps; Bolivar's brother-in-law, or aide-de-camp, or
something of that kind; and which screams so dreadfully at
night that the whole family is disturbed. The Chowchowtow
it is called; is not it, Mrs. Lorraine?"

"The Chowchowtow!" said Mr. Mackaw; "I don't know
it by that name."

"Do not you? I dare say we shall find an account of it in
Spix, however," said Vivian, rising, and taking a volume from
the book-case; "ay! here it is; I will read it to you."

" 'The Chowchowtow is about five feet seven inches in
height from the point of the bill to the extremity of the claws.
Its plumage is of a dingy, yellowish white; its form is elegant,
and in its movements and action a certain pleasing and graceful dignity is observable; but its head is by no means worthy of
the rest of its frame; and the expression of its eye is indicative of the cunning and treachery of its character. The habits
of this bird are peculiar: occasionally most easily domesti-
cated, it is apparently sensible of the slightest kindness; but
its regard can not be depended upon, and for the slightest
inducement, or with the least irritation, it will fly at its feeder.
At other times it seeks perfect solitude, and can only be captured with the utmost skill and perseverance. It generally
feeds three times a day, but its appetite is not rapacious; it
sleeps little, is usually on the wing at sunrise, and proves that
it slumbers but little in the night by its nocturnal and thrilling
shrieks.' "

"What an extraordinary bird! Is that the bird you meant,
Mrs. Felix Lorraine?"

Mr. Mackaw was restless the whole time that Vivian was
reading this interesting passage. At last he burst forth with

an immense deal of science and a great want of construction,
a want which scientific men often experience, always except-
ing those mealy-mouthed professors who lecture "at the
Royal," and get patronized by the blues, the Lavoisiers of
May Fair!

"Chowchowtow, my Lady! five feet seven inches high!
Brazilian bird! When I just remind your Ladyship that the
height of the tallest bird to be found in Brazil, and in mentioning this fact, I mention nothing hypothetical, the tallest
bird does not stand higher than four feet nine. Chowchowtow! Dr. Spix is a name, accurate traveler, don't remember
the passage, most singular bird! Chowchowtow! don't know
it by that name. Perhaps your Ladyship is not aware; I think
you call that gentleman Mr. Grey; perhaps Mr. Grey is not
aware that I am Mr. Mackaw, I arrived late here last night,
whose work in three volumes folio, on Brazilian paroquets,
although I had the honor of seeing his Lordship, is, I trust,
a sufficient evidence that I am not speaking at random on this
subject; and consequently, from the lateness of the hour, could
not have the honor of being introduced to your Ladyship."

"Mr. Mackaw!" thought Vivian. "The deuce you are!
Oh! why did not I say a Columbian cassowary, or a Peruvian
penguin, or a Chilian condor, or a Guatemalan goose, or a
Mexican mastard; anything but Brazilian. Oh! unfortunate
Vivian Grey!"

The Marchioness, who was quite overcome with this scientific appeal, raised her large, beautiful, sleepy eyes from a
delicious compound of French roll and new milk, which she
was working up in a Sèvres saucer for Julie; and then, as
usual, looked to Vivian for assistance.

"Mr. Grey, you know everything; tell Mr. Mackaw about
a bird."

"Is there any point on which you differ from Spix in his
account of the Chowchowtow, Mr. Mackaw?"

"My dear sir, I don't follow him at all. Dr. Spix is a
most excellent man, a most accurate traveler, quite a name;
but, to be sure, I've only read his work in our own tongue;
and I fear from the passage you have just quoted, five feet
seven inches high! in Brazil! it must be an imperfect version.
I say that four feet nine is the greatest height I know. I don't

speak without some foundation for my statement. The only bird I know above that height is the Paraguay cassowary; which, to be sure, is sometimes found in Brazil. But the description of your bird, Mr. Grey, does not answer that at all. I ought to know. I do not speak at random. The only living specimen of that extraordinary bird, the Paraguay cassowary, in this country, is in my possession. It was sent me by Bompland, and was given to him by the Dictator of Paraguay himself. I call it, in compliment, Doctor Francia. I arrived here so late last night, only saw his Lordship, or I would have had it on the lawn this morning."

"Oh, then, Mr. Mackaw," said Vivian, "that was the bird which screamed last night!"

"Oh, yes! oh, yes! Mr. Mackaw," said Mrs. Felix Lorraine.

"Lady Carabas!" continued Vivian, "it is found out. It is Mr. Mackaw's particular friend, his family physician, whom he always travels with, that awoke us all last night."

"Is he a foreigner?" asked the Marchioness, looking up.

"My dear Mr. Grey, impossible! the Doctor never screams."

"Oh! Mr. Mackaw, Mr. Mackaw!" said Vivian.

"Oh! Mr. Mackaw, Mr. Mackaw!" said Mrs. Felix Lorraine.

"I tell you he never screams," reiterated the man of science; "I tell you he can't scream; he's muzzled."

"Oh, then, it must have been the Chowchowtow."

"Yes; I think it must have been the Chowchowtow."

"I should very much like to hear Spix's description again," said Mr. Mackaw, "only I fear it is troubling you too much, Mr. Grey."

"Read it yourself, my dear sir," said Vivian, putting the book into his hand, which was the third volume of "Tremaine."

Mr. Mackaw looked at the volume, and turned it over, and sidewise, and upside downward: the brain of a man who has written three folios on paroquets is soon puzzled. At first, he thought the book was a novel; but then, an essay on predestination, under the title of Memoirs of a Man of Refinement, rather puzzled him; then he mistook it for an Oxford reprint of Pearson on the Creed; and then he stumbled on rather a warm scene in an old Chateau in the south of France.

Before Mr. Mackaw could gain the power of speech the door opened, and entered, who? Dr. Francia.

Mr. Mackaw's traveling companion possessed the awkward accomplishment of opening doors, and now strutted in, in quest of his beloved master. Affection for Mr. Mackaw was not, however, the only cause which induced this entrance.

The household of Chateau Desir, unused to cassowaries, had neglected to supply Dr. Francia with his usual breakfast, which consisted of half a dozen pounds of rump steaks, a couple of bars of hard iron, some pig lead, and brown stout. The consequence was the Dictator was sadly famished.

All the ladies screamed; and then Mrs. Felix Lorraine admired the Doctor's violet neck, and the Marchioness looked with an anxious eye on Julie, and Miss Graves, as in duty bound, with an anxious eye on the Marchioness.

There stood the Doctor, quite still, with his large yellow eye fixed on Mr. Mackaw. At length he perceived the cold pasty, and his little black wings began to flutter on the surface of his immense body.

"Che, che, che, che!" said the ornithologist, who did not like the symptoms at all: "Che, che, che, che, don't be frightened, ladies! you see he's muzzled; che, che, che, che, now, my dear doctor, now, now, now, Franky, Franky, Franky, now go away, go away, that's a dear doctor, che, che, che che!"

But the large yellow eye grew more flaming and fiery, and the little black wings grew larger and larger; and now the left leg was dashed to and fro with a fearful agitation. Mackaw looked agonized. What a whirr! Francia is on the table! All shriek, the chairs tumble over the ottomans, the Sévres china is in a thousand pieces, the muzzle is torn off and thrown at Miss Graves; Mackaw's wig is dashed in the clotted cream, and devoured on the spot; and the contents of the boiling urn are poured over the beauteous and beloved Julie!

CHAPTER VIII

THE HONORABLE CYNTHIA COURTOWN TO VIVIAN GREY, ESQ.

"Alburies, Oct., 18—.

"DEAR GREY—We have now been at Alburies for a fortnight. Nothing can be more delightful. Here is everybody in the world that I wish to see, except yourself. The
Knightons, with as many outriders as usual: Lady Julia and
myself are great allies; I like her amazingly. The Marquess
of Grandgoût arrived here last week with a most delicious
party; all the men who write 'John Bull.' I was rather disappointed at the first sight of Stanislaus Hoax. I had expected, I do not know why, something juvenile and squibbish,
when lo! I was introduced to a corpulent individual, with his
coat buttoned up to his chin, looking dull, gentlemanlike, and
apoplectic. However, on acquaintance, he came out quite rich,
sings delightfully, and improvises like a prophet, ten thousand
times more entertaining than Pistrucci. We are sworn friends;
and I know all the secret history of 'John Bull.' There is
not much, to be sure, that you did not tell me yourself; but
still there are some things. I must not trust them, however, to
paper, and therefore pray dash down to Alburies immediately;
I shall be most happy to introduce you to Lord Devildrain.
There *was* an interview. What think you of that? Stanislaus told me all, circumstantially, and after dinner; I do not
doubt that it is quite true. What would you give for the secret
history of the 'rather yellow, rather yellow,' chanson? I dare
not tell it you. It came from a quarter that will quite astound
you, and in a very elegant, small, female hand. You remember Lambton did stir very awkwardly in the Lisbon business.
Stanislaus wrote all the songs that appeared in the first number, except that; but he never wrote a single line of prose for
the first three months: it all came from Vivida Vis.

"I like the Marchioness of Grandgoût so much! I hope he

will be elevated in the peerage: he looks as if he wanted it so! Poor dear man!

"Oh! do you know I have discovered a liaison between Bull and Blackwood. I am to be in the next Noctes; I forget the words of the chorus exactly, but Courtown is to rhyme with port down, or something of that kind, and then they are to dash their glasses over their heads, give three cheers, and adjourn to whiskey toddy and the Chaldee chamber. How delightful!

"The Prima Donnas are at Cheltenham, looking most respectable. Do you ever see the 'Age'? It is not proper for me to take it in. Pray send me down your numbers, and tell me all about it. Is it true that his Lordship paragraphizes a little?

"I have not heard from Ernest Clay, which I think very odd. If you write to him, mention this, and tell him to send me word how Dormer Stanhope behaves at mess. I understand there has been a mêlée, not much; merely a rouette; do get it all out of him.

"Colonel Delmington is at Cheltenham, with the most knowing beard you can possibly conceive; Lady Julia rather patronizes him. Lady Doubtful has been turned out of the rooms; fifty challenges in consequence and one duel; missed fire, of course.

"I have heard from Alhambra; he has been wandering about in all directions. He has been to the Lakes, and is now at Edinburgh. He likes Southey. He gave the laureate a quantity of hints for his next volume of the Peninsular War, but does not speak very warmly of Wordsworth: gentlemanly man, but only reads his own poetry.

"Here has been a cousin of yours about us; a young barrister going the circuit; by name Hargrave Grey. The name attracted my notice, and due inquiries having been made and satisfactorily answered, I patronized the limb of law. Fortunate for him! I got him to all the fancy balls and picnics that were going on. He was in heaven for a fortnight, and at length, having overstayed his time, he left us, also leaving his bag and only brief behind him. They say he is ruined for life. Write soon.   Yours ever,

"CYNTHIA COURTOWN."

ERNEST CLAY, ESQ., TO VIVIAN GREY, ESQ.

"October, 18—.

"DEAR GREY—I am sick of key-bugles and country-balls!
All the girls in the town are in love with me, or my foraging
cap. I am very much obliged to you for your letter to Kennet, which procured everything I wanted. The family turned
out bores, as you had prepared me. I never met such a clever
family in my life; the father is summoning up courage to favor
the world with a volume of sermons; and Isabella Kennet
most satisfactorily proved to me, after an argument of two
hours, which for courtesy's sake I fought very manfully,
that Sir Walter Scott was not the author of 'Waverley';
and then she vowed, as I have heard fifty young literary
ladies vow before, that she had 'seen the "Antiquary" in
manuscript.'

"There has been a slight row to diversify the monotony
of our military life. Young Premium, the son of the celebrated
loan-monger, has bought in; and Dormer Stanhope, and one
or two others equally fresh, immediately anticipated another
Battier business; but, with the greatest desire to make a fool
of myself, I have a natural repugnance to mimicking the
foolery of others; so with some little exertion, and very fortunately for young Premium, I got the tenth voted vulgar, on
the score of curiosity, and we were civil to the man. As it
turned out, it was all very well, for Premium is a quiet, gentlemanlike fellow enough, and exceedingly useful. He will
keep extra grooms for the whole mess, if they want it. He is
very grateful to me for what does not deserve any gratitude,
and for what gave me no trouble; for I did not defend him
from any feeling of kindness: and both the Mounteneys, and
young Stapylton Toad, and Augustus, being in the regiment,
why, I have very little trouble in commading a majority, if it
come to a division.

"I dined the other day at Old Premium's, who lives near
this town in a magnificent old hall; which, however, is not
nearly splendid enough for a man who is the creditor of every
nation from California to China; and, consequently, the great
Mr. Stucco is building a plaster castle for him in another part
of the park. Glad am I enough that I was prevailed upon to

patronize the Premium; for I think I seldom witnessed a more amusing scene than I did the day I dined there.

"I was ushered through an actual street of servitors, whose liveries were really cloth of gold, and whose elaborately powdered heads would not have disgraced the most ancient mansion in St. James's Square, into a large and crowded saloon. I was, of course, received with miraculous consideration; and the ear of Mrs. Premium seemed to dwell upon the jingling of my spurs (for I am adjutant) as upon exquisite music. It was bona fide evidence of 'the officers being there.'

"Premium is a short, but by no means vulgar-looking man, about fifty, with a high forehead covered with wrinkles, and with eyes deep sunk in his head. I never met a man of apparently less bustle, and of a cooler temperament. He was an object of observation from his very unobtrusiveness. There were, I immediately perceived, a great number of foreigners in the room. They looked much too knowing for Arguelles & Co., and I soon found that they were members of the different embassies, or missions of the various Governments to whose infant existence Premium is foster-father. There were two striking figures in Oriental costume, who were shown to me as the Greek Deputies; not that you are to imagine that they always appear in this picturesque dress. It was only as a particular favor, and to please Miss Premium (there, Grey, my boy! there is a quarry!), that the illustrious envoys appeared habited this day in their national costume.

"You would have enjoyed the scene. In one part of the room was a naval officer, just hot from the mines of Mexico, and lecturing eloquently on the passing of the Cordillera. In another was a man of science, dilating on the miraculous powers of a newly-discovered amalgamation process to a knot of merchants, who, with bent brows and eager eyes, were already forming a company for its adoption. Here floated the latest anecdote of Bolivar; and there a murmur of some new movement of Cochrane's. And then the perpetual babble about 'rising states,' and 'new loans,' and 'enlightened views,' and 'juncture of the two oceans,' and 'liberal principles,' and 'steamboats to Mexico,' and the earnest look which every one had in the room. How different to the vacant gaze that we have been accustomed to! I was really particularly struck by the circumstance. Every one at Premium's looked full of some great plan, as if the fate of empires was on his very breath. I hardly knew whether they were most like conspirators, or gamblers, or the lions of a public dinner, conscious of a universal gaze, and consequently looking proportionately interesting. One circumstance particularly struck me: as I was watching the acute countenance of an individual, who young Premium informed me was the Chilian minister, and who was listening with great attention to a dissertation from Captain Tropic, the celebrated traveler, on the feasibility of a railroad over the Andes, I observed a great sensation among those around me; every one shifting, and shuffling, and staring, and assisting in that curious and confusing ceremony called 'making way.' Even Premium appeared a little excited when he came forward with a smile on his face to receive an individual, apparently a foreigner, and who stepped on with great though gracious dignity. Being curious to know who this great man was, I found that this was an ambassador, the representative of a recognized state.

" 'Pon my honor, when I saw all this, I could not refrain from moralizing on the magic of wealth; and when I just remembered the embryo plot of some young Hussar officers to cut the son of the magician, I rather smiled; but while I, with even greater reverence than all others, was making way for his Excellency, I observed Mrs. Premium looking at my spurs. 'Farewell, Philosophy!' thought I; 'Puppyism forever!'

"Dinner was at last announced, and the nice etiquette which was observed between recognized states and non-recognized states was really excessively amusing: not only the ambassador would take precedence of the mere political agent, but his Excellency's private secretary was equally tenacious as to the agent's private secretary. At length we were all seated: the spacious dining-room was hung round with portraits of most of the successful revolutionary leaders, and over Mr. Premium was suspended a magnificent portrait of Bolivar. If you could but have seen the plate! By Jove! I have eaten off the silver of most of the first families in England, yet never in my life did it enter into my imagination that it was possible for the most ingenious artist that ever existed to repeat a crest half so often in a tablespoon as in that of Premium. The crest is a bubble, and really the effect produced by it is most ludicrous.

"I was very much struck at table by the appearance of an individual who came in very late, but who was evidently, by his bearing, no insignificant personage. He was a tall man, with a long hooked nose and high cheek bones, and with an eye (were you ever at the Old Bailey? there you may see its fellow); his complexion looked as if it had been accustomed to the breezes of many climes, and his hair, which had once been red, was now silvered, or rather iron-grayed, not by age. Yet there was in his whole bearing, in his slightest actions, even in the easy, desperate air with which he took a glass of wine, an indefinable something (you know what I mean) which attracted your unremitting attention to him. I was not wrong in my suspicions of his celebrity; for, as Miss Premium, whom I sat next to, whispered, 'he was quite a lion.' It was Lord Oceanville. What he is after no one knows. Some say he is going to Greece, others whisper an invasion of Paraguay, and others, of course, say other things; perhaps equally correct. I think he is for Greece. I know he is one of the most extraordinary men I ever met with. I am getting prosy. Good-by! Write soon. Any fun going on? How is Cynthia? I ought to have written. How is Mrs. Felix Lorraine? She is a deuced odd woman!

"Yours faithfully,
"Ernest Clay."

Hargrave Grey, Esq., to Vivian Grey, Esq.

"October, 18—.

"Dear Vivian—You ought not to expect a letter from me. I can not conceive why you do not occasionally answer your correspondents' letters, if correspondents they may be called. It is really a most unreasonable habit of yours; any one but myself would quarrel with you.

"A letter from Baker met me at this place, and I find that the whole of that most disagreeable and annoying business is arranged. From the promptitude, skill, and energy which are apparent in the whole affair, I suspect I have to thank the very gentleman whom I was just going to quarrel with. You are

a good fellow, Vivian, after all. For want of a brief, I sit down
to give you a sketch of my adventures on this my first circuit.

"This circuit is a cold and mercantile adventure, and I am
disappointed in it. Not so either, for I looked for but little to
enjoy. Take one day of my life as a specimen; the rest are
mostly alike. The sheriff's trumpets are playing; one, some
tune of which I know nothing, and the other no tune at all. I
am obliged to turn out at eight. It is the first day of the Assize,
so there is some chance of a brief, being a new place. I push
my way into court through files of attorneys, as civil to the
rogues as possible, assuring them there is plenty of room,
though I am at the very moment gasping for breath, wedged
in in a lane of well-lined waistcoats. I get into court, take my
place in the quietest corner, and there I sit, and pass other
men's fees and briefs like a twopenny postman, only without
pay. Well! 'tis six o'clock, dinner-time, at the bottom of the
table, carve for all, speak to none, nobody speaks to me, must
wait till last to sum up, and pay the bill. Reach home quite
devoured by spleen, after having heard every one abused who
happened to be absent.

"I traveled to this place with Manners, whom I believe
you know, and amused myself by getting from him an account
of my fellows, anticipating, at the same time, what in fact
happened; to wit, that I should afterward get his character
from them. It is strange how freely they deal with each other;
that is, the person spoken of being away. I would not have
had you see our Stanhope for half a hundred pounds; your
jealousy would have been so excited. To say the truth, we
are a little rough; our mane wants pulling and our hoofs
trimming, but we jog along without performing either operation; and, by dint of rattling the whip against the splash-
board, using all one's persuasion of hand and voice, and jerking
the bit in his mouth, we do contrive to get into the circuit town,
usually, just about the time that the sheriff and his *posse comi-
tatus* are starting to meet my Lord the King's Justice: and that
is the worst of it; for their horses are prancing and pawing
coursers just out of the stable, sleek skins and smart drivers.
We begin to be knocked up just then, and our appearance is
the least brilliant of any part of the day. Here I had to pass
through a host of these powdered, scented fops; and the mul-

titude who had assembled to gaze on the nobler exhibition rather scoffed at our humble vehicle. As Manners had just then been set down to find the inn and lodging, I could not jump out and leave our equipage to its fate, so I settled my cravat, and seemed not to mind it, only I did.

"But I must leave off this nonsense, and attend to his Lordship's charge, which is now about to commence. I have not been able to get you a single good murder, although. I have kept a sharp lookout, as you desired me; but there is a chance of a first-rate one at ——n.

"I am quite delighted with Mr. Justice St. Prose. He is at this moment in a most entertaining passion, preparatory to a 'conscientious' summing up; and in order that his ideas may not be disturbed, he has very liberally ordered the doorkeeper to have the door oiled immediately, at his own expense. Now for my Lord the King's Justice.

" 'Gentlemen of the Jury:

" 'The noise is insufferable, the heat is intolerable, the doorkeepers let the people keep shuffling in, the ducks in the corner are going quack, quack, quack, here's a little girl being tried for her life, and the judge can't hear a word that's said. Bring me my black cap, and I'll condemn her to death instantly.'

" 'You can't, my Lord,' shrieks the infant sinner; 'it's only for petty larceny.'

"I have just got an invite from the Kearneys. Congratulate me.

"Dear Vivian, yours faithfully,
"HARGRAVE GREY."

LADY SCROPE TO VIVIAN GREY, ESQ.

"Ormsby Park, Oct., 18—.

"MY DEAR VIVIAN—By desire of Sir Berdmore, I have to request the fulfilment of a promise, upon the hope of which being performed I have existed through this dull month. Pray, my dear Vivian, come to us immediately. Ormsby has at present little to offer for your entertainment. We have had that unendurable bore Vivacity Dull with us for a whole fortnight. A report of the death of the Lord Chancellor, or a rumor of the production of a new tragedy, has carried him up to town; but whether it be to ask for the seals, or to indite an ingenious prologue to a play which will be condemned the first night, I can not inform you. I am quite sure he is capable of doing either. However, we shall have other deer in a few days.

"I believe you have never met the Mounteneys. They have never been at Hallesbrooke since you have been at Desir. They are coming to us immediately. I am sure you will like them very much. Lord Mounteney is one of those kind, easy-minded, accomplished men, who, after all, are nearly the pleasantest society one ever meets. Rather wild in his youth, but with his estate now unincumbered, and himself perfectly domestic. His lady is an unaffected, agreeable woman. But it is Caroline Mounteney whom I wish you particularly to meet. She is one of those delicious creatures who, in spite of not being married, are actually conversable. Spirited, without any affectation or brusquerie; beautiful, and knowing enough to be quite conscious of it; perfectly accomplished, and yet never annoying you with tattle about Bochsa, and Ronzi de Begnis, and D'Egville.

"We also expect the Delmonts, the most endurable of the Anglo-Italians that I know. Mrs. Delmont is not always dropping her handkerchief like Lady Gusto, as if she expected a miserable cavalier *servente* to be constantly upon his knees; or giving those odious expressive looks, which quite destroy my nerves whenever I am under the same roof as that horrible Lady Soprano. There is a little too much talk, to be sure, about Roman churches, and newly-discovered Mosaics, and Abbate Maii, but still we can not expect perfection. There are reports going about that Ernest Clay is either ruined or going to be married. Perhaps both are true. Young Premium has nearly lost his character by driving a square-built, striped green thing, drawn by one horse. Ernest Clay got him through this terrible affair. What can be the reasons of the Sieur Ernest's excessive amiability?

"Both the young Mounteneys are with their regiment, but

Aubrey Vere is coming to us, and I have half a promise from
——; but I know you never speak to unmarried men, so why
do I mention them? Let me, I beseech you, my dear Vivian,
have a few days of you to myself before Ormsby is full, and
before you are introduced to Caroline Mounteney. I did not
think it was possible that I could exist so long without seeing
you; but you really must not try me too much, or I shall quarrel with you. I have received all your letters, which are very,
very agreeable; but I think rather, rather impudent. Adieu!
"HARRIETTE SCROPE."

HORACE GREY, ESQ., TO VIVIAN GREY, ESQ.

"Paris, Oct., 18—.

"MY DEAR VIVIAN—I have received yours of the 9th, and
have read it with mixed feelings of astonishment and sorrow.

"You are now, my dear son, a member of what is called
the great world; society formed on anti-social principles. Apparently you have possessed yourself of the object of your
wishes; but the scenes you live in are very movable; the characters you associate with are all masked; and it will always
be doubtful whether you can retain that long which has been
obtained by some slippery artifice. Vivian, you are a juggler;
and the deceptions of your sleight-of-hand tricks depend upon
instantaneous motions.

"When the selfish combine with the selfish, bethink you
how many projects are doomed to disappointment! how many
cross-interests baffle the parties at the same time joined together without ever uniting. What a mockery is their love!
but how deadly are their hatreds! All this great society, with
whom so young an adventurer has trafficked, abate nothing of
their price in the slavery of their service and the sacrifice of
violated feelings. What sleepless nights has it cost you to
win over the disobliged, to conciliate the discontented, to cajole
the contumacious! You may smile at the hollow flatteries, answering to flatteries as hollow, which, like bubbles when they
touch, dissolve into nothing; but tell me, Vivian, what has the
self-tormentor felt at the laughing treacheries which force a
man down into self-contempt?

"Is it not obvious, my dear Vivian, that true Fame and true

Happiness must rest upon the imperishable social affections? I do not mean that coterie celebrity which paltry minds accept as Fame; but that which exists independent of the opinions or the intrigues of individuals: nor do I mean that glittering show of perpetual converse with the world which some miserable wanderers call Happiness; but that which can only be drawn from the sacred and solitary fountain of your own feelings.

"Active as you have now become in the great scenes of human affairs, I would not have you be guided by any fanciful theories of morals or of human nature. Philosophers have amused themselves by deciding on human actions by systems; but, as these systems are of the most opposite natures, it is evident that each philosopher, in reflecting his own feelings in the system he has so elaborately formed, has only painted his own character.

"Do not, therefore, conclude, with Hobbes and Mandeville, that man lives in a state of civil warfare with man; nor, with Shaftesbury, adorn with a poetical philosophy our natural feelings. Man is neither the vile nor the excellent being which he sometimes imagines himself to be. He does not so much act by system as by sympathy. If this creature can not always feel for others, he is doomed to feel for himself; and the vicious are, at least, blessed with the curse of remorse.

"You are now inspecting one of the worst portions of society in what is called the great world (St. Giles's is bad, but of another kind), and it may be useful, on the principle that the actual sight of brutal ebriety was supposed to have inspired youth with the virtue of temperance; on the same principle that the Platonist, in the study of deformity, conceived the beautiful. Let me warn you not to fall into the usual error of youth in fancying that the circle you move in is precisely the world itself. Do not imagine that there are not other beings, whose benevolent principle is governed by finer sympathies, by more generous passions, and by those nobler emotions which really constitute all our public and private virtues. I give you this hint, lest, in your present society, you might suppose these virtues were merely historical.

"Once more, I must beseech you not to give loose to any elation of mind. The machinery by which you have attained this unnatural result must be so complicated that in the very tenth hour you will find yourself stopped in some part where you never counted on an impediment; and the want of a slight screw or a little oil will prevent you from accomplishing your magnificent end.

"We are, and have been, very dull here. There is every probability of Madame de Genlis writing more volumes than ever. I called on the old lady, and was quite amused with the enthusiasm of her imbecility. Chateaubriand is getting what you call a bore; and the whole city is mad about a new opera by Boieldieu. Your mother sends her love, and desires me to say that the salmi of woodcocks, à la Lucullus which you write about, does not differ from the practice here in vogue. How does your cousin Hargrave prosper on his circuit? The Delmingtons are here, which makes it very pleasant for your mother, as well as for myself; for it allows me to hunt over the old bookshops at my leisure. There are no new books worth sending you, or they would accompany this; but I would recommend you to get Meyer's new volume from Treüttel and Wurtz and continue to make notes as you read it. Give my compliments to the Marquess, and believe me,

"Your affectionate father,

"HORACE GREY."

CHAPTER IX

IT was impossible for any human being to behave with more kindness than the Marquess of Carabas did to Vivian Grey after that young gentleman's short conversation with Mrs. Felix Lorraine in the conservatory. The only feeling which seemed to actuate the Peer was an eager desire to compensate, by his present conduct, for any past misunderstanding, and he loaded his young friend with all possible favor. Still Vivian was about to quit Chateau Desir; and in spite of all that had passed he was extremely loth to leave his noble friend under the guardianship of his female one.

About this time, the Duke and Duchess of Juggernaut, the very pink of aristocracy, the wealthiest, the proudest, the most ancient, and most pompous couple in Christendom, honored

Chateau Desir with their presence for two days; only two days, making the Marquess's mansion a convenient resting-place in one of their princely progresses to one of their princely castles.

Vivian contrived to gain the heart of her Grace by his minute acquaintance with the Juggernaut pedigree; and having taken the opportunity, in one of their conversations, to describe Mrs. Felix Lorraine as the most perfect specimen of divine creation with which he was acquainted, at the same time the most amusing and the most amiable of women, that lady was honored with an invitation to accompany her Grace to Hima-laya Castle. As this was the greatest of all possible honors, and as Desir was now very dull, Mrs. Felix Lorraine accepted the invitation, or rather obeyed the command, for the Marquess would not hear of a refusal, Vivian having dilated in the most energetic terms on the opening which now presented itself of gaining the Juggernaut. The coast being thus cleared, Vivian set off the next day for Sir Berdmore Scrope's.

BOOK IV

CHAPTER I

THE important hour drew nigh. Christmas was to be passed by the Carabas family, the Beaconsfields, the Scropes, and the Clevelands at Lord Courtown's villa at Richmond; at which place, on account of its vicinity to the metropolis, the Viscount had determined to make out the holidays, notwithstanding the Thames entered his kitchen windows, and the "Donna del Lago" was acted in the theatre with real water, Cynthia Courtown performing Elena, paddling in a punt.

"Let us order our horses, Cleveland, round to the Piccadilly gate, and walk through the Guards. I must stretch my legs. That bore, Horace Buttonhole, captured me in Pall Mall East, and has kept me in the same position for upward of half an hour. I shall make a note to blackball him at the Athenæum. How is Mrs. Cleveland?"

"Extremely well. She goes down to Buckhurst Lodge with Lady Carabas. Is not that Lord Lowersdale?"

"His very self. He is going to call on Vivida Vis, I have no doubt. Lowersdale is a man of very considerable talent; much more than the world gives him credit for."

"And he doubtless finds a very able counselor in Monsieur le Secrétaire?"

"Can you name a better one?"

"You rather patronize Vivida, I think, Grey?"

"Patronize him! he is my political pet!"

"And yet Kerrison tells me you reviewed the Suffolk papers in the 'Edinburgh.'"

"So I did; what of that? I defended them in 'Blackwood.'"

"This, then, is the usual method of you literary gentlemen. Thank God! I never could write a line."

"York House rises proudly; if York House be its name."

"This confounded Catholic Question is likely to give us a great deal of trouble, Grey. It is perfect madness for us to advocate the cause of the 'six millions of hereditary bondsmen'; and yet, with not only the Marchese, but even Courtown and Beaconsfield committed, it is, to say the least, a very delicate business."

"Very delicate, certainly; but there are some precedents, I suspect, Cleveland, for the influence of a party being opposed to measures which the heads of that party had pledged themselves to adopt."

"Does old Gifford still live at Pimlico, Grey?"

"Still."

"He is a splendid fellow, after all."

"Certainly, a mind of great powers, but bigoted."

"Oh, yes! I know exactly what you are going to say. It is the fashion, I am aware, to abuse the old gentleman. He is the Earl of Eldon of literature; not the less loved because a little vilified. But, when I just remember what Gifford has done; when I call to mind the perfect and triumphant success of everything he has undertaken; the 'Anti-Jacobin,' the 'Baviad' and 'Mæviad,' the 'Quarterly'; all palpable hits, on the very jugular; I hesitate before I speak of William Gifford in any other terms, or in any other spirit, than those of admiration and of gratitude.

"And to think, Grey, that the Tory Administration and the Tory party of Great Britain should never, by one single act, or in a single instance, have indicated that they were in the least aware that the exertions of such a man differed in the slightest degree from those of Hunt and Hone! Of all the delusions which flourish in this mad world, the delusion of that man is the most frantic who voluntarily, and of his own accord, supports the interest of a party. I mention this to you because it is the rock on which all young politicians strike. Fortunately, you enter life under different circumstances from those which usually attend most political débutants. You have your connections formed and your views ascertained. But if, by any chance, you find yourself independent and unconnected, never, for a moment, suppose that you can accomplish your objects by coming forward, unsolicited, to fight the battle of a party. They will cheer your successful exertions, and then smile at your youthful zeal; or, crossing themselves for the unexpected succor, be too cowardly to reward their unexpected champion. No, Grey; make them fear you, and they will kiss your feet. There is no act of treachery or meanness of which a political party is not capable; for in politics there is no honor.

"As to Gifford, I am surprised at their conduct toward him, although I know better than most men of what wood a minister is made, and how much reliance may be placed upon the gratitude of a party: but Canning; from Canning I certainly did expect different conduct."

"Oh, Canning! I love the man: but as you say, Cleveland, ministers have short memories, and Canning's—that was Antilles that just passed us; apropos to whom I quite rejoice that the Marquess has determined to take such a decided course on the West India Question."

"Oh, yes! curse your East India sugar."

"To be sure; slavery and sweetmeats forever!"

"But, aside with joking, Grey, I really think, that if any man of average ability dare rise in the House, and rescue many of the great questions of the day from what Dugald Stuart or Disraeli would call the spirit of Political Religionism, with which they are studiously mixed up, he would not fail to make a great impression upon the House, and a still greater one upon the country."

"I quite agree with you; and certainly I should recommend commencing with the West India Question. Singular state of affairs when even Canning can only insinuate his opinion when the very existence of some of our most valuable colonies is at stake, and when even his insinuations are only indulged with an audience on the condition that he favors the House with an introductory discourse of twenty minutes on "the divine Author of our faith," and an éloge of equal length on the 'Génie du Christianisme,' in a style worthy of Chateaubriand."

"Miserable work, indeed! I have got a pamphlet on the West India Question sent me this morning. Do you know any raving lawyer, any mad Master in Chancery, or something of the kind, who meddles in these affairs?"

"Oh! Stephen! a puddle in the storm! He is for a crusade for the regeneration of the Antilles; the most forcible of feebles, the most energetic of drivellers; Velluti acting Pietro l'Eremita."

"Do you know, by any chance, whether Southey's 'Vindiciæ' is out yet? I wanted to look it over during the holidays."

"Not out, though it has been advertised some time; but what do you expect?"

"Nay, it is an interesting controversy, as controversies go. Not exactly Milton and Salmasius; but fair enough."

"I do not know. It has long degenerated into a mere personal bickering between the Laureate and Butler. Southey is, of course, reveling in the idea of writing an English work with a Latin title; and that, perhaps, is the only circumstance for which the controversy is prolonged."

"But Southey, after all, is a man of splendid talents."

"Doubtless; the most philosophical of bigots, and the most poetical of prose writers."

"Apropos to the Catholic Question, there goes Colonial Bother'em, trying to look like Prince Metternich; a decided failure."

"What can keep him in town?"

"Writing letters, I suppose. Heaven preserve me from receiving any of them!"

"Is it true, then, that his letters are of the awful length that is whispered?"

"True! Oh! they are something beyond all conception! Perfect epistolary Boa Constrictors. I speak with feeling, for I have myself suffered under their voluminous windings."

"Have you seen his quarto volume: 'The Cure for the Catholic Question'?"

"Yes."

"If you have it, lend it to me. What kind of thing is it?"

"Oh! what should it be! ingenious and imbecile. He advises the Catholics, in the old nursery language, to behave like good boys; to open their mouths and shut their eyes, and see what God will send them."

"Well, that is the usual advice. Is there nothing more characteristic of the writer?"

"What think you of a proposition of making Jockey of Norfolk Patriarch of England, and of an ascertained *credo* for our Catholic fellow-subjects? Ingenious, is not it?"

"Have you see Puff's new volume of Ariosto?"

"I have. What could possibly have induced Mr. Partenopex Puff to have undertaken such a duty? Mr. Puff is a man destitute of poetical powers, possessing no vigor of language, and gifted with no happiness of expression. His translation is hard, dry, and husky, as the outside of a cocoanut. I am amused to see the excellent tact with which the public has determined not to read his volumes, in spite of the incessant exertions of a certain set to ensure their popularity; but the time has gone by when the smug coterie could create a reputation."

"Do you think the time ever existed, Cleveland?"

"What could have seduced Puff into being so ambitious? I suppose his admirable knowledge of Italian; as if a man were entitled to strike a die for the new sovereign merely because he was aware how much alloy might legally debase its carats of pure gold."

"I never can pardon Puff for that little book on Cats. The idea was admirable; but, instead of one of the most delightful volumes that ever appeared, to take up a dull, tame compilation from Bingley's Animal Biography!"

"Yes! and the impertinence of dedicating such a work to the Officers of His Majesty's Household troops! Considering the quarter from whence it proceeded, I certainly did not expect much, but still I thought that there was to be some little *esprit*. The poor Guards! how nervous they must have been at the announcement! What could have been the point of that dedication?"

"I remember a most interminable proser, who was blessed with a very sensible-sounding voice, and who, on the strength of that, and his correct and constant emphases, was considered by the world for a great time as a sage. At length it was discovered that he was quite the reverse. Mr. Puff's wit is very like this man's wisdom. You take up one of his little books, and you fancy from its title page that it is going to be very witty; as you proceed you begin to suspect that the man is only a wag, and then, surprised at not "seeing the point," you have a shrewd suspicion that he is a great hand at dry humor. It is not till you have closed the volume that you wonder who it is that has had the hardihood to intrude such imbecility upon an indulgent world."

"Come, come! Mr. Puff is a worthy gentleman. Let him cease to dusk the radiancy of Ariosto's sunny stanzas, and I shall be the first man who will do justice to his merits. He certainly tattles prettily about tenses and terminations, and is not an inelegant grammarian."

"Our literature, I think, is at a low ebb."

"There is nothing like a fall of stocks to affect what it is the fashion to style the Literature of the present day, a fungous production which has flourished from the artificial state of our society, the mere creature of our imaginary wealth. Everybody being very rich, has afforded to be very literary, books being considered a luxury almost as elegant and necessary as ottomans, bonbons, and pier-glasses. Consols at 100 were the origin of all book societies. The Stockbrokers' ladies took off the quarto travels and the hot-pressed poetry. They were the patronesses of your patent ink and your wire-wove paper. That is all past. Twenty per cent difference in the value of our public securities from this time last year, that little incident has done more for the restoration of the old English feeling than all the exertions of Church and State united. There is nothing like a fall in Consols to bring the blood of our good people of England into cool order. It is your grand state medicine, your veritable Doctor Sangrado!

"A fall in stocks! and halt to 'the spread of knowledge!' and 'the progress of liberal principles' is like that of a man too late for post-horses. A fall in stocks! and where are your London Universities, and your Mechanics' Institutes, and your new Docks? Where your philosophy, your philanthropy, and your competition? National prejudices revive as national prosperity decreases. If the Consols were at 60 we should be again bellowing, God save the King! eating roast beef, and damning the French."

"And you imagine literature is equally affected, Grey?"

"Clearly. We were literary because we were rich. Amid the myriad of volumes which issue monthly from the press, what one was not written for the mere hour? It is all very well to buy mechanical poetry and historical novels when our purses have a plethora; but now, my dear fellow, depend upon it, the game is up. We have no scholars now, no literary recluses, no men who ever appear to think. 'Scribble, scribble, scribble,' as the Duke of Cumberland said to Gibbon, should be the motto of the mighty 'nineteenth century.'"

"Southey, I think, Grey, is an exception."

"By no means. Southey is a political writer, a writer for a particular purpose. All his works, from those in three volumes quarto to those in one duodecimo, are alike political pamphlets."

"We certainly want a master-spirit to set us right, Grey. We want Byron."

"There was a man! And that such a man should be lost to us at the very moment that he had begun to discover why it had pleased the Omnipotent to endow him with such powers!"

"If one thing were more characteristic of Byron's mind than another, it was his strong, shrewd, common sense; his pure, unalloyed sagacity."

"You knew him, I think, Cleveland?"

"Well, I was slightly acquainted with him when in England; slightly, however, for I was then very young. But many years afterward I met him in Italy. It was at Pisa, just before he left that place for Genoa. I was then very much struck at the alteration in his appearance."

"Indeed."

"Yes; his face was swollen, and he was getting fat. His hair was gray, and his countenan.. had lost that spiritual expression which it once eminently possessed. His teeth were decaying; and he said that if ever he came to England it would be to consult Wayte about them. I certainly was very much struck at his alteration for the worse. Besides, he was dressed in the most extraordinary manner."

"Slovenly?"

"Oh, no, no, no! in the most dandified style that you can conceive; but not that of an English dandy either. He had on a magnificent foreign foraging cap, which he wore in the room, but his gray curls were quite perceptible; and a frogged surtout; and he had a large gold chain round his neck, and pushed into his waistcoat pocket. I imagined, of course, that a glass was attached to it; but I afterward found that it bore nothing but a quantity of trinkets. He had also another gold chain tight round his neck, like a collar."

"How odd! And did you converse much with him?"

"I was not long at Pisa, but we never parted, and there was only one subject of conversation, England, England, England. I never met a man in whom the *maladie du pays* was so strong. Byron was certainly at this time restless and discontented. He was tired of his dragoon captains and pensioned poetasters, and he dared not come back to England with what he considered a tarnished reputation. His only thought was of some desperate exertion to clear himself: it was for this he went to Greece. When I was with him he was in correspondence with some friends in England about the purchase of a large tract of land in Colombia. He affected a great admiration of Bolivar."

"Who, by the bye, is a great man."

"Assuredly."

"Your acquaintance with Byron must have been one of the gratifying incidents of your life, Cleveland?"

"Certainly; I may say with Friar Martin, in Goetz of Berlichingen, 'The sight of him touched my heart. It is a pleasure to have seen a great man.'"

"Hobhouse was a faithful friend to him?"

"His conduct has been beautiful; and Byron had a thorough affection for him, in spite of a few squibs and a few drunken speeches, which damned good-natured friends have always been careful to repeat."

"The loss of Byron can never be retrieved. He was indeed a real man; and when I say this, I award him the most splendid character which human nature need aspire to. At least, I, for my part, have no ambition to be considered either a divinity or an angel; and truly, when I look round upon the creatures alike effeminate in mind and body of which the world is, in general, composed, I fear that even my ambition is too exalted. Byron's mind was like his own ocean, sublime in its yesty madness, beautiful in its glittering summer brightness, mighty in the lone magnificence of its waste of waters, gazed upon from the magic of its own nature, yet capable of representing, but as in a glass darkly, the natures of all others."

"Hyde Park is greatly changed since I was a dandy, Vivian. Pray, do the Misses Otranto still live in that house?"

"Yes; blooming as ever."

"It is the fashion to abuse Horace Walpole, but I really think him the most delightful writer that ever existed. I wonder who is to be the Horace Walpole of the present century? some one, perhaps, we least suspect."

"Vivida Vis, think you?"

"More than probable. I will tell you who ought to be writing Memoirs—Lord Dropmore. Does my Lord Manfred keep his mansion there, next to the Misses Otranto?"

"I believe so, and lives there."

"I knew him in Germany; a singular man, and not understood. Perhaps he does not understand himself. I see our horses."

"I will join you in an instant, Cleveland. I just want to speak one word to Osborne, whom I see coming down here. Well, Osborne, I must come and knock you up one of these mornings. I have got a commission for you from Lady Julia Knighton, to which you must pay particular attention."

"Well, Mr. Grey, how does Lady Julia like the bay mare?"

"Very much, indeed; but she wants to know what you have done about the chestnut."

"Oh! put it off, sir, in the prettiest style, on young Mr. Feoffment, who has just married, and taken a house in Gower Street. He wanted a bit of blood; hope he likes it!"

"Hope he does, Jack. There is a particular favor which you can do me, Osborne, and which I am sure you will. Ernest Clay; you know Ernest Clay; a most excellent fellow is Ernest Clay, you know, and a great friend of yours, Osborne; I wish you would just step down to Connaught Place, and look at those bays he bought of Harry Mountenay. He is in a little trouble, and we must do what we can for him; you know he is an excellent fellow, and a great friend of yours. Thank you, I knew you would. Good-morning; remember Lady Julia. So you really fitted young Feoffment with the chestnut; well, that was admirable! Good-morning."

"I do not know whether you care for these things at all, Cleveland, but Premium, a famous millionaire, has gone this morning, for I know not how much! Half the new world will be ruined; and in this old one a most excellent fellow, my friend Ernest Clay. He was engaged to Premium's daughter, his last resource, and now, of course, it is all up with him."

"I was at college with his brother, Augustus Clay. He is a nephew of Lord Mountenay's, is he not?"

"The very same. Poor fellow! I do not know what we must do for him. I think I shall advise him to change his name to Clay-*ville;* and if the world ask him the reason of the euphonious augmentation, why, he can swear it was to distinguish himself from his brothers. Too many roués of the same name will never do. And now spurs to our steeds! for we are going at least three miles out of our way, and I must collect my senses and arrange my curls before dinner, for I have to flirt with at least three fair ones."

CHAPTER II

THESE conversations play the very deuce with one's story. We had intended to have commenced this book with something quite terrific, a murder or a marriage; and all our great ideas have ended in a lounge. After all, it is, perhaps, the most natural termination. In life, surely man is not always as monstrously busy as he appears to be in novels and romances. We are not always in action, not always making speeches, or making money, or making war, or making love. Occasionally we talk, about the weather generally; sometimes about ourselves; oftener about our friends; as often about our enemies, at least, those who have any; which, in my opinion, is the vulgarest of all possessions.

But we must get on.

Mr. Cleveland and Mrs. Felix Lorraine again met, and the gentleman scarcely appeared to be aware that this meeting was not their first. The lady sighed and remonstrated. She reproached Mr. Cleveland with passages of letters. He stared, and deigned not a reply to an artifice which he considered equally audacious and shallow. There was a scene. Vivian was forced to interfere; but as he deprecated all explanation, his interference was of little avail; and, as it was ineffectual for one party and uncalled for by the other, it was, of course, not encouraged. The presence of Mrs. Cleveland did not tend to assist Mrs. Felix in that self-control which, with all her wildness, she could appositely practice. In the presence of the Clevelands she was fitful, capricious, perplexing; sometimes impertinent, sometimes humble; but always ill at ease, and never charming.

Peculiar, however, as was her conduct in this particular relation, it was in all others, at this moment, most exemplary. Her whole soul seemed concentrated in the success of the approaching struggle. No office was too mechanical for her attention, or too elaborate for her enthusiastic assiduity. Her attentions were not confined merely to Vivian and the Marquess, but were lavished with equal generosity on their colleagues. She copied letters for Sir Berdmore, and composed letters for Lord Courtown, and construed letters to Lord Beaconsfield; they, in return, echoed her praises to her delighted relative, who was daily congratulated on the possession of "such a fascinating sister-in-law."

"Well, Vivian," said Mrs. Lorraine, to that young gentleman, the day previous to his departure from Buckhurst Lodge, "you are going to leave me behind you."

"Indeed!"

"Yes! I hope you will not want me. I am very annoyed at not being able to go to town with you, but Lady Courtown is so pressing! and I have really promised so often to stay a week with her, that I thought it was better to make out my promise at once than in six months hence."

"Well! I am exceedingly sorry, for you really are so useful! and the interest you take in everything is so encouraging, that I very much fear we shall not be able to get on without you. The important hour draws nigh."

"It does, indeed, Vivian; and I assure you that there is no person awaiting it with intenser interest than myself. I little thought," she added, in a low but distinct voice, "I little thought, when I first reached England, that I should ever again be interested in anything in this world."

Vivian was silent, for he had nothing to say.

"Vivian!" very briskly resumed Mrs. Lorraine, "I shall get you to frank all my letters for me. I shall never trouble the Marquess again. Do you know, it strikes me you will make a very good speaker!"

"You flatter me exceedingly; suppose you give me a few lessons."

"But you must leave off some of your wicked tricks, Vivian! You must not improvise parliamentary papers!"

"Improvise papers, Mrs. Lorraine! What can you mean?"

"Oh! nothing. I never mean anything."

"But you must have had some meaning."

"Some meaning! Yes, I dare say I had; I meant—I meant; do you think it will rain to-day?"

"Every prospect of a hard frost. I never knew before that I was an improvisatore."

"Nor I. Have you heard from papa lately? I suppose he is quite in spirits at your success?"

"My father is a man who seldom gives way to any elation of mind."

"Ah, indeed! a philosopher, I have no doubt, like his son."

"I have no claims to the title of philosopher, although I have had the advantage of studying in the school of Mrs. Felix Lorraine."

"What do you mean? If I thought you meant to be impertinent, I really would; but I excuse you; I think the boy means well."

"The boy 'means nothing; he never means anything.'"

"Come, Vivian! we are going to part. Do not let us quarrel the last day. There, there is a sprig of myrtle for you!

> " 'What! not accept my foolish flower?
> Nay, then, I am indeed unblest!'

and now you want it all! Unreasonable young man! If I were not the kindest lady in the land I should tear this sprig into a thousand pieces sooner; but come, my child! you shall have it. There! it looks quite imposing in your button-hole. How handsome you look to-day!"

"How agreeable you are! I love compliments!"

"Ah, Vivian! will you never give me credit for anything but a light and callous heart? Will you never be convinced that—that—but why make this humiliating confession? Oh! no, let me be misunderstood forever! The time may come when Vivian Grey will find that Amalia Lorraine was—"

"Was what, madam?"

"You shall choose the word, Vivian."

"Say, then, my friend."

" 'Tis a monosyllable full of meaning, and I will not quarrel with it. And now, adieu! Heaven prosper you! Believe me, that my first thoughts and my last are for you and of you!"

CHAPTER III

"THIS is very kind of you, Grey! I was afraid my note might not have caught you. You have not breakfasted? Really I wish you would take up your quarters in Carabas House, for I want you now every moment."

"What is the urgent business of this morning?"

"Oh! I have seen Bromley."

"Hah!"

"And everything most satisfactory. I did not go into detail; I left that for you: but I ascertained sufficient to convince me that management is now alone required."

"Well, my Lord, I trust that will not be wanting."

"No, Vivian; you have opened my eyes to the situation in which fortune has placed me. The experience of every day only proves the truth and soundness of your views. Fortunate, indeed, was the hour in which we met."

"My Lord, I do trust that it was a meeting which neither of us will live to repent."

"Impossible! my dear friend. I do not hesitate to say that I would not change my present lot for that of any Peer of this realm; no, not for that of his Majesty's most favored counselor. What! with my character and my influence, and my connections, I to be a tool! I, the Marquess of Carabas! I say nothing of my own powers; but, as you often most justly and truly observe, the world has had the opportunity of judging of them; and I think I may recur, without vanity, to the days in which my voice had some weight in the Royal Councils. And, as I have often remarked, I have friends, I have you, Vivian. My career is before you. I know what I should have done at your age; not to say what I did do. I to be a tool! The very last person that ought to be a tool. But I see my error: you have opened my eyes, and blessed be the hour in which we met. But we must take care how we act, Vivian;

we must be wary; eh! Vivian, wary, wary. People must know what their situations are; eh! Vivian?"

"Exceedingly useful knowledge; but I do not exactly understand the particular purport of your Lordship's last observation."

"You do not, eh?" asked the Peer; and he fixed his eyes as earnestly and expressively as he possibly could upon his young companion. "Well, I thought not. I was positive it was not true," continued the Marquess in a murmur.

"What, my Lord?"

"Oh! nothing, nothing; people talk at random, at random, at random. I feel confident you quite agree with me; eh! Vivian?"

"Really, my Lord, I fear I am unusually dull this morning."

"Dull! no, no; you quite agree with me. I feel confident you do. People must be taught what their situations are; that is what I was saying, Vivian. My Lord Courtown," added the Marquess, in a whisper, "is not to have everything his own way; eh! Vivian?"

"Oh, oh!" thought Vivian; "this, then, is the result of that admirable creature, Mrs. Felix Lorraine, staying a week with her dear friend, Lady Courtown.—My Lord, it would be singular if, in the Carabas party, the Carabas interest was not the predominant one."

"I knew you thought so. I could not believe for a minute that you could think otherwise; but some people take such strange ideas into their heads, I can not account for them. I felt confident what would be your opinion. My Lord Courtown is not to carry everything before him in the spirit that I have lately observed; or rather, in the spirit which I understand, from very good authority, is exhibited. Eh! Vivian; that is your opinion, is not it?"

"Oh! my dear Marquess, we must think alike on this, as on all points."

"I knew it. I felt confident as to your sentiments upon this subject. I can not conceive why some people take such strange ideas into their heads! I knew that you could not disagree with me upon this point. No, no, no; my Lord Courtown must feel which is the predominant interest, as you so well express it. How choice your expressions always are! I do not know how it is, but you always hit upon the right expression, Vivian. The predominant interest, the pre-dom-i-nant in-ter-est. To be sure. What! with my high character and connections, with my stake in society, was it to be expected that I, the Marquess of Carabas, was going to make any move which compromised the predominancy of my interests? No, no, no, my Lord Courtown; the predominant interest must be kept predominant; eh! Vivian?"

"To be sure, my Lord; explicitness and decision will soon arrange any *désagrémens.*"

"I have been talking to Lady Carabas, Vivian, upon the expediency of her opening the season early. I think a course of parliamentary dinners would produce a good effect. It gives a tone to a political party."

"Certainly; the science of political gastronomy has never been sufficiently studied."

"Egad! Vivian, I am in such spirits this morning. This business of Bromley so delights me; and finding you agree with me about Lord Courtown, I was confident as to your sentiments on that point. But some people take such strange ideas into their heads! To be sure, to be sure, the predominant interest, mine—that is to say, yours, Vivian—is the predominant interest. I have no idea of the predominant interest not being predominant; that would be singular! I knew you would agree with me; we always agree. 'Twas a lucky hour when we met. Two minds so exactly alike! I was just your very self when I was young; and as for you, my career is before you."

Here entered Mr. Sadler with the letters.

"One from Courtown. I wonder if he has seen Mounteney. Mounteney is a very good-natured fellow, and I think might be managed. Ah! I wish you could get hold of him, Vivian; you would soon bring him round. What it is to have brains, Vivian!" and here the Marquess shook his head very pompously, and at the same time tapped very significantly on his left temple. "Hah! what, what is all this? Here, read it, read it, man; I have no head to-day."

Vivian took the letter, and his quick eye dashed through its contents in a second. It was from Lord Courtown, and dated far in the country. It talked of private communications, and premature conduct, and the suspicious, not to say dishonorable, behavior of Mr. Vivian Grey: it trusted that such conduct was not sanctioned by his Lordship, but "nevertheless obliged to act with decision, regretted the necessity," etc., etc., etc., etc. In short, Lord Courtown had deserted, and recalled his pledge as to the official appointment promised to Mr. Cleveland, "because that promise was made while he was the victim of delusions created by the representations of Mr. Grey."

"What can all this mean, my Lord?"

The Marquess swore a fearful oath, and threw another letter.

"This is from Lord Beaconsfield, my Lord," said Vivian, with a face pallid as death, "and apparently the composition of the same writer; at least, it is the same tale, the same *refacimento* of lies, and treachery, and cowardice, doled out with diplomatic *politesse*. But I will off to ——shire instantly. It is not yet too late to save everything. This is Wednesday; on Thursday afternoon I shall be at Norwood Park. Thank God! I came this morning."

The face of the Marquess, who was treacherous as the wind, seemed already to indicate "Adieu! Mr. Vivian Grey!" but that countenance exhibited some very different passions when it glanced over the contents of the next epistle. There was a tremendous oath and a dead silence. His Lordship's florid countenance turned as pale as that of his companion. The perspiration stole down in heavy drops. He gasped for breath!

"Good God! my Lord, what is the matter?"

"The matter!" howled the Marquess, "the matter! That I have been a vain, weak, miserable fool!" and then there was another oath, and he flung the letter to the other side of the table.

It was the official *congé* of the Most Noble Sydney Marquess of Carabas. His Majesty had no longer any occasion for his services. His successor was Lord Courtown!

We will not affect to give any description of the conduct of the Marquess of Carabas at this moment. He raved, he stamped, he blasphemed! but the whole of his abuse was leveled against his former "monstrous clever" young friend; of whose character he had so often boasted that his own was the prototype, but who was now an adventurer, a swindler, a scoundrel, a liar, a base, deluding, flattering, fawning villain, etc., etc., etc., etc.

"My Lord!" said Vivian.

"I will not hear you; out on your fair words! They have duped me enough already. That I, with my high character and connections! that I, the Marquess of Carabas, should have been the victim of the arts of a young scoundrel!"

Vivian's fist was once clinched, but it was only for a moment. The Marquess leaned back in his chair with his eyes shut. In the agony of the moment a projecting tooth of his upper jaw had forced itself through his under lip, and from the wound the blood was flowing freely over his dead white countenance. Vivian left the room.

CHAPTER IV

HE stopped one moment on the landing-place, ere he was about to leave the house forever.

"'Tis all over! and so, Vivian Grey, your game is up! and to die, too, like a dog! a woman's dupe! Were I a despot, I should perhaps satiate my vengeance upon this female fiend with the assistance of the rack, but that can not be; and, after all, it would be but a poor revenge in one who has worshiped the Empire of the Intellect to vindicate the agony I am now enduring upon the base body of a woman. No! 'tis not all over. There is yet an intellectual rack of which few dream: far, far more terrific than the most exquisite contrivances of Parysatis. Jacinte," said he to a female attendant that passed, "is your mistress at home?"

"She is, sir."

"'Tis well," said Vivian, and he sprang upstairs.

"Health to the lady of our love!" said Vivian Grey, as he entered the elegant boudoir of Mrs. Felix Lorraine. "In spite of the easterly wind, which has spoiled my beauty for the season, I could not refrain from inquiring after your prosperity before I went to the Marquess. Have you heard the news?"

"News! no; what news?"

" 'Tis a sad tale," said Vivian, with a melancholy voice.

"Oh! then, pray do not tell it me. I am in no humor for sorrow to-day. Come! a bon-mot, or a calembourg, or exit, Mr. Vivian Grey."

"Well, then, good-morning! I am off for a black crape or a Barcelona kerchief. Mrs. Cleveland is dead."

"Dead!" exclaimed Mrs. Lorraine.

"Dead! She died last night, suddenly. Is it not horrible?"

"Shocking!" exclaimed Mrs. Lorraine, with a mournful voice and an eye dancing with joy. "Why, Mr. Grey, I do declare you are weeping."

"It is not for the departed!"

"Nay, Vivian! for Heaven's sake, what is the matter?"

"My dear Mrs. Lorraine!" but here the speaker's voice was choked with grief, and he could not proceed.

"Pray compose yourself."

"Mrs. Felix Lorraine, can I speak with you half an hour, undisturbed?"

"By all means. I will ring for Jacinte. Jacinte! mind I am not at home to any one. Well, what is the matter?"

"Oh! madam, I must pray your patience; I wish you to shrive a penitent."

"Good God! Mr. Grey! for Heaven's sake be explicit."

"For Heaven's sake, for your sake, for my soul's sake, I would be explicit; but explicitness is not the language of such as I am. Can you listen to a tale of horror? can you promise me to contain yourself?"

"I will promise anything. Pray, pray, proceed."

But in spite of her earnest solicitations her companion was mute.

At length he rose from his chair, and leaning on the chimneypiece, buried his face in his hands and wept.

"Vivian," said Mrs. Lorraine, "have you seen the Marquess yet?"

"Not yet," he sobbed; "I am going to him, but I am in no humor for business this morning."

"Compose yourself, I beseech you. I will hear everything. You shall not complain of an inattentive or an irritable auditor. Now, my dear Vivian, sit down and tell me all." She led him to a chair, and then, after stifling his sobs, with a broken voice he proceeded.

"You will recollect, madam, that accident made me acquainted with certain circumstances connected with yourself and Mr. Cleveland. Alas! actuated by the vilest of sentiments, I conceived a violent hatred against that gentleman, a hatred only to be equaled by my passion for you; but I find difficulty in dwelling upon the details of this sad story of jealousy and despair."

"Oh! speak, speak! compensate for all you have done by your present frankness; be brief, be brief."

"I will be brief," said Vivian, with earnestness: "I will be brief. Know then, madam, that in order to prevent the intercourse between you and Mr. Cleveland from proceeding I obtained his friendship, and became the confidant of his heart's sweetest secret. Thus situated, I suppressed the letters with which I was intrusted from him to you, and, poisoning his mind, I accounted for your silence by your being employed in other correspondence; nay, I did more; with the malice of a fiend, I boasted of—; nay, do not stop me; I have more to tell."

Mrs. Felix Lorraine, with compressed lips and looks of horrible earnestness, gazed in silence.

"The result of all this you know; but the most terrible part is to come; and, by a strange fascination, I fly to confess my crimes at your feet, even while the last minutes have witnessed my most heinous one. Oh! madam, I have stood over the bier of the departed; I have mingled my tears with those of the sorrowing widower, his young and tender child was on my knee, and as I kissed his innocent lips, methought it was but my duty to the departed to save the father from his mother's rival—" He stopped.

"Yes, yes, yes," said Mrs. Felix Lorraine, in a low whisper.

"It was then, even then, in the hour of his desolation, that I mentioned your name, that it might the more disgust him; and while he wept over his virtuous and sainted wife, I dwelt on the vices of his rejected mistress."

Mrs. Lorraine clasped her hands, and moved restlessly on her seat.

"Nay! do not stop me; let me tell all. 'Cleveland,' said I, 'if ever you become the husband of Mrs. Felix Lorraine, re-

member my last words: it will be well for you if your frame
be like that of Mithridates of Pontus, and proof against—
poison.' "

"And did you say this?" shrieked the woman.

"Even these were my words."

"Then may all evil blast you!" She threw herself on the
sofa; her voice was choked with the convulsions of her passion, and she writhed in fearful agony.

Vivian Grey, lounging in an arm-chair in the easiest of
postures, and with a face brilliant with smiles, watched his
victim with the eye of a Mephistopheles.

She slowly recovered, and, with a broken voice, poured
forth her sacred absolution to the relieved penitent.

"You wonder I do not stab you; hah! hah! hah! there is
no need for that! the good powers be praised that you refused
the draught I once proffered. Know, wretch, that your race
is run. Within five minutes you will breathe a beggar and
an outcast. Your golden dreams are over, your cunning plans
are circumvented, your ambitious hopes are crushed forever,
you are blighted in the very spring of your life. Oh, may
you never die! May you wander forever, the butt of the
world's malice; and may the slow-moving finger of scorn
point where'er you go at the ruined Charlatan!"

"Hah, hah! is it so? Think you that Vivian Grey would
fall by a woman's wile? Think you that Vivian Grey could
be crushed by such a worthless thing as you? Know, then,
that your political intrigues have been as little concealed from
me as your personal ones; I have been acquainted with all.
The Marquess has himself seen the Minister, and is more firmly
established in his pride of place than ever. I have myself seen
our colleagues, whom you tampered with, and their hearts are
still true, and their purpose still fixed. All, all prospers; and
ere five days are passed 'the Charlatan' will be a Senator."

The shifting expression of Mrs. Lorraine's countenance,
while Vivian was speaking, would have baffled the most cunning painter. Her complexion was capricious as the chame-
leon's, and her countenance was so convulsed that her features
seemed of all shapes and sizes. One large vein protruded
nearly a quarter of an inch from her forehead, and the dank
light which gleamed in her tearful eye was like an unwhole-

some meteor quivering in a marsh. When he ended she
sprang from the sofa, and, looking up and extending her arms
with unmeaning wildness, she gave one loud shriek and
dropped like a bird shot on the wing; she had burst a blood-
vessel.

Vivian raised her on the sofa and paid her every possible
attention. There is always a medical attendant lurking about
the mansions of the noble, and to this worthy and the attendant
Jacinte Vivian delivered his patient.

Had Vivian Grey left the boudoir a pledged bridegroom
his countenance could not have been more triumphant; but he
was laboring under unnatural excitement; for it is singular
that when, as he left the house, the porter told him that Mr.
Cleveland was with his Lord, Vivian had no idea at the
moment what individual bore that name. The fresh air of
the street revived him, and somewhat cooled the bubbling
of his blood. It was then that the man's information struck
upon his senses.

"So, poor Cleveland!" thought Vivian; "then he knows
all!" His own misery he had not yet thought of; but when
Cleveland occurred to him, with his ambition once more
balked, his high hopes once more blasted, and his honorable
soul once more deceived; when he thought of his fair wife, and
his infant children, and his ruined prospects, a sickness came
over his heart, he grew dizzy, and fell.

"And the gentleman's ill, I think," said an honest Irish-
man; and, in the fulness of his charity, he placed Vivian on
a doorstep.

"So it seems," said a genteel passenger in black; and he
snatched, with great *sangfroid*, Vivian's watch. "Stop thief!"
hallooed the Hibernian. Paddy was tripped up. There was
a row, in the midst of which Vivian Grey crawled to a hotel.

CHAPTER V

I N half an hour Vivian was at Mr. Cleveland's door.

"My master is at the Marquess of Carabas's, sir; he will not return, but is going immediately to Richmond, where Mrs. Cleveland is staying."

Vivian immediately wrote to Mr. Cleveland. "If your master have left the Marquess's, let this be forwarded to him at Richmond immediately."

"CLEVELAND!

"You know all. It would be mockery were I to say that at this moment I am not thinking of myself. I am a ruined man in body and in mind. But my own misery is nothing; I can die, I can go mad, and who will be harmed? But you! I had wished that we should never meet again; but my hand refuses to trace the thoughts with which my heart is full, and I am under the sad necessity of requesting you to see me once more. We have been betrayed, and by a woman; but there has been revenge. Oh, what revenge!

"VIVIAN GREY."

When Vivian left Mr. Cleveland's he actually did not know what to do with himself. Home, at present, he could not face, and so he continued to wander about, quite unconscious of locality. He passed in his progress many of his acquaintance, who, from his distracted air and rapid pace, imagined that he was intent on some important business. At length he found himself in one of the most sequestered parts of Kensington Gardens. It was a cold, frosty day, and as Vivian flung himself upon one of the summer seats the snow drifted from off the frozen board; but Vivian's brow was as burning hot as if he had been an inhabitant of Sirius. Throwing his arms on a small garden table he buried his face in his hands and wept as men can but once weep in this world.

O, thou sublime and most subtle philosopher, who, in thy lamp-lit cell, art speculating upon the passions which thou hast never felt! O, thou splendid and most admirable poet, who, with cunning words, art painting with a smile a tale of woe! tell me what is Grief, and solve me the mystery of Sorrow.

Not for himself, for after the first pang he would have whistled off his high hopes with the spirit of a Ripperda, not even for Cleveland—for at this moment, it must be confessed, his thoughts were not for his friend—did Vivian Grey's soul struggle as if it were about to leave its fleshy chamber. We said he wept as men can weep but once in this world, and yet it would have been impossible for him to have defined what, at that fearful moment, was the cause of his heart's sorrow. Incidents of childhood of the most trivial nature, and until this moment forgotten, flashed across his memory; he gazed on the smile of his mother, he listened to the sweet tones of his father's voice, and his hand clinched, with still more agonized grasp, his rude resting-place, and the scalding tears dashed down his cheek in still more ardent torrents. He had no distinct remembrance of what had so lately happened; but characters flitted before him as in a theatre, in a dream, dim and shadowy, yet full of mysterious and undefinable interest; and then there came a horrible idea across his mind that his glittering youth was gone and wasted; and then there was a dark whisper of treachery, and dissimulation, and dishonor; and then he sobbed as if his very heart were cracking. All his boasted philosophy vanished; his artificial feelings fled him. Insulted Nature reasserted her long-spurned authority, and the once proud Vivian Grey felt too humble even to curse himself. Gradually his sobs became less convulsed and his brow more cool; and, calm from very exhaustion, he sat for upward of an hour motionless.

At this moment there issued, with their attendant, from an adjoining shrubbery, two beautiful children. They were so exceedingly lovely that the passenger would have stopped to gaze upon them. The eldest, who yet was very young, was leading his sister hand in hand with slow and graceful steps,

mimicking the courtesy of men. But when his eye caught
Vivian's the boy uttered a loud cry of exultation, and rushed,
with the eagerness of infantile affection, to his gentle and
favorite playmate. They were the young Clevelands. With
what miraculous quickness will man shake off the outward
semblance of grief when his sorrow is a secret! The mighty
merchant, who knows that in four-and-twenty hours the world
must be astounded by his insolvency, will walk in the front
of his confident creditor as if he were the lord of a thousand
argosies; the meditating suicide will smile on the arm of a
companion as if to breathe in this sunny world were the most
ravishing and rapturous bliss. We cling to our stations in our
fellow-creatures' minds and memories; we know too well the
frail tenure on which we are in this world great and considered personages. Experience makes us shrink from the
specious sneer of sympathy; and when we are ourselves
falling, bitter Memory whispers that we have ourselves been
neglectful.

And so it was that even unto these infants Vivian Grey
dared not appear other than a gay and easy-hearted man; and
in a moment he was dancing them upon his knee, and playing
with their curls, and joining in their pretty prattle, and pressing their small and fragrant lips.

It was night when he paced down ———. He passed his
club; that club to become a member of which had once been
the object of his high ambition, and to gain which privilege
had cost such hours of canvassing, such interference of noble
friends, and the incurring of favors from so many people,
"which never could be forgotten!"

A desperate feeling actuated him, and he entered the Club-
house. He walked into the great saloon and met some fifty
"most particular friends," all of whom asked him "how the
Marquess did," or "have you seen Cleveland?" and a thousand
other as comfortable queries.

At length, to avoid these disagreeable rencontres, and indeed to rest himself, he went to a smaller and more private room. As he opened the door his eyes lighted upon
Cleveland.

He was standing with his back to the fire. There were
only two other persons in the room; one was a friend of Cleve-

land's, and the other an acquaintance of Vivian's. The latter
was writing at the table.

When Vivian saw Cleveland he would have retired, but he
was bid to "come in" in a voice of thunder.

As he entered he instantly perceived that Cleveland was
under the influence of wine. When in this situation, unlike
other men, Mr. Cleveland's conduct was not distinguished by
any of the little improprieties of behavior by which a man is
always known by his friends "to be very drunk." He neither
reeled, nor hiccuped, nor grew maudlin. The effect of drinking upon him was only to increase the intensity of the sensation by which his mind was at the moment influenced. He did
not even lose the consciousness of identity of persons. At this
moment it was clear to Vivian that Cleveland was under the
influence of the extremest passion; his eyes rolled widely,
and seemed fixed only upon vacancy. As Vivian was no
friend to scenes before strangers he bowed to the two gentlemen and saluted Cleveland with his wonted cordiality; but his
proffered hand was rudely repelled.

"Away!" exclaimed Cleveland, in a furious tone; "I have
no friendship for traitors."

The two gentlemen stared, and the pen of the writer
stopped.

"Cleveland!" said Vivian, in an earnest whisper, as he
came up close to him; "for God's sake contain yourself. I
have written you a letter which explains all; but—"

"Out! out upon you. Out upon your honeyed words and
your soft phrases! I have been their dupe too long;" and
he struck Vivian.

"Sir John Poynings!" said Vivian, with a quivering lip,
turning to the gentleman who was writing at the table, "we
were school-fellows; circumstances have prevented us from
meeting often in after-life; but I now ask you, with the frankness of an old acquaintance, to do me the sad service of accompanying me in this quarrel, a quarrel which I call Heaven to
witness is not of my seeking."

The Baronet, who was in the Guards, and, although a
great dandy, quite a man of business in these matters, immediately rose from his seat and led Vivian to a corner of the
room. After some whispering he turned round to Mr. Cleve-

land, and bowed to him with a very significant look. It was
evident that Cleveland comprehended his meaning, for, though
he was silent, he immediately pointed to the other gentleman,
his friend, Mr. Castleton.

"Mr. Castleton," said Sir John, giving his card, "Mr. Grey
will accompany me to my rooms in Pall Mall; it is now ten
o'clock; we shall wait two hours, in which time I hope to
hear from you. I leave time, and place, and terms to yourself. I only wish it to be understood that it is the particular
desire of my principal that the meeting should be as speedy
as possible."

About eleven o'clock the communication from Mr. Castleton arrived. It was quite evident that Cleveland was sobered,
for in one instance Vivian observed that the style was corrected
by his own hand. The hour was eight the next morning, at
——— Common, about six miles from town.

Poynings wrote to a professional friend to be on the
ground at half-past seven, and then he and Vivian retired.

Did you ever fight a duel? No! nor send a challenge
either? Well! you are fresh, indeed! 'Tis an awkward business, after all, even for the boldest. After an immense deal of
negotiation, and giving your opponent every opportunity of
coming to an honorable understanding, the fatal letter is at
length signed, sealed, and sent. You pass your mornings at
your second's apartments, pacing his drawing-room with a
quivering lip and uncertain step. At length he enters with an
answer; and while he reads you endeavor to look easy, with a
countenance merry with the most melancholy smile. You have
no appetite for dinner, but you are too brave not to appear at
table; and you are called out after the second glass by the
arrival of your solicitor, who comes to alter your will. You
pass a restless night, and rise in the morning as bilious as a
Bengal general. Urged by impending fate, you make a desperate effort to accommodate matters; but in the contest
between your pride and your terror you at the same time prove
that you are a coward and fail in the negotiation. You both
fire and miss, and then the seconds interfere, and then you
shake hands: everything being arranged in the most honorable
manner and to the mutual satisfaction of both parties. The
next day you are seen pacing Bond Street with an erect front

and a flashing eye, with an air at once dandyish and heroical, a mixture at the same time of Brummell and the Duke of Wellington.

It was a fine February morning. Sir John drove Vivian to the ground in his cabriolet.

"Nothing like a cab, Grey, for the business you are going on: you glide along the six miles in such style that it actually makes you quite courageous. I remember once going down, on a similar purpose, in a post and pair, and 'pon my soul, when I came to the ground, my hand shook so that I could scarcely draw. But I was green, then. Now, when I go in my cab, with Philidor with his sixteen-mile-an-hour paces, egad! I wing my man in a trice; and take all the parties home to Pall Mall, to celebrate the event with a grilled bone, Havanas, and Regent's punch. Ah! there! that is Cleveland that we have just passed going to the ground in a chariot: he is a dead man, or my name is not Poynings."

"Come, Sir John; no fear of Cleveland's dying," said Vivian, with a smile.

"What? You mean to fire in the air, and all that sort of thing? Sentimental, but slip-slop!"

The ground is measured, all is arranged. Cleveland, a splendid shot, fired first. He grazed Vivian's elbow. Vivian fired in the air. The seconds interfered. Cleveland was implacable, and, "in the most irregular manner," as Sir John declared, insisted upon another shot. To the astonishment of all he fired quite wild. Vivian shot at random, and his bullet pierced Cleveland's heart. Cleveland sprang nearly two yards from the ground and then fell upon his back. In a moment Vivian was at the side of his fallen antagonist, but the dying man "made no sign"; he stared wildly, and then closed his eyes forever!

CHAPTER VI

WHEN Vivian Grey remembered his existence he found himself in bed. The curtains of his couch were closed; but as he stared around him they were softly withdrawn, and a face that recalled everything to his recollection gazed upon him with a look of affectionate anxiety.

"My father!" exclaimed Vivian; but the finger pressed on the parental lip warned him to silence. His father knelt by his side, and then the curtains were again closed.

Six weeks, unconsciously to Vivian, had elapsed since the fatal day, and he was now recovering from the effects of a fever from which his medical attendants had supposed he never could have rallied. And what had been the past? It did indeed seem like a hot and feverish dream. Here was he once more in his own quiet room, watched over by his beloved parents; and had there then ever existed such beings as the Marquess, and Mrs. Lorraine, and Cleveland, or were they only the actors in a vision? "It must be so," thought Vivian; and he jumped up in his bed and stared wildly around him. "And yet it was a horrid dream! Murder, horrible murder! and so real, so palpable! I muse upon their voices as upon familiar sounds, and I recall all the events, not as the shadowy incidents of sleep, that mysterious existence in which the experience of a century seems caught in the breathing of a second, but as the natural and material consequences of time and stirring life. O, no! it is too true!" shrieked the wretched sufferer, as his eye glanced upon a despatch-box which was on the table, and which had been given to him by Lord Carabas; "it is true! it is true! Murder! murder!" He foamed at the mouth, and sank exhausted on his pillow.

But the human mind can master many sorrows, and, after a desperate relapse and another miraculous rally, Vivian Grey rose from his bed.

"My father, I fear that I shall live!"

"Hope, rather, my beloved."

"Oh! why should I hope?" and the sufferer's head sank upon his breast.

"Do not give way, my son; all will yet be well, and we shall all yet be happy," said the father, with streaming eyes.

"Happy! oh, not in this world, my father!"

"Vivian, my dearest, your mother visited you this morning, but you were asleep. She was quite happy to find you slumbering so calmly."

"And yet my dreams were not dreams of joy. O, my mother! you were wont to smile upon me; alas! you smiled upon your sorrow."

"Vivian, my beloved! you must indeed restrain your feelings. At your age life can not be the lost game you think it. A little repose, and I shall yet see my boy the honor to society which he deserves to be."

"Alas! my father, you know not what I feel. The springiness of my mind has gone. O man, what a vain fool thou art! Nature has been too bountiful to thee. She has given thee the best of friends, and thou valuest not the gift of exceeding price until the griefs are past even friendship's cure. O, my father! why did I leave thee?" and he seized Mr. Grey's hand with convulsive grasp.

Time flew on, even in this house of sorrow. "My boy," said Mr. Grey to his son one day, "your mother and I have been consulting together about you; and we think, now that you have somewhat recovered your strength, it may be well for you to leave England for a short time. The novelty of travel will relieve your mind without too much exciting it; and if you can manage by the autumn to settle down anywhere within a thousand miles of England, why, we will come and join you, and you know that will be very pleasant. What say you to this little plan?"

In a few weeks after this proposition had been made Vivian Grey was in Germany. He wandered for some months in that beautiful land of rivers among which flows the Rhine, matchless in its loveliness; and at length the pilgrim shook the dust off his feet at Heidelberg, in which city Vivian proposed taking up his residence. It is, in truth, a place of surpassing loveliness, where all romantic wildness of German scenery is blended with the soft beauty of the Italian. An immense plain, which, in its extent and luxuriance, reminds you of the fertile tracts of Lombardy, is bordered on one side by the Bergstrasse Mountains, and on the other by the range of the Vosges. Situate on the river Neckar, in a ravine of the Bergstrasse, amid mountains covered with vines, is Heidelberg; its ruined castle backing the city, and still frowning from one of the most commanding heights. In the middle of the broad plain may be distinguished the shining spires of Mannheim, Worms, and Frankenthal; and pouring its rich stream through this luxuriant land, the beautiful and abounding Rhine receives the tribute of the Neckar. The range of the Vosges forms the extreme distance.

To the little world of the little city of which he was now a habitant Vivian Grey did not appear a broken-hearted man. He lived neither as a recluse nor a misanthrope. He became extremely addicted to field sports, especially to hunting the wild boar; for he feared nothing so much as thought, and dreaded nothing so much as the solitude of his own chamber. He was an early riser to escape from hideous dreams; and at break of dawn he wandered among the wild passes of the Bergstrasse; or, climbing a lofty ridge, was a watcher for the rising sun; and in the evening he sailed upon the starlit Neckar.

BOOK V

CHAPTER I

THOU rapid Aar! thy waves are swollen by the snows of a thousand hills; but for whom are thy leaping waters fed? Is it for the Rhine?

Calmly, O placid Neckar! does thy blue stream glide through thy vine-clad vales; but calmer seems thy course when it touches the rushing Rhine!

How fragrant are the banks which are cooled by thy dark-green waters, thou tranquil Main! but is not the perfume sweeter of the gardens of the Rhine?

Thou impetuous Nah! I lingered by thine islands of night-ingales, and I asked thy rushing waters why they disturbed the music of thy groves? They told me they were hastening to the Rhine!

Red Moselle! fierce is the swell of thy spreading course; but why do thy broad waters blush when they meet the Rhine?

Thou delicate Meuse! how clear is the current of thy limpid wave; as the wife yields to the husband do thy pure waters yield to the Rhine!

And thou, triumphant and imperial River, flushed with the tribute of these vassal streams! thou art thyself a tributary, and hastenest even in the pride of conquest to confess thine own vassalage! But no superior stream exults in the homage of thy servile waters: the Ocean, the eternal Ocean, alone comes forward to receive thy kiss! not as a conqueror, but as a parent, he welcomes with proud joy his gifted child, the offspring of his honor; thy duty, his delight; thy tribute, thine own glory!

Once more upon thy banks, most beauteous Rhine! In the spring-time of my youth I gazed on thee, and deemed thee matchless. Thy vine-enamored mountains, thy spreading waters, thy traditionary crags, thy shining cities, the spark-

ling villages of thy winding shores, thy antique convents, thy
gray and silent castles, the purple glories of thy radiant grape,
the vivid tints of thy teeming flowers, the fragrance of thy
sky, the melody of thy birds, whose carols tell the pleasures
of their sunny woods; are they less lovely now, less beautiful,
less sweet?

The keen emotions of our youth are often the occasion of
our estimating too ardently; but the first impression of beauty,
though often overcharged, is seldom supplanted: and as the
first great author which he reads is reverenced by the boy as
the most immortal, and the first beautiful woman that he meets
is sanctified by him as the most adorable; so the impressions
created upon us by those scenes of nature which first realize
the romance of our reveries never escape from our minds,
and are ever consecrated in our memories; and thus some
great spirits, after having played their part on the theatre of
the world, have retired from the blaze of courts and cities
to the sweet seclusion of some spot with which they have
accidentally met in the earliest years of their career.

But we are to speak of one who had retired from the world
before his time.

Upward of a year had elapsed since Vivian Grey left
England. The mode of life which he pursued at Heidelberg
for many months has already been mentioned. He felt himself a broken-hearted man, and looked for death, whose delay
was no blessing; but the feelings of youth which had misled
him in his burning hours of joy equally deceived him in his
days of sorrow. He lived; and in the course of time found
each day that life was less burdensome. The truth is, that
if it be the lot of man to suffer, it is also his fortune to
forget. Oblivion and Sorrow share our being, as Darkness
and Light divide the course of time. It is not in human nature
to endure extremities, and sorrows soon destroy either us or
themselves. Perhaps the fate of Niobe is no fable, but a type
of the callousness of our nature. There is a time in human
suffering when succeeding sorrows are but like snow falling
on an iceberg. It is indeed horrible to think that our peace of
mind should arise, not from a retrospection of the past, but from
a forgetfulness of it; but, though this peace be produced at
the best by a mental opiate, it is not valueless; and Oblivion,

after all, is a just judge. As we retain but a faint remembrance of our felicity, it is but fair that the smartest stroke of sorrow should, if bitter, at least be brief. But in feeling that he might yet again mingle in the world, Vivian Grey also felt that he must meet mankind with different feelings, and view their pursuits with a different interest. He woke from his secret sorrow in as changed a state of being as the water nymph from her first embrace; and he woke with a new possession, not only as miraculous as Undine's soul, but gained at as great a price, and leading to as bitter results. The nymph woke to new pleasures and to new sorrows; and, innocent as an infant, she deemed mankind a god, and the world a paradise. Vivian Grey discovered that this deity was but an idol of brass, and this Garden of Eden but a savage waste; for, if the river nymph had gained a soul, he had gained Experience.

Experience, mysterious spirit! whose result is felt by all, whose nature is described by none. The father warns the son of thy approach, and sometimes looks to thee as his offspring's cure and his own consolation. We hear of thee in the nursery, we hear of thee in the world, we hear of thee in books; but who has recognized thee until he was thy subject, and who has discovered the object of so much fame until he has kissed thy chain? To gain thee is the work of all and the curse of all; thou art at the same time necessary to our happiness and destructive of our felicity; thou art the savior of all things and the destroyer of all things; our best friend and our bitterest enemy; for thou teachest us truth, and that truth is despair. Ye youth of England, would that ye could read this riddle!

To wake from your bright hopes, and feel that all is vanity, to be roused from your crafty plans and know that all is worthless, is a bitter, but your sure, destiny. Escape is impossible; for despair is the price of conviction. How many centuries have fled since Solomon, in his cedar palaces, sung the vanity of man! Though his harp was golden and his throne of ivory, his feelings were not less keen, and his conviction not less complete. How many sages of all nations have, since the monarch of Jerusalem, echoed his sad philosophy! yet the vain bubble still glitters and still allures, and must forever.

The genealogy of Experience is brief; for Experience is the child of Thought, and Thought is the child of Action. We can not learn men from books, nor can we form, from written descriptions, a more accurate idea of the movements of the human heart than we can of the movements of nature. A man may read all his life, and form no conception of the rush of a mountain torrent, or the waving of a forest of pines in a storm; and a man may study in his closet the heart of his fellow-creatures forever, and have no idea of the power of ambition, or the strength of revenge.

It is when we have acted ourselves, and have seen others acting; it is when we have labored ourselves under the influence of our passions, and have seen others laboring; it is when our great hopes have been attained or have been balked; it is when, after having had the human heart revealed to us, we have the first opportunity to think; it is then that the whole truth lights upon us; it is then that we ask of ourselves whether it be wise to endure such anxiety of mind, such agitation of spirit, such harrowing of the soul, to gain what may cease to interest to-morrow, or for which, at the best, a few years of enjoyment can alone be afforded; it is then that we waken to the hollowness of all human things; it is then that the sayings of sages and the warnings of prophets are explained and understood; it is then that we gain Experience.

Vivian Grey was now about to join, for the second time, the great and agitated crowd of beings who are all intent in the search after that undiscoverable talisman, Happiness. That he entertained any hope of being the successful inquirer is not to be imagined. He considered that the happiest moment in human life is exactly the sensation of a sailor who has escaped a shipwreck, and that the mere belief that his wishes are to be indulged is the greatest bliss enjoyed by man.

How far his belief was correct, how he prospered in this his second venture on the great ocean of life, it is our business to relate. There were moments when he wished himself neither experienced nor a philosopher; moments when he looked back to the lost paradise of his innocent boyhood, those glorious hours when the unruffled river of his Life mirrored the cloudless heaven of his Hope!

CHAPTER II

VIVIAN pulled up his horse as he ascended through the fine beech wood which leads immediately to the city of Frankfort from the Darmstadt road. The crowd seemed to increase every moment, but as they were all hastening the same way, his progress was not much impeded. It was Frankfort fair; and all countenances were expressive of that excitement which we always experience at great meetings of our fellow-creatures; whether the assemblies be for slaughter, pleasure, or profit, and whether or not we ourselves join in the banquet, the battle, or the fair. At the top of the hill is an old Roman tower, and from this point the flourishing city of Frankfort, with its picturesque Cathedral, its numerous villas, and beautiful gardens in the middle of the fertile valley of the Main, burst upon Vivian's sight. On crossing the bridge over the river, the crowd became almost impassable, and it was with the greatest difficulty that Vivian steered his way through the old narrow winding streets, full of tall ancient houses, with heavy casements and notched gable ends. These structures did not, however, at the present moment, greet the traveler with their usual sombre and antique appearance: their outside walls were, in most instances, covered with pieces of broad cloth of the most showy colors, red, blue, and yellow predominating. These standards of trade were not merely used for the purpose of exhibiting the quality of the articles sold in the interior, but also of informing the curious traveler the name and nation of their adventurous owners. Inscriptions in German, French, Russian, English, Italian, and even Hebrew, appeared in striking characters on each woolen specimen; and, as if these were not sufficient to attract the attention of the passenger, an active apprentice, or assistant, commented in eloquent terms on the peculiar fairness and honesty of his master. The public squares and other open spaces, and indeed

every spot which was secure from the hurrying wheels of the
heavy old-fashioned coaches of the Frankfort aristocracy and
the spirited pawings of their sleek and long-tailed coach-
horses, were covered with large and showy booths, which
groaned under the accumulated treasures of all countries.
French silks and French clocks rivaled Manchester cottons
and Sheffield cutlery, and assisted to attract or entrap the
gazer, in company with Venetian chains, Neapolitan coral,
and Vienna pipeheads: here was the booth of a great book-
seller, who looked to the approaching Leipsic fair for some
consolation for his slow sale and the bad taste of the people
of Frankfort; and there was a dealer in Bologna sausages,
who felt quite convinced that in some things the taste of the
Frankfort public was by no means to be lightly spoken of.
All was bustle, bargaining, and business. There were quarrels and conversation in all languages; and Vivian Grey,
although he had no chance either of winning or losing money,
was amused.

At last Vivian gained the High Street; and here, though
the crowd was not less, the space was greater; and so in time
he arrived at the grand hotel of "the Roman Emperor," where
he stopped. It was a long time before he could be informed
whether Baron Julius von Konigstein at present honored that
respectable establishment with his presence; for, although
Vivian did sometimes succeed in obtaining an audience of a
hurrying waiter, that personage, when in a hurry, has a
peculiar habit of never attending to a question which a traveler
addresses to him. In this dilemma Vivian was saluted by a
stately-looking personage above the common height. He was
dressed in a very splendid uniform of green and gold, covered
with embroidery, and glittering with frogs. He wore a
cocked hat adorned with a flowing parti-colored plume, and
from his broad golden belt was suspended a weapon of
singular shape and costly workmanship. This personage was
as stiff and stately as he was magnificent. His eyes were
studiously preserved from the profanation of meeting the
ground, and his well-supported neck seldom condescended to
move from its perpendicular position. His coat was buttoned
to the chin and over the breast, with the exception of one
small aperture which was elegantly filled up by a delicate white

cambric handkerchief, very redolent of rich perfumes. This gorgeous gentleman, who might have been mistaken for an elector of the German Empire, had the German Empire been in existence, or the governor of the city at least, turned out to be the chasseur of the Baron von Konigstein; and with his courtly assistance Vivian soon found himself ascending the staircase of the Roman Emperor.

Vivian was ushered into an apartment, in which he found three or four individuals at breakfast. A middle-aged man of distinguished appearance, in a splendid chamber robe, sprang up from a many-cushioned easy-chair and seized his hand as he was announced.

"My dear Mr. Grey! I have left notes for you at the principal hotels. And how is Eugene? wild blood for a student, but an excellent heart, and you have been so kind to him! He feels under such particular obligations to you. Will you breakfast? Ah! I see you smile at my supposing a horseman unbreakfasted. And have you ridden here from Heidelberg this morning? Impossible! Only from Darmstadt! I thought so! You were at the opera then last night. And how is the little Signora? We are to gain her, though! trust the good people of Frankfort for that! Pray be seated, but really I am forgetting the commonest rules of breeding. Next to the pleasure of having friends is that of introducing them to each other. Prince, you will have great pleasure in being introduced to my friend, Mr. Grey: Mr. Grey! Prince Salvinski! my particular friend, Prince Salvinski. The Count von Altenburgh! Mr. Grey! my very particular friend, the Count von Altenburgh. And the Chevalier de Bœffleurs! Mr. Grey! my most particular friend, the Chevalier de Bœffleurs."

Baron Julius von Konigstein was minister to the Diet of Frankfort from a first-rate German Power. In person he was short, but delicately formed; his head a little bald, but as he was only five-and-thirty, this could scarcely be from age; and his remaining hair, black, glossy, and curling, proved that their companion ringlets had not been long lost. His features were small, but not otherwise remarkable, except a pair of liquid black eyes, of great size, which would have hardly become a Stoic, and which gleamed with great meaning and perpetual animation.

"I understand, Mr. Grey, that you are a regular philosopher. Pray, who is the favorite master? Kant or Fichte? or is there any other new star who has discovered the origin of our essence, and proved the non-necessity of eating? Count, let me help you to a little more of these *saucisses aux choux*. I am afraid, from Eugene's account, that you are almost past redemption; and I am sorry to say that, although I am very desirous of being your physician and effecting your cure, Frankfort will supply me with very few means to work your recovery. If you could but get me an appointment once again to your delightful London, I might indeed produce some effect; or were I even at Berlin, or at your delicious Vienna, Count Altenburgh! (the Count bowed); or at that Paradise of women, Warsaw, Prince Salvinski!! (the Prince bowed); or at Paris, Chevalier!!! (the Chevalier bowed); why, then, indeed, you should have some difficulty in finding an excuse for being in low spirits with Julius von Konigstein! But Frankfort, eh De Bœffleurs?"

"Oh! Frankfort!" sighed the French Chevalier, who was also attached to a mission in this very city, and who was thinking of his own gay Boulevards and his brilliant Tuileries.

"We are mere citizens here!" continued the Baron, taking a long pinch of snuff, "mere citizens! Do you snuff?" and here he extended to Vivian a gold box, covered with the portrait of a crowned head, surrounded with diamonds. "A present from the King of Sardinia, when I negotiated the marriage of the Duke of —— and his niece, and settled the long-agitated controversy about the right of anchovy fishing on the left shore of the Mediterranean.

"But the women," continued the Baron, "the women; that is a different thing. There is some amusement among the little bourgeoisie, who are glad enough to get rid of their commercial beaux; whose small talk, after a waltz, is about bills of exchange, mixed up with a little patriotism about their free city, and some chatter about what they call 'the fine arts'; their awful collections of 'the Dutch school'; school forsooth! a cabbage by Gerard Dow! and a candlestick by Mieris! And now will you take a basin of soup, and warm yourself, while his Highness continues his account of being frozen to death this spring at the top of Mont Blanc: how was it, Prince?"

"Your Highness has been a great traveler?" said Vivian.

"I have seen a little of most countries. These things are interesting enough when we are young; but when we get a little more advanced in life the novelty wears off, and the excitement ceases. I have been in all quarters of the globe. In Europe I have seen everything except the miracles of Prince Hohenlohe. In Asia, everything except the ruins of Babylon. In Africa, I have seen everything but Timbuctoo; and, in America, everything except Croker's Mountains."

Next to eating, music is the business in which an Austrian is most interested, and Count von Altenburgh, having had the misfortune of destroying, for the present, one great source of his enjoyment, became now very anxious to know what chance there existed of his receiving some consolation from the other. Pushing his plate briskly from him, he demanded with an anxious air:

"Can any gentleman inform me what chance there is of the Signora coming?"

"No news to-day," said the Baron, with a mournful look; "I am almost in despair. What do you think of the last notes that have been interchanged?"

"Very little chance," said the Chevalier de Bœffleurs, shaking his head. "Really these burghers, with all their affected enthusiasm, have managed the business exceedingly bad. No opera can possibly succeed that is not conducted by a committee of noblemen."

"Certainly!" said the Baron; "we are sure then to have the best singers, and be in the 'Gazette' the same season."

"Which is much better, I think, Von Konigstein, than paying our bills and receiving no pleasure."

"But," continued the Baron, "these clumsy burghers, with their affected enthusiasm, as you well observe; who could have contemplated such novices in diplomacy! Whatever may be the issue, I can at least lay my head upon my pillow and feel that I have done my duty. Did not I, De Bœffleurs, first place the negotiation on a basis of acknowledged feasibility and mutual benefit? Who drew the protocol, I should like to know? Who baffled the intrigues of the English Minister, the Lord Amelius Fitzfudge Boroughby? Who sat up one whole night with the Signora's friend, the Russian Envoy,

Baron Squallonoff, and who was it that first arranged about the extra chariot?" and here the representative of a first-rate German Power looked very much like a resigned patriot, who feels that he deserves a ribbon.

"No doubt of it, my dear Von Konigstein," echoed the French Chargé d'Affaires, "and I think, whatever may be the result, that I, too, may look back to this negotiation with no ungratified feelings. Had the arrangement been left as I had wished, merely to the Ministers of the Great Powers, I am confident that the Signora would have been singing this night in our Opera House."

"What is the grand point of difference at present?" asked the Austrian.

"A terrific one," said the Baron; "the lady demanded twenty covers, two tables, two carriages, one of which I arranged should be a chariot; that at least the town owes to me; and, what else? merely a town mansion and establishment. Exerting myself day and night, these terms were at length agreed to by the municipality, and the lady was to ride over from Darmstadt to sign and seal. In the course of her ride she took a cursed fancy to the country villa of a great Jew banker, and since that moment the arrangement has gone off. We have offered her everything; the commandant's country castle; his lady's country farm; the villa of the director of the Opera; the retreat of our present prima donna; all in vain. We have even hinted at a temporary repose in a neighboring royal residence; but all useless. The banker and the Signora are equally intractable, and Frankfort is in despair."

"She ought to have signed and sealed at Darmstadt," said the Count, very indignantly.

"To be sure! they should have closed upon her caprice, and taken her when she was in the fancy."

"Talking of Opera girls," commenced the Polish Prince, "I remember the Countess Katszinski—"

"Your highness has nothing upon your plate," quickly retorted the Baron, who was in no humor for a story.

"Nothing more, I thank you," continued the Prince: "as I was saying, I remember the Countess Katszinski—" but just at this moment the door opened, and Ernstorff entered and handed a despatch to the Baron, recommending it to his Excellency's particular attention.

"Business, I suppose," said the Plenipotentiary; "it may wait till to-morrow."

"From M. Clarionet, your Excellency."

"From M. Clarionet!" eagerly exclaimed the Baron, and tore open the epistle. "Gentlemen! congratulate me, congratulate yourselves, congratulate Frankfort": and the diplomatist, overcome, leaned back in his chair. "She is ours, Salvinski! she is ours, Von Altenburgh! she is ours; my dear De Bœffleurs! Mr. Grey, you are most fortunate; the Signora has signed and sealed; all is arranged; she sings to-night! What a fine spirited body is this Frankfort municipality! what elevation of soul! what genuine enthusiasm! eh, De Bœffleurs?"

"Most genuine!" exclaimed the Chevalier, who hated German music with all his heart, and was now humming an air from "La Dame Blanche."

"But mind, my dear friend, this is a secret, a cabinet secret; the municipality are to have the gratification of announcing the event to the city in a public decree; it is but fair. I feel that I have only to hint to secure your silence."

At this moment, with a thousand protestations of secrecy, the party broke up, each hastening to have the credit of first spreading the joyful intelligence through the circles, and of depriving the Frankfort senate of their hard-earned gratification. The Baron, who was in high spirits, ordered the carriage to drive Vivian round the ramparts, where he was to be introduced to some of the most fashionable beauties, previous to the evening triumph.

CHAPTER III

VIVIAN passed a week very agreeably at Frankfort. In
the Baron and his friends he found the companions that
he had need of; their conversation and pursuits diverted his
mind without engaging his feelings, and allowed him no pause
to brood. There were moments, indeed, when he found in the
Baron a companion neither frivolous nor uninstructive. His
Excellency had traveled in most countries, and had profited by
his travels. His taste for the fine arts was equaled by his
knowledge of them; and his acquaintance with many of the
most eminent men of Europe enriched his conversation with
a variety of anecdotes, to which his lively talents did ample
justice. He seemed fond at times of showing Vivian that he
was not a mere artificial man of the world, destitute of all
feelings, and thinking only of himself; he recurred with satisfaction to moments of his life when his passions had been in
full play; and, while he acknowledged the errors of his youth
with candor, he excused them with grace. In short, Vivian
and he became what the world calls friends; that is to say,
they were men who had no objection to dine in each other's
company, provided the dinner were good; assist each other in
any scrape, provided no particular personal responsibility were
incurred by the assistant; and live under the same roof, provided each were master of his own time. Vivian and the Baron,
indeed, did more than this; they might have been described as
particular friends, for his Excellency had persuaded our hero
to accompany him for the summer to the Baths of Ems, a
celebrated German watering-place, situate in the duchy of
Nassau, in the vicinity of the Rhine.

On the morrow they were to commence their journey.
The fair of Frankfort, which had now lasted nearly a month,
was at its close. A bright sunshiny afternoon was stealing into

twilight, when Vivian, escaping from the principal street and
the attractions of the Braunfels, or chief shops under the Exchange, directed his steps to some of the more remote and
ancient streets. In crossing a little square his attention was
excited by a crowd which had assembled round a conjurer,
who, from the top of a small cart, which he had converted into
a stage, was haranguing, in front of a green curtain, an audience with great fervency, and apparently with great effect; at
least Vivian judged so from the loud applauses which constantly burst forth. The men pressed nearer, shouted, and
clapped their hands; and the anxious mothers struggled to
lift their brats higher in the air, that they might early form a
due conception of the powers of magic, and learn that the
maternal threats which were sometimes extended to them at
home were not mere idle boasting. Altogether, the men with
their cocked hats, stiff holiday coats, and long pipes; the
women with their glazed gowns of bright fancy patterns, close
lace caps, or richly-chased silver headgear; and the children
with their gaping mouths and long heads of hair, offered
quaint studies for a German or Flemish painter. Vivian became also one of the audience, and not an uninterested one.

The appearance of the conjurer was peculiar. He was not
much more than five feet high, but so slightly formed that he
reminded you rather of the boy than the dwarf. The upper
part of his face was even delicately molded; his sparkling black
eyes became his round forehead, which was not too much covered by his short glossy black hair; his complexion was clear,
but quite olive; his nose was very small and straight, and contrasted singularly with his enormous mouth, the thin bluish lips
of which were seldom closed, and consequently did not conceal
his large square teeth, which, though very white, were set
apart, and were so solid that they looked almost like double
teeth. This enormous mouth, which was supported by large
jawbones, attracted the attention of the spectator so keenly
that it was some time before you observed the prodigious size
of the ears, which also adorned this extraordinary countenance.
The costume of this being was not less remarkable than his
natural appearance. He wore a complete under-dress of pliant
leather, which fitted close up to his throat and down to his
wrists and ankles, where it was clasped with large fastenings,

either of gold or some gilt material. This, with the addition of a species of hussar jacket of green cloth, which was quite unadorned with the exception of its vivid red lining, was the sole covering of the conjurer; who, with a light cap and feather in his hand, was now haranguing the spectators. The object of his discourse was a panegyric of himself and a satire on all other conjurers. He was the only conjurer, the real one, a worthy descendant of the magicians of old.

"Were I to tell that broad-faced Herr," continued the conjurer, "who is now gaping opposite to me, that this rod is the rod of Aaron, mayhap he would call me a liar; yet were I to tell him that he was the son of his father, he would not think it wonderful! And yet, can he prove it? My friends, if I am a liar, the whole world is a liar, and yet any one of you who'll go and proclaim that on the Braunfels will get his skull cracked. Every truth is not to be spoken, and every lie is not to be punished. I have told you that it is better for you to spend your money in seeing my tricks than in swigging schnapps in the chimney corner; and yet, my friends, this may be a lie. I have told you that the profits of this whole night shall be given to some poor and worthy person in this town; and perhaps I shall give them to myself. What then! I shall speak the truth; and you will perhaps crack my skull. Is this a reward for truth? Oh, generation of vipers! My friends, what is truth? who can find it in Frankfort? Suppose I call upon you, Mr. Baker, and sup with you this evening; you will receive me as a neighborly man should, tell me to make myself at home, and do as I like. Is it not so? I see you smile, as if my visit would make you bring out one of the bottles of your best Asmannshäuser!"

Here the crowd laughed out; for we are always glad when there is any talk of another's hospitality being put to the test, although we stand no chance of sharing in the entertainment ourselves. The baker looked foolish, as all men singled out in a crowd do.

"Well, well," continued the conjurer, "I have no doubt his wine would be as ready as your tobacco, Mr. Smith; or a waffle from your basket, my honest cake-seller;" and so saying, with a long thin wand the conjurer jerked up the basket of an itinerant and shouting pastry-cook, and immediately began to thrust the contents into his mouth with a rapidity ludicrously miraculous. The laugh now burst out again, but the honest baker joined in it this time with an easy spirit.

"Be not disconcerted, my little custard-monger; if thou art honest, thou shalt prosper. Did I not say that the profits of this night were for the most poor and the most honest? If thy stock in trade were in thy basket, my raspberry-puff, verily thou art not now the richest here; and so, therefore, if thy character be a fair one, that is to say, if thou only cheat five times a day, and give a tenth of thy cheatery to the poor, thou shalt have the benefit. I ask thee again, what is truth? If I sup with the baker, and he tells me to do what I like with all that is his, and I kiss his wife, he will kick me out; yet to kiss his wife might be my pleasure, if her breath were sweet. I ask thee again, what is truth? Truth, they say, lies in a well; but perhaps this is a lie. How do we know that truth is not in one of these two boxes?" asked the conjurer, placing his cap on his head, and holding one small snuff-box to a tall, savage-looking, one-eyed Bohemian, who, with a comrade, had walked over from the Austrian garrison at Mentz.

"I see but one box," growled the soldier.

"It is because thou hast only one eye, friend; open the other, and thou shalt see two," said the conjurer, in a slow, malicious tone, with his neck extended, and his hand with the hateful box outstretched in it.

"Now, by our black Lady of Altoting, I'll soon stop thy prate, chitterling!" bellowed the enraged Bohemian.

"Murder! the protection of the free city against the Emperor of Austria, the King of Bohemia, Hungary, and Lombardy!" and the knave retreated to the very extremity of the stage, and affecting agitating fear, hid himself behind the green curtain, from a side of which his head was alone visible, or rather an immense red tongue, which wagged in all shapes at the unlucky soldier, except when it retired to the interior of his mouth, to enable him to reiterate "Murder!" and invoke the privileges of the free city of Frankfort.

When the soldier was a little cooled, the conjurer again came forward, and, having moved his small magical table to a corner, and lighted two tapers, one of which he placed at each side of the stage, he stripped off his hussar jacket, and began to imitate a monkey; an animal which, by the faint light, in his singular costume, he very much resembled. How amusing were his pranks! He first plundered a rice plantation, and then he cracked cocoanuts; then he washed his face and arranged his toilet with his right paw; and finally he ran a race with his own tail, which humorous appendage to his body was very wittily performed for the occasion by a fragment of an old tarred rope. His gambols were so diverting that they even extracted applause from his enemy, the one-eyed sergeant; and, emboldened by the acclamations, from monkeys the conjurer began to imitate men. He first drank like a Dutchman, and having reeled round with a thousand oaths, to the manifold amusement of the crowd, he suddenly began to smoke like a Prussian. Nothing could be more admirable than the look of complacent and pompous stolidity with which he accompanied each puff of his pipe. The applause was continued; and the one-eyed Bohemian sergeant, delighted at the ridicule which was heaped on his military rival, actually threw the mimic some *groschen.*

"Keep thy pence, friend," said the conjurer; "thou wilt soon owe me more; we have not yet closed accounts. My friends, I have drank like a Dutchman; I have smoked like a Prussian; and now I will eat like an Austrian!" and here the immense mouth of the actor seemed distended even a hundred degrees bigger, while with gloating eyes and extended arms he again set to at the half-emptied waffle basket of the unhappy pastry-cook.

"Now, by our black Lady of Altoting, thou art an impudent varlet!" growled the Austrian soldier.

"You are losing your temper again," retorted the glutton, with his mouth full; "how difficult you are to please! Well, then, if the Austrians may not be touched, what say you to a Bohemian! a tall, one-eyed Bohemian sergeant, with an appetite like a hog and a liver like a lizard?"

"Now, by our black Lady of Altoting, this is too much!" and the soldier sprang at the conjurer.

"Hold him!" cried Vivian Grey; for the mob, frightened at the soldier, gave way.

"There is a gentle's voice under a dark cloak!" cried the conjurer; "but I want no assistance;" and so saying, with a dexterous spring the conjurer leaped over the heads of two or three staring children, and lighted on the nape of the sergeant's gigantic neck; placing his forefingers behind each of the soldier's ears, he threatened to slit them immediately if he were not quiet. The sergeant's companion, of course, came to his rescue, but Vivian engaged him, and attempted to arrange matters. "My friends, surely a gay word at a fair is not to meet with military punishment! What is the use of living in the free city of Frankfort, or, indeed, in any other city, if jokes are to be answered with oaths, and a light laugh met with a heavy blow? Avoid bloodshed, if possible, but stand by the conjurer. His business is jibes and jests, and this is the first time that I ever saw Merry Andrew arrested. Come, my good fellows!" said he to the soldiers, "we had better be off; men so important as you and I should not be spectators of these mummeries." The Austrians, who understood Vivian's compliment literally, were not sorry to make a dignified retreat; particularly as the mob, encouraged by Vivian's interference, began to show fight. Vivian also took his departure as soon as he could possibly steal off unnoticed; but not before he had been thanked by the conjurer.

"I knew there was gentle blood under that cloak. If you like to see the Mystery of the Crucifixion, with the Resurrection, and real fireworks, it begins at eight o'clock, and you shall be admitted gratis. I knew there was gentle blood under that cloak, and some day or other, when your Highness is in distress, you shall not want the aid of Essper George."

CHAPTER IV

IT was late in the evening when a britzska stopped at the post-house at Coblentz. The passage-boat from Bingen had just arrived; and a portly judge from the Danube, a tall, gaunt Prussian officer, a sketching English artist, two university students, and some cloth merchants, returning from Frankfort fair, were busily occupied at a long table in the centre of the room, at an ample banquet, in which sauerkraut, cherry-soup, and savory sausages were not wanting. So keen were the appetites of these worthies that the entrance of the new-comers, who seated themselves at a small table in the corner of the room, was scarcely noticed; and for half an hour nothing was heard but the sound of crashing jaws and of rattling knives and forks. How singular is the sight of a dozen hungry individuals intent upon their prey! What a noisy silence! A human voice was at length heard. It proceeded from the fat judge; a man at once convivial, dignified, and economical: he had not spoken for two minutes before his character was evident to every person in the room, although he flattered himself that his secret purpose was concealed from all. Tired with the thin Moselle gratuitously allowed to the table, the judge wished to comfort himself with a glass of more generous liquor; aware of the price of a bottle of good Rüdesheimer, he was desirous of forming a copartnership with one or two gentlemen in the venture; still more aware of his exalted situation, he felt it did not become him to appear in the eyes of any one as an unsuccessful suppliant.

"This Moselle is very thin," observed the judge, shaking his head.

"Very fair table-wine, I think," said the artist, refilling his tumbler, and then proceeding with his sketch, which was a rough likeness, in black chalk, of the worthy magistrate himself.

"Very good wine, I think," swore the Prussian, taking the bottle. With the officer there was certainly no chance.

The cloth merchants mixed even this thin Moselle with water, and therefore they could hardly be looked to as boon companions; and the students were alone left. A German student is no flincher at the bottle, although he generally drinks beer. These gentry, however, were no great favorites with the magistrate, who was a loyal man, of regular habits, and no encourager of brawls, duels, and other still more disgraceful outrages; to all which abominations, besides drinking beer and chewing tobacco, the German student is remarkably addicted; but in the present case what was to be done? He offered the nearest a pinch of snuff, as a mode of commencing his acquaintance and cultivating his complacency. The student dug his thumb into the box, and, with the additional aid of the forefinger sweeping out half its contents, growled out something like thanks, and then drew up in his seat, as if he had too warmly encouraged the impertinent intrusion of a Philistine to whom he had never been introduced.

The cloth merchant, ceasing from sipping his meek liquor, and taking out of his pocket a letter, from which he tore off the back, carefully commenced collecting with his forefinger the particles of dispersed snuff in a small pyramid, which, when formed, was dexterously slid into the paper, then folded up and put into his pocket; the prudent merchant contenting himself for the moment with the refreshment which was afforded to his senses by the truant particles which had remained in his nail.

"Waiter, a bottle of Rüdesheimer!" bellowed the judge; "and if any gentleman or gentlemen would like to join me, they may," he added, in a more subdued tone. No one answered, and the bottle was put down. The judge slowly poured out the bright yellow fluid into a tall bell glass, adorned with a beautiful and encircling wreath of vine leaves; he held the glass a moment before the lamp, for his eye to dwell with still greater advantage on the transparent radiancy of the contents; and then deliberately pouring them down his throat, and allowing them to dwell a moment on his palate, he uttered an emphatic "bah!" and sucking in his breath, leaned back in his chair. The student immediately poured out a glass from the same bottle, and drank it off. The judge gave him a look, and then blessed himself that, though his boon companion was a brute, still he would lessen the expense of the bottle, which nearly amounted to a day's pay; and so he again filled his glass, but this was merely to secure his fair portion. He saw the student was a rapid drinker; and, although he did not like to hurry his own enjoyment, he thought it most prudent to keep his glass well stored by his side.

"I hope your Lordships have had a pleasant voyage," exclaimed a man, entering the room rapidly as he spoke; and, deliberately walking up to the table, he pushed between two of the cloth merchants, who quietly made way; and then placing a small square box before him, immediately opened it, and sweeping aside the dishes and glasses which surrounded him, began to fill their places with cups, balls, rings, and other mysterious-looking matters, which generally accompany a conjurer.

"I hope your Lordships have had a pleasant voyage. I have been thinking of you all the day. (Here the cups were arranged.) Next to myself, I am interested for my friends. (Here the rice was sprinkled.) I came from Fairy-land this morning. (Here the trick was executed.) Will any gentleman lend me a handkerchief? Now, sir, tie any knot you choose: tighter, tighter, tight as you can, tight as you can: now pull! Why, sir, where's your knot?" Here most of the company good-naturedly laughed at a trick which had amused them before a hundred times. But the dignified judge had no taste for such trivial amusements; and, besides, he thought that all this noise spoiled the pleasure of his wine, and prevented him from catching the flavor of his Rüdesheimer. Moreover, the judge was not in a very good humor. The student appeared to have little idea of the rules and regulations of a fair partnership; for not only did he not regulate his draughts by the moderate example of his bottle companion, but actually filled the glass of his university friend, and even offered the precious green flask to his neighbor, the cloth merchant. That humble individual modestly refused the proffer. The unexpected circumstance of having his health drank by a stranger seemed alone to have produced a great impression upon him; and adding a little more water to his already diluted potation, he bowed reverently to the student, who, in return, did not notice him. All these little circumstances prevented the judge from laughing at the performances of our friend Essper George; for we need hardly mention that the conjurer was no other. His ill-humor did not escape the lord of the cups and balls, who, as was his custom, immediately began to torment him.

"Will you choose a card?" asked the magician of the judge, with a most humble look.

"No, sir!"

Essper George looked very penitent, as if he felt he had taken a great liberty by his application; and so, to compensate for his incorrect behavior, he asked the magistrate whether he would have the goodness to lend him his watch. The judge was irate, and determined to give the intruder a set-down.

"I am not one of those who can be amused by tricks that his grandfather knew."

"Grandfather!" shrieked Essper; "what a wonderful grandfather yours must have been! All my tricks are fresh from Fairy-land this morning. Grandfather, indeed! Pray, is this your grandfather?" and here the conjurer, leaning over the table, with a rapid catch drew out from the fat paunch of the judge a long grinning wooden figure, with great staring eyes, and the parrot nose of a pulcinello. The laugh which followed this sleight-of-hand was loud, long, and universal. The judge lost his temper; and Essper George took the opportunity of the confusion to drink off the glass of Rüdesheimer which stood, as we have mentioned, ready charged, at the magistrate's elbow.

The waiter now went round to collect the money of the various guests who had partaken of the boat-supper; and, of course, charged the judge extra for his ordered bottle, bowing at the same time very low, as was proper to so good a customer. These little attentions at inns encourage expenditure. The judge tried at the same time the bottle, which he found empty, and applied to his two boon companions for their quota; but the students affected a sort of brutal surprise at any one having the impudence to imagine that they were going to pay their proportion; and flinging down the money for their own supper on the table, they retired. The magistrate, calling loudly for the landlord, followed them out of the room.

Essper George stood moralizing at the table, and emptying

every glass whose contents were not utterly drained, with the exception of the tumblers of the cloth merchants, of whose liquor he did not approve.

"Poor man! to get only one glass out of his own bottle! Ay! call for M. Maas; threaten as you will. Your grandfather will not help you here. Blood out of a wall and money out of a student come the same day. Ah! is your Excellency here?" said Essper, turning round to our two travelers with affected surprise, although he had observed them the whole time. "Is your Excellency here? I have been looking for you through Frankfort this whole morning. There! it will do for your glass. It is of chamois leather, and I made it myself, from a beast I caught last summer in the valley of the Rhone." So saying, he threw over Vivian's neck a neat chain, or cord, of curiously worked leather.

"Who the devil is this, Grey?" asked the Baron.

"A funny knave, whom I once saved from a thrashing, or something of the kind, which I do him the justice to say he well deserved."

"Who the devil is this?" said Essper George. "Why, that is exactly the same question I myself asked when I saw a tall, pompous, proud fellow, dressed like a peacock on a May morning, standing at the door just now. He looked as if he would pass himself off for an ambassador at least; but I told him that if he got his wages paid he was luckier than most servants. Was I right, your Excellency?"

"Poor Ernstorff!" said the Baron, laughing. "Yes; he certainly gets paid. Here, you are a clever varlet; fill your glass."

"No; no wine. Don't you hear the brawling, and nearly the bloodshed, which are going on upstairs about a sour bottle of Rüdesheimer? and here I see two gentles who have ordered the best wine merely to show that they are masters and not servants of the green peacock, and lo! can not get through a glass. Lord! Lord! what is man? If my fat friend and his grandfather would but come downstairs again, here is liquor enough to make wine and water of the Danube; for he comes from thence by his accent. No, I'll have none of your wine; keep it to throw on the sandy floor, that the dust may not hurt your delicate shoes, nor dirt the hand of the gentleman in green and gold when he cleans them for you in the morning."

Here the Baron laughed again, and, as he bore his impertinence, Essper George immediately became polite.

"Does your Highness go to Ems?"

"We hardly know, my friend."

"Oh! go there, gentlemen. I have tried them all; Aix-la-Chapelle, Spa, Wiesbaden, Carlsbad, Pyrmont, every one of them; but what are these to Ems? There we all live in the same house and eat from the same table. When there I feel that you are all under my protection; I consider you all as my children. Besides, the country, how delightful! the mountains, the valleys, the river, the woods, and then the company so select! No sharpers, no adventurers, no blacklegs: at Ems you can be taken in by no one except your intimate friend. To Ems, by all means. I would advise you, however, to send the gentlemen in the cocked hat on before you to engage rooms; for I can assure you that you will have a hard chance. The baths are very full."

"And how do you get there, Essper?" asked Vivian.

"Those are subjects on which I never speak," answered the conjurer, with a solemn air.

"But have you all your stock-in-trade with you, my good fellow? Where is the Mystery?"

"Sold, sir; sold! I never keep to anything long. Variety is the mother of Enjoyment. At Ems I shall not be a conjurer; but I never part with my box. It takes no more room than one of those medicine chests, which I dare say you have got with you in your carriage, to prop up your couple of shattered constitutions."

"By Jove! you are a merry, impudent fellow," said the Baron; "and if you like to get up behind my britzska, you may."

"No; I carry my own box and my own body, and I shall be at Ems to-morrow in time enough to receive your Lordships."

CHAPTER V

IN a delightful valley of Nassau, formed by the picturesque winding of the Taunus Mountains, and on the banks of the noisy river Lahn, stands a vast brick pile, of irregular architecture, which nearly covers an acre of ground. This building was formerly a favorite palace of the ducal house of Nassau; but the present Prince has thought proper to let out the former residence of his family as a hotel for the accommodation of the company, who in the season frequent this, the most lovely spot in his lovely little duchy. This extensive building contains two hundred and thirty rooms and eighty baths; and these apartments, which are under the management of an official agent, who lives in the "Princely Bathing House," for such is its present dignified title, are to be engaged at fixed prices, which are marked over the doors. All the rooms in the upper story of the Princely Bathing House open on, or are almost immediately connected with, a long corridor, which extends the whole length of the building. The ground floor, besides the space occupied by the baths, also affords a spacious promenade, arched with stone, and, surrounded with stalls, behind which are marshaled vendors of all possible articles which can be required by the necessities of the frequenters of a watering-place. There you are greeted by the jeweler of the Palais Royal and the *marchande de mode* of the Rue de la Paix; the print-seller from Mannheim and the china-dealer from Dresden; and other small speculators in the various fancy articles which abound in Vienna, Berlin, Geneva, Basle, Strasburg, and Lausanne; such as pipes, costumes of Swiss peasantry, crosses of Mont Blanc crystal, and all varieties of national *bijouterie*. All things may here be sold, save those which administer to the nourishment of the body or the pleasure of the palate. Let not those of my readers who have already planned a trip to the sweet vales of the Taunus be frightened by this last sentence. At Ems "eatables and drinkables" are excellent and abounding; but they are solely supplied by the restaurateur, who farms the monopoly from the Duke. This gentleman, who is a pupil of Beauvillier's, and who has conceived an exquisite cuisine, by adding to the lighter graces of French cookery something of the more solid virtues of the German, presides in a saloon of vast size and magnificent decoration, in which, during the season, upward of three hundred persons frequent the table d'hôte. It is the etiquette at Ems that, however distinguished or however humble the rank of the visitors, their fare and their treatment must be alike. In one of the most aristocratic countries in the world the sovereign prince and his tradesman subject may be found seated in the morning at the same board, and eating from the same dish, as in the evening they may be seen staking on the same color at the gaming-table, and sharing in the same interest at the Redoute.

The situation of Ems is delightful. The mountains which form the valley are not, as in Switzerland, so elevated that they confine the air or seem to impede the facility of breathing. In their fantastic forms the picturesque is not lost in the monotonous, and in the rich covering of their various woods the admiring eye finds at the same time beauty and repose. Opposite the ancient palace, on the banks of the Lahn, are the gardens. In these, in a pavilion, a band of musicians seldom cease from enchanting the visitors by their execution of the most favorite specimens of German and Italian music. Numberless acacia arbors and retired sylvan seats are here to be found, where the student or the contemplative may seek refuge from the noise of his more gay companions, and the tedium of eternal conversation. In these gardens, also, are the billiard-room, and another saloon, in which each night meet, not merely those who are interested in the mysteries of rouge et noir, and the chances of roulette, but, in general, the whole of the company, male and female, who are frequenting the baths. In quitting the gardens for a moment, we must not omit mentioning the interesting booth of our friend the restaurateur, where coffee, clear and hot, and exquisite confectionery, are never wanting. Nor should we forget the glittering pennons of the gay boats which glide along the Lahn; nor the handsome donkeys, who, with their white saddles and red bridles, seem not unworthy of the princesses whom they sometimes bear. The gardens, with an alley of lime trees, which are further on, near the banks of the river, afford easy promenades to the sick and debilitated; but the more robust and active need not fear monotony in the valley of the Lahn. If they sigh for the champaign country, they can climb the wild passes of the encircling mountains, and from their tops enjoy the most magnificent views of the Rhineland. There they may gaze on that mighty river, flowing through the prolific plain which at the same time it nourishes and adorns, bounded on each side by mountains of every form, clothed with wood or crowned with castles. Or, if they fear the fatigues of the ascent, they may wander further up the valley, and in the wild dells, romantic forests, and gray ruins of Stein and Nassau conjure up the old times of feudal tyranny when the forest was the only free land, and he who outraged the laws the only one who did not suffer from their authority.

Besides the Princely Bathing House, I must mention that there was another old and extensive building near it, which, in very full seasons, also accommodated visitors on the same system as the palace. At present, this adjoining building was solely occupied by a Russian Grand Duke, who had engaged it for the season.

Such is a slight description of Ems, a place almost of unique character; for it is a watering-place with every convenience, luxury, and accommodation; and yet without shops, streets, or houses.

The Baron and Vivian were fortunate in finding rooms, for the Baths were very full; the extraordinary beauty of the weather having occasioned a very early season. They found themselves at the baths early on the morning after their arrival at Coblentz, and at three o'clock in the same day had taken their places at the dinner table in the great saloon. At the long table upward of two hundred and fifty guests were assembled, of different nations, and of very different characters. There was the cunning, intriguing Greek, who served well his imperial master the Russian. The order of the patron saint of Moscow, and the glittering stars of other nations which sparkled on his green uniform, told how well he had labored for the interest of all other countries except his own; but his clear, pale complexion, his delicately trimmed mustache, his lofty forehead, his arched eyebrow, and his Eastern eye, recalled to the traveler, in spite of his barbarian trappings, the fine countenances of the Ægean, and became a form which apparently might have struggled in Thermopylæ. Next to him was the Austrian diplomatist, the Sosia of all cabinets, in whose gay address and rattling conversation you could hardly recognize the sophistical defender of unauthorized invasion, and the subtle inventor of Holy Alliances and Imperial Leagues. Then came the rich usurer from Frankfort or the prosperous merchant from Hamburg, who, with his wife and daughters, were seeking some recreation from his flourishing counting-house in the sylvan gayeties of a German bathing-place. Flirting with these was an adventurous dancing-master from Paris, whose profession at present was kept in the background, and whose well-curled black hair, diamond pin, and frogged coat hinted at the magnifico incog, and also enabled him, if he did not choose in time to follow his own profession, to pursue another one, which he had also studied, in the profitable mystery of the Redoute. There were many other individuals, whose commonplace appearance did not reveal a character which perhaps they did not possess. There were officers in all uniforms, and there were some uniforms without officers. But all looked perfectly *comme il faut,* and on the whole very select; and if the great persons endeavored for a moment to forget their dignity, still these slight improprieties were amply made up by the affected dignity of those little persons who had none to forget.

"And how like you the baths of Ems?" the Baron asked of Vivian. "We shall get better seats to-morrow, and perhaps be among those whom you shall know. I see many friends and some agreeable ones. In the meantime, you must make a good dinner to-day, and I will amuse you, and assist your digestion, by putting you up to some of the characters with whom you are dining."

At this moment a party entered the room, who were rather late in their appearance, but who attracted the attention of Vivian. The group consisted of three persons; a very good-looking young man, who supported on each arm a female. The lady on his right arm was apparently of about five-and-twenty years of age. She was of majestic stature; her complexion of untinged purity. Her features were like those conceptions of Grecian sculptors which, in moments of despondency, we sometimes believe to be ideal. Her full eyes were of the same deep blue as the mountain lake, and gleamed from under their long lashes as that purest of waters beneath its fringing sedge. Her light-brown hair was braided from her high forehead, and hung in long full curls over her neck; the mass gathered up into a Grecian knot, and confined by a bandeau of cameos. She wore a dress of black velvet, whose folding drapery was confined round a waist which was in exact symmetry with the proportions of her full bust and the polished roundness of her bending neck. The countenance of the lady was dignified, without any expression of pride, and reserved, without any of the harshness of austerity. In gazing on her the enraptured spectator for a moment believed that Minerva had forgotten her severity, and had entered into a delightful rivalry with Venus.

Her companion was much younger, not so tall, and of slender form. The long tresses of her chestnut hair shaded her oval face. Her small, aquiline nose, bright hazel eyes, delicate mouth, and the deep color of her lips, were as remarkable as the transparency of her complexion. The flush of her cheek was singular; it was of a brilliant pink: you may find it in the lip of an Indian shell. The blue veins played beneath her arched forehead, like lightning beneath a rainbow. She was dressed in white, and a damask rose, half hid in her clustering hair, was her only ornament. This lovely creature glided by Vivian Grey almost unnoticed, so fixed was his gaze on her companion. Yet, magnificent as was the style of Lady Madeleine Trevor, there were few who preferred even her commanding graces to the softer beauties of Violet Fane.

This party, having passed Vivian, proceeded to the top of the room, where places had been kept for them. Vivian's eye watched them till they were lost among surrounding visitors: their peculiar loveliness could not deceive him.

"English, no doubt," observed he to the Baron; "who can they be?"

"I have not the least idea; that is, I do not exactly know. I think they are English," answered the Baron, in so confused a manner that Vivian rather stared. After musing a moment, the Baron recovered himself.

"The unexpected sight of a face we feel that we know, and yet can not immediately recognize, is extremely annoying; it is almost agitating. They are English. The lady in black is Lady Madeleine Trevor; I knew her in London."

"And the gentleman?" asked Vivian: "is the gentleman Mr. Trevor?"

"No; Trevor, poor Trevor, is dead, I think; is, I am sure, dead. That, I am confident, is not he. He was of the —— family, and was in office when I was in England. It was in my diplomatic capacity that I first became acquainted with him. Lady Madeleine was, and, as you see, is a charming woman; a very charming woman is Lady Madeleine Trevor."

"And the young lady with her?"

"And the young lady with her, I can not exactly say; I do not exactly know. Her face is familiar to me, and yet I can not remember her name. She must have been very young, as you may see, when I was in England; she can not now be above eighteen. Miss Fane must therefore have been very young when I was in England. Miss Fane; how singular I should have recalled her name! that is her name! Violet Fane, a cousin, or some relation, of Lady Madeleine: good family. Will you have some soup?"

Whether it were from not being among his friends or some other cause, the Baron was certainly not in his usual spirits this day at dinner. Conversation, which with him was generally as easy as it was brilliant, like a fountain at the same time sparkling and fluent, was evidently constrained. For a few minutes he talked very fast, and was then uncommunicative, absent, and dull. He, moreover, drank a great deal of wine, which was not his custom; but the grape did not inspire him. Vivian found amusement in his next neighbor, a forward, bustling man, clever in his talk, very fine, but rather vulgar. He was the manager of a company of Austrian actors, and had come to Ems on the chance of forming an engagement for his troupe, who generally performed at Vienna. He had been successful in his adventure, the Archduke having engaged the whole band at the New House, and in a few days the troupe were to arrive; at which time the manager was to drop the character of a traveling gentleman, and cease to dine at the table d'hôte of Ems. From this man Vivian learned that Lady Madeleine Trevor had been at the baths for some time before the season commenced: that at present hers was the party which, from its long stay and eminent rank, gave the tone to the amusements of the place; the influential circle which those who have frequented watering-places have often observed, and which may be seen at Ems, Spa, or Pyrmont, equally as at Harrowgate, Tunbridge Wells, or Cheltenham.

CHAPTER VI

WHEN dinner was finished the party broke up, and most of them assembled in the gardens. The Baron, whose countenance had assumed its wonted cheerfulness, and who excused his previous dulness by the usual story of a sudden headache, proposed to Vivian to join the promenade. The gardens were very full, and the Baron recognized many of his acquaintances.

"My dear Colonel, who possibly expected to meet you here? Why! did you dine in the saloon? I only arrived this morning. This is my friend, Mr. Grey; Colonel von Trumpetson."

"An Englishman, I believe?" said the Colonel, bowing. He was a starch militaire, with a blue frock coat buttoned up to his chin, a bald head with a few gray hairs, and long, thin mustaches like a mandarin's. "An Englishman, I believe; pray, sir, will you inform me whether the household troops in England wear the Marbœuf cuirass?"

"Sir!" said Vivian.

"I esteem myself particularly fortunate in thus meeting with an English gentleman. It was only at dinner to-day that a controversy arose between Major von Musquetoon and the Prince of Buttonstein on this point. As I said to the Prince, you may argue forever, for at present we can not decide the fact. How little did I think when I parted from the Major that in a few minutes I should be able to settle the question beyond a doubt. I esteem myself particularly fortunate in meeting with an Englishman."

"I regret to say, Colonel, that the question is one that I can not decide."

"Sir, I wish you good-morning," said the Colonel, very dryly; and, staring keenly at Vivian, he walked away.

"He is good enough to fight, I suppose," said the Baron, with a smile and shrug of the shoulders, which seemed to return thanks to Providence for having been educated in the civil service.

At this moment Lady Madeleine Trevor, leaning on the arm of the same gentleman, passed, and the Baron bowed. The bow was coldly returned.

"You know her Ladyship, then, well?"

"I did know her," said the Baron; "but I see from her bow that I am at present in no very high favor. The truth is, she is a charming woman, but I never expected to see her in Germany, and there was some little commission of hers which I neglected, some little order for Eau de Cologne, or a message about a worked pocket-handkerchief, which I utterly forgot: and then, I never wrote! and you know, Grey, that these little sins of omission are never forgiven by women."

"My dear friend, De Konigstein, one pinch! one pinch!" chirped out a little, old, odd-looking man, with a *poudré* head, and dressed in a costume in which the glories of the *vieille cour* seemed to retire with reluctance. A diamond ring twinkled on the snuffy hand, which was encircled by a rich ruffle of dirty lace. The brown coat was not modern, and yet not quite such a one as was worn by its master when he went to see the king dine in public at Versailles before the Revolution: large silver buckles still adorned the well-polished shoes; and silk stockings, whose hue was originally black, were picked out with clock-work of gold.

"My dear Marquis, I am most happy to see you; will you try the boulangero?"

"With pleasure! A-a-h! what a box! a Louis-Quatorze, I think?"

"Oh, no! by no means so old."

"Pardon me, my dear De Konigstein; I think a Louis-Quatorze."

"I bought it in Sicily."

"A-a-h!" slowly exclaimed the little man, shaking his head.

"Well, good afternoon," said the Baron, passing on.

"My dear De Konigstein, one pinch; you have often said you have a particular regard for me."

"My dear Marquis!"

"A-a-h! I thought so; you have often said you would serve me, if possible."

"My dear Marquis, be brief."

"A-a-h! I will. There's a cursed crusty old Prussian officer here; one Colonel de Trumpetson."

"Well, what can I do? you are surely not going to fight him!'"

"A-a-h! no, no; I wish you to speak to him."

"Well, what?"

"He takes snuff."

"What is that to me?'

"He has got a box."

"Well!"

"It is a Louis-Quatorze; could not you get it for me?"

"Good-morning to you," said the Baron, pulling on Vivian.

"You have had the pleasure, Grey, of meeting this afternoon two men who have each only one idea. Colonel von Trumpetson and the Marquis de la Tabatière are equally tiresome. But are they more tiresome than any other man who always speaks on the same subject? We are more irritable, but not more wearied, with a man who is always thinking of the pattern of a button-hole, or the shape of a snuff-box, than with one who is always talking about pictures, or chemistry, or politics. The true bore is that man who thinks the world is only interested in one subject, because he himself can only comprehend one."

Here Lady Madeleine passed again, and this time the Baron's eyes were fixed on the ground.

A buzz and a bustle at the other end of the gardens, to which the Baron and Vivian were advancing, announced the entry of the Grand Duke. His Imperial Highness was a tall

man, with a quick, piercing eye, which was prevented from
giving to his countenance the expression of intellect, which it
otherwise would have done, by the dull and almost brutal effect
of his flat, Calmuck nose. He was dressed in a plain green
uniform, adorned by a single star; but his tightened waist, his
stiff stock, and the elaborate attention which had evidently
been bestowed upon his mustache, denoted the military fop.
The Grand Duke was accompanied by three or four stiff and
stately-looking personages, in whom the severity of the mar-
tinet seemed sunk in the servility of the aide-de-camp.

The Baron bowed very low to the Prince as he drew near,
and his Highness, taking off his cocked hat with an appearance of cordial condescension, made a full stop. The silent
gentlemen in the rear, who had not anticipated this suspense
in their promenade, almost foundered on the heels of their
royal master; and, frightened at the imminency of the profanation, forgot their stiff pomp in a precipitate retreat of half
a yard.

"Baron," said his Highness, "why have I not seen you at
the New House?"

"I have but this moment arrived, may it please your Imperial Highness."

"Your companion," continued the Grand Duke, pointing
very graciously to Vivian.

"My intimate friend, my fellow-traveler, and an Englishman. May I have the honor of presenting Mr. Grey to your
Imperial Highness?"

"Any friends of the Baron von Konigstein I shall always
feel great pleasure in having presented to me. Sir, I feel
great pleasure in having you presented to me. Sir, you ought
to be proud of the name of Englishman; sir, the English are
a noble nation; sir, I have the highest respect for the English
nation!"

Vivian of course bowed very low; and of course made a
very proper speech on the occasion, which, as all speeches of
that kind should be, was very dutiful and quite inaudible.

"And what news from Berlin, Baron? let us move on," and
the Baron turned with the Grand Duke. The silent gentlemen, settling their mustaches, followed in the rear. For
about half an hour, anecdote after anecdote, scene after scene,

caricature after caricature, were poured out with prodigal expenditure for the amusement of the Prince, who did nothing during the exhibition but smile, stroke his whiskers, and at the end of the best stories fence with his forefinger at the Baron's side, with a gentle laugh, and a mock shake of the head, and an "Eh! Von Konigstein, you're too bad!" Here Lady Madeleine Trevor passed again, and the Grand Duke's hat nearly touched the ground. He received a most gracious bow.

"Finish the story about Salvinski, Baron, and then I will present you for a reward to the most lovely creature in existence, a countrywoman of your friend, Lady Madeleine Trevor."

"I have the honor of a slight acquaintance with her," said the Baron; "I had the pleasure of knowing her in England."

"Indeed! Fortunate mortal! I see she has stopped, talking to some stranger. Let us turn and join her."

The Grand Duke and the two friends accordingly turned, and of course the silent gentlemen in the rear followed with due precision.

"Lady Madeleine!" said the Grand Duke, "I flattered myself for a moment that I might have had the honor of presenting to you a gentleman for whom I have a great esteem; but he has proved to me that he is more fortunate than myself, since he had the honor before me of an acquaintance with Lady Madeleine Trevor."

"I have not forgotten Baron von Konigstein," said her Ladyship, with a serious air. "May I ask his Highness how he prospered in his negotiation with the Austrian troupe?"

"Perfectly successful! Inspired by your Ladyship's approbation, my steward has really done wonders. He almost deserves a diplomatic appointment for the talent which he has shown; but what should I do without Cracowsky? Lady Madeleine, can you conceive what I should do without Cracowsky?"

"Not in the least."

"Cracowsky is everything to me. It is impossible to say what Cracowsky is to me. I owe everything to Cracowsky. To Cracowsky I owe being here." The Grand Duke bowed very low, for this eulogium on his steward also conveyed a

compliment to her Ladyship. The Grand Duke was certainly
right in believing that he owed his summer excursion to Ems
to his steward. That wily Pole regularly every year put his
Imperial master's summer excursion up to auction, and according to the biddings of the proprietors of the chief baths
did he take care that his master regulated his visit. The restaurateur of Ems, in collusion with the official agent of the
Duke of Nassau, were fortunate this season in having the
Grand Duke knocked down to them.

"May I flatter myself that Miss Fane feels herself better?"
asked the Grand Duke.

"She certainly does feel herself better, but my anxiety
about her does not decrease. In her illness apparent conva-
lescence is sometimes as alarming as suffering."

The Grand Duke continued by the side of Lady Madeleine
for about twenty minutes, seizing every opportunity of uttering, in the most courtly tone, inane compliments; and then
trusting that he might soon have her Ladyship's opinion respecting the Austrian troupe at the New House, and that Von
Konigstein and his English friend would not delay letting him
see them there, his Imperial Highness, followed by his silent
suite, left the gardens.

"I am afraid Lady Madeleine must have almost mistaken
me for a taciturn lord chamberlain," said the Baron, occupy-
ing immediately the Grand Duke's vacated side.

"Baron von Konigstein must be very changed if silence
be imputed to him as a fault," said Lady Madeleine.

"Baron von Konigstein is very much changed since last
he had the pleasure of conversing with Lady Madeleine
Trevor; more changed than she will perhaps believe; more
changed than he can sometimes himself believe. I hope that
he will not be less acceptable to Lady Madeleine Trevor because he is no longer rash, passionate, and unthinking; because he has learned to live more for others and less for
himself."

"Baron von Konigstein does indeed appear changed, since,
by his own account, he has become, in a very few years, a
being in whose existence philosophers scarcely believe, a perfect man."

"My self-conceit has been so often reproved by you that

I will not apologize for a quality which I almost flattered myself I no longer possessed; but you will excuse, I am sure, one who, in zealous haste to prove himself amended, has, I fear, almost shown that he has deceived himself."

Some strange thoughts occurred to Vivian while this conversation was taking place. "Is this a woman to resent the neglect of an order for Eau de Cologne? My dear Von Konigstein, you are a very pleasant fellow, but this is not the way men apologize for the non-purchase of a pocket-handkerchief!"

"Have you been long at Ems?" inquired the Baron, with an air of great deference.

"Nearly a month; we are traveling in consequence of the ill-health of a relation. It was our intention to have gone on to Pisa, but our physician, in consequence of the extreme heat of the summer, is afraid of the fatigue of traveling, and has recommended Ems. The air between these mountains is very soft and pure, and I have no reason to regret at present that we have not advanced further on our journey."

"The lady who was with your party at dinner is, I fear, your invalid. She certainly does not look like one. I think," said the Baron, with an effort, "I think that her face is not unknown to me. It is difficult, even after so many years, to mistake Miss—"

"Fane," said Lady Madeleine, firmly; for it seemed that the Baron required a little assistance at the end of his sentence.

"Ems," returned his Excellency, with great rapidity of utterance, "Ems is a charming place, at least to me. I have, within these few years, quite recurred to the feelings of my boyhood; nothing to me is more disgustingly wearisome than the gay bustle of a city. My present diplomatic appointment at Frankfort ensures a constant life among the most charming scenes of nature. Naples, which was offered to me, I refused. Eight years ago, I should have thought an appointment at Naples a Paradise on earth."

"You must indeed be changed."

"How beautiful is the vicinity of the Rhine! I have passed within these three days, for almost the twentieth time in my life, through the Rheingau; and yet how fresh, and lovely, and novel seemed all its various beauties! My young traveling companion is enthusiastic about this gem of Germany. He is one of your Ladyship's countrymen. Might I take the liberty of presenting to you Mr. Grey?"

Lady Madeleine, as if it could now no longer be postponed, introduced to the two gentlemen her brother, Mr. St. George. This gentleman, who, during the whole previous conversation, had kept his head in a horizontal position, looking neither to the right nor to the left, and apparently unconscious that any one was conversing with his sister, because, according to the English custom, he was not introduced, now suddenly turned round, and welcomed his acquaintance with cordiality.

"Mr. Grey," asked her Ladyship, "are you of Dorsetshire?"

"My mother is a Dorsetshire woman; her family name is Vivian, which name I also bear."

"Then I think we are longer acquainted than we have been introduced. I met your father at Sir Hargrave Vivian's last Christmas. He spoke of you in those terms that make me glad that I have met his son. You have been long from England, I think?"

"Nearly a year and a half."

The Baron had resigned his place by Lady Madeleine, and was already in close conversation with Mr. St. George, from whose arm Lady Madeleine was disengaged. No one acted the part of Asmodeus with greater spirit than his Excellency; and the secret history of every person whose secret history could be amusing delighted Mr. St. George.

"There," said the Baron, "goes the son of an unknown father; his mother followed the camp, and her offspring was early initiated in the mysteries of military petty larceny. As he grew up he became the most skilful plunderer that ever rifled the dying of both sides. Before he was twenty he followed the army as a petty chapman, and amassed an excellent fortune by reacquiring after a battle the very goods and trinkets which he had sold at an immense price before it. Such a wretch could do nothing but prosper, and in due time the sutler's brat became a commissary-general. He made millions in a period of general starvation, and cleared at least a hundred thousand dollars by embezzling the shoe leather during a retreat. He is now a baron, covered with orders, and his daughters are married to some of our first nobles. There goes a Polish Count who is one of the greatest gamblers in Christendom. In the same season he lost to a Russian general, at one game of chess, his chief castle and sixteen thousand acres of woodland; and recovered himself on another game, on which he won of a Turkish Pasha one hundred and eighty thousand leopard skins. The Turk, who was a man of strict honor, paid the Count by embezzling the tribute in kind of the province he governed; and as on quarter-day he could not, of course, make up his accounts with the Divan, he joined the Greeks."

While the Baron was entertaining Mr. St. George, the conversation between Lady Madeleine and Vivian proceeded.

"Your father expressed great disappointment to me at his being prevented paying you a visit. Do you not long to see him?"

"More than I can express. Did you think him in good spirits?"

"Generally so; as cheerful as all fathers can be without their only son."

"Did he complain, then, of my absence?"

"He regretted it."

"I linger in Germany with the hope of seeing him; otherwise I should have now been much further south. Do you find Sir Hargrave as amusing as ever?"

"When is he otherwise than the most delightful of old men? Sir Hargrave is one of my great favorites. I should like to persuade you to return and see them all. Can not you fancy Chester Grange very beautiful now? Albert!" said her Ladyship, turning to her brother, "what is the number of our apartments? Mr. Grey, the sun has now disappeared, and I fear the night air among these mountains. We have hardly yet summer nights, though we certainly have summer days. We shall be happy to see you at our rooms." So saying, bowing very cordially to Vivian and coldly to the Baron, Lady Madeleine left the gardens.

"There goes the most delightful woman in the world," said the Baron; "how fortunate that you know her! for really, as you might have observed, I have no great claims on her indulgent notice. I was certainly very wild in England; but then

young men, you know, Grey! and I did not leave a card, or
call, before I went; and the English are very stiff and precise
about those things; and the Trevors had been very kind to
me. I think we had better take a little coffee now; and then,
if you like, we will just stroll into the REDOUTE."

In a brilliantly illuminated saloon, adorned with Corinthian
columns and casts from some of the most famous antique
statues, assembled, between nine and ten o'clock in the evening, many of the visitors at Ems. On each side of the room
was placed a long narrow table, one of which was covered
with green baize, and unattended; while the variously-colored
leathern surface of the other was closely surrounded by an
interested crowd. Behind this table stood two individuals of
different appearance. The first was a short, thick man, whose
only business was dealing certain portions of playing cards
with quick succession one after the other: and as the fate of
the table was decided by this process, did his companion, a
very tall, thin man, throw various pieces of money upon certain stakes, which were deposited by the bystanders on different parts of the table; or, which was much oftener the case,
with a silver rake with a long ebony handle, sweep into a
large inclosure near him the scattered sums. This inclosure
was called the Bank, and the mysterious ceremony in which
these persons were assisting was the celebrated game of rouge
et noir. A deep silence was strictly preserved by those who
immediately surrounded the table; no voice was heard save
that of the little, short, stout dealer, when, without an expression of the least interest, he seemed mechanically to announce
the fate of the different colors. No other sound was heard,
except the jingle of the dollars and Napoleons, and the omi-
nous rake of the tall, thin banker. The countenances of those
who were hazarding their money were grave and gloomy:
their eyes were fixed, their brows contracted, and their lips
projected; and yet there was an evident effort visible to show
that they were both easy and unconcerned. Each player held
in his hand a small piece of pasteboard, on which, with a steel
pricker, he marked the run of the cards, in order, from his
observations, to regulate his own play. The rouge et noir
player imagines that chance is not capricious. Those who
were not interested in the game promenaded in two lines

within the tables, or, seated in recesses between the pillars, formed small parties for conversation.

"I suppose we must throw away a dollar or two," said the Baron, as he walked up to the table.

"My dear De Konigstein, one pinch!"

"Ah! Marquess, what fortune to-night?"

"Bad! I have lost my Napoleon: I never risk further. There is that cursed crusty old De Trumpetson, persisting, as usual, in his run of bad luck; because he never will give in. Trust me, my dear De Konigstein, it will end in his ruin; and then, if there be a sale of his effects, I shall, perhaps, get his snuff-box; a-a-h!"

"Come, shall I throw down a couple of Napoleons on joint account. I do not care much for play myself; but I suppose, at Ems, we must make up our minds to lose a few Louis. Here! now, for the red; joint account, mind!"

"Done."

"There's the Grand Duke! Let us go and make our bow; we need not stick at the table as if our whole soul were staked with our crown-pieces." So saying, the gentlemen walked up to the top of the room.

"Why, Grey! Surely no, it can not be, and yet it is. De Bœffleurs, how d'ye do?" said the Baron, with a face beaming with joy and a hearty shake of the hand. "My dear fellow, how did you manage to get off so soon? I thought you were not to be here for a fortnight: we only arrived ourselves to-day."

"Yes; but I have made an arrangement which I did not anticipate; and so I posted after you at once. Whom do you think I have brought with me?"

"Who?"

"Salvinski."

"Ah! And the Count?"

"Follows immediately. I expect him to-morrow or next day. Salvinski is talking to the Grand Duke; and see, he beckons to me. I suppose I am going to be presented."

The Chevalier moved forward, followed by the Baron and Vivian.

"Any friend of Prince Salvinski I shall always have great pleasure in having presented to me. Chevalier, I feel great pleasure in having you presented to me. Chevalier, you ought to be proud of the name of Frenchman. Chevalier, the French are a great nation. Chevalier, I have the highest respect for the French nation."

"The most subtile diplomatist," thought Vivian, as he recalled to mind his own introduction, "would be puzzled to decide to which interest his Imperial Highness leans."

The Grand Duke now entered into conversation with the Prince and most of the circle who surrounded him. As his Imperial Highness was addressing Vivian, the Baron let slip our hero's arm, and, taking that of the Chevalier de Bœffleurs, began walking up and down the room with him, and was soon engaged in animated conversation. In a few minutes the Grand Duke, bowing to his circle, made a move, and regained the side of a Saxon lady, from whose interesting company he had been disturbed by the arrival of Prince Salvinski; an individual of whose long stories and dull romances the Grand Duke had, from experience, a particular dread: but his Highness was always very courteous to the Poles.

"Grey, I have despatched De Bœffleurs to the house, to instruct his servant and Ernstorff to do the impossible, in order that our rooms may be all together. You will be delighted with De Bœffleurs when you know him, and I expect you to be great friends. By the bye, his unexpected arrival has quite made us forget our venture at rouge et noir. Of course we are too late now for anything; even if we had been fortunate, our stake, remaining on the table, is, of course, lost: we may as well, however, walk up." So saying, the Baron reached the table.

"That is your Excellency's stake! that is your Excellency's stake!" exclaimed many voices as he came up.

"What is the matter, my friends?" asked the Baron, calmly.

"There has been a run on the red! there has been a run on the red! and your Excellency's stake has doubled each time. It has been 4, 8, 16, 32, 64, 128, 256, and now it is 512!" quickly rattled a little thin man in spectacles, pointing at the same time to his unparalleled line of punctures. This was one of those officious, noisy little men who are always ready to give you unasked information, and who are never so happy as when they are watching over the interest of some stranger, who never thanks them for their unnecessary solicitude.

Vivian, in spite of his philosophy, felt the excitement of the moment. He looked at the Baron, whose countenance, however, was unmoved.

"It seems," said he, coolly, "we are in luck."

"The stake, then, is not all your own?" eagerly asked the little man in spectacles.

"No; part of it is yours, sir," answered the Baron, dryly.

"I am going to deal," said the short, thick man behind. "Is the board cleared?"

"Your Excellency, then, allows the stake to remain?" inquired the tall, thin banker, with affected nonchalance.

"Oh! certainly," said the Baron, with real nonchalance.

"Three, eight, fourteen, twenty-four, thirty-four. Rouge 34—"

All crowded nearer; the table was surrounded five or six deep, for the wonderful run of luck had got wind, and nearly the whole room were round the table. Indeed, the Grand Duke and Saxon lady, and of course the silent suite, were left alone at the upper part of the room. The tall banker did not conceal his agitation. Even the short, stout dealer ceased to be a machine. All looked anxious except the Baron. Vivian looked at the table; his Excellency watched, with a keen eye, the little dealer. No one even breathed as the cards descended. "Ten, twenty (here the countenance of the banker brightened), twenty-two, twenty-five, twenty-eight, thirty-one; noir 31. The bank's broke: no more play to-night. The roulette table opens immediately."

In spite of the great interest which had been excited, nearly the whole crowd, without waiting to congratulate the Baron, rushed to the opposite side of the room, in order to secure places at the roulette table.

"Put these five hundred and twelve Napoleons into a bag," said the Baron. "Grey, this is your share. With regard to the other half, Mr. Herrmann, what bills have you got?"

"Two on Gogel of Frankfort for two hundred and fifty each, and these twelve Napoleons will make it right," said the tall banker, as he opened a large black pocketbook, from which he took out two small bits of paper. The Baron examined them, and after having seen them indorsed, put them into his pocket, not forgetting the twelve Napoleons; and then taking Vivian's arm, and regretting extremely that he should have the trouble of carrying such a weight, he wished Mr. Hermann a very good-night and success at his roulette, and walked with his companion quietly home. Thus passed a day at Ems!

CHAPTER VII

ON the following morning, Vivian met with his friend, Essper George, behind a small stall in the Bazaar.

"Well, my Lord, what do you wish? Here are Eau de Cologne, violet soap, and watch-ribbons; a smelling bottle of Ems crystal; a snuff-box of fig-tree wood. Name your price: the least trifle that can be given by a man who breaks a bank must be more than my whole stock-in-trade is worth."

"I have not paid you yet, Essper, for my glass chain. There is your share of my winnings, the fame of which, it seems, has reached even you!" added Vivian, with a pleased air.

"I thank you, sir, for the Nap; but I hope I have not offended by alluding to a certain event, which shall be passed over in silence," continued Essper George, with a look of mock solemnity. "I really think you have but a faint appetite for good fortune. They deserve her most who value her least."

"Have you any patrons at Ems, Essper, that have induced you to fix on this place in particular for your speculations? Here, I should think, you have many active rivals," said Vivian, looking round the various stalls.

"I have a patron here who has never deceived, and who will never desert me; I want no other; and that's myself. Now here comes a party: could you just tell me the name of that tall lady now?"

"If I tell you it is Lady Madeleine Trevor, what will it profit you?"

Before Vivian could well finish his sentence Essper had drawn out a long horn from beneath his small counter, and sounded a blast which echoed through the arched passages.

The attention of every one was excited, and no part of the following speech was lost:

"The celebrated Essper George, fresh from Fairy-land, dealer in pomatum and all sorts of perfumery, watches, crosses, Ems crystal, colored prints, Dutch toys, Dresden china, Venetian chains, Neapolitan coral, French crackers, chamois bracelets, tame poodles, and Cherokee corkscrews, mender of mandolins and all other musical instruments, to Lady Madeleine Trevor, has just arrived at Ems, where he only intends to stay two or three days, and a few more weeks besides. Now, gracious lady, what do you wish?"

"And who," said Lady Madeleine, smiling, "is this?"

"The celebrated Essper George, just—" again commenced the conjurer; but Vivian prevented the repetition.

"He is an odd knave, Lady Madeleine, that I have met with before, at other places. I believe I may add an honest one. What say you, Essper?"

"More honest than moonlight, gracious lady, for that deceives every one; and less honest than self-praise, for that deceives no one."

"My friend, you have a ready wit."

"My wit is like a bustling servant, gracious lady; always ready when not wanted, and never present at a pinch."

"Come, I must have a pair of your chamois bracelets. How sell you them?"

"I sell nothing; all here is gratis to beauty, virtue, and nobility: and these are my only customers."

"Thanks will not supply a stock-in-trade though, Essper," said Vivian.

"Very true! but my customers are apt to leave some slight testimonies behind them of the obligations which they are under to me; and these, at the same time, are the prop of my estate and the proof of their discretion. But who comes here?" said Essper, drawing out his horn. The sight of this instrument reminded Lady Madeleine how greatly the effect of music is heightened by distance, and she made a speedy retreat, yielding her place to a family procession of a striking character.

Three daughters abreast, flanked by two elder sons, formed the first file. The father, a portly, prosperous-looking man, followed, with his lady on his arm. Then came two nursery maids, with three children between the tender ages of five and six. The second division of the grand army, consisting of three younger sons, immediately followed. This was commanded by a tutor. A governess and two young daughters then advanced: and then came the extreme rear, the sutlers of the camp, in the persons of two footmen in rich liveries, who each bore a basket on his arm, filled with various fancy articles, which had been all purchased during the promenade of this nation through only part of the bazaar.

The trumpet of Essper George produced a due effect upon the great party. The commander-in-chief stopped at his little stall, and, as if this were the signal for general attack and plunder, the files were immediately broken up. Each individual dashed at his prey, and the only ones who struggled to maintain a semblance of discipline were the nursery maids, the tutor, and the governess, who experienced the greatest difficulty in suppressing the early taste which the detachment of light infantry indicated for booty. But Essper George was in his element: he joked, he assisted, he exhibited, he explained; tapped the cheeks of the children and complimented the elder ones; and finally, having parted at a prodigious profit with nearly his whole stock, paid himself out of a large and heavy purse, which the portly father, in his utter inability to comprehend the complicated accounts and the debased currency, with great frankness deposited in the hands of the master of the stall, desiring him to settle his own claims.

"I hope I may be allowed to ask after Miss Fane," said Vivian.

"She continues better; we are now about to join her in the Limewalk. If you will join our morning stroll, it will give us much pleasure."

Nothing in the world could give Vivian greater pleasure; he felt himself impelled to the side of Lady Madeleine; and only regretted his acquaintance with the Baron because he felt conscious that there was some secret cause which prevented that intimacy from existing between his Excellency and the Trevor party which his talents and his position would otherwise have easily produced.

"By the bye," said Lady Madeleine, "I do not know whether

10

I may be allowed to congratulate you upon your brilliant success at the Redoute last night. It is fortunate that all have not to regret your arrival at Ems so much as poor Mr. Hermann."

"The run was extraordinary. I am only sorry that the goddess should have showered her favors on one who neither deserves nor desires them; for I have no wish to be rich; and as I never lost by her caprices, it is hardly fair that I should gain by them."

"You do not play, then, much?"

"I never played in my life till last night. Gambling has never been one of my follies, although my catalogue of errors is fuller, perhaps, than most men's."

"I think Baron von Konigstein was your partner in the exploit?"

"He was; and apparently as little pleased at the issue as myself."

"Indeed! Have you known the Baron long?"

"We are only friends of a week. I have been living, ever since I was in Germany, a very retired life. A circumstance of a most painful nature drove me from England; a circumstance of which I can hardly flatter myself, and can hardly wish, that you should be ignorant."

"I learned the sad history from one who, while he spoke the truth, spoke of the living sufferer in terms of the fondest affection."

"A father!" said Vivian, agitated, "a father can hardly be expected to be impartial."

"Such a father as yours may. I only wish that he was with us now, to assist me in bringing about what he must greatly desire, your return to England."

"It can not be. I look back to the last year which I spent in that country with feelings of such disgust, I look forward to a return to that country with feelings of such repugnance that—but I feel I am trespassing beyond all bounds in touching on these subjects."

"I promised your father that in case we met I would seek your society. I have suffered too much myself not to understand how dangerous and how deceitful is the excess of grief. You have allowed yourself to be overcome by that which

Providence intended as a lesson of instruction, not as a sentence of despair. In your solitude you have increased the shadow of those fantasies of a heated brain which converse with the pure sunshine of the world would have enabled you to dispel."

"The pure sunshine of the world, Lady Madeleine! would that it had ever lighted me! My youth flourished in the unwholesome sultriness of a blighted atmosphere, which I mistook for the resplendent brilliancy of a summer day. How deceived I was, you may judge, not certainly from finding me here; but I am here because I have ceased to suffer only in having ceased to hope."

"You have ceased to hope, because hope and consolation are not the companions of solitude, which are of a darker nature. Hope and consolation spring from the social affections. Converse with the world will do more for you than all the arguments of philosophers. I hope yet to find you a believer in the existence of that good which we all worship and all pursue. Happiness comes when we least expect it, and to those who strive least to obtain it; as you were fortunate yesterday at the Redoute, when you played without an idea of winning."

They were in the Limewalk: gay sounds greeted them, and Miss Fane came forward from a light-hearted band to welcome her cousin. She had to propose a walk to the New Spring, which she was prepared for Lady Madeleine to resist on the ground of her cousin's health. But Miss Fane combated all the objections with airy merriment, and with a bright resource that never flagged. As she bent her head slightly to Vivian, ere she hastened back to her companions to announce the success of her mission, it seemed to him that he had never beheld so animated and beaming a countenance, or glanced upon a form of such ineffable and sparkling grace.

"You would scarcely imagine, Mr. Grey, that we are traveling for my cousin's health, nor do her physicians, indeed, give us any cause for serious uneasiness; yet I can not help feeling at times great anxiety. Her flushed cheek and the alarming languor which succeeds any excitement make me fear her complaint may be more deeply seated than they are willing to acknowledge."

"They were saying the other day that the extraordinary heat of this season must end in an earthquake, or some great convulsion of nature. That would bring languor."

"We are willing to adopt any reasoning that gives us hope, but her mother died of consumption."

CHAPTER VIII

WHEN the walking party returned home they found a crowd of idle servants assembled opposite the house, round a group of equipages, consisting of two enormous crimson carriages, a britzska, and a large caravan, on all which vehicles the same coat of arms was ostentatiously blazoned.

"Some new guests!" said Miss Fane.

"It must be the singular party that we watched this morning in the bazaar," said Lady Madeleine. "Violet! I have such a curious character to introduce you to, a particular friend of Mr. Grey, who wishes very much to have the honor of your acquaintance, MR. ESSPER GEORGE."

"These carriages, then, belong to him?"

"Not exactly," said Vivian.

In an hour's time the party again met at dinner in the saloon. By the joint exertions of Ernstorff and Mr. St. George's servants, the Baron, Vivian, and the Chevalier de Bœffleurs were now seated next to the party of Lady Madeleine Trevor.

"My horses fortunately arrived from Frankfort this morning," said the Baron. "Mr. St. George and myself have been taking a ride very far up the valley. Has your Ladyship yet been to the Castle of Nassau?"

"We have not. The expedition has been one of those plans often arranged and never executed."

"You should go. The ruin is one of the finest in Germany. An expedition to Nassau Castle would be a capital foundation for a picnic. Conceive a beautiful valley, discovered by a knight, in the Middle Ages, following the track of a stag. How romantic! The very incident vouches for its sweet seclusion. Can not you imagine the wooded mountains, the old gray ruin, the sound of the unseen river? What more should we want, except agreeable company, fine music, and the best provisions, to fancy ourselves in Paradise?"

"I wish the plan were practicable," said Mr. St. George.

"I take the whole arrangement upon myself; there is not a difficulty. The ladies shall go on donkeys, or we might make a water excursion of it part of the way, and the donkeys can meet us at the pass near Stein, and then the gentlemen may walk; and if you fear the water at night, why, then the carriages may come round: and if your own be too heavy for mountain roads, my britzska is always at your command. You see there is not a difficulty."

"Not a difficulty," said Mr. St. George. "Madeleine, we only wait your consent."

"I think we had better put off the execution of our plan till June is a little more advanced. We must have a fine summer night for Violet."

"Well, then, I hold the whole party present engaged to follow my standard whenever I have permission from authority to unfold it," said the Baron, bowing to Lady Madeleine: "and lest, on cool reflection, I shall not possess influence enough to procure the appointment, I shall, like a skilful orator, take advantage of your feelings, which gratitude for this excellent plan must have already enlisted in my favor, and propose myself as Master of the Ceremonies." The Baron's eye caught Lady Madeleine's as he uttered this, and something like a smile, rather of pity than derision, lighted up her face.

Here Vivian turned round to give some directions to an attendant, and to his annoyance found Essper George standing behind his chair.

"Is there anything you want, sir?"

"Who ordered you here?"

"My duty."

"In what capacity do you attend?"

"As your servant, sir?"

"I insist upon your leaving the room directly.

"Ah! my friend, Essper George," said Lady Madeleine, "are you there? What is the matter?"

"This, then, is Essper George!" said Violet Fane. "What kind of being can he possibly be? What indeed is the matter?"

"I am merely discharging a servant at a moment's warning, Miss Fane; and if you wish to engage his constant attendance upon yourself, I have no objection to give him a character for the occasion."

"What do you want, Essper?" said Miss Fane.

"Merely to see whether your walk this morning had done your appetites any good," answered Essper, looking disconsolate; "and so I thought I might make myself useful at the same time. And though I do not bring on the soup in a cocked hat, and carve the venison with a *couteau-de-chasse*," continued he, bowing very low to Ernstorff, who, standing stiff behind his master's chair, seemed utterly unaware that any other person in the room could experience a necessity; "still I can change a plate or hand the wine without cracking the first or drinking the second."

"And very good qualities, too!" said Miss Fane. "Come, Essper, you shall put your accomplishments into practice immediately; change my plate."

This Essper did with dexterity and quiet, displaying at the same time a small white hand, on the back of which was marked a comet and three daggers. As he had the discretion not to open his mouth, and performed all his duties with skill, his intrusion in a few minutes was not only pardoned, but forgotten.

"There has been a great addition to the visitors to-day, I see," said Mr. St. George. "Who are the new-comers?"

"I will tell you all about them," said the Baron. "This family is one of those whose existence astounds the Continent much more than any of your mighty dukes and earls, whose fortunes, though colossal, can be conceived, and whose rank is understood. Mr. Fitzloom is a very different personage, for thirty years ago he was a journeyman cotton-spinner. Some miraculous invention in machinery entitled him to a patent, which has made him one of the great proprietors of England. He has lately been returned a Member for a manufacturing town, and he intends to get over the first two years of his parliamentary career by successively monopolizing the accommodation of all the principal cities of France, Germany, Switzerland, and Italy, and by raising the price of provisions and post-horses through a track of five thousand miles. My information is authentic, for I had a casual acquaintance with him in England. There was some talk of a contract for supplying our army from England, and I saw Fitzloom often on the subject. I have spoken to him to-day. This is by no means the first of the species that we have had in Germany. I can assure you that the plain traveler feels seriously the inconvenience of following such a caravan; their money flows with such unwise prodigality that real liberality ceases to be valued; and many of your nobility have complained to me that in their travels they are now often expostulated with on account of their parsimony, and taunted with the mistaken extravagance of a stocking-maker or a porter-brewer."

"What pleasure can such people find in traveling?" wondered Mr. St. George.

"As much pleasure and more profit than half the young men of the present day," replied a middle-aged English gentleman, who was a kinsman of the St. Georges, and called them cousins. "In my time traveling was undertaken on a very different system to what it is now. The English youth then traveled to frequent, what Lord Bacon says are 'especially to be seen and observed, the Courts of Princes.' You all travel now, it appears, to look at mountains and catch cold in spouting trash on lakes by moonlight."

"But, my dear sir!" said the Baron, "although I grant you that the principal advantages of travel must be the opportunity which it affords us of becoming acquainted with human nature, knowledge, of course, chiefly gained where human beings most congregate, great cities, and, as you say, the Courts of Princes; still, one of its great benefits is that it enlarges a man's experience, not only of his fellow-creatures in particular, but of nature in general. Many men pass through life without seeing a sunrise: a traveler can not. If human experience be gained by seeing men in their undress, not only when they are conscious of the presence of others, natural experience is only to be acquired by studying nature at all periods, not merely when man is busy and the beasts asleep."

"But what is the use of this deep experience of nature? Men are born to converse with men, not with stocks and stones. He who has studied Le Sage will be more happy and more successful in this world than the man who muses over Rousseau."

"I agree with you. I have no wish to make man an anchorite. But as to the benefit of a thorough experience of nature, it appears to me to be evident. It increases our stock of ideas."

"So does everything."

"But it does more than this. It calls into being new emotions, it gives rise to new and beautiful associations; it creates that salutary state of mental excitement which renders our ideas more lucid and our conclusions more sound. Can we too much esteem a study which at the same time stimulates imagination and corrects the judgment?"

"Do not you think that a communion with nature is calculated to elevate the soul," said Lady Madeleine, "to—?"

"So is reading your Bible. A man's soul should always be elevated. If not, he might look at mountains forever, but I should not trust him a jot more."

"But, sir," continued the Baron, with unusual warmth, "I am clear that there are cases in which the influence of nature has worked what you profess to treat as an impossiblity or a miracle. I am myself acquainted with an instance of a peculiar character. A few years ago, a gentleman of high rank found himself exposed to the unhappy suspicion of being connected with some dishonorable transactions which took place in the highest circles of England. Unable to find any specific charge which he could meet, he added one to the numerous catalogue of those unfortunate beings who have sunk in society, the victims of a surmise. He quitted England, and, disgusted with the world, became the profligate which he had been falsely believed to be. At the house of Cardinal ——, at Naples, celebrated for its revels, this gentleman became a constant guest. He entered with a mad eagerness into every species of dissipation, although none gave him pleasure, and his fortune, his health, and the powers of his mind were all fast vanishing. One night of frantic dissipation a mock election of Master of the Sports was proposed, and the hero of my tale had the splendid gratification of being chosen by unanimous consent to this new office. About two o'clock of the same night he left the palace of the Cardinal, with an intention of returning; his way on his return led by the Chiaja. It was one of those nights which we witness only in the south. The blue and brilliant sea was sleeping beneath a cloudless sky; and the moon not only shed her light over the orange and lemon trees, which, springing from their green banks of myrtle, hung over the water, but added fresh lustre to the white domes and glittering towers of the city, and flooded Vesuvius and the distant coast with light as far even as Capua. The individual of whom I am speaking had passed this spot on many nights when the moon was not less bright, the waves not less silent, and the orange trees not less sweet; but to-night something irresistible impelled him to stop. What a contrast to the artificial light and heat and splendor of the palace to which he was returning! He mused in silence. Would it not be wiser to forget the world's injustice in gazing on a moonlit ocean than in discovering in the illumined halls of Naples the baseness of the crowd which forms the world's power? To enjoy the refreshing luxury of a fanning breeze which now arose he turned and gazed on the other side of the bay; upon his right stretched out the promontory of Pausilippo; there were the shores of Baiæ. But it was not only the loveliness of the land which now overcame his spirit; he thought of those whose fame had made us forget even the beauty of these shores in associations of a higher character and a more exalted nature. He remembered the time when it was his only wish to be numbered among them. How had his early hopes been fulfilled! What just account had he rendered to himself and to his country; that country that had expected so much, that self that had aspired even to more!

"Day broke over the city and found him still pacing the Chiaja; he did not return to the Cardinal's palace, and in two days he had left Naples. I can myself, from personal experience, aver that this individual is now a useful and honorable member of society. The world speaks of him in more flattering terms."

The Baron spoke with energy and animation. Miss Fane, who had been silent, and who certainly had not encouraged by any apparent interest the previous conversation of the Baron, listened to this anecdote with eager attention; but the effect it produced upon Lady Madeleine Trevor was remarkable.

Soon after this the party broke up. The promenade followed; the Grand Duke, his complements and courtiers; then came the Redoute. Mr. Hermann bowed low as the gentlemen walked up to the table. The Baron whispered Vivian that it was "expected" that they should play, and give the tables a chance of winning back their money. Vivian staked with the carelessness of one who wishes to lose; as is often the case under such circumstances, he again left the Redoute a considerable winner. He parted with the Baron at his Excellency's door and proceeded to the next, which was his own. Here he stumbled over something at the doorway which appeared like a large bundle; he bent down with his light to examine it, and found Essper George lying on his back with his eyes half-open. It was some moments before Vivian perceived he was asleep; stepping gently over him, he entered his apartment.

CHAPTER IX

WHEN Vivian rose in the morning a gentle tap at his door announced the presence of an early visitor, who, being desired to enter, appeared in the person of Essper George.

"Do you want anything, sir?" asked Essper, with a submissive air.

Vivian stared at him for a moment, and then ordered him to come in.

"I had forgotten, Essper, until this moment, that on returning to my room last night I found you sleeping at my door. This also reminds me of your conduct in the saloon yesterday; and as I wish to prevent the repetition of such improprieties, I shall take this opportunity of informing you, once for all, that if you do not in future conduct yourself with more discretion, I must apply to the Maitre d'Hotel. Now, sir, what do you want?"

Essper was silent, and stood with his hands crossed on his breast, and his eyes fixed on the ground.

"If you do not want anything, quit the room immediately."

Here the singular being began to weep.

"Poor fellow!" thought Vivian, "I fear, with all thy wit and pleasantry, thou art, after all, but one of those *capriccios* which Nature sometimes indulges in, merely to show how superior is her accustomed order to eccentricities, even accompanied with rare powers."

"What is your wish, Essper?" continued Vivian, in a kinder tone. "If there be any service that I can do you, you will not find me backward. Are you in trouble? you surely are not in want?"

"No!" sobbed Essper; "I wish to be your servant." Here he hid his face in his hands.

"My servant! why, surely it is not very wise to seek dependence upon any man. I am afraid that you have been keeping company too much with the lackeys that are always loitering about these bathing-places. Ernstorff's green livery and sword, have they not turned your brain. Essper?"

"No, no, no! I am tired of living alone."

"But remember, to be a servant, you must be a person of regular habits and certain reputation. I have myself a good opinion of you, but I have myself seen very little of you, though more than any one here, and I am a person of a peculiar turn of mind. Perhaps there is not another individual in this house who would even allude to the possibility of engaging a servant without a character."

"Does the ship ask the wind for a character when he bears her over the sea without hire and without reward? and shall you require a character from me when I request to serve you without wages and without pay?"

"Such an engagement, Essper, it would be impossible for me to enter into, even if I had need of your services, which at present I have not. But I tell you frankly that I see no chance of your suiting me. I should require an attendant of steady habits and experience; not one whose very appearance would attract attention when I wished to be unobserved, and acquire a notoriety for the master which he detests. I warmly advise you to give up all idea entering into a state of life for

which you are not in the least suited. Believe me, your stall
will be a better friend than a master. Now leave me."

Essper remained one moment with his eyes still fixed on
the ground; then walking very rapidly up to Vivian, he
dropped on his knee, kissed his hand, and disappeared.

Mr. St. George breakfasted with the Baron, and the gentlemen called on Lady Madeleine early in the morning to propose a drive to Stein Castle; but she excused herself, and
Vivian followong her example, the Baron and Mr. St. George
"patronized" the Fitzlooms, because there was nothing else to
do. Vivian again joined the ladies in their morning walk, but
Miss Fane was not in her usual high spirits. She complained
more than once of her cousin's absence; and this, connected
with some other circumstances, gave Vivian the first impression that her feelings toward Mr. St. George were not merely
those of a relation. As to the Chevalier de Bœffleurs, Vivian
soon found that it was utterly impossible to be on intimate
terms with a being without an idea. The Chevalier was certainly not a very fit representative of the gay, gallant, mer-
curial Frenchman: he rose very late, and employed the whole
of the morning in reading the French journals and playing
billiards alternately with Prince Salvinski and Count von
Altenburgh.

These gentlemen, as well as the Baron, Vivian, and Mr.
St. George, were to dine this day at the New House.

They found assembled at the appointed hour a party of
about thirty individuals. The dinner was sumptuous, the
wines superb. At the end of the banquet the company adjourned to another room, where play was proposed and immediately commenced. His Imperial Highness did not join in
the game, but, seated in a corner of the apartment, was surrounded by his aides-de-camp, whose business was to bring
their master constant accounts of the fortunes of the table
and the fate of his bets. His Highness did not stake.

Vivian soon found that the game was played on a very different scale at the New House to what it was at the Redoute.
He spoke most decidedly to the Baron of his detestation of
gambling, and expressed his unwillingness to play; but the
Baron, although he agreed with him in his sentiments, advised him to conform for the evening to the universal custom.

As he could afford to lose, he consented, and staked boldly.
This night very considerable sums were lost and won; but
none returned home greater winners than Mr. St. George and
Vivian Grey.

CHAPTER X

THE first few days of an acquaintance with a new scene of
life and with new characters generally appear to pass very
slowly; not certainly from the weariness which they induce,
but rather from the keen attention which every little circumstance commands. When the novelty has worn off, when we
have discovered that the new characters differ little from all
others we have met before, and that the scene they inhabit is
only another variety of the great order we have so often observed, we relapse into our ancient habits of inattention; we
think more of ourselves, and less of those we meet; and musing our moments away in reverie, or in a vain attempt to cheat
the coming day of the monotony of the present one, we begin
to find that the various vested hours have bounded and are
bounding away in a course at once imperceptible, uninteresting, and unprofitable. Then it is that, terrified at our nearer
approach to the great river whose dark windings it seems the
business of all to forget, we start from our stupor to mourn
over the rapidity of that collective sum of past time every
individual hour of which we have in turn execrated for its
sluggishness.

Vivian had now been three weeks at Ems, and the presence
of Lady Madeleine Trevor and her cousin alone induced him
to remain. Whatever the mystery existing between Lady
Madeleine and the Baron, his efforts to attach himself to her
party had been successful. The great intimacy subsisting between the Baron and her brother materially assisted in bringing about this result. For the first fortnight the Baron was
Lady Madeleine's constant attendant in the evening promenade, and sometimes in the morning walk; and though there
were few persons whose companionship could be preferred
to that of Baron von Konigstein, still Vivian sometimes regretted that his friend and Mr. St. George had not continued

their rides. The presence of the Baron seemed always to have an unfavorable influence upon the spirits of Miss Fane, and the absurd and evident jealousy of Mr. St. George prevented Vivian from finding in her agreeable conversation some consolation for the loss of the sole enjoyment of Lady Madeleine's exhilarating presence. Mr. St. George had never met Vivian's advances with cordiality, and he now treated him with studied coldness.

The visits of the gentlemen to the New House had been frequent. The saloon of the Grand Duke was open every evening, and in spite of his great distaste for the fatal amusement which was there invariably pursued, Vivian found it impossible to decline frequently attending without subjecting his motives to painful misconception. His extraordinary fortune did not desert him, and rendered his attendance still more a duty. The Baron was not so successful as on his first evening's venture at the Redoute; but Mr. St. George's star remained favorable. Of Essper Vivian had seen little. In passing through the Bazaar one morning, which he seldom did, he found, to his surprise, that the former conjurer had doffed his quaint costume, and was now attired in the usual garb of men of his condition of life. As Essper was busily employed at the moment, Vivian did not stop to speak to him; but he received a respectful bow. Once or twice, also, he had met Essper in the Baron's apartments; and he seemed to have become a very great favorite with the servants of his Excellency and the Chevalier de Bœffleurs, particularly with his former butt, Ernstorff, to whom he now behaved with great deference.

For the first fortnight the Baron's attendance on Lady Madeleine was constant. After this time he began to slacken in his attentions. He first disappeared from the morning walks, and yet he did not ride; he then ceased from joining the party at Lady Madeleine's apartments in the evening, and never omitted increasing the circle at the New House for a single night. The whole of the fourth week the Baron dined with his Imperial Highness. Although the invitation had been extended to all the gentlemen from the first, it had been agreed that it was not to be accepted, in order that the ladies should not find their party in the saloon less numerous or less agreeable. The Baron was the first to break through a rule which he had himself proposed, and Mr. St. George and the Chevalier de Bœffleurs soon followed his example.

"Mr. Grey," said Lady Madeleine one evening as she was about to leave the gardens, "we shall be happy to see you to-night, if you are not engaged."

"I fear that I am engaged," said Vivian; for the receipt of some letters from England made him little inclined to enter into society.

"Oh, no! you can not be," said Miss Fane: "pray come! I know you only want to go to that terrible New House. I wonder what Albert can find to amuse him there; I fear no good. Men never congregate together for any beneficial purpose. I am sure, with all his gastronomical affectations, he would not, if all were right, prefer the most exquisite dinner in the world to our society. As it is, we scarcely see him a moment. I think that you are the only one who has not deserted the saloon. For once, give up the New House."

Vivian smiled at Miss Fane's wrath, and could not persist in his refusal, although she did dilate most provokingly on the absence of her cousin. He therefore soon joined them.

"Lady Madeleine is assisting me in a most important work, Mr. Grey. I am making drawings of the Valley of the Rhine. I know that you are acquainted with the scenery; you can, perhaps, assist me with your advice about this view of Old Hatto's Castle."

Vivian was so completely master of every spot in the Rhineland that he had no difficulty in suggesting the necessary alterations. The drawings were vivid representations of the scenery which they professed to depict, and Vivian forgot his melancholy as he attracted the attention of the fair artist to points of interest unknown or unnoticed by the guide-books and the diaries.

"You must look forward to Italy with great interest, Miss Fane?"

"The greatest! I shall not, however, forget the Rhine, even among the Apennines."

"Our intended fellow-travelers, Lord Mounteney and his family, are already at Milan," said Lady Madeleine to Vivian;

"we were to have joined their party. Lady Mounteney is a Trevor."

"I have had the pleasure of meeting Lord Mounteney in England, at Sir Berdmore Scrope's: do you know him?"

"Slightly. The Mounteneys pass the winter at Rome, where I hope we shall join them. Do you know the family intimately?"

"Mr. Ernest Clay, a nephew of his Lordship's, I have seen a great deal of; I suppose, according to the adopted phraseology, I ought to describe him as my friend, although I am ignorant where he is at present; and although, unless he is himself extremely altered, there scarcely can be two persons who now more differ in their pursuits and tempers than ourselves."

"Ernest Clay! is he a friend of yours? He is at Munich, attached to the Legation. I see you smile at the idea of Ernest Clay drawing up a protocol!"

"Madeleine, you have never read me Caroline Mounteney's letter, as you promised," said Miss Fane; "I suppose full of raptures; 'the Alps and Apennines, the Pyrenæan, and the River Po?'"

"By no means; the whole letter is filled with an account of the ballet at La Scala, which, according to Caroline, is a thousand times more interesting than Mont Blanc or the Simplon."

"One of the immortal works of Vigano, I suppose," said Vivian; "he has raised the ballet of action to an equality with tragedy. I have heard my father mention the splendid effect of his 'Vestale' and his 'Otello.'"

"And yet," said Violet, "I do not like 'Othello' to be profaned. It is not for operas and ballets. We require the thrilling words."

"It is very true; yet Pasta's acting in the opera was a grand performance; and I have myself seldom witnessed a more masterly effect produced by any actor in the world than I did a fortnight ago, at the Opera at Darmstadt, by Wild in 'Othello.'"

"I think the history of Desdemona is the most affecting of all tales," said Miss Fane.

"The violent death of a woman, young, lovely, and innocent, is assuredly the most terrible of tragedies," observed Vivian.

"I have often asked myself," said Miss Fane, "which is the most terrible destiny for the young to endure: to meet death after a life of anxiety and suffering, or suddenly to be cut off in the enjoyment of all things that make life delightful."

"For my part," said Vivian, "in the last instance, I think that death can scarcely be considered an evil. How infinitely is such a destiny to be preferred to that long apprenticeship of sorrow, at the end of which we are generally as unwilling to die as at the commencement!"

"And yet," said Miss Fane, "there is something fearful in the idea of sudden death."

"Very fearful," muttered Vivian, "in some cases;" for he thought of one whom he had sent to his great account before his time.

"Violet, my dear!" said Lady Madeleine, "have you finished your drawing of the Bingenloch?" But Miss Fane would not leave the subject.

"Very fearful in all cases, Mr. Grey. How few of us are prepared to leave this world without warning! And if from youth, or sex, or natural disposition, a few may chance to be better fitted for the great change than their companions, still I always think that in those cases in which we view our fellow-creatures suddenly departing from this world, apparently without a bodily or mental pang, there must be a moment of suffering which none of us can understand; a terrible consciousness of meeting death in the very flush of life; a moment of suffering which, from its intense and novel character, may appear an eternity of anguish. I have always looked upon such an end as the most fearful of dispensations."

"Violet, my dear," said her Ladyship, "let us talk no more of death. You have been silent a fortnight. I think to-night you may sing." Miss Fane rose and sat down to the instrument.

It was a lively air, calculated to drive away all melancholy feelings, and cherishing sunny views of human life. But Rossini's muse did not smile to-night upon her who invoked its gay spirit; and ere Lady Madeleine could interfere Violet

Fane had found more congenial emotions in one of Weber's prophetic symphonies.

Oh, Music! miraculous art, that makes the poet's skill a jest, revealing to the soul inexpressible feelings by the aid of inexplicable sounds! A blast of thy trumpet, and millions rush forward to die; a peal of thy organ, and uncounted nations sink down to pray. Mighty is thy threefold power!

First, thou canst call up all elemental sounds, and scenes, and subjects, with the definiteness of reality. Strike the lyre! Lo! the voice of the winds, the flash of the lightning, the swell of the wave, the solitude of the valley!

Then thou canst speak to the secrets of a man's heart as if by inspiration. Strike the lyre! Lo! our early love, our treasured hate, our withered joy, our flattering hope!

And, lastly, by thy mysterious melodies thou canst recall man from all thought of this world and of himself, bringing back to his soul's memory dark but delightful recollections of the glorious heritage which he has lost, but which he may win again. Strike the lyre! Lo! Paradise, with its palaces of inconceivable splendor and its gates of unimaginable glory!

When Vivian left the apartment of Lady Madeleine he felt no inclination to sleep, and, instead of retiring to rest, he bent his steps toward the gardens. It was a rich summer night; the air, recovered from the sun's scorching rays, was cool, not chilling. The moon was still behind the mountains; but the dark-blue heavens were studded with innumerable stars, whose tremulous light quivered on the face of the river. All human sounds had ceased to agitate; and the note of the nightingale and the rush of the waters banished monotony without disturbing reflection. But not for reflection had Vivian Grey deserted his chamber: his heart was full, but of indefinable sensations, and, forgetting the world in the intenseness of his emotions, he felt too much to think.

How long he had been pacing by the side of the river he knew not, when he was awakened from his reverie by the sound of voices. He looked up, and saw lights moving at a distance. The party at the New House had just broke up. He stopped beneath a branching elm-tree for a moment, that the sound of his steps might not attract their attention, and at this very instant the garden gate opened and closed with great violence. The figure of a man approached. As he passed Vivian the moon rose up from above the brow of the mountain, and lighted up the countenance of the Baron. Despair was stamped on his distracted features.

CHAPTER XI

ON the evening of the next day there was to be a grand fête given at the New House by his Imperial Highness. The ladies would treasure their energies for the impending ball, and the morning was to pass without an excursion. Only Lady Madeleine, whom Vivian met taking her usual early promenade in the gardens, seemed inclined to prolong it, and even invited him to be her companion. She talked of the fête, and she expressed a hope that Vivian would accompany their party; but her air was not festive, she seemed abstracted and disturbed, and her voice more than once broke off abruptly at the commencement of a sentence which it seemed she had not courage to finish.

At length she said suddenly, "Mr. Grey, I can not conceal any longer that I am thinking of a very different subject from the ball. As you form part of my thoughts, I shall not hesitate to disburden my mind to you. I wish not to keep you in suspense. It is of the mode of life which I see my brother, which I see you, pursuing here that I wish to speak," she added with a tremulous voice. "May I speak with freedom?"

"With the most perfect unreserve and confidence."

"You are aware that Ems is not the first place at which I have met Baron von Konigstein."

"I am not ignorant that he has been in England."

"It can not have escaped you that I acknowledged his acquaintance with reluctance."

"I should judge, with the greatest."

"And yet it was with still more reluctance that I prevailed upon myself to believe you were his friend. I experienced great relief when you told me how short and accidental had been your acquaintance. I have experienced great pain in witnessing to what that acquaintance has led; and it is with extreme sorrow for my own weakness, in not having had courage to speak to you before, and with a hope of yet benefiting you, that I have been induced to speak to you now."

"I trust there is no cause either for your sorrow or your fear; but much, much cause for my gratitude."

"I have observed the constant attendance of yourself and my brother at the New House with the utmost anxiety. I have seen too much not to be aware of the danger which young men, and young men of honor, must always experience at such places. Alas! I have seen too much of Baron von Konigstein not to know that at such places especially his acquaintance is fatal. The evident depression of your spirits yesterday determined me on a step which I have for the last few days been considering. I can learn nothing from my brother. I fear that I am even now too late; but I trust that, whatever may be your situation, you will remember, Mr. Grey, that you have friends; that you will decide on nothing rash."

"Lady Madeleine," said Vivian, "I will not presume to express the gratitude which your generous conduct allows me to feel. This moment repays me for a year of agony. I affect not to misunderstand your meaning. My opinion, my detestation of the gaming table, has always been, and must always be, the same. I do assure you this, and all things, upon my honor. Far from being involved, my cheek burns while I confess that I am master of a considerable sum acquired by this unhallowed practice. You are aware of the singular fortune which awaited my first evening at Ems; that fortune was continued at the New House the very first day I dined there, and when, unexpectedly, I was forced to play. That fatal fortune has rendered my attendance at the New House necessary. I found it impossible to keep away without subjecting myself to painful observations. My depression of yesterday was occasioned by the receipt of letters from England. I am ashamed of having spoken so much about myself, and so little about those for whom you are more interested. So far as I can judge, you have no cause, at present, for any uneasiness with regard to Mr. St. George. You may, perhaps, have observed that we are not very intimate, and therefore I can not speak with any precision as to the state of his fortunes; but I

have reason to believe that they are by no means unfavorable.
And as for the Baron—"

"Yes, yes!"

"I hardly know what I am to infer from your observations
respecting him. I certainly should infer something extremely
bad, were not I conscious that, after the experience of five
weeks, I, for one, have nothing to complain of him. The
Baron, certainly, is fond of play; plays high, indeed. He has
not had equal fortune at the New House as at the Redoute;
at least I imagine so, for he has given me no cause to believe,
in any way, that he is a loser."

"If you could only understand the relief I feel at this moment, I am sure you would not wonder that I prevailed upon
myself to speak to you. It may still be in my power, however,
to prevent evil."

"Yes, certainly! I think the best course now would be to
speak to me frankly respecting Von Konigstein; and, if you
are aware of anything which has passed in England of a
nature—"

"Stop!" said Lady Madeleine, agitated. Vivian was silent,
and some moments elapsed before his companion again spoke.
When she did her eyes were fixed on the ground, and her tones
were low; but her voice was calm and steady.

"I am going to accept, Mr. Grey, the confidence which you
have proffered me; but I do not affect to conceal that I speak,
even now, with reluctance; an effort, and it will soon be over.
It is for the best." Lady Madeleine paused one moment, and
then resumed with a firm voice:

"Upward of six years have now passed since Baron von
Konigstein was appointed Minister to London from the Court
of ——. Although apparently young for such an important
mission, he had already distinguished himself as a diplomatist;
and with all the advantages of brilliant talents, various accomplishments, rank, reputation, person, and a fascinating
address, I need not tell you that he immediately became of
consideration, even in the highest circles. Mr. Trevor—I was
then just married—was at this period in office, and was constantly in personal communication with the Baron. They
became intimate, and he was our constant guest. He had the
reputation of being a man of pleasure. He was one for whose

indiscretions there might be some excuse; nor had anything ever transpired which could induce us to believe that Baron von Konigstein could be guilty of anything but an indiscretion. At this period a relation and former ward of Mr. Trevor's, a young man of considerable fortune, and one whom we all fondly loved, resided in our family. We considered him as our brother. With this individual Baron von Konigstein formed a strong friendship; they were seldom apart. Our relation was not exempted from the failings of young men. He led a dissipated life; but he was very young; and as, unlike most relations, we never allowed any conduct on his part to banish him from our society, we trusted that the contrast which his own family afforded to his usual companions would in time render his habits less irregular. We had now known Baron von Konigstein for upward of a year and a half, intimately. Nothing had transpired during this period to induce Mr. Trevor to alter the opinion which he had entertained of him from the first; he believed him to be a man of honor, and, in spite of a few imprudences, of principle. Whatever might have been my own opinion of him at this period, I had no reason to doubt the natural goodness of his disposition; and though I could not hope that he was one who would assist us in our plans for the reformation of Augustus, I still was not sorry to believe that in the Baron he would at least find a companion very different from the unprincipled and selfish beings by whom he was too often surrounded. Something occurred at this time which placed Baron von Konigstein, according to his own declaration, under lasting obligations to myself. In the warmth of his heart he asked if there was any real and important service which he could do me. I took advantage of the moment to speak to him about our young friend; I detailed to him all our anxieties; he anticipated all my wishes, and promised to watch over him, to be his guardian, his friend, his real friend. Mr. Grey," continued her Ladyship, "I struggle to restrain my feelings; but the recollections of this period of my life are so painful that for a moment I must stop to recover myself."

For a few minutes they walked on in silence. Vivian did not speak; and when his companion resumed her tale, he, unconsciously, pressed her arm.

"I try to be brief. About three months after the Baron had given me the pledge which I mentioned, Mr. Trevor was called up at an early hour one morning with the intelligence that his late ward was supposed to be at the point of death at a neighboring hotel. He instantly repaired to him, and on the way the fatal truth was broken to him: our friend had committed suicide! He had been playing all night with one whom I can not now name." Here Lady Madeleine's voice died away, but with a struggle she again spoke firmly.

"I mean with the Baron, some foreigners also, and an Englishman, all intimate friends of Von Konigstein, and scarcely known to the deceased. Our friend had been the only sufferer; he had lost his whole fortune, and more than his fortune: and, with a heart full of despair and remorse, had, with his own hand, terminated his life. The whole circumstances were so suspicious that they attracted public attention, and Mr. Trevor spared no exertion to bring the offenders to justice. The Baron had the hardihood to call upon us the next day; of course, in vain. He wrote violent letters, protesting his innocence; that he was asleep during most of the night, and accusing the others who were present of a conspiracy. The unhappy business now attracted very general interest. Its consequence on me was an alarming illness of a most unfortunate kind; I was therefore prevented from interfering, or, indeed, knowing anything that took place; but my husband informed me that the Baron was involved in a public correspondence; that the accused parties recriminated, and that finally he was convinced that Von Konigstein, if there were any difference, was, if possible, the most guilty. However this might be, he soon obtained his recall from his own Government. He wrote to us both before he left England; but I was too ill to hear of his letters, until Mr. Trevor informed me that he had returned them unopened. And now, I must give utterance to that which as yet has always died upon my lips, the unhappy victim was the brother of Miss Fane!"

"And Mr. St. George," said Vivian, "knowing all this, which surely he must have done; how came he to tolerate, for an instant, the advances of such a man?"

"My brother," said Lady Madeleine, "is a very good young man, with a kind heart and warm feelings; but my brother has not much knowledge of the world, and he is too honorable himself ever to believe that what he calls a gentleman can be dishonest. My brother was not in England when the unhappy event took place, and of course the various circumstances have not made the same impression upon him as upon us. He has heard of the affair only from me; and young men too often imagine that women are apt to exaggerate in matters of this nature, which, of course, few of us can understand. The Baron had not the good feeling, or perhaps had not the power, connected as he was with the Grand Duke, to affect ignorance of our former acquaintance, or to avoid a second one. I was obliged formally to present him to my brother. I was quite perplexed how to act. I thought of writing to him the next morning, impressing upon him the utter impossiblity of our acquaintance being renewed: but this proceeding involved a thousand difficulties. How was a man of his distinction, a man who not only from his rank, but from his disposition, is always a remarkable and a remarked character, wherever he may be; how could he account to the Grand Duke, and to his numerous friends, for his not associating with a party with whom he was perpetually in contact. Explanations, and worse, must have been the consequence. I could hardly expect him to leave Ems; it was, perhaps, out of his power: and for Miss Fane to leave Ems at this moment was most strenuously prohibited by her physician. While I was doubtful and deliberating, the conduct of Baron von Konigstein himself prevented me from taking any step whatever. Feeling all the awkwardness of his situation, he seized, with eagerness, the opportunity of becoming intimate with a member of the family whom he had not before known. His amusing conversation, and insinuating address, immediately enlisted the feelings of my brother in his favor. You know yourself that the very morning after their introduction they were riding together. As they became more intimate, the Baron boldly spoke to Albert, in confidence, of his acquaintance with us in England, and of the unhappy circumstances which led to its termination. Albert was deceived by this seeming courage and candor. He has become the Baron's friend, and has adopted his version of the unhappy story; and as the Baron has had too much delicacy to allude to the affair in a defence of himself to me, he calculated that the representations of Albert, who, he was conscious, would not preserve the confidence which he has always intended him to betray, would assist in producing in my mind an impression in his favor. The Neapolitan story which he told the other day at dinner was of himself. I confess to you, that though I have not for a moment doubted his guilt, still I was weak enough to consider that his desire to become reconciled to me was at least an evidence of a repentant heart; and the Neapolitan story deceived me. Actuated by these feelings, and acting as I thought wisest under existing circumstances, I ceased to discourage his advances. Your acquaintance, which we all desired to cultivate, was perhaps another reason for enduring his presence. His subsequent conduct has undeceived me: I am convinced now, not only of his former guilt, but also that he is not changed; and that, with his accustomed talent, he has been acting a part which for some reason or other he has no longer any object in maintaining."

"And Miss Fane," said Vivian, "she must know all?"

"She knows nothing in detail; she was so young at the time that we had no difficulty in keeping the particular circumstances of her brother's death, and the sensation which it excited, a secret from her. As she grew up, I have thought it proper that the mode of his death should no longer be concealed from her; and she has learned from some incautious observations of Albert enough to make her look upon the Baron with terror. It is for Violet," continued Lady Madeleine, "that I have the severest apprehensions. For the last fortnight her anxiety for her cousin has produced an excitement which I look upon with more dread than anything that can happen to her. She has entreated me to speak to Albert, and also to you. The last few days she has become more easy and serene. She accompanies us to-night; the weather is so beautiful that the night air is scarcely to be feared; and a gay scene will have a favorable influence upon her spirit. Your depression last night did not, however, escape her notice. Once more let me say how I rejoice at hearing what you have told me. I unhesitatingly believe all that you have said. Watch Albert. I have no fear for yourself."

CHAPTER XII

THE company at the Grand Duke's fête was most select;
that is to say, it consisted of everybody who was then at
the Baths: those who had been presented to his Highness having the privilege of introducing any number of their friends;
and those who had no friend to introduce them purchasing
tickets at an enormous price from Cracowsky, the wily Polish
Intendant. The entertainment was imperial; no expense and
no exertion were spared to make the hired lodging-house look
like a hereditary palace; and for a week previous to the great
evening the whole of the neighboring town of Wiesbaden, the
little capital of the duchy, had been put under contribution.
What a harvest for Cracowsky! What a commission from the
restaurateur for supplying the refreshments! What a per-
centage on hired mirrors and dingy hangings!

The Grand Duke, covered with orders, received every one
with the greatest condescension, and made to each of his guests
a most flattering speech. His suite, in new uniforms, simultaneously bowed directly the flattering speech was finished.

"Madame von Furstenburg, I feel the greatest pleasure in
seeing you. My greatest pleasure is to be surrounded by my
friends. Madame von Furstenburg, I trust that your amiable
and delightful family are quite well. [The party passed on.]
Cravatischeff!" continued his Highness, inclining his head
round to one of his aides-de-camp, "Cravatischeff! a very
fine woman is Madame von Furstenburg. There are few
women whom I more admire than Madame von Furstenburg.

"Prince Salvinski, I feel the greatest pleasure in seeing
you. My greatest pleasure is to be surrounded by my friends.
Póland honors no one more than Prince Salvinski. Cravatischeff! a remarkable bore is Prince Salvinski. There are few
men of whom I have a greater terror than Prince Salvinski.

"Baron von Konigstein, I feel the greatest pleasure in see-

ing you. My greatest pleasure is to be surrounded by my
friends. Baron von Konigstein, I have not yet forgotten the
story of the fair Venetian. Cravatischeff! an uncommonly
pleasant fellow is Baron von Konigstein. There are few
men whose company I more enjoy than Baron von Konigstein's.

"Count von Altenburgh, I feel the greatest pleasure in seeing you. My greatest pleasure is to be surrounded by my
friends. You will not forget to give me your opinion of my
Austrian troupe. Cravatischeff! a very good billiard player is
Count von Altenburgh. There are few men whose play I
would sooner bet upon than Count von Altenburgh's.

"Lady Madeleine Trevor, I feel the greatest pleasure in
seeing you. My greatest pleasure is to be surrounded by my
friends. Miss Fane, your servant; Mr. St. George, Mr. Grey.
Cravatischeff! a most splendid woman is Lady Madeleine
Trevor. There is no woman whom I more admire than Lady
Madeleine Trevor! and Cravatischeff! Miss Fane, too! a remarkably fine girl is Miss Fane."

The great saloon of the New House afforded excellent accommodation for the dancers. It opened on the gardens, which,
though not very large, were tastefully laid out, and were this
evening brilliantly illuminated. In the smaller saloon the Austrian troupe amused those who were not fascinated by waltz
or quadrille with acting proverbs: the regular dramatic performance was thought too heavy a business for the evening.
There was sufficient amusement for all; and those who did
not dance, and to whom proverbs were no novelty, walked and
talked, stared at others, and were themselves stared at; and
this, perhaps, was the greatest amusement of all. Baron von
Konigstein did certainly to-night look neither like an unsuccessful gamester nor a designing villain. Among many who
were really amusing he was the most so, and, apparently without the least consciousness of it, attracted the admiration of all.
To the Trevor party he had attached himself immediately, and
was constantly at Lady Madeleine's side, introducing to her,
in the course of the evening, his own and Mr. St. George's
particular friends, Mr. and Mrs. Fitzloom. Among many
smiling faces Vivian Grey's was clouded; the presence of the
Baron annoyed him. When they first met he was conscious

that he was stiff and cool. One moment's reflection convinced him of the folly of his conduct, and he made a struggle to be very civil. In five minutes' time he had involuntarily insulted the Baron, who stared at his friend, and evidently did not comprehend him.

"Grey," said his Excellency, very quietly, "you are not in a good humor to-night. What is the matter? This is not at all a temper to come to a fête in. What! won't Miss Fane dance with you?" asked the Baron, with an arch smile.

"I wonder what can induce your Excellency to talk such nonsense!"

"Your Excellency! by Jove, that's good! What the deuce is the matter with the man? It is Miss Fane, then, eh?"

"Baron von Konigstein, I wish you to understand—"

"My dear fellow, I never could understand anything. I think you have insulted me in a most disgraceful manner, and I positively must call you out, unless you promise to dine at my rooms with me to-morrow, to meet De Bœffleurs."

"I can not."

"Why not? You have no engagement with Lady Madeleine, I know, for St. George has agreed to come."

"Yes?"

"De Bœffleurs leaves Ems next week. It is sooner than he expected, and I wish to have a quiet evening together before he goes. I should be very vexed if you were not there. We have scarcely been enough together lately. What with the New House in the evening, and riding parties in the morning, and those Fitzloom girls, with whom St. George is playing a most foolish game—he will be taken in now if he is not on his guard—we really never meet, at least not in a quiet friendly way; and so now, will you come?"

"St. George is positively coming?"

"Oh, yes! positively; do not be afraid of his gaining ground on the little Violet in your absence."

"Well, then, my dear Von Konigstein, I will come."

"Well, that is yourself again. It made me quite unhappy to see you look so sour and melancholy; one would have thought that I was some bore, Salvinski at least, by the way you spoke to me. Well, mind you; it is a promise, good. I must go and say just one word to the lovely little Saxon girl; by the bye,

Grey, one word before I am off. List to a friend; you are on
the wrong scent about Miss Fane; St. George, I think, has no
chance there, and now no wish to succeed. The game is
your own, if you like; trust my word, she is an angel.
The good powers prosper you!" So saying, the Baron
glided off.

Mr. St. George had danced with Miss Fane the only quadrille in which Lady Madeleine allowed her to join. He was
now waltzing with Aurelia Fitzloom, and was at the head of
a band of adventurous votaries of Terpsichore; who, wearied
with the commonplace convenience of a saloon, had ventured
to invoke the muse on the lawn.

"A most interesting sight, Lady Madeleine!" said Mr.
Fitzloom, as he offered her his arm, and advised their instant
presence as patrons of the "Fête du Village," for such Baron
von Konigstein had most happily termed it. "A delightful
man, that Baron von Konigstein, and says such delightful
things! Fête du Village! how very good!"

"That is Miss Fitzloom, then, whom my brother is waltzing with?" asked Lady Madeleine.

"Not exactly, my Lady," said Mr. Fitzloom, "not exactly
Miss Fitzloom, rather Miss Aurelia Fitzloom, my third daughter; our third eldest, as Mrs. Fitzloom sometimes says; for
really it is necessary to distinguish, with such a family as ours,
you know."

"Let us walk," said Miss Fane to Vivian, for she was now
leaning upon his arm; "the evening is deliciously soft, but even
with the protection of a cashmere I scarcely dare venture to
stand still. Lady Madeleine seems very much engaged at present. What amusing people these Fitzlooms are!"

"Mrs. Fitzloom; I have not heard her voice yet."

"No; Mrs. Fitzloom does not talk. Albert says she makes
it a rule never to speak in the presence of a stranger. She
deals plenteously, however, at home in domestic apophthegms.
If you could but hear him imitating them all! Whenever she
does speak, she finishes all her sentences by confessing that she
is conscious of her own deficiencies, but that she has taken care
to give her daughters the very best education. They are what
Albert calls fine girls, and I am glad he has made friends with
them; for, after all, he must find it rather dull here. By the

bye, Mr. Grey, I am afraid that you can not find this evening very amusing; the absence of a favorite pursuit always makes a sensible void, and these walls must remind you of more piquant pleasures than waltzing with fine London ladies, or promenading up a dull terrace with an invalid."

"I assure you that you are quite misinformed as to the mode in which I generally pass my evenings."

"I hope I am!" said Miss Fane, in rather a serious tone. "I wish I could also be mistaken in my suspicions of the mode in which Albert spends his time. He is sadly changed. For the first month that we were here he seemed to prefer nothing in the world to our society, and now—I was nearly saying that we had not seen him for one single evening these three weeks. I can not understand what you find at this house of such absorbing interest. Although I know you think I am much mistaken in my suspicions, still I feel very anxious. I spoke to Albert to-day, but he scarcely answered me; or said that which it was a pleasure for me to forget."

"Mr. St. George should feel highly gratified in having excited such an interest in the mind of Miss Fane."

"He should not feel more gratified than all who are my friends; for all who are such I must ever experience the liveliest interest."

"How happy must those be who feel that they have a right to count Miss Fane among their friends!"

"I have the pleasure then, I assure you, of making many happy, and among them Mr. Grey."

Vivian was surprised that he did not utter some complimentary answer; but, he knew not why, the words would not come; and instead of speaking, he was thinking of what had been spoken.

"How brilliant are these gardens!" said Vivian, looking at the sky.

"Very brilliant!" said Miss Fane, looking on the ground. Conversation seemed nearly extinct and yet neither offered to turn back.

"Good heavens! you are ill," exclaimed Vivian, when, on accidentally turning to his companion, he found she was in tears. Shall we go back, or will you wait here? Can I fetch anything? I fear you are very ill!"

"No, not very ill, but very foolish; let us walk on," and, sighing, she seemed suddenly to recover.

"I am ashamed of this foolishness; what can you think? But I am so agitated, so nervous. I hope you will forget—I hope—"

"Perhaps the air has suddenly affected you. Shall we go in? Nothing has been said, nothing happened; no one has dared to say or do anything to annoy you? Speak, dear Miss Fane, the, the—" the words died on Vivian's lips, yet a power he could not understand urged him to speak—"the, the, the Baron?"

"Ah!" almost shrieked Miss Fane. "Stop one second; an effort, and I must be well; nothing has happened, and no one has done or said anything; but it is of something that should be said, of something that should be done, that I was thinking, and it overcame me."

"Miss Fane," said Vivian, "if there be anything which I can do or devise, any possible way that I can exert myself in your service, speak with the most perfect confidence; do not fear that your motives will be misconceived, that your purpose will be misinterpreted, that your confidence will be misunderstood. You are addressing one who would lay down his life for you, who is willing to perform all your commands, and forget them when performed. I beseech you to trust me; believe me, that you shall not repent."

She answered not, but holding down her head, covered her face with her small white hand; her lovely face which was crimsoned with her flashing blood. They were now at the end of the terrace; to return was impossible. If they remained stationary, they must be perceived and joined. What was to be done? He led her down a retired walk still further from the house. As they proceeded in silence, the bursts of the music and the loud laughter of the joyous guests became fainter and fainter, till at last the sounds died away into echo, and echo into silence.

A thousand thoughts dashed through Vivian's mind in rapid succession; but a painful one, a most painful one to him, to any man, always remained the last. His companion would not speak; yet to allow her to return home without freeing her mind of the fearful burden which evidently overwhelmed it was impossible. At length he broke a silence which seemed to have lasted an age.

"Do not believe that I am taking advantage of an agitating moment to extract from you a confidence which you may repent. I feel assured that I am right in supposing that you have contemplated in a calmer moment the possibility of my being of service to you; that, in short, there is something in which you require my assistance, my co-operation; an assistance, a co-operation, which, if it produce any benefit to you, will make me at length feel that I have not lived in vain. No feeling of false delicacy shall prevent me from assisting you in giving utterance to thoughts which you have owned it is absolutely necessary should be expressed. Remember that you have allowed me to believe that we are friends; do not prove by your silence that we are friends only in name."

"I am overwhelmed; I can not speak. My face burns with shame; I have miscalculated my strength of mind; perhaps my physical strength; what, what must you think of me?" She spoke in a low and smothered voice.

"Think of you! everything which the most devoted respect dare think of an object which it reverences. Do not believe that I am one who would presume an instant on my position, because I have accidentally witnessed a young and lovely woman betrayed into a display of feeling which the artificial forms of cold society can not contemplate and dare to ridicule. You are speaking to one who also has felt; who, though a man, has wept; who can comprehend sorrow; who can understand the most secret sensations of an agitated spirit. Dare to trust me. Be convinced that hereafter, neither by word nor look, hint nor sign, on my part, shall you feel, save by your own wish, that you have appeared to Vivian Grey in any other light than in the saloons we have just quitted."

"Generous man, I dare trust anything to you that I dare trust to human being; but—" here her voice died away.

"It is a painful thing for me to attempt to guess your thoughts; but if it be of Mr. St. George that you are thinking, have no fear respecting him; have no fear about his present situation. Trust to me that there shall be no anxiety for his future one. I will be his unknown guardian, his unseen friend; the promoter of your wishes, the protector of your—"

"No, no," said Miss Fane, with firmness, and looking quickly up, as if her mind were relieved by discovering that all this time Vivian had never imagined she was thinking of him. "No, no, you are mistaken; it is not of Mr. St. George, of Mr. St. George only, that I am thinking. I am much better now; I shall be able in an instant to speak; be able, I trust, to forget how foolish, how very foolish I have been."

"Let us walk on," continued Miss Fane, "let us walk on; we can easily account for our absence if it be remarked; and it is better that it should be all over. I feel quite well, and shall be able to speak quite firmly now."

"Do not hurry; there is no fear of our absence being remarked, Lady Madeleine is so surrounded."

"After what has passed, it seems ridiculous in me to apologize, as I had intended, for speaking to you on a graver subject than what has generally formed the point of conversation between us. I feared that you might misunderstand the motives which have dictated my conduct. I have attempted not to appear agitated, and I have been overcome. I trust that you will not be offended if I recur to the subject of the New House. Do not believe that I ever would have allowed my fears, my girlish fears, so to have overcome my discretion; so to have overcome, indeed, all propriety of conduct on my part as to have induced me to have sought an interview with you, to moralize to you about your mode of life. No, no; it is not of this that I wish to speak, or rather that I will speak. I will hope, I will pray, that Albert and yourself have never found in that which you have followed as an amusement the source, the origin, the cause of a single unhappy or even anxious moment; Mr. Grey, I will believe all this."

"Dearest Miss Fane, believe it with confidence. Of St. George, I can with sincerity aver that it is my firm opinion that, far from being involved, his fortune is not in the slightest degree injured. Believe me, I will not attempt to quiet you now, as I would have done at any other time, by telling you that you magnify your fears, and allow your feelings to exaggerate the danger which exists. There has been danger. There is danger; play, high play, has been and is pursued at this New House, but Mr. St. George has never been a loser; and if the exertions of man can avail, never shall, at least unfairly. As to the other individual, whom you have honored by the interest which you have professed in his welfare, no one can more thoroughly detest any practice which exists in this world than he does the gaming-table."

"Oh! you have made me so happy! I feel so persuaded that you have not deceived me! the tones of your voice, your manner, your expression, convince me that you have been sincere, and that I am happy, at least for the present."

"Forever, I trust, Miss Fane."

"Let me now prevent future misery. Let me speak about that which has long dwelt on my mind like a nightmare, about that which I did fear it was almost too late to speak. Not of your pursuit, not even of that fatal pursuit, do I now think, but of your companion in this amusement, in all amusements! it is he, he whom I dread, whom I look upon with horror, even to him, I can not say, with hatred!"

"The Baron?" said Vivian, calmly.

"I can not name him. Dread him, fear him, avoid him! it is he that I mean, he of whom I thought that you were the victim. You must have been surprised, you must have wondered at our conduct toward him. Oh! when Lady Madeleine turned from him with coldness, when she answered him in tones which to you might have appeared harsh, she behaved to him, in comparison to what is his due, and what we sometimes feel to be our duty, with affection, actually with affection and regard. No human being can know what horror is until he looks upon a fellow-creature with the eyes that I look upon that man." She leaned upon Vivian's arm with her whole weight, and even then he thought she must have sunk; neither spoke. How solemn is the silence of sorrow!

"I am overcome," continued Miss Fane; "the remembrance of what he has done overwhelms me. I can not speak it; the recollection is death; yet you must know it. That you might know it, I have before attempted. I wished to have spared myself the torture which I now endure. You must know it. I will write; ay! that will do. I will write; I can not speak now; it is impossible; but beware of him; you are so young."

"I have no words now to thank you, dear Miss Fane, for this. Had I been the victim of Von Konigstein, I should have been repaid for all my misery by feeling that you regretted its infliction; but I trust that I am in no danger: though young, I fear that I am one who must not count his time by calendars. 'An aged interpreter, though young in days.' Would that I could be deceived! Fear not for your cousin. Trust to one whom you have made think better of this world, and of his fellow-creatures."

The sound of approaching footsteps, and the light laugh of pleasure, told of some who were wandering like themselves.

"We had better return," said Miss Fane; "I fear that Lady Madeleine will observe that I look unwell. Some one approaches! No, they pass only the top of the walk." It was Mr. St. George and Aurelia Fitzloom.

Quick flew the brilliant hours; and soon the dance was over, and the music mute.

It was late when Vivian retired. As he opened his door he was surprised to find lights in his chamber. The figure of a man appeared seated at the table. It moved; it was Essper George.

CHAPTER XIII

THE reader will remember that Vivian had agreed to dine, on the day after the fête, with the Baron, in his private apartments. This was an arrangement which, in fact, the custom of the house did not permit; but the irregularities of great men who are attended by chasseurs are occasionally winked at by a supple *maître d'hôtel*. Vivian had reasons for not regretting his acceptance of the invitation; and he never shook hands with the Chevalier de Bœffleurs, apparently, with greater cordiality than on the day on which he met him at dinner at the Baron von Konigstein's. Mr. St. George had not arrived.

"Past five!" said the Baron; "riding out, I suppose, with the Fitzlooms. Aurelia is certainly a fine girl; but I should think that Lady Madeleine would hardly approve the connection. The St. Georges have blood in their veins; and would, I suppose, as soon think of marrying a Fitzloom as we Germans should of marrying a woman without a *von* before her name. We are quite alone, Grey, only the Chevalier and St. George. I had an idea of asking Salvinski, but he is such a regular steam-engine, and began such a long story last night about his interview with the King of Ashantee, that the bare possibility of his taking it into his head to finish it to-day frightened me. You were away early from the Grand Duke's last night. The business went off well."

"Very well, indeed!" said the Chevalier de Bœffleurs, completing by this speech the first dozen of words which he had uttered since his stay at Ems.

"I think that last night Lady Madeleine Trevor looked perfectly magnificent; and a certain lady, too, Grey, eh? Here is St. George. My dear fellow, how are you? Has the fair Aurelia recovered from the last night's fatigues? Now, Ernstorff, dinner as soon as possible."

The Baron made up to-day, certainly, for the silence of his friend the Chevalier. He outdid himself. Story after story, adventure after adventure, followed each other with exciting haste. In fact, the Baron never ceased talking the whole dinner, except when he refreshed himself with wine, which he drank copiously. A nice observer would, perhaps, have considered the Baron's high spirits artificial, and his conversation an effort. Yet his temper, though lively, was generally equable; and his ideas, which always appeared to occur easily, were usually thrown out in fluent phraseology. The dinner was long, and a great deal of wine was drank; more than most of the parties present for a long time had been accustomed to. About eight o'clock the Chevalier proposed going to the Redoute, but the Baron objected.

"Let us have an evening all together: surely we have had enough of the Redoute. In my opinion one of the advantages of the fête is, that there is no New House to-night. Conversation is a novelty. On a moderate calculation I must have told you to-day at least fifty original anecdotes. I have done my duty. It is the Chevalier's turn now. Come, De Bœffleurs, a choice one!"

"I remember a story Prince Salvinski once told me."

"No, no, that is too bad; none of that Polish bear's romances; if we have his stories, we may as well have his company."

"But it is a very curious story," continued the Chevalier, with a little animation.

"Oh! so is every story, according to the storier."

"I think, Von Konigstein, you imagine no one can tell a story but yourself," said De Bœffleurs, actually indignant. Vivian had never heard him speak so much before, and really began to believe that he was not quite an automaton.

"Let us have it!" said St. George.

"It is a story told of a Polish nobleman, a Count somebody: I never can remember their crack-jaw names. Well! the point is this," said the silent little Chevalier, who apparently already repented of the boldness of his offer, and, misdoubting his powers, wished to begin with the end of his tale: "the point is this, he was playing one day at ecarté with the Governor of Wilna; the stake was trifling, but he had a bet, you see, with the Governor of a thousand roubles; a bet with the Governor's secretary, never mind the amount, say two hundred and fifty, you see; then, he went on the turn-up with the Commandant's wife; and took the pips on the trumps with the Archbishop of Warsaw. To understand the point of the story, you see, you must have a distinct conception how the game stood. You see, St. George, there was the bet with the Governor, one thousand roubles; the Governor's secretary, never mind the amount, say two hundred and fifty; turn-up with the Commandant's lady, and the pips with the Archbishop of Warsaw. Proposed three times, one for the king, the Governor drew ace; the Governor was already three and the ten. When the Governor scored king, the Archbishop gave the odds, drew knave queen one hand. The Count offered to propose fourth time. Governor refused. King to six, ace fell to knave, queen cleared on. Governor lost, besides bets with the whole état-major; the Secretary gave his bill; the Commandant's lady pawned her jewels; and the Archbishop was done on the pips!"

"By Jove, what a Salvinski!"

"How many trumps had the Governor?" asked St. George.
"Three," said the Chevalier.

"Then it is impossible: I do not believe the story; it could not be."

"I beg your pardon," said the Chevalier; "you see the Governor had—"

"By Jove, don't let us have it all over again!" said the Baron. "Well! if this be your model for an after-dinner anecdote, which ought to be as piquant as an anchovy toast, I will never complain of your silence in future."

"The story is a true story," said the Chevalier; "have you got a pack of cards, Von Konigstein? I will show it you."

"There is not such a thing in the room," said the Baron.

"Well, I never heard of a room without a pack of cards before," said the Chevalier. "I will send for one to my own apartments."

"Perhaps Ernstorff has got a pack. Here, Ernstorff, have you got a pack of cards? That's well; bring it immediately."

The cards were brought, and the Chevalier began to fight his battle over again; but could not satisfy Mr. St. George. "You see, there was the bet with the Governor, and the pips, as I said before, with the Archbishop of Warsaw."

"My dear De Bœffleurs, let's have no more of this. If you like to have a game of ecarté with St. George, well and good; but as for quarreling the whole evening about some blundering lie of Salvinski's, it really is too much. You two can play and I can talk to Don Vivian, who, by the bye, is rather of the rueful countenance to-night. Why, my dear fellow, I have not heard your voice this evening: frightened by the fate of the Archbishop of Warsaw, I suppose?"

"Ecarté is so devilish dull," said St. George; "and it is such a trouble to deal."

"I will deal for both, if you like," said De Bœffleurs; "I am used to dealing."

"Oh! no, I won't play ecarté; let us have something in which we can all join."

"Rouge-et-noir," suggested the Chevalier, in a careless tone, as if he had no taste for the amusement.

"There is not enough, is there?" asked St. George.

"Oh! two are enough, you know."

"Well, I don't care; rouge-et-noir then, let us have rouge-et-noir. Von Konigstein, what say you to rouge-et-noir? De Bœffleurs says we can play it here very well. Come, Grey."

"Oh! rouge-et-noir, rouge-et-noir," said the Baron; "have not you both had rouge-et-noir enough? Am I not to be allowed one holiday? Well, anything to please you; so rouge-et-noir, if it must be so."

"If all wish it, I have no objection," said Vivian.

"Well, then, let us sit down; Ernstorff has, I dare say, another pack of cards, and St. George will be dealer; I know he likes that ceremony."

"No, no; I appoint the Chevalier."

"Very well," said De Bœffleurs, "the plan will be for two to bank against the table; the table to play on the same color by joint agreement. You can join me, Von Konigstein, and pay or receive with me, from Mr. St. George and Grey."

"I will bank with you, if you like, Chevalier," said Vivian.

"Oh! certainly; that is if you like. But perhaps the Baron is more used to banking; you perhaps don't understand it."

"Perfectly; it appears to me to be very simple."

"No, don't you bank, Grey," said St. George. "I want you to play with me against the Chevalier and the Baron; I like your luck."

"Luck is very capricious, remember."

"Oh, no, I like your luck; don't bank."

"Be it so."

Playing commenced. An hour elapsed, and the situation of none of the parties was materially different from what it had been when they began the game. Vivian proposed leaving off; but Mr. St. George avowed that he felt very fortunate, and that he had a presentiment that he should win. Another hour elapsed, and he had lost considerably. Eleven o'clock: Vivian's luck had also deserted him. Mr. St. George was losing desperately. Midnight: Vivian had lost back half his gains on the season. St. George still more desperate, all his coolness had deserted him. He had persisted obstinately against a run on the red; then floundered and got entangled in a seesaw, which alone cost him a thousand.

Ernstorff now brought in refreshments; and for a moment they ceased playing. The Baron opened a bottle of champagne; and St. George and the Chevalier were stretching their legs and composing their minds in very different ways, the first in walking rapidly up and down the room, and the other by lying very quietly at his full length on the sofa; Vivian was employed in building houses with the cards.

"Grey," said the Chevalier de Bœffleurs, "I can not imagine why you do not for a moment try to forget the cards: that is the only way to win. Never sit musing over the table."

But Grey was not to be persuaded to give up building his pagoda: which, now many stories high, like a more celebrated but scarcely more substantial structure, fell with a crash. Vivian collected the scattered cards into two divisions.

"Now!" said the Baron, seating himself, "for St. George's revenge."

The Chevalier and the greatest sufferer took their places.

"Is Ernstorff coming in again, Baron?" asked Vivian.

"No! I think not."

"Let us be sure; it is disagreeable to be disturbed at this time of night."

"Lock the door, then," said St. George.

"A very good plan," said Vivian; and he locked it accordingly.

"Now, gentlemen," said Vivian, rising from the table, and putting both packs of cards into his pocket; "now, gentlemen, I have another game to play." The Chevalier started on his chair, the Baron turned pale, but both were silent. "Mr. St. George," continued Vivian, "I think that you owe the Chevalier de Bœffleurs about four thousand Napoleons, and to Baron von Konigstein something more than half that sum. I have to inform you that it is unnecessary for you to satisfy the claims of either of these gentlemen, which are founded neither in law nor in honor."

"Mr. Grey, what am I to understand?" asked the quiet Chevalier de Bœffleurs, with the air of a wolf and the voice of a lion.

"Understand, sir!" answered Vivian, sternly, "that I am not one who will be bullied by a blackleg."

"Grey! good God! what do you mean?" asked the Baron.

"That which it is my duty, not my pleasure, to explain, Baron von Konigstein."

"If you mean to insinuate," burst forth the Chevalier.

"I mean to insinuate nothing. I leave insinuations and innuendoes to *chevaliers d'industrie*. I mean to prove everything."

Mr. St. George did not speak, but seemed as utterly astounded and overwhelmed as Baron von Konigstein himself, who, with his arm leaning on the table, his hands clasped, and the forefinger of his right hand playing convulsively on his left, was pale as death, and did not even breathe.

"Gentlemen," said Vivian, "I shall not detain you long, though I have much to say that is to the purpose. I am perfectly cool, and, believe me, perfectly resolute. Let me recommend to you all the same temperament; it may be better for you. Rest assured, that if you flatter yourselves that I am one to be pigeoned and then bullied, you are mistaken. In one word, I am aware of everything that has been arranged for the reception of Mr. St. George and myself this evening. Your marked cards are in my pocket, and can only be obtained by you with my life. Here are two of us against two; we are equally matched in number, and I, gentlemen, am armed. If I were not, you would not dare to go to extremities. Is it not, then, the wisest course to be temperate, my friends?"

"This is some vile conspiracy of your own, fellow," said De Bœffleurs: "marked cards, indeed! a pretty tale, forsooth! The Ministers of a first-rate Power playing with marked cards! The story will gain credit, and on the faith of whom? An adventurer that no one knows, who, having failed this night in his usual tricks, and lost money which he can not pay, takes advantage of the marked cards, which he has not succeeded in introducing, and pretends, forsooth, that they are those which he has stolen from our table; our own cards being, previously to his accusation, concealed in a secret pocket."

The impudence of the fellow staggered even Vivian. As for Mr. St. George, he stared like a wild man. Before Vivian could answer him the Baron had broken silence. It was with the greatest effort that he seemed to dig his words out of his breast.

"No, no; this is too much! It is all over! I am lost; but I will not add crime to crime. Your courage and your fortune have saved you, Mr. Grey, and your friend from the designs of villains. And you! wretch," said he, turning to De Bœffleurs, "sleep now in peace; at length you have undone me." He leaned on the table and buried his face in his hands.

"Chicken-hearted fool!" said the Chevalier; "is this the end of all your promises and all your pledges? But remember, sir! remember. I have no taste for scenes. Good-night, gentlemen. Baron, I expect to hear from you."

"Stop, sir!" said Vivian; "no one leaves this room without my permission."

"I am at your service, sir, when you please," said the Chevalier.

"It is not my intention to detain you long, sir; far from it. I have every inclination to assist you in your last exit from this room; had I time, it should not be by the door. As it is, go! in the devil's name." So saying he hurled the adventurous Frenchman half down the corridor.

"Baron von Konigstein," said Vivian, turning to the Baron, "you have proved yourself, by your conduct this evening, to be a better man than I imagined you. I confess that I thought you had been much too accustomed to such scenes to be sensible of the horror of detection."

"Never!" said the Baron, with emphasis, with energy. The firm voice and manner in which he pronounced this single word wonderfully contrasted with his delivery when he had last spoken; but his voice immediately died away.

" 'Tis all over! I have no wish to excite your pity, gentlemen, or to gain your silence, by practicing upon your feelings. Be silent. I am not the less ruined, not the less disgraced, not the less utterly undone. Be silent; my honor, all the same, in four-and-twenty hours, has gone forever. I have no motive, then, to deceive you. You must believe what I speak; even what *I* speak, the most degraded of men. I say again, *never,* never, never, never, never was my honor before sullied, though guilty of a thousand follies. You see before you, gentlemen, the unhappy victim of circumstances; of circumstances which he has in vain struggled to control, to which he has at length fallen a victim. I am not pretending, for a moment, that my crimes are to be accounted for by an inexorable fate, and not to be expiated by my everlasting misery. No, no! I have been too weak to be virtuous; but I have been tried, tried most bitterly. I am the most unfortunate of men; I was not born to be a villain. Four years have passed since I was banished from the country in which I was honored, my prospects in life blasted, my peace of mind destroyed; and all because a crime was committed of any participation in which I am as innocent as yourselves. Driven in despair to wander, I tried in the wild dissipation of Naples to forget my existence and my misery. I found my fate in the person of this vile Frenchman, who never since has quitted me. Even after two years of madness in that fatal place, my natural disposition rallied; I struggled to save myself; I quitted it. I was already involved to De Bœffleurs; I became still more so, in gaining from him the means of satisfying all claims against me. Alas! I found I had sold myself to a devil, a very devil, with a heart like an adder's. Incapable of a stray generous sensation, he has looked upon mankind during his whole life with the eyes of a bully of a gaming-house. I still struggled to free myself from this man; and I indemnified him for his advances by procuring him a place in the mission to which, with the greatest difficulty and perseverance, I had at length obtained my appointment. In public life I yet hoped to forget my private misery. At Frankfort I felt that, though not happy, I might be calm. I determined never again even to run the risk of enduring the slavery of debt. I foreswore, with the most solemn oaths, the gaming table; and had it not been for the perpetual sight of De Bœffleurs, I might, perhaps, have felt at ease; though the remembrance of my blighted prospects, the eternal feeling that I experienced of being born for nobler ends, was quite sufficient perpetually to imbitter my existence. The second year of my Frankfort appointment I was tempted to this unhappy place. The unexpected sight of faces which I had known in England, though they called up the most painful associations, strengthened me, nevertheless, in my resolution to be virtuous. My unexpected fortune at the Redoute, the first night, made me forget all my resolves, and has led to all this misery. I make my sad tale brief. I got involved at the New House: De Bœffleurs once more assisted me, though his terms were most severe. Yet, yet again, I was mad enough, vile enough, to risk what I did not possess. I lost to Prince Salvinski and a Russian gentleman a considerable sum on the night before the fête. It is often the custom at the New House, as you know, among men who are acquainted, to pay and receive all losses which are considerable on the next night of meeting. The fête gave me breathing time: it was not necessary to redeem my pledge till the fourth night. I rushed to De Bœffleurs; he refused to assist me, alleging his own losses and his previous advance. What was to be done? No possibility of making any arrangement with Salvinski. Had he won of me as others have done, an arrangement, though painful, would perhaps have been possible; but, by a singular fate, whenever I have chanced to be successful, it is of this man that I have won. De Bœffleurs, then, was the only chance. He was inexorable. I prayed to him; I promised him everything; I offered him any terms; in vain! At length, when he had worked me up to the last point of despair, he whispered hope. I listened; let me be quick! why finish? You know I fell!" The Baron again covered his face, and appeared perfectly overwhelmed.

"By God! it is too horrible," said St. George. "Grey, let us do something for him."

"My dear St. George," said Vivian, "be calm. You are taken by surprise. I was prepared for all this. Believe me, it is better for you to leave us. I recommend you to retire, and meet me in the morning. Breakfast with me at eight; we can then arrange everything."

Vivian's conduct had been so decisive, and evidently so well matured, that St. George felt that, in the present case, it was for him only to obey, and he retired with wonder still expressed on his countenance; for he had not yet, in the slightest degree, recovered from the first surprise.

"Baron von Konigstein," said Vivian to the unhappy man, "we are alone. Mr. St. George has left the room: you are freed from the painful presence of the cousin of Captain Fane."

"You know all, then!" exclaimed the Baron quickly, looking up, "or you have read my secret thoughts. How wonderful! at that very moment I was thinking of my friend. Would I had died with him! You know all, then; and now you must believe me guilty. Yet, at this moment of annihilating sorrow, when I can gain nothing by deceit, I swear; and if I swear falsely, may I fall down a livid corpse at your feet; I swear that I was guiltless of the crime for which I suffered, guiltless as yourself. What may be my fate I know not. Probably a few hours, and all will be over. Yet, before we part, sir, it would be a relief; you would be doing a generous service to a dying man to bear a message from me to one with whom you are acquainted; to one whom I can not now name."

"Lady Madeleine Trevor?"

"Again you have read my thoughts! Lady Madeleine! Is it she who told you of my early history?"

"All that I know is known to many."

"I must speak! If you have time, if you can listen for half an hour to a miserable being, it would be a consolation to me. I should die with ease if I thought that Lady Madeleine could believe me innocent of that first great offence."

"Your Excellency may address anything to me, if it be your wish, even at this hour of the night. It may be better; after what has passed, we neither of us can sleep, and this business must be arranged at once."

"My object is, that Lady Madeleine should receive from me at this moment, at a time when I can have no interest to deceive, an account of the particulars of her cousin's and my friend's death. I sent it written after the horrid event; but she was ill, and Trevor, who was very bitter against me, returned the letters unopened. For four years I have never traveled without these rejected letters; this year I have them not. But you could convey to Lady Madeleine my story, as now given to you; to you at this terrible moment."

"Speak on!"

"I must say one word of my connection with the family to enable you fully to understand the horrid event, of which, if, as I believe, you only know what all know, you can form but a most imperfect conception. When I was Minister at the Court of London I became acquainted, became, indeed, intimate, with Mr. Trevor, then in office, the husband of Lady Madeleine. She was just married. Of myself at that time, I may say that, though depraved, I was not heartless, and that there were moments when I panted to be excellent. Lady Madeleine and myself became friends; she found in me a companion who not only respected her talents and delighted in her conversation, but one who in return was capable of instructing, and was overjoyed to amuse her. I loved her; but when I loved her I ceased to be a libertine. At first I thought that nothing in the world could have tempted me to have allowed her for an instant to imagine that I dared to look upon her in any other light than as a friend; but the negligence, the coldness of Trevor, the overpowering mastery of my own passions, drove me one day past the line, and I wrote that which I dared not utter. It never entered into my mind for an instant to insult such a woman with the commonplace sophistry of a ribald. No! I loved her with all my spirit's strength. I would have sacrificed all my views in life, my ambition, my family, my fortune, my country, to have gained her; and I told her this in terms of respectful adoration. I worshiped the divinity, even while I attempted to profane the altar. When I had sent this letter I was in despair. Conviction of the insanity of my conduct flashed across my mind. I expected never to see her again. There came an answer; I opened it with the greatest agitation; to my surprise, an appointment. Why trouble you with a detail of my feelings, my mad hope, my dark despair! The moment for the interview arrived. I was received neither with affection nor anger. In sorrow she spoke. I listened in despair. I was more madly in love with her than ever. That very love made me give her such evidences of a contrite spirit that I was pardoned. I rose with a resolution to be virtuous, with a determination to be her friend: then I made the fatal promise which you know of, to be doubly the friend of a man whose friend I already was. It was then that I pledged myself to Lady Madeleine to be the guardian spirit of her cousin." Here the Baron, overpowered by his emotions, leaned back in his chair and ceased to speak. In a few minutes he resumed.

"I did my duty; by all that's sacred, I did my duty! Night and day I was with young Fane. A hundred times he was on the brink of ruin; a hundred times I saved him. One day, one never-to-be-forgotten day, one most dark and damnable day, I called on him, and found him on the point of joining a coterie of desperate character. I remonstrated with him, I entreated, I supplicated him not to go; in vain. At last he

agreed to forego his engagement on condition that I dined
with him. There were important reasons that day for my not
staying with him; yet every consideration vanished when I
thought of her for whom I was exerting myself. He was
frantic this day; and, imagining that there was no chance of
his leaving his home, I did not refuse to drink freely, to drink
deeply! My doing so was the only way to keep him at home.
As we were passing down Pall Mall we met two foreigners
of distinction and a noble of your country; they were men of
whom we both knew little. I had myself introduced Fane to
the foreigners a few days before, being aware that they were
men of high rank. After some conversation they asked us to
join them at supper at the house of their English friend. I
declined; but nothing could induce Fane to refuse them, and I
finally accompanied him. Play was introduced after supper:
I made an ineffectual struggle to get Fane home, but I was
too full of wine to be energetic. After losing a small sum I
got up from the table, and, staggering to a sofa, fell fast
asleep. Even as I passed Fane's chair in this condition, my
master-thought was evident, and I pulled him by the shoulder:
all was useless; I woke to madness!" It was terrible to
witness the anguish of Von Konigstein.

"Could you not clear yourself?" asked Vivian, for he felt
it necessary to speak.

"Clear myself! Everything told against me. The villains were my friends, not the sufferer's; I was not injured.
My dining with him was part of the conspiracy; he was
intoxicated previous to his ruin. Conscious of my innocence,
quite desperate, but confiding in my character, I accused the
guilty trio; they recriminated and answered, and without
clearing themselves convinced the public that I was their dis-
satisfied and disappointed tool. I can speak no more."

It is awful to witness sudden death; but, oh! how much
more awful it is to witness in a moment the moral fall of a
fellow-creature! How tremendous is the quick succession
of mastering passions! The firm, the terrifically firm, the
madly resolute denial of guilt; that eagerness of protesta-
tion which is a sure sign of crime, then the agonizing suspense before the threatened proof is produced, the hell of
detection, the audible anguish of sorrow, the curses of re-

morse, the silence of despair! Few of us, unfortunately, have passed through life without having beheld some instance of this instantaneous degradation of human nature. But, oh! how terrible is it when the confessed criminal has been but a moment before our friend! What a contrast to the laugh of joyous companionship is the quivering tear of an agonized frame! how terrible to be prayed to by those whose wishes a moment before we lived only to anticipate!

"Von Konigstein," said Vivian, after a long silence, "I feel for you. Had I known this I would have spared both you and myself this night of misery; I would have prevented you from looking back to this day with remorse. You have suffered for that of which you were not guilty; you shall not suffer now for what has passed. Much would I give to see you freed from that wretched knave, whose vile career I was very nearly tempted this evening to have terminated forever. I shall make the communication you desire, and I will endeavor that it shall be credited; as to the transactions of this evening, the knowledge of them can never transpire to the world. It is the interest of De Bœffleurs to be silent; if he speak no one will credit the tale of such a creature, who, if he speak truth, must proclaim his own infamy. And now for the immediate calls upon your honor; in what sum are you indebted to Prince Salvinski and his friend?"

"Thousands! two, three thousand."

"I shall then have an opportunity of ridding myself of that the acquisition of which, to me, has been a matter of great sorrow. Your honor is saved. I will discharge the claims of Salvinski and his friend."

"Impossible! I can not allow—"

"Stop; in this business I must command. Surely there can be no feelings of delicacy between us two now. If I gave you the treasures of the Indies you would not be under so great an obligation to me as you are already: I say this with pain. I recommend you to leave Ems to-morrow; public business will easily account for your sudden departure. And now, your character is yet safe, you are yet in the prime of life, you have vindicated yourself from that which has preyed upon your mind for years; cease to accuse your fate!" Vivian was about to leave the room when the Baron started from his seat and seized his hand. He would have spoken, but the words died upon his lips, and before he could recover himself Vivian had retired.

CHAPTER XIV

THE sudden departure of Baron von Konigstein from the Baths excited great surprise and sorrow; all wondered at the cause, and all regretted the effect. The Grand Duke missed his good stories, the rouge-et-noir table his constant presence, and Monsieur le Restaurateur gave up, in consequence, an embryo idea of a fête and fireworks for his own benefit, which agreeable plan he had trusted that, with his Excellency's generous co-operation as patron, he should have no difficulty in carrying into execution. But no one was more surprised, and more regretted the absence of his Excellency, than his friend Mr. Fitzloom. What could be the reason? Public business, of course; indeed he had learned as much, confidentially, from Cracowsky. He tried Mr. Grey, but could elicit nothing satisfactory; he pumped Mr. St. George, but produced only the waters of oblivion; Mr. St. George was gifted, when it suited his purpose, with a most convenient want of memory. There must be something in the wind, perhaps a war. Was the independence of Greece about to be acknowledged, or the dependence of Spain about to be terminated? What first-rate Power had marched a million of soldiers into the land of a weak neighbor, on the mere pretence of exercising the military? What patriots had had the proud satisfaction of establishing a constitutional government without bloodshed, to be set aside in the course of the next month in the same manner? Had a conspiracy for establishing a republic in Russia been frustrated by the timely information of the intended first Consuls? Were the janizaries learning mathematics, or had Lord Cochrane taken Constantinople in the James Watt steam-packet? One of these many events must have happened; but which? At length Fitzloom decided on a general war. England must interfere either to defeat the ambition of France or to curb the rapacity of Russia, or to check the arrogance of Austria, or to regenerate Spain, or to redeem Greece, or to protect Portugal, or to shield the Brazils, or to uphold the Bible Societies, or to consolidate the Greek Church, or to monopolize the commerce of Mexico, or to disseminate the principles of free trade, or to keep up her high character, or to keep up the price of corn. England must interfere. In spite of his conviction, however, Fitzloom did not alter the arrangements of his tour; he still intended to travel for two years. All he did was to send immediate orders to his broker in England to sell two millions of consols. The sale was of course effected, the example followed, stocks fell ten per cent, the exchange turned, money became scarce. The public funds of all Europe experienced a great decline, smash went the country banks, consequent runs on London, a dozen Baronets failed in one morning, Portland Place deserted, the cause of infant Liberty at a terrific discount, the Greek loan disappeared like a vapor in a storm, all the new American States refused to pay their dividends, manufactories deserted, the revenue in a decline, the country in despair, Orders in Council, meetings of Parliament, change of Ministry, and new loan! Such were the terrific consequences of a diplomatist turning blackleg! The secret history of the late distress is a lesson to all modern statesmen. Rest assured that in politics, however tremendous the effects, the causes are often as trifling.

Vivian found his reception by the Trevor party, the morning after the memorable night, a sufficient reward for all his anxiety and exertion. St. George, a generous, open-hearted young man, full of gratitude to Vivian, and regretting his previous want of cordiality toward him, now delighted in doing full justice to his coolness, courage, and ability. Lady Madeleine said a great deal in the most graceful and impressive manner; but Miss Fane scarcely spoke. Vivian, however, read in her eyes her approbation and her gratitude.

"And now, how came you to discover the whole plot, Mr. Grey?" asked Lady Madeleine, "for we have not yet heard. Was it at the table?"

"They would hardly have had recourse to such clumsy instruments as would have given us the chance of detecting the conspiracy by casual observation. No, no; we owe our preservation and our gratitude to one whom we must hereafter count among our friends. I was prepared, as I told you, for everything; and though I had seen similar cards to those with which they played only a few hours before, it was with difficulty that I satisfied myself at the table that the cards we lost by were prepared, so wonderful is the contrivance!"

"But who is the unknown friend?" said Miss Fane, with great eagerness.

"I must have the pleasure of keeping you all in suspense," said Vivian: "can not any of you guess?"

"None, none, none!"

"What say you, then, to—Essper George?"

"Is it possible?"

"It is the fact that he, and he alone, is our preserver. Soon after my arrival at this place this singular being was seized with the unaccountable fancy of becoming my servant. You all remember his unexpected appearance one day in the saloon. In the evening of the same day, I found him sleeping at the door of my room; and, thinking it high time that he should be taught more discretion, I spoke to him very seriously the next morning respecting his troublesome and eccentric conduct. It was then that I learned his wish. I objected, of course, to engaging a servant of whose previous character I was ignorant, and of which I could not be informed, and one whose peculiar habits would render both himself and his master notorious. While I declined his services, I also advised him most warmly to give up all idea of deserting his present mode of life, for which I thought him extremely well suited. The consequence of my lecture was, what you all perceived with surprise, a great change in Essper's character. He became serious, reserved, and retiring, and commenced his career as a respectable character by throwing off his quaint costume. In a short time, by dint of making a few bad bargains, he ingratiated himself with Ernstorff, Von Konigstein's pompous chasseur. His object in forming this connection was to gain an opportunity of becoming acquainted with the duties of a gentleman's servant, and in this he has succeeded. About a week since, he purchased from Ernstorff a large quantity of cast-off apparel of the Baron's, and other perquisites of a great man's valet; among these were some playing cards which had been borrowed one evening in great haste from the servant of that rascal De Bœffleurs, and never returned. On accidentally examining these cards, Essper detected they were marked. The system on which the marks are formed and understood is so simple and novel that it was long before I could bring myself to believe that his suspicions were founded even on a probability. At length, however, he convinced me. It is at ·Vienna, he tells me, that he has met with these cards before. The marks are all on the rim of the cards; and an experienced dealer, that is to say, a blackleg, can with these marks produce any results and combinations which may suit his purpose. Essper tells me that De Bœffleurs is even more skilled in sleight-of-hand than himself. From Ernstorff, Essper learned on the day of the fête that Mr. St. George was to dine with the Chevalier at the Baron's apartments on the morrow, and that there was a chance that I should join them. He suspected that villany was in the wind, and when I retired to my room at a late hour on the night of the fête, I there met him, and it was then that he revealed to me everything which I have told you. Am I not right, then, in calling him our preserver?"

"What can be done for him?" said Lady Madeleine.

"His only wish is already granted; he is my servant. That he will serve me diligently and faithfully I have no doubt. I only wish that he would accept or could appreciate a more worthy reward."

"Can man be more amply rewarded," said Miss Fane, "than by choosing his own remuneration? I think he has shown in his request his accustomed talent. I must go and see him this moment."

"Say nothing of what has passed; he is prepared for silence from all parties."

A week, a happy week, passed over, and few minutes of the day found Vivian absent from the side of Violet Fane; and now he thought again of England, of his return to that country under very different circumstances to what he had ever contemplated. Soon, very soon, he trusted to write to his father, to announce to him the revolution in his wishes, the consummation of his hopes. Soon, very soon, he trusted that he should hail his native cliffs, a reclaimed wanderer, with a matured mind and a contented spirit, his sorrows forgotten, his misanthropy laid aside.

CHAPTER XV

IT was about a week after the departure of the Baron that two young Englishmen, who had been college friends of Mr. St. George, arrived at the Baths. These were Mr. Anthony St. Leger and Mr. Adolphus St. John. In the academic shades of Christchurch these three gentlemen had been known as "All Saints." Among their youthful companions they bore the more martial style of "The Three Champions," St. George, St. John, and St. Anthony.

St. John and St. Anthony had just completed the grand tour, and, after passing the Easter at Rome, had returned through the Tyrol from Italy. Since then they had traveled over most parts of Germany; and now, in the beginning of July, found themselves at the Baths of Ems. Two years' travel had not produced any very beneficial effect on either of these sainted personages. They had gained, by visiting the capitals of all Europe, only a due acquaintance with the follies of each; and the only difference that could be observed in their conduct on their return was, that their affectation was rather more fantastical, and therefore more amusing.

"*Corpo di Bacco,* my champion! who ever thought of meeting thee, thou holy saint! By the eyebrow of Venus, my spirit rejoiceth!" exclaimed St. Anthony, whose peculiar affectation was an adoption in English of the Italian oaths.

"This is the sweetest spot, St. Anthony, that we have found since we left Paradiso; that is, St. George, in the vulgar, since we quitted Italia. 'Italia! O Italia!' I forget the rest; probably you remember it. Certainly, a most sweet spot this, quite a Gaspar!"

Art was the peculiar affectation of St. John; he was, indeed, quite a patron of the Belle Arti, had scattered his orders through the studios of most of the celebrated sculptors of Italy, and spoke on all subjects and all things only with a

view to their capability of forming material for the painter.
According to the school of which Mr. St. John was a disciple,
the only use of the human passions is, that they produce situations for the historical painter; and Nature, according to these
votaries of the τὸ καλὸν, is only to be valued as affording hints
for the more perfect conceptions of a Claude or a Salvator.

"By the girdle of Venus, a devilish fine woman!" exclaimed
St. Anthony.

"A splendid bit!" ejaculated St. John; "touched in with
freedom, a grand tournure, great gout in the swell of the neck.
What a study for Retsch!"

"In the name of the Graces, who is it, *mio Santo?*"

"Ay! name *la bellissima Signora.*"

"The 'fine bit,' St. John, is my sister."

"The devil!"

"*Diavolo!*"

"Will you introduce us, most holy man?"

This request from both, simultaneously arranging their
mustaches.

The two saints were accordingly, in due time, introduced;
but finding the attention of Miss Fane always engrossed, and
receiving some not very encouraging responses from Lady
Madeleine, they voted her Ladyship cursedly satirical; and
passing a general censure on the annoying coldness of En-
glishwomen, they were in four-and-twenty hours attached to
the suite of the Miss Fitzlooms, to whom they were introduced by St. George as his particular friends, and were received with the most flattering consideration.

"By the aspect of Diana! fine girls," swore St. Anthony.

"Truly most gorgeous coloring! quite Venetian! Aurelia
is a perfect Giorgione!" said St. John.

"Madeleine," said St. George, one morning, to his sister,
"have you any objection to make up a party with the Fitzlooms
to pass a day at Nassau? You know we have often talked
of it; and as Violet is so well now, and the weather so delightful, there surely can be no objection. The Fitzlooms are very
agreeable people; and though you do not admire the Santi,
still, upon my word, when you know them a little more, you
will find them very pleasant fellows, and they are extremely
good-natured; and just the fellows for such a party. Do not

refuse me. I have set my mind upon your joining the party. Pray nod assent; thank you. Now I must go and arrange everything. Let us see: there are seven Fitzlooms; for we can not count on less than two boys; yourself, Grey, Violet, and myself, four; the Santi; quite enough, a most delightful party. Half a dozen servants and as many donkeys will manage the provisions. Then three light carriages will take us all. 'By the wand of Mercury!' as St. Anthony would vow, admirably planned!"

"By the breath of Zephyr! a most lovely day, Miss Fane," said St. Anthony, on the morning of the intended excursion.

"Quite a Claude!" said St. John.

"Almost as beautiful as an Italian winter day, Mr. St. Leger?" asked Miss Fane.

"Hardly!" said St. Anthony, with a serious air; for he imagined the question to be quite genuine.

The carriages are at the door; into the first ascended Mrs. Fitzloom, two daughters, and the traveling saints. The second bore Lady Madeleine, Mr. Fitzloom, and his two sons; the third division was formed of Mr. St. George and Aurelia Fitzloom, Miss Fane and Vivian.

Away, away, rolled the carriages; the day was beautiful, the sky was without a cloud, and a mild breeze prevented the heat of the sun from being overpowering. All were in high spirits; for St. George had made a capital master of the ceremonies, and had arranged the company in the carriages to their mutual satisfaction. St. Anthony swore, by the soul of Psyche! that Augusta Fitzloom was an angel; and St. John was in equal raptures with Araminta, who had an expression about the eyes which reminded him of Titian's Flora. Mrs. Fitzloom's natural silence did not disturb the uninterrupted jargon of the Santi, whose foppery elicited loud and continued approbation from the fair sisters. The mother sat admiring these sprigs of noble trees. The young Fitzlooms, in crimson cravats, conversed with Lady Madeleine with a delightful military air; and their happy parent, as he gazed upon them with satisfied affection, internally promised them both a commission in a crack regiment.

The road from Ems to Nassau winds along the banks of the Lahn, through two leagues of delightful scenery; at the end of which, springing up from the peak of a bold and richly wooded mountain, the lofty tower of the ancient castle of Nassau meets your view. Winding walks round the sides of the mountain lead through all the varieties of sylvan scenery, and command in all points magnificent views of the surrounding country. These finally bring you to the old castle, whose spacious chambers, though now choked up with masses of gray ruin or covered with underwood, still bear witness to the might of their former lord! the powerful Baron whose sword gained for his posterity a throne.

All seemed happy; none happier than Violet Fane. Never did she look so beautiful as to-day, never was she so animated, never had she boasted that her pulse beat more melodious music, or her lively blood danced a more healthful measure. After examining all the antique chambers of the castle, and discovering, as they flattered themselves, secret passages, and dark dungeons, and hidden doors, they left this interesting relic of the Middle Ages; and soon, by a gradual descent through delightful shrubberies, they again found themselves at the bottom of the valley. Here they visited the modern chateau of Baron von Stein, one of the most enlightened and able politicians that Germany has ever produced. As minister of Prussia, he commenced those reforms which the illustrious Hardenberg perfected. For upward of five centuries the family of Stein have retained their territorial possessions in the valley of the Lahn. Their family castle, at present a ruin, and formerly a fief of the House of Nassau, is now only a picturesque object in the pleasure-grounds of the present lord.

The noon had passed some hours before the delighted wanderers complained of fatigue, and by that time they found themselves in a pleasant green glade on the skirts of the forest of Nassau. It was nearly environed by mountains, covered with hanging woods, which shaded the beautiful valley, and gave it the appearance of a sylvan amphitheatre. From a rocky cleft in these green mountains a torrent, dashing down with impetuous force, and whose fall was almost concealed by the cloud of spray which it excited, gave birth to a small and gentle river, whose banks were fringed with beautiful trees, which prevented the sun's darts from piercing its coldness, by bowing their fair heads over its waters. From their extending branches Nature's choristers sent forth many a lovely lay

Of God's high praise, and of their loves' sweet teen.

Near the banks of this river, the servants, under the active direction of Essper George, had prepared a banquet for the party. The cloth had been laid on a raised work of wood and turf, and rustic seats of the same material surrounded the picturesque table. It glowed with materials, and with colors to which Veronese alone could have done justice: pasties, and birds, and venison, and groups of fish, gleamy with prismatic hues, while amid pyramids of fruit rose goblets of fantastic glass, worthy of the famous wines they were to receive.

"Well!" said Miss Fane, "I never will be a member of an adventurous party like the present of which Albert is not manager."

"I must not take the whole credit upon myself, Violet; St. John is butler, and St. Leger my vice-chamberlain."

"Well, I can not praise Mr. St. John till I have tasted the *malvoisie* which he has promised; but as for the other part of the entertainment, Mr. St. Leger, I am sure this is a temptation which it would be a sin, even in St. Anthony, to withstand."

"By the body of Bacchus, very good!" swore Mr. St. Leger.

"These mountains," said Mr. St. John, "remind me of one of Gaspar's cool valleys. The party, indeed, give it a different character, quite a Watteau!"

"Now, Mrs. Fitzloom," said St. George, who was in his element, "let me recommend a little of this pike! Lady Madeleine, I have sent you some lamb. Miss Fitzloom, I hope St. Anthony is taking care of you. Wrightson, plates to Mr. St. Leger. Holy man, and much beloved! send Araminta some chicken. Grey has helped you, Violet? Aurelia, this is for you. William Pitt Fitzloom, I leave you to yourself. George Canning Fitzloom, take care of the ladies near you. Essper George! Where is Essper? St. John, who is your deputy in the wine department? Wrightson! bring those long green bottles out of the river, and put the champagne underneath the willow. Will your Ladyship take some light claret? Mrs. Fitzloom, you must use your tumbler; nothing but tumblers allowed, by Miss Fane's particular request!"

"St. George, thou holy man!" said Miss Fane, "methinks you are very impertinent. You shall not be my patron saint if you say such words."

For the next hour there was nothing heard save the calling of servants, the rattling of knives and forks, the drawing of corks, and continued bursts of laughter, which were not occasioned by any brilliant observations, either of the Saints, or any other persons, but merely the result of an exuberance of spirits on the part of every one present.

"Well, Aurelia," said Lady Madeleine, "do you prefer our present mode of life to feasting in an old hall, covered with banners and battered shields, and surrounded by mysterious corridors and dark dungeons?" Aurelia was so flattered by the notice of Lady Madeleine that she made her no answer; probably because she was intent on a plover's egg.

"I think we might all retire to this valley," said Miss Fane, "and revive the feudal times with great success. Albert might take us to Nassau Castle, and you, Mr. Fitzloom, might refortify the old tower of Stein. With two sons, however, who are about to enter the Guards, I am afraid we must be your vassals. Then what should we do? We could not have wood parties every day; I suppose we should get tired of each other. No! that does seem impossible; do not you all think so?"

Omnes, "Impossible!"

"We must, however, have some regular pursuit, some cause of constant excitement, some perpetual source of new emotions. New ideas, of course, we must give up; there would be no going to London for the season, for new opinions to astound country cousins on our return. Some pursuit must be invented; we all must have something to do. I have it! Albert shall be a tyrant."

"I am very much obliged to you, Violet."

"Yes! a cruel, unprincipled, vindictive, remorseless tyrant, with a long black beard, I can not tell how long, about twenty thousand times longer than Mr. St. Leger's mustaches."

"By the beard of Jove!" swore St. Anthony, as he almost started from his seat, and arranged with his thumb and forefinger the delicate Albanian tuft of his upper lip, "by the beard of Jove, Miss Fane, I am obliged to you."

"Well, then," continued Violet, "Albert being a tyrant, Lady Madeleine must be an unhappy, ill-used, persecuted woman, living on black bread and green water, in an unknown dungeon. My part shall be to discover her imprisonment. Sounds of strange music attract my attention to a part of the castle which I have not before frequented. There I shall distinctly hear a female voice chanting the 'Bridesmaids' Chorus,' with Erard's double pedal accompaniment. By the aid of the confessors of the two families, two drinking, rattling, impertinent, most corrupt, and most amusing friars, to wit, our sainted friends—"

Here both Mr. St. Leger and Mr. St. John bowed low to Miss Fane.

"A most lively personage is Miss Fane," whispered St. Anthony to his neighbor, Miss Fitzloom, "great style!"

"Most amusing, delightful girl, great style! rather a display to-day, I think."

"Oh, decidedly! and devilish personal, too; some people wouldn't like it. I have no doubt she will say something about you next."

"Oh, I shall be very surprised indeed if she does! It may be very well to you, but Miss Fane must be aware—"

Before this pompous sentence could be finished an incident occurred which prevented Miss Fane from proceeding with her allotment of characters, and rendered unnecessary the threatened indignation of Miss Fitzloom.

Miss Fane, as we mentioned, suddenly ceased speaking; the eyes of all were turned in the direction in which she was gazing as if she had seen a ghost.

"What are you looking up at, Violet?" asked St. George.

"Did not you see anything? did not any of you see anything?"

"None, none!"

"Mr. Grey, surely you must have seen it!"

"I saw nothing."

"It could not be fancy; impossible. I saw it distinctly. I can not be in a dream. See there! again, on that topmost branch. It moves!"

Some odd shrill sounds, uttered in the voice of a Pulcinello, attracted the notice of them all; and lo! high in the air, behind a lofty chestnut tree, the figure of a Pulcinello did appear, hopping and vaulting in the unsubstantial air. Now it sent forth another shrill, piercing sound, and now, with both its hands, it patted and complacently stroked its ample paunch; dancing all the time with unremitting activity, and wagging its queer head at the astounded guests.

"Who, what can it be?" cried all. The Misses Fitzloom shrieked, and the Santi seemed quite puzzled.

"Who, what can it be?"

Ere time could be given for any one to hazard a conjecture, the figure had advanced from behind the trees, and had spanned in an instant the festal board, with two enormous stilts, on which they now perceived it was mounted. The Misses Fitzloom shrieked again. The figure imitated their cries in his queer voice, and gradually raising one enormous stilt up into the air, stood only on one support, which was planted behind the lovely Araminta.

"Oh! inimitable Essper George!" exclaimed Violet Fane.

Here Signor Punch commenced a song, which he executed in the tone peculiar to his character, and in a style which drew applauses from all; and then, with a hop, step, and a jump, he was again behind the chestnut tree. In a moment he advanced without his stilts toward the table. Here, on the turf, he again commenced his antics; kicking his nose with his right foot, and his hump with his left one; executing splendid somersets, and cutting every species of caper, and never ceasing for a moment from performing all his movements to the inspiring music of his own melodious voice. At last, jumping up very high in the air, he fell as if all his joints were loosened, and the Misses Fitzloom, imagining that his bones were really broken, shrieked again. But now Essper began the wonderful performance of a dead body possessed by a devil, and in a minute his shattered corpse, apparently without the assistance of any of its members, began to jump and move about the ground with miraculous rapidity. At length it disappeared behind the chestnut tree.

"I really think," said Mr. St. George, "it is the most agreeable day I ever passed in all my life."

"Decidedly!" said St. Anthony. "St. John, you remember

our party to Pæstum with Lady Calabria M'Crater and the Marquis of Agrigentum. It was nothing to this! Nothing! Do you know I thought that rather dull."

"Yes, too elaborate; too highly finished; nothing of the *pittore improvvisatore*. A party of this kind should be more sketchy in its style; the outline more free, and less detail."

"Essper is coming out to-day," said Vivian to Miss Fane, "after a long and, I venture to say, painful forbearance. However, I hope you will excuse him. It seems to amuse us."

"I think it is delightful. See! here he comes again."

He now appeared in his original costume; the one in which Vivian first met him at the fair. Bowing, he threw his hand carelessly over his mandolin, and having tried the melody of its strings, sang with great taste and a sweet voice—sweeter from its contrast with its previous shrill tones—a very pretty romance. All applauded him very warmly, and no one more than Miss Fane.

"Ah! inimitable Essper George, how can we sufficiently thank you! How well he plays! and his voice is quite beautiful. Oh! could not we dance? would not it be delightful? and he could play on his guitar. Think of the delicious turf!"

Omnes, "Delightful! delightful!" They rose from the table.

"Violet, my dear," asked Lady Madeleine, "what are you going to do?"

"By the toe of Terpsichore!" as Mr. St. Leger would say, "I am going to dance."

"But remember, to-day you have done so much! let us be moderate; though you feel so much better, still think what a change to-day has been from your usual habits!"

"But, dearest Lady Madeleine, think of dancing on the turf, and I feel so well!"

"By the Graces! I am for the waltz," said St. Anthony.

"It has certainly a very free touch to recommend it," said St. John.

"No, no," said Violet; "let us all join in a country dance." But the Misses Fitzloom preferred a quadrille.

The quadrille was soon formed: Violet made up for not dancing with Vivian at the Grand Duke's. She was most animated and kept up a successful rivalry with Mr. St. Leger, who evidently prided himself, as Mr. Fitzloom observed, "on his light fantastic toe." Now he pirouetted like Paul, and now he attitudinized like Albert; and now Miss Fane eclipsed all his exertions by her inimitable imitations of Ronzi Vestris's rushing and arrowy manner. St. Anthony, in despair, but quite delighted, revealed a secret which had been taught him by a Spanish dancer at Milan; but then Miss Fane vanquished him forever with the *pas de Zephyr* of the exquisite Fanny Bias.

The day was fast declining when the carriages arrived; the young people were in no humor to return; and as, when they had once entered the carriage, the day seemed finished forever, they proposed walking part of the way home. Lady Madeleine made little objection to Violet joining the party, as after the exertion that Miss Fane had been making, a drive in an open carriage might be dangerous; and yet the walk was too long, but all agreed that it would be impossible to shorten it; and, as Violet declared that she was not in the least fatigued, the lesser evil was therefore chosen. The carriages rolled off; at about half way from Ems, the two empty ones were to wait for the walking party. Lady Madeleine smiled with fond affection as she waved her hand to Violet the moment before she was out of sight.

"And now," said St. George, "good people all, instead of returning by the same road, it strikes me that there must be a way through this little wood; you see there is an excellent path. Before the sun is set we shall have got through it, and it will bring us out, I have no doubt, by the old cottage which you observed, Grey, when we came along. I saw a gate and path there; just where we first got sight of Nassau Castle; there can be no doubt about it. You see it is a regular right-angle, and besides varying the walk, we shall at least gain a quarter of an hour, which, after all, as we have to walk nearly three miles, is an object. It is quite clear, if I have a head for anything, it is for finding my way."

"I think you have a head for everything," said Aurelia Fitzloom, in a soft sentimental whisper; "I am sure we owe all our happiness to-day to you!"

"If I have a head for everything, I have a heart only for one person!"

As every one wished to be convinced, no one offered any

argument in opposition to Mr. St. George's view of the case; and some were already in the wood.

"Albert," said Miss Fane, "I do not like walking in the wood so late; pray come back."

"Oh, nonsense, Violet! come. If you do not like to come, you can walk by the road; you will meet us round by the gate, it is only five minutes' walk." Ere he had finished speaking, the rest were in the wood, and some had advanced. Vivian strongly recommended Violet not to join them; he was sure that Lady Madeleine would not approve of it; he was sure that it was very dangerous, extremely; and, by the bye, while he was talking, which way had they gone? he did not see them. He hallooed; all answered, and a thousand echoes besides. "We certainly had better go by the road, we shall lose our way if we try to follow them; nothing is so puzzling as walking in woods; we had much better keep to the road." So by the road they went.

The sun had already sunk behind the mountains, whose undulating forms were thrown into dark shadow against the crimson sky. The thin crescent of the new moon floated over the eastern hills, whose deep woods glowed with the rosy glories of twilight. Over the peak of a purple mountain glittered the solitary star of evening. As the sun dropped, universal silence seemed to pervade the whole face of nature. The voice of the birds was stilled; the breeze, which had refreshed them during the day, died away, as if its office were now completed; and none of the dark sounds and sights of hideous Night yet dared to triumph over the death of Day. Unseen were the circling wings of the fell bat; unheard the screech of the waking owl; silent the drowsy hum of the shade-born beetle! What heart has not acknowledged the influence of this hour, the sweet and soothing hour of twilight! the hour of love, the hour of adoration, the hour of rest! when we think of those we love, only to regret that we have not loved more dearly; when we remember our enemies only to forgive them!

And Vivian and his beautiful companion owned the magic of this hour, as all must do, by silence. No word was spoken, yet is silence sometimes a language. They gazed, and gazed again, and their full spirits held due communion with the starlit sky, and the mountains and the woods, and the soft shadows of the increasing moon. Oh! who can describe what the o'er-charged spirit feels at this sacred hour, when we almost lose the consciousness of existence, and our souls seem to struggle to pierce futurity! In the forest of the mysterious Odenwald, in the solitudes of the Bergstrasse, had Vivian at this hour often found consolation for a bruised spirit, often in adoring nature had forgotten man. But now, when he had never felt nature's influence more powerful; when he had never forgotten man and man's world more thoroughly; when he was experiencing emotions which, though undefinable, he felt to be new; he started when he remembered that all this was in the presence of a human being! Was it Hesperus he gazed upon, or something else that glanced brighter than an evening star? Even as he thought that his gaze was fixed on the countenance of nature, he found that his eyes rested on the face of nature's loveliest daughter!

"Violet! dearest Violet!"

As in some delicious dream the sleeper is awakened from his bliss by the sound of his own rapturous voice, so was Vivian roused by these words from his reverie, and called back to the world which he had forgotten. But ere a moment had passed, he was pouring forth in a rapid voice, and incoherent manner, such words as men speak only once. He spoke of his early follies, his misfortunes, his misery; of his matured views, his settled principles, his plans, his prospects, his hopes, his happiness, his bliss; and when he had ceased, he listened, in his turn, to some small still words, which made him the happiest of human beings. He bent down, he kissed the soft silken cheek which now he could call his own. Her hand was in his; her head sank upon his breast. Suddenly she clung to him with a strong grasp. "Violet! my own, my dearest; you are overcome. I have been rash, I have been imprudent. Speak, speak, my beloved! say, you are not ill!"

She spoke not, but clung to him with a fearful strength, her head still upon his breast, her full eyes closed. Alarmed, he raised her off the ground, and bore her to the riverside. Water might revive her. But when he tried to lay her a moment on the bank, she clung to him gasping, as a sinking person clings to a stout swimmer. He leaned over her; he did not attempt to disengage her arms; and, by degrees, by very slow degrees, her grasp loosened. At last her arms gave way and fell by his side, and her eyes partly opened.

"Thank God! Violet, my own, my beloved, say you are better!"

She answered not, evidently she did not know him, evidently she did not see him. A film was on her sight, and her eye was glassy. He rushed to the waterside, and in a moment he had sprinkled her temples, now covered with a cold dew. Her pulse beat not, her circulation seemed suspended. He rubbed the palms of her hands, he covered her delicate feet with his coat; and then rushing up the bank into the road, he shouted with frantic cries on all sides. No one came, no one was near. Again, with a cry of fearful anguish, he shouted as if a hyena were feeding on his vitals. No sound; no answer. The nearest cottage was above a mile off. He dared not leave her. Again he rushed down to the waterside. Her eyes were still open, still fixed. Her mouth also was no longer closed. Her hand was stiff, her heart had ceased to beat. He tried with the warmth of his own body to revive her. He shouted, he wept, he prayed. All, all in vain. Again he was in the road, again shouting like an insane being. There was a sound. Hark! It was but the screech of an owl!

Once more at the riverside, once more bending over her with starting eyes, once more the attentive ear listening for the soundless breath. No sound! not even a sigh! Oh! what would he have given for her shriek of anguish! No change had occurred in her position, but the lower part of her face had fallen; and there was a general appearance which struck him with awe. Her body was quite cold, her limbs stiffened. He gazed, and gazed, and gazed. He bent over her with stupor rather than grief stamped on his features. It was very slowly that the dark thought came over his mind, very slowly that the horrible truth seized upon his soul. He gave a loud shriek, and fell on the lifeless body of VIOLET FANE!

BOOK V

CHAPTER I

THE green and bowery summer had passed away. It was midnight when two horsemen pulled up their steeds beneath a wide oak; which, with other lofty trees, skirted the side of a winding road in an extensive forest in the south of Germany.

"By heavens!" said one, who apparently was the master, "we must even lay our cloaks, I think, under this oak; for the road winds again, and assuredly can not lead now to our village."

"A starlit sky in autumn can scarcely be the fittest curtain for one so weak as you, sir; I should recommend traveling on, if we keep on our horses' backs till dawn."

"But if we are traveling in a directly contrary way to our *voiturier*, honest as we may suppose him to be, if he find in the morning no paymaster for his job, he may with justice make free with our baggage. And I shall be unusually mistaken if the road we are now pursuing does not lead back to the city."

"City, town, or village, you must sleep under no forest tree, sir. Let us ride on. It will be hard if we do not find some huntsman's or ranger's cottage; and for aught we know a neat snug village, or some comfortable old manor-house, which has been in the family for two centuries; and where, with God's blessing, they may chance to have wine as old as the bricks. I know not how you may feel, sir, but a ten hours' ride when I was only prepared for half the time, and that, too, in an autumn night, makes me somewhat desirous of renewing my acquaintance with the kitchen fire."

"I could join you in a glass of hock and a slice of veni-

son, I confess, my good fellow; but in a nocturnal ride I am no
longer your match. However, if you think it best, we will
prick on our steeds for another hour. If it be only for them,
I am sure we must soon stop."

"Ay! do, sir; and put your cloak well round you; all is for
the best. You are not, I guess, a Sabbath-born child?"

"That am I not, but how would that make our plight worse
than it is? Should we be further off supper?"

"Nearer, perhaps, than you imagine; for we should then
have a chance of sharing the spoils of the Spirit Hunter."

"Ah! Essper, is it so?"

"Truly yes, sir; and were either of us a Sabbath-born
child, by holy cross! I would not give much for our chance
of a down bed this night."

Here a great horned owl flew across the road.

"Were I in the north," said Essper, "I would sing an Ave
Marie against the STUT-OZEL."

"What call you that?" asked Vivian.

" 'Tis the great bird, sir; the great horned owl, that always
flies before the Wild Hunter. And truly, sir, I have passed
through many forests in my time, but never yet saw I one
where I should sooner expect to hear a midnight bugle. If
you will allow me, sir, I will ride by your side. Thank God,
at least, it is not the Walpurgis night!"

"I wish to Heaven it were!" said Vivian, "and that we were
on the Brocken. It must be highly amusing!"

"Hush! hush! it is lucky we are not in the Hartz; but we
know not where we are, nor who at this moment may be
behind us."

And here Essper began pouring forth a liturgy of his own,
half Catholic and half Calvinistic, quite in character with the
creed of the country through which they were traveling.

"My horse has stumbled," continued Essper, "and yours,
sir, is he not shying? There is a confounded cloud over the
moon, but I have no sight in the dark if that mass before you
be not a devil's-stone. The Lord have mercy upon our sinful
souls!"

"Peace! Essper," said Vivian, who was surprised to find
him really alarmed; "I see nothing but a block of granite, no
uncommon sight in a German forest."

"It is a devil's-stone, I tell you, sir; there has been some church here, which he has knocked down in the night. Look! is it the moss-people that I see? As sure as I am a hungry sinner, the Wild One is out a-hunting to-night."

"More luck for us if we meet him. His dogs, as you say, may gain us a supper. I think our wisest course will be to join the cry."

"Hush! hush! you would not talk so if you knew what your share of the spoils might be. Ay! if you did, sir, your cheek would be paler, and your very teeth would chatter. I knew one man who was traveling in the forest, just as we are now; it was about this time; and he believed in the Wild Huntsman about as much as you, that is, he liked to talk of the Spirit, merely to have the opportunity of denying that he believed in him; which showed, as I used to say, that his mind was often thinking of it. He was a merry knave, and as firm a hand for a boar-spear as ever I met with, and I have met many. We used to call him, before the accident, Left-handed Hans, but they call him now, sir, the Child-Hunter. Oh! it is a very awful tale, and I would sooner tell it in blazing hall than in free forest. You did not hear any sound to the left, did you?"

"Nothing but the wind, Essper; on with your tale, my man."

"It is a very awful tale, sir, but I will make short work of it. You see, sir, it was a night just like this; the moon was generally hid, but the stars prevented it from ever being pitch dark. And so, sir, he was traveling alone; he had been up to the castle of the baron, his master; you see, sir, he was head-ranger to his lordship, and he always returned home through the forest. What he was thinking of, I can not say, but most likely of no good; when all on a sudden he heard the baying of hounds in the distance. Now directly he heard it—I have heard him tell the story a thousand times—directly he heard it, it struck him that it must be the Spirit Huntsman; and though there were many ways to account for the hounds, still he never for a moment doubted that they were the hell-dogs. The sounds came nearer and nearer. Now I tell you this, because if ever, which the Holy Virgin forbid! if ever you meet the Wild Huntsman, you will know how to act: conduct yourself always with propriety, make no noise, but behave like a gentleman, and don't put the dogs off the scent; stand aside, and let him pass. Don't talk; he has no time to lose; for if he hunt after daybreak, a night's sport is forfeited for every star left in the morning sky. So, sir, you see nothing puts him in a greater passion than to lose his time in answering impertinent questions. Well, sir, Left-Handed Hans stood by the roadside. The baying of the dogs was so distinct that he felt that in a moment the Wild One would be up: his horse shivered like a sallow in a storm. He heard the tramp of the Spirit-steed: they came in sight. As the tall figure of the Huntsman passed; I can not tell you what it was; it might have been; Lord, forgive me for thinking what it might have been! but a voice from behind Hans, a voice so like his own that for a moment he fancied that he had himself spoken, although he was conscious that his lips had been firmly closed the whole time; a voice from the roadside, just behind poor Hans, mind, said, 'Good sport, Sir Huntsman, 'tis an odd light to track a stag!' The poor man, sir, was all of an ague; but how much greater was his horror when the tall Huntsman stopped! He thought that he was going to be eaten up on the spot, at least: not at all. 'My friend!' said the Wild One, in the kindest voice imaginable; 'my friend, would you like to give your horse a breathing with us?' Poor Hans was so alarmed that it never entered into his head for a single moment to refuse the invitation, and instantly he was galloping by the side of the Wild Huntsman. Away they flew! away! away! away! over bog and over mere; over ditch and over hedge; away! away! away! and the Ranger's horse never failed, but kept by the side of the Wild Spirit without the least distress; and yet it is very singular that Hans was about to sell this very beast only a day before for a matter of five crowns: you see, he only kept it just to pick his way at night from the castle to his own cottage. Well, it is very odd, but Hans soon lost all fear, for the sport was so fine and he had such a keen relish for the work that, far from being alarmed, he thought himself one of the luckiest knaves alive. But the oddest thing all this time was that Hans never caught sight for one moment of either buck or boar, although he saw by the dogs' noses that there was something keen in the wind, and although he felt that if the hunted

beast were like any that he had himself ever followed before,
it must have been run down with such dogs quicker than a
priest could say a paternoster. At last, for he had grown
quite bold, says Hans to the Wild Huntsman, 'The beasts run
quick o' nights, sir, I think; it has been a long time, I ween, ere
I scampered so far, and saw so little!' Do you know that the
old gentleman was not the least affronted, but said, in the pleasantest voice imaginable, 'A true huntsman should be patient,
Hans; you will see the game quick; look forward, man! what
see you?' And sure enough, your Highness, he did look forward. It was near the skirts of the forest, there was a green
glade before them, and very few trees, and therefore he could
see far ahead. The moon was shining very bright, and sure
enough, what did he see? Running as fleet over the turf as a
rabbit was a child. The little figure was quite black in the
moonlight, and Hans could not catch its face: in a moment the
hell-dogs were on it. Hans quivered like a windy reed, and the
Wild One-laughed till the very woods echoed. 'How like you
hunting moss-men?' asked the Spirit. Now when Hans found
it was only a moss-man, he took heart again, and said in a
shaking voice that 'It is rare good sport in good company';
and then the Spirit jumped off his horse, and said, 'Now,
Hans, you must watch me well, for I am little used to bag
game.' He said this with a proudish air, as much as to hint
that, had not he expected Hans, he would not have rode out
this evening without his groom. So the Wild One jumped on
his horse again, and put the bag before him. It was nearly
morning when Hans found himself at the door of his own
cottage and, bowing very respectfully to the Spirit Hunter,
he thanked him for the sport, and begged his share of the
night's spoil. This was all in joke, but Hans had heard that
'talk to the devil, and fear the last word'; and so he was determined, now that they were about to part, not to appear to
tremble, but to carry it off with a jest. 'Truly, Hans,' said the
Huntsman, 'thou art a bold lad, and to encourage thee to
speak to wild huntsmen again, I have a mind to give thee for
thy pains the whole spoil. Take the bag, knave, a moss-man
is good eating; had I time I would give thee a receipt for
sauce'; and, so saying, the Spirit rode off, laughing very
heartily. Well, sir, Hans was so anxious to examine the con-

tents of the bag, and see what kind of thing a moss-man really was, for he had only caught a glimpse of him in the chase, that instead of going to bed immediately, and saying his prayers, as he should have done, he lighted a lamp and undid the string; and what think you he took out of the bag? As sure as I am a born sinner, his own child!"

" 'Tis a wonderful tale," said Vivian; "and did the unfortunate man tell you this himself?"

"Often and often. I knew Left-handed Hans well. He was ranger, as I said, to a great lord; and was quite a favorite, you see. For some reason or other he got out of favor. Some said that the Baron had found him out a-poaching, and that he used to ride his master's horses a-night. Whether this be true or not, who can say? But, howsoever, Hans went to ruin; and instead of being a flourishing active lad, he was turned out, and went a-begging all through Saxony; and he always told this story as the real history of his misfortunes. Some say he is not as strong in his head as he used to be. However, why should we say it is not a true tale? What is that?" almost shrieked Essper.

Vivian listened, and heard distinctly the distant baying of hounds.

" 'Tis he!" said Essper; "now don't speak, sir, don't speak! and if the devil make me join him, as may be the case, for I am but a cock-brained thing, particularly at midnight, don't be running after me from any foolish feeling, but take care of yourself, and don't be chattering. To think you should come to this, my precious young master!"

"Cease your blubbering! Do you think that I am to be frightened by the idiot tales of a parcel of old women, and the lies of a gang of detected poachers? Come, sir, ride on. We are, most probably, near some huntsman's cottage. That distant baying is the sweetest music I have heard in a long while."

"Don't be rash, sir; don't be rash. If you were to give me fifty crowns now, I could not remember a single line of a single prayer. Ave Marie! it always is so when I most want it. Paternoster! and whenever I have need to remember a song, sure enough I am always thinking of a prayer. '*Unser vater, der du bist im himmel, sanctificado se el tu nombra; il tuo regno venga.'"* Here Essper George was proceeding with a scrap of modern Greek, when the horsemen suddenly came upon one of those broad green vistas which we often see in forests, and which are generally cut, either for the convenience of hunting, or carting wood. It opened on the left side of the road; and at the bottom of it, though apparently at a great distance, a light was visible.

"So much for your Wild Huntsman, friend Essper! I shall be much disappointed if here are not quarters for the night. And see! the moon comes out, a good omen!"

After ten minutes' canter over the noiseless turf, the travelers found themselves before a large and many-windowed mansion. The building formed the furthest side of a quadrangle, which you entered through an ancient and massy gate, on each side of which was a small building, of course the lodges. Essper soon found that the gate was closely fastened; and though he knocked often and loudly, it was with no effect. That the inhabitants of the mansion had not yet retired was certain, for lights were moving in the great house; and one of the lodges was not only very brilliantly illuminated, but full, as Vivian was soon convinced, of clamorous if not jovial guests.

"Now, by the soul of my unknown father!" said the enraged Essper, "I will make these saucy porters learn their duty. What ho! there; what ho! within! within!" But the only answer he received was the loud reiteration of a rude and roaring chorus, which, as it was now more distinctly and audibly enunciated, evidently for the purpose of enraging the travelers, they detected to be something to the following effect:

> "Then a prayer to St. Peter, a prayer to St. Paul!
> A prayer to St. Jerome, a prayer to them all!
> A prayer to each one of the saintly stock
> But devotion alone, devotion to Hock!"

"A right good burden!" said Essper. The very words had made him recover his temper, and ten thousand times more desirous of gaining admittance. He was off his horse in a moment, and scrambling up the wall with the aid of the iron stanchions, he clambered up to the window. The sudden appearance of his figure startled the inmates of the lodge, and one of them soon staggered to the gate.

"What want you, ye noisy and disturbing varlets? What want you, ye most unhallowed rogues, at such a place, and at such an hour? If you be thieves, look at our bars (here a hiccup). If you be poachers, our master is engaged, and ye may slay all the game in the forest (another hiccup); but if ye be good men and true—"

"We are!" halloed Essper, eagerly.

"You are!" said the porter, in a tone of great surprise; "then you ought to be ashamed of yourselves for disturbing holy men at their devotions!"

"Is this the way," said Essper, "to behave, ye shameless rascals, to a noble and mighty Prince, who happens to have lost his way in your abominable forest, but who, though he has parted with his suite, has still in his pocket a purse full of ducats? Would ye have him robbed by any others but yourselves? Is this the way you behave to a Prince of the Holy Roman Empire, a Knight of the Golden Fleece, and a most particular friend of your own master? Is this the way to behave to his secretary, who is one of the merriest fellows living, can sing a jolly song with any of you, and so bedevil a bottle of Geisenheimer with lemons and brandy that for the soul of ye you wouldn't know it from the greenest Tokay? Out, out on ye! you know not what you have lost!"

Ere Essper had finished more than one stout bolt had been drawn, and the great key had already entered the stouter lock.

"Most honorable sirs!" hiccuped the porter, "in our Lady's name enter. I had forgot myself, for in these autumn nights it is necessary to anticipate the cold with a glass of cheering liquor; and, God forgive me! if I did not mistake your most mighty Highnesses for a couple of forest rovers, or small poachers at least. Thin entertainment here, kind sir (here the last bolt was withdrawn); a glass of indifferent liquor and a prayer-book. I pass the time chiefly these cold nights with a few holy-minded friends at our devotions. You heard us at our prayers, honorable lords!

> " 'A prayer to St. Peter, a prayer to St. Paul!
> A prayer to St. Jerome, a prayer to them all!' "

Here the devout porter most reverently crossed himself.

> " 'A prayer to each one of the saintly stock,
> But devotion alone, devotion to Hock!' "

added Essper George; "you forget the best part of the burden, my honest friend."

"Oh!" said the porter, with an arch smile, as he opened the lodge door; "I am glad to find that your honorable Excellencies have a taste for hymns!"

The porter led them into a room, at a round table in which about half a dozen individuals were busily engaged in discussing the merits of various agreeable liquors. There was an attempt to get up a show of polite hospitality to Vivian as he entered, but the man who offered him his chair fell to the ground in an unsuccessful struggle to be courteous; and another one, who had filled a large glass for his guest on his entrance, offered him, after a preliminary speech of incoherent compliments, the empty bottle by mistake. The porter and his friends, although they were all drunk, had sense enough to feel that the presence of a Prince of the Holy Empire, a Chevalier of the Golden Fleece, and the particular friend of their master, was not exactly a fit companion for themselves, and was rather a check on the gay freedom of equal companionship; and so, although the exertion was not a little troublesome, the guardian of the gate reeled out of the room to inform his honored lord of the sudden arrival of a stranger of distinction. Essper George immediately took his place, and ere the master of the lodge had returned the noble secretary had not only given a choice toast, sung a choice song, and been hailed by the grateful plaudits of all present, but had proceeded in his attempt to fulfil the pledge which he had given at the gate to the very letter by calling out lustily for a bottle of Geisenheimer, lemons, brandy, and a bowl.

"Fairly and softly, my little son of Bacchus," said the porter as he re-entered, "fairly and softly, and then thou shalt want nothing; but remember I have to perform my duties unto the noble Lord, my master, and also to the noble Prince, your master. If thou wilt follow me," continued the porter, reeling as he bowed with the greatest consideration to Vivian; "if thou wilt follow me, most high and mighty sir,

my master will be right glad to have the honor of drinking
your health. And as for you, my friends, fairly and softly say
I again. We will talk of the Geisenheimer anon. Am I to be
absent from the first brewing? No, no! fairly and softly; you
can drink my health when I am absent in cold liquor, and say
those things which you could not well say before my face.
But mind, my most righteous and well-beloved, I will have
no flattery. Flattery is the destruction of all good fellowship;
it is like a qualmish liqueur in the midst of a bottle of wine.
Speak your minds, say any little thing that comes first, as
thus, 'Well, for Hunsdrich, the porter, I must declare that I
never heard evil word against him'; or 'A very good leg has
Hunsdrich, the porter, and a tight-made lad altogether; no
enemy with the girls, I warrant me'; or thus, 'Well, for a
good-hearted, good-looking, stout-drinking, virtuous, honorable, handsome, generous, sharp-witted knave, commend me to
Hunsdrich the porter'; but not a word more, my friends, not
a word more, no flattery. Now, sir, I beg your pardon."

The porter led the way through a cloistered walk, until
they arrived at the door of a great mansion, to which they
ascended by a lofty flight of steps; it opened into a large
octagonal hall, the sides of which were covered with fowling-
pieces, stags' heads, *couteaux de chasse,* boar-spears, and huge
fishing nets. Passing through this hall, they ascended a noble
staircase, on the first landing-place of which was a door, which
Vivian's conductor opened, and ushering him into a large
and well-lighted chamber, withdrew. From the centre of this
room descended a magnificently cut chandelier, which threw
a graceful light upon a sumptuous banquet table, at which
were seated eight very singular-looking personages. All of
them wore hunting-dresses of various shades of straw-colored
cloth, with the exception of one, who sat on the left hand of
the master of the feast, and the color of whose costume was
a rich crimson purple. From the top to the bottom of the
table extended a double file of wine-glasses and goblets, of all
sizes and all colors. There you might see brilliant relics of
that ancient ruby-glass, the vivid tints of which seem lost to
us forever. Next to these were marshaled goblets of Venetian manufacture, of a cloudy, creamy white; then came the
huge hock glass of some ancient Primate of Mentz, nearly a

yard high, towering above its companions, as the church, its former master, predominated over the simple laymen of the Middle Ages. Why should we forget a set of most curious and antique drinking-cups of painted glass, on whose rare surfaces were emblazoned the Kaiser and ten electors of the old Empire?

Vivian bowed to the party and stood in silence, while they stared a scrutinizing examination. At length the master of the feast spoke. He was a very stout man, with a prodigious paunch, which his tightened dress set off to great advantage. His face, and particularly his forehead, were of great breadth. His eyes were set far apart. His long ears hung down almost to his shoulders; yet, singular as he was, not only in these, but in many other respects, everything was forgotten when your eyes lighted on his nose. It was the most prodigious nose that Vivian ever remembered not only seeing, but hearing or even reading of. In fact, it was too monstrous for a dream. This mighty nose seemed to hang almost to its owner's chest.

"Be seated," said this personage, in no unpleasing voice, and he pointed to the chair opposite to him. Vivian took the vacated seat of the Vice-President, who moved himself to the right. "Be seated, and whoever you may be, welcome! If our words be few, think not that our welcome is scant. We are not much given to speech, holding it for a principle that if a man's mouth be open, it should be for the purpose of receiving that which cheers a man's spirit; not of giving vent to idle words, which, so far as we have observed, produce no other effect save filling the world with crude and unprofitable fantasies, and distracting our attention when we are on the point of catching those flavors which alone make the world endurable. Therefore, briefly, but heartily, welcome! Welcome, Sir Stranger, from us and from all; and first from us, the Grand Duke of Johannisberger." Here his Highness rose, and pulled out a large ruby tumbler from the file. Each of those present did the same, without, however, rising, and the late Vice-President, who sat next to Vivian, invited him to follow their example.

The Grand Duke of Johannisberger brought forward, from beneath the table, an ancient and exquisite bottle of that choice liquor from which he took his exhilarating title. The cork was drawn, and the bottle circulated with rapidity; and in three minutes the ruby glasses were filled and emptied, and the Grand Duke's health quaffed by all present.

"Again, Sir Stranger," continued the Grand Duke, "briefly, but heartily, welcome! welcome from us and welcome from all; and first from us, and now from the Archduke of Hochheimer!"

The Archduke of Hochheimer was a thin, sinewy man, with long, carroty hair, eyelashes of the same color, but of a remarkable length; and mustaches which, though very thin, were so long that they met under his chin. Vivian could not refrain from noticing the extreme length, whiteness, and apparent sharpness of his teeth. The Archduke did not speak, but, leaning under the table, soon produced a bottle of Hochheimer. He then took from the file one of the Venetian glasses of clouded white. All followed his example; the bottle was sent round, his health was pledged, and the Grand Duke of Johannisberger again spoke:

"Again, Sir Stranger, briefly, but heartily, welcome! Welcome from us, and welcome from all; and first from us, and now from the Elector of Steinberg!"

The Elector of Steinberg was a short but very broadbacked, strong-built man. Though his head was large, his features were small, and appeared smaller from the immense quantity of coarse, shaggy, brown hair which grew over almost every part of his face and fell down upon his shoulders. The Elector was as silent as his predecessor, and quickly produced a bottle of Steinberger. The curious drinking cups of painted glass were immediately withdrawn from the file, the bottle was sent round, the Elector's health was pledged, and the Grand Duke of Johannisberger again spoke:

"Again, Sir Stranger, briefly, but heartily, welcome! Welcome from us, and welcome from all; and first from us, and now from the Margrave of Rüdesheimer!"

The Margrave of Rüdesheimer was a slender man of elegant appearance. As Vivian watched the glance of his speaking eye, and the half-satirical and half-jovial smile which played upon his features, he hardly expected that he would be as silent as his predecessors. But the Margrave spoke no word. He gave a kind of shout of savage exultation as he smacked his lips after dashing off his glass of Rüdesheimer; and scarcely noticing the salutations of those who drank his health, he threw himself back in his chair, and listened seemingly with a smile of derision, while the Grand Duke of Johannisberger again spoke:

"Again, Sir Stranger, briefly, but heartily, welcome! Welcome from us, and welcome from all; and first from us, and now from the Landgrave of Grafenberg."

The Landgrave of Grafenberg was a rude, awkward-looking person, who, when he rose from his seat, stared like an idiot, and seemed utterly ignorant of what he ought to do. But his quick companion, the Margrave of Rüdesheimer, soon thrust a bottle of Grafenberger into the Landgrave's hand, and with some trouble and bustle the Landgrave extracted the cork; and then helping himself sat down, forgetting either to salute, or to return the salutations of those present.

"Again, Sir Stranger, briefly, but heartily, welcome! Welcome from us, and welcome from all; and first from us, and now from the Palsgrave of Geisenheim!"

The Palsgrave of Geisenheim was a dwarf in spectacles. He drew the cork from his bottle like lightning, and mouthed at his companions even while he bowed to them.

"Again, Sir Stranger, briefly, but heartily, welcome! Welcome from us, and welcome from all; and first from us, and now from the Count of Markbrunnen!"

The Count of Markbrunnen was a sullen-looking personage, with lips protruding nearly three inches beyond his nose. From each side of his upper jaw projected a large tooth.

"Thanks to Heaven!" said Vivian, as the Grand Duke again spoke; "thanks to Heaven, here is our last man!"

"Again, Sir Stranger, briefly, but heartily, welcome! Welcome from us, and welcome from all; and first from us, and now from the Baron of Asmannshausen!"

The Baron of Asmannshausen sat on the left hand of the Grand Duke of Johannisberger, and was dressed, as we have before said, in a unique costume of crimson purple. The Baron stood, without his boots, about six feet eight. He was a sleek man, with a head not bigger than a child's, and a pair of small, black, beady eyes, of singular brilliancy. The Baron introduced a bottle of the only red wine that the Rhine boasts; but which, for its fragrant and fruity flavor and its brilliant tint, is perhaps not inferior to the sunset glow of Burgundy.

"And now," continued the Grand Duke, "having introduced you to all present, sir, we will begin drinking."

Vivian had submitted to the introductory ceremonies with the good grace which becomes a man of the world; but the coolness of this last observation recalled our hero's wandering senses; and, at the same time, alarmed at discovering that eight bottles of wine had been discussed by the party merely as a preliminary, and emboldened by the contents of one bottle which had fallen to his own share, he had the courage to confront the Grand Duke of Johannisberger in his own castle.

"Your wine, most noble Lord, stands in no need of my commendation; but as I must mention it, let it not be said that I ever mentioned it without praise. After a ten hours' ride, its flavor is as grateful to the palate as its strength is refreshing to the heart; but though old Hock, in homely phrase, is styled meat and drink, I confess to you that, at this moment, I stand in need of even more solid sustenance than the juice of the sunny hill."

"A traitor!" shrieked all present, each with his right arm stretched out, glass in hand; "a traitor!"

"No traitor," answered Vivian, "noble and right thirsty lords, but one of the most hungry mortals that ever yet famished."

The only answer that he received for some time was a loud and ill-boding murmur. The long whisker of the Archduke of Hochheimer curled with renewed rage; audible, though suppressed, was the growl of the hairy Elector of Steinberg; fearful the corporeal involutions of the tall Baron of Asmannshausen; and savagely sounded the wild laugh of the bright-eyed Margrave of Rüdesheimer.

"Silence, my Lords!" said the Grand Duke. "Forget we that ignorance is the stranger's portion, and that no treason can exist among those who are not our sworn subjects? Pity

we rather the degeneracy of this bold-spoken youth, and in
the plenitude of our mercy let us pardon his demand! Know
ye, unknown knight, that you are in the presence of an august
society who are here met at one of their accustomed con-
vocations, whereof the purport is the frequent quaffing of
those most glorious liquors of which the sacred Rhine is the
great father. We profess to find a perfect commentary on
the Pindaric laud of the strongest element in the circumstance
of the banks of a river being the locality where the juice of
the grape is most delicious, and holding, therefore, that water
is strongest because, in a manner, it giveth birth to wine, we
also hold it as a sacred element, and consequently most relig-
iously refrain from refreshing our bodies, with that sanctified
and most undrinkable fluid. Know ye that we are the children of the Rhine, the conservators of his flavors, profound in
the learning of his exquisite aroma, and deep students in the
mysteries of his inexplicable näre. Professing not to be
immortal, we find in the exercise of the chase a noble means
to preserve that health which is necessary for the performance
of the ceremonies to which we are pledged. At to-morrow's
dawn our bugle sounds, and thou, stranger, may engage the
wild boar at our side; at to-morrow's noon the castle bell will
toll, and thou, stranger, may eat of the beast which thou hast
conquered; but to feed after midnight, to destroy the power of
catching the delicate flavor, to annihilate the faculty of detecting the undefinable näre, is heresy, most rank and damnable
heresy! Therefore at this hour soundeth no plate or platter,
jingleth no knife or culinary instrument, in the PALACE OF
THE WINES. Yet, in consideration of thy youth, and that
on the whole thou hast tasted thy liquor like a proper man,
from which we augur the best expectations of the manner
in which thou wilt drink it, we feel confident that our brothers
of the goblet will permit us to grant thee the substantial solace
of a single shoeing horn."

"Let it be a Dutch herring, then," said Vivian, "and as
you have souls to be saved grant me one slice of bread."

"It can not be," said the Grand Duke; "but as we are
willing to be indulgent to bold hearts, verily, we will wink at
the profanation of a single toast; but you must order an anchovy
one, and give secret instructions to the waiting man to forget

the fish. It must be counted as a second shoeing horn, and you will forfeit for the last a bottle of Markbrunnen.

"And now, illustrious brothers," continued the Grand Duke, "let us drink 1726."

All present gave a single cheer, in which Vivian was obliged to join, and they honored with a glass of the very year the memory of a celebrated vintage.

"1748!" said the Grand Duke.

Two cheers and the same ceremony.

1766 and 1779 were honored in the same manner, but when the next toast was drank, Vivian almost observed in the countenances of the Grand Duke and his friends the signs of incipient insanity.

"1783!" hallooed the Grand Duke in a tone of the most triumphant exultation, and his mighty proboscis, as it snuffed the air, almost caused a whirlwind round the room. Hochheimer gave a roar, Steinberg a growl, Rüdesheimer a wild laugh, Markbrunnen a loud grunt, Grafenberg a bray, Asmannshausen's long body moved to and fro with wonderful agitation, and little Geisenheim's bright eyes glistened through their glasses as if they were on fire. How ludicrous is the incipient inebriety of a man who wears spectacles!

Thanks to an excellent constitution, which recent misery, however, had somewhat shattered, Vivian bore up against all these attacks; and when they had got down to 1802, from the excellency of his digestion and the inimitable skill with which he emptied many of the latter glasses under the table, he was, perhaps, in better condition than any one in the room.

And now rose the idiot Grafenberg; Rüdesheimer all the time, with a malicious smile, faintly pulling him down by the skirt of his coat, as if he were desirous of preventing an exposure which his own advice had brought about. He had been persuading Grafenberg the whole evening to make a speech.

"My Lord Duke," brayed the jackass; and then he stopped dead, and looked round the room with an unmeaning stare.

"Hear, hear, hear!" was the general cry; but Grafenberg seemed astounded at any one being desirous of hearing his voice, or for a moment seriously entertaining the idea that he could have anything to say; and so he stared again, and again, and again, till at last Rüdesheimer, by dint of kicking his shins under the table, the Margrave the whole time seeming perfectly motionless, at length extracted a sentence from the asinine Landgrave.

"My Lord Duke!" again commenced Grafenberg, and again he stopped.

"Go on!" shouted all.

"My Lord Duke! Rüdesheimer is treading on my toes!"

Here little Geisenheim gave a loud laugh of derision, in which all joined except surly Markbrunnen, whose lips protruded an extra inch beyond their usual length when he found that all were laughing at his friend. The Grand Duke at last procured silence.

"Shame! shame! mighty Princes! Shame! shame! noble Lords! Is it with this irreverent glee, these scurvy flouts and indecorous mockery, that you would have this stranger believe that we celebrate the ceremonies of our Father Rhine? Shame, I say; and silence! It is time that we should prove to him that we are not merely a boisterous and unruly party of swilling varlets, who leave their brains in their cups. It is time that we should do something to prove that we are capable of better and worthier things. What ho! my Lord of Geisenheim! shall I speak twice to the guardian of the horn of the Fairy King?"

The little dwarf instantly jumped from his seat and proceeded to the end of the room, where, after having bowed three times with great reverence before a small black cabinet made of vine wood, he opened it with a golden key, and then with great pomp and ceremony bore its contents to the Grand Duke. That chieftain took from the little dwarf the horn of a gigantic and antediluvian elk. The cunning hand of an ancient German artificer had formed this curious relic into a drinking-cup. It was exquisitely polished, and cased in the interior with silver. On the outside the only ornaments were three richly chased silver rings, which were placed nearly at equal distances. When the Grand Duke had carefully examined this most precious horn, he held it up with great reverence to all present, and a party of devout Catholics could not have paid greater homage to the elevated Host than

did the various guests to the horn of the Fairy King. Even
the satanic smile on Rüdesheimer's countenance was for a
moment subdued, and all bowed. The Grand Duke then delivered the mighty cup to his neighbor, the Archduke of
Hochheimer, who held it with both hands until his Royal
Highness had emptied into it, with great care, three bottles
of Johannisberger. All rose: the Grand Duke took the goblet
in one hand, and with the other he dexterously put aside his
most inconvenient and enormous nose. Dead silence prevailed, save the roar of the liquor as it rushed down the Grand
Duke's throat, and resounded through the chamber like the
distant dash of a waterfall. In three minutes the Chairman
had completed his task, the horn had quitted his mouth, his
nose had again resumed its usual situation, and as he handed
the cup to the Archduke, Vivian thought that a material
change had taken place in his countenance since he had
quaffed his last draught. His eyes seemed more apart; his
ears seemed broader and longer; and his nose visibly length-
ened. The Archduke, before he commenced his draught,
ascertained with great scrupulosity that his predecessor had
taken his fair share by draining the horn as far as the first
ring; and then he poured off with great rapidity his own
portion. But though, in performing the same task, he was
quicker than the master of the party, the draught not only
apparently, but audibly, produced upon him a much more
decided effect than it had on the Grand Duke; for when the
second ring was drained the Archduke gave a loud roar of
exultation, and stood up for some time from his seat, with his
hands resting on the table, over which he leaned, as if he were
about to spring upon his opposite neighbor. The cup was now
handed across the table to the Baron of Asmannshausen. His
Lordship performed his task with ease; but as he withdrew
the horn from his mouth, all present, except Vivian, gave
a loud cry of "Supernaculum!" The Baron smiled with great
contempt, as he tossed, with a careless hand, the great horn
upside downward, and was unable to shed upon his nail even
the one excusable pearl. He handed the refilled horn to the
Elector of Steinberg, who drank his portion with a growl;
but afterward seemed so pleased with the facility of his
execution that, instead of delivering it to the next bibber, the

Palsgrave of Markbrunnen, he commenced some clumsy attempts at a dance of triumph, in which he certainly would have proceeded, had not the loud grunts of the surly and thick-lipped Markbrunnen occasioned the interference of the President. Supernaculum now fell to the Margrave of Rüdesheimer, who gave a loud and long-continued laugh as the dwarf of Geisenheim filled the horn for the third time.

While this ceremony was going on, a thousand plans had occurred to Vivian for his escape; but all, on second thought, proved impracticable. With agony he had observed that supernaculum was his miserable lot. Could he but have foisted it on the idiot Grafenberg, he might, by his own impudence and the other's stupidity, have escaped. But he could not flatter himself that he should be successful in bringing about this end, for he observed with dismay that the malicious Rüdesheimer had not for a moment ceased watching him with a keen and exulting glance. Geisenheim performed his task; and ere Vivian could ask for the goblet, Rüdesheimer, with a fell laugh, had handed it to Grafenberg. The greedy ass drank his portion with ease, and indeed drank far beyond his limit. The cup was in Vivian's hand, Rüdesheimer was roaring supernaculum louder than all; Vivian saw that the covetous Grafenberg had providentially rendered his task comparatively light; but even as it was, he trembled at the idea of drinking at a single draught more than a pint of most vigorous and powerful wine.

"My Lord Duke," said Vivian, "you and your companions forget that I am little used to these ceremonies; that I am yet uninitiated in the mysteries of the näre. I have endeavored to prove myself no chicken-hearted, water-drinking craven, and I have more wine within me at this moment than any man yet bore without dinner. I think, therefore, that I have some grounds for requesting indulgence, and I have no doubt that the good sense of yourself and your friends—"

Ere Vivian could finish, he almost fancied that a well-stocked menagerie had been suddenly emptied in the room. Such roaring, and such growling, and such hissing, could only have been exceeded on some grand feast day in the recesses of a Brazilian forest. Asnannshausen looked as fierce

as a boa constrictor before dinner. The proboscis of the
Grand Duke heaved to and fro like the trunk of an enraged
elephant. Hochheimer glared like a Bengal tiger about to
spring upon its prey. Steinberg growled like a Baltic bear.
In Markbrunnen Vivian recognized the wild boar he had himself often hunted. Grafenberg brayed like a jackass, and
Geisenheim chattered like an ape. But all was forgotten and
unnoticed when Vivian heard the fell and frantic shouts of
the laughing hyena, the Margrave of Rüdesheimer! Vivian,
in despair, dashed the horn of Oberon to his mouth. One
pull, a gasp, another desperate draught; it was done! and
followed by a supernaculum almost superior to the exulting
Asmannshausen's.

A loud shout hailed the exploit, and when the shout had
subsided into silence the voice of the Grand Duke of Johannisberger was again heard:

"Noble Lords and Princes! I congratulate you on the
acquisition of a congenial co-mate, and the accession to our
society of one who, I now venture to say, will never disgrace
the glorious foundation; but who, on the contrary, with heav-
en's blessing and the aid of his own good palate, will, it is
hoped, add to our present knowledge of flavors by the detection of new ones, and by illustrations drawn from frequent
study and constant observation of the mysterious näre. In
consideration of his long journey and his noble achievement,
I do propose that we drink but very lightly to-night, and
meet by two hours after to-morrow's dawn under the moss-
man's oak. Nevertheless, before we part, for the refreshment of our own good bodies, and by way of reward and act
of courtesy to this noble and accomplished stranger, let us
pledge him in some foreign grape of fame, to which he may
perhaps be more accustomed than unto the ever preferable
juices of our Father Rhine." Here the Grand Duke nodded
to little Geisenheim, who in a moment was at his elbow.

It was in vain that Vivian remonstrated, excused himself
from joining, or assured them that their conduct had already
been so peculiarly courteous, that any further attention was
at present unnecessary. A curiously-cut glass, which on a
moderate calculation Vivian reckoned would hold at least
three pints, was placed before each guest; and a basket, con-

taining nine bottles of sparkling champagne, *première qualité,* was set before his Highness.

"We are no bigots, noble stranger," said the Grand Duke, as he took one of the bottles, and scrutinized the cork with a very keen eye; "we are no bigots, and there are moments when we drink champagne, nor is Burgundy forgotten, nor the soft Bordeaux, nor the glowing grape of the sunny Rhone!" His Highness held the bottle at an oblique angle with the chandelier. The wire is loosened, whirr! The exploded cork whizzed through the air, extinguished one of the burners of the chandelier, and brought the cut drop which was suspended under it rattling down among the glasses on the table. The President poured the foaming fluid into his great goblet, and bowing to all around, fastened on its contents with as much eagerness as Arabs hasten to a fountain.

The same operation was performed as regularly and as skilfully by all except Vivian. Eight burners were extinguished; eight diamond drops had fallen clattering on the table; eight human beings had finished a miraculous carouse, by each drinking off a bottle of sparkling champagne. It was Vivian's turn. All eyes were fixed on him with the most perfect attention. He was now, indeed, quite desperate; for had he been able to execute a trick which long practice alone could have enabled any man to perform, he felt conscious that it was quite out of his power to taste a single drop of the contents of his bottle. However, he loosened his wire and held the bottle at an angle with the chandelier; but the cork flew quite wild, and struck with great force the mighty nose of Johannisberger.

"A forfeit!" cried all.

"Treason, and a forfeit!" cried the Margrave of Rüdesheimer.

"A forfeit is sufficient punishment," said the President, who, however, still felt the smarting effect of the assault on his proboscis. "You must drink Oberon's horn full of champagne," he continued.

"Never!" said Vivian. "Enough of this. I have already conformed in a degree which may injuriously affect my health with your barbarous humors; but there is moderation even in excess. And so, if you please, my Lord, your servant may show me to my apartment, or I shall again mount my horse."

"You shall not leave this room," said the President, with great firmness.

"Who shall prevent me?" asked Vivian.

"I will, all will!"

"Now, by heavens! a more insolent and inhospitable old ruffian did I never meet. By the wine you worship, if one of you dare touch me, you shall rue it all your born days; and as for you, sir, if you advance one step toward me, I will take that sausage of a nose of yours and hurl you half round your own castle!"

"Treason!" shouted all, and looked to the chair.

"Treason!" said enraged majesty. The allusion to the nose had done away with all the constitutional doubts which had been sported so moderately at the commencement of the evening.

"Treason!" howled the President: "instant punishment!"

"What punishment?" asked Asmannshausen.

"Drown him in the new butt of Moselle," recommended Rüdesheimer. The suggestion was immediately adopted. Every one rose: the little Geisenheim already had hold of Vivian's shoulder; and Grafenberg, instigated by the cowardly but malicious Rüdesheimer, was about to seize him by the neck. Vivian took the dwarf and hurled him at the chandelier, in whose brazen chains the little being got entangled, and there remained. An unexpected cross-buttocker floored the incautious and unscientific Grafenberg; and following up these advantages, Vivian laid open the skull of his prime enemy, the retreating Margrave of Rüdesheimer, with the assistance of the horn of Oberon, which flew from his hand to the other end of the room, from the force of which it rebounded from the cranium of the enemy. All the rest were now on the advance; but giving a vigorous and unexpected push to the table, the Johannisberger and Asmannshausen were thrown over, and the nose of the former got entangled with the awkward windings of the Fairy King's horn. Taking advantage of this move, Vivian rushed to the door. He escaped, but had not time to secure the lock against the enemy, for the stout Elector of Steinberg was too quick for him. He dashed down the stairs with extraordinary agility; but just as he had gained the large octagonal hall, the whole of his late boon companions, with the exception of the dwarf of Geisenheim, who was left in the chandelier, were visible in full chase. Escape was impossible, and so Vivian, followed by the seven nobles, headed by their President, described with all possible rapidity a circle round the hall. He gave himself up for lost; but, luckily for him, it never occurred to one of his pursuers to do anything but follow their leader; and as, therefore, they never dodged Vivian, and as, also, he was a much fleeter runner than the fat President, whose pace, of course, regulated the progress of his followers, the party might have gone on at this rate until all of them had dropped from fatigue, had not the occurrence of a ludicrous incident prevented this consummation.

The hall door was suddenly dashed open, and Essper George rushed in, followed in full chase by Hunsdrich and the guests of the lodge, who were the servants of Vivian's pursuers. Essper darted in between Rüdesheimer and Markbrunnen, and Hunsdrich and his friends following the same tactics as their lords and masters, without making any attempt to surround and hem in the object of their pursuit, merely followed him in order, describing, but in a contrary direction, a lesser circle within the eternal round of the first party. It was only proper for the servants to give their masters the wall. In spite of their very disagreeable and dangerous situation, it was with difficulty that Vivian refrained from laughter, as he met Essper regularly every half minute at the foot of the great staircase. Suddenly, as Essper passed, he took Vivian by the waist, and with a single jerk placed him on the stairs; and then, with a dexterous dodge, he brought Hunsdrich, the porter, and the Grand Duke in full contact.

"I have got you at last," said Hunsdrich, seizing hold of his Grace of Johannisberger by the ears, and mistaking him for Essper.

"I have got you at last," said his master, grappling, as he supposed, with Vivian. Both struggled: their followers pushed on with impetuous force, the battle was general, the overthrow universal. In a moment all were on the ground; and if any less inebriated or more active individual attempted to rise, Essper immediately brought him down with a boar-spear.

"Give me that large fishing-net," said Essper to Vivian; "quick, quick."

Vivian pulled down a large coarse net, which covered nearly five sides of the room. It was immediately unfolded and spread over the fallen crew. To fasten it down with half a dozen boar-spears, which they drove into the floor, was the work of a moment. Essper had one pull at the proboscis of the Grand Duke of Johannisberger before he hurried Vivian away; and in ten minutes they were again on their horses' backs and galloping through the starlit wood.

CHAPTER II

IT is the hour before the laboring bee has left his golden hive; not yet the blooming day buds in the blushing East; not yet has the victorious Lucifer chased from the early sky the fainting splendor of the stars of night. All is silent, save the light breath of morn waking the slumbering leaves. Even now a golden streak breaks over the gray mountains. Hark to shrill chanticleer! As the cock crows the owl ceases. Hark to shrill chanticleer's feathered rival! The mountain lark springs from the sullen earth, and welcomes with his hymn the coming day. The golden streak has expanded into a crimson crescent, and rays of living fire flame over the rose-enameled East. Man rises sooner than the sun, and already sound the whistle of the plowman, the song of the mower, and the forge of the smith; and hark to the bugle of the hunter, and the baying of his deep-mouthed hound. The sun is up, the generating sun! and temple, and tower, and tree, the massy wood, and the broad field, and the distant hill, burst into sudden light; quickly upcurled is the dusky mist from the shining river; quickly is the cold dew drunk from the raised heads of the drooping flowers!

A canter by a somewhat clearer light than the one which had so unfortunately guided himself and his companion to

the Palace of the Wines soon carried them again to the skirts
of the forest, and at this minute they are emerging on the
plain from yonder dark wood.

"By heavens! Essper, I can not reach the town this morning. Was ever anything more unfortunate. A curse on those
drunken fools. What with no rest and no solid refreshment,
and the rivers of hock that are flowing within me, and the
infernal exertion of running round that vile hall, I feel fairly
exhausted, and could at this moment fall from my saddle. See
you no habitation, my good fellow, where there might be a
chance of a breakfast and a few hours' rest? We are now
well out of the forest. Oh! surely there is smoke from
behind those pines; some good wife, I trust, is by her chimney
corner."

"If my sense be not destroyed by the fumes of that mulled
Geisenheimer, which still haunts me, I could swear that the
smoke is the soul of a burning weed."

"A truce to your jokes, good Essper; I really am very ill.
A year ago I could have laughed at our misfortunes, but now
it is very different; and, by heavens, I must have breakfast! so
stir, exert yourself, and, although I die for it, let us canter
up to the smoke."

"No, dear master, I will ride on before. Do you follow
gently, and if there be a pigeon in the pot in all Germany, I
swear by the patron saint of every village for fifty miles round,
provided they be not heretics, that you shall taste of its breast-
bone this morning."

The smoke did issue from a chimney, but the door of the
cottage was shut.

"Hilloa, within!" shouted Essper; "who shuts the sun out
on a September morning?"

The door was at length slowly opened, and a most ill-
favored and inhospitable-looking dame demanded, in a sullen
voice, "What's your will?"

"You pretty creature!" said Essper, who was still a little
tipsy.

The door would have been shut in his face had not he
darted into the house before the woman was aware.

"Truly, a neat and pleasant dwelling! and you would have
no objection, I guess, to give a handsome young gentleman

some little sop of something just to remind him, you know, that it isn't dinner-time."

"We give no sops here: what do you take us for? and so, my handsome young gentleman, be off, or I shall call the good man."

"Why, I am not the handsome young gentleman; that is my master! who, if he were not half-starved to death, would fall in love with you at first sight."

"Your master; is he in the carriage?"

"Carriage! no; on horseback."

"Travelers?"

"To be sure, dear dame; travelers true."

"Travelers true, without luggage, and at this time of morn! Methinks, by your looks, queer fellows, that you are travelers whom it may be wise for an honest woman not to meet."

"What! some people have an objection, then, to a forty kreutzer piece on a sunny morning?"

So saying, Essper, in a careless manner, tossed a broad piece in the air, and made it ring on a fellow coin, as he caught it in the palm of his hand when it descended.

"Is that your master?" asked the woman.

"Ay, is it! and the prettiest piece of flesh I have seen this month, except yourself."

"Well! if the gentleman likes bread he can sit down here," said the woman, pointing to a bench, and throwing a sour black loaf upon the table.

"Now, sir!" said Essper, wiping the bench with great care, "lie you here and rest yourself. I have known a marshal sleep upon a harder sofa. Breakfast will be ready immediately."

"If you can not eat what you have, you may ride where you can find better cheer."

"What is bread for a traveler's breakfast? But I dare say my lord will be contented; young men are so easily pleased when there is a pretty girl in the case; you know that, you wench! you do, you little hussy; you are taking advantage of it."

Something like a smile lighted up the face of the sullen woman when she said, "There may be an egg in the house, but I don't know."

"But you will soon, you dear creature! What a pretty

foot!" bawled Essper after her, as she left the room. "Now confound this hag; if there be not meat about this house may I keep my mouth shut at our next dinner. What's that in the corner? a boar's tusk! Ay, ay! a huntsman's cottage; and when lived a huntsman on black bread before! Oh! bless your bright eyes for these eggs, and this basin of new milk."

So saying, Essper took them out of her hand and placed them before Vivian.

"I was saying to myself, my pretty girl, when you were out of the room, 'Essper George, good cheer, say thy prayers, and never despair; come what may. you will fall among friends at last, and how do you know that your dream mayn't come true after all? Didn't you dream that you breakfasted in the month of September with a genteel young woman with gold earrings? and is not she standing before you now? and did not she do everything in the world to make you comfortable? Did not she give you milk and eggs, and when you complained that you and meat had been but slack friends of late, did not she open her own closet, and give you as fine a piece of hunting beef as was ever set before a Jagd Junker?"

"I think you will turn me into an innkeeper's wife at last," said the dame, her stern features relaxing into a smile; and while she spoke she advanced to the great closet, Essper George following her, walking on his toes, lolling out his enormous tongue, and stroking his mock paunch. As she opened it he jumped upon a chair and had examined every shelf in less time than a pistol could flash. "White bread! fit for a countess; salt! worthy of Poland; boar's head!! no better at Troyes; and hunting beef!!! my dream is true!" and he bore in triumph to Vivian, who was nearly asleep, the ample round of salt and pickled beef well stuffed with all kinds of savory herbs.

It was nearly an hour before noon ere the travelers had remounted. Their road again entered the forest which they had been skirting for the last two days. The huntsmen were abroad; and the fine weather, his good meal and seasonable rest, and the inspiriting sounds of the bugle made Vivian feel recovered from his late fatigues.

"That must be a true-hearted huntsman, Essper, by the sound of his bugle. I never heard one played with more spirit.

Hark! how fine it dies away in the wood; fainter and fainter, yet how clear! It must be now half a mile distant."

"I hear nothing so wonderful," said Essper, putting the two middle fingers of his right hand before his mouth and sounding a note so clear and beautiful, so exactly imitative of the fall which Vivian had noticed and admired, that for a moment he imagined that the huntsman was at his elbow.

"Thou art a cunning knave! do it again." This time Essper made the very wood echo. In a few minutes a horseman galloped up; he was as spruce a cavalier as ever pricked gay steed on the pliant grass. He was dressed in a green military uniform, and a gilt bugle hung by his side; his spear told them that he was hunting the wild boar. When he saw Vivian and Essper he suddenly pulled up his horse and seemed astonished.

"I thought that his Highness had been here," said the huntsman.

"No one has passed us, sir," said Vivian.

"I could have sworn that his bugle sounded from this very spot," said the huntsman. "My ear seldom deceives me."

"We heard a bugle to the right, sir," said Essper.

"Thanks, my friends," and the huntsman was about to gallop off.

"May I ask the name of his Highness?" said Vivian. "We are strangers in this country."

"That may certainly account for your ignorance," said the huntsman; "but no one who lives in this land can be unacquainted with his Serene Highness the Prince of Little Lilliput, my illustrious master. I have the honor," continued the huntsman, "of being Jagd Junker, or Gentilhomme de la Chasse to his Serene Highness."

"'Tis an office of great dignity," said Vivian, "and one that I have no doubt you admirably perform; I will not stop you, sir, to admire your horse."

The huntsman bowed courteously and galloped off.

"You see, sir," said Essper George, "that my bugle has deceived even the Jagd Junker, or Gentilhomme de la Chasse of his Serene Highness the Prince of Little Lilliput himself;" so saying, Essper again sounded his instrument.

"A joke may be carried too far, my good fellow," said

Vivian. "A true huntsman like myself must not spoil a brother's sport, so silence your bugle."

Now again galloped up the Jagd Junker, or Gentilhomme de la Chasse of his Serene Highness the Prince of Little Lilliput. He pulled up his horse again, apparently as much astounded as ever.

"I thought that his Highness had been here," said the huntsman.

"No one has passed us," said Vivian.

"We heard a bugle to the right," said Essper George.

"I am afraid his Serene Highness must be in distress. The whole suite are off the scent. It must have been his bugle, for the regulations of this forest are so strict that no one dare sound a blast but his Serene Highness." Away galloped the huntsman.

"Next time I must give you up, Essper," said Vivian.

"One more blast, good master!" begged Essper, in a supplicating voice. "This time to the left; the confusion will be then complete."

"I command you not," and so they rode on in silence. But it was one of those days when Essper could neither be silent nor subdued. Greatly annoyed at not being permitted to play his bugle, he amused himself imitating the peculiar sound of every animal that he met; a young fawn and various birds already followed him, and even a squirrel had perched on his horse's neck. And now they came to a small farmhouse, which was situated in the forest: the yard here offered great amusement to Essper. He neighed, and half a dozen horses' heads immediately appeared over the hedge; another neigh, and they were following him in the road. A dog rushed out to seize the dangerous stranger and recover his charge, but Essper gave an amicable bark, and in a second the dog was jumping by his side and engaged in earnest and friendly conversation. A loud and continued grunt soon brought out the pigs, and meeting three or four cows returning home, a few lowing sounds soon seduced them from keeping their appointment with the dairymaid. A stupid jackass, who stared with astonishment at the procession, was saluted with a lusty bray, which immediately induced him to swell the ranks; and, as Essper passed the poultry-yard, he so deceitfully informed its inhabitants that they were about to be fed, that broods of ducks and chickens were immediately after him. The careful hens were terribly alarmed at the danger which their offspring incurred from the heels and hoofs of the quadrupeds; but while they were in doubt and despair a whole flock of stately geese issued in solemn pomp from another gate of the farmyard, and commenced a cackling conversation with the delighted Essper. So contagious is the force of example, and so great was the confidence which the hens placed in these pompous geese, who were not the first fools whose solemn air has deceived a few old females, that as soon as they perceived them in the train of the horsemen they also trotted up to pay their respects at his levée.

But it was not a moment for mirth; for rushing down the road with awful strides appeared two sturdy and enraged husbandmen, one armed with a pike and the other with a pitchfork, and accompanied by a frantic female, who never for a moment ceased hallooing "Murder, rape, and fire!" everything but "theft."

"Now, Essper, here's a pretty scrape!"

"Stop, you rascals!" hallooed Adolph, the herdsman.

"Stop, you gang of thieves!" hallooed Wilhelm, the plowman.

"Stop, you bloody murderers!" shrieked Phillippa, the indignant mistress of the dairy and the poultry-yard.

"Stop, you villains!" hallooed all three. The villains certainly made no attempt to escape, and in half a second the enraged household of the forest farmer would have seized on Essper George; but just at this crisis he uttered loud sounds in the respective language of every bird and beast about him, and suddenly they all turned round and counter-marched. Away rushed the terrified Adolph, the herdsman, while one of his own cows was on his back. Still quicker scampered off the scared Wilhelm, the plowman, while one of his own steeds kicked him in his rear. Quicker than all these, shouting, screaming, shrieking, dashed back the unhappy mistress of the hen-roost, with all her subjects crowding about her; some on her elbow, some on her head, her lace cap destroyed, her whole dress disordered. The movements of the crowd were so quick that they were soon out of sight.

"A trophy!" called out Essper, as he jumped off his horse and picked up the pike of Adolph, the herdsman.

"A boar-spear, or I am no huntsman," said Vivian: "give it me a moment!" He threw it up into the air, caught it with ease, poised it with the practiced skill of one well used to handle the weapon, and with the same delight imprinted on his countenance as greets the sight of an old friend.

"This forest, Essper, and this spear, make me remember. days when I was vain enough to think that I had been suffi- ciently visited with sorrow. Ah! little did I then know of human misery, although I imagined I had suffered so much!"

As he spoke, the sounds of a man in distress were heard from the right side of the road.

"Who calls?" cried Essper. A shout was the only answer. There was no path, but the underwood was low, and Vivian took his horse, an old forester, across it with ease. Essper's jibbed; Vivian found himself in a small green glade of about thirty feet square. It was thickly surrounded with lofty trees, save at the point where he had entered; and at the furthest corner of it, near some gray rocks, a huntsman was engaged in a desperate contest with a wild boar.

The huntsman was on his right knee, and held his spear with both hands at the furious beast. It was an animal of ex- traordinary size and power. Its eyes glittered like fire. On the turf to its right a small gray mastiff, of powerful make, lay on its back, bleeding profusely, with its body ripped open. Another dog, a fawn-colored bitch, had seized on the left ear of the beast; but the under-tusk of the boar, which was nearly a foot long, had penetrated the courageous dog, and the poor creature writhed in agony, even while it attempted to wreak its revenge upon its enemy. The huntsman was nearly exhausted. Had it not been for the courage of the fawn- colored dog, which, clinging to the boar, prevented it making a full dash at the man, he must have been gored. Vivian was off his horse in a minute, which, frightened at the sight of the wild boar, dashed again over the hedge.

"Keep firm, sir!" said he; "do not move. I will amuse him behind, and make him turn."

A graze of Vivian's spear on its back, though it did not

materially injure the beast, for there the boar is nearly invulnerable, annoyed it; and dashing off the fawn-colored dog with great force, it turned on its new assailant. Now there are only two places in which the wild boar can be assailed with any effect; and these are just between the eyes and between the shoulders. Great caution, however, is necessary in aiming these blows, for the boar is very adroit in transfixing the weapon on his snout or his tusks; and if once you miss, particularly if you are not assisted by dogs, which Vivian was not, 'tis all over with you; for the enraged animal rushes in like lightning, and gored you must be.

But Vivian was fresh and cool. The animal suddenly stood still and eyed its new enemy. Vivian was quiet, for he had no objection to give the beast an opportunity of retreating to its den. But retreat was not its object; it suddenly darted at the huntsman, who, however, was not off his guard, though unable, from a slight wound in his knee, to rise. Vivian again annoyed the boar at the rear, and the animal soon returned to him. He made a feint, as if he were about to strike his pike between its eyes. The boar, not feeling a wound which had not been inflicted, and very irritated, rushed at him, and he buried his spear a foot deep between its shoulders. The beast made one fearful struggle and then fell down quite dead. The fawn-colored bitch, though terribly wounded, gave a loud bark; and even the other dog, which Vivian thought had been long dead, testified its triumphant joy by an almost inarticulate groan. As soon as he was convinced that the boar was really dead, Vivian hastened to the huntsman, and expressed his hope that he was not seriously hurt.

"A trifle, which our surgeon, who is used to these affairs, will quickly cure. Sir! we owe you our life!" said the huntsman, with great dignity, as Vivian assisted him in rising from the ground. He was a tall man, of distinguished appearance; but his dress, which was the usual hunting costume of a German nobleman, did not indicate his quality.

"Sir, we owe you our life!" repeated the stranger; "five minutes more, and our son must have reigned in Little Lilliput."

"I have the honor, then, of addressing your Serene Highness. Far from being indebted to me, I feel that I ought to apologize for having so unceremoniously joined your sport."

"Nonsense, man! We have killed in our time too many of these gentry to be ashamed of owning that, had it not been for you, one of them would at last have revenged the species. But many as are the boars that we have killed or eaten, we never saw a more furious or powerful animal than the present. Why, sir, you must be one of the best hands at the spear in all Christendom!"

"Indifferently good, your Highness: your Highness forgets that the animal was already exhausted by your assault."

"Why, there is something in that; but it was neatly done, man; it was neatly done. You are fond of the sport, we think?"

"I have had some practice, but illness has so weakened me that I have given up the forest."

"Pity! and on a second examination we observe that you are no hunter. This coat is not for the free forest; but how came you by the pike?"

"I am traveling to the next post town, to which I have sent on my luggage. I am getting fast to the south; and as for this pike, my servant got it this morning from some peasant in a brawl, and was showing it to me when I heard your Highness call. I really think now that Providence must have sent it. I certainly could not have done you much service with my riding whip. Hilloa! Essper, where are you?"

"Here, noble sir! here, here. Why, what have you got there? The horses have jibbed, and will not stir. I can stay no longer; they may go to the devil!" So saying, Vivian's valet dashed over the underwood, and leaped at the foot of the Prince.

"In God's name, is this thy servant?" asked his Highness.

"In good faith am I," said Essper; "his valet, his cook, and his secretary, all in one; and also his Jagd Junker, or *Gentilhomme de la Chasse,* as a puppy with a bugle horn told me this morning."

"A merry knave!" said the Prince; "and talking of a puppy with a bugle horn reminds us how unaccountably we have been deserted to-day by a suite that never yet were wanting. We are indeed astonished. Our bugle, we fear, has turned traitor." So saying, the Prince executed a blast with great skill, which Vivian immediately recognized as the one which Essper George had imitated.

"And now, my good friend," said the Prince, "we can not hear of your passing through our land without visiting our good castle. We would that we could better testify the obligation that we feel under to you in any other way than by the offer of a hospitality which all gentlemen, by right, can command. But your presence would, indeed, give us sincere pleasure. You must not refuse us. Your looks, as well as your prowess, prove your blood; and we are quite sure no cloth merchant's order will suffer by your not hurrying to your proposed point of destination. We are not wrong, we think, though your accent is good, in supposing that we are conversing with an English gentleman. But here they come."

As he spoke, three or four horsemen, at the head of whom was the young huntsman whom the travelers had met in the morning, sprang into the glade.

"Why, Arnelm!" said the Prince, "when before was the Jagd Junker's ear so bad that he could not discover his master's bugle, even though the wind were against him?"

"In truth, your Highness, we have heard bugles enough this morning. Who is violating the forest laws we know not; but that another bugle is sounding, and played—St. Hubert forgive me for saying so—with as great skill as you Highness, is certain. Myself, Von Neuweid, and Lintz have been galloping over the whole forest. The rest, I doubt not, will be up directly." The Jagd Junker blew his own bugle.

In the course of five minutes, about twenty other horsemen, all dressed in the same uniform, had arrived; all complaining of their wild chases after the Prince in every other part of the forest.

"It must be the Wild Huntsman himself!" swore an old hand. This solution of the mystery satisfied all.

"Well, well!" said the Prince; "whoever it may be, had it not been for the timely presence of this gentleman, you must have changed your green jackets for mourning coats, and our bugle would have sounded no more in the forest of our fathers. Here, Arnelm! cut up the beast, and remember that the left shoulder is the quarter of honor, and belongs to this stranger, not less honored because unknown."

All present took off their caps and bowed to Vivian, who took this opportunity of informing the Prince who he was.

"And now," continued his Highness, "Mr. Grey will accompany us to our castle; nay, sir, we can take no refusal. We will send on to the town for your luggage. Arnelm, do you look to this. And, honest friend," said the Prince, turning to Essper George, "we commend you to the special care of our friend Von Neuwied; and so, gentlemen, with stout hearts and spurs to your steeds, to the castle."

CHAPTER III

THE cavalcade proceeded for some time at a brisk but irregular pace, until they arrived at a less wild and wooded part of the forest. The Prince of Little Lilliput reined in his steed as he entered a broad avenue of purple beeches, at the end of which, though at a considerable distance, Vivian perceived the towers and turrets of a Gothic edifice glittering in the sunshine.

"Welcome to Turriparva!" said his Highness.

"I assure your Highness," said Vivian, "that I view with no unpleasant feeling the prospect of a reception in any civilized mansion; for to say the truth, for the last eight-and-forty hours Fortune has not favored me either in my researches after a bed, or that which some think still more important than repose."

"Is it so?" said the Prince. "Why, we should have thought by your home-thrust this morning that you were as fresh as the early lark. In good faith, it was a pretty stroke! And whence come you, then, good sir?"

"Know you a most insane and drunken idiot who styles himself the Grand Duke of Johannisberger?"

"No, no!" said the Prince, staring in Vivian's face earnestly, and then laughing. "And you have actually fallen among that mad crew. A most excellent adventure! Arnelm!

why, man, where art thou? Ride up! Behold in the person of
this gentleman a new victim to the overwhelming hospitality
of our Uncle of the Wines. And did they confer a title on you
on the spot? Say, 'art thou Elector, or Palsgrave, or Baron;
or, failing in thy devoirs, as once did our good cousin Arnelm,
confess that thou wert ordained with becoming reverence the
Archprimate of Puddledrink. Eh! Arnelm, is not that the style
thou bearest at the Palace of the Wines?"

"So it would seem, your Highness. I think the title was
conferred on me the same night that your Highness mistook
the Grand Duke's proboscis for Oberon's horn, and committed
treason not yet pardoned."

"Good! good! thou hast us there. Truly a good memory
is often as ready a friend as a sharp wit. Wit is not thy strong
point, friend Arnelm; and yet it is strange that in the sharp
encounter of ready tongues and idle *logomachies* thou hast
sometimes the advantage. But, nevertheless, rest assured, good
cousin Arnelm, that wit is not thy strong point."

"It is well for me that all are not of the same opinion as
your Serene Highness," said the young Jagd Junker, somewhat
nettled; for he prided himself on his repartees.

The Prince was much diverted with Vivian's account of
his last night's adventure; and our hero learned from his Highness that his late host was no less a personage than the cousin
of the Prince of Little Lilliput, an old German Baron who
passed his time, with some neighbors of congenial temperament, in hunting the wild boar in the morning and speculating
on the flavors of the fine Rhenish wines during the rest of the
day. "He and his companions," continued the Prince, "will
enable you to form some idea of the German nobility half a
century ago. The debauch of last night was the usual carouse
which crowned the exploits of each day when we were
a boy. The revolution has rendered all these customs obsolete.
Would that it had not sent some other things equally out
of fashion!"

At this moment the Prince sounded his bugle, and the gates
of the castle, which were not more than twenty yards distant,
were immediately thrown open. The whole cavalcade set
spurs to their steeds, and dashed at full gallop over the hollow-
sounding drawbridge into the courtyard of the castle. A crowd

of serving-men, in green liveries, instantly appeared, and Arnelm and Von Neuwied, jumping from their saddles, respectively held the stirrup and the bridle of the Prince as he dismounted.

"Where is Master Rodolph?" asked his Highness, with a loud voice.

"So please your Serene Highness, I am here!" answered a very thin treble; and, bustling through the surrounding crowd, came forward the owner of the voice. Master Rodolph was not much above five feet high, but he was nearly as broad as he was long. Though more than middle-aged, an almost infantile smile played upon his broad fair face, to which his small turn-up nose, large green goggle-eyes, and unmeaning mouth gave no expression. His long hair hung over his shoulders, the flaxen locks in some places maturing into gray. In compliance with the taste of his master, this most unsportsmanlike-looking steward was clad in a green jerkin, on the right arm of which was embroidered a giant's head, the crest of the Little Lilliputs.

"Truly, Rodolph, we have received some scratch in the chase to-day, and need your assistance. The best of surgeons, we assure you, Mr. Grey, if you require one: and look you that the blue chamber be prepared for this gentleman; and we shall have need of our cabinet this evening. See that all this be done, and inform Prince Maximilian that we would speak with him. And look you, Master Rodolph, there is one in this company—what call you your servant's name, sir? Essper George! 'tis well: look you, Rodolph, see that our friend Essper George be well provided for. We know that we can trust him to your good care. And now, gentlemen, at sunset we meet in the Giants' Hall." So saying, his Highness bowed to the party; and taking Vivian by the arm, and followed by Arnelm and Von Neuwied, he ascended a staircase which opened into the court, and then mounted into a covered gallery which ran round the whole building. The interior wall of the gallery was alternately ornamented with stags' heads or other trophies of the chase, and coats of arms blazoned in stucco. The Prince did the honors of the castle to Vivian with great courtesy. The armory and the hall, the knights' chamber, and even the donjon-keep, were all examined; and when Vivian had sufficiently admired the antiquity of the structure and the beauty of the situation, the Prince, having proceeded down a long corridor, opened the door into a small chamber, which he introduced to Vivian as his cabinet. The furniture of this room was rather quaint, and not unpleasing. The wainscot and ceiling were painted alike, of a light-green color, and were richly carved and gilt. The walls were hung with green velvet, of which material were also the chairs, and a sofa, which was placed under a large and curiously cut looking-glass. The lower panes of the windows of this room were of stained glass, of vivid tints; but the upper panes were untinged, in order that the light should not be disturbed which fell through them upon two magnificent pictures; one a hunting-piece, by Schneiders, and the other a portrait of an armed chieftain on horseback, by Lucas Cranach.

And now the door opened, and Master Rodolph entered, carrying in his hand a white wand, and bowing very reverently as he ushered in servants bearing a cold collation. As he entered, it was with difficulty that he could settle his countenance into the due and requisite degree of gravity; and so often was the fat steward on the point of bursting into laughter, as he arranged the setting out of the refreshments on the table, that the Prince, with whom he was at the same time both a favorite and a butt, at last noticed his unusual and unmanageable risibility.

"Why, Rodolph, what ails thee? Hast thou just discovered the point of some good saying of yesterday?"

The steward could now contain his laughter no longer, and he gave vent to his emotion in a most treble "He! he! he!"

"Speak, man, in the name of St. Hubert, and on the word of as stout a huntsman as ever yet crossed horse. Speak, we say; what ails thee?"

"He! he! he! in truth, a most comical knave! I beg your Serene Highness's ten thousand most humble pardons, but, in truth, a more comical knave did I never see. How call you him? Essper George, I think; he! he! he! In truth, your Highness was right when you styled him a merry knave; in truth, a most comical knave; he! he! a very funny knave! He says, your Highness, that I am like a snake in a consumption! he! he! he! In truth, a most comical knave!"

"Well, Rodolph, so long as you do not quarrel with his

jokes, they shall pass as true wit. But why comes not our son? Have you bidden the Prince Maximilian to our presence?"

"In truth have I, your Highness; but he was engaged at the moment with Mr. Sievers, and therefore he could not immediately attend my bidding. Nevertheless, he bade me deliver to your Serene Highness his dutiful affection, saying that he would soon have the honor of bending his knee unto your Serene Highness."

"He never said any such nonsense. At least, if he did, he must be changed since last we hunted."

"In truth, your Highness, I can not aver, upon my conscience as a faithful steward, that such were the precise words and exact phraseology of his Highness the Prince Maximilian. But in the time of the good Prince, your father, whose memory be ever blessed, such were the words and style of message which I was schooled and instructed by Mr. von Lexicon, your Serene Highness's most honored tutor, to bear unto the good Prince your father, whose memory be ever blessed, when I had the great fortune of being your Serene Highness's most particular page, and it fell to my lot to have the pleasant duty of informing the good Prince your father, whose memory be ever blessed—"

"Enough! but Sievers is not Von Lexicon, and Maximilian, we trust, is—"

"Papa! papa! dearest papa!" shouted a young lad, as he dashed open the door, and, rushing into the room, threw his arms round the Prince's neck.

"My darling!" said the father, forgetting at this moment of genuine feeling the pompous plural in which he had hitherto spoken of himself. The Prince fondly kissed his child. The boy was about ten years of age, exquisitely handsome. Courage, not audacity, was imprinted on his noble features.

"Papa! may I hunt with you to-morrow?"

"What says Mr. Sievers?"

"Oh! Mr. Sievers says I am excellent; I assure you, upon my honor, he does. I heard you come home; but though I was dying to see you, I would not run out till I had finished my Roman History. I say, papa! what a grand fellow Brutus was; what a grand thing it is to be a patriot! I intend to be a

patriot myself, and to kill the Grand Duke of Reisenburg.
Who is that?"

"My friend, Max, Mr. Grey. Speak to him."

"I am happy to see you at Turriparva, sir," said the boy,
bowing to Vivian with dignity. "Have you been hunting with
his Highness this morning?"

"I can hardly say I have."

"Max, I have received a slight wound to-day. Do not look
alarmed; it is slight. I only mention it because, had it not
been for this gentleman, it is very probable you would never
have seen your father again. He has saved my life!"

"Saved your life! saved my papa's life!" said the young
Prince, seizing Vivian's hand. "Oh! sir, what can I do for
you? Mr. Sievers!" said the boy, with eagerness, to a gentleman who entered the room; "Mr. Sievers! here is a young
lord who has saved papa's life!"

Mr. Sievers was a tall, thin man, about forty, with a clear
sallow complexion, a high forehead, on which a few wrinkles
were visible, bright keen eyes, and a quantity of gray curling
hair, which was combed back off his forehead, and fell down
over his shoulders. He was introduced to Vivian as the
Prince's particular friend; and then he listened, apparently
with interest, to his Highness's narrative of the morning's adventure, his danger, and his rescue. Young Maximilian never
took his large, dark-blue eyes off his father while he was speaking, and when he had finished the boy rushed to Vivian and
threw his arms round his neck. Vivian was delighted with the
affection of the child, who whispered to him in a low voice,
"I know what you are!"

"What, my young friend?"

"Ah! I know."

"But tell me!"

"You thought I should not find out: you are a patriot!"

"I hope I am," said Vivian; "but traveling in a foreign
country is hardly a proof of it. Perhaps you do not know that
I am an Englishman."

"An Englishman!" said the child, with an air of great disappointment. "I thought you were a patriot! I am one. Do
you know I will tell you a secret. You must promise not to
tell, though. Promise, upon your word. Well, then," said the

urchin, whispering with great energy in Vivian's ear through his hollow fist, "I hate the Grand Duke of Reisenburg, and I mean to stab him to the heart." So saying, the little Prince grated his teeth with an expression of bitter detestation.

"What the deuce is the matter with the child!" thought Vivian; but at this moment his conversation with him was interrupted.

"Am I to believe this young gentleman, my dear Sievers," asked the Prince, "when he tells me that his conduct has met your approbation?"

"Your son, Prince," answered Mr. Sievers, "can only speak truth. His excellence is proved by my praising him to his face."

The young Maximilian, when Mr. Sievers had ceased speaking, stood blushing, with his eyes fixed on the ground; and the delighted parent, catching his child up in his arms, embraced him with unaffected fondness.

"And now, all this time Master Rodolph is waiting for his patient. By St. Hubert, you can none of you think me very ill! Your pardon, Mr. Grey, for leaving you. My friend Sievers will, I am sure, be delighted to make you feel at ease at Turriparva. Max, come with me!"

Vivian found in Mr. Sievers an interesting companion; nothing of the pedant and much of the philosopher. Their conversation was of course chiefly on topics of local interest, anecdotes of the castle and the country, of Vivian's friends, the drunken Johannisberger and his crew, and such matters; but there was a keenness of satire in some of Mr. Sievers's observations which was highly amusing, and enough passed to make Vivian desire opportunities of conversing with him at greater length, and on subjects of greater interest. They were at present disturbed by Essper George entering the room to inform Vivian that his luggage had arrived from the village, and that the blue chamber was now prepared for his presence.

"We shall meet, I suppose, in the hall, Mr. Sievers?"

"No; I shall not dine there. If you remain at Turriparva, which I trust you will, I shall be happy to see you in my room. If it have no other inducement to gain it the honor of your visit, it has here, at least, the recommendation of singularity;

there is, at any rate, no other chamber like it in this good castle."

The business of the toilet is sooner performed for a hunting party in a German forest than for a state dinner at Chateau Desir, and Vivian was ready before he was summoned.

"His Serene Highness has commenced his progress toward the hall," announced Essper George to Vivian in a treble voice, and bowing with ceremony as he offered to lead the way, with a white wand waving in his right hand.

"I shall attend his Highness," said his master; "but before I do, if that white wand be not immediately laid aside it will be broken about your back."

"Broken about my back! what, the wand of office, sir, of your steward! Master Rodolph says that, in truth, a steward is but half himself who hath not his wand: methinks when his rod of office is wanting, his Highness of Lilliput's steward is but unequally divided. In truth, he is stout enough to be Aaron's wand that swallowed up all the rest. But has your nobleness any serious objection to my carrying a wand? It gives such an air!"

The Giants' Hall was a Gothic chamber of imposing appearance; the oaken rafters of the curiously carved roof rested on the grim heads of gigantic figures of the same material. These statues extended the length of the hall on each side; they were elaborately sculptured and highly polished, and each one held in its outstretched arm a blazing and aromatic torch. Above them, small windows of painted glass admitted a light which was no longer necessary at the banquet to which we are now about to introduce the reader. Over the great entrance doors was a gallery, from which a band of trumpeters, arrayed in ample robes of flowing scarlet, sent forth many a festive and martial strain. More than fifty individuals, all wearing hunting dresses of green cloth on which the giant's head was carefully emblazoned, were already seated in the hall when Vivian entered: he was conducted to the upper part of the chamber, and a seat was allotted him on the left hand of the Prince. His Highness had not arrived, but a chair of state, placed under a crimson canopy, denoted the style of its absent owner; and a stool, covered with velvet of the same regal color, and glistening with gold lace, announced that the presence of Prince Maximilian was expected. While Vivian was musing in astonishment at the evident affectation of royal pomp which pervaded the whole establishment of the Prince of Little Lilliput, the trumpeters in the gallery suddenly commenced a triumphant flourish. All rose as the princely procession entered the hall: first came Master Rodolph twirling his white wand with the practiced pride of a drum-major, and looking as pompous as a turkey-cock in a storm; six footmen in splendid liveries, two by two, immediately followed him. A page heralded the Prince Maximilian, and then came the Serene father; the Jagd Junker, and four or five other gentlemen of the court, formed the suite.

His Highness ascended the throne, Prince Maximilian was on his right, and Vivian had the high honor of the left hand; the Jagd Junker seated himself next to our hero. The table was profusely covered, chiefly with the sports of the forest, and the celebrated wild boar was not forgotten. Few minutes had elapsed ere Vivian perceived that his Highness was always served on bended knee; surprised at this custom, which even the mightiest and most despotic monarchs seldom exact, and still more surprised at the contrast which all this state afforded to the natural ease and affable amiability of the Prince, Vivian ventured to ask his neighbor Arnelm whether the banquet of to-day was in celebration of any particular event of general or individual interest.

"By no means," said the Jagd Junker, "this is the usual style of the Prince's daily meal, except that to-day there is, perhaps, rather less state and fewer guests than usual, in consequence of many of our fellow-subjects having left us with the purpose of attending a great hunting party, which is now holding in the dominions of his Highness's cousin, the Duke of Micromegas."

When the more necessary but, as most hold, the less delightful part of banqueting was over, and the numerous serving-men had removed the more numerous dishes of wild boar, red deer, roebuck, and winged game, a stiff Calvinistic-looking personage rose and delivered a long and most grateful grace, to which the sturdy huntsmen listened with a due mixture of piety and impatience. When his starch reverence, who in his black coat looked among the huntsmen very like (as Essper

George observed) a blackbird among a set of moulting canaries, had finished, an old man, with long snow-white hair and a
beard of the same color, rose from his seat, and, with a glass
in his hand, bowing first to his Highness with great respect and
then to his companions with an air of condescension, gave in
a stout voice, "The Prince!" A loud shout was immediately
raised, and all quaffed with rapture the health of a ruler
whom evidently they adored. Master Rodolph now brought
forward an immense silver goblet full of some crafty compound, from its odor doubtless delicious. The Prince held
the goblet by its two massy handles, and then said in a
loud voice:

"My friends, the Giant's head! and he who sneers at its
frown may he rue its bristles!"

The toast was welcomed with a cry of triumph. When
the noise had subsided the Jagd Junker rose, and prefacing
the intended pledge by a few observations as remarkable for
the delicacy of their sentiments as the elegance of their expression, he gave, pointing to Vivian, "The Guest! and may the
Prince never want a stout arm at a strong push!" The sentiment was again echoed by the lusty voices of all present, and
particularly by his Highness. As Vivian shortly returned
thanks and modestly apologized for the German of a foreigner,
he could not refrain from remembering the last time when he
was placed in the same situation; it was when the treacherous
Lord Courtown had drank success to Mr. Vivian Grey's
maiden speech in a bumper of claret at the political orgies of
Chateau Desir. Could he really be the same individual as the
daring youth who then organized the crazy councils of those
ambitious, imbecile graybeards? What was he then? What
had happened since? What was he now? He turned from the
comparison with feelings of sickening disgust, and it was with
difficulty that his countenance could assume the due degree of
hilarity which befitted the present occasion.

"Truly, Mr. Grey," said the Prince, "your German would
pass current at Weimar. Arnelm, good cousin Arnelm, we
must trouble thy affectionate duty to marshal and regulate
the drinking devoirs of our kind subjects to-night; for by the
advice of our trusty surgeon, Master Rodolph, of much fame,
we shall refrain this night from our accustomed potations, and

betake ourselves to the solitude of our cabinet; a solitude in good sooth, unless we can persuade you to accompany us, kind sir," said the Prince, turning to Mr. Grey. "Methinks eight-and-forty hours without rest, and a good part spent in the mad walls of our cousin of Johannisberger, are hardly the best preparatives for a drinking bout, unless, after Oberon's horn, ye may fairly be considered to be in practice. Nevertheless, I advise the cabinet and a cup of Rodolph's coffee. What sayest thou?"

Vivian acceded to the Prince's proposition with eagerness; and, accompanied by Prince Maximilian, and preceded by the little steward, who, surrounded by his serving-men, very much resembled a planet eclipsed by his satellites, they left the hall.

" 'Tis almost a pity to shut out the moon on such a night," said the Prince, as he drew a large green velvet curtain from the windows of the cabinet.

" 'Tis a magnificent night!" said Vivian; "how fine the effect of the light is upon the picture of the warrior. The horse seems quite living, and its fierce rider actually frowns upon us."

"He may well frown," said the Prince of Little Lilliput, in a voice of deep melancholy; and he hastily redrew the curtain. In a moment he started from the chair on which he had just seated himself, and again admitted the moonlight. "Am I really afraid of an old picture? No, no; it has not yet come to that."

This was uttered in a distinct voice, and of course excited the astonishment of Vivian, who, however, had too much discretion to evince his surprise, or to take any measure by which his curiosity might be satisfied.

His companion seemed instantly conscious of the seeming singularity of his expression.

"You are surprised at my words, good sir," said his Highness, as he paced very rapidly up and down the small chamber; "you are surprised at my words; but, sir, my ancestor's brow was guarded by a diadem!"

"Which was then well won, Prince, and is now worthily worn."

"By whom? where? how?" asked the Prince, in a rapid

voice. "Maximilian," continued his Highness, in a more subdued tone; "Maximilian, my own love, leave us; go to Mr. Sievers. God bless you, my only boy. Good-night!"

"Good-night, dearest papa, and down with the Grand Duke of Reisenburg!"

"He echoes the foolish zeal of my fond followers," said the Prince, as his son left the room. "The idle parade to which their illegal loyalty still clings; my own manners, the relics of former days; habits will not change like stations; all these have deceived you, sir. You have mistaken me for a monarch; I should be one. A curse light on me the hour I can mention it without a burning blush. Oh, shame! shame on the blood of my father's son! Can my mouth own that I once was one? Yes, sir! you see before you the most injured, the least enviable of human beings. I am a mediatized Prince!"

Vivian had resided too long in Germany to be ignorant of the meaning of this title, with which, perhaps, few of our readers may be acquainted. A mediatized prince is an unhappy victim of those Congresses which, among other good and evil, purged with great effect the ancient German political system. By the regulations then determined on that country was freed at one fell swoop from the vexatious and harassing dominion of the various petty princes who exercised absolute sovereignties over little nations of fifty thousand souls. These independent sovereigns became subjects; and either swelled, by their mediatization, the territories of some already powerful potentate, or transmuted into a state of importance some more fortunate petty ruler than themselves, whose independence, through the exertions of political intrigue or family influence, had been preserved inviolate. In most instances, the concurrence of these little rulers in their worldly degradation was obtained by a lavish grant of official emoluments or increase of territorial possessions; and the mediatized Prince, instead of being an impoverished and uninfluential sovereign, became a wealthy and powerful subject. But so dominant in the heart of man is the love of independent dominion that even with these temptations few of the petty princes could have been induced to have parted with their cherished sceptres, had they not been conscious that, in case of contumacy, the resolutions of a Diet would have been enforced by the armies of an emperor. As it is, few of them have yet given up the outward and visible signs of regal sway. The throne is still preserved and the tiara still revered. They seldom frequent the courts of their sovereigns, and scarcely condescend to notice the attentions of their fellow nobility. Most of them expend their increased revenues in maintaining the splendor of their little courts at their ancient capitals, or in swelling the ranks of their retainers at their solitary forest castles.

The Prince of Little Lilliput was the first mediatized sovereign that Vivian had ever met. At another time, and under other circumstances, he might have smiled at the idle parade and useless pomp which he had this day witnessed, or moralized on that weakness of human nature which seemed to consider the inconvenient appendages of a throne as the great end for which power was to be coveted; but at the present moment he only saw a kind and, as he believed, estimable individual disquieted and distressed. It was painful to witness the agitation of the Prince, and Vivian felt it necessary to make some observations which, from his manner, expressed more than they meant.

"Sir," said his Highness, "your sympathy consoles me. Do not imagine that I can misunderstand it; it does you honor. You add by this to the many favors you have already conferred on me by saving my life and accepting my hospitality. I sincerely hope that your departure hence will be postponed to the last possible moment. Your conversation and your company have made me pass a more cheerful day than I am accustomed to. All here love me; but, with the exception of Sievers, I have no companion; and although I esteem his principles and his talents, there is no congeniality in our tastes, or in our tempers. As for the rest, a more devoted band can not be conceived; but they think only of one thing, the lost dignity of their ruler; and although this concentration of their thoughts on one subject may gratify my pride, it does not elevate my spirits. But this is a subject on which in future we will not converse. One of the curses of my unhappy lot is, that a thousand circumstances daily occur which prevent me forgetting it."

The Prince rose from the table, and pressing with his

right hand on part of the wall, the door of a small closet sprang open; the interior was lined with crimson velvet. He took out of it a cushion of the same regal material, on which reposed, in solitary magnificence, a golden coronet of antique workmanship.

"The crown of my fathers," said his Highness, as he placed the treasure with great reverence on the table, "won by fifty battles and lost without a blow! Yet in my youth I was deemed no dastard; and I have shed more blood for my country in one day than he who claims to be my suzerain in the whole of his long career of undeserved prosperity. Ay, this is the curse; the ancestor of my present sovereign was that warrior's serf!" The Prince pointed to the grim chieftain, whose stout helmet Vivian now perceived was encircled by a crown similar to the one which was now lying before him. "Had I been the subject, had I been obliged to acknowledge the sway of a Cæsar, I might have endured it with resignation. Had I been forced to yield to the legions of an emperor, a noble resistance might have consoled me for the clanking of my chains. But to sink without a struggle, the victim of political intrigue; to become the bondsman of one who was my father's slave; for such was Reisenburg, even in my own remembrance, our unsuccessful rival; this was too bad. It rankles in my heart, and unless I can be revenged I shall sink under it. To have lost my dominions would have been nothing. But revenge I will have! It is yet in my power to gain for an enslaved people the liberty I have myself lost. Yes! the enlightened spirit of the age shall yet shake the quavering councils of the Reisenburg cabal. I will, in truth I have already seconded the just, the unanswerable demands of an oppressed and insulted people; and, ere six months are over, I trust to see the convocation of a free and representative council in the capital of the petty monarch to whom I have been betrayed. The chief of Reisenburg has, in his eagerness to gain his grand ducal crown, somewhat overstepped the mark.

"Besides myself, there are no less than three other powerful princes whose dominions have been devoted to the formation of his servile duchy. We are all animated by the same spirit, all intent upon the same end. We have all used, and are using, our influence as powerful nobles to gain for our fellow-subjects their withheld rights; rights which belong to them as men, not merely as Germans. Within this week I have forwarded to the Residence a memorial subscribed by myself, my relatives, the other princes, and a powerful body of discontented nobles, requesting the immediate grant of a constitution similar to those of Wurtemburg and Bavaria. My companions in misfortune are inspirited by my joining them. Had I been wise I should have joined them sooner; but until this moment I have been the dupe of the artful conduct of an unprincipled Minister. My eyes, however, are now open. The Grand Duke and his crafty counselor, whose name shall not profane my lips, already tremble. Part of the people, emboldened by our representations, have already refused to answer an unconstitutional taxation. I have no doubt that he must yield. Whatever may be the inclination of the Courts of Vienna or St. Petersburg, rest assured that the liberty of Germany will meet with no opponent except political intrigue; and that Metternich is too well acquainted with the spirit which is now only slumbering in the bosom of the German nation to run the slightest risk of exciting it by the presence of foreign legions. No, no! that mode of treatment may do very well for Naples, or Poland, or Spain; but the moment that a Croat or a Cossack shall encamp upon the Rhine or the Elbe, for the purpose of supporting the unadulterated tyranny of their newfangled Grand Dukes, that moment Germany becomes a great and united nation. The greatest enemy of the prosperity of Germany is the natural disposition of her sons; but that disposition, while it does now, and may forever, hinder us from being a great people, will at the same time infallibly prevent us from ever becoming a degraded one."

At this moment, this moment of pleasing anticipation of public virtue and private revenge, Master Rodolph entered, and prevented Vivian from gaining any details of the history of his host. The little round steward informed his master that a horseman had just arrived, bearing for his Highness a despatch of importance, which he insisted upon delivering into the Prince's own hands.

"Whence comes he?" asked his Highness.

"In truth, your Serene Highness, that were hard to say, inasmuch as the messenger refuses to inform us."

"Admit him."

A man whose jaded looks proved that he had traveled far that day was soon ushered into the room, and, bowing to the Prince, delivered to him in silence a letter.

"From whom comes this?" asked the Prince.

"It will itself inform your Highness," was the only answer.

"My friend, you are a trusty messenger, and have been well trained. Rodolph, look that this gentleman be well lodged and attended."

"I thank your Highness," said the messenger, "but I do not tarry here. I wait no answer, and my only purpose in seeing you was to perform my commission to the letter, by delivering this paper into your own hands."

"As you please, sir; you must be the best judge of your own time; but we like not strangers to leave our gates while our drawbridge is yet echoing with their entrance steps."

The Prince and Vivian were again alone. Astonishment and agitation were visible on his Highness's countenance as he threw his eye over the letter. At length he folded it up, put it into his breast-pocket, and tried to resume conversation; but the effort was both evident and unsuccessful. In another moment the letter was again taken out, and again read with not less emotion than accompanied its first perusal.

"I fear I have wearied you, Mr. Grey," said his Highness; "it was inconsiderate in me not to remember that you require repose."

Vivian was not sorry to have an opportunity of retiring, so he quickly took the hint, and wished his Highness agreeable dreams.

CHAPTER IV

NO one but an adventurous traveler can know the luxury of sleep. There is not a greater fallacy in the world than the common creed that sweet sleep is labor's guerdon. Mere regular, corporeal labor may certainly procure us a good, sound, refreshing slumber, disturbed often by the con- sciousness of the monotonous duties of the morrow; but how sleep the other great laborers of this laborious world? Where is the sweet sleep of the politician? After hours of fatigue in his office and hours of exhaustion in the House, he gains his pillow; and a brief, feverish night, disturbed by the triumph of a cheer and the horrors of a reply. Where is the sweet sleep of the poet? We all know how harassing are the common dreams which are made up of incoherent images of our daily life, in which the actors are individuals that we know, and whose conduct generally appears to be regulated by principles which we can comprehend. How much more enervating and destroying must be the slumber of that man who dreams of an imaginary world! waking, with a heated and excited spirit, to mourn over some impressive incident of the night, which is nevertheless forgotten, or to collect some inexplicable plot which has been revealed in sleep, and has fled from the memory as the eyelids have opened. Where is the sweet sleep of the artist? of the lawyer? Where, in-deed, of any human being to whom to-morrow brings its necessary duties? Sleep is the enemy of Care, and Care is the constant companion of regular labor, mental or bodily.

But your traveler, your adventurous traveler, careless of the future, reckless of the past, with a mind interested by the world, from the immense and various character which that world presents to him, and not by his own stake in any petty or particular contingency; wearied by delightful fatigue, daily occasioned by varying means and from varying causes; with the consciousness that no prudence can regulate the fortunes of the morrow, and with no curiosity to discover what those fortunes may be, from a conviction that it is utterly impossible to ascertain them; perfectly easy whether he lie in a mountain hut or a royal palace; and reckless alike of the terrors and chances of storm and bandits, seeing that he has as fair a chance of meeting both with security and enjoyment; this is the fellow who, throwing himself upon a down couch or his mule's pack-saddle, with equal eagerness and equal sang-froid, sinks into a repose, in which he is never reminded by the remembrance of an appointment or an engagement for the next day, a duel, a marriage, or a dinner, the three perils of man, that he has the misfortune of being mortal; and wakes not to combat care, but only to feel that he is fresher and more vigorous than he was the night before; and that, come what come may, he is, at any rate, sure this day of seeing different faces, and of improvising his unpremeditated part upon a different scene.

We have now both philosophically accounted and politely apologized for the loud and unfashionable snore which sounded in the blue chamber about five minutes after Vivian Grey had entered that most comfortable apartment. In about twelve hours' time he was scolding Essper George for having presumed to wake him so early, quite unconscious that he had enjoyed anything more than a twenty minutes' doze.

"I should not have come in, sir, only they are all out. They were off by six o'clock this morning, sir; most part at least. The Prince has gone; I do not know whether he went with them, but Master Rodolph has given me— I breakfasted with Master Rodolph. Holy Virgin! what quarters we have got into!"

"To the point; what of the Prince?"

"His Highness has left the castle, and desired Master Rodolph; if your Grace had only seen Master Rodolph tipsy last night; he rolled about like a turbot in a tornado."

"What of the Prince?"

"The Prince desired this letter to be given to you, sir."

Vivian read the note, which supposed that, of course, he would not wish to join the chase this morning, and regretted that the writer was obliged to ride out for a few hours to visit a neighboring nobleman, but requested the pleasure of his guest's company at a private dinner in the cabinet on his return.

After breakfast Vivian called on Mr. Sievers. He found that gentleman busied in his library.

"You never hunt, I suppose, Mr. Sievers?"

"Never. His Highness, I apprehend, is out this morning; the beautiful weather continues; surely we never had such a season. As for myself, I almost have given up my indoor pursuits. The sun is not the light of study. Let us take our caps and have a stroll."

The gentlemen accordingly left the library, and proceeding through a different gate to that by which Vivian had entered the castle, they came upon a part of the forest in which the timber and brushwood had been in a great measure cleared away; large clumps of trees being left standing on an artificial lawn, and newly-made roads winding about in pleasing irregularity until they were all finally lost in the encircling woods.

"I think you told me," said Mr. Sievers, "that you had been long in Germany. What course do you think of taking from here?"

"Straight to Vienna."

"Ah! a delightful place. If, as I suppose to be the case, you are fond of dissipation and luxury, Vienna is to be preferred to any city with which I am acquainted. And intellectual companions are not wanting there, as some have said. There are one or two houses in which the literary soirées will yield to few in Europe; and I prefer them to most, because there is less pretension and more ease. The Archduke John is a man of considerable talents, and of more considerable acquirements. An excellent geologist! Are you fond of geology?"

"I am not in the least acquainted with the science."

"Naturally so; at your age, if, in fact, we study at all, we are fond of fancying ourselves moral philosophers, and our study is mankind. Trust me, my dear sir, it is a branch of research soon exhausted; and in a few years you will be very glad, for want of something else to do, to meditate upon stones. See now," said Mr. Sievers, picking up a stone, "to what associations does this little piece of quartz give rise! I am already an antediluvian, and instead of a stag bounding by that wood I witness the moving mass of a mammoth. I live in other worlds, which, at the same time, I have the advantage of comparing with the present. Geology is indeed a magnificent study. What excites more the imagination? What exercises more the reason? Can you conceive anything sublimer than the gigantic shadows and the grim wreck of an antediluvian world? Can you devise any plan which will more brace our powers, and develop our mental energies, than the formation of a perfect chain of inductive reasoning to account for these phenomena? What is the boasted communion which the vain poet holds with nature compared with conversation which the geologist perpetually carries on with the elemental world? Gazing on the strata of the earth, he reads the fate of his species. In the undulations of the mountains is revealed to him the history of the past; and in the strength of rivers and the powers of the air he discovers the fortunes of the future. To him, indeed, that future, as well as the past and the present, are alike matter for meditation: for the geologist is the most satisfactory of antiquarians, the most interesting of philosophers, and the most inspired of prophets; demonstrating that which has past by discovery, that which is occurring by observation, and that which is to come by induction. When you go to Vienna I will give you a letter to Frederick Schlegel; we were fellow-students, and are friends, though for various reasons we do not at present meet; nevertheless a letter from me will command respect. I will recommend you, however, before you go on to Vienna, to visit Reisenburg."

"Indeed! from the Prince's account, I should have thought that there was little to interest me there."

"His Highness is not an impartial judge. You are probably acquainted with the disagreeable manner in which he is connected with that Court. Far from his opinion being correct, I should say there are few places in Germany more worthy of a visit than the little Court near us; and above all things my advice is that you should not pass it over."

"I am inclined to follow it. You are right in supposing that I am not ignorant that his Highness has the misfortune of being a mediatized Prince; but what is the exact story about him? I have heard some odd rumors, some —"

"It is a curious story, but I am afraid you will find it rather long. Nevertheless, if you really visit Reisenburg, it may be of use to you to know something of the singular characters you will meet there. In the first place, you say you know that Little Lilliput is a mediatized Prince, and, of course, are precisely aware what that title means. About fifty years ago, the rival of the illustrious family in whose chief castle we are both of us now residing was the Margrave of Reisenburg, another petty Prince with territories not so extensive as those of our friend, and with a population more limited; perhaps fifty thousand souls, half of whom were drunken cousins. The old Margrave of Reisenburg, who then reigned, was a perfect specimen of the old-fashioned German Prince; he did nothing but hunt and drink and think of the quarterings of his immaculate shield, all duly acquired from some Vandal ancestor as barbarous as himself. His little Margravate was misgoverned enough for a great empire. Half of his nation, who were his real people, were always starving, and were unable to find crown pieces to maintain the extravagant expenditure of the other moiety, the cousins; who, out of gratitude to their fellow-subjects for their generous support, harassed them with every species of excess. Complaints were of course made to the Margrave, and loud cries for justice resounded at the palace gates. This Prince was an impartial chief magistrate; he prided himself upon his 'invariable' principles of justice, and he allowed nothing to influence his decisions. His plan for arranging all differences had the merit of being brief; and if brevity be the soul of wit, it certainly was most unreasonable in his subjects to consider his judgments no joke. He always counted the quarterings in the shields of the respective parties, and decided accordingly. Imagine the speedy redress gained by a muddy-veined peasant against one of the cousins; who, of course, had as many quarterings as the Margrave himself. The defendant was regularly acquitted. At length, a man's house having been burned down out of mere joke in the night, the owner had the temerity in the morning to accuse one of the privileged, and to produce, at the same time, a shield with exactly one more quartering than the reigning shield itself contained. The Margrave was astounded, the people in raptures, and the cousins in despair. The complainant's shield was examined and counted, and not a flaw discovered. What a dilemma! The chief magistrate consulted with the numerous branches of his family, and the next morning the complainant's head was struck off for high treason, for daring to have one more quartering than his monarch!

"In this way they passed the time about fifty years since in Reisenburg; occasionally, for the sake of variety, declaring war against the inhabitants of Little Lilliput, who, to say the truth, in their habits and pursuits did not materially differ from their neighbors. The Margrave had one son, the present Grand Duke. A due reverence of the great family shield, and a full acquaintance with the invariable principles of justice, were early instilled into him; and the royal stripling made such rapid progress, under the tuition of his amiable parent, that he soon became highly popular with all his relations. At length his popularity became troublesome to his father; and so the old Margrave sent for his son one morning, and informed him that he had dreamed the preceding night that the air of Reisenburg was peculiarly unwholesome for young persons, and therefore he begged him to get out of his dominions as soon as possible. The young Prince had no objection to see something of the world. He flew to a relative whom he had never before visited. The nobleman was one of those individuals who anticipate their age, which, by the bye, Mr. Grey, none but noblemen should do; for he who anticipates his century is generally persecuted when living, and is always pilfered when dead. Howbeit, this relation was a philosopher; all about him thought him mad; he, in return, thought all about him fools. He sent the Prince to a university, and gave him for a tutor a young man about ten years older than his pupil. This person's name was Beckendorff. You will hear more of him.

"About three years after the sudden departure of the young Prince, the old Margrave his father and the then reigning Prince of Little Lilliput shot each other through the head in a drunken brawl, after a dinner given in honor of a proclamation of peace between the two countries. The cousins were not much grieved, as they anticipated a fit successor in their

15

former favorite. Splendid preparations were made for the reception of the inheritor of the family shield, and all Reisenburg was poured out to witness the triumphant entrance of their future monarch. At last two horsemen in plain dresses, and on indifferent steeds, rode up to the palace gates, dismounted, and without making any inquiry ordered the attendance of some of the chief nobility in the presence chamber. One of them, a young man, without any preparatory explanation, introduced the Reisenburg chieftains to his companion as his Prime Minister, and commanded them immediately to deliver up their portefeuilles and golden keys to Mr. Beckendorff. The nobles were in dismay, and so astounded that they made no resistance, though the next morning they started in their beds when they remembered that they had delivered their insignia of office to a man without a von before his name. They were soon, however, roused from their sorrow and their stupor, by receiving a peremptory order to quit the palace; and as they retired from the walls which they had long considered as their own, they had the mortification of meeting crowds of the common people, their slaves and their victims, hurrying with joyful countenances and triumphant looks to the palace of their Prince, in consequence of an energetic proclamation for the redress of grievances, and an earnest promise to decide cases in future without examining the quarterings of the parties. In a week's time the cousins were all adrift. At length they conspired, but the conspiracy was tardy, they found their former servants armed, and they joined in an unequal struggle; for their opponents were alike animated with hopes of the future and with revenge for the past. The cousins got well beaten, and this was not the worst; for Beckendorff took advantage of this unsuccessful treason, which he had himself fomented, and forfeited all their estates; destroying in one hour the system which had palsied for so many years the enemies of his master's subjects. In time many of the chief nobility were restored to their honors and estates; but the power with which they were again invested was greatly modified, and the privileges of the Commons greatly increased. At this moment the French Revolution broke out. The French crossed the Rhine and carried all before them; and the Prince of Little Lilliput, among other true Germans, made a bold but fruitless resistance. The Margrave of Reisenburg, on the contrary, received the enemy with open arms; he raised a larger body of troops than his due contingent, and exerted himself in every manner to second the views of the Great Nation. In return for his services he was presented with the conquered principality of Little Lilliput and some other adjoining lands; and the Margravate of Reisenburg, with an increased territory and population, and governed with consummate wisdom, began to be considered the most flourishing of the petty states in the quarter of the empire to which it belonged. On the contrary, our princely and patriotic friend, mortified by the degenerate condition of his country and the prosperity of his rival house, quitted Little Lilliput, and became one of those emigrant princes who abounded during the first years of the Revolution in the northern courts of Europe. Napoleon soon appeared upon the stage; and vanquished Austria, with the French dictating at the gates of her capital, was no longer in a condition to support the dignity of the Empire. The policy of the Margrave of Reisenburg was as little patriotic and quite as consistent as before. Beckendorff became the constant and favored counselor of the French Emperor. It was chiefly by his exertions that the celebrated Confederation of the Rhine was carried into effect. The institution of this body excited among many Germans, at the time, loud expressions of indignation; but I believe few impartial and judicious men now look upon that league as any other than one in the formation of which consummate statesmanship was exhibited. In fact, it prevented the subjugation of Germany by France, and by flattering the pride of Napoleon saved the decomposition of our Empire. But how this might be it is not at present necessary for us to inquire. Certain it was that the pupil of Beckendorff was amply repaid for the advice and exertions of his master and his Minister; and when Napoleon fell the brows of the former Margrave were encircled with a grand ducal crown, and his duchy, while it contained upward of a million and a half of inhabitants, numbered in its limits some of the most celebrated cities in Germany and many of Germany's most flourishing provinces. But Napoleon fell. The Prince of Little Lilliput and his companions in patriotism and mis-

fortune returned from their exile panting with hope and vengeance. A Congress was held to settle the affairs of agitated
Germany. Where was the Grand Duke of Reisenburg? His
hard-earned crown tottered on his head.   Where was his
crafty Minister, the supporter of revolutionary France, the
friend of its Imperial enslaver, the constant enemy of the
House of Austria? At the very Congress which, according
to the expectations of the exiled Princes, was to restore them
to their own dominions, and to reward their patriotic loyalty
with the territories of their revolutionary brethren; yes! at
this very Congress was Beckendorff; not as a suppliant, not
as a victim, but seated at the right hand of Metternich, and
watching, with parental affection, the first interesting and
infantile movements of that most prosperous of political bant-
lings, the Holy Alliance. You may well imagine that the Military Grand Duke had a much better chance in political negotiation than the emigrant Prince. In addition to this, the
Grand Duke of Reisenburg had married, during the war, a
Princess of a powerful House; and the allied Sovereigns were
eager to gain the future aid and constant co-operation of a
mind like Beckendorff's. The Prince of Little Lilliput, the
patriot, was rewarded for his conduct by being restored to his
forfeited possessions; and the next day he became the subject of his former enemy, the Grand Duke of Reisenburg, the
traitor. What think you of Monsieur Beckendorff?"

   "One of the most interesting characters I have long heard
of. But his pupil appears to be a man of mind."

   "You shall hear.   I should, however, first mention that
while Beckendorff has not scrupled to resort to any measures
or adopt any opinions in order to further the interests of his
monarch and his country, he has in every manner shown that
personal agrandizement has never been his object. He lives in
retirement, with scarcely an attendant, and his moderate official stipend amply supports his more moderate expenditure.
The subjects of the Grand Duke may well be grateful that
they have a Minister without relations and without favorites.
The Grand Duke is, unquestionably, a man of talents; but
at the same time, perhaps, one of the most weak-minded men
that ever breathed. He was fortunate in meeting with Beckendorff early in life; and as the influence of the Minister has

not for a moment ceased over the mind of the monarch, to
the world the Grand Duke of Reisenburg has always appeared to be an individual of a strong mind and consistent
conduct. But when you have lived as much and as intimately
in his Court as I have done, you will find how easily the world
may be deceived. Since the close connection which now exists
between Reisenburg and Austria took place, Beckendorff has,
in a great degree, revived the ancient privileges of blood and
birth. A Minister who has sprung from the people will always
conciliate the aristocracy. Having no family influence of his
own, he endeavors to gain the influence of others; and it often
happens that merit is never less considered than when merit
has made the Minister. A curious instance of this occurs in
a neighboring State. There the Premier, decidedly a man
of great talents, is of as humble an origin as Beckendorff.
With no family to uphold him, he supports himself by a lavish
division of all the places and patronage of the State among the
nobles. If the younger son or brother of a peer dare to sully
his oratorical virginity by a chance observation in the Lower
Chamber, the Minister, himself a real orator, immediately
rises to congratulate, in pompous phrase, the House and the
country on the splendid display which has made this night
memorable, and on the decided advantages which must accrue
both to their own resolutions and the national interests from
the future participation of his noble friend in their delibera-
tions. All about him are young nobles, quite unfit for the
discharge of their respective duties. His private secretary is
unable to coin a sentence, almost to direct a letter; but he is
noble! The secondary officials can not be trusted even in the
least critical conjunctures; but they are noble! And the Prime
Minister of a powerful empire is forced to rise early and be
up late; not to meditate on the present fortunes or future
destinies of his country, but by his personal exertions to compensate for the inefficiency and expiate the blunders of his
underlings, whom his unfortunate want of blood has forced
him to overwhelm with praises which they do not deserve,
and duties which they can not discharge. I do not wish you
to infer that the policy of Beckendorff has been actuated by
the feelings which influence the Minister whom I have noticed,
from whose conduct in this very respect his own materially

differs. On the contrary, his connection with Austria is, in all probability, the primary great cause. However this may be, certain it is that all offices about the Court and connected with the army (and I need not remind you that at a small German Court these situations are often the most important in the State) can only be filled by the nobility; nor can any person who has the misfortune of not inheriting the magical monosyllable *von* before his name, the shibboleth of nobility and the symbol of territorial pride, violate by their unhallowed presence the sanctity of Court dinners, or the as sacred ceremonies of a noble fête. But while a monopoly of these offices, which for their due performance require only a showy exterior or a schooled address, is granted to the nobles, all those State charges which require the exercise of intellect are now chiefly filled by the bourgeoisie. At the same time, however, that both our Secretaries of State, many of our Privy Councilors, war Councilors, forest Councilors, and finance Councilors, are to be reckoned among the second class, still not one of these exalted individuals, who from their situations are necessarily in constant personal communication with the Sovereign, ever see that Sovereign except in his Cabinet and his Council-chamber. Beckendorff himself, the Premier, is the son of a peasant; and of course not noble. Nobility, which has been proffered him, not only by his own monarch, but by most of the sovereigns of Europe, he has invariably refused; and consequently never appears at Court. The truth is, that, from disposition, he is little inclined to mix with men; and he has taken advantage of his want of an escutcheon completely to exempt himself from all those duties of etiquette which his exalted situation would otherwise have imposed upon him. None can complain of the haughtiness of the nobles when, ostensibly, the Minister himself is not exempted from their exclusive regulations. If you go to Reisenburg, you will not therefore see Beckendorff, who lives, as I have mentioned, in solitude, about thirty miles from the capital; communicating only with his royal master, the foreign Ministers, and one or two official characters of his own country. I was myself an inmate of the Court for upward of two years. During that time I never saw the Minister; and, with the exception of some members of the royal family and the characters I have mentioned, I never knew one person who had even caught a glimpse of the individual who may indeed be said to be regulating their destinies.

"It is at the Court, then," continued Mr. Sievers, "when he is no longer under the control of Beckendorff, and in those minor points which are not subjected to the management or influenced by the mind of the Minister, that the true character of the Grand Duke is to be detected. Indeed it may really be said that the weakness of his mind has been the origin of his fortune. In his early youth his pliant temper adapted itself without a struggle to the barbarous customs and the brutal conduct of his father's Court; that same pliancy of temper prevented him opposing with bigoted obstinacy the exertions of his relation to educate and civilize him; that same pliancy of temper allowed him to become the ready and the enthusiastic disciple of Beckendorff. Had the pupil, when he ascended the throne, left his master behind him, it is very probable that his natural feelings would have led him to oppose the French; and at this moment, instead of being the first of the second-rate powers of Germany, the Grand Duke of Reisenburg might himself have been a mediatized Prince. As it was, the same pliancy of temper which I have noticed enabled him to receive Napoleon, when an Emperor, with outstretched arms; and at this moment does not prevent him from receiving, with equal rapture, the Imperial Archduchess, who will soon be on her road from Vienna to espouse his son; for, to crown his career, Beckendorff has successfully negotiated a marriage between a daughter of the House of Austria and the Crown Prince* of Reisenburg. It is generally believed that the next step of the Diet will be to transmute the father's Grand Ducal coronet into a Regal crown; and perhaps, my good sir, before you reach Vienna, you may have the supreme honor of being presented to his Majesty the King of Reisenburg."

"But when you talk only of the pupil's pliancy of temper,

---

* Hereditary Prince is the correct style of the eldest son of a German Grand Duke. I have not used a title which would not be understood by the English reader. Crown Prince is also a German title; but, in strictness, only assumed by the son of a King.

am I to suppose that in mentioning his talents you were speaking ironically?"

"By no means! The Grand Duke is a scholar; a man of refined taste, a patron of the fine arts, a lover of literature, a promoter of science, and what the world would call a philosopher. His judgment is sound, and generally correct, his powers of discrimination acute, and his knowledge of mankind greater than that of most sovereigns; but with all these advantages he is cursed with such a wavering and indecisive temper that when, which is usually the case, he has come to a right conclusion, he can never prevail upon himself to carry his theory into practice; and with all his acuteness, his discernment, and his knowledge of the world, his mind is always ready to receive any impression from the person who last addresses him, though he himself be fully aware of the inferiority of his adviser's intellect to his own, or the imperfection of that adviser's knowledge. Never for a moment out of the sight of Beckendorff, the royal pupil has made an admirable political puppet, since his talents have always enabled him to understand the part which the Minister had forced him to perform. Thus the world has given the Grand Duke credit, not only for the possession of great talents, but almost for as much firmness of mind and decision of character as his Minister. But since his long agitated career has become calm and tranquil, and Beckendorff, like a guardian spirit, has ceased to be ever at his elbow, the character of the Grand Duke of Reisenburg begins to be understood. His Court has been, and still is, frequented by all the men of genius in Germany, who are admitted without scruple, even if they be not noble. But the astonishing thing is that the Grand Duke is always surrounded by every species of political and philosophical quack that you can imagine. Discussions on a free press, on the reformation of the criminal code, on the abolition of commercial duties, and such like interminable topics, are perpetually resounding within the palace of this arbitrary Prince; and the people, fired by the representations of the literary and political journals with which Reisenburg abounds, and whose bold speculations on all subjects elude the vigilance of the censor, by being skilfully amalgamated with a lavish praise of the royal character, are perpetually flattered with the speedy hope of becoming freemen. Suddenly, when all are expecting the grant of a charter or the institution of Chambers, Mr. Beckendorff rides up from his retreat to the Residence, and the next day the whole crowd of philosophers are swept from the royal presence, and the censorship of the press becomes so severe that for a moment you would fancy that Reisenburg, instead of being, as it boasts itself, the modern Athens, had more right to the title of the modern Bœotia. The people, who enjoy an impartial administration of equal laws, who have flourished, and are flourishing, under the wise and moderate rule of their new monarch, have in fact no inclination to exert themselves for the attainment of constitutional liberty in any other way than by their voices.' Their barbarous apathy astounds the philosophers; who, in despair, when the people tell them that they are happy and contented, artfully remind them that their happiness depends on the will of a single man; and that, though the present character of the monarch may guarantee present felicity, still they should think of their children, and not less exert themselves for the insurance of the future. These representations, as constantly reiterated as the present system will allow, have at length produced an effect; and political causes of a peculiar nature, combining their influence with these philosophical exertions, have of late frequently frightened the Grand Duke, who, in despair, would perhaps grant a Constitution if Beckendorff would allow him. But the Minister is conscious that the people would not be happier, and do not in fact require one: he looks with a jealous and an evil eye on the charlatanism of all kinds which is now so prevalent at Court: he knows, from the characters of many of these philosophers and patriots, that their private interest is generally the secret spring of their public virtue; that if the Grand Duke, moved by their entreaties or seduced by their flattery, were to yield a little, he would soon be obliged to grant all to their demands and their threats; and finally, Beckendorff has, of late years, so completely interwoven the policy of Reisenburg with that of Austria that he feels that the rock on which he has determined to found the greatness of his country must be quitted forever if he yield one jot to the caprice or the weakness of his monarch."

"But Beckendorff," said Vivian; "why can he not crush in

the bud the noxious plant which he so much dreads? Why does the press speak in the least to the people? Why is the Grand Duke surrounded by any others except pompous Grand Marshals and empty-headed Lord Chamberlains? I am surprised at this indifference, this want of energy!"

"My dear sir, there are reasons for all things. Rest assured that Beckendorff is not a man to act incautiously or weakly. The Grand Duchess, the mother of the Crown Prince, has been long dead. Beckendorff, who, as a man, has the greatest contempt for women, as a statesman looks to them as the most precious of political instruments; it was his wish to have married the Grand Duke to the young Princess who is now destined for his son, but for once in his life he failed in influencing his pupil. The truth was, and it is to this cause that we must trace the present disorganized state of the Court, and indeed of the Duchy, that the Grand Duke had secretly married a lady to whom he had long been attached. This lady was a Countess, and his subject; and, as it was impossible by the laws of the kingdom that any one but a member of the reigning family could be allowed to share the throne, his Royal Highness had recourse to a plan which is not uncommon in this country, and espoused the lady with his left hand. The ceremony, which we call here a morganatic marriage, you have, probably, heard of before. The favored female is, to all intents and purposes, the wife of the monarch, and shares everything except his throne. She presides at Court, but neither she nor her children assume the style of majesty, although in some instances the latter have been created princes, and acknowledged as heirs-apparent when there has been a default in the lineal royal issue. The lady of whom we are speaking, according to the usual custom, has assumed a name derivative from that of her royal husband; and as the Grand Duke's name is Charles, she is styled Madame Carolina."

"And what kind of lady is Madame Carolina?" asked Vivian.

"Philosophical! piquant! Parisian! a genius, according to her friends; who, as in fact she is a Queen, are of course the whole world. Though a German by family, she is a Frenchwoman by birth. Educated in the spiritual saloons of the French metropolis, she has early imbibed superb ideas of the perfectibility of man, and of the 'science' of conversation, on both which subjects you will not be long at Court ere you hear her descant; demonstrating by the brilliancy of her ideas the possibility of the one, and by the fluency of her language her acquaintance with the other. She is much younger than her husband, and, though not exactly a model for Phidias, a fascinating woman. Variety is the talisman by which she commands all hearts and gained her monarch's. She is only consistent in being delightful; but, though changeable, she is not capricious. Each day displays a new accomplishment as regularly as it does a new costume; but as the acquirement seems only valued by its possessor as it may delight others, so the dress seems worn, not so much to gratify her own vanity as to please her friends' tastes. Genius is her idol; and with her genius is found in everything. She speaks in equal raptures of an opera dancer and an epic poet. Her ambition is to converse on all subjects; and by a judicious management of a great mass of miscellaneous reading, and by indefatigable exertions to render herself mistress of the prominent points of the topics of the day, she appears to converse on all subjects with ability. She takes the liveliest interest in the progress of mind, in all quarters of the globe; and imagines that she should, at the same time, immortalize herself and benefit her species, could she only establish a 'Quarterly Review' in Ashantee and a scientific 'Gazette' at Timbuctoo. Notwithstanding her sudden elevation no one has ever accused her of arrogance, or pride, or ostentation. Her liberal principles and her enlightened views are acknowledged by all. She advocates equality in her circle of privileged nobles, and is enthusiastic on the rights of man in a country where justice is a favor. Her boast is to be surrounded by men of genius, and her delight to correspond with the most celebrated persons of all countries. She is herself a literary character of no mean celebrity. Few months have elapsed since enraptured Reisenburg hailed from her glowing pen two neat octavos, bearing the title of 'Memoirs of the Court of Charlemagne,' which give an interesting and accurate picture of the age, and delight the modern public with vivid descriptions of the cookery, costume, and conversation of the eighth century. You smile, my friend, at Madame Carolina's production. Do not you agree with me that it requires no mean talent to convey a picture of the bustle of a levée during the Middle Ages? Conceive Sir Oliver looking in at his club! and fancy the small talk of Roland during a morning visit! Yet even the fame of this work is to be eclipsed by Madame's forthcoming quarto of 'Haroun al Raschid and His Times.' This, it is whispered, is to be a chef-d'œuvre, enriched by a chronological arrangement, by a celebrated Oriental scholar, of all the anecdotes in the Arabian Nights relating to the Caliph. It is, of course, the sun of Madame's patronage that has hatched into noxious life the swarm of sciolists who now infest the Court, and who are sapping the husband's political power while they are establishing the wife's literary reputation. So much for Madame Carolina! I need hardly add that during your short stay at Court you will be delighted with her. If ever you know her as well as I do, you will find her vain, superficial, heartless; her sentiment a system, her enthusiasm exaggeration, and her genius merely a clever adoption of the profundity of others."

"And Beckendorff and the lady are not friendly?" asked Vivian, who was delighted with his communicative companion.

"Beckendorff's is a mind that such a woman can not comprehend. He treats her with contempt, and, if possible, views her with hatred, for he considers that she has degraded the character of his pupil; while she, on the contrary, wonders by what magic spell he exercises such influence over the conduct of her husband. At first Beckendorff treated her and her circle of *illuminati* with contemptuous silence; but in politics nothing is contemptible. The Minister, knowing that the people were prosperous and happy, cared little for projected constitutions, and less for metaphysical abstractions; but some circumstances have lately occurred which, I imagine, have convinced him that for once he has miscalculated. After the arrangement of the German States, when the Princes were first mediatized, an attempt was made, by means of a threatening league, to obtain for these political victims a very ample share of the power and patronage of the new State of Reisenburg. This plan failed from the lukewarmness and indecision of our good friend of Little Lilliput, who, between ourselves, was prevented from joining the alliance by the intrigues of Beck-

GEORGE CHRISTIAN FREDERICK,
LEOPOLD I
KING OF THE BELGIANS
BORN 1790; DIED 1865
PROTOTYPE OF THE PRINCE OF LITTLE LILLIPUT

"I have well weighed, at least I have endeavored well to weigh, all the circumstances and contingencies which such a circumstance would involve; and the result of my reflection is that I will look to you as a friend and adviser, feeling assured that . . . no temptation exists which can induce you to betray or deceive me."

—Prince of Little Lilliput, page 351.

LEOPOLD I OF BELGIUM

Vivian Grey   See preceding page

endorff. Beckendorff secretly took measures that the Prince should be promised that, in case of his keeping backward, he should obtain more than would fall to his lot by leading the van. The Prince of Little Lilliput and his peculiar friends accordingly were quiet, and the attempt of the other chieftains failed. It was then that his Highness found he had been duped. Beckendorff would not acknowledge the authority, and, of course, did not redeem the pledge, of his agent. The effect that this affair produced upon the Prince's mind you can conceive. Since then he has never frequented Reisenburg, but constantly resided either at his former capital, now a provincial town of the Grand Duchy, or at this castle; viewed, you may suppose, with no very cordial feeling by his companions in misfortune. But the thirst of revenge will inscribe the bitterest enemies in the same muster-roll; and the Princes, incited by the bold carriage of Madame Carolina's philosophical protégés, and induced to believe that Beckendorff's power is on the wane, have again made overtures to our friend, without whose powerful assistance they feel that they have but little chance of success. Observe how much more men's conduct is influenced by circumstances than principles! When these persons leagued together before it was with the avowed intention of obtaining a share of the power and patronage of the State: the great body of the people, of course, did not sympathize in that which, after all, to them was a party quarrel, and by the joint exertions of open force and secret intrigue the Court triumphed. But now these same individuals come forward, not as indignant Princes demanding a share of the envied tyranny, but as ardent patriots advocating a people's rights. The public, though I believe that in fact they will make no bodily exertion to acquire a constitutional freedom the absence of which they can only abstractedly feel, have no objection to attain that which they are assured will not injure their situation, provided it be by the risk and exertions of others. So far, therefore, as clamor can support the Princes, they have the people on their side; and as upward of three hundred thousand of the Grand Ducal subjects are still living on their estates, and still consider themselves as their serfs, they trust that some excesses from this great body may incite the rest of the people to similar outrages. The natural disposition of mankind to imitation, particularly when the act to be imitated is popular, deserves attention. The Court is divided; for the exertions of Madame and the bewitching influence of Fashion have turned the heads even of graybeards: and to give you only one instance, his Excellency the Grand Marshal, protégé of the House of Austria, and a favorite of Metternich, the very person to whose interests, and as a reward for whose services, our princely friend was sacrificed by the Minister, has now himself become a pupil in the school of modern philosophy, and drivels out, with equal ignorance and fervor, enlightened notions on the most obscure subjects. In the midst of all this confusion, the Grand Duke is timorous, dubious, and uncertain. Beckendorff has a difficult game to play; he may fall at last. Such, my dear sir, are the tremendous consequences of a weak Prince marrying a blue-stocking!"

"And the Crown Prince, Mr. Sievers, how does he conduct himself at this interesting moment? or is his mind so completely engrossed by the anticipation of his Imperial alliance that he has no thought for anything but his approaching bride."

"The Crown Prince, my dear sir, is neither thinking of his bride nor of anything else: he is a hunch-backed idiot. Of his deformity I have myself been a witness; and though it is difficult to give an opinion of the intellect of a being with whom you have never interchanged a syllable, nevertheless his countenance does not contradict the common creed. I say the common creed, Mr. Grey, for there are moments when the Crown Prince of Reisenburg is spoken of by his future subjects in a very different manner. Whenever any unpopular act is committed, or any unpopular plan suggested by the Court or the Grand Duke, then whispers are immediately afloat that a future Brutus must be looked for in their Prince; then it is generally understood that his idiocy is only assumed; and what woman does not detect, in the glimmerings of his lack-lustre eye, the vivid sparks of suppressed genius! In a short time the cloud blows over the Court, dissatisfaction disappears, and the moment that the monarch is again popular the unfortunate Crown Prince again becomes the uninfluential object of pity or derision. All immediately forget that his idiocy is only assumed; and what woman ever ceases from deploring the unhappy lot of the future wife of their impuissant Prince! Such, my dear sir, is the way of mankind! At the first glance it would appear that in this world monarchs, on the whole, have it pretty well their own way; but reflection will soon enable us not to envy their situations; and speaking as a father, which unfortunately I am not, should I not view with disgust that lot in life which necessarily makes my son my enemy? The Crown Prince of all countries is only a puppet in the hands of the people, to be played against his own father."

CHAPTER V

THE Prince returned home at a late hour, and immediately inquired for Vivian. During dinner, which he hastily despatched, it did not escape our hero's attention that his Highness was unusually silent, and, indeed, agitated.

"When we have finished our meal, my good friend," at length said the Prince, "I very much wish to consult with you on a most important business." Since the explanation of last night, the Prince in private conversation had dropped his regal plural.

"I am ready at once," said Vivian.

"You will think it strange, Mr. Grey, when you become acquainted with the nature of my communication; you will justly consider it most strange, most singular, that I should choose for a confidant and a counselor in an important business a gentleman with whom I have been acquainted so short a time as yourself. But, sir, I have well weighed, at least I have endeavored well to weigh, all the circumstances and contingencies which such a confidence would involve; and the result of my reflection is, that I will look to you as a friend and adviser, feeling assured that, both from your situation and your disposition, no temptation exists which can induce you to betray or to deceive me." Though the Prince said this with an appearance of perfect sincerity, he stopped and looked earnestly in his guest's face, as if he would read his secret thoughts, or were desirous of now giving him an opportunity of answering.

"So far as the certainty of your confidence being respected," answered Vivian, "I trust your Highness may communicate to me with the most assured spirit. But while my ignorance of men and affairs in this country will ensure you from any treachery on my part, I very much fear that it will also preclude me from affording you any advantageous advice or assistance."

"On that head," replied the Prince, "I am, of course, the best judge. The friend whom I need is a man not ignorant of the world, with a cool head and an impartial mind. Though young, you have said and told me enough to prove that you are not unacquainted with mankind. Of your courage I have already had a convincing proof. In the business in which I require your assistance freedom from national prejudices will materially increase the value of your advice; and, therefore, I am far from being unwilling to consult a person ignorant, according to your own phrase, of men and affairs in this country. Moreover, your education as an Englishman has early led you to exercise your mind on political subjects; and it is in a political business that I require your aid."

"Am I fated always to be the dry nurse of an embryo faction!" thought Vivian; and he watched earnestly the countenance of the Prince. In a moment he expected to be invited to become a counselor of the leagued Princes. Either the lamp was burning dim, or the blazing wood fire had suddenly died away, or a mist was over Vivian's eyes; but for a moment he almost imagined that he was sitting opposite his old friend the Marquess of Carabas. The Prince's phrase had given rise to a thousand agonizing associations: in an instant Vivian had worked up his mind to a pitch of nervous excitement.

"Political business?" said Vivian, in an agitated voice. "You could not address a more unfortunate person. I have seen, Prince, too much of politics ever to wish to meddle with them again."

"You are too quick, my good friend," continued his Highness. "I may wish to consult you on political business, and yet have no intention of engaging you in politics, which, indeed, is quite a ridiculous idea. But I see that I was right in supposing that these subjects have engaged your attention."

"I have seen, in a short time, something of the political

world," answered Vivian, who was almost ashamed of his previous emotion; "and I thank Heaven daily that I have no chance of again having any connection with it."

"Well, well! that is as it may be. Nevertheless, your experience is only another inducement to me to request your assistance. Do not fear that I wish to embroil you in politics; but I hope you will not refuse, although almost a stranger, to add to the great obligations which I am already under to you, and give me the benefit of your opinion."

"Your Highness may speak with perfect unreserve, and reckon upon my delivering my genuine sentiments."

"You have not forgotten, I venture to believe," said the Prince, "our short conversation of last night?"

"It was of too interesting a nature easily to escape my memory."

"Before I can consult you on the subject which at present interests me, it is necessary that I should make you a little acquainted with the present state of public affairs here, and the characters of the principal individuals who control them."

"So far as an account of the present state of political parties, the history of the Grand Duke's career, and that of his Minister, Mr. Beckendorff, and their reputed characters, will form part of your Highness's narrative, by so much may its length be curtailed and your trouble lessened; for I have at different times picked up, in casual conversation, a great deal of information on these topics. Indeed, you may address me, in this respect, as you would any German gentleman who, not being himself personally interested in public life, is, of course, not acquainted with its most secret details."

"I did not reckon on this," said the Prince, in a cheerful voice. "This is a great advantage, and another reason that I should no longer hesitate to develop to you a certain affair which now occupies my mind. To be short," continued the Prince, "it is of the letter which I so mysteriously received last night, and which, as you must have remarked, very much agitated me; it is on this letter that I wish to consult you. Bearing in mind the exact position, the avowed and public position, in which I stand, as connected with the Court, and having a due acquaintance, which you state you have, with the character of Mr. Beckendorff, what think you of this letter?"

So saying, the Prince leaned over the table, and handed to Vivian the following epistle:

"To His Highness the Prince of Little Lilliput

"I am commanded by his Royal Highness to inform your Highness that his Royal Highness has considered the request which was signed by your Highness and other noblemen, and presented by you to his Royal Highness in a private interview. His Royal Highness commands me to state that that request will receive his most attentive consideration. At the same time, his Royal Highness also commands me to observe that, in bringing about the completion of a result desired by all parties, it is difficult to carry on the necessary communications merely by written documents; and his Royal Highness has therefore commanded me to submit to your Highness the advisability of taking some steps in order to further the possibility of the occurrence of an oral interchange of the sentiments of the respective parties. Being aware, from the position which your Highness has thought proper at present to maintain, and from other causes which are of too delicate a nature to be noticed in any other way except by allusion, that your Highness may feel difficulty in personally communicating with his Royal Highness without consulting the wishes and opinions of the other Princes; a process to which, it must be evident to your Highness, his Royal Highness feels it impossible to submit; and, at the same time, desirous of forwarding the progress of those views which his Royal Highness and your Highness may conjunctively consider calculated to advance the well-being of the State, I have to submit to your Highness the propriety of considering the propositions contained in the inclosed paper; which, if your Highness keep unconnected with this communication, the purport of this letter will be confined to your Highness.

"Propositions

"1st. That an interview shall take place between your Highness and myself, the object of which shall be the consideration of measures by which, when adopted, the various interests now in agitation shall respectively be regarded.

"2d. That this interview shall be secret; your Highness be incognito.

"If your Highness be disposed to accede to the first proposition, I beg to submit to you that, from the nature of my residence, its situation, and other causes, there will be no fear that any suspicion of the fact of Mr. von Philipson acceding to the two propositions will gain notoriety. This letter will be delivered into your own hands. If Mr. von Philipson determine on acceding to these propositions, he is most probably aware of the general locality in which my residence is situated; and proper measures will be taken that, if Mr. von Philipson honor me with a visit, he shall not be under the necessity of attracting attention by inquiring the way to my house. It is wished that the fact of the second proposition being acceded to should only be known to Mr. von Philipson and myself; but if to be perfectly unattended be considered as an insuperable objection, I consent to his being accompanied by a single friend. I shall be alone.

"BECKENDORFF."

"Well!" said the Prince, as Vivian finished the letter.

"The best person," said Vivian, "to decide upon your Highness consenting to this interview is yourself."

"That is not the point on which I wish to have the benefit of your opinion; for I have already consented. I rode over this morning to my cousin, the Duke of Micromegas, and despatched from his residence a trusty messenger to Beckendorff. I have agreed to meet him, and to-morrow; but on the express terms that I should not be unattended. Now, then," continued the Prince, with great energy; "now, then, will you be my companion?"

"I!" said Vivian.

"Yes; you, my good friend! you. I should consider myself as safe if I were sleeping in a burning house as I should be were I with Beckendorff alone. Although this is not the first time that we have communicated, I have never yet seen him; and I am fully aware, if the approaching interview were known to my friends, they would consider it high time that my son reigned in my stead. But I am resolved to be firm, to be inflexible. My course is plain. I am not to be again duped by him, which," continued the Prince, much confused, "I will not conceal that I have been once."

"But I!" said Vivian; "I; what good can I possibly do? It appears to me that, if Beckendorff is to be dreaded as you describe, the presence or the attendance of no friend can possibly save you from his crafty plans. But surely, if any one attend you, why not be accompanied by a person whom you have known long, and who knows you well; on whom you can confidently rely, and who may be aware, from a thousand signs and circumstances which will never attract my attention, at what particular and pressing moment you may require prompt and energetic assistance. Such is the companion you want; and surely such a one you may find in Arnelm, Von Neuwied—"

"Arnelm! Von Neuwied!" said the Prince; "the best hands at sounding a bugle or spearing a boar in all Reisenburg! Excellent men, forsooth! to guard their master from the diplomatic deceits of the wily Beckendorff! Moreover, were they to have even the slightest suspicion of my intended movement, they would commit rank treason out of pure loyalty, and lock me up in my own cabinet! No, no! they will never do: I want a companion of experience and knowledge of the world, with whom I may converse with some prospect of finding my wavering firmness strengthened, or my misled judgment rightly guided, or my puzzled brain cleared; modes of assistance to which the worthy Jagd Junker is but little accustomed, however quickly he might hasten to my side in a combat or the chase."

"If these, then, will not do, surely there is one man in this castle who, although he may not be a match for Beckendorff, can be foiled by few others. Mr. Sievers?" said Vivian, with an inquiring eye.

"Sievers!" exclaimed the Prince, with great eagerness; "the very man! firm, experienced, and sharp-witted; well schooled in political learning, in case I required his assistance in arranging the terms of the intended Charter or the plan of the intended Chambers; for these, of course, are the points on which Beckendorff wishes to consult. But one thing I am determined on: I positively pledge myself to nothing while under Beckendorff's roof. He doubtless anticipates, by my visit, to grant the liberties of the people on his own terms: perhaps Mr. Beckendorff, for once in his life, may be mistaken. I am not to be deceived twice, and I am determined not to yield the point of the Treasury being under the control of the Senate. That is the part of the harness which galls; and to preserve themselves from this rather inconvenient regulation, without question, my good friend Beckendorff has hit upon this plan."

"Then Mr. Sievers will accompany you?" asked Vivian, calling the Prince's attention to the point of consultation.

"The very man for it, my dear friend! but although Beckendorff, most probably respecting my presence, and taking into consideration the circumstances under which we meet, would refrain from consigning Sievers to a dungeon, still, although the Minister invites this interview, and although I have no single inducement to conciliate him, yet it would scarcely be correct, scarcely dignified on my part, to prove, by the presence of my companion, that I had for a length of time harbored an individual who, by Beckendorff's own exertions, was banished from the Grand Duchy. It would look too much like bravado."

"Oh!" said Vivian; "is it so? And pray of what was Mr. Sievers guilty?"

"Of high treason against one who was not his sovereign."

"How is that?"

"Sievers, who is a man of considerable talents, was for a long time a professor in one of our great Universities. The publication of many able works procured him a reputation which induced Madame Carolina to use every exertion to gain his attendance at Court; and a courtier in time the professor became. At Reisenburg Mr. Sievers was the great authority on all subjects: philosophical, literary, and political. In fact, he was the fashion; and, at the head of the great literary journal which is there published, he terrified admiring Germany with his profound and piquant critiques. Unfortunately, like some men as good, he was unaware that Reisenburg was not an independent state; and so, on the occasion of Austria attacking Naples, Mr. Sievers took the opportunity of attacking Austria. His article, eloquent, luminous, profound, revealed the dark colors of the Austrian policy, as an artist's lamp brings out the murky tints of Spagnoletto. Every one admired Sievers's bitter sarcasms, enlightened views, and indignant eloquence. Madame Carolina crowned him with laurel in the midst of her coterie, and it is said that the Grand Duke sent him a snuff-box. In a short time the article reached Vienna, and in a still shorter time Mr. Beckendorff reached the Residence, and insisted on the author being immediately given up to the Austrian Government. Madame Carolina was in despair, the Grand Duke in doubt, and Beckendorff threatened to resign if the order were not signed. A kind friend, perhaps his Royal Highness himself, gave Sievers timely notice, and•by rapid flight he reached my castle, and demanded my hospitality. He has lived here ever since, and has done me a thousand services, not the least of which is the education which he has given my son, my glorious Maximilian."

"And Beckendorff," asked Vivian; "has he always been aware that Sievers was concealed here?"

"That I can not answer: had he been, it is not improbable that he would have winked at it; since it never has been his policy unnecessarily to annoy a mediatized Prince, or without great occasion to let us feel that our independence is gone; I will not, with such a son as I have, say, forever."

"Mr. Sievers of course, then, can not visit Beckendorff," said Vivian.

"That is clear," said the Prince; "and I therefore trust that now you will no longer refuse my first request."

It was impossible for Vivian to deny the Prince any longer; and indeed he had no objection (as his Highness could not be better attended) to seize the singular and unexpected opportunity which now offered itself of becoming acquainted with an individual respecting whom his curiosity was much excited. It was a late hour ere the Prince and his friend retired, having arranged everything for the morrow's journey, and conversed on the probable subjects of the approaching interview at great length.

CHAPTER VI

ON the following morning, before sunrise, the Prince's valet roused Vivian from his slumbers. According to the appointment of the preceding evening, Vivian repaired in due time to a certain spot in the park. The Prince reached it at the same moment. A mounted groom, leading two English horses of showy appearance, and each having a traveling case strapped on the back of its saddle, awaited them. His Highness mounted one of the steeds with skilful celerity, although Arnelm and Von Neuwied were not there to do honor to his bridle and his stirrup.

"You must give me an impartial opinion of your courser, my dear friend," said the Prince to Vivian; "for if you deem it worthy of being bestridden by you, my son requests that you will do him the honor of accepting it. If so, call it Max; and provided it be as thoroughbred as the donor, you need not change it for Bucephalus."

"Not unworthy of the son of Ammon!" said Vivian, as he touched the spirited animal with the spur, and proved its fiery action on the springing turf.

A man never feels so proud or so sanguine as when he is bounding on the back of a fine horse. Cares fly with the first curvet, and the very sight of a spur is enough to prevent one committing suicide.

When Vivian and his companion had proceeded about five miles, the Prince pulled up, and giving a sealed letter to the groom, he desired him to leave them. The Prince and Vivian amused themselves by endeavoring to form some conception of the person, manners, and habits of the remarkable man to whom they were on the point of paying so interesting a visit.

"I expect," said Vivian, "to be received with folded arms, and a brow lowering with the overwhelming weight of a brain meditating for the control of millions. His letter has prepared us for the mysterious, but not very amusing, style of his conversation. He will be perpetually on his guard not to commit himself; and although public business, and the receipt of papers, by calling him away, will occasionally give us an opportunity of being alone, still I regret that I did not put up in my case some interesting volume, which would have allowed me to feel less tedious those hours during which you will necessarily be employed with him in private consultation."

After a ride of five hours, the horsemen arrived at a small village.

"Thus far I think I have well piloted you," said the Prince: "but I confess my knowledge here ceases; and though I shall disobey the diplomatic instructions of the great man, I must even ask some old woman the way to Mr. Beckendorff's."

While they were hesitating as to whom they should address, an equestrian, who had already passed them on the road, though at some distance, came up, and inquired, in a voice which Vivian recognized as that of the messenger who had brought Beckendorff's letter to Turriparva, whether he had the honor of addressing Mr. von Philipson. Neither of the gentlemen answered, for Vivian of course expected the Prince to reply; and his Highness was, as yet, so unused to his incognito that he had actually forgotten his own name. But it was evident that the demandant had questioned rather from system than by way of security, and he waited patiently until the Prince had collected his senses and assumed sufficient gravity of countenance to inform the horseman that he was the person in question. "What, sir, is your pleasure?"

"I am instructed to ride on before you, sir, that you may not mistake your way;" and without waiting for an answer the laconic messenger turned his steed's head and trotted off.

The travelers soon left the high road and turned up a wild turf path, not only inaccessible to carriages, but even requiring great attention from horsemen. After much winding and some floundering, they arrived at a light gate, which apparently opened into a shrubbery.

"I will take your horses here, gentlemen," said the guide; and getting off his horse, he opened the gate. "Follow this path, and you can meet with no difficulty." The Prince and

Vivian accordingly dismounted, and the guide immediately gave a loud shrill whistle.

The path ran, for a short way, through the shrubbery, which evidently was a belt encircling the grounds. From this the Prince and Vivian emerged upon a lawn, which formed on the furthest side a terrace, by gradually sloping down to the margin of the river. It was inclosed on the other side, and white pheasants were feeding in its centre. Following the path which skirted the lawn, they arrived at a second gate, which opened into a garden, in which no signs of the taste at present existing in Germany for the English system of picturesque pleasure-grounds were at all visible. The walk was bounded on both sides by tall borders, or rather hedges, of box, cut into the shape of battlements; the sameness of these turrets being occasionally varied by the immovable form of some trusty warder, carved out of yew or laurel. Raised terraces and arched walks, aloes and orange trees mounted on sculptured pedestals, columns of cypress and pyramids of bay, whose dark foliage strikingly contrasted with the marble statues, and the white vases shining in the sun, rose in all directions in methodical confusion. The sound of a fountain was not wanting, and large beds of beautiful flowers abounded. Proceeding through a lofty berçeau, occasional openings in whose curving walks allowed effective glimpses of a bust or a statue, the companions at length came in sight of the house. It was a long, uneven, low building, evidently of ancient architecture. Numerous stacks of tall and fantastically shaped chimneys rose over three thick and heavy gables, which reached down further than the middle of the elevation, forming three compartments, one of them including a large and modern bow window, over which clustered in profusion the sweet and glowing blossoms of the clematis and the pomegranate. Indeed, the whole front of the house was so completely covered with a rich scarlet creeper that it was difficult to ascertain of what materials it was built. As Vivian was admiring a white peacock, which, attracted by their approach, had taken the opportunity of unfurling its wheeling train, a man came forward from the bow window.

In height he was about five feet eight, and of a spare but well-proportioned figure. He had little hair, which was powdered, and dressed in a manner to render more remarkable the elevation of his conical and polished forehead. His long piercing black eyes were almost closed, from the fulness of their upper lids. His cheek was sallow, his nose aquiline, his mouth compressed. His ears, which were uncovered, were so small that it would be wrong to pass them over unnoticed; as, indeed, were his hands and feet, in form quite feminine. He was dressed in a coat and waistcoat of black velvet, the latter part of his costume reaching to his thighs; and in a buttonhole of his coat was a large bunch of tuberose. The broad collar of his exquisitely plaited shirt, though tied round with a wide black ribbon, did not conceal a neck which agreed well with his beardless chin, and would not have misbecome a woman. In England we should have called his breeches buckskin. They were of a pale yellow leather, and suited his large and spur-armed cavalry boots, which fitted closely to the legs they covered, reaching over the knees of the wearer. A ribbon round his neck, tucked into his waistcoat pocket, was attached to a small French watch. He swung in his right hand the bow of a violin; and in the other, the little finger of which was nearly hid by a large antique ring, he held a white handkerchief strongly perfumed with violets. Notwithstanding the many feminine characteristics which I have noticed, either from the expression of the eyes or the formation of the mouth, the countenance of this individual generally conveyed an impression of firmness and energy. This description will not be considered ridiculously minute by those who have never had an opportunity of becoming acquainted with the person of so celebrated a gentleman as MR. BECKENDORFF.

He advanced to the Prince with an air which seemed to proclaim that, as his person could not be mistaken, the ceremony of introduction was unnecessary. Bowing in a ceremonious and courtly manner to his Highness, Mr. Beckendorff, in a weak but not unpleasing voice, said that he was "honored by the presence of Mr. von Philipson." The Prince answered his salutation in a manner equally ceremonious and equally courtly; for having no mean opinion of his own diplomatic abilities, his Highness determined that neither by an excess of coldness nor cordiality on his part should the Minister gather the slightest indication of the temper in which he had attended the interview. You see that even the bow of a diplomatist is a serious business!

"Mr. Beckendorff," said his Highness, "my letter doubtless informed you that I should avail myself of your permission to be accompanied. Let me have the honor of presenting to you my friend Mr. Grey, an English gentleman."

As the Prince spoke, Beckendorff stood with his arms crossed behind him, and his chin resting upon his chest, but his eyes at the same time so raised as to look his Highness full in the face. Vivian was so struck by his posture and the expression of his countenance that he nearly omitted to bow when he was presented. As his name was mentioned, the Minister gave him a sharp, sidelong glance, and moving his head slightly, invited his guests to enter the house. The gentlemen accordingly complied with his request. Passing through the bow window, they found themselves in a well-sized room, the sides of which were covered with shelves filled with richly-bound books. There was nothing in the room which gave the slightest indication that the master of the library was any other than a private gentleman. Not a book, not a chair was out of its place. A purple inkstand of Sèvres and a highly-tooled morocco portfolio of the same color reposed on a marqueterie table, and that was all. No papers, no despatches, no red tape, and no red boxes. Over an ancient chimney, lined with china tiles, on which were represented grotesque figures, cows playing the harp, monkeys acting monarchs, and tall figures all legs, flying with rapidity from pursuers who were all head; over this chimney were suspended some curious pieces of antique armor, among which an Italian dagger, with a chased and jeweled hilt, was the most remarkable and the most precious.

"This," said Mr. Beckendorff, "is my library."

"What a splendid poniard!" said the Prince, who had no taste for books; and he immediately walked up to the chimney-piece. Beckendorff followed him, and taking down the admired weapon from its resting-place, proceeded to lecture on its virtues, its antiquity, and its beauty. Vivian seized this opportunity of taking a rapid glance at the contents of the library. He anticipated interleaved copies of Machiavelli, Vattel, and Montesquieu; and the lightest works that he expected to

meet with were the lying memoirs of some intriguing cardinal
or the deluding apology of an exiled minister. To his surprise, he found that, without an exception, the collection consisted of poetry and romance. Somewhat surprised, Vivian
looked with a curious eye on the unlettered backs of a row of
mighty folios on a corner shelf. "These," he thought, "at
least must be royal ordinances, and collected state papers."
The sense of propriety struggled for a moment with the passion
of curiosity; but nothing is more difficult for the man who
loves books than to refrain from examining a volume which he
fancies may be unknown to him. From the jeweled dagger
Beckendorff had now got to an enameled breast-plate. Two
to one he should not be observed; and so, with a desperate
pull, Vivian extracted a volume; it was a herbal! He tried
another; it was a collection of dried insects!

"And now," said Mr. Beckendorff, "I will show you my
drawing-room."

He opened a door at the further end of the library, and
introduced them to a room of a different character. The sun,
which was shining brightly, lent additional brilliancy to the
rainbow-tinted birds of paradise, the crimson macaws, and
the green paroquets that glistened on the Indian paper, which
covered not only the walls, but also the ceiling of the room.
Over the fireplace a black frame, projecting from the wall, and
mournfully contrasting with the general brilliant appearance
of the apartment, inclosed a picture of a beautiful female; and
bending over its frame, and indeed partly shadowing the countenance, was the withered branch of a tree. A harpsichord and
several cases of musical instruments were placed in different
parts of the room; and suspended by broad black ribbons from
the wall, on each side of the picture, were a guitar and a tam-
bourine. On a sofa of unusual size lay a Cremona; and as Mr.
Beckendorff passed the instrument he threw by its side the
bow, which he had hitherto carried in his hand.

"We may as well now take something," said Mr. Beckendorff, when his guests had sufficiently admired the room; "my
pictures are in my dining-room; let us go there."

So saying, and armed this time not only with his bow but
also with his violin, he retraced his steps through the library,
and crossing a small passage which divided the house into two

compartments, he opened the door into his dining-room. The moment they entered the room their ears were saluted, and indeed their senses ravished, by what appeared to be a concert of a thousand birds; yet none of the winged choristers were to be seen, and not even a single cage was visible. The room, which was simply furnished, appeared at first rather gloomy; for, though lighted by three windows, the silk blinds were all drawn.

"And now," said Mr. Beckendorff, raising the first blind, "you shall see my pictures. At what do you estimate this Breughel?"

The window, which was of stained green glass, gave to the landscape an effect similar to that generally produced by the artist mentioned. The Prince, who was already puzzled by finding one who at the same time was both his host and his enemy so different a character from what he had conceived, and who, being by temper superstitious, considered that this preliminary false opinion of his was rather a bad omen, did not express any great admiration of the gallery of Mr. Beckendorff; but Vivian, who had no ambitious hopes or fears to affect his temper, and who was amused by the character with whom he had become so unexpectedly acquainted, good-naturedly humored the fantasies of the Minister, and said that he preferred his picture to any Breughel he had ever seen.

"I see you have a fine taste," said Mr. Beckendorff, with a serious air, but in a courteous tone; "you shall see my Claude!"

The rich yellow tint of the second window gave to the fanciful garden all that was requisite to make it look Italian.

"Have you ever been in Italy, sir?" asked Beckendorff.

"I have not."

"You have, Mr. von Philipson?"

"Never south of Germany," answered the Prince, who was hungry, and eyed with a rapacious glance the capital luncheon which he saw prepared for him.

"Well, then, when either of you go, you will, of course, not miss the Lago Maggiore. Gaze on Isola Bella at sunset, and you will not view so fair a scene as this! And now, Mr. von Philipson," said Beckendorff, "do me the favor of giving me your opinion of this Honthorst?"

His Highness would rather have given his opinion of the dish of game which still smoked upon the table, but which he was mournfully convinced would not smoke long. "But," thought he, "this is the last!" and so he admired the effect produced by the flaming panes, to which Beckendorff swore that no piece ever painted by Gerard Honthorst, for brilliancy of coloring and boldness of outline, could be compared. "Besides," continued Beckendorff, "mine are all animated pictures. See that cypress, waving from the breeze which is now stirring, and look! look at this crimson peacock! look! Mr. von Philipson."

"I am looking, Mr. von—I beg pardon, Mr. Beckendorff," said the Prince, with great dignity, making this slight mistake in the name, either from being unused to converse with such low people as had not the nominal mark of nobility, or to vent his spleen at being so unnecessarily kept from the refreshment which he so much required.

"Mr. von Philipson," said Beckendorff, suddenly turning round, "all my fruits and all my vegetables are from my own garden. Let us sit down and help ourselves."

The only substantial food at table was a great dish of game. The vegetables and the fruits were numerous and superb; and there really appeared to be a fair prospect of the Prince of Little Lilliput making as good a luncheon as if the whole had been conducted under the auspices of Master Rodolph himself, had it not been for the melody of the unseen vocalists, which, probably excited by the sounds of the knives and plates, too evidently increased every moment. But this inconvenience was soon removed by Mr. Beckendorff rising and giving three loud knocks on the door opposite to the one by which they had entered. Immediate silence ensued.

"Clara will change your plate, Mr. von Philipson," said Beckendorff.

Vivian eagerly looked up, not with the slightest idea that the entrance of Clara would prove that the mysterious picture in the drawing-room was a portrait, but, it must be confessed, with a little curiosity to view the first specimen of the sex who lived under the roof of Mr. Beckendorff. Clara was a hale old woman, with rather an acid expression of countenance, prim in her appearance, and evidently precise in her manners. She placed a bottle and two wine-glasses with long thin stems on the table; and having removed the game and changed the plates, she disappeared.

"Pray, what wine is this, Mr. Beckendorff?" eagerly asked the Prince.

"I really don't know. I never drink wine."

"Not know! I never tasted such Tokay in my life!"

"Probably," said Mr. Beckendorff; "I think it was a present from the Emperor. I have never tasted it."

"My dear sir, take a glass!" said the Prince, his naturally jovial temper having made him completely forget whom he was addressing, and the business he had come upon.

"I never drink wine; I am glad you like it; I have no doubt Clara has more."

"No, no, no! we must be moderate," said the Prince, who, though a great admirer of a good luncheon, had also a due respect for a good dinner, and consequently had no idea, at this awkward hour in the day, of preventing himself from properly appreciating the future banquet. Moreover, his Highness, taking into consideration the manner in which the game had been dressed, and the marks of refinement and good taste which seemed to pervade every part of the establishment of Mr. Beckendorff, did not imagine that he was much presuming when he conjectured that there was a fair chance of his dinner being something superior.

The sudden arrival and appearance of some new and unexpected guests through the mysterious portal on which Mr. Beckendorff by his three knocks had previously produced such a tranquillizing effect, and which he had now himself opened, explained the character of the apartment, which, from its unceasing melody, had so much excited the curiosity of his guests. These new visitors were a crowd of piping bullfinches, Virginia nightingales, trained canaries, Java sparrows, and Indian lories; which, freed from their cages of golden wire by their fond master, had fled, as was their custom, from his superb aviary to pay their respects and compliments at his daily levée.

"I am glad to see that you like birds, sir," said Beckendorff to Vivian; for our hero, good-naturedly humoring the tastes of his host, was impartially dividing the luxuries of a peach among a crowd of gaudy and greedy little sparrows. "You shall see my favorites," continued Beckendorff; and tapping rather loudly on the table, he held out the forefinger of each hand. Two bullfinches recognized the signal, and immediately hastened to their perch.

"My dear!" trilled out one little songster, and it raised its speaking eyes to its delighted master.

"My love!" warbled the other, marking its affection by looks equally personal.

As these monosyllables were repeated, Beckendorff, with sparkling eyes, triumphantly looked round at Vivian, as if the frequent reiteration were a proof of the sincerity of the affection of these singular friends.

At length, to the Prince's relief, Mr. Beckendorff's feathered friends, having finished their dessert, were sent back to their cages, with a strict injunction not to trouble their master at present with their voices, an injunction which was obeyed to the letter; and when the door was closed few persons could have been persuaded that the next room was an aviary.

"I am proud of my peaches, Mr. von Philipson," said Beckendorff, recommending the fruit to his guest's attention; then rising from the table, he threw himself on the sofa, and began humming a tune in a low voice. Presently he took up his Cremona, and, using the violin as a guitar, accompanied himself in a beautiful air, but not in a more audible tone. While Mr. Beckendorff was singing he seemed unconscious that any person was in the room; and the Prince, who was not very fond of music, certainly gave him no hint, either by his approbation or his attention, that he was listened to. Vivian, however, like most unhappy men, loved music; and actuated by his feeling, and the interest which he began to take in the character of Mr. Beckendorff, he could not, when that gentleman had finished his air, refrain from very sincerely saying "encore!"

Beckendorff started and looked round, as if he were for the first moment aware that any being had heard him.

"Encore!" said he, with a kind of sneer; "who ever could sing or play the same thing twice! Are you fond of music, sir?"

"Very much so, indeed. I fancied I recognized that air. You are an admirer, I imagine, of Mozart?"

"I never heard of him; I know nothing of those gentry. But if you really like music, I will play you something worth listening to."

Mr. Beckendorff began a beautiful air very *adagio*, gradually increasing the time in a kind of variation, till at last his execution became so rapid that Vivian, surprised at the mere mechanical action, rose from his chair in order better to examine the player's management and motion of his bow. Exquisite as were the tones, enchanting as were the originality of his variations and the perfect harmony of his composition, it was nevertheless extremely difficult to resist smiling at the contortions of his face and figure. Now, his body bending to the strain, he was at one moment with his violin raised in the air, and the next instant with the lower nut almost resting upon his foot. At length, by well-proportioned degrees, the air died away into the original soft cadence; and the player, becoming completely entranced in his own performance, finished by sinking back on the sofa, with his bow and violin raised over his head. Vivian would not disturb him by his applause. An instant after, Mr. Beckendorff, throwing down the instrument, rushed through an open window into the garden.

As soon as Beckendorff was out of sight, Vivian looked at the Prince; and his Highness, elevating his eyebrows, screwing up his mouth, and shrugging his shoulders, altogether presented a comical picture of a puzzled man.

"Well, my dear friend," said he, "this is rather different from what we expected."

"Very different; but much more amusing."

"Humph!" said the Prince, slowly; "I do not think it exactly requires a ghost to tell us that Mr. Beckendorff is not in the habit of going to Court. I do not know how he is accustomed to conduct himself when he is honored by a visit from the Grand Duke; but I am quite sure that, as regards his treatment of myself, to say the least, the incognito is well observed."

"Mr. von Philipson," said the gentleman of whom they were speaking, putting his head in at the window, "you shall see my blue passion-flower. We will take a walk round the garden."

The Prince gave Vivian a look which seemed to suppose they must go, and accordingly they stepped into the garden.

"You do not see my garden in its glory," said Mr. Beckendorff, stopping before the bow window of the library. "This spot is my strong point; had you been here earlier in the year, you might have admired with me my invaluable crescents of tulips; such colors! such brilliancy! so defined! And last year I had three king-tulips; their elegantly formed, creamy cups I have never seen equaled. And then my double variegated ranunculuses; my hyacinths of fifty bells, in every tint, single and double; and my favorite stands of auriculas, so large and powdered that the color of the velvet leaves was scarcely discoverable! The blue passion-flower is, however, now beautiful. You see that summer-house, sir," continued he, turning to Vivian; "the top is my observatory. You will sleep in that pavilion to-night, so you had better take notice how the walk winds."

The passion-flower was trained against the summer-house in question.

"There," said Mr. Beckendorff; and he stood admiring with outstretched arms; "the latter days of its beauty, for the autumn frosts will soon stop its flower. Pray, Mr. von Philipson, are you a botanist?"

"Why," said the Prince, "I am a great admirer of flowers, but I can not exactly say that—"

"Ah! no botanist. The flower of this beautiful plant continues only one day, but there is a constant succession from July to the end of the autumn; and if this fine weather continue— Pray, sir, how is the wind?"

"I really can not say," said the Prince; "but I think the wind is either—"

"Do you know, sir?" continued Beckendorff to Vivian.

"I think, sir, that it is—"

"Westerly. Well! If this weather continue, the succession may still last another month. You will be interested to know, Mr. von Philipson, that the flower comes out at the same joint with the leaf, on a peduncle nearly three inches long; round the centre of it are two radiating crowns; look, look, sir! the inner inclining toward the centre column; now examine this well, and I will be with you in a moment." So saying, Mr. Beckendorff, running down the walk, jumped over the railing, and in a moment was coursing across the lawn, toward the river, in a chase after a dragon-fly.

Mr. Beckendorff was soon out of sight, and after lingering half an hour in the vicinity of the blue passion-flower, the Prince proposed to Vivian that they should quit the spot. "So far as I can observe," continued his Highness, "we might as well quit the house. No wonder that Beckendorff's power is on the wane, for he appears to me to be growing childish. Surely he could not always have been this frivolous creature!"

"I really am so astonished," said Vivian, "that it is quite out of my power to assist your Highness in any supposition. But I should recommend you not to be too hasty in your movements. Take care that staying here does not affect the position which you have taken up, or retard the progress of any measures on which you have determined, and you are safe. What will it injure you if, with the chance of achieving the great and patriotic purpose to which you have devoted your powers and energies, you are subjected for a few hours to the caprices, or even rudeness, of any man whatever? If Beckendorff be the character which the world gives him credit to be, I do not think he can imagine that you are to be deceived twice; and if he do imagine so, we are convinced that he will be disappointed. If, as you have supposed, not only his power is on the wane, but his intellect also, four-and-twenty hours will convince us of the fact; for in less than that time your Highness will necessarily have conversation of a more important nature with him. I recommend, therefore, that we continue here to-day, although," added Vivian, smiling, "I have to sleep in his observatory."

After walking in the gardens about an hour, the Prince and Vivian again went into the house, imagining that Beckendorff might have returned by another entrance; but he was not there. The Prince was much annoyed; and Vivian, to amuse himself, had recourse to the library. After re-examining the armor, looking at the garden through the painted windows, conjecturing who might be the original of the mysterious picture and what could be the meaning of the withered branch, the Prince was fairly worn out. The precise dinner hour he did not know; and notwithstanding repeated exertions, he had hitherto been unable to find the blooming Clara. He could not flatter himself, however, that there were less than two hours to kill before the great event took place; and so, heartily wishing himself back again at Turriparva, he prevailed upon Vivian to throw aside his book and take another walk.

This time they extended their distance, stretched out as far as the river, and explored the adjoining woods; but of Mr. Beckendorff they saw and heard nothing. At length they again returned: it was getting dusk. They found the bow window of the library closed. They again entered the dining-room, and, to their surprise, found no preparations for dinner. This time the Prince was more fortunate in his exertions to procure an interview with Madam Clara, for that lady almost immediately entered the room.

"Pray, my good madam," inquired the Prince, "has your master returned?"

"Mr. Beckendorff is in the library, sir," said the old lady, pompously.

"Indeed! we do not dine in this room, then?"

"Dine, sir!" said the good dame, forgetting her pomposity in her astonishment.

"Yes, dine," said the Prince.

"Mr. Beckendorff never takes anything after his noon meal."

"Am I to understand, then, that we are to have no dinner?" asked his Highness, angry and agitated.

"Mr. Beckendorff never takes anything after his noon meal, sir; but I am sure that if you and your friend are hungry, sir, I hope there is never a want in this house."

"My good lady, I am hungry, very hungry, indeed; and if your master—I mean Mr. von, that is, Mr. Beckendorff—has such a bad appetite that he can satisfy himself with picking, once a day, the breast of a pheasant; why, if he expect his friends to be willing or even able to live on such fare, the least that I can say is that he is much mistaken; and so, therefore, my good friend Grey, I think we had better order our horses and be off."

"No occasion for that, I hope," said Mrs. Clara, rather

alarmed at the Prince's passion; "no want, I trust, ever here, sir; and I make no doubt you will have dinner as soon as possible; and so, sir, I hope you will not be hasty."

"Hasty! I have no wish to be hasty; but as for disarranging the whole economy of the house, and getting up an extemporaneous meal for me, I can not think of it. Mr. Beckendorff may live as he likes, and if I stay here I am contented to live as he does. I do not wish him to change his habits for me, and I shall take care that, after to-day, there will be no necessity for his doing so. However, absolute hunger can make no compliments; and therefore I will thank you, my good madam, to let me and my friend have the remains of that cold game, if they be still in existence, on which we lunched, or, as you term it, took our noon meal, this morning; and which, if it were your own cooking, Mrs. Clara, I assure you, as I observed to my friend at the time, did you infinite credit."

The Prince, although his gentlemanlike feelings had, in spite of his hunger, dictated a deprecation of Mrs. Clara's making a dinner merely for himself, still thought that a seasonable and deserved compliment to the lady might assist in bringing about a result which, notwithstanding his politeness, he much desired; and that was the production of another specimen of her culinary accomplishments. Having behaved, as he considered, with moderation and dignified civility, he was, it must be confessed, rather astounded when Mrs. Clara, duly acknowledging his compliment by her courtesy, was sorry to inform him that she dared give no refreshment in this house without Mr. Beckendorff's special order.

"Special order! Why! surely your master will not grudge me the cold leg of a pheasant?"

"Mr. Beckendorff is not in the habit of grudging anything," answered the housekeeper, with offended majesty.

"Then why should he object?" asked the Prince.

"Mr. Beckendorff is the best judge, sir, of the propriety of his own regulations."

"Well, well!" said Vivian, more interested for his friend than himself, "there is no difficulty in asking Mr. Beckendorff?"

"None in the least, sir," answered the housekeeper, "when he is awake."

"Awake!" said the Prince, "why! is he asleep now?"

"Yes, sir, in the library."

"And how long will he be asleep?" asked the Prince, with eagerness.

"It is uncertain; he may be asleep for hours, he may wake in five minutes; all I can do is to watch."

"But, surely in a case like the present, you can wake your master?"

"I could not wake Mr. Beckendorff, sir, if the house were on fire. No one can enter the room when he is asleep."

"Then how can you possibly know when he is awake?"

"I shall hear his violin immediately, sir."

"Well, well! I suppose it must be so. I wish we were in Turriparva; that is all I know. Men of my station have no business to be paying visits to the sons of the Lord knows who! peasants, shopkeepers, and pedagogues!"

As a fire was blazing in the dining-room, which Mrs. Clara informed them Mr. Beckendorff never omitted having every night in the year, the Prince and his friend imagined that they were to remain there, and they consequently did not attempt to disturb the slumbers of their host. Resting his feet on the hobs, his Highness, for the fiftieth time, declared that he wished he had never left Turriparva; and just when Vivian was on the point of giving up in despair the hope of consoling him, Mrs. Clara entered and proceeded to lay the cloth.

"Your master is awake, then?" asked the Prince, very quickly.

"Mr. Beckendorff has been long awake, sir! and dinner will be ready immediately."

His Highness's countenance brightened; and in a short time the supper appearing, the Prince, again fascinated by Mrs. Clara's cookery and Mr. Beckendorff's wine, forgot his chagrin, and regained his temper.

In about a couple of hours Mr. Beckendorff entered.

"I hope that Clara has given you wine you like, Mr. von Philipson?"

"The same bin, I will answer for that."

Mr. Beckendorff had his violin in his hand, but his dress was much changed. His great boots being pulled off, exhibited the white silk stockings which he invariably wore; and his coat had given place to the easier covering of a brocade dressing-gown. He drew a chair round the fire, between the Prince and Vivian. It was a late hour, and the room was only lighted by the glimmering coals, for the flames had long died away. Mr. Beckendorff sat for some time without speaking, gazing earnestly on the decaying embers. Indeed, before many minutes had elapsed, complete silence prevailed; for both the endeavors of the Prince and of Vivian to promote conversation had been unsuccessful. At length the master of the house turned round to the Prince, and pointing to a particular mass of coal, said, "I think, Mr. von Philipson, that is the completest elephant I ever saw. We will ring the bell for some coals, and then have a game of whist."

The Prince was so surprised by Mr. Beckendorff's remark that he was not sufficiently struck by the strangeness of his proposition, and it was only when he heard Vivian professing his ignorance of the game that it occurred to him that to play at whist was hardly the object for which he had traveled from Turriparva.

"An Englishman not know whist!" said Mr. Beckendorff: "ridiculous! you do know it. Let us play! Mr. von Philipson, I know, has no objection."

"But, my good sir," said the Prince, "although previous to conversation I may have no objection to join in a little amusement, still it appears to me that it has escaped your memory that whist is a game which requires the co-operation of four persons."

"Not at all! I take dummy! I am not sure it is not the finest way of playing the game."

The table was arranged, the lights brought, the cards produced, and the Prince of Little Lilliput, greatly to his surprise, found himself playing whist with Mr. Beckendorff. Nothing could be more dull. The Minister would neither bet nor stake, and the immense interest which he took in every card that was played ludicrously contrasted with the rather sullen looks of the Prince and the very sleepy ones of Vivian. Whenever Mr. Beckendorff played for dummy he always looked with the most searching eye into the next adversary's face, as if he would read his cards in his features. The first rubber lasted an hour and a half, three long games, which

Mr. Beckendorff, to his triumph, hardly won. In the first game of the second rubber Vivian blundered; in the second he revoked; and in the third, having neglected to play, and being loudly called upon, and rated both by his partner and Mr. Beckendorff, he was found to be asleep. Beckendorff threw down his hand with a loud dash, which roused Vivian from his slumber. He apologized for his drowsiness; but said that he was so sleepy that he must retire. The Prince, who longed to be with Beckendorff alone, winked approbation of his intention.

"Well!" said Beckendorff, "you spoiled the rubber. I shall ring for Clara. Why you all are so fond of going to bed I can not understand. I have not been to bed these thirty years."

Vivian made his escape; and Beckendorff, pitying his degeneracy, proposed to the Prince, in a tone which seemed to anticipate that the offer would meet with instantaneous acceptation, double dummy. This, however, was too much.

"No more cards, sir, I thank you," said the Prince; "if, however, you have a mind for an hour's conversation, I am quite at your service."

"I am obliged to you; I never talk. Good-night, Mr. von Philipson."

Mr. Beckendorff left the room. His Highness could contain himself no longer. He rang the bell.

"Pray, Mrs. Clara," said he, "where are my horses?"

"Mr. Beckendorff will have no quadruped within a mile of the house, except Owlface."

"How do you mean? Let me see the man-servant."

"The household consists only of myself, sir."

"Why! where is my luggage, then?"

"That has been brought up, sir; it is in your room."

"I tell you I must have my horses."

"It is quite impossible to-night, sir. I think, sir, you had better retire. Mr. Beckendorff may not be home again these six hours."

"What! is your master gone out?"

"Yes, sir, he is just gone out to take his ride."

"Why! where is his horse kept, then?"

"It is Owlface, sir."

"Owlface, indeed! What! is your master in the habit of riding out at night?"

"Mr. Beckendorff rides out, sir, just when it happens to suit him."

"It is very odd I can not ride out when it happens to suit me! However, I will be off to-morrow; and so, if you please, show me my bedroom at once."

"Your room is the library, sir."

"The library! Why, there is no bed in the library."

"We have no beds, sir; but the sofa is made up."

"No beds! Well! it is only for one night. You are all mad, and I am as mad as you for coming here."

CHAPTER VII

THE morning sun peeping through the window of the little summer-house roused its inmate at an early hour; and finding no signs of Mr. Beckendorff and his guest having yet arisen from their slumbers, Vivian took the opportunity of strolling about the gardens and the grounds. Directing his way along the margin of the river, he soon left the lawn and entered some beautiful meadows, whose dewy verdure glistened in the brightening beams of the early sun. Crossing these, and passing through a gate, he found himself in a rural road, whose lofty hedge-rows, rich with all the varieties of wild fruit and flower, and animated with the cheering presence of the busy birds chirping from every bough and spray, altogether presented a scene which reminded him of the soft beauties of his own country. With some men, to remember is to be sad, and unfortunately for Vivian Grey, there were few objects which with him did not give rise to associations of a painful nature. The strange occurrences of the last few days had recalled, if not revived, the feelings of his boyhood. His early career flitted across his mind. He would have stifled the remembrance with a sigh, but man is the slave of Memory. For a moment he mused over Power; but then he, shuddering, shrank from the wearing anxiety, the consuming care, the eternal vigilance, the constant contrivance, the agonizing suspense, the distracting vicissitudes of his past career. Alas! it is our nature to sicken, from our birth, after some object of unattainable felicity, to struggle through the freshest years of our life in an insane pursuit after some indefinite good, which does not even exist! But sure and quick is the dark hour which cools our doting frenzy in the frigid waves of the ocean of oblivion! We dream of immortality until we die. Ambition! at thy proud and fatal altar we whisper the secrets of our mighty thoughts, and breathe the aspirations of our inexpressible desires. A clouded flame licks up the offering of our ruined souls, and the sacrifice vanishes in the sable smoke of Death.

But where are his thoughts wandering? Had he forgotten that day of darkest despair? There had that happened to him which had happened to no other man. He was roused from his reverie by the sound of a trotting horse. He looked up, but the winding road prevented him at first from seeing the steed which evidently was approaching. The sound came nearer and nearer, and at length, turning a corner, Mr. Beckendorff came in sight. He was mounted on a strong-built, rough, and ugly pony, with an obstinate mane, which, defying the exertions of the groom, fell in equal divisions on both sides of its bottle neck, and a large white face, which, combined with its blinking vision, had earned for it the euphonious title of Owlface. Both master and steed must have traveled hard and far, for both were covered with dust and mud from top to toe, from mane to hoof. Mr. Beckendorff seemed surprised at meeting Vivian, and pulled up his pony as he reached him.

"An early riser, I see, sir. Where is Mr. von Philipson?"

"I have not yet seen him, and imagined that both he and yourself had not yet risen."

"Hum! how many hours is it to noon?" asked Mr. Beckendorff, who always spoke astronomically.

"More than four, I imagine."

"Pray do you prefer the country about here to Turriparva?"

"Both, I think, are beautiful."

"You live at Turriparva?" asked Mr. Beckendorff.

"As a guest," answered Vivian.

"Has it been a fine summer at Turriparva?"

"I believe everywhere."

"I am afraid Mr. von Philipson finds it rather dull here?"

"I am not aware of it."

"He seems a very—?" said Beckendorff, looking keenly in his companion's face. But Vivian did not supply the desired phrase; and so the Minister was forced to finish the sentence himself, "a very gentlemanlike sort of man?" A low bow was the only response.

"I trust, sir, I may indulge the hope," continued Mr. Beckendorff, "that you will honor me with your company another day."

"You are exceedingly obliging!"

"Mr. von Philipson is fond, I think, of a country life?" said Beckendorff.

"Most men are."

"I suppose he has no innate objection to live occasionally in a city."

"Few have."

"You probably have known him long?"

"Not long enough to wish our acquaintance at an end."

"Hum!"

They proceeded in silence for some moments, and then Beckendorff again turned round, and this time with a direct question:

"I wonder if Mr. von Philipson can make it convenient to honor me with his company another day. Can you tell me?"

"I think the best person to inform you of that would be his Highness himself," said Vivian, using his friend's title purposely to show Mr. Beckendorff how ridiculous he considered his present use of the incognito.

"You think so, sir, do you?" answered Beckendorff, sarcastically.

They had now arrived at the gate by which Vivian had reached the road.

"Your course, sir," said Mr. Beckendorff, "lies that way. I see, like myself, you are no great talker. We shall meet at breakfast." So saying, the Minister set spurs to his pony, and was soon out of sight.

When Vivian reached the house, he found the bow window

of the library thrown open, and as he approached he saw
Mr. Beckendorff enter the room and bow to the Prince. His
Highness had passed a good night in spite of not sleeping in a
bed, and he was at this moment commencing a delicious breakfast. His ill-humor had consequently vanished. He had
made up his mind that Beckendorff was mad; and although
he had given up all the secret and flattering hopes which he
had dared to entertain when the interview was first arranged,
he nevertheless did not regret his visit, which on the whole
had been amusing, and had made him acquainted with the
person and habits, and, as he believed, the intellectual powers
of a man with whom, most probably, he should soon be
engaged in open hostility. Vivian took his seat at the breakfast table, and Beckendorff stood conversing with them with
his back to the fireplace, and occasionally, during the pauses
of conversation, pulling the strings of his violin with his
fingers. It did not escape Vivian's observation that the Minister was particularly courteous and even attentive to the
Prince; and that he endeavored by his quick and more communicative answers, and occasionally by a stray observation,
to encourage the good humor visible on the cheerful countenance of his guest.

"Have you been long up, Mr. Beckendorff?" asked the
Prince; for his host had resumed his dressing-gown and
slippers.

"I generally see the sun rise."

"And yet you retire late! Out riding last night, I understand?"

"I never go to bed."

"Indeed," said the Prince. "Well, for my part, without my
regular rest I am nothing. Have you breakfasted, Mr. Beckendorff?"

"Clara will bring my breakfast immediately."

The dame accordingly soon appeared, bearing a tray with
a basin of boiling water and one large thick biscuit. This
Mr. Beckendorff, having well soaked in the hot fluid, eagerly
devoured; and then taking up his violin, amused himself until
his guests had finished their breakfast.

When Vivian had ended his meal he left the Prince and
Beckendorff alone, determined that his presence should not

be the occasion of the Minister any longer retarding the commencement of business. The Prince, who by a private glance had been prepared for his departure, immediately took the opportunity of asking Mr. Beckendorff, in a decisive tone, whether he might flatter himself that he could command his present attention to a subject of importance. Mr. Beckendorff said that he was always at Mr. von Philipson's service; and drawing a chair opposite him, the Prince and Mr. Beckendorff now sat on each side of the fireplace.

"Hem!" said the Prince, clearing his throat; and he looked at Mr. Beckendorff, who sat with his heels close together, his toes out square, his hands resting on his knees, which, as well as his elbows, were turned out, his shoulders bent, his head reclined, and his eyes glancing.

"Hem!" said the Prince of Little Lilliput. "In compliance, Mr. Beckendorff, with your wish, developed in the communication received by me on the —— inst., I assented in my answer to the arrangement then proposed; the object of which was, to use your own words, to facilitate the occurrence of an oral interchange of the sentiments of various parties interested in certain proceedings, by which interchange it was anticipated that the mutual interests might be respectively considered and finally arranged. Prior, Mr. Beckendorff, to either of us going into any detail upon those points of probable discussion, which will, in all likelihood, form the fundamental features of this interview, I wish to recall your attention to the paper which I had the honor of presenting to his Royal Highness, and which is alluded to in your communication of the —— inst. The principal heads of that document I have brought with me, abridged in this paper."

Here the Prince handed to Mr. Beckendorff a MS. pamphlet, consisting of several sheets closely written. The Minister bowed very graciously as he took it from his Highness's hand, and then, without even looking at it, laid it on the table.

"You, sir, I perceive," continued the Prince, "are acquainted with its contents; and it will therefore be unnecessary for me at present to expatiate upon their individual expediency, or to argue for their particular adoption. And, sir, when we observe the progress of the human mind, when we take into consideration the quick march of intellect, and the wide expansion of enlightened views and liberal principles; when we take a bird's-eye view of the history of man from the earliest ages to the present moment, I feel that it would be folly in me to conceive for an instant that the measure developed and recommended in that paper will not finally receive the approbation of his Royal Highness. As to the exact origin of slavery, Mr. Beckendorff, I confess that I am not, at this moment, prepared distinctly to speak. That the Divine Author of our religion was its decided enemy, I am informed, is clear. That the slavery of ancient times was the origin of the feudal service of a more modern period, is a point on which men of learning have not precisely made up their minds. With regard to the exact state of the ancient German people, Tacitus affords us a great deal of most interesting information. Whether or not certain passages which I have brought with me marked in the Germania are incontestable evidences that our ancestors enjoyed or understood the practice of a wise and well-regulated representative system, is a point on which I shall be happy to receive the opinion of so distinguished a statesman as Mr. Beckendorff. In stepping forward, as I have felt it my duty to do, as the advocate of popular rights and national privileges, I am desirous to prove that I have not become the votary of innovation and the professor of revolutionary doctrines. The passages of the Roman author in question, and an ancient charter of the Emperor Charlemagne, are, I consider, decisive and sufficient precedents for the measures which I have thought proper to sanction by my approval, and to support by my influence. A minister, Mr. Beckendorff, must take care that in the great race of politics the minds of his countrymen do not leave his own behind them. We must never forget the powers and capabilities of man. On this very spot, perhaps, some centuries ago, savages clothed in skins were committing cannibalism in a forest. We must not forget, I repeat, that it is the business of those to whom Providence has allotted the responsible possession of power and influence (that it is their duty, our duty, Mr. Beckendorff), to become guardians of our weaker fellow-creatures; that all power is a trust; that we are accountable for its exercise; that from the people, and for the people, all springs, and all must exist; and that, unless we conduct ourselves with the requisite wisdom, prudence, and propriety, the whole system of society will be disorganized; and this country, in particular, will fall a victim to that system of corruption and misgovernment which has already occasioned the destruction of the great kingdoms mentioned in the Bible, and many other states besides, Greece, Rome, Carthage, etc."

Thus ended the peroration of a harangue consisting of an incoherent arrangement of imperfectly-remembered facts and misunderstood principles! all gleaned by his Highness from the enlightening articles of the Reisenburg journals. Like Brutus, the Prince of Little Lilliput paused for a reply.

"Mr. von Philipson," said his companion, when his Highness had finished, "you speak like a man of sense." Having given this answer, Mr. Beckendorff rose from his seat and walked straight out of the room.

The Prince at first took the answer for a compliment; but Mr. Beckendorff not returning, he began to have a faint idea that he was neglected. In this uncertainty he rang the bell for his friend Clara.

"Mrs. Clara! where is your master?"

"Just gone out, sir."

"How do you mean?"

"He has gone out with his gun, sir."

"You are quite sure he has gone out?"

"Quite sure, sir. I took him his coat and boots myself."

"I am to understand, then, that your master has gone out?"

"Yes, sir; Mr. Beckendorff has gone out. He will be home for his noon meal."

"That is enough! Grey!" called out the indignant Prince, darting into the garden.

"Well, my dear Prince," said Vivian, "what can possibly be the matter?"

"The matter! Insanity can be the only excuse; insanity can alone account for his preposterous conduct. We have seen enough of him. The repetition of absurdity is only wearisome. Pray assist me in getting our horses immediately."

"Certainly, if you wish it; but remember you brought me here as your friend and counselor. As I have accepted the trust, I can not help being sensible of the responsibility. Before, therefore, you finally resolve upon departure, pray let me be fully acquainted with the circumstances which have impelled you to this sudden resolution."

"Willingly, my good friend, could I only command my temper; and yet to fall into a passion with a madman is almost a mark of madness. But his manner and his conduct are so provoking and so puzzling that I can not altogether repress my irritability. And that ridiculous incognito! Why, I sometimes begin to think that I really am Mr. von Philipson! An incognito forsooth! for what? to deceive whom? His household apparently only consists of two persons, one of whom has visited me in my own castle; and the other is a cross old hag, who would not be able to comprehend my rank if she were aware of it. But to the point! When you left the room I was determined to be trifled with no longer, and I asked him in a firm voice and very marked manner whether I might command his immediate attention to important business. He professed to be at my service. I opened the affair by taking a cursory, yet definite, review of the principles in which my political conduct had originated and on which it was founded. I flattered myself that I had produced an impression. Sometimes we are in a better cue for these expositions than at others, and to-day I was really unusually felicitous. My memory never deserted me. I was at the same time luminous and profound; and while I was guided by the philosophical spirit of the present day, I showed, by my various reading, that I respected the experience of antiquity. In short, I was satisfied with myself; and with the exception of one single point about the origin of slavery, which unfortunately got entangled with the feudal system, I could not have got on better had Sievers himself been at my side. Nor did I spare Mr. Beckendorff; but, on the contrary, I said a few things which, had he been in his senses, must, I imagine, have gone home. Do you know, I finished by drawing his own character, and showing the inevitable effects of his ruinous policy: and what do you think he did?"

"Left you in a passion?"

"Not at all. He seemed much struck by what I had said, and apparently understood it. I have heard that in some species of insanity the patient is perfectly able to comprehend everything addressed to him, though at that point his sanity ceases, and he is unable to answer or to act. This must be Beckendorff's case; for no sooner had I finished than he rose up immediately, and, saying that I spoke like a man of sense, abruptly quitted the room. The housekeeper says he will not be at home again till that infernal ceremony takes place called the noon meal. Now, do not you advise me to be off as soon as possible?"

"It will require some deliberation. Pray, did you not speak to him last night?"

"Ah! I forgot that I had not been able to speak to you since then. Well! last night, what do you think he did? When you were gone, he had the insolence to congratulate me on the opportunity then afforded of playing double dummy; and when I declined his proposition, but said that if he wished to have an hour's conversation I was at his service, he coolly told me that he never talked, and bade me good-night! Did you ever know such a madman? He never goes to bed. I only had a sofa. How the deuce did you sleep?"

"Well and safely, considering that I was in a summer-house without lock or bolt."

"Well! I need not ask you now as to your opinion of our immediately getting off. We shall have, however, some trouble about our horses, for he will not allow a quadruped near the house, except some monster of an animal that he rides himself; and, by St. Hubert! I can not find out where our steeds are. What shall we do?" But Vivian did not answer. "What are you thinking of?" continued his Highness. "Why don't you answer?"

"Your Highness must not go," said Vivian, shaking his head.

"Not go! Why so?"

"Depend upon it, you are wrong about Beckendorff. That he is a humorist there is no doubt; but it appears to me to be equally clear that his queer habits and singular mode of life are not of late adoption. What he is now he must have been these ten, perhaps these twenty years, perhaps more; of this there are a thousand proofs about us. As to the overpowering cause which has made him the character he appears at present, it is needless for us to inquire; probably some incident in his private life in all likelihood connected with the mysterious picture. Let us be satisfied with the effect. If the case be as I state it, in his private life and habits, Beckendorff must have been equally incomprehensible and equally singular at the very time that, in his public capacity, he was producing such brilliant results as at the present moment. Now then, can we believe him to be insane? I anticipate your objections. I know you will enlarge upon the evident absurdity of his inviting his political opponent to his house for a grave consultation on the most important affairs, and then treating him as he has done you, when it must be clear to him that you can not be again duped, and when he must feel that, were he to amuse you for as many weeks as he has days, your plans and your position would not be injuriously affected. Be it so; probably a humorist like Beckendorff can not, even in the most critical moment, altogether restrain the bent of his capricious inclinations. However, my dear Prince, I will lay no stress upon this point. My opinion, indeed my conviction, is that Beckendorff acts from design. I have considered his conduct well, and I have observed all that you have seen, and more than you have seen, and keenly; depend upon it that since you assented to the interview Beckendorff has been obliged to shift his intended position for negotiation; some of the machinery has gone wrong. Fearful, if he had postponed your visit, you should imagine that he was only again amusing you, and consequently would listen to no future overtures, he has allowed you to attend a conference for which he is not prepared. That he is making desperate exertions to bring the business to a point is my firm opinion; and you would perhaps agree with me were you as convinced as I am that, since we parted last night, our host has been to Reisenburg and back again."

"To Reisenburg and back again!"

"Ay! I rose this morning at an early hour, and imagining that both you and Beckendorff had not yet made your appearance, I escaped from the grounds, intending to explore part of the surrounding country. In my stroll I came to a narrow winding road, which I am convinced lies in the direction toward Reisenburg; there, for some reason or other, I loitered more than an hour, and very probably should have been too late for breakfast had not I been recalled to myself by the approach of a horseman. It was Beckendorff, covered with dust and mud; his horse had been evidently hard ridden. I did not think much of it at the time, because I supposed he might have been out for three or four hours and hard worked, but I nevertheless was struck by his appearance; and when you mentioned that he went out riding at a late hour last night, it immediately occurred to me that had he come home at one or two o'clock it was not very probable that he would have gone out again at four or five. I have no doubt that my conjecture is correct; Beckendorff has been to Reisenburg."

"You have placed this business in a new and important light," said the Prince, his expiring hopes reviving; "what then do you advise me to do?"

"To be quiet. If your own view of the case be right, you can act as well to-morrow or the next day as this moment; on the contrary, if mine be the correct one, a moment may enable Beckendorff himself to bring affairs to a crisis. In either case I should recommend you to be silent, and in no manner to allude any more to the object of your visit. If you speak you only give opportunities to Beckendorff of ascertaining your opinions and your inclinations; and your silence, after such frequent attempts on your side to promote discussion upon business, will soon be discovered by him to be systematic. This will not decrease his opinion of your sagacity and firmness. The first principle of negotiation is to make your adversary respect you."

After long consultation the Prince determined to follow Vivian's advice; and so firmly did he adhere to his purpose that when he met Mr. Beckendorff at the noon meal, he asked him, with a very unembarrassed voice and manner, "what sport he had had in the morning."

The noon meal again consisted of a single dish, as exquisitely dressed, however, as the preceding one. It was a haunch of venison.

"This is my dinner, gentlemen," said Beckendorff; "let it be your luncheon. I have ordered your dinner at sunset."

After having eaten a slice of the haunch, Mr. Beckendorff rose from the table and said, "We will have our wine in the drawing-room, Mr. von Philipson, and then you will not be disturbed by my birds."

He left the room.

To the drawing-room, therefore, his two guests soon adjourned; they found him busily employed with his pencil. The Prince thought it must be a chart, or a fortification at least, and was rather surprised when Mr. Beckendorff asked him the magnitude of Mirac in Boötes; and the Prince confessing his utter ignorance of the subject, the Minister threw aside his unfinished planisphere and drew his chair to them at the table. It was with satisfaction that his Highness perceived a bottle of his favorite Tokay; and with no little astonishment he observed that to-day there were three wine-glasses placed before them. They were of peculiar beauty, and almost worthy, for their elegant shapes and great antiquity, of being included in the collection of the Grand Duke of Johannisberger.

After exhausting their bottle, in which they were assisted to the extent of one glass by their host, who drank Mr. von Philipson's health with cordiality, they assented to Mr. Beckendorff's proposition of visiting his fruitery.

To the Prince's great relief, dinner-time soon arrived; and having employed a couple of hours on that meal very satisfactorily, he and Vivian adjourned to the drawing-room, having previously pledged their honor to each other that nothing should again induce them to play dummy whist. Their resolutions and their promises were needless. Mr. Beckendorff, who was sitting opposite the fire when they came into the room, neither by word nor motion acknowledged that he was aware of their entrance. Vivian found refuge in a book; and the Prince, after having examined and re-examined the brilliant birds that figured on the drawing-room paper, fell asleep upon the sofa. Mr. Beckendorff took down the guitar, and accompanied himself in a low voice for some time; then he suddenly ceased, and stretching out his legs, and supporting his thumbs in the armholes of his waistcoat, he leaned back in his chair and remained motionless, with his eyes fixed upon the picture. Vivian, in turn, gazed upon this singular being and the fair pictured form which he seemed to idolize. Was he, too, unhappy? Had he, too, been bereft in the hour of his proud and perfect joy? Had he, too, lost a virgin bride? His agony overcame him, the book fell from his hand, and he sighed aloud! Mr. Beckendorff started, and the Prince awoke. Vivian, confounded, and unable to overpower his emotions, uttered some hasty words, explanatory, apologetical, and contradictory, and retired. In his walk to the summer-house a man passed him. In spite of a great cloak, Vivian recognized him as their messenger and guide; and his ample mantle did not conceal his riding boots and the spurs which glistened in the moonlight.

It was an hour past midnight when the door of the summer-house softly opened and Mr. Beckendorff entered. He started when he found Vivian still undressed, and pacing up and down the little chamber. The young man made an effort, when he witnessed an intruder, to compose a countenance whose agitation could not be concealed.

"What, are you up again?" said Mr. Beckendorff. "Are you ill?"

"Would I were as well in mind as in body! I have not yet been to rest. We can not command our feelings at all moments, sir; and at this, especially, I felt that I had a right to count upon being alone."

"I exceedingly regret that I have disturbed you," said Mr. Beckendorff, in a kind voice, and in a manner which responded to the sympathy of his tone. "I thought that you had been long asleep. There is a star which I can not exactly make out. I fancy it must be a comet, and so I ran to the observatory; but let me not disturb you;" and Mr. Beckendorff was retiring.

"You do not disturb me, sir. I can not sleep: pray ascend."

"Never mind the star. But if you really have no inclination to sleep, let us sit down and have a little conversation; or perhaps we had better take a stroll. It is a warm night." As he spoke, Mr. Beckendorff gently put his arm within Vivian's, and led him down the steps.

"Are you an astronomer, sir?" asked Beckendorff.

"I can tell the Great Bear from the Little Dog; but I confess that I look upon the stars rather in a poetical than a scientific spirit."

"Hum! I confess I do not."

"There are moments," continued Vivian, "when I can not

refrain from believing that these mysterious luminaries have more influence over our fortunes than modern times are disposed to believe. I feel that I am getting less sceptical, perhaps I should say more credulous, every day; but sorrow makes us superstitious."

"I discard all such fantasies," said Mr. Beckendorff; "they only tend to enervate our mental energies and paralyze all human exertion. It is the belief in these, and a thousand other deceits I could mention, which teaches man that he is not the master of his own mind, but the ordained victim or the chance sport of circumstances, that makes millions pass through life unimpressive as shadows, and has gained for this existence the stigma of a vanity which it does not deserve."

"I wish that I could think as you do," said Vivian; "but the experience of my life forbids me. Within only these last two years my career has, in so many instances, indicated that I am not the master of my own conduct; that no longer able to resist the conviction which is hourly impressed on me, I recognize in every contingency the preordination of my fate."

"A delusion of the brain!" said Beckendorff, quickly. "Fate, Destiny, Chance, particular and special Providence; idle words! Dismiss them all, sir! A man's fate is his own temper; and according to that will be his opinion as to the particular manner in which the course of events is regulated. A consistent man believes in Destiny, a capricious man in Chance."

"But, sir, what is a man's temper? It may be changed every hour. I started in life with very different feelings from those which I profess at this moment. With great deference to you, I imagine that you mistake the effect for the cause; for surely temper is not the origin, but the result of those circumstances of which we are all the creatures."

"Sir, I deny it. Man is not the creature of circumstances. Circumstances are the creatures of men. We are free agents, and man is more powerful than matter. I recognize no intervening influence between that of the established course of nature and my own mind. Truth may be distorted, may be stifled, be suppressed. The invention of cunning deceits may, and in most instances does, prevent man from exercising his own powers. They have made him responsible to a realm of shadows, and a suitor in a court of shades. He is ever dreading authority which does not exist, and fearing the occurrence of penalties which there are none to enforce. But the mind that dares to extricate itself from these vulgar prejudices, that proves its loyalty to its Creator by devoting all its adoration to His glory; such a spirit as this becomes a master-mind, and that master-mind will invariably find that circumstances are its slaves."

"Mr. Beckendorff, yours is a bold philosophy, of which I myself was once a votary. How successful in my service you may judge by finding me a wanderer."

"Sir! your present age is the age of error; your whole system is founded on a fallacy: you believe that a man's temper can change. I deny it. If you have ever seriously entertained the views which I profess; if, as you lead me to suppose, you have dared to act upon them, and failed; sooner or later, whatever may be your present conviction and your present feelings, you will recur to your original wishes and your original pursuits. With a mind experienced and matured, you may in all probability be successful; and then I suppose, stretching your legs in your easy-chair, you will at the same moment be convinced of your own genius, and recognize your own Destiny!"

"With regard to myself, Mr. Beckendorff, I am convinced of the erroneousness of your views. It is my opinion that no one who has dared to think can look upon this world in any other than a mournful spirit. Young as I am, nearly two years have elapsed since, disgusted with the world of politics, I retired to a foreign solitude. At length, with passions subdued, and, as I flatter myself, with a mind matured, convinced of the vanity of all human affairs, I felt emboldened once more partially to mingle with my species. Bitter as my lot had been, I had discovered the origin of my misery in my own unbridled passions; and, tranquil and subdued, I now trusted to pass through life as certain of no fresh sorrows as I was of no fresh joys. And yet, sir, I am at this moment sinking under the infliction of unparalleled misery; misery which I feel I have a right to believe was undeserved. But why expatiate to a stranger on sorrow which must be secret? I deliver myself up to my remorseless Fate."

"What is grief?" said Mr. Beckendorff; "if it be excited by

the fear of some contingency, instead of grieving, a man should exert his energies and prevent its occurrence. If, on the contrary, it be caused by an event, that which has been occasioned by anything human, by the co-operation of human circumstances, can be, and invariably is, removed by the same means. Grief is the agony of an instant; the indulgence of grief the blunder of a life. Mix in the world, and in a month's time you will speak to me very differently. A young man, you meet with disappointment; in spite of all your exalted notions of your own powers, you immediately sink under it. If your belief of your powers were sincere, you should have proved it by the manner in which you have struggled against adversity, not merely by the mode in which you labored for advancement. The latter is but a very inferior merit. If, in fact, you wish to succeed, success, I repeat, is at your command. You talk to me of your experience; and do you think that my sentiments are the crude opinions of an unpracticed man? Sir! I am not fond of conversing with any person, and therefore far from being inclined to maintain an argument in a spirit of insincerity merely for the sake of a victory of words. Mark what I say: it is truth. No Minister ever yet fell but from his own inefficiency. If his downfall be occasioned, as it generally is, by the intrigues of one of his own creatures, his downfall is merited for having been the dupe of a tool which in all probability he should never have employed. If he fall through the open attacks of his political opponents, his downfall is equally deserved for having occasioned by his impolicy the formation of a party, for having allowed it to be formed, or for not having crushed it when formed. No conjuncture can possibly occur, however fearful, however tremendous it may appear, from which a man, by his own energy, may not extricate himself, as a mariner by the rattling of his cannon can dissipate the impending waterspout!"

CHAPTER VIII

IT was on the third day of the visit to Mr. Beckendorff, just as that gentleman was composing his mind after his noon meal with his favorite Cremona, and in a moment of rapture raising his instrument high in air, that the door was suddenly dashed open, and Essper George rushed into the room.

The intruder, the moment that his eye caught Vivian, flew to his master, and, seizing him by the arm, commenced and continued a loud shout of exultation, accompanying his scream the whole time by a kind of quick dance, which, though not quite as clamorous as the Pyrrhic, nevertheless completely drowned the scientific harmony of Mr. Beckendorff.

So astounded were the three gentlemen by this unexpected entrance that some moments elapsed ere either of them found words at his command. At length the master of the house spoke.

"Mr. von Philipson, I beg the favor of being informed who this person is?"

The Prince did not answer, but looked at Vivian in great distress; and just as our hero was about to give Mr. Beckendorff the requisite information, Essper George, taking up the parable himself, seized the opportunity of explaining the mystery.

"Who am I? who are you? I am an honest man, and no traitor; and if all were the same, why, then, there would be no rogues in Reisenburg. Who am I? A man. There's an arm! there's a leg! Can you see through a wood by twilight? If so, yours is a better eye than mine. Can you eat an unskinned hare, or dine on the haunch of a bounding stag? If so, your teeth are sharper than mine. Can you hear a robber's footstep when he's kneeling before murder? or can you listen to the snow falling on Midsummer's day? If so, your ears are finer than mine. Can you run with a chamois? can you wrestle with a bear? can you swim with an otter? If so, I'm your match. How many cities have you seen? How many knaves have you gulled? Which is dearest, bread or justice? Why do men pay more for the protection of life than life itself? Is cheatery a staple at Constantinople, as it is at Vienna? and what's the difference between a Baltic merchant and a Greek pirate? Tell me all this, and I will tell you who went in mourning in the moon at the death of the last comet. Who am I, indeed!"

The embarrassment of the Prince and Vivian while Essper George addressed to Mr. Beckendorff these choice queries was indescribable. Once Vivian tried to check him, but in vain. He did not repeat his attempt, for he was sufficiently employed in restraining his own agitation and keeping his own countenance; for in spite of the mortification and anger that Essper's appearance had excited in him, still an unfortunate but innate taste for the ludicrous did not allow him to be perfectly insensible to the humor of the scene. Mr. Beckendorff listened quietly till Essper had finished; he then rose.

"Mr. von Philipson," said he, "as a personal favor to yourself, and to my own great inconvenience, I consented that in this interview you should be attended by a friend. I did not reckon upon your servant, and it is impossible that I can tolerate his presence for a moment. You know how I live, and that my sole attendant is a female. I allow no male servants within this house. Even when his Royal Highness honors me with his presence he is unattended. I desire that I am immediately released from the presence of this buffoon."

So saying, Mr. Beckendorff left the room.

"Who are you?" said Essper, following him, with his back bent, his head on his chest, and his eyes glancing. The imitation was perfect.

"Essper," said Vivian, "your conduct is inexcusable, the mischief that you have done irreparable, and your punishment shall be severe."

"Severe! Why, what day did my master sell his gratitude

for a silver groschen? Is this the return for finding you out, and saving you from a thousand times more desperate gang than that Baron at Ems? Severe indeed will be your lot when you are in a dungeon in Reisenburg Castle, with black bread for roast venison and sour water for Rhenish!"

"Why, what are you talking about?"

"Talking about! About treason, and arch traitors, and an old scoundrel who lives in a lone lane, and dares not look you straight in the face. Why, his very blink is enough to hang him without trial!"

"Essper, cease immediately this rhodomontade, and then in distinct terms inform his Highness and myself of the causes of this unparalleled intrusion."

The impressiveness of Vivian's manner produced a proper effect; and except that he spoke somewhat affectedly slow and ridiculously precise, Essper George delivered himself with great clearness.

"You see, sir, you never let me know that you were going to leave, and so when I found that you did not come back, I made bold to speak to Mr. Arnelm when he came home from hunting; but I could not get enough breath out of him to stop a ladybird on a rose-leaf. I did not much like it, your honor, for I was among strangers, and so were you, you know. Well, then, I went to Master Rodolph: he was very kind to me, and seeing me in low spirits, and thinking me, I suppose, in love, or in debt, or that I had done some piece of mischief, or had something or other preying on my mind, he comes to me, and says, 'Essper,' said he; you remember Master Rodolph's voice, sir?"

"To the point. Never let me hear Master Rodolph's name again."

"Yes, sir. Well, well! he said to me, 'Come and dine with me in my room;' says I, 'I will.' A good offer should never be refused, unless we have a better one at the same time. Whereupon, after dinner, Master Rodolph said to me, 'We will have a bottle of Burgundy for a treat.' You see, sir, we were rather sick of the Rhenish. Well, sir, we were free with the wine; and Master Rodolph, who is never easy except when he knows everything, must be trying, you see, to get out of me what it was that made me so down in the mouth. I, seeing this, thought I would put off the secret to another bottle; which being produced, I did not conceal from him any longer what was making me so low. 'Rodolph,' said I, 'I do not like my young master going out in this odd way: he is of a temper to get into scrapes, and I should like very much to know what he and the Prince (saving your Highness's presence) are after. They have been shut up in that cabinet these two nights, and though I walked by the door pretty often, devil a bit of a word ever came through the keyhole; and so you see, Rodolph,' said I, 'it requires a bottle or two of Burgundy to keep my spirits up.' Well, your Highness, strange to say, no sooner had I spoken than Master Rodolph put his head across the little table; we dined at the little table on the right hand of the room as you enter—"

"Go on."

"I am going on. Well! he put his head across the little table, and said to me in a low whisper, cocking his odd-looking eye at the same time, 'I tell you what, Essper, you are a deuced sharp fellow!' and so, giving a shake of his head and another wink of his eye, he was quiet. I smelled a rat, but I did not begin to pump directly; but after the third bottle, 'Rodolph,' said I, 'with regard to your last observation' (for we had not spoken lately, Burgundy being too fat a wine for talking), 'we are both of us sharp fellows. I dare say, now, you and I are thinking of the same thing.' 'No doubt of it,' said Rodolph. And so, sir, he agreed to tell me what he was thinking of, on condition that I should be equally frank afterward. Well, then, he told me that there were sad goings on at Turriparva."

"The deuce!" said the Prince.

"Let him tell his story," said Vivian.

"Sad goings on at Turriparva! He wished that his Highness would hunt more and attend less to politics; and then he told me, quite confidentially, that his Highness the Prince, and Heaven knows how many other Princes besides, had leagued together, and were going to dethrone the Grand Duke, and that his master was to be made King, and he, Master Rodolph, Prime Minister. Hearing all this, and duly allowing for a tale over a bottle, I made no doubt, as I find to be the case, that you, good master, were about to be led into some mischief; and as I know that conspiracies are always unsuccessful, I have done my best to save my master; and I beseech you, upon my knees, to get out of the scrape as soon as you possibly can." Here Essper George threw himself at Vivian's feet, and entreated him to quit the house immediately.

"Was ever anything so absurd and so mischievous!" ejaculated the Prince; and then he conversed with Vivian for some time in a whisper. "Essper," at length Vivian said, "you have committed one of the most perfect and most injurious blunders that you could possibly perpetrate. The mischief which may result from your imprudent conduct is incalculable. How long is it since you have thought proper to regulate your conduct on the absurd falsehoods of a drunken steward? His Highness and myself wish to consult in private; but on no account leave the house. Now mind me; if you leave this house without my permission, you forfeit the little chance which remains of being retained in my service."

"Where am I to go, sir?"

"Stay in the passage."

"Suppose (here he imitated Beckendorff) comes to me."

"Then open the door and come into this room."

"Well," said the Prince, when the door was at length shut, "one thing is quite clear. He does not know who Beckendorff is."

"So far satisfactory; but I feel the force of your Highness's observations. It is a most puzzling case. To send him back to Turriparva would be madness: the whole affair would be immediately revealed over another bottle of Burgundy with Master Rodolph; in fact, your Highness's visit would be a secret to no one in the country, your host would be soon discovered, and the evil consequences are incalculable. I know no one to send him to at Reisenburg; and if I did, it appears to me that the same objections equally apply to his proceeding to that city as to his returning to Turriparva. What is to be done? Surely some demon must have inspired him. We can not now request Beckendorff to allow him to stay here; and if we did, I am convinced, from his tone and manner, that nothing could induce him to comply with our wish. The only course to be pursued is certainly an annoying one; but, so far as I can judge, it is the only mode by which very serious mischief can be prevented. Let me proceed forthwith to Reisenburg with Essper. Placed immediately under my eye, and solemnly adjured by me to silence, I think I can answer, particularly when I give him a gentle hint of the station of Beckendorff, for his preserving the confidence with which it will now be our policy partially to intrust him. It is, to say the least, awkward and distressing to leave you alone; but what is to be done? It does not appear that I can now be of any material service to you. I have assisted you as much as, and more than, we could reasonably have supposed it would have been in my power to have done, by throwing some light upon the character and situation of Beckendorff. With the clew to his conduct which my chance meeting with him yesterday morning has afforded us, the only point for your Highness to determine is as to the length of time you will resolve to wait for his communication. As to your final agreement together, with your Highness's settled views and decided purpose, all the difficulty of negotiation will be on his side. Whatever, my dear Prince," continued Vivian, with a significant voice and marked emphasis, "whatever, my dear Prince, may be your secret wishes, be assured that to attain them in your present negotiation you have only to be firm. Let nothing divert you from your purpose, and the termination of this interview must be gratifying to you."

The Prince of Little Lilliput was very disinclined to part with his shrewd counselor, who had already done him considerable service, and he strongly opposed Vivian's proposition. His opposition, however, like that of most other persons, was unaccompanied by any suggestion of his own. And as both agreed that something must be done, it of course ended in the Prince being of opinion that Vivian's advice must be followed. The Prince was really much affected by this sudden and unexpected parting with one for whom, though he had known him so short a time, he began to entertain a sincere regard. "I owe you my life," said the Prince, "and perhaps more than my life; and here we are about suddenly to part, never to meet again. I wish I could get you to make Turriparva your home. You should have your own suite of rooms, your own horses, your own servants, and never feel for an instant that you were not master of all around you. In truth," continued the Prince, with great earnestness, "I wish, my dear friend, you would really think seriously of this. You know you could visit Vienna, and even Italy, and yet return to me. Max would be delighted to see you: he loves you already; and Sievers and his library would be at your command. Agree to my proposition, dear friend."

"I can not express to your Highness how sensible I am of your kindness. Your friendship I sincerely value and shall never forget; but I am too unhappy and unlucky a being to burden any one with my constant presence. Adieu! or will you go with me to Beckendorff?"

"Oh, go with you by all means! But," said the Prince, taking a ruby ring of great antiquity off his finger, "I should feel happy if you would wear this for my sake."

The Prince was so much affected at the thought of parting with Vivian that he could scarcely speak. Vivian accepted the ring with a cordiality which the kind-hearted donor deserved; and yet our hero unfortunately had had rather too much experience of the world not to be aware that, most probably, in less than another week, his affectionate friend would not be able to recall his name under an hour's recollection. Such are friends! The moment that we are not at their side we are neglected, and the moment that we die we are forgotten!

They found Mr. Beckendorff in his library. In apprising Mr. Beckendorff of his intention of immediately quitting his roof, Vivian did not omit to state the causes of his sudden departure. These not only accounted for the abruptness of his movement, but also gave Beckendorff an opportunity of preventing its necessity, by allowing Essper to remain. But the opportunity was not seized by Mr. Beckendorff. The truth was, that gentleman had a particular wish to see Vivian out of his house. In allowing the Prince of Little Lilliput to be attended during the interview by a friend, Beckendorff had prepared himself for the reception of some brawny Jagd Junker, or some thick-headed chamberlain, who he reckoned would act rather as an incumbrance than an aid to his opponent. It was with great mortification, therefore, that he found him accompanied by a shrewd, experienced, wary, and educated Englishman. A man like Beckendorff soon discovered that Vivian Grey's was no common mind. His conversation with him of the last night had given him some notion of his powers, and the moment that Beckendorff saw Essper George enter the house he determined that he should be the cause of Vivian leaving it. There was also another and weighty reason for Mr. Beckendorff desiring that the Prince of Little Lilliput should at this moment be left to himself.

"Mr. Grey will ride on to Reisenburg immediately," said the Prince, "and, my dear friend, you may depend upon having your luggage by the day after to-morrow. I shall be at Turriparva early to-morrow, and it will be my first care."

This was said in a loud voice, and both gentlemen watched Mr. Beckendorff's countenance as the information was given; but no emotion was visible.

"Well, sir, good-morning to you," said Mr. Beckendorff; "I am sorry you are going. Had I known it sooner I would have given you a letter. Mr. von Philipson," said Beckendorff, "do me the favor of looking over that paper." So saying, Mr. Beckendorff put some official report into the Prince's hand; and while his Highness's attention was attracted by this sudden request, Mr. Beckendorff laid his finger on Vivian's arm, and said in a lower tone, "I shall take care that you find a powerful friend at Reisenburg!"

BOOK VII

CHAPTER I

AS Vivian left the room Mr. Beckendorff was seized with an unusual desire to converse with the Prince of Little Lilliput, and his Highness was consequently debarred the consolation of walking with his friend as far as the horses. At the little gate Vivian and Essper encountered the only male attendant who was allowed to approach the house of Mr. Beckendorff. As Vivian quietly walked his horse up the rough turf road, he could not refrain from recurring to his conversation of the previous night; and when he called to mind the adventures of the last six days, he had new cause to wonder at, and perhaps to lament over, his singular fate. In that short time he had saved the life of a powerful Prince, and being immediately signaled out, without any exertion on his part, as the object of that Prince's friendship, the moment he arrives at his castle, by a wonderful contingency, he becomes the depositary of state secrets, and assists in a consultation of importance with one of the most powerful Ministers in Europe. And now the object of so much friendship, confidence, and honor, he is suddenly on the road to the capital of the State of which his late host is the Prime Minister and his friend the chief subject, without even the convenience of a common letter of introduction; and with little prospect of viewing, with even the usual advantages of a common traveler, one of the most interesting of European Courts.

When he had proceeded about half-way up the turf lane he found a private road to his right, which, with that spirit of adventure for which Englishmen are celebrated, he immediately resolved must not only lead to Reisenburg, but also carry him to that city much sooner than the regular highroad. He had not advanced far up this road before he came to the gate at which he had parted with Beckendorff on the morning that gentleman had roused him so unexpectedly from his reverie in a green lane. He was surprised to find a horseman dismounting at the gate. Struck by this singular circumstance, the appearance of the stranger was not unnoticed. He was a tall and well-proportioned man, and as the traveler passed he stared Vivian so fully in the face that our hero did not fail to remark his handsome countenance, the expression of which, however, was rather vacant and unpleasing. He was dressed in a riding-coat exactly similar to the one always worn by Beckendorff's messenger, and had Vivian not seen him so distinctly he would have mistaken him for that person. The stranger was rather indifferently mounted, and carried his cloak and a small portmanteau at the back of his saddle.

"I suppose it is the butler," said Essper George, who now spoke for the first time since his dismissal from the room. Vivian did not answer him; not because he entertained any angry feeling on account of his exceedingly unpleasant visit. By no means: it was impossible for a man like Vivian Grey to cherish an irritated feeling for a second. But he did not exchange a syllable with Essper George, merely because he was not in the humor to speak. He could not refrain from musing on the singular events of the last few days; and, above all, the character of Beckendorff particularly engrossed his meditation. Their conversation of the preceding night excited in his mind new feelings of wonder, and revived emotions which he thought were dead or everlastingly dormant. Apparently, the philosophy on which Beckendorff had regulated his career, and by which he had arrived at his pitch of greatness, was exactly the same with which he himself, Vivian Grey, had started in life; which he had found so fatal in its consequences; which he believed to be so vain in its principles. How was this? What radical error had he committed? It required little consideration. Thirty, and more than thirty, years had passed over the head of Beckendorff ere the world felt his power, or indeed was conscious of his existence. A deep student, not only of man in detail, but of man in groups; not only of individuals, but of nations; Beckendorff had hived up his ample knowledge of all subjects which could interest his fellow-creatures, and when that opportunity which in this world occurs to all men occurred to Beckendorff he was prepared. With acquirements equal to his genius, Beckendorff depended only upon himself, and succeeded. Vivian Grey, with a mind inferior to no man's, dashed on the stage, in years a boy, though in feelings a man. Brilliant as might have been his genius, his acquirements necessarily were insufficient. He could not depend only upon himself; a consequent necessity arose to have recourse to the assistance of others; to inspire them with feelings which they could not share, and humor and manage the petty weaknesses which he himself could not experience. His colleagues were, at the same time, to work for the gratification of their own private interests, the most palpable of all abstract things; and to carry into execution a great purpose, which their feeble minds, interested only by the first point, cared not to comprehend. The unnatural combination failed, and its originator fell. To believe that he could recur again to the hopes, the feelings, the pursuits of his boyhood, he felt to be the vainest of delusions. It was the expectation of a man like Beckendorff, whose career, though difficult, though hazardous, had been uniformly successful; of a man who mistook cares for grief, and anxiety for sorrow.

The travelers entered the city at sunset. Proceeding through an ancient and unseemly town, full of long, narrow, and ill-paved streets, and black, unevenly built houses, they ascended the hill, on the top of which was situated the new and residence town of Reisenburg. The proud palace, the white squares, the architectural streets, the new churches, the elegant opera house, the splendid hotels, and the gay public gardens, full of busts, vases, and statues, and surrounded by an iron railing cast out of the cannon taken from both sides during the war by the Reisenburg troops, and now formed into pikes and fasces, glittering with gilded heads: all these, shining in the setting sun, produced an effect which, at any time and in any place, would have been beautiful and striking; but on the present occasion were still more so, from the remarkable contrast they afforded to the ancient, gloomy, and filthy town through which Vivian had just passed, and where, from the lowness of its situation, the sun had already set. There was as much difference between the old and new town of Reisenburg as between the old barbarous Margrave and the new and noble Grand Duke.

On the second day after his arrival at Reisenburg, Vivian received the following letter from the Prince of Little Lilliput. His luggage did not accompany the epistle.

"MY DEAR FRIEND—By the time you have received this I shall have returned to Turriparva. My visit to a certain gentleman was prolonged for one day. I never can convey to you by words the sense I entertain of the value of your friendship and of your services; I trust that time will afford me opportunities of testifying it by my actions. I return home by the same road by which we came; you remember how excellent the road was, as indeed are all the roads in Reisenburg; that must be confessed by all. I fear that the most partial admirers of the old régime can not say as much for the convenience of traveling in the time of our fathers. Good roads are most excellent things, and one of the first marks of civilization and prosperity. The Emperor Napoleon, who, it must be confessed, had, after all, no common mind, was celebrated for his roads. You have doubtless admired the Route Napoleon on the Rhine, and if you travel into Italy I am informed that you will be equally, and even more, struck by the passage over the Simplon and the other Italian roads. Reisenburg has certainly kept pace with the spirit of the time; nobody can deny that; and I confess to you that the more I consider the subject it appears to me that the happiness, prosperity, and content of a state are the best evidences of the wisdom and beneficent rule of a government. Many things are very excellent in theory which are quite the reverse in practice, and even ludicrous. And while we should do our most to promote the cause and uphold the interests of rational liberty, still, at the same time, we should ever be on our guard against the crude ideas and revolutionary systems of those who are quite inexperienced in that sort of particular knowledge which is necessary for all statesmen. Nothing is so easy as to make things look fine on paper; we should never forget that: there is a great difference between high-sounding generalities and laborious details. Is it reasonable to expect that men who have passed their lives dreaming in colleges and old musty studies should be at all calculated to take the head of affairs, or know what measures those at the head of affairs ought to adopt? I think not. A certain personage, who by the bye is one of the most clear-headed and most perfect men of business that I ever had the pleasure of being acquainted with; a real practical man, in short; he tells me that Professor Skyrocket, whom you will most likely see at Reisenburg, wrote an article in the 'Military Quarterly Review,' which is published there, on the probable expenses of a war between Austria and Prussia, and forgot the commissariat altogether. Did you ever know anything so ridiculous? What business have such fellows to meddle with affairs of state? They should certainly be put down: that, I think, none can deny. A liberal spirit in government is certainly a most excellent thing; but we must always remember that liberty may degenerate into licentiousness. Liberty is certainly an excellent thing, that all admit; but, as a certain person very well observed, so is physic, and yet it is not to be given at all times, but only when the frame is in a state to require it. People may be as unprepared for a wise and discreet use of liberty as a vulgar person may be for the management of a great estate unexpectedly inherited; there is a great deal in this, and, in my opinion, there are cases in which to force liberty down a people's throat is presenting them, not with a blessing, but a curse. I shall send your luggage on immediately; it is very probable that I may be in town at the end of the week, for a short time. I wish much to see and to consult you, and therefore hope that you will not leave Reisenburg before you see

"Your faithful and obliged friend,

"LITTLE LILLIPUT."

Two days after the receipt of this letter Essper George ran into the room with a much less solemn physiognomy than he had thought proper to assume since his master's arrival at Reisenburg.

"Lord, sir! whom do you think I have just met?"

"Whom?" asked Vivian with eagerness, for, as is always the case when such questions are asked us, he was thinking of every person in the world except the right one. "It might be—"

"To think that I should see him!" continued Essper.

"It is a man, then," thought Vivian; "who is it at once, Essper?"

"I thought you would not guess, sir! It will quite cure you to hear it—Master Rodolph!"

"Master Rodolph!"

"Ay! and there's great news in the wind."

"Which of course you have confidentially extracted from him. Pray let us have it."

"The Prince of Little Lilliput is coming to Reisenburg," said Essper.

"Well! I had some idea of that before," said Vivian.

"Oh! then you know it all, sir, I suppose," said Essper, with a look of great disappointment.

"I know nothing more than I have mentioned," said his master.

"What! do you not know, sir, that the Prince has come over; that he is going to live at Court; and be, Heaven knows what! That he is to carry a staff every day before the Grand Duke at dinner; does not my master know that?"

"I know nothing of all this; and so tell me in plain German what the case is."

"Well, then," continued Essper, "I suppose you do not know that his Highness the Prince is to be his Excellency the Grand Marshal, that unfortunate but principal officer of state having received his dismissal yesterday. They are coming up immediately. Not a moment is to be lost, which seems to me very odd. Master Rodolph is arranging everything; and he has this morning purchased from his master's predecessor his palace, furniture, wines, and pictures; in short, his whole establishment: the late Grand Marshal consoling himself for his loss of office, and revenging himself on his successor, by selling him his property at a hundred per cent profit. However, Master Rodolph seems quite contented with his bargain; and your luggage is come, sir. His Highness, the Prince, will be in town at the end of the week; and all the men are to be put in new livery. Mr. Arnelm is to be his Highness's chamberlain, and Von Neuwied master of the horse. So you see, sir, you were right; and that old puss in boots was no traitor, after all. Upon my soul, I did not much believe you, sir, until I heard all this good news."

CHAPTER II

ABOUT a week after his arrival at Reisenburg, as Vivian was at breakfast, the door opened, and Mr. Sievers entered.

"I did not think that our next meeting would be in this city," said Mr. Sievers, smiling.

"His Highness, of course, informed me of your arrival," said Vivian, as he greeted him cordially.

"You, I understand, are the diplomatist whom I am to thank for finding myself again at Reisenburg. Let me, at the same time, express my gratitude for your kind offices to me, and congratulate you on the brilliancy of your talents for negotiation. Little did I think, when I was giving you, the other day, an account of Mr. Beckendorff, that the information would have been of such service to you."

"I am afraid you have nothing to thank me for; though, certainly, had the office of arranging the terms between the parties devolved on me, my first thoughts would have been for a gentleman for whom I have so much regard and respect as Mr. Sievers."

"Sir! I feel honored: you already speak like a finished courtier. Pray, what is to be your office?"

"I fear Mr. Beckendorff will not resign in my favor; and my ambition is so exalted that I can not condescend to take anything under the Premiership."

"You are not to be tempted by a Grand Marshalship!" said Mr. Sievers. "You hardly expected, when you were at Turriparva, to witness such a rapid termination of the patriotism of our good friend. I think you said you have seen him since your arrival: the interview must have been piquant!"

"Not at all. I immediately congratulated him on the judicious arrangements which had been concluded; and, to relieve his awkwardness, took some credit to myself for having partially assisted in bringing about the result. The subject was not again mentioned, and I dare say never will be."

"It is a curious business," said Sievers. "The Prince is a man who, rather than have given me up to the Grand Duke; me, with whom he was not connected, and who, of my own accord, sought his hospitality; sooner, I repeat, than have delivered me up, he would have had his castle razed to the ground and fifty swords through his heart; and yet, without the slightest compunction, has this same man deserted, with the greatest coolness, the party of which, ten days ago, he was the zealous leader. How can you account for this, except it be, as I have long suspected, that in politics there positively is no feeling of honor? Every one is conscious that not only himself, but his colleagues and his rivals, are working for their own private purpose; and that however a party may apparently be assisting in bringing about a result of common benefit, that nevertheless, and in fact, each is conscious that he is the tool of another. With such an understanding, treason is an expected affair; and the only point to consider is, who shall be so unfortunate as to be the deserted, instead of the deserter. It is only fair to his Highness to state that Beckendorff gave him incontestable evidence that he had had a private interview with every one of the mediatized Princes. They were the dupes of the wily Minister. In these negotiations he became acquainted with their plans and characters, and could estimate the probability of their success. The golden bribe, which was in turn dandled before the eyes of all, had been always reserved for the most powerful, our friend. His secession and the consequent desertion of his relatives destroy the party forever; while, at the same time, that party have not even the consolation of a good conscience to uphold them in their adversity; but feel that in case of their clamor, or of any attempt to stir up the people by their hollow patriotism, it is in the power of the Minister to expose and crush them forever."

"All this," said Vivian, "makes me the more rejoice that our friend has got out of their clutches; he will make an excellent Grand Marshal; and you must not forget, my dear sir, that he did not forget you. To tell you the truth, although I did not flatter myself that I should benefit during my stay at

Reisenburg by his influence, I am not the least surprised at
the termination of our visit to Mr. Beckendorff. I have seen
too many of these affairs not to have been quite aware, the
whole time, that it would require very little trouble, and very
few sacrifices on the part of Mr. Beckendorff, to quash the
whole cabal. By the bye, our visit to him was highly amusing; he is a singular man."

"He has had, nevertheless," said Sievers, "a difficult part
to play. Had it not been for you, the Prince would have
perhaps imagined that he was only trifling with him again,
and terminated the interview abruptly and in disgust. Having brought the Grand Duke to terms, and having arranged
the interview, Beckendorff of course imagined that all was
finished. The very day that you arrived at his house he had
received despatches from his Royal Highness, recalling his
promise, and revoking Beckendorff's authority to use his un-
limited discretion in this business. The difficulty then was to
avoid discussion with the Prince, with whom he was not prepared to negotiate; and, at the same time, without letting his
Highness out of his sight, to induce the Grand Duke to resume his old view of the case. The first night that you were
there Beckendorff rode up to Reisenburg, saw the Grand
Duke, was refused, through the intrigues of Madame Carolina, the requested authority, and resigned his power. When
he was a mile on his return, he was summoned back to the
palace; and his Royal Highness asked, as a favor from his
tutor, four-and-twenty hours' consideration. This Beckendorff granted, on the condition that, in case the Grand Duke
assented to the terms proposed, his Royal Highness should
himself be the bearer of the proposition; and that there should
be no more written promises to recall, and no more written
authorities to revoke. The terms were hard, but Beckendorff
was inflexible. On the second night of your visit a messenger
arrived with a despatch, advising Beckendorff of the intended
arrival of his Royal Highness on the next morning. The
ludicrous intrusion of your amusing servant prevented you
from being present at the great interview, in which I understand Beckendorff for the moment laid aside all his caprices.
Our friend acted with great firmness and energy. He would
not be satisfied even with the personal pledge and written

promise of the Grand Duke, but demanded that he should receive the seals of office within a week; so that, had the Court not been sincere, his situation with his former party would not have been injured. It is astonishing how very acute even a dull man is when his own interests are at stake! Had his Highness been the agent of another person, he would probably have committed many blunders, have made disadvantageous terms, or perhaps have been thoroughly duped. Self-interest is the finest eye-water."

"And what says Madame Carolina to all this?"

"Oh! according to custom, she has changed already, and thinks the whole business admirably arranged. His Highness is her grand favorite, and my little pupil Max her pet. I think, however, on the whole, the boy is fondest of the Grand Duke, whom, if you remember, he was always informing you in confidence that he intended to assassinate. And as for your obedient servant," said Sievers, bowing, "here am I once more the Aristarchus of her coterie. Her friends, by the bye, view the accession of the Prince with no pleased eyes; and, anticipating that his juncture with the Minister is only a prelude to their final dispersion, they are compensating for the approaching termination of their career by unusual violence and fresh fervor, stinging like mosquitoes before a storm, conscious of their impending destruction from the clearance of the atmosphere. As for myself, I have nothing more to do with them. Liberty and philosophy are fine words; but until I find men are prepared to cultivate them both in a wiser spirit I shall remain quiet. I have no idea of being banished and imprisoned because a parcel of knaves are making a vile use of the truths which I disseminate. In my opinion, philosophers have said enough; now let men act. But all this time I have forgotten to ask you how you like Reisenburg."

"I can hardly say; with the exception of yesterday, when I rode Max round the ramparts, I have not been once out of the hotel. But to-day I feel so well that, if you are disposed for a lounge, I should like it above all things."

"I am quite at your service; but I must not forget that I am the bearer of a missive to you from his Excellency the Grand Marshal. You are invited to join the Court dinner to-day, and be presented—"

"Really, my dear sir, an invalid—"

"Well! if you do not like it, you must make your excuses to him; but it really is the pleasantest way of commencing your acquaintance at Court, and only allowed to distingués; among which, as you are the friend of the new Grand Marshal, you are of course considered. No one is petted so much as the political apostate, except, perhaps, a religious one; so at present we are all in high feather. You had better dine at the palace to-day. Everything quite easy; and, by an agreeable relaxation of state, neither swords, bags, nor trains are necessary. Have you seen the palace? I suppose not. We will look at it, and then call on the Prince."

The gentlemen accordingly left the hotel; and proceeding down the principal street of the New Town, they came into a large square, or Place d'Armes. A couple of regiments of infantry were exercising in it.

"A specimen of our standing army," said Sievers. "In the war time, this little State brought thirty thousand highly-disciplined and well-appointed troops into the field. This efficient contingent was, at the same time, the origin of our national prosperity and our national debt. For we have a national debt, sir! I assure you we are proud of it, and consider it the most decided sign of being a great people. Our force in times of peace is, of course, much reduced. We have, however, still eight thousand men, who are perfectly unnecessary. The most curious thing is, that, to keep up the patronage of the Court and please the nobility, though we have cut down our army two-thirds, we have never reduced the number of our generals; and so, at this moment, among our eight thousand men, we count upon forty general officers, being one to every two hundred privates. We have, however, which perhaps you would not suspect, one military genius among our multitude of heroes. The Count von Sohnspeer is worthy of being one of Napoleon's marshals. Who he is no one exactly knows; some say an illegitimate son of Beckendorff. Certain it is that he owes his nobility to his sword; and as certain is it that he is to be counted among the very few who share the Minister's confidence. Von Sohnspeer has certainly performed a thousand brilliant exploits; yet, in my opinion, the not least splendid day of his life was that of the battle of Leipsic. He was on the side of the French, and fought against the Allies with desperate fury. When he saw that all was over, and the Allies triumphant, calling out "Germany forever!" he dashed against his former friends, and captured from the flying Gauls a hundred pieces of cannon. He hastened to the tent of the Emperors with his blood-red sword in his hand, and at the same time congratulated them on the triumph of their cause, and presented them with his hard-earned trophies. The manœuvre was perfectly successful; and the troops of Reisenburg, complimented as true Germans, were pitied for their former unhappy fate in being forced to fight against their fatherland, and were immediately enrolled in the allied army; as such, they received a due share of all the plunder. He is a grand genius, young Master von Sohnspeer!"

"Decidedly! Worthy of being a companion of the fighting bastards of the Middle Ages. This is a fine square."

"Very grand indeed! Precedents for some of the architectural combinations could hardly be found at Athens or Rome; nevertheless the general effect is magnificent. Do you admire this plan of making every elevation of an order consonant with the purpose of the building? See, for instance, on the opposite side of the square is the palace. The Corinthian order, which is evident in all its details, suits well the character of the structure. It accords with royal pomp and elegance, with fêtes and banquets, and interior magnificence. On the other hand, what a happy contrast is afforded to this gorgeous structure by the severe simplicity of this Tuscan Palace of Justice. The School of Arts, in the furthest corner of the square, is properly entered through an Ionic portico. Let us go into the palace. Here not only does our monarch reside, but (an arrangement which I much admire) here are deposited, in a gallery worthy of the treasures it contains, our superb collection of pictures. They are the private property of his Royal Highness; but, as is usually the case under despotic Princes, the people, equally his property, are flattered by the collection being styled the 'Public Gallery.'"

The hour of the Court dinner at Reisenburg was two o'clock, about which time, in England, a man first remembers the fatal necessity of shaving; though, by the bye, this allusion is not a very happy one, for in this country shaving is a ceremony at present somewhat obsolete. At two o'clock, however, our hero, accompanying the Grand Marshal and Mr. Sievers, reached the palace. In the saloon were assembled various guests, chiefly attached to the Court. Immediately after the arrival of our party, the Grand Duke and Madame Carolina, followed by their chamberlains and ladies in waiting, entered. The little Prince Maximilian strutted in between his Royal Highness and his fair Consort, having hold of a hand of each. The urchin was much changed in appearance since Vivian first saw him; he was dressed in the complete uniform of a captain of the Royal Guards, having been presented with a commission on the day of his arrival at Court. A brilliant star glittered on his scarlet coat, and paled the splendor of his golden epaulets. The duties, however, of the princely captain were at present confined to the pleasing exertion of carrying the bon-bon box of Madame Carolina, the contents of which were chiefly reserved for his own gratification. In the Grand Duke Vivian was not surprised to recognize the horseman whom he had met in the private road on the morning of his departure from Mr. Beckendorff's; his conversation with Sievers had prepared him for this. Madame Carolina was in appearance Parisian of the highest order: that is to say, an exquisite figure and an indescribable tournure, an invisible foot, a countenance full of esprit and intelligence, without a single regular feature, and large and very bright black eyes. Madame's hair was of the same color, and arranged in the most effective manner. Her cashmere would have graced the Feast of Roses, and so engrossed your attention that it was long before you observed the rest of her costume, in which, however, traces of a creative genius were immediately visible; in short, Madame Carolina was not fashionable, but fashion herself. In a subsequent chapter, at a ball which we have in preparation, we will make up for this brief notice of her costume by publishing her Court dress. For the sake of our fair readers, however, we will not pass over the ornament in her hair. The comb which supported her elaborate curls was invisible, except at each end, whence it threw a large Psyche's wing of golden web, the eyes of which were formed of rubies encircled with turquoises.

The Royal party made a progress round the circle. Madame Carolina first presented her delicate and faintly-rouged cheek to the humpbacked Crown Prince, who scarcely raised his eyes from the ground as he performed the accustomed courtesy. One or two Royal relatives, who were on a visit at the palace, were honored by the same compliment. The Grand Duke bowed graciously and gracefully to every individual; and his lady accompanied the bow by a speech, which was at the same time personal and piquant. The first great duty of a monarch is to know how to bow skilfully! nothing is more difficult and nothing more important. A Royal bow may often quell a rebellion and sometimes crush a conspiracy. It should at the same time be both general and individual; equally addressed to the company assembled, and to every single person in the assembly. Our own sovereign bows to perfection. His bow is eloquent, and will always render an oration on his part unnecessary; which is a great point, for harangues are not regal. Nothing is more undignified than to make a speech. It is from the first an acknowledgment that you are under the necessity of explaining, or conciliating, or convincing, or confuting; in short, that you are not omnipotent, but opposed.

The bow of the Grand Duke of Reisenburg was a first-rate bow, and always produced a great sensation with the people, particularly if it were followed up by a proclamation for a public fête or fireworks; then his Royal Highness's popularity was at its height. But Madame Carolina, after having by a few magic sentences persuaded the whole room that she took a peculiar interest in the happiness of every individual present, has reached Vivian, who stood next to his friend the Grand Marshal. He was presented by that great officer, and received most graciously. For a moment the room thought that his Royal Highness was about to speak; but he only smiled. Madame Carolina, however, said a great deal; and stood not less than sixty seconds complimenting the English nation, and particularly the specimen of that celebrated people who now had the honor of being presented to her. No one spoke more in a given time than Madame Carolina; and as, while the eloquent words fell from her deep red lips, her bright eyes were invariably fixed on those of the person she addressed, what she did say, as invariably, was very effective. Vivian had only time to give a nod of recognition to his friend

Max, for the company, arm-in-arm, now formed into a procession to the dining saloon. Vivian was parted from the Grand Marshal, who, as the highest officer of state present, followed immediately after the Grand Duke. Our hero's companion was Mr. Sievers. Although it was not a state dinner, the party, from being swelled by the suites of the royal visitors, was numerous; and as the Court occupied the centre of the table, Vivian was too distant to listen to the conversation of Madame, who, however, he well perceived, from the animation of her countenance, was delighted and delighting. The Grand Duke spoke little, but listened, like a lover of three days, to the accents of his accomplished consort. The arrangement of a German dinner promotes conversation. The numerous dishes are at once placed upon the table; and when the curious eye has well examined their contents, the whole dinner, untouched, disappears. Although this circumstance is rather alarming to a novice, his terror soon gives place to self-congratulation when he finds the banquet reappear, each dish completely carved and cut up.

"Not being Sunday," said Mr. Sievers, "there is no opera to-night. We are to meet again, I believe, at the palace, in a few hours, at Madame Carolina's soirée. In the meantime, you had better accompany his Excellency to the public gardens; that is the fashionable drive. I shall go home and smoke a pipe."

The circle of the public gardens of Reisenburg exhibited exactly, although upon a smaller scale, the same fashions and the same frivolities, the same characters and the same affectations, as the Hyde Park of London, or the Champs Elysées of Paris, the Prater of Vienna, the Corso of Rome or Milan, or the Cascine of Florence. There was the female leader of *ton*, hated by her own sex and adored by the other, and ruling both; ruling both by the same principle of action, and by the influence of the same quality which creates the arbitress of fashion in all countries, by courage to break through the conventional customs of an artificial class, and by talents to ridicule all those who dare follow her innovating example; attracting universal notice by her own singularity, and at the same time conciliating the support of those from whom she dares to differ, by employing her influence in preventing others from violating their laws. The arbitress of fashion is one who is allowed to be singular, in order that she may suppress singularity; she is exempted from all laws; but, by receiving the dictatorship, she ensures the despotism. Then there was that mysterious being whose influence is perhaps even more surprising than the dominion of the female despot of manners, for she wields a power which can be analyzed and comprehended; I mean the male authority in coats, cravats, and chargers; who, without fortune and without rank, and sometimes merely through the bold obtrusion of a fantastic taste, becomes the glass of fashion in which even royal dukes and the most aristocratic nobles hasten to adjust themselves, and the mold by which the ingenious youth of a whole nation is enthusiastically formed. There is a Brummell in every country.

Vivian, who, after a round or two with the Grand Marshal, had mounted Max, was presented by the young Count von Bernstorff, the son of the Grand Chamberlain, to whose care he had been specially commended by the Prince, to the lovely Countess von S——. The examination of this high authority was rigid and her report satisfactory. When Vivian quitted the side of her britzska half a dozen dandies immediately rode up to learn the result, and, on being informed, they simultaneously cantered up to young Von Bernstorff, and requested to have the honor of being introduced to his highly interesting friend. All these exquisites wore white hats lined with crimson, in consequence of the head of the all-influential Emilius von Aslingen having, on the preceding day, been kept sacred from the profaning air by that most tasteful covering. The young lords were loud in their commendations of this latest evidence of Von Aslingen's happy genius, and rallied with unmerciful spirit the unfortunate Von Bernstorff for not having yet mounted the all-perfect chapeau. Like all Von Aslingen's introductions, it was as remarkable for good taste as for striking singularity; they had no doubt it would have a great run, exactly the style of thing for a hot autumn, and it suited so admirably with the claret-colored riding coat which Madame considered Von Aslingen's chef-d'œuvre. Inimitable Von Aslingen! As they were in these raptures, to Vivian's delight and to their dismay, the object of their admiration appeared. Our hero was, of course, anxious to see so interesting a character; but he could scarcely believe that he, in fact, beheld the ingenious introducer of white and crimson hats, and the still happier inventor of those chef-d'œuvres, claret-colored riding coats, when his attention was directed to a horseman who wore a peculiarly high heavy black hat and a frogged and furred frock, buttoned up, although it was a most sultry day, to his very nose. How singular is the slavery of fashion! Notwithstanding their mortification, the unexpected costume of Von Aslingen appeared only to increase the young lords' admiration of his character and accomplishments; and instead of feeling that he was an insolent pretender, whose fame originated in his insulting their tastes, and existed only by their sufferance, all cantered away with the determination of wearing on the next day, even if it were to cost them each a calenture, furs enough to keep a man warm during a winter party at St. Petersburg; not that winter parties ever take place there; on the contrary, before the winter sets in, the Court moves on to Moscow, which, from its situation and its climate, will always, in fact, continue the real capital of Russia.

The royal carriage, drawn by six horses and backed by three men servants, who would not have disgraced the fairy equipage of Cinderella, has now left the gardens.

CHAPTER III

MADAME CAROLINA held her soirée in her own private apartments, the Grand Duke himself appearing in the capacity of a visitor. The company was numerous and brilliant. His Royal Highness, surrounded by a select circle, dignified one corner of the saloon; Madame Carolina at the other end of the room, in the midst of poets, philosophers, and politicians, in turn decided upon the most interesting and important topics of poetry, philosophy, and politics. Boston, and Zwicken, and whist interested some, and puzzles and other ingenious games others. A few were above conversing, or gambling, or guessing; superior intelligences, who would neither be interested nor amused, among these Emilius von Aslingen was most prominent. He leaned against a door in full uniform, with his vacant eyes fixed on no object. The others were only awkward copies of an easy original; and among these, stiff or stretching, lounging on a chaise-lounge or posted against the wall, Vivian's quick eye recognized more than one of the unhappy votaries of white hats lined with crimson.

When Vivian made his bow to the Grand Duke he was surprised by his Royal Highness coming forward a few steps from the surrounding circle and extending to him his hand. His Royal Highness continued conversing with him for upward of a quarter of an hour; expressed the great pleasure he felt at seeing at his Court a gentleman of whose abilities he had the highest opinion; and, after a variety of agreeable compliments (compliments are doubly agreeable from crowned heads), the Grand Duke retired to a game of Boston with his royal visitors. Vivian's reception made a sensation through the room. Various rumors were immediately afloat.

"Who can he be?"

"Don't you know? Oh! most curious story. Killed a boar as big as a bonasus, which was ravaging half Reisenburg, and saved the lives of his Excellency the Grand Marshal and his whole suite."

"What is that about the Grand Marshal and a boar as big as a bonasus? Quite wrong; natural son of Beckendorff; know it for a fact. Don't you see he is being introduced to Von Sohnspeer! brothers, you know, managed the whole business about the leagued Princes; not a son of Beckendorff, only a particular friend; the son of the late General ——, I forget his name exactly. Killed at Leipsic, you know; that famous general; what was his name? that very famous general; don't you remember? Never mind; well! he is his son; father particular friend of Beckendorff; college friend; brought up the orphan; very handsome of him! They say he does handsome things sometimes."

"Ah! well, I've heard so too; and so this young man is to be the new under-secretary! very much approved by the Countess von S——."

"No, it can't be! your story is quite wrong. He is an Englishman."

"An Englishman! no!"

"Yes, he is. I had it from Madame; high rank incog.; going to Vienna; secret mission."

"Something to do with Greece, of course; independence recognized?"

"Oh! certainly; pay a tribute to the Porte, and governed by a hospodar. Admirable arrangement! have to support their own government and a foreign one besides!"

It was with pleasure that Vivian at length observed Mr. Sievers enter the room, and extricating himself from the enlightened and enthusiastic crowd who were disserting round the tribunal of Madame, he hastened to his amusing friend.

"Ah! my dear sir, how glad I am to see you! I have, since we met last, been introduced to your fashionable ruler, and some of her most fashionable slaves. I have been honored by a long conversation with his Royal Highness, and have listened to some of the most eloquent of the Carolina coterie. What a Babel! there all are, at the same time, talkers and listeners. To what a pitch of perfection may the 'science' of conversation be carried! My mind teems with original ideas, to which I can annex no definite meaning. What a variety of contradictory theories, which are all apparently sound! I begin to suspect that there is a great difference between reasoning and reason!"

"Your suspicion is well founded, my dear sir," said Mr. Sievers; "and I know no circumstance which would sooner prove it than listening for a few minutes to this little man in a snuff-colored coat near me. But I will save you from so terrible a demonstration. He has been endeavoring to catch my eye these last ten minutes, and I have as studiously avoided seeing him. Let us move."

"Willingly; who may this fear-inspiring monster be?"

"A philosopher," said Mr. Sievers, "as most of us call ourselves here; that is to say, his profession is to observe the course of Nature; and if by chance he can discover any slight deviation of the good dame from the path which our ignorance has marked out as her only track, he claps his hands, cries εὔρηκα! and is dubbed 'illustrious' on the spot. Such is the world's reward for a great discovery, which generally, in a twelvemonth's time, is found out to be a blunder of the philosopher, and not an eccentricity of Nature. I am not underrating those great men who, by deep study, or rather by some mysterious inspiration, have produced combinations and effected results which have materially assisted the progress of civilization and the security of our happiness. No, no! to them be due adoration. Would that the reverence of posterity could be some consolation to these great spirits for neglect and persecution when they lived! I have invariably observed of great natural philosophers that if they lived in former ages they were persecuted as magicians, and in periods which profess to be more enlightened they have always been ridiculed as quacks. The succeeding century the real quack arises. He adopts and develops the suppressed, and despised, and forgotten discovery of his unfortunate predecessor! and Fame trumpets this resurrection-man of science with as loud a blast of rapture as if, instead of being merely the accidental animator of the corpse, he were the cunning artist himself who had devised and executed the miraculous machinery which the other had only wound up."

"But in this country," said Vivian, "surely you have no reason to complain of the want of moral philosophers, or of the respect paid to them. The country of Kant—of—"

"Yes, yes! we have plenty of metaphysicians, if you mean them. Watch that lively-looking gentleman who is stuffing *kalte schale* so voraciously in the corner. The leader of the Idealists, a pupil of the celebrated Fichte! To gain an idea of his character, know that he out-Herods his master; and Fichte is to Kant what Kant is to the unenlightened vulgar. You can now form a slight conception of the spiritual nature of our friend who is stuffing *kalte schale*. The first principle of his school is to reject all expressions which incline in the slightest degree to substantiality. Existence is, in his opinion, a word too absolute. Being, principle, essence, are terms scarcely sufficiently ethereal even to indicate the subtle shadowings of his opinions. Some say that he dreads the contact of all real things, and that he makes it the study of his life to avoid them. Matter is his great enemy. When you converse with him you lose all consciousness of this world. My dear sir," continued Mr. Sievers, "observe how exquisitely Nature revenges herself upon these capricious and fantastic children. Believe me, Nature is the most brilliant of wits; and that no repartees that were ever inspired by hate, or wine, or beauty, ever equaled the calm effects of her indomitable power upon those who are rejecting her authority. You understand me? Methinks that the best answer to the idealism of M. Fichte is to see his pupil devouring *kalte schale!*"

"And this is really one of your great lights?"

"Verily! His works are the most famous and the most unreadable in all Germany. Surely you have heard of his 'Treatise on Man'? A treatise on a subject in which every one is interested, written in a style which no one can understand."

"You think, then," said Vivian, "that posterity may rank the German metaphysicians with the later Platonists?"

"I hardly know; they are a body of men not less acute, but I doubt whether they will be as celebrated. In this age of print, notoriety is more attainable than in the age of manuscript; but lasting fame certainly is not. That tall thin man in black that just bowed to me is the editor of one of our great Reisenburg reviews. The journal he edits is one of the most successful periodical publications ever set afloat. Among its contributors may assuredly be classed many men of eminent talents; yet to their abilities the surprising success and influence of this work is scarcely to be ascribed. It is the result rather of the consistent spirit which has always inspired its masterly critics. One principle has ever regulated its management; it is a simple rule, but an effective one: every author is reviewed by his personal enemy. You may imagine the point of the critic; but you would hardly credit, if I were to inform you, the circulation of the review. You will tell me that you are not surprised, and talk of the natural appetite of our species for malice and slander. Be not too quick. The rival of this review, both in influence and in sale, is conducted on as simple a principle, but not a similar one. In this journal every author is reviewed by his personal friend; of course, perfect panegyric. Each number is flattering as a lover's tale; every article an eloge. What say you to this? These are the influential literary and political journals of Reisenburg. There was yet another; it was edited by an eloquent scholar; all its contributors were, at the same time, brilliant and profound. It numbered among its writers some of the most celebrated

names in Germany; its critics and articles were as impartial as
they were able, as sincere as they were sound; it never paid
the expense of the first number. As philanthropists and admirers of our species, my dear sir, these are gratifying results;
they satisfactorily demonstrate that mankind have no innate
desire for scandal, calumny, and backbiting; it only proves that
they have an innate desire to be gulled and deceived."

"And who is that?" said Vivian.

"That is Von Chronicle, our great historical novelist.
When I first came to Reisenburg, now eight years ago, the
popular writer of fiction was a man, the most probable of whose
numerous romances was one in which the hero sold his shadow
to a demon over the dice-box; then married an unknown
woman in a churchyard; afterward wedded a river nymph;
and, having committed bigamy, finally stabbed himself, to
enable his first wife to marry his own father. He and his
works are quite obsolete; and the star of his genius, with those
of many others, has paled before the superior brilliancy of that
literary comet, Mr. von Chronicle. According to Von Chronicle, we have all, for a long time, been under a mistake. We
have ever considered that the first point to be studied in novel
writing is character: miserable error! It is costume. Variety
of incident, novelty, and nice discrimination of character;
interest of story, and all those points which we have hitherto
looked upon as necessary qualities of a fine novel, vanish before the superior attractions of variety of dresses, exquisite
descriptions of the cloak of a signor, or the trunk-hose of a
serving man.

"Amuse yourself while you are at Reisenburg by turning
over some volumes which every one is reading; Von Chronicle's last great historical novel. The subject is a magnificent
one, Rienzi; yet it is strange that the hero only appears in the
first and the last scenes. You look astonished. Ah! I see you
are not a great historical novelist. You forget the effect which
is produced by the contrast of the costume of Master Nicholas,
the notary in the quarter of the Jews, and that of Rienzi, the
tribune, in his robe of purple, at his coronation in the Capitol.
Conceive the effect, the contrast. With that coronation Von
Chronicle's novel terminates; for, as he well observes, after
that, what is there in the career of Rienzi which would afford

matter for the novelist? Nothing! All that afterward occurs is a mere contest of passions and a development of character; but where is a procession, a triumph, or a marriage?

"One of Von Chronicle's great characters in this novel is a Cardinal. It was only last night that I was fortunate enough to have the beauties of the work pointed out to me by the author himself. He entreated, and gained my permission to read to me what he himself considered 'the great scene.' I settled myself in my chair, took out my handkerchief, and prepared my mind for the worst. While I was anticipating the terrors of a heroine he introduced me to his Cardinal. Thirty pages were devoted to the description of the prelate's costume. Although clothed in purple, still, by a skilful ad justment of the drapery, Von Chronicle managed to bring in six other petticoats. I thought this beginning would never finish, but to my surprise, when he had got to the seventh petticoat, he shut his book, and leaning over the table, asked me what I thought of his 'great scene.' 'My friend,' said I, 'you are not only the greatest historical novelist that ever lived, but that ever will live.'"

"I shall certainly get 'Rienzi,' " said Vivian; "it seems to me to be an original work."

"Von Chronicle tells me that he looks upon it as his masterpiece, and that it may be considered as the highest point of perfection to which his system of novel-writing can be carried. Not a single name is given in the work, down even to the rabble, for which he has not contemporary authority; but what he is particularly proud of are his oaths. Nothing, he tells me, has cost him more trouble than the management of the swearing; and the Romans, you know, are a most profane nation. The great difficulty to be avoided was using the ejaculations of two different ages. The 'bloods' of the sixteenth century must not be confounded with the 'zounds' of the seventeenth. Enough of Von Chronicle! The most amusing thing," continued Mr. Sievers, "is to contrast this mode of writing works of fiction with the prevalent and fashionable method of writing works of history. Contrast the 'Rienzi' of Von Chronicle with the 'Haroun Al Raschid' of Madame Carolina. Here we write novels like history, and history like novels: all our facts are fancy, and all our imagination reality." So saying,

Mr. Sievers rose, and wishing Vivian good-night, quitted the room. He was one of those prudent geniuses who always leave off with a point.

Mr. Sievers had not left Vivian more than a minute when the little Prince Maximilian came up and bowed to him in a condescending manner. Our hero, who had not yet had an opportunity of speaking with him, thanked him cordially for his handsome present, and asked him how he liked the Court.

"Oh, delightful! I pass all my time with the Grand Duke and Madame:" and here the young apostate settled his military stock and arranged the girdle of his sword. "Madame Carolina," continued he, "has commanded me to inform you that she desires the pleasure of your attendance."

The summons was immediately obeyed, and Vivian had the honor of a long conversation with the interesting Consort of the Grand Duke. He was, for a considerable time, complimented by her enthusiastic panegyric of England, her original ideas of the character and genius of Lord Byron, her veneration for Sir Humphry Davy, and her admiration of Sir Walter Scott. Not remiss was Vivian in paying, in his happiest manner, due compliments to the fair and royal authoress of the Court of Charlemagne. While she spoke his native tongue, he admired her accurate English; and while she professed to have derived her imperfect knowledge of his perfect language from a study of its best authors, she avowed her belief of the impossibility of ever speaking it correctly without the assistance of a native. Conversation became more interesting.

When Vivian left the palace he was not unmindful of an engagement to return there the next day, to give a first lesson in English pronunciation to Madame Carolina.

CHAPTER IV

VIVIAN duly kept his appointment with Madame Carolina. The chamberlain ushered him into a library, where Madame Carolina was seated at a large table covered with books and manuscripts. Her costume and her countenance were equally engaging. Fascination was alike in her smile, and her sash, her bow, and her buckle. What a delightful pupil to perfect in English pronunciation! Madame pointed, with a pride pleasing to Vivian's feelings as an Englishman, to her shelves, graced with the most eminent of English writers. Madame Carolina was not like one of those admirers of English literature whom you often meet on the Continent: people who think that Beattie's "Minstrel" is our most modern and fashionable poem; that the "Night Thoughts" is the masterpiece of our literature; and that Richardson is our only novelist. Oh, no! Madame Carolina would not have disgraced Mayfair. She knew "Childe Harold" by rote, and had even peeped into "Don Juan." Her admiration of the "Edinburgh" and "Quarterly Reviews" was great and similar. To a Continental liberal, indeed, even the Toryism of the "Quarterly" is philosophy: and not an Under-Secretary ever yet massacred a radical innovator without giving loose to some sentiments and sentences which are considered rank treason in the meridian of Vienna.

After some conversation, in which Madame evinced eagerness to gain details about the persons and manners of our most eminent literary characters, she naturally began to speak of the literary productions of other countries; and in short, ere an hour was passed, Vivian Grey, instead of giving a lesson in English pronunciation to the Consort of the Grand Duke of Reisenburg, found himself listening, in an easy chair, and with folded arms, to a long treatise by that lady *de l'Esprit de Conversation*. It was a most brilliant dissertation. Her kindness in reading it to him was most particular; nevertheless, for unexpected blessings we are not always sufficiently grateful.

Another hour was consumed by the treatise. How she refined! what unexpected distinctions! what exquisite discrimination of national character! what skilful eulogium of her own! Nothing could be more splendid than her elaborate character of a repartee; it would have sufficed for an epic poem. At length Madame Carolina ceased *de l'Esprit de Conversation,* and Vivian was successful in concealing his weariness and in testifying his admiration. "The evil is over," thought he; "I may as well gain credit for my good taste." The lesson in English pronunciation, however, was not yet terminated. Madame was charmed with our hero's uncommon discrimination and extraordinary talents. He was the most skilful and the most agreeable critic with whom she had ever been acquainted. How invaluable must the opinion of such a person be to her on her great work! No one had yet seen a line of it; but there are moments when we are irresistibly impelled to seek a confidant; that confidant was before her. The morocco case was unlocked, and the manuscript of "Haroun Al Raschid" revealed to the enraptured eye of Vivian Grey.

"I flatter myself," said Madame Carolina, "that this work will create a great sensation; not only in Germany. It abounds, I think, with interesting story, engaging incidents, and animated and effective descriptions. I have not, of course, been able to obtain any new matter respecting his Sublimity the Caliph. Between ourselves, I do not think this very important. So far as I have observed, we have matter enough in this world on every possible subject already. It is manner in which the literature of all nations is deficient. It appears to me that the great point for persons of genius now to direct their attention to is the expansion of matter. This I conceive to be the great secret; and this must be effected by the art of picturesque writing. For instance, my dear Mr. Grey, I will open the 'Arabian Nights' Entertainments,' merely for an exemplification, at the one hundred and eighty-fifth night; good! Let us attend to the following passage:

" 'In the reign of the Caliph Haroun Al Raschid, there was at Bagdad a druggist, called Alboussan Ebn Thaher, a very rich, handsome man. He had more wit and politeness than people of his profession ordinarily have. His integrity, sincerity, and jovial humor made him beloved and sought after by all sorts of people. The Caliph, who knew his merit, had entire confidence in him. He had so great an esteem for him that he intrusted him with the care to provide his favored ladies with all the things they stood in need of. He chose for them their clothes, furniture, and jewels, with admirable taste. His good qualities and the favor of the Caliph made the sons of Emirs and other officers of the first rank be always about him. His house was the rendezvous of all the nobility of the Court.' "

"What capabilities lurk in this dry passage!" exclaimed Madame Carolina; "I touch it with my pen, and transform it into a chapter. It shall be one of those that I will read to you. The description of Alboussan alone demands ten pages. There is no doubt that his countenance was Oriental: The tale says that he was handsome: I paint him with his Eastern eye, his thin arched brow, his fragrant beard, his graceful mustache. The tale says he was rich: I have authorities for the costume of men of his dignity in contemporary writers. In my history he appears in an upper garment of green velvet, and loose trousers of pink satin; a jeweled dagger lies in his golden girdle; his slippers are of the richest embroidery; and he never omits the bath of roses daily. On this system, which in my opinion elicits truth, for by it you are enabled to form a conception of the manners of the age; on this system I proceed throughout the paragraph. Conceive my account of his house being the 'rendezvous of all the nobility of the Court.' What a brilliant scene! what variety of dress and character! what splendor! what luxury! what magnificence! Imagine the detail of the banquet; which, by the bye, gives me an opportunity of inserting, after the manner of your own Gibbon, 'a dissertation on sherbet.' What think you of the art of picturesque writing?"

"Admirable!" said Vivian; "Von Chronicle himself—"

"How can you mention the name of that odious man!" almost shrieked Madame Carolina, forgetting the dignity of her semi-regal character in the jealous feelings of the author. "How can you mention him! A scribbler without a spark, not only of genius, but even of common invention. A miserable fellow, who seems to do nothing but clothe and amplify, in his own fantastic style, the details of a parcel of old chronicles!"

Madame's indignation reminded Vivian of a true but rather vulgar proverb of his own country; and he extricated himself from his very awkward situation with a dexterity worthy of his former years.

"Von Chronicle himself," said Vivian; "Von Chronicle himself, as I was going to observe, will be the most mortified of all on the appearance of your work. He can not be so blinded by self-conceit as to fail to observe that your history is a thousand times more interesting than his fiction. Ah! Madame, if you can thus spread enchantment over the hitherto weary page of history, what must be your work of imagination!"

CHAPTER V

VIVIAN met Emilius von Aslingen in his ride through the gardens. As that distinguished personage at present patronized the English nation, and astounded the Reisenburg natives by driving an English mail, riding English horses, and ruling English grooms, he deigned to be exceedingly courteous to our hero, whom he had publicly declared at the soirée of the preceding night to be "very good style." Such a character from such a man raised Vivian even more in the estimation of the Reisenburg world than his flattering reception by the Grand Duke and his cordial greeting by Madame Carolina.

"Shall you be at the Grand Marshal's to-night?" asked Vivian.

"Ah! that is the new man, the man who was mediatized, is not it?"

"The Prince of Little Lilliput."

"Yes!" drawled out Mr. von Aslingen. "I shall go if I have courage enough; but they say his servants wear skins, and he has got a tail."

. The ballroom was splendidly illuminated. The whole of the Royal Family was present, and did honor to their new officer of state; his Royal Highness all smiles and his Consort all diamonds. Stars and uniforms, ribbons and orders, abounded. The diplomatic body wore the dresses of their respective Courts. Emilius von Aslingen, having given out in the morning that he should appear as a captain in the Royal Guards, the young lords and fops of fashion were consequently ultra military. They were not a little annoyed when, late in the evening, their model lounged in, wearing the rich scarlet uniform of a Knight of Malta, of which newly revived order Von Aslingen, who had served half a campaign against the Turks, was a member.

The Royal Family had arrived only a few minutes: dancing had not yet commenced. Vivian was at the top of the room, honored by the notice of Madame Carolina, who complained of his yesterday's absence from the palace. Suddenly the universal hum and buzz which are always sounding in a crowded room were stilled; and all present, arrested in their conversation and pursuits, stood with their heads turned toward the great door. Thither also Vivian looked, and, wonderstruck, beheld—Mr. Beckendorff. His singular appearance, for, with the exception of his cavalry boots, he presented the same figure as when he first came forward to receive the Prince of Little Lilliput and Vivian on the lawn, immediately attracted universal attention; but in this crowded room there were a few who, either from actual experience or accurate information, were not ignorant that this personage was the Prime Minister. The report spread like wildfire. Even the etiquette of a German ballroom, honored as it was by the presence of the Court, was no restraint to the curiosity and wonder of all present. Yes! even Emilius von Aslingen raised his glass to his eye. But great as was Vivian's astonishment, it was not only occasioned by this unexpected appearance of his former host. Mr. Beckendorff was not alone: a woman was leaning on his left arm. A quick glance in a moment convinced Vivian that she was not the original of the mysterious picture. The companion of Beckendorff was very young. Her full voluptuous growth gave you, for a moment, the impression that she was somewhat low in stature; but it was only for a moment, for the lady was by no means short. Her beauty it is impossible to describe. It was of a kind that baffles all phrases, nor have I a single simile at command to make it more clear or more confused. Her luxurious form, her blond complexion, her silken hair, would have all become the languishing Sultana; but then her eyes, they banished all idea of the Seraglio, and were the most decidedly European, though the most brilliant, that ever glanced; eagles might have proved their young at them. To a countenance which otherwise would have been calm, and perhaps pensive, they gave an expression of extreme vivacity and unusual animation, and perhaps of restlessness and arrogance; it might have been courage. The lady was dressed in the costume of a Chanoinesse of a *Couvent des dames* nobles; an institution to which Protestant and Catholic ladies are alike admitted. The orange-colored cordon of her canonry was slung gracefully over her plain black silk dress, and a diamond cross hung below her waist.

Mr. Beckendorff and his fair companion were instantly welcomed by the Grand Marshal; and Arnelm and half a dozen Chamberlains, all in new uniforms, and extremely agitated, did their utmost, by their exertions in clearing the way, to prevent the Prime Minister of Reisenburg from paying his respects to his Sovereign. At length, however, Mr. Beckendorff reached the top of the room, and presented the young lady to his Royal Highness, and also to Madame Carolina. Vivian had retired on their approach, and now found himself among a set of young officers, idolators of Von Aslingen, and of white hats lined with crimson. "Who can she be?" was the universal question. Though all by the query acknowledged their ignorance, yet it is singular that, at the same time, every one was prepared with a response to it. Such are the sources of accurate information!

"And that is Beckendorff, is it?" exclaimed the young Count of Eberstein; "and his daughter, of course! Well; there is nothing like being a plebeian and a Prime Minister! I suppose Beckendorff will bring an anonymous friend to Court next."

"She can not be his daughter," said Bernstorff. "To be a Chanoinesse of that order, remember, she must be noble."

"Then she must be his niece," answered the young Count of Eberstein. "I think I do remember some confused story

about a sister of Beckendorff who ran away with some Wurtemburg Baron. What was that story, Gernsbach?"

"No, it was not his sister," said the Baron of Gernsbach;
"it was his aunt, I think."

"Beckendorff's aunt; what an idea! As if he ever had an
aunt! Men of his calibre make themselves out of mud. They
have no relations. Well, never mind; there was some story, I
am sure, about some woman or other. Depend upon it that
this girl is the child of that woman, whether she be aunt, niece,
or daughter. I shall go and tell every one that I know the
whole business; this girl is the daughter of some woman or
other." So saying, away walked the young Count of Eberstein, to disseminate in all directions the important conclusion at which his logical head had allowed him to arrive.

"Von Weinbren," said the Baron of Gernsbach, "how can
you account for this mysterious appearance of the Premier?"

"Oh! when men are on the decline they do desperate things.
I suppose it is to please the *renegado.*"

"Hush! there's the Englishman behind you."

"*On dit,* another child of Beckendorff."

"Oh, no! secret mission."

"Ah! indeed."

"Here comes Von Aslingen! Well, great Emilius! how
solve you this mystery?"

"What mystery? Is there one?"

"I allude to this wonderful appearance of Beckendorff."

"Beckendorff! what a name! Who is he?"

"Nonsense! the Premier."

"Well!"

"You have seen him, of course; he is here. Have you just
come in?"

"Beckendorff here!" said Von Aslingen, in a tone of affected horror; "I did not know that the fellow was to be
visited. It is all over with Reisenburg. I shall go to Vienna
to-morrow."

But hark! the sprightly music calls to the dance; and first
the stately Polonaise, an easy gradation between walking and
dancing. To the surprise of the whole room and the indignation of many of the high nobles, the Crown Prince of Reisenburg led off the Polonaise with the unknown fair one. Such

an attention to Beckendorff was a distressing proof of present power and favor. The Polonaise is a dignified promenade, with which German balls invariably commence. The cavaliers, with an air of studied grace, offer their right hands to their fair partners; and the whole party, in a long file, accurately follow the leading couple through all their scientific evolutions, as they wind through every part of the room. Waltzes in sets speedily followed the Polonaise; and the unknown, who was now an object of universal attention, danced with Count von Sohnspeer, another of Beckendorff's numerous progeny, if the reader remember. How scurvily are poor single gentlemen who live alone treated by the candid tongues of their fellow-creatures! The commander-in-chief of the Reisenburg troops was certainly a partner of a different complexion from the young lady's previous one. The Crown Prince had undertaken his duty with reluctance, and had performed it without grace; not a single word had he exchanged with his partner during the promenade, and his genuine listlessness was even more offensive than affected apathy. Von Sohnspeer, on the contrary, danced in the true Vienna style, and whirled like a dervish. All our good English prejudices against the soft, the swimming, the sentimental, melting, undulating, dangerous waltz would quickly disappear if we only executed the dreaded manœuvres in the true Austrian style. One might as soon expect our daughters to get sentimental in a swing.

Vivian did not choose to presume upon his late acquaintance with Mr. Beckendorff, as it had not been sought by that gentleman, and he consequently did not pay his respects to the Minister. Mr. Beckendorff continued at the top of the room, standing between the state chairs of his Royal Highness and Madame Carolina, and occasionally addressing an observation to his Sovereign and answering one of the lady's. Had Mr. Beckendorff been in the habit of attending balls nightly he could not have exhibited more perfect nonchalance. There he stood, with his arms crossed behind him, his chin resting on his breast, and his raised eyes glancing!

"My dear Prince," said Vivian to the Grand Marshal, "you are just the person I wanted to speak to. How came you to invite Beckendorff, and how came he to accept the invitation?"

"My dear friend," said his Highness, shrugging his shoulders, "wonders will never cease. I never invited him; I should just as soon have thought of inviting old Johannisberger."

"Were not you aware, then, of his intention?"

"Not in the least! you should rather say attention; for, I assure you, I consider it a most particular one. It is quite astonishing, my dear friend, how I mistook that man's character. He really is one of the most gentlemanlike, polite, and excellent persons I know; no more mad than you are! And as for his power being on the decline, we know the nonsense of that!"

"Better than most persons, I suspect. Sievers, of course, is not here?"

"No! you have heard about him, I suppose?"

"Heard! heard what?"

"Not heard! well, he told me yesterday, and said he was going to call upon you directly to let you know."

"Know what?"

"He is a very sensible man, Sievers; and I am very glad at last that he is likely to succeed in the world. All men have their little imprudences, and he was a little too hot once. What of that? He has come to his senses, so have I; and I hope you will never lose yours!"

"But pray, my dear Prince, tell me what has happened to Sievers."

"He is going to Vienna immediately, and will be very useful there, I have no doubt. He has got a good place, and I am sure he will do his duty. They can not have an abler man."

"Vienna! that is the last city in the world in which I should expect to find Mr. Sievers. What place can he have? and what services can he perform there?"

"Many! He is to be Editor of the 'Austrian Observer,' and Censor of the Austrian Press. I thought he would do well at last. All men have their imprudent day. I had. I can not stop now. I must go and speak to the Countess von S——."

As Vivian was doubting whether he should most grieve or laugh at this singular termination of Mr. Sievers's career, his arm was suddenly touched, and on turning round he found it was by Mr. Beckendorff.

"There is another strong argument, sir," said the Minister, without any of the usual phrases of recognition; "there is another strong argument against your doctrine of Destiny." And then Mr. Beckendorff, taking Vivian by the arm, began walking up and down part of the saloon with him; and in a few minutes, quite forgetting the scene of the discussion, he was involved in metaphysics. This incident created another great sensation, and whispers of 'secret mission,' 'Secretary of State,' 'decidedly a son,' etc., etc., etc., were in an instant afloat in all parts of the room.

The approach of his Royal Highness extricated Vivian from an argument which was as profound as it was interminable; and as Mr. Beckendorff retired with the Grand Duke into a recess in the ballroom, Vivian was requested by Von Neuwied to attend his Excellency the Grand Marshal.

"My dear friend," said the Prince, "I saw you talking with a certain person. I did not say anything to you when I passed you before; but, to tell you the truth now, I was a little annoyed that he had not spoken to you. I knew you were as proud as Lucifer, and would not salute him yourself; and between ourselves I had no great wish you should, for, not to conceal it, he did not even mention your name. But the reason of this is now quite evident, and you must confess he is remarkably courteous. You know, if you remember, we thought that incognito was a little affected; rather annoying, if you recollect. I remember in the green lane you gave him a gentle cut about it. It was spirited, and I dare say did good. Well! what I was going to say about that is this; I dare say now, after all," continued his Excellency, with a knowing look, "a certain person had very good reasons for that; not that he ever told them to me, nor that I have the slightest idea of them; but when a person is really so exceedingly polite and attentive, I always think he would never do anything disagreeable without a cause; and it was exceedingly disagreeable, if you remember, my dear friend. I never knew to whom he was speaking. Von Philipson indeed! Well! we did not think, the day we were floundering down that turf road, that it would end in this. Rather a more brilliant scene than the Giants' Hall at Turriparva, I think, eh? But all men have their imprudent days; the best way is to forget them. There was poor Sievers; who ever did more imprudent things than he? and now it is likely he will do very well in the world, eh?

What I want of you, my dear friend, is this. There is that girl who came with Beckendorff; who the deuce she is, I don't know: let us hope the best! We must pay her every attention. I dare say she is his daughter. You have not forgotten the portrait. Well! we all were gay once. All men have their imprudent day; why should not Beckendorff? Speaks rather in his favor, I think. Well, this girl, his Royal Highness very kindly made the Crown Prince walk the Polonaise with her; very kind of him, and very proper. What attention can be too great for the daughter or friend of such a man! a man who, in two words, may be said to have made Reisenburg. For what was Reisenburg before Beckendorff? Ah! what? Perhaps we were happier then, after all; and then there was no Royal Highness to bow to; no person to be condescending, except ourselves. But never mind! we will forget. After all, this life has its charms. What a brilliant scene! but this girl, every attention should be paid her. The Crown Prince was so kind as to walk the Polonaise with her. And Von Sohnspeer; he is a brute, to be sure; but then he is a Field Marshal. Now, I think, considering what has taken place between Beckendorff and yourself, and the very distinguished manner in which he recognized you; I think that after all this, and considering everything, the etiquette is for you, particularly as you are a foreigner, and my personal friend; indeed, my most particular friend, for in fact I owe everything to you, my life, and more than my life; I think, I repeat, considering all this, that the least you can do is to ask her to dance with you; and I, as the host, will introduce you. I am sorry, my dear friend," contined his Excellency, with a look of great regret, "to introduce you to—; but we will not speak about it. We have no right to complain of Mr. Beckendorff. No person could possibly behave to us in a manner more gentlemanlike."

After an introductory speech in his Excellency's happiest manner, and in which a eulogium of Vivian and a compliment to the fair unknown got almost as completely entangled as the origin of slavery and the history of the feudal system in his more celebrated harangue, Vivian found himself waltzing with the anonymous beauty. The Grand Marshal, during the process of introduction, had given the young lady every opportunity of declaring her name; but every opportunity was thrown away. "She must be incog.," whispered his Excellency: "Miss von Philipson, I suppose?"

Vivian was not a little desirous of discovering the nature of the relationship or connection between Beckendorff and his partner. The rapid waltz allowed no pause for conversation; but after the dance Vivian seated himself at her side, with the determination of not quickly deserting it. The lady did not even allow him the satisfaction of commencing the conversation; for no sooner was she seated than she begged to know who the person was with whom she had previously waltzed. The history of Count von Sohnspeer amused her; and no sooner had Vivian finished his anecdote than the lady said, "Ah! I see you are an amusing person. Now tell me the history of everybody in the room."

"Really," said Vivian, "I fear I shall forfeit my reputation of being amusing very speedily, for I am almost as great a stranger at this Court as you appear to be yourself. Count von Sohnspeer is too celebrated a personage at Reisenburg to have allowed even me to be long ignorant of his history; and as for the rest, so far as I can judge, they are most of them as obscure as myself, and not nearly as interesting as you are!"

"Are you an Englishman?" asked the lady.

"I am."

"I supposed so, both from your traveling and your appearance: I think the English countenance very peculiar."

"Indeed! we do not flatter ourselves so at home."

"Yes! it is peculiar," said the lady, in a tone which seemed to imply that contradiction was unusual; "and I think that you are all handsome! I admire the English, which in this part of the world is singular; the South, you know, is generally *francisé*."

"I am aware of that," said Vivian. "There, for instance, pointing to a pompous-looking personage who at that moment strutted by; "there, for instance, is the most *francisé* person in all Reisenburg! that is our Grand Chamberlain. He considers himself a felicitous copy of Louis the Fourteenth! He allows nothing in his opinions and phrases but what is orthodox. As it generally happens in such cases, his orthodoxy is rather obsolete."

"Who is that Knight of Malta?" asked the lady.

"The most powerful individual in the room," answered Vivian.

"Who can he be?" asked the lady, with eagerness.

"Behold him, and tremble!" rejoined Vivian: "for with him it rests to decide whether you are civilized or a savage; whether you are to be abhorred or admired; idolized or despised. Nay, do not be alarmed! there are a few heretics, even in Reisenburg, who, like myself, value from conviction, and not from fashion, and who will be ever ready, in spite of a Von Aslingen anathema, to evince our admiration where it is due."

The lady pleaded fatigue as an excuse for not again dancing; and Vivian did not quit her side. Her lively remarks, piquant observations, and singular questions highly amused him; and he was flattered by the evident gratification which his conversation afforded her. It was chiefly of the principal members of the Court that she spoke: she was delighted with Vivian's glowing character of Madame Carolina, whom she said she had this evening seen for the first time. Who this unknown could be was a question which often occurred to him; and the singularity of a man like Beckendorff suddenly breaking through his habits and outraging the whole system of his existence, to please a daughter, or niece, or female cousin, did not fail to strike him.

"I have the honor of being acquainted with Mr. Beckendorff," said Vivian. This was the first time that the Minister's name had been mentioned.

"I perceived you talking with him," was the answer.

"You are staying, I suppose, at Mr. Beckendorff's?"

"Not at present."

"You have, of course, been at his retreat; delightful place!"

"Yes!"

"Are you an ornithologist?" asked Vivian, smiling.

"Not at all scientific; but I, of course, can now tell a lory from a Java sparrow, and a bullfinch from a canary. The first day I was there, I never shall forget the surprise I experienced, when, after the noon meal being finished, the aviary door was opened. After that I always let the creatures out myself; and one day I opened all the cages at once. If you could but have witnessed the scene! I am sure you would have been quite delighted with it. As for poor Mr. Beckendorff, I thought even he would have gone out of his mind; and when I brought in the white peacock he actually left the room in despair. Pray how do you like Madame Clara and Owlface too? Which do you think the most beautiful? I am no great favorite with the old lady. Indeed, it was very kind of Mr. Beckendorff to bear with everything as he did: I am sure he is not much used to lady visitors."

"I trust that your visit to him will not be very short?"

"My stay at Reisenburg will not be very long," said the young lady, with rather a grave countenance. "Have you been here any time?"

"About a fortnight; it was a mere chance my coming at all. I was going on straight to Vienna."

"To Vienna, indeed! Well, I am glad you did not miss Reisenburg; you must not quit it now. You know that this is not the Vienna season?"

"I am aware of it; but I am such a restless person that I never regulate my movements by those of other people."

"But surely you find Reisenburg agreeable?"

"Very much so; but I am a confirmed wanderer."

"Why are you?" asked the lady, with great naïveté.

Vivian looked grave; and the lady, as if she were sensible of having unintentionally occasioned him a painful recollection, again expressed her wish that he should not immediately quit the Court, and trusted that circumstances would not prevent him from acceding to her desire.

"It does not even depend upon circumstances," said Vivian; "the whim of the moment is my only principle of action, and therefore I may be off to-night, or be here a month hence."

"Oh! pray stay then," said his companion eagerly; "I expect you to stay now. If you could only have an idea what a relief conversing with you is, after having been dragged by the Crown Prince and whirled by that Von Sohnspeer! Heigho! I could almost sigh at the very remembrance of that doleful Polonaise."

The lady ended with a faint laugh a sentence which apparently had been commenced in no light vein. She did not cease speaking, but continued to request Vivian to remain at Reisenburg at least as long as herself. Her frequent requests were perfectly unnecessary, for the promise had been pledged at the first hint of her wish; but this was not the only time during the evening that Vivian had remarked that his interesting companion occasionally talked without apparently being sensible that she was conversing.

The young Count of Eberstein, who, to use his own phrase, was "sadly involved," and consequently desirous of being appointed a Forest Councilor, thought that he should secure his appointment by condescending to notice the person whom he delicately styled "the Minister's female relative." To his great mortification and surprise, the honor was declined; and "the female relative," being unwilling to dance again, but perhaps feeling it necessary to break off her conversation with her late partner, it having already lasted an unusual time, highly gratified his Excellency the Grand Marshal by declaring that she would dance with Prince Maximilian. "This, to say the least, was very attentive of Miss von Philipson."

Little Max, who had just tact enough to discover that to be the partner of the fair incognita was the place of honor of the evening, now considered himself by much the most important personage in the room. In fact, he was only second to Emilius von Aslingen. The evident contest which was ever taking place between his natural feelings as a boy and his acquired habits as a courtier made him an amusing companion. He talked of the Gardens and the Opera in a style not unworthy of the young Count of Eberstein. He thought that Madame Carolina was as charming as usual to-night; but, on the contrary, that the Countess von S—— was looking rather ill, and this put him in mind of her ladyship's new equipage; and then, apropos to equipages, what did his companion think of the new fashion of the Hungarian harness? His lively and kind companion encouraged the boy's tattle; and, emboldened by her good nature, he soon forgot his artificial speeches, and was quickly rattling on about Turriparva, and his horses, and his dogs, and his park, and his guns, and his grooms. Soon after the waltz, the lady, taking the arm of the young Prince, walked up to Mr. Beckendorff. He received her with great attention, and led her to Madame Carolina, who rose, seated Mr. Beckendorff's "female relative" by her side, and evidently said something extremely agreeable.

CHAPTER VI

VIVIAN had promised Madame Carolina a second English lesson on the day after the Grand Marshal's fête. The progress which the lady had made, and the talent which the gentleman had evinced during the first, had rendered Madame the most enthusiastic of pupils, and Vivian, in her estimation, the ablest of instructors. Madame Carolina's passion was patronage: to discover concealed merit, to encourage neglected genius, to reveal the mysteries of the world to a novice in mankind, or, in short, to make herself very agreeable to any one whom she fancied to be very interesting, was the great business and the great delight of her existence. No sooner had her eyes lighted on Vivian Grey than she determined to patronize. His country, his appearance, the romantic manner in which he had become connected with the Court, all pleased her lively imagination. She was intuitively acquainted with his whole history, and in an instant he was the hero of a romance, of which the presence of the principal character compensated, we may suppose, for the somewhat indefinite details. His taste and literary acquirements completed the spell by which Madame Carolina was willingly enchanted. A Low Dutch professor, whose luminous genius rendered unnecessary the ceremony of shaving; and a dumb dwarf, in whose interesting appearance was forgotten its perfect idiocy; a prosy improvisatore, and a South American savage, were all superseded by the appearance of Vivian Grey.

As Madame Carolina was, in fact, a charming woman, our hero had no objection to humor her harmless foibles; and not contented with making notes in an interleaved copy of her "Charlemagne," he even promised to read "Haroun Al Raschid" in manuscript. The consequence of his courtesy and the reward of his taste was unbounded favor. Apartments in the palace were offered him, and declined; and when Madame

Carolina had become acquainted with sufficient of his real history to know that, on his part, neither wish nor necessity existed to return immediately to his own country, she tempted him to remain at Reisenburg by an offer of a place at Court; and doubtless, had he been willing, Vivian might in time have become a Lord Chamberlain, or perhaps even a Field Marshal.

On entering the room the morning in question he found Madame Carolina writing. At the end of the apartment a lady ceased, on his appearance, humming an air to which she was dancing, and at the same time imitating castanets. Madame received Vivian with expressions of delight, saying also, in a peculiar and confidential manner, that she was just sealing up a packet for him, the preface of "Haroun"; and then she presented him to "the Baroness"! The lady who was lately dancing came forward. It was his unknown partner of the preceding night. "The Baroness" extended her hand to Vivian, and unaffectedly expressed her great pleasure at seeing him again.

Vivian trusted that she was not fatigued by the fête and asked after Mr. Beckendorff. Madame Carolina was busily engaged at the moment in duly securing the precious preface. The Baroness said that Mr. Beckendorff had returned home, but that Madame Carolina had kindly insisted upon her staying at the palace. She was not the least wearied. Last night had been one of the most agreeable she had ever spent; at least she supposed she ought to say so: for if she had experienced a tedious or mournful feeling for a moment, it was hardly for what was then passing so much as for—"

"Pray, Mr. Grey," said Madame Carolina, interrupting them, "have you heard about our new ballet?"

"No."

"I do not think you have ever been to our Opera. Tomorrow is Opera night, and you must not be again away. We pride ourselves here very much upon our Opera."

"We estimate it even in England," said Vivian, "as possessing perhaps the most perfect orchestra now organized."

"The orchestra is perfect. His Royal Highness is such an excellent musician, and he has spared no trouble or expense in forming it: he has always superintended it himself. But

I confess I admire our ballet department still more. I expect you to be delighted with it. You will perhaps be gratified to know that the subject of our new splendid ballet, which is to be produced to-morrow, is from a great work of your illustrious poet, my Lord Byron."

"From which?"

" 'The Corsair.' Ah! what a sublime work! what passion! what energy! what knowledge of feminine feeling! what contrast of character! what sentiments! what situations! I wish this were Opera night; Gulnare! my favorite character; beautiful! How do you think they will dress her?"

"Are you an admirer of our Byron?" asked Vivian of the Baroness.

"I think he is a very handsome man. I once saw him at the carnival at Venice."

"But his works; his grand works! *ma chère petite*," said Madame Carolina, in her sweetest tone; "you have read his works?"

"Not a line," answered the Baroness, with great naïveté; "I never saw them."

"*Pauvre enfant!*" said Madame Carolina; "I will employ you, then, while you are here."

"I never read," said the Baroness; "I can not bear it. I like poetry and romances, but I like somebody to read to me."

"Very just," said Madame Carolina; "we can judge with greater accuracy of the merit of a composition when it reaches our mind merely through the medium of the human voice. The soul is an essence, invisible and indivisible. In this respect the voice of man resembles the principle of his existence; since few will deny, though there are some materialists who will deny everything, that the human voice is both impalpable and audible only in one place at the same time. Hence, I ask, is it illogical to infer its indivisibility? The soul and the voice, then, are similar in two great attributes; there is a secret harmony in their spiritual construction. In the early ages of mankind a beautiful tradition was afloat that the soul and the voice were one and the same. We may perhaps recognize in this fanciful belief the effect of the fascinating and imaginative philosophy of the East; that mysterious portion of the globe," continued Madame Carolina, "from which we should frankly confess that we derive everything: for the South is but the pupil of the East, through the mediation of Egypt. Of this opinion," said Madame with fervor, "I have no doubt: of this opinion," continued the lady with enthusiasm, "I have boldly avowed myself a votary in a dissertation appended to the second volume of 'Haroun': for this opinion I would die at the stake! Oh, lovely East! why was I not Oriental! Land where the voice of the nightingale is never mute! Land of the cedar and the citron, the turtle and the myrtle, of ever-blooming flowers and ever-shining skies! Illustrious East! Cradle of Philosophy! My dearest Baroness, why do not you feel as I do? From the East we obtain everything!"

"Indeed!" said the Baroness, with simplicity; "I thought we only got shawls."

This puzzling answer was only noticed by Vivian; for the truth is, Madame Carolina was one of those individuals who never attend to any person's answers. Always thinking of herself, she only asked questions that she herself might supply the responses. And now having made, as she flattered herself, a splendid display to her favorite critic, she began to consider what had given rise to her oration. Lord Byron and the ballet again occurred to her; and as the Baroness, at least, was not unwilling to listen, and as she herself had no manuscript of her own which she particularly wished to be perused, she proposed that Vivian should read to them part of "The Corsair," and in the original tongue. Madame Carolina opened the volume at the first prison scene between Gulnare and Conrad. It was her favorite. Vivian read with care and feeling. Madame was in raptures, and the Baroness, although she did not understand a single syllable, seemed almost equally delighted. At length Vivian came to this passage:

"My love stern Seyd's! Oh, no, no, not my love!
Yet much this heart, that strives no more, once strove
To meet his passion; but it would not be.
I felt, I feel, love dwells with, with the free,
I am a slave, a favor'd slave at best,
To share his splendor, and seem very blest!
Oft must my soul the question undergo,
Of, 'Dost thou love?' and burn to answer, 'No!'
Oh! hard it is that fondness to sustain,
And struggle not to feel averse in vain;

But harder still the heart's recoil to bear,
And hide from one, perhaps another there;
He takes the hand I give not nor withhold,
Its pulse nor checked nor quickened, calmly cold:
And when resign'd, it drops a lifeless weight
From one I never loved enough to hate.
No warmth these lips return by his imprest,
And chill'd remembrance shudders o'er the rest.
Yes, had I ever prov'd that passion's zeal,
The change to hatred were at least to feel:
But still he goes unmourn'd, returns unsought,
And oft when present, absent from my thought.
Or when reflection comes, and come it must,
I fear that henceforth 'twill but bring disgust:
I am his slave; but, in despite of pride,
'Twere worse than bondage to become his bride."

"Superb!" said Madame, in a voice of enthusiasm; "how true! what passion! what energy! what sentiments! what knowledge of feminine feeling! Read it again, I pray: it is my favorite passage."

"What is this passage about?" asked the Baroness, with some anxiety; "tell me."

"I have a French translation, *ma mignonne*," said Madame; "you shall have it afterward."

"No! I detest reading," said the young lady, with an imperious air; "translate it to me at once."

"You are rather a self-willed beauty!" thought Vivian; "but your eyes are so brilliant that nothing must be refused you!" and so he translated it.

On its conclusion Madame was again in raptures. The Baroness was not less affected, but she said nothing. She appeared agitated; she changed color, raised her beautiful eyes with an expression of sorrow, looked at Vivian earnestly, and then walked to the other end of the room. In a few moments she returned to her seat.

"I wish you would tell me the story," she said, with earnestness.

"I have a French translation, *ma belle!*" said Madame Carolina; "at present I wish to trouble Mr. Grey with a few questions." Madame Carolina led Vivian into a recess.

"I am sorry we are troubled with this sweet little savage; but I think she has talent, though evidently quite uneducated. We must do what we can for her. Her ignorance of all breeding is amusing, but then I think she has a natural elegance. We shall soon polish her. His Royal Highness is so anxious that every attention should be paid to her. Beckendorff, you know, is a man of the greatest genius." (Madame Carolina had lowered her tone about the Minister since the Prince of Little Lilliput's apostasy.) "The country is greatly indebted to him. This, between ourselves, is his daughter. At least I have no doubt of it. Beckendorff was once married, to a lady of great rank; died early; beautiful woman, very interesting! His Royal Highness had a great regard for her. The Premier, in his bereavement, turned humorist, and has brought up this lovely girl in the oddest possible manner; nobody knows where. Now that he finds it necessary to bring her forward, he, of course, is quite at a loss. His Royal Highness has applied to me. There was a little coldness before between the Minister and myself. It is now quite removed. I must do what I can for her. I think she must marry Von Sohnspeer, who is no more Beckendorff's son than you are: or young Eberstein, or young Bernstorff, or young Gernsbach. We must do something for her. I offered her last night to Emilius von Aslingen; but he said that, unfortunately, he was just importing a savage or two of his own from the Brazils, and consequently was not in want of her."

A chamberlain now entered, to announce the speedy arrival of his Royal Highness. The Baroness, without ceremony, expressed her great regret that he was coming, as now she should not hear the wished-for story. Madame Carolina reproved her, and the reproof was endured rather than submitted to.

His Royal Highness entered, and was accompanied by the Crown Prince. He greeted the young lady with great kindness; and even the Crown Prince, inspired by his father's unusual warmth, made a shuffling kind of bow and a stuttering kind of speech.

Vivian was about to retire on the entrance of the Grand Duke, but Madame Carolina prevented him from going, and his Royal Highness, turning round, very graciously seconded her desire, and added that Mr. Grey was the very gentleman with whom he was desirous of meeting.

"I am anxious," said he to Vivian, in rather a low tone, "to make Reisenburg agreeable to Mr. Beckendorff's fair friend. As you are one of the few who are honored by his intimacy, and are familiar with some of our state secrets," added the Grand Duke with a smile, "I am sure it will give you pleasure to assist me in the execution of my wishes."

His Royal Highness proposed that the ladies should ride; and he himself, with the Crown Prince and Mr. Grey, would attend them. Madame Carolina expressed her willingness; but the Baroness, like all forward girls unused to the world, suddenly grew at the same time both timid and disobliging. She looked sullen and discontented, and coolly said that she did not feel in the humor to ride for at least these two hours. To Vivian's surprise, even the Grand Duke humored her fancy, and declared that he should then be happy to attend them after the Court dinner. Until that time Vivian was amused by Madame, and the Grand Duke exclusively devoted himself to the Baroness. His Royal Highness was in his happiest mood, and his winning manners and elegant conversation soon chased away the cloud which, for a moment, had settled on the young lady's fair brow.

CHAPTER VII

THE Grand Duke of Reisenburg was an enthusiastic lover of music, and his people were consequently music mad. The whole city were fiddling day and night, or blowing trumpets, oboes, and bassoons. Sunday, however, was the most harmonious day in the week. The Opera amused the Court and the wealthiest citizens, and few private houses could not boast their family concert or small party of performers. In the tea-gardens, of which there were many in the suburbs of the city, bearing the euphonious, romantic, and fashionable titles of Tivoli, Arcadia, and Vauxhall, a strong and amateur orchestra was never wanting. Strolling through the city on a Sunday afternoon, many a pleasing picture of innocent domestic enjoyment might be observed. In the arbor of a garden a very stout man, with a fair, broad, good-natured, solid German

face, may be seen perspiring under the scientific exertion of the
French horn; himself wisely disembarrassed of the needless
incumbrance of his pea-green coat and showy waistcoat, which
lies neatly folded by his side; while his large and sleepy blue
eyes actually gleam with enthusiasm. His daughter, a soft
and delicate girl, touches the light guitar; catching the notes
of the music from the opened opera, which is placed before the
father on a massy music-stand. Her voice joins in melody
with her mother, who, like all German mothers, seems only her
daughter's self, subdued by an additional twenty years. The
bow of one violin is handled with the air of a master by an
elder brother; while a younger one, a university student,
grows sentimental over the flute. The same instrument is also
played by a tall and tender-looking young man in black, who
stands behind the parents, next to the daughter, and occasionally looks off his music-book to gaze on his young mistress's
eyes. He is a clerk in a public office; and on next Michaelmas
day, if he succeed, as he hopes, in gaining a small addition to
his salary, he will be still more entitled to join in the Sunday
family concert. Such is one of the numerous groups, the sight
of which must, assuredly, give pleasure to every man who
delights in seeing his fellow-creatures refreshed after their
weekly labors by such calm and rational enjoyment. We
would gladly linger among such scenes; and, moreover,
the humors of a guinguette are not unworthy of our attention; but we must introduce the reader to a more important party.

The Court chapel and the Court dinner are over. We are
in the Opera-house of Reisenburg; and, of course, rise as the
Royal party enters. The house, which is of moderate size, was
fitted up with splendor: we hardly know whether we should say
with great taste; for, although not merely the scenery, but
indeed every part of the house, was painted by eminent artists,
the style of the ornaments was rather patriotic than tasteful.
The house had been built immediately after the war, at a
period when Reisenburg, flushed with the success of its thirty
thousand men, imagined itself to be a great military nation.
Trophies, standards, cannon, eagles, consequently appeared
in every corner of the Opera-house; and quite superseded
lyres, and timbrels, and tragic daggers, and comic masks. The

royal box was constructed in the form of a tent, and held nearly fifty persons. It was exactly in the centre of the house, its floor over the back of the pit and its roof reaching to the top of the second circle; its crimson hangings were restrained by ropes of gold, and the whole was surmounted by a large and radiant crown. The house was merely lighted by a chandelier from the centre.

The Opera for the evening was Rossini's "Otello." As soon as the Grand Duke entered the overture commenced, his Royal Highness coming forward to the front of the box and himself directing the musicians, keeping time earnestly with his right hand, in which was a long black opera-glass. This he occasionally used, but merely to look at the orchestra, not, assuredly, to detect a negligent or inefficient performer; for in the schooled orchestra of Reisenburg it would have been impossible even for the eagle eye of his Royal Highness, assisted as it was by his long black opera-glass, or for his fine ear, matured as it was by the most complete study, to discover there either inattention or feebleness. The house was perfectly silent; for when the Monarch directs the orchestra the world goes to the Opera to listen. Perfect silence at Reisenburg, then, was etiquette and the fashion. Between the acts of the Opera, however, the Ballet was performed; and then everybody might talk, and laugh, and remark as much as they chose.

The Grand Duke prided himself as much upon the accuracy of his scenery and dresses and decorations as upon the exquisite skill of his performers. In truth, an Opera at Reisenburg was a spectacle which could not fail to be interesting to a man of taste. When the curtain drew up the first scene presented a view of old Brabantio's house. It was accurately copied from one of the sumptuous structures of Scamozzi, or Sansovino, or Palladio, which adorn the Grand Canal of Venice. In the distance rose the domes of St. Mark and the lofty Campanile. Vivian could not fail to be delighted with this beautiful work of art, for such indeed it should be styled. He was more surprised, however, but not less pleased, on the entrance of Othello himself. In England we are accustomed to deck this adventurous Moor in the costume of his native country; but is this correct? The Grand Duke of Reisenburg thought not.

Othello was an adventurer; at an early age he entered, as many foreigners did, into the service of Venice. In that service he rose to the highest dignities, became General of her armies and of her fleets, and finally the Viceroy of her favorite kingdom. Is it natural to suppose that such a man should have retained, during his successful career, the manners and dress of his original country? Ought we not rather to admit that, had he done so, his career would, in fact, not have been successful? In all probability, he imitated to affectation the manners of the country which he had adopted. It is not probable that in such or in any age the turbaned Moor would have been treated with great deference by the common Christian soldier of Venice; or, indeed, that the scandal of a heathen leading the armies of one of the most powerful of European States would have been tolerated for an instant by indignant Christendom. If Shylock even, the Jew merchant, confined to his quarter, and herding with his own sect, were bearded on the Rialto, in what spirit would the Venetians have witnessed their doge and nobles, whom they ranked above kings, holding equal converse, and loading with the most splendid honors of the Republic a follower of Mahomet? Such were the sentiments of the Grand Duke of Reisenburg on this subject, a subject interesting to Englishmen; and I confess I think that they are worthy of attention. In accordance with his opinions, the actor who performed Othello appeared in the full dress of a Venetian *magnifico* of the Middle Ages; a fit companion for Cornaro, or Grimani, or Barberigo, or Foscari.

The first act of the Opera was finished. The Baroness expressed to Vivian her great delight at its being over, as she was extremely desirous of learning the story of the ballet, which she had not yet been able to acquire. His translation of yesterday had greatly interested her. Vivian shortly gave her the outline of the story of Conrad. She listened with much attention, but made no remark.

The ballet at Reisenburg was not merely a vehicle for the display of dancing. It professed by gesture and action, aided by music, to influence the minds of the spectators not less than the regular drama. Of this exhibition dancing was a casual ornament, as it is of life. It took place therefore only on fitting occasions, and grew out, in a natural manner, from some event in the history represented. For instance, suppose the story of "Otello" the subject of the ballet. The dancing, in all probability, would be introduced at a grand entertainment given in celebration of the Moor's arrival at Cyprus. All this would be in character. Our feelings would not be outraged by a husband chassezing forward to murder his wife, or by seeing the pillow pressed over the innocent Desdemona by the impulse of a pirouette. In most cases, therefore, the chief performers in this species of spectacle are not even dancers. This, however, may not always be the case. If Diana be the heroine, poetical probability will not be offended by the goddess joining in the chaste dance with her huntress nymphs; and were the Bayadere of Goethe made the subject of a ballet, the Indian dancing girl would naturally be the heroine both of the drama and the poem. There are few performances more affecting than the serious pantomime of a master. In some of the most interesting situations it is in fact even more natural than the oral drama, logically it is more perfect; for the soliloquy is actually thought before us, and the magic of the representation not destroyed by the sound of the human voice at a moment when we all know man never speaks.

The curtain again rises. Sounds of revelry and triumph are heard from the Pirate Isle. They celebrate recent success. Various groups, accurately attired in the costume of the Greek islands, are seated on the rocky foreground. On the left rises Medora's tower, on a craggy steep; and on the right gleams the blue Ægean. A procession of women enters. It heralds the presence of Conrad and Medora; they honor the festivity of their rude subjects. The pirates and the women join in the national dance; and afterward eight warriors, completely armed, move in a warlike measure, keeping time to the music with their bucklers and clattering sabres. Suddenly the dance ceases; a sail is in sight. The nearest pirates rush to the strand, and assist the disembarkation of their welcome comrades. The commander of the vessel comes forward with an agitated step and gloomy countenance. He kneels to Conrad and delivers him a scroll, which the chieftain reads with suppressed agitation. In a moment the faithful Juan is at his side, the contents of the scroll revealed, the dance broken up, and preparations made to sail in an hour's time to the city of the Pacha. The stage is cleared, and Conrad and Medora are alone. The mysterious leader is wrapped in the deepest abstraction. He stands with folded arms, and eyes fixed on the yellow sand. A gentle pressure on his arm calls him back to recollection; he starts, and turns to the intruder with a gloomy brow. He sees Medora, and his frown sinks into a sad smile. "And must we part again! this hour, this very hour; it can not be!" She clings to him with agony, and kneels to him with adoration. No hope! no hope! a quick return promised with an air of foreboding fate. His stern arm encircles her waist. He chases the heavy tear from her fair cheek, and while he bids her be glad in his absence with her handmaids peals the sad thunder of the signal gun. She throws herself upon him. The frantic quickness of her motion strikingly contrasts with the former stupor of her appearance. She will not part. Her face is buried in his breast; her long fair hair floats over his shoulders. He is almost unnerved; but at this moment the ship sails on; the crew and their afflicted wives enter; the page brings to Lord Conrad his cloak, his carbine, and his bugle. He tears himself from her embrace, and without daring to look behind him bounds over the rocks, and is in the ship. The vessel moves, the wives of the pirates continue on the beach, waving their scarfs to their desolate husbands. In the foreground Medora, motionless, stands rooted to the strand, and might have inspired Phidias with a personification of Despair.

In a hall of unparalleled splendor stern Seyd reclines on innumerable pillows, placed on a carpet of golden cloth. His bearded chiefs are ranged around. The chambers are brilliantly illuminated, and an opening at the further end of the apartments exhibits a portion of the shining city and the glittering galleys. Gulnare, covered with a silver veil, which reaches even to her feet, is ushered into the presence of the Pacha. Even the haughty Seyd rises to honor his beautiful favorite. He draws the precious veil from her blushing features and places her on his right hand. The dancing girls now appear, and then are introduced the principal artists. Now takes place the scientific part of the ballet; and here might Bias, or

Noblet, or Ronzi Vestris, or her graceful husband, or the classical Albert, or the bounding Paul, vault without stint, and attitudinize without restraint, and not in the least impair the effect of the tragic tale. The Dervise, of course, appears; the galleys, of course, are fired; and Seyd, of course, retreats. A change in the scenery gives us the blazing Harem, the rescue of its inmates, the deliverance of Gulnare, the capture of Conrad.

It is the prison scene. On a mat, covered with irons, lies the forlorn Conrad. The flitting flame of a solitary lamp hardly reveals the heavy bars of the huge grate that forms the entrance to his cell. For some minutes nothing stirs. The mind of the spectator is allowed to become fully aware of the hopeless misery of the hero. His career is ended, secure is his dungeon, trusty his guards, overpowering his chains. To-morrow he wakes to be impaled. A gentle noise, so gentle that the spectator almost deems it unintentional, is now heard. A white figure appears behind the dusky gate; is it a guard or a torturer? The gate softly opens, and a female comes forward. Gulnare was represented by a girl with the body of a Peri and the soul of a poetess. The Harem Queen advances with an agitated step; she holds in her left hand a lamp, and in the girdle of her light dress is a dagger. She reaches with a soundless step the captive. He is asleep. Ay! he sleeps, while thousands are weeping over his ravage or his ruin; and she, in restlessness, is wandering here! A thousand thoughts are seen coursing over her flushed brow; she looks to the audience, and her dark eye asks why this Corsair is so dear to her. She turns again, and raises the lamp with her long white arm, that the light may fall on the captive's countenance. She gazes, without moving, on the sleeper, touches the dagger with a slow and tremulous hand, and starts from the contact with terror. She again touches it; it is drawn from her vest; it falls to the ground. He wakes; he stares with wonder; he sees a female not less fair than Medora. Confused, she tells him her station; she tells him that her pity is as certain as his doom. He avows his readiness to die; he appears undaunted, he thinks of Medora, he buries his face in his hands. She grows pale as he avows he loves—another. She can not conceal her own passion. He, wondering, confesses that he supposed her love was his enemy's, was Seyd's. Gulnare shudders at the name; she draws herself up to her full stature, she smiles in bitterness:

"My love stern Seyd's! Oh, no, no, not my love!"

The acting was perfect. The house burst into unusual shouts of admiration. Madame Carolina applauded with her little finger on her fan. The Grand Duke himself gave the signal for applause. Vivian never felt before that words were useless. His hand was suddenly pressed. He turned round; it was the Baroness. She was leaning back in her chair; and though she did her utmost to conceal her agitated countenance, a tear coursed down her cheek big as the miserable Medora's!

CHAPTER VIII

ON the evening of the Opera arrived at Court part of the suite of the young Archduchess, the betrothed of the Crown Prince of Reisenburg. These consisted of an old gray-headed General, who had taught her Imperial Highness the manual exercise; and her tutor and confessor, an ancient and toothless Bishop. Their youthful mistress was to follow them in a few days; and this arrival of such a distinguished portion of her suite was the signal for the commencement of a long series of sumptuous festivities. After interchanging a number of compliments and a few snuff-boxes, the new guests were invited by his Royal Highness to attend a Review, which was to take place the next morning, of five thousand troops and fifty Generals.

The Reisenburg army was the best appointed in Europe. Never were men seen with breasts more plumply padded, mustaches better trained, or such spotless gaiters. The Grand Duke himself was a military genius, and had invented a new cut for the collars of the Cavalry. His Royal Highness was particularly desirous of astonishing the old gray-headed governor of his future daughter by the skilful evolutions and imposing appearance of his legions. The affair was to be of the most refined nature, and the whole was to be concluded by a mock battle, in which the spectators were to be treated by a display of the most exquisite evolutions and complicated movements which human beings ever yet invented to destroy others or to escape destruction. Field Marshal Count von Sohnspeer, the Commander-in-Chief of all the Forces of his Royal Highness the Grand Duke of Reisenburg, condescended, at the particular request of his Sovereign, to conduct the whole affair himself.

At first it was rather difficult to distinguish between the army and the staff; for Darius, in the Straits of Issus, was not more sumptuously and numerously attended than Count von Sohnspeer. Wherever he moved he was followed by a train of waving plumes and radiant epaulets, and foaming chargers and shining steel. In fact, he looked like a large military comet. Had the fate of Reisenburg depended on the result of the day, the Field Marshal, and his Generals, and Aides-de-camp, and Orderlies, could not have looked more agitated and more in earnest. Von Sohnspeer had not less than four horses in the field, on every one of which he seemed to appear in the space of five minutes. Now he was dashing along the line of the Lancers on a black charger, and now round the column of the Cuirassiers on a white one. He exhorted the Tirailleurs on a chestnut, and added fresh courage to the ardor of the Artillery on a bay.

It was a splendid day. The bands of the respective regiments played triumphant tunes as each marched on the field. The gradual arrival of the troops was picturesque. Distant music was heard, and a corps of Infantry soon made its appearance. A light bugle sounded, and a body of Tirailleurs issued from the shade of a neighboring wood. The kettle-drums and clarions heralded the presence of a troop of Cavalry; and an advanced guard of Light Horse told that the Artillery were about to follow. The arms and standards of the troops shone in the sun; military music sounded in all parts of the field; unceasing was the bellow of the martial drum and the blast of the blood-stirring trumpet. Clouds of dust ever and anon excited in the distance denoted the arrival of a regiment of Cavalry. Even now one approaches; it is the Red Lancers. How gracefully their Colonel, the young Count of Eberstein, bounds on his barb! Has Theseus turned Centaur? His spur and bridle seem rather the emblems of sovereignty than the instruments of government: he neither chastises nor directs. The rider moves without motion, and the horse judges without guidance. It would seem that the man had borrowed the beast's body, and the beast the man's mind. His regiment has formed upon the field, their stout lances erected like a young and leafless grove; but although now in line, it is with difficulty that they can subject the spirit of their warlike steeds. The trumpet has caught the ear of the horses; they stand with open nostrils, already breathing war ere they can see an enemy; and now dashing up one leg, and now the other, they seem to complain of Nature that she has made them of anything earthly.

The troops have all arrived; there is an unusual bustle in the field. Von Sohnspeer is again changing his horse, giving directions while he is mounting to at least a dozen Aides-de-camp. Orderlies are scampering over every part of the field. Another flag, quite new, and of large size, is unfurled by the Field Marshal's pavilion. A signal gun! the music in the whole field is hushed: a short silence of agitating suspense, another gun, and another! All the bands of all the regiments burst forth at the same moment into the national air: the Court dash into the field!

Madame Carolina, the Baroness, the Countess von S——, and some other ladies, wore habits of the uniform of the Royal Guards. Both Madame and the Baroness were perfect horse-women; and the excited spirits of Mr. Beckendorff's female relative, both during her ride and her dashing run over the field, amid the firing of cannon and the crash of drums and trumpets, strikingly contrasted with her agitation and depression of the preceding night.

"Your Excellency loves the tented field, I think!" said Vivian, who was at her side.

"I love war! it is a diversion for kings!" was the answer. "How fine the breast-plates and helmets of those Cuirassiers glisten in the sun!" continued the lady. "Do you see Von Sohnspeer? I wonder if the Crown Prince be with him!"

"I think he is."

"Indeed! Ah! can he interest himself in anything? He

seemed Apathy itself at the Opera last night. I never saw him smile, or move, and have scarcely heard his voice! but if he love war, if he be a soldier, if he be thinking of other things than a pantomime and a ball, 'tis well! very well for his country! Perhaps he is a hero?"

At this moment the Crown Prince, who was of Von Sohnspeer's staff, slowly rode up to the Royal party.

"Rodolph!" said the Grand Duke, "do you head your regiment to-day?"

"No," was the muttered answer.

The Grand Duke moved his horse to his son, and spoke to him in a low tone, evidently with earnestness. Apparently he was expostulating with him; but the effect of the royal exhortation was only to render the Prince's brow more gloomy, and the expression of his withered features more sullen and more sad. The Baroness watched the father and son as they were conversing with keen attention. When the Crown Prince, in violation of his father's wishes, fell into the party, and allowed his regiment to be headed by the Lieutenant-Colonel, the young lady raised her lustrous eyes to heaven with that same expression of sorrow or resignation which had so much interested Vivian on the morning that he had translated to her the moving passage in "The Corsair."

But the field is nearly cleared, and the mimic war has commenced. On the right appears a large body of Cavalry, consisting of Cuirassiers and Dragoons. A vanguard of Light Cavalry and Lancers, under the command of the Count of Eberstein, is ordered out, from this body, to harass the enemy, a strong body of Infantry supposed to be advancing. Several squadrons of Light Horse immediately spring forward; they form themselves into line, they wheel into column, and endeavor, by well-directed manœuvres, to outflank the strong wing of the advancing enemy. After succeeding in executing all that was committed to them, and after having skirmished in the van of their own army, so as to give time for all necessary dispositions of the line of battle, the vanguard suddenly retreats between the brigades of the Cavalry of the line; the prepared battery of cannon is unmasked; and a tremendous concentric fire opened on the line of the advancing foe. Taking advantage of the confusion created by this unexpected salute of his Artillery, Von Sohnspeer, who commands the Cavalry, gives the word to "Charge!"

The whole body of Cavalry immediately charge in masses; the extended line of the enemy is as immediately broken. But the Infantry, who are commanded by one of the royal relatives and visitors, the Prince of Pike and Powdren, dexterously form into squares, and commence a masterly retreat in square battalions. At length they take up a more favorable position than the former one. They are again galled by the Artillery, who have proportionately advanced, and again charged by the Cavalry in their huge masses. And now the squares of Infantry partially give way. They admit the Cavalry, but the exulting Horse find, to their dismay, that the enemy are not routed, but that there are yet inner squares formed at salient angles. The Cavalry for a moment retire, but it is only to give opportunity to their Artillery to rake the obstinate foes. The execution of the battery is fearful. Headed by their Commander, the whole body of Cuirassiers and Dragoons again charge with renewed energy and concentrated force. The Infantry are thrown into the greatest confusion, and commence a rout, increased and rendered irremediable by the Lancers and Hussars, the former vanguard, who now, seizing on the favorable moment, again rush forward, increasing the effect of the charge of the whole army, overtaking the fugitives with their lances, and securing the prisoners.

The victorious Von Sohnspeer, followed by his staff, now galloped up to receive the congratulations of his Sovereign.

"Where are your prisoners, Field Marshal?" asked his Royal Highness, with a flattering smile.

"What is the ransom of our unfortunate guest?" asked Madame Carolina.

"I hope we shall have another affair," said the Baroness, with a flushed face and glowing eyes.

But the Commander-in-Chief must not tarry to bandy compliments. He is again wanted in the field. The whole troops have formed in line. Some most scientific evolutions are now executed. With them we will not weary the reader, nor dilate on the comparative advantages of forming *en cremaillière* and *en echiquier;* nor upon the duties of tirailleurs, nor upon concentric fires and eccentric movements, nor upon

20

deploying, nor upon enfilading, nor upon oblique fronts, nor upon *échellons*. The day finished by the whole of the troops again forming in line and passing in order before the Commander-in-Chief to give him an opportunity of observing their discipline and inspecting their equipments.

The review being finished, Count von Sohnspeer and his staff joined the Royal party; and after walking their horses round the field, they proceeded to his pavilion, where refreshments were prepared for them. The Field Marshal, flattered by the interest which the young Baroness had taken in the business of the day, and the acquaintance which she evidently possessed of the more obvious details of military tactics, was inclined to be particularly courteous to her; but the object of his admiration did not encourage attentions by which half the ladies of the Court would have thought themselves as highly honored as by those of the Grand Duke himself; so powerful a person was the Field Marshal, and so little inclined by temper to cultivate the graces of the fair sex.

"In the tent keep by my side," said the Baroness to Vivian. "Although I am fond of heroes, Von Sohnspeer is not to my taste. I know not why I flatter you so by my notice, for I suppose, like all Englishmen, you are not a soldier? I thought so. Never mind! you ride well enough for a field marshal. I really think I could give you a commission without much stickling of my conscience. No, no! I should like you nearer the lady's: she blushed deeply, looked down upon her horse's that is to say, when I am entitled to have one."

As Vivian acknowledged the young Baroness's compliment by becoming emotion, and vowed that an office near her person would be the consummation of all his wishes, his eye caught the lady's: she blushed deeply, looked down upon her horse's neck, and then turned away her head.

Von Sohnspeer's pavilion excellently became the successful leader of the army of Reisenburg. Trophies taken from all sides decked its interior. The black eagle of Austria formed part of its roof, and the brazen eagle of Gaul supported part of the side. The gray-headed General looked rather grim when he saw a flag belonging to a troop which perhaps he had himself once commanded. He vented his indignation to the toothless Bishop, who crossed his breast with his fingers, covered with diamonds, and preached temperance and moderation in inarticulate sounds.

During the collation the conversation was principally military. Madame Carolina, who was entirely ignorant of the subject of discourse, enchanted all the officers present by appearing to be the most interested person in the tent. Nothing could exceed the elegance of her eulogium of "*petit guerre.*" The old gray General talked much about the "good old times," by which he meant the thirty years of plunder, bloodshed, and destruction, which were occasioned by the French Revolution. He gloated on the recollections of horror, which he feared would never occur again. The Archduke Charles and Prince Schwartzenburg were the gods of his idolatry, and Nadasti's hussars and Wurmser's dragoons the inferior divinities of his bloody heaven. One evolution of the morning, a discovery made by Von Sohnspeer himself, in the deploying of cavalry, created a great sensation; and it was settled that it would have been of great use to Desaix and Clairfait in the Netherlands affair of some eight-and-twenty years ago, and was not equaled even by Seidlitz's cavalry in the affair with the Russians at Zorndorff. In short, every "affair" of any character during the late war was fought over again in the tent of Field Marshal von Sohnspeer. At length from the Archduke Charles and Prince Schwartzenburg, the old gray-headed General got to Polybius and Monsieur Folard; and the Grand Duke, now thinking that the "affair" was taking too serious a turn, broke up the party. Madame Carolina and most of the ladies used their carriages on their return. They were nearly fifteen miles from the city; but the Baroness, in spite of the most earnest solicitation, would remount her charger.

They cantered home, the Baroness in unusual spirits, Vivian thinking very much of his fair companion. Her character puzzled him. That she was not the lovely simpleton that Madame Carolina believed her to be, he had little doubt. Some people have great knowledge of society and little of mankind. Madame Carolina was one of these. She viewed her species through only one medium. That the Baroness was a woman of acute feeling, Vivian could not doubt. Her conduct at the Opera, which had escaped every one's attention, made this evident. That she had seen more of the world than her previous

conversation had given him to believe was equally clear by
her conduct and conversation this morning. He determined to
become more acquainted with her character. Her evident partiality to his company would not render the execution of his
purpose very difficult. At any rate, if he discovered nothing,
it was something to do: it would at least amuse him.

In the evening he joined a large party at the palace. He
looked immediately for the Baroness. She was surrounded by
the dandies. Their attentions she treated with contempt, and
ridiculed their compliments without mercy. Without obtrud-
ing himself on her notice, Vivian joined her circle, and witnessed her demolition of the young Count of Eberstein with
great amusement. Emilius von Aslingen was not there; for
having made the interesting savage the fashion, she was no
longer worthy of his attention, and consequently deserted. The
young lady soon observed Vivian; and saying, without the
least embarrassment, that she was delighted to see him, she
begged him to share her *chaise-longue*. Her envious levée
witnessed the preference with dismay; and as the object of
their attention did not now notice their remarks, even by her
expressed contempt, one by one fell away. Vivian and the
Baroness were left alone, and conversed much together. The
lady displayed, on every subject, engaging ignorance, and requested information on obvious topics with artless naïveté.
Vivian was convinced that her ignorance was not affected, and
equally sure that it could not arise from imbecility of intellect;
for while she surprised him by her crude questions, and her
want of acquaintance with all those topics which generally form
the staple of conversation, she equally amused him with her
poignant wit, and the imperious and energetic manner in
which she instantly expected satisfactory information on every
possible subject.

CHAPTER IX

O N the day after the review a fancy-dress ball was to be given at Court. It was to be an entertainment of a peculiar nature. The lively genius of Madame Carolina, wearied of the commonplace effect generally produced by this species of amusement, in which usually a stray Turk and a wandering Pole looked sedate and singular among crowds of Spanish girls, Swiss peasants, and gentlemen in uniforms, had invented something novel. Her idea was ingenious. To use her own sublime phrase, she determined that the party should represent "an age"! Great difficulty was experienced in fixing upon the century which was to be honored. At first a poetical idea was started of having something primeval, perhaps antediluvian; but Noah, or even Father Abraham, were thought characters hardly sufficiently romantic for a fancy-dress ball, and consequently the earliest postdiluvian ages were soon under consideration. Nimrod, or Sardanapalus, were distinguished personages, and might be well represented by the Master of the Staghounds, or the Master of the Revels; but then the want of an interesting lady character was a great objection. Semiramis, though not without style in her own way, was not sufficiently Parisian for Madame Carolina. New ages were proposed and new objections started; and so the "Committee of Selection," which consisted of Madame herself, the Countess von S——, and a few other dames of fashion, gradually slid through the four great empires. Athens was not aristocratic enough, and then the women were nothing. In spite of her admiration of the character of Aspasia, Madame Carolina somewhat doubted the possibility of persuading the ladies of the Court of Reisenburg to appear in the characters of ἑταῖραι. Rome presented great capabilities, and greater difficulties. Finding themselves, after many days' sitting and study, still very far from coming to a decision, Madame called in the aid of the Grand Duke, who proposed "something national." The proposition was plausible; but, according to Madame Carolina, Germany, until her own time, had been only a land of barbarism and barbarians; and therefore in such a country, in a national point of view, what could there be interesting? The Middle Ages, as they are usually styled, in spite of the Emperor Charlemagne, "that oasis in the desert of barbarism," to use her own eloquent and original image, were her particular aversion. "The age of chivalry is past!" was as constant an exclamation of Madame Carolina as it was of Mr. Burke. "The age of chivalry is past; and very fortunate that it is. What resources could they have had in the age of chivalry? an age without either moral or experimental philosophy; an age in which they were equally ignorant of the doctrine of association of ideas and of the doctrine of electricity; and when they were as devoid of a knowledge of the incalculable powers of the human mind as of the incalculable powers of steam!" Had Madame Carolina been the consort of an Italian grand duke, selection would not be difficult; and, to inquire no further, the court of the Medici alone would afford them everything they wanted. But Germany never had any character, and never produced nor had been the resort of illustrious men and interesting persons. What was to be done? The age of Frederick the Great was the only thing; and then that was so recent, and would offend the Austrians: it could not be thought of.

At last, when the "Committee of Selection" was almost in despair, some one proposed a period which not only would be German, not only would compliment the House of Austria, but, what was of still greater importance, would allow of every contemporary character of interest of every nation, the age of Charles the Fifth! The suggestion was received with enthusiasm, and adopted on the spot. "The Committee of Selection" was immediately dissolved, and its members as immediately formed themselves into a "Committee of Arrangement." Lists of all the persons of any fame, distinction, or notoriety, who had lived either in the empire of Germany, the kingdoms of Spain, Portugal, France, or England, the Italian States, the Netherlands, the Americas, and, in short, in every country in the known world, were immediately formed. Von Chronicle, rewarded for his last historical novel by a ribbon and the title of Baron, was appointed secretary to the "Committee of Costume." All guests who received a card of invitation were desired, on or before a certain day, to send in the title of their adopted character and a sketch of their intended dress, that their plans might receive the sanction of the ladies of the "Committee of Arrangement," and their dresses the approbation of the secretary of costume. By this method the chance and inconvenience of two persons selecting and appearing in the same character were destroyed and prevented. After exciting the usual jealousies, intrigues, dissatisfaction, and ill-blood, by the influence and imperturbable temper of Madame Carolina, everything was arranged; Emilius von Aslingen being the only person who set both the Committees of Arrangement and Costume at defiance, and treated the repeated applications of their respected secretary with contemptuous silence. The indignant Baron von Chronicle entreated the strong interference of the "Committee of Arrangement," but Emilius von Aslingen was too powerful an individual to be treated by others as he treated them. Had the fancy-dress ball of the Sovereign been attended by all his subjects, with the exception of this Captain in his Guards, the whole affair might have been a failure; would have been dark in spite of the glare of ten thousand lamps and the glories of all the jewels of his state; would have been dull, although each guest were wittier than Pasquin himself; and very vulgar, although attended by lords of as many quarterings as the ancient shield of his own antediluvian house! All, therefore, that the ladies of the "Committee of Arrangement" could do was to inclose to the rebellious Von Aslingen a list of the expected characters, and a resolution passed, in consequence of his contumacy, that no person or persons was, or were, to appear as either or any of these characters, unless he, or they, could produce a ticket, or tickets, granted by a member of the "Committee of Arrangement," and countersigned by the secretary of the "Committee of Costume." At the same time that these vigorous measures were resolved on, no persons spoke of Emilius von Aslingen's rebellious conduct in terms of greater admiration than the ladies of the Committee themselves. If possible, he in consequence became even a more influential and popular personage than before, and his conduct procured him almost the adoration of persons who, had they dared to imitate him, would have been instantly crushed, and would have been banished society principally by the exertions of the very individual whom they had the presumption to mimic.

. In the gardens of the palace was a spacious amphitheatre, cut out in green seats, for the spectators of the plays which, during the summer months, were sometimes performed there by the Court. There was a stage in the same taste, with rows of trees for side-scenes, and a great number of arbors and summer-rooms, surrounded by lofty hedges of laurel, for the actors to retire and dress in. Connected with this "Rural Theatre," for such was its title, were many labyrinths, and groves, and arched walks, in the same style. More than twelve large fountains were in the immediate vicinity of this theatre. At the end of one walk a sea-horse spouted its element through its nostrils; and in another, Neptune turned an Ocean out of a vase. Seated on a rock, Arcadia's half-goat god, the deity of silly sheep and silly poets, sent forth trickling streams through his rustic pipes; and in the centre of a green grove, an enamoured Salmacis, bathing in a pellucid basin, seemed watching for her Hermaphrodite.

It was in this rural theatre and its fanciful confines that Madame Carolina and her councillors resolved that their magic should, for a night, not only stop the course of time, but recall past centuries. It was certainly rather late in the year for choosing such a spot for the scene of their enchantment; but the season, as we have often had occasion to remark in the course of these volumes, was singularly fine; and indeed at this moment the nights were as warm, and as clear from mist and dew, as they are during an Italian midsummer.

But it is eight o'clock; we are already rather late. Is that a figure by Holbein, just started out of the canvas, that I am about to meet? Stand aside! It is a page of the Emperor Charles the Fifth! The Court is on its way to the theatre. The theatre and the gardens are brilliantly illuminated. The effect of the thousands of colored lamps, in all parts of the foliage, is very beautiful. The moon is up, and a million stars! If it be not quite as light as day, it is just light enough for pleasure. You could not perhaps indorse a bill of exchange, or engross a parchment, by this light; but then it is just the light to read a love-letter by, and do a thousand other things besides.

All hail to the Emperor! we would give his costume, were it not rather too much in the style of the Von Chronicles. Reader! you have seen a portrait of Charles by Holbein; very well; what need is there of a description? No lack was there in this gay scene of massy chains and curious collars, nor of cloth of gold, nor of cloth of silver! No lack was there of trembling plumes and costly hose! No lack was there of crimson velvet, and russet velvet, and tawny velvet, and purple velvet, and plunket velvet, and of scarlet cloth, and green taffeta, and cloth of silk embroidered! No lack was there of garments of estate, and of quaint chemews, nor of short crimson cloaks, covered with pearls and precious stones! No lack was there of party-colored splendor, of purple velvet embroidered with white, and white satin dresses embroidered with black! No lack was there of splendid coifs of damask, or kerchiefs of fine Cyprus; nor of points of Venice silver of ducat fineness, nor of garlands of friars' knots, nor of colored satins, nor of bleeding hearts embroidered on the bravery of dolorous lovers, nor of quaint sentences of wailing gallantry! But for the details, are they not to be found in those much-neglected and much-plundered persons, the old chroniclers? and will they not sufficiently appear in the most inventive portion of the next great historical novel?

The Grand Duke looked the Emperor. Our friend the Grand Marshal was Francis the First; and Arnelm and Von Neuwied figured as the Marshal of Montmorency and the Marshal Lautrec. The old toothless Bishop did justice to Clement the Seventh; and his companion, the ancient General, looked grim as Pompeo Colonna. A prince of the House of Nassau, one of the royal visitors, represented his adventurous ancestor the Prince of Orange. Von Sohnspeer was that haughty and accomplished rebel, the Constable of Bourbon. The young Baron Gernsbach was worthy of the seraglio, as he stalked along as Solyman the Magnificent, with all the family jewels belonging to his dowager mother shining in his superb turban. Our friend the Count of Eberstein personified chivalry, in the person of Bayard. The younger

Bernstorff, the intimate friend of Gernsbach, attended his sumptuous sovereign as that Turkish Paul Jones, Barbarossa. An Italian Prince was Andrew Doria. The Grand Chamberlain, our *francisé* acquaintance, and who affected a love of literature, was the Protestant Elector of Saxony. His train consisted of the principal litterateurs of Reisenburg. The Editor of the "Attack-all Review," who originally had been a Catholic, but who had been skilfully converted some years ago, when he thought Catholicism was on the decline, was Martin Luther, an individual whom, both in his apostasy and fierceness, he much and only resembled: on the contrary, the Editor of the "Praise-all Review" appeared as the mild and meek Melanchthon. Mr. Sievers, not yet at Vienna, was Erasmus. Ariosto, Guicciardini, Ronsard, Rabelais, Machiavelli, Pietro Aretino, Garcilasso de la Vega, Sannazaro, and Paracelsus, afforded names to many nameless critics. Two Generals, brothers, appeared as Cortes and Pizarro. The noble Director of the Gallery was Albert Durer, and his deputy Hans Holbein. The Court painter, a wretched mimic of the modern French school, did justice to the character of Correggio; and an indifferent sculptor looked sublime as Michael Angelo.

Von Chronicle had persuaded the Prince of Pike and Powdren, one of his warmest admirers, to appear as Henry the Eighth of England. His Highness was one of those true North German patriots who think their own country a very Garden of Eden, and verily believe that original sin is to be finally put an end to in a large sandy plain between Berlin and Hanover. The Prince of Pike and Powdren passed his whole life in patriotically sighing for the concentration of all Germany into one great nation, and in secretly trusting that, if ever the consummation took place, the North would be rewarded for their condescending union by a monopoly of all the privileges of the Empire. Such a character was of course extremely desirous of figuring to-night in a style peculiarly national. The persuasions of Von Chronicle, however, prevailed, and induced his Highness of Pike and Powdren to dismiss his idea of appearing as the ancient Arminus, although it was with great regret that the Prince gave up his plan of personating his favorite hero, with hair

down to his middle and skins up to his chin. Nothing would
content Von Chronicle but that his kind patron should represent a crowned head; anything else was beneath him. The
patriotism of the Prince disappeared before the flattery of
the novelist, like the bloom of a plum before the breath of
a boy, when he polishes the powdered fruit ere he devours it.
No sooner had his Highness agreed to be changed into bluff
Harry than the secret purpose of his adviser was immediately
detected. No Court confessor, seduced by the vision of a red
hat, ever betrayed the secrets of his sovereign with greater
fervor than did Von Chronicle labor for the Cardinal's costume, which was the consequence of the Prince of Pike and
Powdren undertaking the English monarch. To-night, proud
as was the part of the Prince as regal Harry, his strut was a
shamble compared with the imperious stalk of Von Chronicle
as the arrogant and ambitious Wolsey. The Cardinal in Rienzi
was nothing to him; for to-night Wolsey had as many pages
as the other had petticoats!

But, most ungallant of scribblers! *Place aux dames!*
Surely Madame Carolina, as the beautiful and accomplished
Margaret of Navarre, might well command, even without a
mandate, your homage and your admiration! The lovely Queen
seemed the very goddess of smiles and repartee; young Max,
as her page, carried at her side a painted volume of her own
poetry. The arm of the favorite sister of Francis, who it
will be remembered once fascinated even the Emperor, was
linked in that of Cæsar's natural daughter, her beautiful name-
sake, the bright-eyed Margaret of Austria. Conversing with
these royal dames, and indeed apparently in attendance upon
them, was a young gallant of courtly bearing, and attired in a
fantastic dress. It is Clement Marot, "the Poet of Princes and
the Prince of Poets," as he was styled by his own admiring
age; he offers to the critical inspection of the nimble-witted
Navarre a few lines in celebration of her beauty and the
night's festivity; one of those short Marotique poems once so
celebrated; perhaps a page culled from those gay and airy
psalms which, with characteristic gallantry, he dedicated "to
the Dames of France!" Observe well the fashionable bard!
Marot was a true poet, and in his day not merely read by
queens and honored by courtiers: observe him well; for the

character is supported by our Vivian Grey. It was with great difficulty that Madame Carolina had found a character for her favorite, for the lists were all filled before his arrival at Reisenburg. She at first wished him to appear as some celebrated Englishman of the time, but no character of sufficient importance could be discovered. All our countrymen in contact or connection with the Emperor Charles were churchmen and civilians; and Sir Nicholas Carew and the other fops of the reign of Henry the Eighth, who, after the visit to Paris, were even more ridiculously *francisé* than the Grand Chamberlain of Reisenburg himself, were not, after mature deliberation, considered entitled to the honor of being ranked in Madame Carolina's age of Charles the Fifth.

But who is this, surrounded by her ladies and her chamberlains and her secretaries? Four pages in dresses of cloth of gold, and each the son of a prince of the French blood, support her train; a crown encircles locks gray as much from thought as from time, which require no show of loyalty to prove that they belong to a mother of princes; that ample forehead, aquiline nose, and the keen glance of her piercing eye denote the Queen as much as the regality of her gait and her numerous and splendid train. The young Queen of Navarre hastens to proffer her duty to the mother of Francis, the celebrated Louise of Savoy; and exquisitely did the young and lovely Countess of S—— personate the most celebrated of female diplomatists.

We have forgotten one character; the repeated commands of his father and the constant entreaties of Madame Carolina had at length prevailed upon the Crown Prince to shuffle himself into a fancy dress. No sooner had he gratified them by his hard-wrung consent than Baron von Chronicle called upon him with drawings of the costume of the Prince of Asturias, afterward Philip the Second of Spain. If we for a moment forgot so important a personage as the future Grand Duke, it must have been because he supported his character so ably that no one for an instant believed that it was an assumed one; standing near the side scenes of the amphitheatre, with his gloomy brow, sad eye, protruding under-lip, and arms hanging straight by his sides, he looked a bigot without hope, and a tyrant without purpose.

The first hour is over, and the guests are all assembled. As yet they content themselves with promenading round the amphitheatre; for before they can think of dance or stroll, each of them must be duly acquainted with the other's dress. It was a most splendid scene. The Queen of Navarre has now been presented to the Emperor, and, leaning on his arm, they head the promenade. The Emperor had given the hand of Margaret of Austria to his legitimate son; but the Crown Prince, though he continued in silence by the side of the young Baroness, soon resigned a hand which did not struggle to retain his. Clement Marot was about to fall back into a less conspicuous part of the procession; but the Grand Duke, witnessing the regret of his loved Consort, condescendingly said, "We can not afford to lose our poet"; and so Vivian found himself walking behind Madame Carolina, and on the left side of the young Baroness. Louise of Savoy followed with her son, the King of France; most of the ladies of the Court, and a crowd of officers, among them Montmorency and De Lautrec, after their Majesties. The King of England moves by; his state unnoticed in the superior magnificence of Wolsey. Pompeo Colonna apologizes to Pope Clement for having besieged his holiness in the Castle of St. Angelo. The Elector of Saxony and the Prince of Orange follow. Solyman the Magnificent is attended by his Admiral; and Bayard's pure spirit almost quivers at the whispered treason of the Constable of Bourbon. Luther and Melanchthon, Erasmus and Rabelais, Cortez and Pizarro, Correggio and Michael Angelo, and a long train of dames and dons of all nations, succeed; so long that the amphitheatre can not hold them, and the procession, that all may walk over the stage, makes a short progress through an adjoining summer-room.

Just as the Emperor and the fair Queen are in the middle of the stage, a wounded warrior with a face pale as an eclipsed moon, a helmet on which is painted the sign of his sacred order, a black mantle thrown over his left shoulder, but not concealing his armor, a sword in his right hand and an outstretched crucifix in his left, rushes on the scene. The procession suddenly halts; all recognize Emilius von Aslingen! and Madame Carolina blushes through her rouge when she perceives that so celebrated, "so interesting a character" as Ignatius Loyola, the Founder of the Jesuits, has not been included in the all-comprehensive lists of her committee.

CHAPTER X

HENRY of England led the Polonaise with Louise of Savoy; Margaret of Austria would not join in it; waltzing quickly followed. The Emperor seldom left the side of the Queen of Navarre, and often conversed with her Majesty's poet. The Prince of Asturias hovered for a moment round his father's daughter, as if he were summoning resolution to ask her to waltz. Once, indeed, he opened his mouth; could it have been to speak? But the young Margaret gave no encouragement to this unusual exertion; and Philip of Asturias, looking, if possible, more sad and sombre than before, skulked away. The Crown Prince left the gardens, and now a smile lighted up every face except that of the young Baroness. The gracious Grand Duke, unwilling to see a gloomy countenance anywhere to-night, turned to Vivian, who was speaking to Madame Carolina, and said, "Gentle poet, would that thou hadst some chanson or courtly compliment to chase the cloud which hovers on the brow of our much-loved daughter of Austria! Your popularity, sir," continued the Grand Duke, dropping his mock heroic vein and speaking in a much lower tone, "your popularity, sir, among the ladies of the Court can not be increased by any panegyric of mine; nor am I insensible, believe me, to the assiduity and skill with which you have complied with my wishes in making our Court agreeable to the relative of a man to whom we owe so much as Mr. Beckendorff. I am informed, Mr. Grey," continued his Royal Highness, "that you have no intention of very speedily returning to your country; I wish that I could count you among my peculiar attendants. If you have an objection to live in the palace without performing your quota of duty to the State, we shall have no difficulty in finding you an office, and clothing you in our official costume. Think of this!" So saying, with a gracious smile, his Royal Highness, leading Madame Carolina, commenced a walk round the gardens.

The young Baroness did not follow them. Solyman the Magnificent, and Bayard the irreproachable, and Barbarossa the pirate, and Bourbon the rebel, immediately surrounded her. Few persons were higher *ton* than the Turkish Emperor and his Admiral; few persons talked more agreeable nonsense than the Knight *sans peur et sans reproche;* no person was more important than the warlike Constable; but their attention, their amusement, and their homage were to-night thrown away on the object of their observance. The Baroness listened to them without interest, and answered them with brevity. She did not even condescend, as she had done before, to enter into a war of words, to mortify their vanity or exercise their wit. She treated them neither with contempt nor courtesy. If no smile welcomed their remarks, at least her silence was not scornful, and the most shallow-headed prater that fluttered around her felt that he was received with dignity and not with disdain. Awed by her conduct, not one of them dared to be flippant, and every one of them soon became dull. The ornaments of the Court of Reisenburg, the arbiters of *ton* and the lords of taste, stared with astonishment at each other when they found, to their mutual surprise, that at one moment, in such a select party, universal silence pervaded. In this state of affairs, every one felt that his dignity required his speedy disappearance from the lady's presence. The Orientals, taking advantage of Bourbon's returning once more to the charge with an often unanswered remark, coolly walked away; the Chevalier made an adroit and honorable retreat by joining a passing party; and the Constable was the only one who, being left in solitude and silence, was finally obliged to make a formal bow and retire discomfited from the side of the only woman with whom he had ever condescended to fall in love. Leaning against the trunk of a tree at some little distance, Vivian Grey watched the formation and dissolution of the young Baroness's levée with lively interest. His eyes met the lady's as she raised them from the ground on Von Sohnspeer quitting her. She immediately beckoned to Vivian, but without her usual smile. He was directly at her side, but she did not speak. At last he said, "This is a most brilliant scene!"

"You think so, do you?" answered the lady, in a tone and

manner which almost made Vivian believe, for a moment, that
his friend Mr. Beckendorff was at his side.

"Decidedly his daughter!" thought he.

"You are not gay to-night?" said Vivian.

"Why should I be?" said the lady, in a manner which would
have made Vivian imagine that his presence was as disagreeable to her as that of Count von Sohnspeer, had not the lady
herself invited his company.

"I suppose the scene is very brilliant," continued the Baroness, after a few moments' silence. "At least all here seem to
think so, except two persons."

"And who are they?" asked Vivian.

"Myself and — the Crown Prince. I am almost sorry
that I did not dance with him. There seems a wonderful
similarity in our dispositions."

"You are pleased to be severe to-night."

"And who shall complain when the first person that I
satirize is myself?"

"It is most considerate in you," said Vivian, "to undertake
such an office; for it is one which you yourself are alone
capable of fulfilling. The only person that can ever satirize
your Excellency is yourself; and I think even then that, in
spite of your candor, your self-examination must please us
with a self-panegyric."

"Nay, a truce to compliments; at least let me hear better
things from you. I can not any longer endure the glare of
these lamps and dresses! Your arm! Let us walk for
a few minutes in the more retired and cooler parts of the
gardens!"

The Baroness and Vivian left the amphitheatre by a different path to that by which the Grand Duke and Madame
Carolina had quitted it. They found the walks quite solitary;
for the royal party, which was small, contained the only persons who had yet left the stage.

Vivian and his companion strolled about for some time, conversing on subjects of casual interest. The Baroness, though
no longer absent, either in her manner or her conversation,
seemed depressed; and Vivian, while he flattered himself that
he was more entertaining than usual, felt, to his mortification,
that the lady was not entertained.

"I am afraid you find it dull here," said he; "shall we return?"

"Oh, no; do not let us return! We have so short a time to be together that we must not allow even one hour to be dull."

As Vivian was about to reply, he heard the joyous voice of young Maximilian; it sounded very near. The royal party was approaching. The Baroness expressed her earnest desire to avoid it; and as to advance or to retreat, in these labyrinthine walks, was almost equally hazardous, they retired into one of those green recesses which we have before mentioned; indeed it was the very evergreen grove in the centre of which the Nymph of the Fountain watched for her loved Carian youth. A shower of moonlight fell on the marble statue, and showed the Nymph in an attitude of consummate skill; her modesty struggling with her desire, and herself crouching in her hitherto pure waters, while her anxious ear listens for the bounding step of the regardless huntsman.

"The air is cooler here," said the Baroness, "or the sound of the falling water is peculiarly refreshing to my senses. They have passed. I rejoice that we did not return; I do not think that I could have remained among those lamps another moment. How singular, actually to view with aversion a scene which appears to enchant all!"

"A scene which I should have thought would have been particularly charming to you," said Vivian; "you are dispirited to-night!"

"Am I?" said the Baroness. "I ought not to be; not to be more dispirited than I ever am. To-night I expected pleasure; nothing has happened which I did not expect, and everything which I did. And yet I am sad! Do you think that happiness can ever be sad? I think it must be so. But whether I am sorrowful or happy I can hardly tell; for it is only within these few days that I have known either grief or joy."

"It must be counted an eventful period in your existence which reckons in its brief hours a first acquaintance with such passions!" said Vivian, with a searching eye and inquiring voice.

"Yes; an eventful period, certainly an eventful period,"

answered the Baroness, with a thoughtful air and in measured words.

"I can not bear to see a cloud upon that brow!" said Vivian. "Have you forgotten how much was to be done to-night? How eagerly you looked forward to its arrival? How bitterly we were to regret the termination of the mimic empire?"

"I have forgotten nothing; would that I had! I will not look grave. I will be gay; and yet, when I remember how soon other mockery besides this splendid pageant must be terminated, why should I look gay? Why may I not weep?"

"Nay, if we are to moralize on worldly felicity, I fear that instead of inspiriting you, which is my wish, I shall prove but a too congenial companion. But such a theme is not for you."

"And why should it be for one who, though he lecture me with such gravity and gracefulness, can scarcely be entitled to play the part of Mentor by the weight of years?" said the Baroness, with a smile; "for one who, I trust, who I should think, as little deserved, and was as little inured to, sorrow as myself!"

"To find that you have cause to grieve," said Vivian, "and to learn from you, at the same time, your opinion of my own lot, prove what I have too often had the sad opportunity of observing, that the face of man is scarcely more genuine and less deceitful than these masquerade dresses which we now wear."

"But you are not unhappy?" asked the Baroness with a quick voice.

"Not now," said Vivian.

His companion seated herself on the marble balustrade which surrounded the fountain; she did not immediately speak again, and Vivian was silent, for he was watching her motionless countenance as her large brilliant eyes gazed with earnestness on the falling water sparkling in the moonlight. Surely it was not the mysterious portrait at Beckendorff's that he beheld!

She turned. She exclaimed in an agitated voice, "O friend! too lately found, why have we met to part?"

"To part, dearest!" said he, in a low and rapid voice, and he gently took her hand; "to part! and why should we part? why—"

"Ask not; your question is agony!" She tried to withdraw her hand, he pressed it with renewed energy, it remained in his, she turned away her head, and both were silent.

"O! lady," said Vivian, as he knelt at her side, "why are we not happy?"

His arm is round her waist, gently he bends his head, their speaking eyes meet, and their trembling lips cling into a kiss!

A seal of love and purity and faith! and the chaste moon need not have blushed as she lighted up the countenances of the lovers.

"O! lady, why are we not happy?"

"We are, we are; is not this happiness, is not this joy, is not this bliss? Bliss," she continued, in a low broken voice, "to which I have no right, no title. Oh! quit, quit my hand! Happiness is not for me!" She extricated herself from his arm, and sprang upon her feet. Alarm, rather than affection, was visible on her agitated features. It seemed to cost her a great effort to collect her scattered senses; the effort was made with pain, but with success.

"Forgive me," she said, in a hurried and indistinct tone; "forgive me! I would speak, but can not, not now at least; we have been long away, too long; our absence will be remarked to-night; to-night we must give up to the gratification of others, but I will speak. For yours, for my own sake, let us, let us go. You know that we are to be very gay to-night, and gay we will be. Who shall prevent us? At least the present hour is our own; and when the future ones must be so sad, why, why trifle with this?"

CHAPTER XI

THE reader is not to suppose that Vivian Grey thought of the young Baroness merely in the rapid scenes which we have sketched. There were few moments in the day in which her image did not occupy his thoughts, and which, indeed, he did not spend in her presence. From the first her character had interested him. His accidental but extraordinary acquaintance with Beckendorff made him view any individual connected with that singular man with a far more curious feeling than could influence the young nobles of the Court, who were ignorant of the Minister's personal character. There was an evident mystery about the character and situation of the Baroness, which well accorded with the eccentric and romantic career of the Prime Minister of Reisenburg. Of the precise nature of her connection with Beckendorff Vivian was wholly ignorant. The world spoke of her as his daughter, and the affirmation of Madame Carolina confirmed the world's report. Her name was still unknown to him; and although during the few moments that they had enjoyed an opportunity of conversing together alone Vivian had made every exertion of which good breeding, impelled by curiosity, is capable, and had devised many little artifices with which a schooled address is well acquainted to obtain it, his exertions had hitherto been unsuccessful. If there was a mystery, the young lady was competent to preserve it; and with all her naïveté, her interesting ignorance of the world, and her evidently uncontrollabe spirit, no hasty word ever fell from her cautious lips which threw any light on the objects of his inquiry. Though impetuous, she was never indiscreet, and often displayed a caution which was little in accordance with her youth and temper. The last night had witnessed the only moment in which her passions seemed for a time to have struggled with, and to have overcome, her judgment; but it was only for a moment. That display of overpowering feeling had cost Vivian a sleepless night; and he is at this instant pacing up and down the chamber of his hotel, thinking of that which he had imagined could exercise his thoughts no more.

She was beautiful; she loved him; she was unhappy! To be loved by any woman is flattering to the feelings of every man, no matter how deeply he may have quaffed the bitter goblet of worldly knowledge. The praise of a fool is incense to the wisest of us; and though we believe ourselves broken-hearted, it still delights us to find that we are loved. The memory of Violet Fane was still as fresh, as sweet, to the mind of Vivian Grey as when he pressed her blushing cheek for the first and only time. To love again, really to love as he had done, he once thought was impossible; he thought so still. The character of the Baroness had interested him from the first. Her ignorance of mankind, and her perfect acquaintance with the polished forms of society; her extreme beauty, her mysterious rank, her proud spirit and impetuous feelings; her occasional pensiveness, her extreme waywardness, had astonished, perplexed, and enchanted him. But he had never felt in love. It never for a moment had entered into his mind that his lonely bosom could again be a fit resting-place for one so lovely and so young. Scared at the misery which had always followed in his track, he would have shuddered ere he again asked a human being to share his sad and blighted fortunes. The partiality of the Baroness for his society, without flattering his vanity, or giving rise to thoughts more serious than how he could most completely enchant for her the passing hour, had certainly made the time passed in her presence the least gloomy which he had lately experienced. At the same moment that he left the saloon of the palace he had supposed that his image quitted her remembrance; and if she had again welcomed him with cheerfulness and cordiality, he had felt that his reception was owing to not being, perhaps, quite as frivolous as the Count of Eberstein, and rather more amusing than the Baron of Gernsbach.

It was therefore with the greatest astonishment that, last night, he had found that he was loved—loved, too, by this beautiful and haughty girl, who had treated the advances of the most distinguished nobles with ill-concealed scorn, and who had so presumed upon her dubious relationship to the bourgeois Minister that nothing but her own surpassing loveliness and her parent's all-engrossing influence could have excused or authorized her conduct.

Vivian had yielded to the magic of the moment, and had returned the feelings apparently no sooner expressed than withdrawn. Had he left the gardens of the palace the Baroness's plighted lover he might perhaps have deplored his rash engagement, and the sacred image of his first and hallowed love might have risen up in judgment against his violated affection; but how had he and the interesting stranger parted? He was rejected, even while his affection was returned; and while her flattering voice told him that he alone could make her happy, she had mournfully declared that happiness could not be hers. How was this? Could she be another's? Her agitation at the Opera, often the object of his thought, quickly occurred to him! It must be so. Ah! another's! and who this rival? this proud possessor of a heart which could not beat for him? Madame Carolina's declaration that the Baroness must be married off was at this moment remembered; her marked observation, that Von Sohnspeer was no son of Beckendorff's, not forgotten. The Field Marshal, too, was the valued friend of the Minister; and it did not fail to occur to Vivian that it was not Von Sohnspeer's fault that his attendance on the Baroness was not as constant as his own. Indeed, the unusual gallantry of the Commander-in-Chief had been the subject of many a joke among the young lords of the Court, and the reception of his addresses by their unmerciful object not unobserved or unspared. But as for poor Von Sohnspeer, what could be expected, as Emilius von Aslingen observed, "from a man whose softest compliment was as long, loud, and obscure as a birthday salute!"

No sooner was the affair clear to Vivian, no sooner was he convinced that a powerful obstacle existed to the love or union of himself and the Baroness, than he began to ask what right the interests of third persons had to interfere between the mutual affection of any individuals. He thought of her in the moonlight garden, struggling with her pure and natural passion. He thought of her exceeding beauty, her exceeding love. He beheld this rare and lovely creature in the embrace of Von Sohnspeer. He turned from the picture in disgust and indignation. She was his. Nature had decreed it. She should be the bride of no other man. Sooner than yield her up he would beard Beckendorff himself in his own retreat, and run every hazard and meet every danger which the ardent imagination of a lover could conceive. Was he madly to reject the happiness which Providence, or Destiny, or Chance had at length offered him? If the romance of boyhood could never be realized, at least with this engaging being for his companion, he might pass through his remaining years in calmness and in peace. His trials were perhaps over. Alas! this is the last delusion of unhappy men!

Vivian called at the Palace, but the fatigues of the preceding night prevented either of the ladies from being visible. In the evening he joined a small and select circle. The party, indeed, only consisted of the Grand Duke, Madame, their visitors, and the usual attendants, himself, and Von Sohnspeer. The quiet of the little circle did not more strikingly contrast with the noise, and glare, and splendor of the last night than did Vivian's subdued reception by the Baroness with her agitated demeanor in the garden. She was cordial, but calm. He found it quite impossible to gain even one moment's private conversation with her. Madame Carolina monopolized his attention, as much to favor the views of the Field Marshal as to discuss the comparative merits of Pope as a moralist and a poet; and Vivian had the mortification of observing his odious rival, whom he now thoroughly detested, discharge without ceasing his royal salutes in the impatient ear of Beckendorff's lovely daughter.

Toward the conclusion of the evening a chamberlain entered the room and whispered his mission to the Baroness. She immediately rose and quitted the apartment. As the party was breaking up she again entered. Her countenance was agitated. Madame Carolina was in the act of being overwhelmed with the compliments of the Grand Marshal, and Vivian seized the opportunity of reaching the Baroness. After a few hurried sentences she dropped her glove. Vivian gave it her. So many persons were round them that it was impossible to converse except on the most common topics. The glove was again dropped.

"I see," said the Baroness, with a meaning look, "that you are but a recreant knight, or else you would not part with a lady's glove so easily."

Vivian gave a rapid glance round the room. No one was observing him, and the glove was immediately concealed. He hurried home, rushed up the staircase of the hotel, ordered lights, locked the door, and with a sensation of indescribable anxiety tore the precious glove from his bosom, seized, opened, and read the inclosed and following note. It was written in pencil, in a hurried hand, and some of the words were repeated:

"I leave the Court to-night. He is here himself. No art can postpone my departure. Much, much I wish to see you; to say, to say to you. He is to have an interview with the Grand Duke to-morrow morning. Dare you come to his place in his absence? You know the private road. He goes by the highroad, and calls in his way on a Forest Counselor: it is the white house by the barrier; you know it! Watch him to-morrow morning; about nine or ten I should think; here, here; and then for heaven's sake let me see you. Dare everything! Fail not! Mind, by the private road: beware the other! You know the ground. God bless you! SYBILLA."

CHAPTER XII

VIVIAN read the note over a thousand times. He could not retire to rest. He called Essper George, and gave him all necessary directions for the morning. About three o'clock Vivian lay down on a sofa, and slept for a few hours. He started often in his short and feverish slumber. His dreams were unceasing and inexplicable. At first Von Sohnspeer was their natural hero; but soon the scene shifted. Vivian was at Ems, walking under the well-remembered lime-trees, and with the Baroness. Suddenly, although it was midday, the sun became large, blood-red, and fell out of the heavens; his companion screamed, a man rushed forward with a drawn sword. It was the idiot Crown Prince of Reisenburg. Vivian tried to oppose him, but without success. The infuriated ruffian sheathed his weapon in the heart of the Baroness. Vivian shrieked, and fell upon her body, and, to his horror, found himself embracing the cold corpse of Violet Fane!

Vivian and Essper mounted their horses about seven o'clock. At eight they had reached a small inn near the Forest Counselor's house, where Vivian was to remain until Essper had watched the entrance of the Minister. It was a few minutes past nine when Essper returned with the joyful intelligence that Owlface and his master had been seen to enter the courtyard. Vivian immediately mounted Max, and telling Essper to keep a sharp watch, he set spurs to his horse.

"Now, Max, my good steed, each minute is golden; serve thy master well!" He patted the horse's neck, the animal's erected ears proved how well it understood its master's wishes; and taking advantage of the loose bridle, which was confidently allowed it, the horse sprang rather than galloped to the Minister's residence. Nearly an hour, however, was lost in gaining the private road, for Vivian, after the caution in the Baroness's letter, did not dare the highroad.

He is galloping up the winding rural lane, where he met Beckendorff on the second morning of his visit. He has reached the little gate, and following the example of the Grand Duke, ties Max at the entrance. He dashes over the meadows; not following the path, but crossing straight through the long and dewy grass, he leaps over the light iron railing; he is rushing up the walk; he takes a rapid glance, in passing, at the little summer-house; the blue passion-flower is still blooming, the house is in sight; a white handkerchief is waving from the drawing-room window! He sees it; fresh wings are added to his course; he dashes through a bed of flowers, frightens the white peacock, darts through the library window, is in the drawing-room.

The Baroness was there: pale and agitated she stood beneath the mysterious picture, with one arm leaning on the old carved mantelpiece. Overcome by her emotions, she did not move forward to meet him as he entered; but Vivian observed neither her constraint nor her agitation.

"Sybilla! dearest Sybilla! say you are mine!"

He seized her hand. She struggled not to disengage herself; her head sank upon her arm, which rested upon his shoulder. Overpowered, she sobbed convulsively. He endeavored to calm her, but her agitation increased; and minutes elapsed ere she seemed to be even sensible of his presence. At length she became more calm, and apparently making a struggle to compose herself, she raised her head and said, "This is very weak: let us walk for a moment about the room!"

At this moment Vivian was seized by the throat with a strong grasp. He turned round; it was Mr. Beckendorff, with a face deadly white, his full eyes darting from their sockets like a hungry snake's, and the famous Italian dagger in his right hand.

"Villain!" said he, in the low voice of fatal passion; "Villain, is this your Destiny?"

Vivian's first thoughts were for the Baroness; and turning his head from Beckendorff, he looked with the eye of anxious love to his companion. But, instead of fainting, instead of being overwhelmed by this terrible interruption, she seemed, on the contrary, to have suddenly regained her natural spirit and self-possession. The blood had returned to her hitherto pale cheek, and the fire to an eye before dull with weeping. She extricated herself immediately from Vivian's encircling arm, and by so doing enabled him to have struggled, had it been necessary, more equally with the powerful grasp of his assailant.

"Stand off, sir!" said the Baroness, with an air of inexpressible dignity, and a voice which even at this crisis seemed to anticipate that it would be obeyed. "Stand off, sir! stand off, I command you!"

Beckendorff for one moment was motionless; he then gave her a look of piercing earnestness, threw Vivian, rather than released him, from his hold, and flung the dagger with a bitter smile into the corner of the room. "Well, madame!" said he, in a choking voice, "you are obeyed!"

"Mr. Grey," continued the Baroness, "I regret that this outrage should have been experienced by you because you have dared to serve me. My presence should have preserved you from this contumely; but what are we to expect from those who pride themselves upon being the sons of slaves! You shall hear further from me." So saying, the lady, bowing to

Vivian, and sweeping by the Minister with a glance of indescribable disdain, quitted the apartment. As she was on the point of leaving the room, Vivian was standing against the wall, with a pale face and folded arms; Beckendorff, with his back to the window, his eyes fixed on the ground; and Vivian, to his astonishment, perceived, what escaped the Minister's notice, that while the lady bade him adieu with one hand she made rapid signs with the other to some unknown person in the garden.

Mr. Beckendorff and Vivian were left alone, and the latter was the first to break silence.

"Mr. Beckendorff," said he, in a calm voice, "considering the circumstances under which you have found me in your house this morning, I should have known how to excuse and to forget any irritable expressions which a moment of ungovernable passion might have inspired. I should have passed them over unnoticed. But your unjustifiable behavior has exceeded that line of demarcation which sympathy with human feelings allows even men of honor to recognize. You have disgraced both me and yourself by giving me a blow. It is, as that lady well styled it, an outrage; an outrage which the blood of any other man but yourself could only obliterate from my memory; but while I am inclined to be indulgent to your exalted station and your peculiar character, I at the same time expect, and now wait for, an apology."

"An apology!" said Beckendorff, now beginning to stamp up and down the room; "an apology! Shall it be made to you, sir, or the Archduchess?"

"The Archduchess!" said Vivian. "Good God! what can you mean! Did I hear you right?"

"I said the Archduchess," answered Beckendorff, with firmness; "a Princess of the House of Austria, and the pledged wife of his Royal Highness the Crown Prince of Reisenburg. Perhaps you may now think that other persons have to apologize?"

"Mr. Beckendorff," said Vivian, "I am overwhelmed; I declare, upon my honor—"

"Stop, sir! you have said too much already—"

"But, Mr. Beckendorff, surely you will allow me to explain—"

"Sir! there is no need of explanation. I know everything; more than you do yourself. You can have nothing to explain to me! and I presume you are now fully aware of the impossibility of again speaking to her. It is at present within an hour of noon. Before sunset you must be twenty miles from the Court; so far you will be attended. Do not answer me; you know my power. A remonstrance only, and I write to Vienna; your progress shall be stopped throughout the South of Europe. For her sake this business will be hushed up. An important and secret mission will be the accredited reason of your leaving Reisenburg. This will be confirmed by your official attendant, who will be an Envoy's Courier. Farewell!"

As Mr. Beckendorff quitted the room, his confidential servant, the messenger of Turriparva, entered, and with the most respectful bow informed Vivian that the horses were ready. In about three hours' time Vivian Grey, followed by the Government messenger, stopped at his hotel. The landlord and waiters bowed with increased obsequiousness on seeing him so attended, and in a few minutes Reisenburg was ringing with the news that his appointment to the Under-Secretaryship of State was now "a settled thing."

BOOK VIII

CHAPTER I

THE landlord of the Grand Hotel of the Four Nations at Reisenburg was somewhat consoled for the sudden departure of his distinguished guest by selling the plenipotentiary a traveling carriage lately taken for a doubtful bill from a gambling Russian General at a large profit. In this convenient vehicle, in the course of a couple of hours after his arrival in the city, was Mr. Vivian Grey borne through the gate of the Allies. Essper George, who had reached the hotel about half an hour after his master, followed behind the carriage on his hack, leading Max. The Courier cleared the road before, and expedited the arrival of the special Envoy of the Grand Duke of Reisenburg at the point of his destination by ordering the horses, clearing the barriers, and paying the postilions in advance. Vivian had never traveled before with such style and speed.

Our hero covered himself up with his cloak and drew his traveling cap over his eyes, though it was one of the hottest days of this singularly hot autumn. Entranced in a reverie, the only figure that occurred to his mind was the young Archduchess, and the only sounds that dwelt on his ear were the words of Beckendorff; but neither to the person of the first nor to the voice of the second did he annex any definite idea.

After some hours' traveling, which to Vivian seemed both an age and a minute, he was roused from his stupor by the door of his calèche being opened. He shook himself as a man does who has awakened from a benumbing and heavy sleep, although his eyes were the whole time wide open. The disturbing intruder was his Courier, who, bowing, with his hat in hand, informed his Excellency that he was now on the frontier of Reisenburg; regretting that he was under the necessity of quitting his Excellency, he begged to present him with his passport. "It is made out for Vienna," continued the messenger. "A private pass, sir, of the Prime Minister, and will entitle you to the greatest consideration."

The carriage was soon again advancing rapidly to the next post-house, when, after they had proceeded about half a mile, Essper George calling loudly from behind, the drivers suddenly stopped. Just as Vivian, to whose tortured mind the rapid movement of the carriage was some relief, for it produced an excitement which prevented thought, was about to inquire the cause of this stoppage, Essper George rode up to the calèche.

"Kind sir!" said he, with a peculiar look, "I have a packet for you."

"A packet! from whom? speak! give it me!"

"Hush! softly, good master. Here am I about to commit rank treason for your sake, and a hasty word is the only reward of my rashness."

"Nay, nay, good Essper, try me not now!"

"I will not, kind sir! but the truth is, I could not give you the packet while that double-faced knave was with us, or even while he was in sight. 'In good truth,' as Master Rodolph was wont to say—!"

"But of this packet?"

" 'Fairly and softly,' good sir! as Hunsdrich the porter said when I would have drunk the mulled wine, while he was on the cold staircase—"

"Essper! do you mean to enrage me?"

" 'By St. Hubert!' as that worthy gentleman the Grand Marshal was in the habit of swearing, I—"

"This is too much; what are the idle sayings of these people to me?"

"Nay, nay, kind sir! they do but show that each of us has his own way of telling a story, and that he who would hear a tale must let the teller's breath come out of his own nostrils."

"Well, Essper, speak on! Stranger things have happened to me than to be reproved by my own servant."

"Nay, kind master! say not a bitter word to me because you have slipped out of a scrape with your head on your shoulders. The packet is from Mr. Beckendorff's daughter."

"Ah! why did you not give it me before?"

"Why do I give it you now? Because I am a fool; that is why. What! you wanted it when that double-faced scoundrel was watching every eyelash of yours as it moved from the breath of a fly? a fellow who can see as well at the back of his head as from his face. I should like to poke out his front eyes, to put him on an equality with the rest of mankind. He it was who let the old gentleman know of your visit this morning, and I suspect that he has been nearer your limbs of late than you have imagined. Every dog has his day, and the oldest pig must look for the knife! The devil was once cheated on Sunday, and I have been too sharp for Puss in Boots and his mousetrap! Prowling about the Forest Counselor's house, I saw your new servant, sir, gallop in, and his old master soon gallop out. I was off as quick as they, but was obliged to leave my horse within two miles of the house, and then trust to my legs. I crept through the shrubs like a land tortoise; but, of course, too late to warn you. However, I was in for the death, and making signs to the young lady, who directly saw that I was a friend—bless her! she is as quick as a partridge—I left you to settle it with papa, and, after all, did that which I suppose you intended, sir, to do yourself; made my way into the young lady's bedchamber."

"Hold your tongue, sir! and give me the packet!"

"There it is, and now we will go on; but we must stay an hour at the next post, if your honor pleases not to sleep there; for both Max and my own hack have had a sharp day's work."

Vivian tore open the packet. It contained a long letter, written on the night of her return to Beckendorff's; she had stayed up the whole night writing. It was to have been forward to Vivian in case of their not being able to meet. In the inclosure were a few hurried lines, written since the catastrophe. They were these: "May this safely reach you! Can you ever forgive me? The inclosed, you will see, was intended for you, in case of our not meeting. It anticipated sorrow; yet what were its anticipations to our reality!"

The Archduchess's letter was evidently written under the influence of agitated feelings. We omit it; because, as the mystery of her character is now explained, a great portion of her communications would be irrelevant to our tale. She spoke of her exalted station as a woman, that station which so many women envy, in a spirit of agonizing bitterness. A royal princess is only the most flattered of state victims. She is a political sacrifice, by which enraged governments are appeased, wavering allies conciliated and ancient amities confirmed. Debarred by her rank and her education from looking forward to that exchange of equal affection which is the great end and charm of female existence, no individual finds more fatally and feels more keenly that pomp is not felicity, and splendor not content.

Deprived of all those sources of happiness which seem inherent in woman, the wife of the Sovereign sometimes seeks in politics and in pleasure a means of excitement which may purchase oblivion. But the political queen is a rare character; she must possess an intellect of unusual power, and her lot must be considered as an exception in the fortunes of female royalty. Even the political queen generally closes an agitated career with a broken heart. And for the unhappy votary of pleasure, who owns her cold duty to a royal husband, we must not forget that even in the most dissipated courts the conduct of the queen is expected to be decorous, and that the instances are not rare where the wife of the monarch has died on the scaffold, or in a dungeon, or in exile, because she dared to be indiscreet where all were debauched. But for the great majority of royal wives, they exist without a passion; they have nothing to hope, nothing to fear, nothing to envy, nothing to want, nothing to confide, nothing to hate, and nothing to love. Even their duties, though multitudinous, are mechanical, and, while they require much attention, occasion no anxiety. Amusement is their moment of greatest emotion, and for them amusement is rare; for amusement is the result of equal companionship. Thus situated, they are doomed to become frivolous in their pursuits and formal in their manners, and the Court chaplain or the Court confessor is the only person who can prove they have a soul, by convincing them that it will be saved.

The young Archduchess had assented to the proposition of marriage with the Crown Prince of Reisenburg without opposition, as she was convinced that requesting her assent was only a courteous form of requiring her compliance. There was nothing outrageous to her feelings in marrying a man whom she had never seen, because her education, from her tenderest years, had daily prepared her for such an event. Moreover, she was aware that, if she succeeded in escaping from the offers of the Crown Prince of Reisenburg, she would soon be under the necessity of assenting to those of some other suitor; and if proximity to her own country, accordance with its sentiments and manners, and previous connection with her own house, were taken into consideration, a union with the family of Reisenburg was even desirable. It was to be preferred, at least, to one which brought with it a foreign husband and a foreign clime, a strange language and strange customs. The Archduchess, a girl of ardent feelings and lively mind, had not, however, agreed to become that all-commanding slave, a Queen, without a stipulation. She required that she might be allowed, previous to her marriage, to visit her future Court incognita. This singular and unparalleled proposition was not easily acceded to; but the opposition with which it was received only tended to make the young Princess more determined to be gratified in her caprice. Her Imperial Highness did not pretend that any end was to be obtained by this unusual procedure, and indeed she had no definite purpose in requesting it to be permitted. It was originally the mere whim of the moment, and had it not been strongly opposed it would not have been strenuously insisted upon. As it was, the young Archduchess persisted, threatened, and grew obstinate; and the gray-headed negotiators of the marriage, desirous of its speedy completion, and not having a more tractable tool ready to supply her place, at length yielded to her bold importunity. Great difficulty, however, was experienced in carrying her wishes into execution. By what means and in what character she was to appear at Court, so as not to excite suspicion or occasion discovery, were often discussed, without being resolved upon. At length it became necessary to consult Mr. Beckendorff. The upper lip of the Prime Minister of Reisenburg curled as the Imperial Minister detailed the caprice and contumacy of the Princess, and treating with the greatest contempt this girlish whim, Mr. Beckendorff ridiculed those by whom it had been humored with no suppressed derision. The consequence of his conduct was an interview with the future Grand Duchess, and the consequence of his interview an unexpected undertaking on his part to arrange the visit according to her Highness's desires.

The Archduchess had not yet seen the Crown Prince; but six miniatures and a whole-length portrait had prepared her for not meeting an Adonis or a Baron Trenck, and that was all; for never had the Correggio of the age of Charles the Fifth better substantiated his claims to the office of Court painter than by these accurate semblances of his Royal Highness, in which his hump was subdued into a Grecian bend, and his lack-lustre eyes seemed beaming with tenderness and admiration. His betrothed bride stipulated with Mr. Beckendorff that the fact of her visit should be known only to himself and the Grand Duke; and before she appeared at Court she had received the personal pledge both of himself and his Royal Highness that the affair should be kept a complete secret from the Crown Prince.

Most probably, on her first introduction to her future husband, all the romantic plans of the young Archduchess to excite an involuntary interest in his heart vanished; but how this may be, it is needless for us to inquire, for that same night introduced another character into her romance for whom she was perfectly unprepared, and whose appearance totally disorganized its plot.

Her inconsiderate, her unjustifiable conduct, in tampering with that individual's happiness and affection was what the young and haughty Archduchess deplored in the most energetic, the most feeling, and the most humble spirit; and anticipating that after this painful disclosure they would never meet again, she declared that for his sake alone she regretted what had passed, and praying that he might be happier than herself, she supplicated to be forgiven and forgotten.

Vivian read the Archduchess's letter over and over again, and then put it in his breast. At first he thought that he had lived to shed another tear; but he was mistaken. In a few minutes he found himself quite roused from his late overwhelming stupor. Remorse or regret for the past, care or caution for the future, seemed at the same moment to have fled from his mind. He looked up to Heaven with a wild smile, half of despair and half of defiance. It seemed to imply that Fate had now done her worst, and that he had at last the satisfaction of knowing himself to be the most unfortunate and unhappy being that ever existed. When a man at the same time believes in and sneers at his destiny we may be sure that he considers his condition past redemption.

CHAPTER II

THEY stopped for an hour at the next post, according to Essper's suggestion. Indeed, he proposed resting there for the night, for both men and beasts much required repose; but Vivian panted to reach Vienna, to which city two days' traveling would now carry him. His passions were so roused, and his powers of reflection so annihilated, that while he had determined to act desperately, he was unable to resolve upon anything desperate. Whether, on his arrival at the Austrian capital, he should plunge into dissipation or into the Danube was equally uncertain. He had some thought of joining the Greeks or Turks, no matter which, probably the latter, or perhaps of serving in the Americas. The idea of returning to England never once entered his mind; he expected to find letters from his father at Vienna, and he almost regretted it; for, in his excessive misery, it was painful to be conscious that a being still breathed who was his friend.

It was a fine moonlight night, but the road was mountainous; and in spite of all the encouragement of Vivian, and all the consequent exertions of the postilion, they were upward of two hours and a half going these eight miles. To get on any further to-night was quite impossible. Essper's horse was fairly knocked up, and even Max visibly distressed. The post-house was fortunately an inn. It was not at a village, and, as far as the travelers could learn, not near one, and its appearance did not promise very pleasing accommodation. Essper, who had scarcely tasted food for nearly eighteen hours, was not highly delighted with the prospect before them. His anxiety, however, was not merely selfish; he was as desirous that his young master should be refreshed by a good night's rest as himself, and anticipating that he should have to exercise his skill in making a couch for Vivian in the carriage, he proceeded to cross-examine the postmaster on the possibility of his accommodating them. The host was a pious-looking personage, in a black velvet cap, with a singularly meek and charitable expression of countenance. · His long black hair was exquisitely braided, and he wore round his neck a collar of pewter medals, all which had been recently sprinkled with holy water and blessed under the petticoat of the saintly Virgin; for the postmaster had only just returned from a pilgrimage to the celebrated shrine of the Black Lady of Altoting.

"Good friend!" said Essper, looking him cunningly in the face, "I fear that we must order horses on; you can hardly accommodate two?"

"Good friend!" answered the innkeeper, and he crossed himself very reverently at the same time, "it is not for man to fear, but to hope."

"If your beds were as good as your adages," said Essper George, laughing, "in good truth, as a friend of mine would say, I would sleep here to-night."

"Prithee, friend," continued the innkeeper, kissing a medal of his collar very devoutly, "what accommodation dost thou lack?"

"Why," said Essper, "in the way of accommodation, little, for two excellent beds will content us; but in the way of refreshment, by St. Hubert! as another friend of mine would swear, he would be a bold man who would engage to be as hungry before his dinner as I shall be after my supper."

"Friend!" said the innkeeper, "Our Lady forbid that thou shouldst leave our walls to-night; for the accommodation, we have more than sufficient; and as for the refreshment, by Holy Mass! we had a priest tarry here last night, and he left his rosary behind. I will comfort my soul, by telling my beads over the kitchen fire. and for every Paternoster my wife shall give thee a rasher of kid, and for every Ave a tumbler of Augsberg, which Our Lady forget me if I did not myself purchase but yesterday se'nnight from the pious fathers of the Convent of St. Florian!"

"I take thee at thy word, honest sir," said Essper. "By

the Creed! I liked thy appearance from the first; nor wilt thou find me unwilling, when my voice has taken its supper, to join thee in some pious hymn or holy canticle. And now for the beds!"

"There is the green room, the best bedroom in my house," said the innkeeper. "Holy Mary forget me if in that same bed have not stretched their legs more valorous generals, more holy prelates, and more distinguished counselors of our Lord the Emperor, than in any bed in all Austria."

"That, then, for my master, and for myself—"

"H-u-m!" said the host, looking very earnestly in Essper's face; "I should have thought that thou wert one more anxious after dish and flagon than curtain and eider-down!"

"By my Mother! I love good cheer," said Essper earnestly, "and want it more at this moment than any knave that ever yet starved; but if thou hast not a bed to let me stretch my legs on after four and twenty hours' hard riding, by holy Virgin! I will have horses on to Vienna."

"Our Black Lady forbid!" said the innkeeper, with a quick voice, and with rather a dismayed look; "said I that thou shouldst not have a bed? St. Florian desert me if I and my wife would not sooner sleep in the chimney-corner than thou shouldst miss one wink of thy slumbers!"

"In one word, have you a bed?"

"Have I a bed? Where slept, I should like to know, the Vice-Principal of the Convent of Molk on the day before the last holy Ascension? The waters were out in the morning; and when will my wife forget what his reverence was pleased to say when he took his leave: 'Good woman!' said he, 'my duty calls me; but the weather is cold; and between ourselves, I am used to great feasts, and I should have no objection, if I were privileged, to stay and to eat again of thy red cabbage and cream!' What say you to that? Do you think we have got beds now? You shall sleep to-night, sir, like an Aulic Councilor!"

This adroit introduction of the red cabbage and cream settled every thing; when men are wearied and famished they have no inclination to be incredulous, and in a few moments Vivian was informed by his servant that the promised accommodation was satisfactory; and having locked up the carriage, and wheeled it into a small outhouse, he and Essper were ushered by their host into a room which, as is usual in small German inns in the South, served at the same time both for kitchen and saloon. The fire was lighted in a platform of brick, raised in the centre of the floor; the sky was visible through the chimney, which, although of a great breadth below, gradually narrowed to the top. A family of wandering Bohemians, consisting of the father and mother and three children, were seated on the platform when Vivian entered; the man was playing on a coarse wooden harp, without which the Bohemians seldom travel. The music ceased as the new guests came into the room, and the Bohemian courteously offered his place at the fire to our hero, who, however, declined disturbing the family group. A small table and a couple of chairs were placed in a corner of the room by the innkeeper's wife, a bustling active dame, who apparently found no difficulty in laying the cloth, dusting the furniture, and cooking the supper at the same time. At this table Vivian and his servant seated themselves; nor, indeed, did the cookery discredit the panegyric of the reverend Vice-Principal of the Convent of Molk.

Alike wearied in mind and body, Vivian soon asked for his bed, which, though not exactly fitted for an Aulic Councillor, as the good host perpetually avowed it to be, nevertheless afforded decent accommodation.

The Bohemian family retired to the hayloft, and Essper George would have followed his master's example, had not the kind mistress of the house tempted him to stay behind by the production of a new platter of rashers; indeed, he never remembered meeting with such hospitable people as the postmaster and his wife. They had evidently taken a fancy to him, and, though extremely wearied, the lively little Essper endeavored, between his quick mouthfuls and long draughts, to reward and encourage their kindness by many a good story and sharp joke. With all these both mine host and his wife were exceedingly amused, seldom containing their laughter, and frequently protesting, by the sanctity of various saints, that this was the pleasantest night and Essper the pleasantest fellow that they had ever met with.

"Eat, eat, my friend!" said his host; "by the Mass! thou

hast traveled far; and fill thy glass, and pledge with me Our Black Lady of Altoting. By Holy Cross! I have hung up this week in her chapel a garland of silk roses, and have ordered to be burned before her shrine three pounds of perfumed wax tapers! Fill again, fill again! and thou too, good mistress; a hard day's work hast thou had; a glass of wine will do thee no harm! join me with our new friend! Pledge we together the Holy Fathers of St. Florian, my worldly patrons and my spiritual pastors; let us pray that his reverence the Sub-Prior may not have his Christmas attack of gout in the stomach, and a better health to poor Father Felix! Fill again, fill again! this Augsburg is somewhat acid; we will have a bottle of Hungary. Mistress, fetch us the bell-glasses, and here to the reverend Vice-Principal of Molk! our good friend; when will my wife forget what he said to her on the morning of last holy Ascension! Fill again, fill again!"

Inspired by the convivial spirit of the pious and jolly post-master, Essper George soon forgot his threatened visit to his bedroom, and ate and drank, laughed and joked, as if he were again with his friend, Master Rodolph; but wearied Nature at length avenged herself for this unnatural exertion, and leaning back in his chair, he was, in the course of an hour, overcome by one of those dead and heavy slumbers, the effect of the united influence of fatigue and intemperance; in short, it was like the midnight sleep of a fox-hunter.

No sooner had our pious votary of the Black Lady of Altoting observed the effect of his Hungary wine than, making a well-understood sign to his wife, he took up the chair of Essper in his brawny arms, and, preceded by Mrs. Postmistress with a lantern, he left the room with his guest. Essper's hostess led and lighted the way to an outhouse, which occasionally served as a coach-house, a stable, and a lumber room. It had no window, and the lantern afforded the only light which exhibited its present contents. In one corner was a donkey tied up, belonging to the Bohemian. Under a hayrack was a large child's cradle; it was of a remarkable size, having been made for twins. Near it was a low wooden sheep-tank, half filled with water, and which had been placed there for the refreshment of the dog and his feathered friends, which were roosting in the rack.

The pious innkeeper very gently lowered to the ground the chair on which Essper was soundly sleeping; and then, having crossed himself, he took up our friend with great tenderness and solicitude, and dexterously fitted him in the huge cradle.

About an hour past midnight Essper George awoke. He was lying on his back, and very unwell; and on trying to move, found that he was rocking. His late adventure was obliterated from his memory; and the strange movement, united with his peculiar indisposition, left him no doubt that he was on board ship! As is often the case when we are tipsy or nervous, Essper had been awakened by the fright of falling from some immense height; and finding that his legs had no sensation, for they were quite benumbed, he concluded that he had fallen down the hatchway, that his legs were broken, and himself jammed in between some logs of wood in the hold, and so he began to cry lustily to those above to come down to his rescue.

"O, Essper George!" thought he, "how came you to set foot on salt timber again! Had not you had enough of it in the Mediterranean and the Turkish seas, that you must be getting aboard this lubberly Dutch galliot! for I am sure she's Dutch by being so low in the water. Well, they may talk of a sea life, but for my part, I never saw the use of the sea. Many a sad heart it has caused, and many a sick stomach has it occasioned! The boldest sailor climbs on board with a heavy soul, and leaps on land with a light spirit. O! thou indifferent ape of Earth! thy houses are of wood and thy horses of canvas; thy roads have no landmarks and thy highways no inns; thy hills are green without grass and wet without showers! and as for food, what art thou, O, bully Ocean! but the stable of horse-fishes, the stall of cow-fishes, the sty of hog-fishes, and the kennel of dog-fishes! Commend me to a fresh-water dish for meagre days! Sea-weeds stewed with chalk may be savory stuff for a merman; but, for my part, give me red cabbage and cream; and as for drink, a man may live in the midst of thee his whole life and die for thirst at the end of it! Besides, thou blasphemous salt lake, where is thy religion? Where are thy churches, thou heretic?" So saying, Essper made a desperate effort to crawl up the hold. His exertion set the cradle rocking with renewed violence; and at last dashing against the sheep-tank, that pastoral piece of furniture was overset, and part of its contents poured upon the inmate of the cradle.

"Sprung a leak in the hold, by St. Nicholas!" bawled out Essper George. "Caulkers ahoy!"

At this moment three or four fowls, roused by the fall of the tank and the consequent shouts of Essper, began fluttering about the rack, and at last perched upon the cradle. "The live-stock got loose!" shouted Essper, "and the breeze getting stiffer every instant! Where is the captain? I will see him. I am not one of the crew; I belong to the Court! I must have cracked my skull when I fell like a lubber down that confounded hatchway! Egad! I feel as if I had been asleep, and been dreaming I was at Court."

The sound of heavy footsteps was now over his head. These noises were at once an additional proof that he was in the hold, and an additional stimulus to his calls to those on deck. In fact, these sounds were occasioned by the Bohemians, who always rose before break of day; and consequently, in a few minutes, the door of the stable opened and the Bohemian, with a lantern in his hand, entered.

"What do you want?" cried Essper.

"I want my donkey."

"You do?" said Essper. "You're the Purser, I suppose, detected keeping a jackass among the poultry! eating all the food of our live-stock, and we having kid every day. Though both my legs are off, I'll have a fling at you!" and so saying, Essper, aided by the light of the lantern, scrambled out of the cradle, and taking up the sheep-tank, sent it straight at the astonished Bohemian's head. The aim was good, and the man fell; more, however, from fright than injury. Seizing his lantern, which had fallen out of his hand, Essper escaped through the stable door and rushed into the house. He found himself in the kitchen. The noise of his entrance roused the landlord and his wife, who had been sleeping by the fire; since, not having a single bed besides their own, they had given that up to Vivian. The countenance of the innkeeper effectually dispelled the clouds which had been fast clearing off from Essper's intellect. Giving one wide stare, and then rubbing his eyes, the truth lighted upon him, and so he sent the Bohemian's lantern at his landlord's head. The postmaster seized the poker and the postmistress a fagot, and as the Bohemian, who had now recovered himself, had entered in the rear, Essper George stood a fair chance of receiving a thorough drubbing, had not his master, roused by the suspicious noises and angry sounds which had reached his room, entered the kitchen with his pistols.

CHAPTER III

AS it was now morning, Vivian did not again retire to rest, but took advantage of the disturbance in the inn to continue his route at an earlier hour than he had previously intended.

Essper, when he found himself safely mounted, lagged behind a few minutes to vent his spleen against the innkeeper's wife.

"May St. Florian confound me, madame!" said Essper, addressing himself to the lady in the window, "if ever I beheld so ugly a witch as yourself! Pious friend! thy chaplet of roses was ill bestowed, and thou needest not have traveled so far to light thy wax tapers at the shrine of the Black Lady at Altoting; for, by the beauty of holiness! an image of ebony is mother of pearl to that soot-face whom thou callest thy wife. Fare thee well! thou couple of saintly sinners! and may the next traveler who tarries in the den of thieves qualify thee for canonization by thy wife's admiring pastor, the cabbage-eating Vice-Principal of Molk!"

Before the end of an hour they had to ford a rivulet running between two high banks. The scenery just here was particularly lovely, and Vivian's attention was so engrossed by it that he did not observe the danger which he was about to incur.

On the left of the road a high range of rocky mountains abruptly descended into an open but broken country, and the other side of the road was occasionally bounded by low undulating hills, partially covered with dwarf woods, not high enough to obstruct the view of the distant horizon. Rocky knolls jutted out near the base of the mountains; and on the top of one of them, overlooked by a gigantic gray peak, stood an ancient and still inhabited feudal castle. Round the base of this insulated rock a rustic village peeped above the encircling nut-woods, its rising smoke softening the hard features of the naked crag. On the side of the village nearest to Vivian a bold sheet of water discharged itself in three separate falls between the ravine of a wooded mountain, and flowing round the village as a fine, broad river, expanded before it reached the foundation of the castled rock into a long and deep lake, which was also fed by numerous streams, the gulleys only of which were now visible down the steep sides of the mountains, their springs having been long dried up.

Vivian's view was interrupted by his sudden descent into the bed of the rivulet, one of the numerous branches of the mountain torrent, and by a crash which as immediately ensued. The spring of his carriage was broken. The carriage fell over, but Vivian sustained no injury; and while Essper George rode forward to the village for assistance, his master helped the postilion to extricate the horses and secure them on the opposite bank. They had done all that was in their power some time before Essper returned; and Vivian, who had seated himself on some tangled beech-roots, was prevented growing impatient by contemplating the enchanting scenery. The postilion, on the contrary, who had traveled this road every day of his life, and who found no gratification in gazing upon rocks, woods, and waterfalls, lighted his pipe and occasionally talked to his horses. So essential an attribute of the beautiful is novelty! Essper at length made his appearance, attended by five or six peasants, dressed in holiday costume, with some fanciful decorations; their broad hats wreathed with wild flowers, their short brown jackets covered with buttons and fringe, and various colored ribbons streaming from their knees.

"Well, sir! the grandson is born the day the grandfather dies! a cloudy morning has often a bright sunset! and though we are now sticking in a ditch, by the aid of St. Florian we may be soon feasting in a castle! Come, my merry men, I did not bring you here to show your ribbons; the sooner you help us out of this scrape the sooner you will be again dancing with the pretty maidens on the green! Lend a hand!"

The calèche appeared to be so much shattered that they only ventured to put in one horse; and Vivian, leaving his carriage in charge of Essper and the postilion, mounted Max and rode to the village, attended by the peasants. He learned from them on the way that they were celebrating the marriage of the daughter of their lord, who, having been informed of the accident, had commanded them to go immediately to the gentleman's assistance, and then conduct him to the castle.

They crossed the river over a light stone bridge of three arches, the keystone of the centre one being decorated with a splendidly sculptured shield.

"This bridge appears to be very recently built?" said Vivian to one of his conductors.

"It was opened, sir, for the first time yesterday, to admit the bridegroom of my young lady, and the foundation stone was laid on the day she was born."

"I see that your good lord was determined that it should be a solid structure?"

"Why, sir, it was necessary that the foundation should be strong, because three succeeding winters it was washed away by the rush of that mountain torrent. Turn this way, if you please, sir, through the village."

Vivian was much struck by the appearance of the little settlement as he rode through it. It did not consist of more than fifty houses, but they were all detached, and each beautifully embowered in trees. The end of the village came upon a large rising green, leading up to the only accessible side of the castle. It presented a most animated scene, being covered with various groups, all intent upon different rustic amusements. An immense pole, the stem of a gigantic fir tree, was fixed nearly in the centre of the green, and crowned with a chaplet, the reward of the most active young man of the village, whose agility might enable him to display his gallantry by presenting it to his mistress, she being allowed to wear it during the remainder of the sports. The middle-aged men were proving their strength by raising weights; while the elders of the village joined in the calmer and more scientific diversion of skittles, which in Austria are played with bowls and pins of very great size. Others were dancing; others sitting under tents, chattering or taking refreshments. Some were walking in pairs, anticipating the speedy celebration of a wedding day happier to them, if less gay to others. Even the tenderest infants on this festive day seemed conscious of some unusual cause of excitement, and many an urchin, throwing himself forward in a vain attempt to catch an elder brother or a laughing sister, tried the strength of his leading-strings, and rolled over, crowing in the soft grass.

At the end of the green a splendid tent was erected, with a large white bridal flag waving from its top, embroidered in gold, with a true-lover's knot. From this pavilion came forth, to welcome the strangers, the lord of the village. He was a tall but thin, bending figure, with a florid, benevolent countenance, and a quantity of long white hair. This venerable person cordially offered his hand to Vivian, regretted his accident, but expressed much pleasure that he had come to partake of their happiness. "Yesterday," continued he, "was my daughter's wedding day, and both myself and our humble friends are endeavoring to forget, in this festive scene, our approaching loss and separation. If you had come yesterday you would have assisted at the opening of my new bridge. Pray, what do you think of it? But I will show it to you myself, which I assure you will give me great pleasure; at present let me introduce you to my family, who will be quite happy to see you. It is a pity that you have missed the Regatta; my daughter is just going to reward the successful candidate. You see the boats upon the lake; the one with the white and purple streamer was the conqueror. You will have the pleasure, too, of seeing my son-in-law; I am sure you will like him; he quite enjoys our sports. We shall have a fête champêtre to-morrow, and a dance on the green to-night."

The old gentleman paused for want of breath, and having stood a moment to recover himself, he introduced his new guests to the inmates of the tent; first, his maiden sister, a softened fac-simile of himself; behind her stood his beautiful and blushing daughter, the youthful bride, wearing on her head a coronal of white roses, and supported by three bridesmaids, the only relief to whose snowy dresses were large bouquets on their left side. The bridegroom was at first shaded by the curtain; but as he came forward Vivian started when he recognized his Heidelberg friend, Eugene von Konigstein!

Their mutual delight and astonishment were so great that for an instant neither of them could speak; but when the old man learned from his son-in-law that the stranger was his most valued and intimate friend, and one to whom he was under great personal obligations, he absolutely declared that he would have the wedding, to witness which appeared to him the height of human felicity, solemnized over again. The bride blushed, the bridesmaids tittered, the joy was universal.

Vivian inquired after the Baron. He learned from Eugene that he had quitted Europe about a month, having sailed as Minister to one of the New American States. "My uncle," continued the young man, "was neither well nor in spirits before his departure. I can not understand why he plagues himself so about politics; however, I trust he will like his new appointment. You found him, I am sure, a delightful companion."

"Come! you two young gentlemen," said the father-in-law, "put off your chat till the evening. The business of the day stops, for I see the procession coming forward to receive the Regatta prize. Now, my dear! where is the scarf? You know what to say? Remember, I particularly wish to do honor to the victor! The sight of all these happy faces makes me feel quite young again. I declare, I think I shall live a hundred years!"

The procession advanced. First came a band of young children strewing flowers, then followed four stout boys carrying a large purple and white banner. The victor, proudly preceding the other candidates, strutted forward, with his hat on one side, a light scull decorated with purple and white ribbons in his right hand, and his left arm round his wife's waist. The wife, a beautiful young woman, to whom were clinging two fat flaxen-headed children, was the most interesting figure in the procession. Her tight dark bodice set off her round full figure, and her short red petticoat displayed her springy foot and ankle. Her neatly braided and plaited hair was partly concealed by a silk cap, covered with gold-spangled gauze, flattened rather at the top, and finished at the back of the head with a large bow. This costly headgear, the highest fashion of her class, was presented to the wearer by the bride, and was destined to be kept for festivals. After the victor and his wife came six girls and six boys, at the side of whom walked a very bustling personage in black, who seemed extremely interested about the decorum of the procession. A long train of villagers succeeded.

"Well!" said the old Lord to Vivian, "this must be a very gratifying sight to you! How fortunate that your carriage broke down just at my castle! I think my dear girl is acquitting herself admirably. Ah! Eugene is a happy fellow, and I have no doubt that she will be happy too. The young sailor receives his honors very properly; they are as nice a family as I know. Observe, they are moving off now to make way for the pretty girls and boys. That person in black is our Abbé, as benevolent, worthy a creature as ever lived! and very clever too; you will see in a minute. Now they are going to give us a little bridal chorus, after the old fashion, and it is all the Abbé's doing. I understand that there is an elegant allusion to my new bridge in it, which I think will please you. Who ever thought that bridge would be opened for my girl's wedding? Well! I am glad that it was not finished before. But we must be silent! You will notice that part about the bridge: it is in the fifth verse, I am told, beginning with something about Hymen, and ending with something about roses."

By this time the procession had formed a semicircle before the tent, the Abbé standing in the middle, with a paper in his hand, and dividing the two bands of choristers. He gave a signal with his cane, and the girls commenced:

Chorus of Maidens.

Hours fly! it is Morn; he has left the bed of love! She follows him with a strained eye when his figure is no longer seen; she leans her head upon her arm. She is faithful to him as the lake to the mountain!

Chorus of Youths.

Hours fly! it is Noon; fierce is the restless sun! While he labors he thinks of her! while he controls others he will obey her! A strong man subdued by love is like a vineyard silvered by the moon!

Chorus of Youths and Maidens.

Hours fly! it is Eve; the soft star lights him to his home; she meets him as his shadow falls on the threshold! she smiles, and their child, stretching forth its tender hands from its mother's bosom, struggles to lisp "Father!"

Chorus of Maidens.

Years glide! it is Youth; they sit within a secret bower. Purity is in her raptured eyes, Faith in his warm embrace. He must fly! He kisses his farewell; the fresh tears are on her cheek! He has gathered a lily with the dew upon its leaves!

Chorus of Youths.

Years glide! it is Manhood. He is in the fierce Camp; he is in the deceitful Court. He must mingle sometimes with others, that he may be always with her! In the false world, she is to him like a green olive among rocks!

Chorus of Youths and Maidens.

Years glide! it is Old Age. They sit beneath a branching elm. As the moon rises on the sunset green, their children dance before them! Her hand is in his; they look upon their children, and then upon each other!

"The fellow has some fancy," said the old Lord, "but given, I think, to conceits. I did not exactly catch the passage about the bridge, but I have no doubt it was all right."

Vivian was now invited to the pavilion, where refreshments were prepared. Here our hero was introduced to many other guests, relations of the family, who were on a visit at the castle, and who had been on the lake at the moment of his arrival.

"This gentleman," said the old Lord, pointing to Vivian, "is my son's friend, and I am quite sure that you are all delighted to see him. He arrived here accidentally, his carriage having fortunately broken down in passing one of the streams. All those rivulets should have bridges built over them! I could look at my new bridge forever. I often ask myself, "Now, how can such a piece of masonry ever be destroyed?" It seems quite impossible, does not it? We all know that everything has an end; and yet, whenever I look at that bridge, I often think that it can only end when all things end."

In the evening they all waltzed upon the green. The large yellow moon had risen, and a more agreeable sight than to witness two or three hundred persons so gayly occupied, and in such a scene, is not easy to imagine. How beautiful was the stern old castle, softened by the moonlight, the illumined lake, the richly silvered foliage of the woods, and the white brilliant cataract!

As the castle was quite full of visitors, its hospitable master had lodged Vivian for the night at the cottage of one of his favorite tenants. Nothing would give greater pleasure to Vivian than this circumstance, nor more annoyance to the worthy old gentleman.

The cottage belonged to the victor in the Regatta, who himself conducted the visitor to his dwelling. Vivian did not press Essper's leaving the revelers, so great an acquisition did he seem to their sports! teaching them a thousand new games, and playing all manner of antics; but perhaps none of his powers surprised them more than the extraordinary facility and freedom with which he had acquired and used all their names. The cottager's pretty wife had gone home an hour before her husband, to put her two fair-haired children to bed and prepare her guest's accommodation for the night. Nothing could be more romantic and lovely than the situation of the cottage. It stood just on the gentle slope of the mountain's base, not a hundred yards from the lower waterfall. It was in the middle of a patch of highly cultivated ground which bore creditable evidence to the industry of its proprietor. Fruit trees, Turkey corn, vines, and flax flourished in luxuriance.

The dwelling itself was covered with myrtle and arbutus, and the tall lemon plant perfumed the window of the sitting-room. The casement of Vivian's chamber opened full on the foaming cataract. The distant murmur of the mighty waterfall, the gentle sighing of the trees, the soothing influence of the moonlight, and the faint sounds occasionally caught of dying revelry, the joyous exclamation of some successful candidate in the day's games, the song of some returning lover, the plash of an oar in the lake; all combined to produce that pensive mood in which we find ourselves involuntarily reviewing the history of our life.

As Vivian was musing over the last harassing months of his burdensome existence he could not help feeling that there was only one person in the world on whom his memory could dwell with solace and satisfaction, and this person was Lady Madeleine Trevor!

It was true that with her he had passed some agonizing hours; but he could not forget the angelic resignation with which her own affliction had been borne, and the soothing converse by which his had been alleviated. This train of thought was pursued till his aching mind sank into indefiniteness. He sat for some little time almost unconscious of existence, till the crying of a child, waked by its father's return, brought him back to the present scene. His thoughts naturally ran to his friend Eugene. Surely this youthful bridegroom might reckon upon happiness! Again Lady Madeleine recurred to him. Suddenly he observed a wonderful appearance in the sky. The moon was paled in the high heavens, and surrounded by luminous rings, almost as vividly tinted as the rainbow, spreading and growing fainter, till they covered nearly half the firmament. It was a glorious and almost unprecedented halo!

CHAPTER IV

THE sun rose red, the air was thick and hot. Anticipating that the day would be very oppressive, Vivian and Essper were on their horses' backs at an early hour. Already, however, many of the rustic revelers were about, and preparations were commencing for the fête champêtre, which this day was to close the wedding festivities. Many and sad were the looks which Essper George cast behind him at the old castle on the lake. "No good luck can come of it!" said he to his horse; for Vivian did not encourage conversation. "O! master of mine, when wilt thou know the meaning of good quarters! To leave such a place, and at such a time! Why, Turriparva was nothing to it! The day before marriage and the hour before death is when a man thinks least of his purse and most of his neighbor. O! man, man, what are thou, that the eye of a girl can make thee so pass all discretion that thou wilt sacrifice for the whim of a moment good cheer enough to make thee last an age!"

Vivian had intended to stop and breakfast after riding about ten miles; but he had not proceeded half that way when, from the extreme sultriness of the morning, he found it impossible to advance without refreshment. Max, also, to his rider's surprise, was much distressed; and, on turning round to his servant, Vivian found Essper's hack panting and puffing, and breaking out, as if, instead of commencing their day's work, they were near reaching their point of destination.

"Why, how now, Essper? One would think that we had been riding all night. What ails the beast?"

"In truth, sir, that which ails its rider; the poor dumb brute has more sense than some who have the gift of speech. Who ever heard of a horse leaving good quarters without much regretting the indiscretion?"

"The closeness of the air is so oppressive that I do not wonder at even Max being distressed. Perhaps when the sun is higher, and has cleared away the vapors, it may be more endurable; as it is, I think we had better stop at once and breakfast here. This wood is as inviting as, I trust, are the contents of your basket!"

"St. Florian devour them!" said Essper, in a very pious voice, "if I agree not with you, sir; and as for the basket, although we have left the land of milk and honey, by the blessing of our Black Lady! I have that within it which would put courage in the heart of a caught mouse. Although we may not breakfast on bridecake and beccaficos, yet is a neat's tongue better than a fox's tail; and I have ever held a bottle of Rhenish to be superior to rain-water, even though the element be filtered through a gutter. Nor, by All Saints! have I forgotten a bottle of Kirschenwasser from the Black Forest, nor a keg of Dantzic brandy, a glass of which, when traveling at night, I am ever accustomed to take after my prayers; for I have always observed that, though devotion doth sufficiently warm up the soul, the body all the time is rather the colder for stopping under a tree to tell its beads."

The travelers accordingly led their horses a few yards into the wood, and soon met, as they had expected, with a small green glade. It was surrounded, except at the slight opening by which they had entered it, with fine Spanish chestnut trees, which now, loaded with their large brown fruit, rich and ripe, clustered in the starry foliage, afforded a retreat as beautiful to the eye as its shade was grateful to their senses. Vivian dismounted, and, stretching out his legs, leaned back against the trunk of a tree; and Essper, having fastened Max and his own horse to some branches, proceeded to display his stores. Vivian was silent, thoughtful, and scarely tasted anything; Essper George, on the contrary, was in unusual and even troublesome spirits, and had not his appetite necessarily produced a few pauses in his almost perpetual rattle, the patience of his master would have been fairly worn out. At length Essper had devoured the whole supply; and as Vivian not only did not encourage his remarks, but even in a peremptory manner had desired his silence, he was fain to amuse himself by trying to catch in his mouth a large brilliant fly which every instant was dancing before him. Two individuals more singularly contrasting in their appearance than the master and the servant could scarcely be conceived; and Vivian, lying with his back against a tree, with his legs stretched out, his arms folded, and his eyes fixed on the ground; and Essper, though seated, in perpetual motion, and shifting his posture with feverish restlessness, now looking over his shoulder for the fly, then making an unsuccessful bite at it, and then, wearied with his frequent failures, amusing himself with acting Punch with his thumbs; altogether presented two figures, which might have been considered as not inapt personifications of the rival systems of Ideality and Materialism.

At length Essper became silent for the sake of variety, and imagining, from his master's example, that there must be some sweets in meditation hitherto undiscovered by him, he imitated Vivian's posture! So perverse is human nature, that the moment Vivian was aware that Essper was perfectly silent, he began to feel an inclination to converse with him.

"Why. Essper!" said he, looking up and smiling, "this is the first time during our acquaintance that I have ever seen thought upon your brow. What can now be puzzling your wild brain?"

"I was thinking, sir," said Essper, with a very solemn look, "that if there were a deceased field-mouse here I would moralize on death."

"What! turned philosopher!"

"Ay! sir, it appears to me," said he, taking up a husk which lay on the turf, "that there is not a nutshell in Christendom which may not become matter for very grave meditation!"

"Can you expound that?"

"Verily, sir, the whole philosophy of life seems to me to consist in discovering the kernel. When you see a courtier out of favor or a merchant out of credit, when you see a soldier without pillage, a sailor without prize money, and a lawyer without papers, a bachelor with nephews, and an old maid with nieces, be assured the nut is not worth the cracking, and send it to the winds, as I do this husk at present."

"Why, Essper!" said Vivian, laughing, "considering that you have taken your degree so lately, you wear the Doctor's cap with authority! Instead of being in your novitiate, one would think that you had been a philosopher long enough to have outlived your system."

"Bless you, sir! for philosophy, I sucked it in with my mother's milk. Nature then gave me the hint, which I have ever since acted on, and I hold that the sum of all learning consists in milking another man's cow. So much for the recent acquisition of my philosophy! I gained it, you see, sir, with the first wink of my eye; and though I lost a great portion of it by sea-sickness in the Mediterranean, nevertheless, since I served your lordship, I have resumed my old habits, and do opine that this vain globe is but a large football, to be kicked and cuffed about by moody philosophers!"

"You must have seen a great deal in your life, Essper," said Vivian.

"Like all great travelers," said Essper, "I have seen more than I remember, and remember more than I have seen."

"Have you any objection to go to the East again?" asked Vivian. "It would require but little persuasion to lead me there."

"I would rather go to a place where the religion is easier; I wish, sir, you would take me to England!"

"Nay, not there with me, if with others."

"With you, or with none."

"I can not conceive, Essper, what can induce you to tie up your fortunes with those of such a sad-looking personage as myself."

"In truth, sir, there is no accounting for fates. My grandmother loved a brindled cat!"

"Your grandmother, Essper! Nothing would amuse me more than to be introduced to your family."

"My family, sir, are nothing more nor less than what all of us must be counted, worms of five feet long, mortal angels, the world's epitome, heaps of atoms which Nature has kneaded with blood into solid flesh, little worlds of living clay, sparks of heaven, inches of earth, Nature's quintessence, moving dust, the little all, smooth-faced cherubim, in whose souls the King of stars has drawn the image of Himself!"

"And how many years has breathed the worm of five feet long that I am now speaking to?"

"Good my Lord, I was no head at calculating from a boy; but I do remember that I am two days older than one of the planets."

"How is that?"

"There was one born in the sky, sir, the day I was christened, with a Turkish crescent."

"Come, Essper," said Vivian, who was rather interested by the conversation; Essper, having, until this morning, skilfully avoided any discourse upon the subject of his birth or family, adroitly turning the conversation whenever it chanced to approach these subjects, and silencing inquiries, if commenced, by some ludicrous and evidently fictitious· answer. "Come, Essper," said Vivian, "I feel by no means in the humor to quit this shady retreat. You and I have now known each other long, and gone through much together. It is but fair that I should become better acquainted with one who, to me, is not only a faithful servant, but what is more valuable, a faithful friend, I might now almost add, my only one. What say you to whiling away a passing hour by giving me some sketch of your curious and adventurous life? If there be anything that you wish to conceal, pass it over; but no invention, nothing but the truth, if you please; the whole truth, if you like."

"Why, sweet sir, as for this odd knot of soul and body, which none but the hand of Heaven could have twined, it was first seen, I believe, near the very spot where we are now sitting; for my mother, when I saw her first and last, lived in Bohemia. She was an Egyptian, and came herself from the Levant. I lived a week, sir, in the Seraglio when I was at Constantinople, and I saw there the brightest women of all countries, Georgians, and Circassians, and Poles; in truth, sir, Nature's masterpieces. And yet, by the Gods of all nations! there was not one of them half so lovely as the lady who gave me this tongue!" Here Essper exhibited at full length the enormous feature which had so much enraged the one-eyed sergeant at Frankfort.

"When I first remember myself," he continued, "I was playing with some other gypsy boys in the midst of a forest. Here was our settlement! It was large and powerful. My mother, probably from her beauty, possessed great influence, particularly among the men; and yet I found not among them all a father. On the contrary, every one of my companions had a man whom he reverenced as his parent, and who taught him to steal; but I was called by the whole tribe the mother-son, and was honest from my first year out of mere wilfulness; at least, if I stole anything, it was always from our own people. Many were the quarrels I occasioned, since, presuming on my mother's love and power, I never called mischief a scrape; but acting just as my fancy took me, I left those who suffered by my conduct to apologize for my ill-behavior. Being thus an idle, unprofitable, impudent, and injurious member of this pure community, they determined one day to cast me out from their bosom; and in spite of my mother's exertions and entreaties, the ungrateful vipers succeeded in their purpose. As a compliment to my parent, they allowed me to tender my resignation, instead of receiving my expulsion. My dear mother gave me a donkey, a wallet, and a ducat, a great deal of advice about my future conduct, and, what was more interesting to me, much information about my birth.

" 'Sweet child of my womb!' said my mother, pressing me to her bosom; 'be proud of thy white hands and straight nose!

Thou gottest them not from me, and thou shalt take them from
whence they came. Thy father is a Hungarian Prince; and
though I would not have parted with thee, had I thought that
thou wouldst ever have prospered in our life, even if he had
made thee his child of the law and lord of his castle, still, as
thou canst not tarry with us, haste thou to him! Give him this
ring and this lock of hair; tell him none have seen them but
the father, the mother, and the child! He will look on them,
and remember the days that are passed; and thou shalt be unto
him as a hope for his lusty years and a prop for his old age.'

"My mother gave me all necessary directions, which I well
remembered, and much more advice, which I directly forgot.

"Although tempted, now that I was a free man, to follow
my own fancy, I still was too curious to see what kind of a
person was my unknown father to deviate either from my
route or my maternal instructions, and in a fortnight's time I
had reached my future Principality.

"The sun sank behind the proud castle of my princely father
as, trotting slowly along upon my humble beast, with my wallet
slung at my side, I approached it through his park. A guard,
consisting of twenty or thirty men in magnificent uniforms,
were lounging at the portal. I— but, sir, sir, what is the meaning of this darkness? I always made a vow to myself that I
never would tell my history. Ah! what ails me?"

A large eagle fell dead at their feet.

"Protect me, master!" screamed Essper, seizing Vivian by
the shoulder; "what is coming? I can not stand; the earth
seems to tremble! Is it the wind that roars and rages? or is
it ten thousand cannon blowing this globe to atoms?"

"It is, it must be the wind!" said Vivian, agitated. "We
are not safe under these trees: look to the horses!"

"I will," said Essper, "if I can stand. Out of the forest!
Ah, look at Max!"

Vivian turned, and beheld his spirited horse raised on his
hind legs, and dashing his fore feet against the trunk of a
tree to which they had tied him. The terrified and furious
creature was struggling to disengage himself, and would
probably have sustained or inflicted some terrible injury, had
not the wind suddenly hushed. Covered with foam, he stood
panting, while Vivian patted and encouraged him. Essper's

less spirited beast had, from the first, crouched upon the earth, covered with sweat, his limbs quivering and his tongue hanging out.

"Master!" said Essper, "what shall we do? Is there any chance of getting back to the castle? I am sure our very lives are in danger. See that tremendous cloud! It looks like eternal night! Whither shall we go? what shall we do?"

"Make for the castle!" said Vivian, mounting.

They had just got into the road when another terrific gust of wind nearly took them off their horses, and blinded them with the clouds of sand which it drove out of the crevices of the mountains.

They looked round on every side, and hope gave way before the scene of desolation. Immense branches were shivered from the largest trees; small ones were entirely stripped of their leaves; the long grass was bowed to the earth; the waters were whirled in eddies out of the little rivulets; birds deserting their nests to seek shelter in the crevices of the rocks, unable to stem the driving air, flapped their wings and fell upon the earth: the frightened animals in the plain, almost suffocated by the impetuosity of the wind, sought safety, and found destruction: some of the largest trees were torn up by the roots; the sluices of the mountain. were filled, and innumerable torrents rushed down the before empty gullies. The heavens now open, and lightning and thunder contended with the horrors of the wind!

In a moment all was again hushed. Dead silence succeeded the bellow of the thunder, the roar of the wind, the rush of the waters, the moaning of the beasts, the screaming of the birds! Nothing was heard save the splash of the agitated lake as it beat up against the black rocks which girt it in.

"Master!" again said Essper, "is this the day of doom?"

"Keep by my side, Essper; keep close, make the best of this pause: let us but reach the village!"

Scarcely had Vivian spoken when greater darkness enveloped the trembling earth. Again the heavens were rent with lightning, which nothing could have quenched but the descending deluge. Cataracts poured down from the lowering firmament. In an instant the horses dashed round; beast and rider, blinded and stifled by the gushing rain, and gasping for breath.

Shelter was nowhere. The quivering beasts reared, and snorted, and sank upon their knees. The horsemen were dismounted. Vivian succeeded in hoodwinking Max, who was still furious; the other horse appeared nearly exhausted. Essper, beside himself with terror, could only hang over his neck.

Another awful calm.

"Courage, Essper!" said Vivian. "We are still safe; look up, man! the storm can not last long thus; and see! I am sure the clouds are breaking."

The heavy mass of vapor which had seemed to threaten the earth with instant destruction suddenly parted. The red and lurid sun was visible, but his light and heat were quenched in the still impending waters.

"Mount, Essper!" said Vivian, "this is our only chance: five minutes' good speed will take us to the village."

Encouraged by his master's example, Essper once more got upon his horse, and the panting animals, relieved by the cessation of the hurricane, carried them at a fair pace toward the village, considering that their road was now impeded by the overflowing of the lake.

"Master!" said Essper, "can not we get out of these waters?"

He had scarcely spoken before a terrific burst, a noise, they knew not what, a rush they could not understand, a vibration which shook them on their horses, made them start back and again dismount. Every terror sank before the appalling roar of the cataract. It seemed that the mighty mountain, unable to support its weight of waters, shook to the foundation. A lake had burst on its summit, and the cataract became a falling ocean. The source of the great deep appeared to be discharging itself over the range of mountains; the great gray peak tottered on its foundations! It shook! it fell! and buried in its ruins the castle, the village, and the bridge!

Vivian with starting eyes beheld the whole washed away; instinct gave him energy to throw himself on the back of his horse: a breath, and he had leaped up the nearest hill! Essper George, in a state of distraction, was madly laughing as he climbed to the top of a high tree: his horse was carried off in the drowning waters, which had now reached the road.

"The desolation is complete!" thought Vivian. At this

moment the wind again rose, the rain again descended, the heavens again opened, the lightning again flashed! An amethystine flame hung upon rocks and waters, and through the raging elements a yellow fork darted its fatal point at Essper's resting-place. The tree fell! Vivian's horse, with a maddened snort, dashed down the hill; his master, senseless, clung to his neck; the frantic animal was past all government; he stood upright in the air, flung his rider, and fell dead!

Here leave we Vivian! It was my wish to have detailed, in the present portion of this work, the singular adventures which befell him in one of the most delightful of modern cities, light-hearted Vienna! But his history has expanded under my pen, and I fear that I have, even now, too much presumed upon an attention which I am not entitled to command. I am, as yet, but standing without the gate of the Garden of Romance. True it is that, as I gaze through the ivory bars of its Golden Portal, I would fain believe that, following my roving fancy, I might arrive at some green retreats hitherto unexplored, and loiter among some leafy bowers where none have lingered before me. But these expectations may be as vain as those dreams of Youth over which all have mourned. The Disappointment of Manhood succeeds to the delusion of Youth: let us hope that the heritage of Old Age is not Despair.